D1713530

Darconville's Cat

ALEXANDER THEROUX

Darconville's Cat

Doubleday & Company, Inc.
Garden City, New York
1981

THEY FLEE FROM ME

They flee from me, that sometime did me seek,
With naked foot stalking in my chamber.
I have seen them, gentle, tame, and meek,
That now are wild, and do not remember
That sometime they put themselves in danger
To take bread at my hand, and now they range,
Busily seeking with a continual change.

Thankèd be fortune it hath been otherwise,
Twenty times better; but once in special,
In thin array, after a pleasant guise,
When her loose gown from her shoulders did fall,
And she me caught in her arms long and small,
And therewith all sweetly did me kiss
And softly said, "Dear heart, how like you this?"

It was no dream: I lay broad waking.
But all is turned, through my gentleness,
Into a strange fashion of forsaking;
And I have leave to go of her goodness,
And she also to use newfangleness.
But since that I so kindely am servèd,
I fain would know what she hath deserved.

Sir THOMAS WYATT

Explicitur

THIS IS A STORY of murder, which, as an act, is as apt to characterize deliverance as it is to corroborate death. There are certain elemental emotions that touch upon powers other and larger than our own discrete wishes might allow—for every consciousness is continuous with a wider self open to the hidden processes and unseen regions created in the soul by the very nature of an *opposite* effort—and while, taken together, each may prove the other simply by contrast, considered separately neither may admit of various shades in the law of whichever whole it finds reigning at the time. That which produces effects within one reality creates another reality itself. I am thinking, specifically, of love and hate.

We cannot distinguish, perhaps, natural from supernatural effects, nor among either know which are favors of God and which are counterfeit operations of the Devil. Who, furthermore, can speak of the incubations of motives? And of love and hate? Are they not too often, in spite of the comparative chaos within us, generally taken to be little more than a set of titles obtained by the mere mechanical manipulation of antonyms? I have no aspiration here to reclaim mystery and paradox from whatever territory they might inhabit, for there is, indeed, often a killing in a kiss, a mercy in the slap that heats your face.

There is, nevertheless, a particular poverty in those alloplasts who, addressing tragedy, seek to subdistinguish motives beyond those we have best, because nearest, at hand, and so it is with love and hate—emotions upon whose necks, whether wrung or wreathed, may be found the oldest fingerprints of man. A simple truth intrudes: the basic instincts of every man to every man are known. But who knows when or where or how? For the answers to such questions, summon Augurello, your personal jurisconsult and theological wiseacre, to teach you about primal reality and then to dispel those complexities and cabals you crouch behind in this sad, psychiatric century you call your own. It is the *anti*-labyrinths of the world that scare. Here is a story for you. Your chair.

A.L.T.

Contents

Contents   xi

Darconville's Cat

I

The Beginning

Delirium is the disease of the night.

—St. PONTEFRACT

DARCONVILLE, the schoolmaster, always wore black. The single tree, however, that shanked out of the front yard he now crossed in long strides showed even more distinct a darkness, a simulacrum of the dread probationary tree—trapfall of all lost love—for coming upon it, gibbet-high and half leafless in the moonlight, was to feel somehow disposed to the general truth that it is a dangerous and pagan notion that beauty palliates evil.

He was alone. It had always seemed axiomatic for him that he be alone: a vow, the linchpin of his art, his praxis.

The imperscrutable winds of autumn, blowing leaves across the porch, had almost stripped the tree, leaving it nearly naked and essential against the moon that shone down on the quiet little town in Virginia. It was late as he let himself into the house and walked up the creaking stairs to his rooms where, pulling a chair to the window, he sat meditatively in that dark chamber like a nomadic gulsar—his black coat still unbuttoned—and was left alone with those odd retrospective prophecies borne in on one at the start of that random moment we, for some reason, choose to call the beginning of a new life.

The night, solemn and beautiful, seemed fashioned to force those who would observe it to look within themselves. He watched awhile and then grew weary. He took a late mixt of some rolls and a bottle of ale and soon dropped asleep on his bed, dreaming out of fallen reason the rhymes received with joy he shaped accordingly. It was only early the following morning that he found on the bedside table next to his pen and unscrewed cap—a huge Moore's Non-Leakable—the open commonplace book in which, having arisen in the middle of the night to do so, he had written a single question: "Who is she?"

II

Darconville

I thought I heard the rustle of a dress, but I don't—I don't see anyone. No, I imagined it.

—*Peter Schlemihl; or, The Man Who Sold His Shadow*

SEPTEMBER: it was the most beautiful of words, he'd always felt, evoking orange-flowers, swallows, and regret. The shutters were open. Darconville stared out into a small empty street, touched with autumnal fog, that looked like the lugubrious frontispiece to a book as yet to be read. His obligate room, its walls several shades of distemper, was spare as the skite of a recluse—a postered bed, several chairs, and an old deal desk he'd just left, confident in the action of moderating powers, to ease his mind of some congested thoughts. He looked at his watch which he kept hung on a nail. The afternoon was to have been spent, as the morning had, writing, but something else was on his mind.

There was an unfinished manuscript, tentatively called *Rumpopulorum,* spread out there, a curious, if speculative, examination of the world of angels, archistrateges, and the archonic wardens of heaven in relation—he appropriated without question the right to know both—to mortal man. The body of material, growing over the last few months, was formidable, its sheets pied with inky corrections and smudged with the additions that overheated his prose and yet brought it all to test.

The human skull, his pencils in its noseholes, that had been ritually placed on that desk a week previous—his first days in the South— seemed appropriate to his life, a reminder, mysteriously elate, of what actually wasn't, something there but not, a memory of man without one, for not only had he more or less withdrawn from the world, long a characteristic of the d'Arconvilles, but the caricatures of mortal vanity were as necessary to his point of view as the unction of religious conventionality was featureless.

Darconville's cat leaped onto the windowsill and peered up, as if collating the thoughts of his master: where were they? How had they come to be here? What reason, in fact, had they to be in this strange place? The young man, however, continued leaning by the window and reviewing what he saw. But there was another view, for behind it, or perhaps beyond somewhere, in vague, half-blind remembrances of wherever he'd been—sources of endless pleasure to him—he dwelled awhile to find himself, looking back in time, surprised at the absence in it of any figure but his own. He felt no particular responsibility to memory but accepted his dreams, to which, living altogether as a twin self in the depths of him, he could speak in inviolable secrecy.

It had long seemed clear, commandmental: to seek out a relatively distant and unembellished part of the world where, in the solitude he arranged for himself—rather like the pilgrim who lives on lentils, pulses, and the tested modes of self-denial—one might apply himself to those deeper mysteries where nameless somethings in their causes slept. He sought the obol of Pasetes, the mallet of Daikoku, the lamp of Aladdin. There were difficulties, often, in the way of carrying out his plans. But he overbore them and, hoping to fall prey to neither fascination nor fatigue, sought only to stem distraction, to learn the secrets beyond the world he felt belonged to him, and to write. It was the Beatitude of Destitution.

Alaric Darconville—insurrect, courteous, liturgical—was twenty-nine years old. He had the pointed medieval face of a pageboy, which showed less of mature steadiness than innocent deliberation, an expensive coloring backlit with a kind of intangible grace, and his eyes, of a strange tragic beauty, dark and filled with studying what's represented by what is, could light up like a monk at jubilee when rounding the verge of a new idea and sparkle up in happy conviction as if to say "Excelsior!" He dreamed, like Astrophel, with his head in the stars. His mind was like one of those Gothic cathedrals of which he was so fond, mysterious within, and filled with light, a brightness at once richer and less real than the light of day, flashing accompaniment, on occasion, to the long satirical tirades of which he was also capable and yet wakefully aware, in gentleness, of what in matters of difficulty he felt should either be removed, pitied, or understood. He was six feet tall. His hair he wore long, like the Renaissance prince at his lyre, and it matched in color his coat of jet which was of an obsolete but distinct cut and as black as the *mundus* where Romans communed with their dead.

The book he was working on—a grimoire, in the old style—recapitulated such communication. He scribbled away in the light of his gooseneck lamp that not only left the rest of the room in darkness but at such times rendered insignificant any matters of consequence beyond that. There was a private quality about him as he worked: a wizard in conical hat conjuring mastertricks; the sacristan jing-jing-jingling the bells of sext; the alchemist, counsel to caliphs, shuttling in a cellar enigmatic beaker to tort for rare demulcents and rubefacients. It was a closed world, his, arresting thoughts for words to work, to skid around, to transubstantiate: the writer is the ponce who introduces Can to Ought. He crafted his writing and loved listening to those tiny explosions when the active brutality of verbs in revolution raced into sweet established nouns to send marching across the page a newly commissioned army of words-on-maneuvers, all decorated in loops, frets, and arrowlike flourishes. Darconville was bedeviled by angels: they stalked and leaguered him by night and day, and, when sitting at his desk, he never failed to acknowledge Stimulator, the angel invoked in the exorcism of ink, for the storm and stress of making something from nothing partook no less of the supernatural than Creation itself. Was doubt the knot in faith's muscle? And yet faith required to fill the desert places of an empty page? Then this was a day in September no different from any others on which he wrote, the mind making up madness, the hand its little prattboy hopping along after it to record what it could of measure—but there was one exception.

Darconville anxiously kept seeing the face of one of his students, someone he had noticed on the first day of class. She was a freshman. He didn't know her name.

He might have spent an inattentive afternoon in consequence but, subdued by what had no charm for him, instead vexed himself to write as a means of serving notice to a mischief he'd been uncertain of now for too many days. Beauty, while it haunted him, also distracted him; unable to resist its appeal, he, however, longed to be above it. There is a will so strong as to recoil upon itself and fall into indecision: a deliberate person's, often, who, otherwise prompt to action, sometimes leaves everything undone—or, better, assumes that whatever has been done is something already charged to an appointed end, relieving him then of calling into question by subsequent thought the meaning of its worth. Did Darconville's mind, then, obsessed and overwhelmed by images and dreams of the supernatural, crave at last for the one thing stranger than all these—the experience of it in fact? It is perhaps easy to believe so.

He was born—of French and Italian parentage—on the reaches of coastal New England where the old Victorian house that was the family seat stands to this day in a small village hard by the sea. It was always a region of spectacular beauty, infinite skies and meadows and ocean, and all aspects of nature there seemed drawn together in a tie of inexpressible benediction. His youthful dreams were always of a supernatural cast, shot through with vision, and nothing whatsoever matter-of-fact could avail against the propagation of his early romantic ideals. It had been instilled in him early—his Venetian grandmother fairly threw her hands over her ears at the suggestion of any aspiration less noble—that the goal of a person's life must naturally afford the light by which the rest of it should be read, a doctrine that paradoxically created in him less a strength against than a disposition to a belief in unreal worlds, a condition somehow making him particularly unsuited for the heartache of real life.

The facts of one's childhood are always important when touching on a genius. Darconville was an ardently religious boy, much attracted to ritual. At six, he won the school ribbon for a drawing of the face of God—it resembled a cat's—and illustrated a juvenile book of his own dramatic making which ended: *"But wait, there is something coming toward me—!"* There were illnesses, and a double pneumonia in childhood following a nearly fatal bout with measles left his lungs imperfect. He would never forget his father who read to him or his mother who kissed him goodnight, for he lost both of them before he was fourteen, whereupon, becoming wayward and discontented with everything else, he cut short his schooling to join the Franciscan Order, less on the advice growing out of the newly assumed regency of his grandmother, though that, than on the investigation of a dream: a nostalgia for vision, if commonly absent in others, then not so for a little boy whose earliest memory was of trying to pick up pieces of moonlight that had fallen through the window onto his bed.

Seminary life in those early years led to strange and unaccountable antipathies. It was not that he didn't feel he fit, but if particulars went well—in everything, save, perhaps, for the occasional youthful temptation he suffered during *lectio divina* while reading Lucretius on the terminology of physical love—general acceptance came hard. He improvised piano arrangements at midnight, claimed he could work curses, and put it about that he believed animals, because of a universal language from which we alone had fallen, could understand us when we spoke. He astonished his fellow students, furthermore, with several rapturous edificial schemes few shared: to rebuild the tomb of St. John at Ephesus; to set up birdhouses for Christ through upstate New York; and to reconstruct—he actually stepped off the dimensions on the ballfield and began to assemble planks—Noah's Ark. Throughout these years he showed a splendid but innocent sense of fun.

Darconville owned a great fat pen he called "The Black Disaster" —an object, he demoted, no other hand dare touch! His classmates were solemnly, ceremoniously, assured it was magic, and it was coveted by all of them only in so far as stealing it might render its owner a less vivid, if not less bumptious, antagonist. He managed never to relinquish it, however, and drew angels all over his copybooks; wrote squibs about some of his colleagues which, signed "Aenigmaticus," he secretly distributed in various library books; and one day, for drawing a fresco—his *capolavoro*—of St. Bernard excom-

municating a multitude of flies at Foigny, where each little creature ingeniously, but undisguisedly, bore the face of one of the college pre-
fects, he was slapped so hard by a certain Father Theophane that it
effected a stammer in him that would be activated, during moments of
confrontation, for the rest of his life. Hostility eventually built up, and
his unconventional conduct became the subject of such unfavorable
comment in the college that it was suggested he leave. A few defended
him. (He believed it was because there had once been a cardinal in his
family, as indeed there had been.) The rest, some silently abusive,
naggingly malevolent, or outright vindictive, more or less concurred in
the bizarre if hard to be seriously taken fiat that he not only vacate the
premises but withdraw, meditate, and summarily impale himself on
the same wretched object that had been the source, in several ways,
less of any black disaster than of their own humorless and over-pious
objections.

As it happened, he never attained to the priesthood—not, however,
because he didn't again try. For try again he did, but failed once
more. And yet with what reckless audacity, with what fierce, uncompromising passion did he always charge and fight and charge again!
Resignation to appointed ends? He was not of an age for that. And as
there hovered before him, always, a sense of disgust in resigning the
soul to the pleasures and idle conveniences of the world, his aspirations, individual and metaphysical, led abruptly to another decision.
He entered a Trappist monastery at eighteen and yet, again, before
long fell into confusion and a particular variety of quarrels there for
which he was never directly responsible but to which, as we've seen,
even the most saintly precincts are liable. The principal agent of the
worst of them was a priggish anathemette named Frater Clement
who, without the gift of reason, much less the gift of faith, had as his
goal not the salvation of his soul but the acquisition in matrimony of a
blond boy, another novice, who thought the world was run and possibly owned by the Order of Cistercians. *His* submission was naïveté,
but Darconville grew impatient with the other's venal disability. And
one afternoon as the monks were proceeding to nones, he snared the
hypocrite by the cowl, pulled him into a side-cloister, and—not without stuttering—adroitly gave him the lecture on spiritual discipline he
found later, much to his own grief, he himself couldn't follow, for he
saw he couldn't forgive Frater Clement, whose jug ears alone at chant
and chapter phosphorized his charity on the spot. Dismal depression

followed. He received the blessing of the Abbot, who repeated the famous words of the old desert fathers: *"fuge, tace, et quiesce"* and, leaving the following day in an egg truck—with one suitcase, a great fat pen, and all his limitations—went bouncing over the hill in the direction of the declining sunshine.

At twenty, in what was probably the climactic event of his life, Darconville discovered writing, the sole subject of his curiosity at this time being words and the possibility of giving expression to them. Now, among those fragile loves to which most men look back with tenderness and passion, certain must be singled out as of special importance: in young Darconville's life it was to be his proud and irrepressible grandmama whose affection for him was always on the increase and who—never once having failed to give fortitude to his individuality, although in quaint deference to his family's nobility on the paternal side she used only his surname in matters of address, a habit he would continue all his life—with rising emphasis that gave words to his inward instincts encouraged him at this critical juncture of his life to go live with her in Venice. At every point she was replete with wise suggestions, the value of which he recognized and the tenor of which he followed. Did he want to write? she had asked and upon the instant answered Darconville, who had but to follow the direction of her raised and superintendent cane to a corner where sat a beautiful desk.

It wasn't long before his grandmother passed away. The palazzo, immediately becoming the object of what had even long before been a curious litigation, was locked up. And so with a certain amount of money earmarked for his education, belated for the clerical years, he took her cat, Spellvexit—his sole companion now—and set sail back to the United States, looking once more for the possibilities of the possible as possible. The spirit of his youthful dreams, long, strangely enough, having retarded his purposes rather than advancing them, he studiedly refused to renounce: of justice and fair play, of living instead of dying, of loving instead of hating. Single virtue, he always believed, was proof against manifold vice. And yet all the caprices and aspects of human life that gratified curiosity and excited surprise in him continued only as incidents on the way to Glory.

Darconville—wherever—quite happily chose to live within his own world, within his own writing, within himself. The thickest, most permanent wall dividing him from his fellow creatures was that of mediocrity. His particular sensibility forbade him to accept unquestioned society's rules and taboos, its situational standards and ethics, syntheses that to him always seemed either too exclusive or too inclusive. His domineering sense of right, as sometimes only he saw it, and his ardent desire to keep to the fastness of his own destiny, set him apart in several ways. Reclusive, he shrank from all avoidable company with others—it was the prerogative of his faith to recognize, and of his character to overpower, objection here—and chose to believe only that somewhere, perhaps on the footing of schoolmaster, he could inoffensively foster sums, if modest, then at least sufficient to allow him the time to write. He sought the land of Nusquamia, a place broadly mapped out in James 4:4, and whether by chance or perchance by intention one day, wasting no time balancing or inquiring, he selected a school for the purpose, was hired, and disappeared again into the arcane. It didn't really have to have a name. In fact, however, it did. It was a town in Virginia, called Quinsyburg.

The train whistle there every evening seemed to beckon dusk, precreating a mood of sudden melancholy in a wail that left its echo behind like the passing tribute of a sigh. And Darconville, while yet amply occupied, was by no means so derogate from the common run of human emotions as not to share, upon hearing it—Spellvexit always looked up—a derivative feeling of loneliness, a disposition compounded, further, not only by the portentous evidences of the season but also by the bleakness of the place upon which it settled. The town was the quotidian co-efficient of limbo: there was no suddenness, no irresistibility, no velocity of extraordinary acts. He found hours and hours of complete solitude there, however, and that became the source, as he wrote, not of oppressive exclusiveness but of organizing anticipations he could accommodate in his work: the mystic's rapture at feeling his phantom self. He had assumed this exile not with the destitution of spirit the prodigal is too often unfairly assigned, nor from any aristocratic weariness a previous life in foreign parts might have induced, but rather to pull the plug of *consequence* from the sump of the world—to avoid the lust of result and the vice of emulation.

There are advantages to being in a backwater, and at the margins, in the less symphonic underground, recriminations were few, ambition didn't mock useful toil, and the bald indices of failure and success became irrelevant. The man beyond the context of hope is equally beyond the context of despair, and the serious vow Darconville had once made to himself, medievally sworn in the old ipsedixitist tradition of silent knights, holy knights, aimed to that still point; so it was with love as with loneliness: to fall in love would make him a pneumatomachian—an opponent of the spirit which, however, to him disposed to it, nightly blew its unfathomable afflatus down the cold reaches of the otherwise impenetrable heavens to quicken man to magic.

It didn't matter where he was. No, the best attitude to the world, he felt, unless the Patristics belied us, was to look beyond it. Darconville was below envy and above want. And what pleasures a place denied to the sight, he hoped, were given necessarily to the imagination. He sought the broom of Eucrates, the sword of Fragarach, the horse of Pacolet. Prosperity, furthermore, had perhaps killed more than adversity, an observance fortified in him by what was not only the d'Arconville motto but also his grandmother's most often repeated if somewhat overly enthusiastic febrifuge: *"Un altro, un altro, gran' Dio, ma più forte!"* And so he had come to this plutonial grey area, a neglected spot, where passersby didn't look for art to happen as it might and when it would—to lose himself for good, in both senses, and realize the apocalypse that is incomprehensible without Patmos. The passion for truth is unsociable. We are in this world *not* to conform to it.

It had grown dark.

Darconville had finished a day's writing, took some cigarettes from his suitcase, still as yet unpacked, and walked through the disheveled light down the flight of stairs to the porch—the night was positively beautiful—when past the hedges, through the rustling leaves by the large tree, he thought he saw a girl, looking apprehensively side to side, walk quickly across the street like a tapered dream-bird in fragile but pronounced strides and then disappear. But he noticed something else. He reached down to pick up from the doorstep a small round object, studded with a hundred cloves, its pure odor a sweet orange like September. It was a pomander ball. Darconville, by matchlight, slipped the accompanying card out of its tiny envelope. It read simply: "For the fairest."

They were the three words that had started the Trojan War.

III

Quinsyburg, Va.

Death hath not only particular stars in Heaven, but malevolent
Places on Earth, which single out our Infirmities and strike at
our weaker Parts.

—Sir Thomas Browne, *A Letter to a Friend*

RULE A LINE from Charlottesville, directly through Scottsville and
its lazy river, and draw it down—a straight 180°—into the southside,
fixing it to a terminal in the heart of Prince Edward County, Va.
Follow scale to measure the low point. Now, drive that sixty miles of
narrow godforsaken road past old huts and shacks, scrub pines and
blasted forests into a desolation the crossed boundaries of which,
though not silent to your eyes, one feels more in the depth of imagination, the kind of anxiety, a foreboding, of a guilt within not traceable
to a fact without; turn then and trail slowly on a wind across a

tableland of sallow weeds and sunken dingles into flat tobacco country where the absence of perspective seems as if offered in awful proof of what suddenly, crouching in a perfect and primitive isolation, becomes a town. Stop your car. Your hesitations are real. You can hear yourself breathing. You can hear your hands move. You are in Quinsyburg.

It is immediately a terrible letdown, a dislocation, solitary in the framework of its rigid and iconoclastic literalness, which yet sits in the exact center of the Commonwealth of Virginia, a state commemoratively named—if we may charitably disregard for a moment her biological interludes with everyone from the royal dancing master to the beetle-faced Duke of Anjou*—after the twenty-third British sovereign, Elizabeth I, she of the judas wig: bastard, usurper, excommunicate, baldpate, heretic, murderess, schismatic, and willing copulatrix. The sharp and instinctive disappointment you feel, that this must be the capital city of all failure, wrongheadedness, and provinciality, does not subside—it increases, intensifies, heightens. The approach that announces with sadder and sadder emphasis its sterility leads only to a confirmation of its deeper afflictions: for it amounts to, infringes on, nothing, shares nothing with the prospect of the sky but, deathshot with monotony, lies like a shroud wrapped around itself as if, so determined, it refuses to be inhabited by even so much as the relative humanity of a corpse. It is infinitely liker hell than earth, the proper place to feel the first hint of the decay of the fall. It appears to have extracted from beauty the piety given to it and, keeping that, dismissed the rest as ignominious accident to build a town. A sign tells you where.

The place—nothing surrounded by nowhere—is rigorously confined within its own settled limits, huddled, as if on its knees searching the corners of its rural conscience for some sin of omission or commission whereby, to ratify the truth of natural depravity, every pleasure, every recreation, every trifle scratched out of the dust might then be magnified into a great offense, and less for its severe white churches than a general mood of dissent do you feel that the deepest solicitudes of its inhabitants must have nothing to feed on except by what either outraged godliness or gave the devil his due. Crete had no owls,

---

* Greetings here might also be extended to Alençon; Charles Blount; Hatton; De Vere; Heneage; Sir Walter Raleigh; Admiral Thomas Seymour; Robert Dudley, Earl of Leicester; Eric, King of Sweden; Robert Devereux, Earl of Essex; Archduke Charles of Austria; and any number of others.

Thebes no swallows, Ithaca no hares, Pontus no asses, Scythia no swine. Quinsyburg had no hope. It is overpowering to realize and worse suddenly to accept, you fight it, and only the muteness of apprehension stifles an immediate impulse to cry out in despair, "Of all the loveless, lifeless things that quail beneath the wrath of God, commend Quinsyburg to it!"

IV

He Enters the House of Rimmon

My child, how didst thou come beneath the murky darkness,
being still alive?

—*Odyssey*, XI, 155–156

MISS THELMA TRAPPE, spinster, had a pitted nose. An ex-schoolmistress from Quinsy College, having been forced because of age to retire, she could often be seen walking eccentrically up and down the streets of the neighborhood in her wide straw hats, peering over her spectacles and repeating like a mantra to the sun, "Let me suffer, just keep shining. Let me suffer, just keep shining."

One Saturday morning, she simply walked over to Darconville, who was sitting on a porchswing, and with her little pyewacket of a head turned sweetly to the side asked him, as he was new there, would he care to see the town? A little walking tour, perhaps?

It was the first friend Darconville had made in Quinsyburg. An exile herself, she had come down from New Hampshire many years ago, stayed on to teach, and now lived by herself in rented rooms at the top of the hill where the loneliness, she said, always seemed worse. She wore a dress like a teepee, loved frequently to quote from her favorite literary piece, "Mrs. Battle's Opinions on Whist," and although she once had red hair and fair skin, with the passage of time and more than periodic though secret infusions of parsnip wine they had reversed, creating a face rather like a crabapple. It was a glorious day, and so they went off together on the jaunt, exchanging confidences freely from the very start.

Quinsyburg was the county seat. The old courthouse stood behind a short lawn in the square. The place hadn't changed much since the long-gone days of the Civil War, and its townsfolk—ardent lifelong drys—lived out their small agonies or quietly went to the dogs in the proper behind-the-curtains manner of shabby genteel respectability. There was an odor of decay there, of custom, of brittle endurance, a sort of banality, with yet something sinister, waiting below the bleak checkerwork of vacant yards, used-car lots, gas stations, and the pan-moronium of faded motels (the "Bide-A-Wee," the "Sleepy Hollow," etc.), to the rooms of which, studiously obliterative of every trace of pretense, came the intrepid Polos and pan-animated wanderers of America who, in point of fact, had usually taken the wrong road, missed the right bus, blinked the incidentals of a highway sign, or somehow got delayed or waylaid at the eleventh hour. It was a little world unpardonably misled by fundamentalist drivel, a stronghold of biblicism, and one drowned in the swamp of its execrable simplicities. Nowhere could be found anything in the way of adornment. It was a place that liked its coffee black, its flapjacks dry, its adjectives few, its cheeses hard, its visits short, its melodies whistleable, and its dreams in black and white—preferably the latter.

Darconville was amused to find Miss Trappe setting a good pace, her hat so large, wagging, that she looked like a tip under a plate. " 'I like a thorough-paced partner,' " quoted Miss Trappe, "as Mrs. Battle would say." They crossed through the nicer part of town, an area of well-treed properties and rows of colonnaded houses, handsomely appointed in old brick that served also the formal front walks, chimneys, and no-longer-used slave quarters out back. The patrician section of Quinsyburg was small.

This was not the doo-dah South of the Camptown Races, good bourbon, and the smell of honeysuckle in old shambling yards where at dusk one heard the sound of risible Negroes pocking out "Dixie" on hand-hewn banjos. It was far more dreadful and far less eloquent: a kind of cimmeria, a serviceable huggermugger of old wooden tobacco sheds; auction barns; too many hardware stores; a dismal shoe factory; and a run-down dairy bar into whose neon "foot-long hotdog" sign, at night, sizzled bugs blown in by the stale breezes of the dung-drab Appomattox River which sludged along its fosses of spatterdock and alligator weed and milfoil. The freight train Darconville had heard but hadn't yet seen chugged through town once in a while on its way to Cincinnati, but as it had long ago stopped taking on passengers, the station had fallen into disrepair. The town came to an abrupt halt at both ends, a foolish watertank marking the limits on one side and the other giving way to a region of fat-farms and open fields which, several times a year, suddenly sprouted up tents soon to be all faffed up with the trivialities of the camp-meeting and the chatauqua harangue, the county fair and the vote-rousing picnic. But these were *special* events.

During most of the year, the brass-jewelry tastes of its citizens—you knew them by string ties, brutal haircuts, and snap-brim hats, with fishhooks and lures, advertising things like "Funk's Hybrid" or "Wirthmore Feeds"—ran to little more than a general enthusiasm for church bake-offs, barbershop gossip, and all that hand-me-down bumpkinry touching on Bryanism, vice-crusading, and prohibition. It was a town nonascriptive, nonchalant, and nonentitative, one of those places that lent itself to uneasy jokes or gave rise to dismissive quips, like "I spent a whole week there one Sunday" or "It'd be a great place to live if you were dead" or "I visited there once, but it was closed."

"Look," pointed Miss Trappe, coming to a halt. "I never see him without thinking, for some reason, of my father." The statue of a sinople-green Confederate soldier, so common in Southern communities, stood above them on a granite pediment, surrounded by cannonballs, with a dapper Van Dyke beard, a bandolier, a rifle-at-the-ready, and a chivalric squint into the heart of the legitimacy of states' rights, honoring those who died—so read the inscription—"in a just and holy cause." He was the Defender of State Sovereignty. He stood there in all weather, unphased by birdlime or pigeons. He never flinched. "My father left us, you know. I was only a child, but almost died of shame.

Oh yes, but that was long ago, and, besides," she sighed, "that, as they say, was in another country."

The main buildings of Quinsy College could now be seen across the street, a cloister of white columns running along by way of a portico. Disquisiting, somewhat abstractly, on the college's history, Miss Trappe stepped off the sidewalk. Suddenly leaping back to the curb— peevishly screeching, *"You!"*—she saved her toes, just, as a green pickup truck with an armament rack at the back window whipped out onto High St. and raced toward Main, pedal to the metal. The driver, an underscullion with a face like a knife, called out something vile.

Miss Trappe and Darconville continued walking, a strange little mock-up—a skeptical Dante, a wizened Beatrice—in a most un-paradisaical world: a matchbox-sized theatre, an ice-cream shop, and the old Timberlake Hotel, with its chintz curtains, upon whose shaded veranda sat several cut-to-the-pattern townies slumped in black-lacquered wicker chairs and several careworn arteriopaths, hunched up like angry hawks, fussily presiding over a game of dominoes. "Percy," came a squawk, "you ain't got enough strength to pull a greasy string out of a goose's ass." A slam followed. "Move!" Miss Trappe shook her head. "I had a brother," she said, out of the blue, "who always played chess with me. We wouldn't *consider* dominoes." She paused. "He married, lost his wife to another, took to drink—" A distinct sorrow came into her eyes.

"And is he—"

Miss Trappe made a cataphatic nod. "By his own hand. He was twenty." She sighed and stumped along. " 'The rigor of the game,' " she said, "as Mrs. Battle would say."

They came to Quinsyburg's main street. It was a contingent, down both sides, of shoulder-to-shoulder shops, a frontage dull and repetitious but saved from the blight of uniformity by cute mercantile jingles painted on each window—the poetic effusions of various local struld-brugs and place-proud retailers—which in small towns, for some pe-culiar reason, become such a rich source of humor: United Dixiebelle Cup Co. ("Even Our Name Begins with You"); Quinsyburg Bedding Co. ("We Give You a Lot of Bunk"); The Old Dominion Outlet ("If Your Clothes Aren't Becoming to You, You Should Be Coming to Us"); Stars 'N' Bars Exterminating Co. ("All Our Patients Die"); Piedmont Travel Service ("Please Go Away"); Southside Rug and

Linoleum ("The Best Floor Show in Town"); The Virginia Shook Co. ("We'll Stave You In"); The Quinsyburg Gun Shop ("The First to Last"); and The Prince Edward Lumber Co. ("May We Strike a Cord for You?")

The Southern town, a parody of itself, is the prototype from which every other one is copied. Where is the one, for instance, that doesn't have a radio announcer named Don Dale; a private white academy; Muddy Creek; a chili-dog emporium; the State theatre; Jaycees with berry-knotted ties; a sheriff called "Goober"; something like the ol' Shuckcorn Place (it's always supposed to be haunted by J. E. B. Stuart); a popular delivery boy-cum-halfwit named Willis Foster; and a local NRA enclave that meets upstairs in the gunshop every Friday night to tell lies and make up stories about niggers, nymphomania, and New York City?

Darconville and Miss Trappe took time for tea at the Seldom Inn ("A Place to Remember for Cares to Forget")—a popular meeting place downtown for the professional tie-and-jacket faction (booths) who rotated matchbooks and told loud interminable tales ánd various peckerwoods (stools) who gripcruppered their coffee cups from the non-handle side and stared into a stippled wall-mirror at their chinless faces and pointed ears. The jukebox was blaring country music— Kitty Wells, "Honky Tonk Angels"—making it impossible to talk, so Darconville and Miss Trappe together watched through the window as the Quinsyburg townsfolk passed by, peculiar people on the hop, remarkably alike all, with faces like the trolls on German beer mugs, the curious result, perhaps, of poultry-like inbreeding (farmers, farmers' daughters, farmers' daughters' farmers) that had trans-mogrified a once vital eighteenth-century Protestant Celtic stock into a hedgecreeping lower-class breed of joltheads and jusqu' aubouts and then metastasized into one huge gene pool which seemed to reach from the bulletheaded truckers of Mississippi to the triple-named sena-tors of Virginia, slackjawed and malplasmic to a one. It seemed an orgy of kin, with everybody anybody's cousin.

It was a burlesque subordinating individuality to a constant reference of type. *Quaeritis habitantes?* Rotarians; wood-hewing gibeonites; 32° Masons and their ball-jars; pushing tradesmen; zelators and zelatrices; Odd Fellows of indecipherable worth; Hem-erobaptists; racist Elks (B!P!O.E.) and their shovelmouthed wives,

usually named Lorinda or Moxone; psalm-snufflers; longnosed um-
brella-carrying joykillers; widows with applepandowdy faces; Vol-
steaders; rattle-toothed almsters; gout-footed Shriners; tiny birdheaded
clerks in red suspenders; supposititious chamberers of commerce; pul-
lulating boosters; and cretinous, peasant-like Colin Clouts on every
street corner who slunched against poles squinting and chewing down
toothpicks in a slow watchful rhythm.

Growing depressed, Miss Trappe suggested she resume showing
Darconville the town she simultaneously warned him against, arguing,
convincingly, that a writer in staying too long would go mad there.
The suicide rate in Quinsyburg, she said, was—she stopped and, in
the reflection of a window, retied under her chin the wide straw hat.

"High?"

The crabapple wrinkled. "Astronomical."

I will stay here for only a year, thought Darconville, and try to do
my work. He told Miss Trappe he'd take the chance, but she told him
that Mrs. Battle said chance is nothing. And yet, he reasoned, wasn't
the price for privacy anonymity? *Un altro, un altro, gran' Dio, ma più
forte.*

They now stood in front of the Wyanoid Baptist Church, a plain
white affair with the usual homiletic menu out front and at the peak
of its steeple, spiritual guerdon to a whole community, a weathervane
in the shape of a metal cricket (has anyone ever figured that one
out?).

Quinsyburg, Va. was one of those places where pulpit and drum ec-
clesiastick were beat with a fist instead of a stick, and whatever the
persuasion—whether Wycliffites, Old Order Dunkers, Stundo-
Baptists, or the International Church of the Foursquare Gospel—
religion was religion as long as it had been scoured of any whim or
wishet that flirted with Rome or ritual or racial equality. It was, in
fact, a reactionary little town filled with stiff-nosed Galatians, circuit-
riders, and reformers with upsidedown bibles, all looking up hill and
down dale for a chance to save someone's soul. The place teemed with
Presbyters Writ Large, and on every Sunday this very church, become
a hotbed of tracasseries and dissent, swelled to overflowing with singing, ringing wonglers, diehards from the U.D.C. looking for fellowship, and hundreds of bag-in-hand geriatrics with voices like hoopoes
who preferred their theology muscular, their ministers mousy, and
their church quite definitely in the majority.

Darconville bent forward to read the little marquee—and cocked an eyebrow. It read:

Sermon
"Did God Wink?" (Acts 17:30)
W. C. Cloogy, Pastor and Evangelist
Wyanoid Baptist Church
Bethel of Blessings

God help us, thought Darconville, who quite frankly, if somewhat surprisingly, had yet to be convinced that the Edict of Nantes hadn't perhaps caused more trouble on earth than original sin.

Darconville and Miss Trappe hadn't gone two feet when a woman came suddenly shooting out of the side-door of the church. She looked like the wife of a manciple, frazzled, with shocked eyes. Clutching a fistful of pamphlets, she identified herself as an evangelist's helper and quickly began batsqueaking about God's love, in support of which topic she swiftly presented to each one of her little tracts: "Crumbs from My Table" by W. C. Cloogy, Evangelist. As all three stood there, two bewildered, the third—intense with eyeshine—spontaneously improvised a wee sermonette on The Deluge, she playing Noah, her voice the animals it knew, and the air was soon filled with a most ingenious array of barks, oinks, croaks, snarls, cheeps, and moos, all articulating the same curious complaint, that this world was too corrupt and wretched to live in, the unavoidable implication of which seemed to be that the lesser creatures of this earth shared, if not the same size or shape, then at least the same agony and accent. And when, she asked, would they make their assent to faith? Did they know Jesus for their personal savior? Were they willing to be born again?

And, pray, were they in need of revival?

Revival? The word sprouted a capital letter. It was bad enough, thought Darconville, to suggest anything to perfect strangers, but to dare to suggest one of those punk kick-ups and premillennial antihomologoumena? He had a sudden vision of all those bible-thumping wompsters, unscrupulous sharpers, and pigeon-faced decretalicides who, having weaseled into the narrow existentialate of the American South, had for so long impunitively burked reason, honesty, and truth and set up false gods to whom, like rats toward platters of meazled pork, the illiterate *faex populi* had swarmed only to be bilked, beg-

gared, and buccaneered right on the spot. Was that religion? Miss
Trappe, agreeing, said she would rather take her own life—at least
that way, she added, she would not need to be scared anymore about
what would happen if she didn't. They walked away in silence.

Then Miss Trappe adjusted her spectacles, waited until her optic
axes grew coincident, and took one last painful look to the far end of
Main St. She shook her head.

"You know," she said, "a thought just crossed my feeble old mind,
dear."

"Yes?"

"Well," offered Miss Trappe, "the act of committing suicide may
be very easy."

Darconville gently took her arm.

"When you do it," she said, shrugging and looking up at him with
eyes pale as air, "just simply pretend it isn't you!"

There was nothing Darconville could find to say, search his heart
though he might. They slipped behind the courthouse and walked
through an alley past the Quinsyburg jail where, high above their
heads, they both noticed a series of black fists gripping the bars of the
grills. A lonesome song drifted from one of the cells across the afternoon.

> "What a beautiful mornin' that will be,
>   Let my people go;
> When time breaks up in eternity,
>   Let my people go."

Miss Trappe halted again on the edge of a thought, the shadow of
the building darkening her face. She looked up at him like Van Eyck's
pinchfaced Arnolfini in horizontal hat, and as Darconville again took
her arm—the skin seemed to crumble between his fingers, like burial
earth—she stared past him and placed a finger on her chin.

"And you know, the strangest thing of all is," said she, "you may
not even have to pretend."

It was clear, Darconville now saw, that from her lugubrious pro-
nouncements Miss Trappe had seen to more terrible depths than the
town at first glance afforded, and, asking her various questions, he
began to learn more of what oppressed her. Quinsyburg was a closed
account. It was a place, apparently, reduced to total irrelevance, to

terms that, while having fallen to the category of the tedious and the negligible, were yet maintained in the hollowness of their churchianity, the religion, deportmentalized and moralistic, of the Prodigal Son's brother, and reinforced in a terrible irony of reciprocity by the cynical and nonconformist whingeings of Luther, Melanchthon, Bucer, Pomeranus, Knox, Flacius Illyricus, and various other sons of revolt. If it seemed, at first, the kind of town that customarily salted its appeal with a sort of grassroots neighborliness, the notion didn't last. Insiders were in, outsiders out. When and if friendship were shown, she said, it was the type of loving-kindness that uncomfortably verged on tyranny. They wanted not so much to convince you of their opinions as to deprive you of your own, and typical of so many other one-crop regions that had taprooted out of the normal world—pockets of homogeneity bypassed by culture and change—most of its townsfolk were in the grip of an acute xenophobia that filled the vocabularies of their villageois language with a repetition of paranoid they/them pronouns and convinced them that beyond the particular borders of their town spread the etceterated sloughs of godlessness where people drank swipes, backslid, and gambled away their wives. They stuck together in the same way that piranhas, seeing certain maculate spots of identification, would not attack each other. Politically, the community was so far to the Right it jimmied the Left. In terms of actual religious belief, Quinsyburg's, oxymoronically, was in fact a *civic* faith, for spiritual obligation had devolved to the concept of good citizenry, a *quo ad sacra* invariably performed as an endorsement for, and in the name of, the American Way of Life. Knowledge to them was the parent of malice. Ideas they met with derision, truth with suspicion, and differences with fear. For any other way of life one couldn't raise their temperatures a therm. They lived, they knew, the way it was done, and the devil, the great disturber of our faith in this world, couldn't raise in the townsfolk there one scruple whatsoever leading to alternatives. They will be there yesterday. They were there tomorrow. They are.

Miss Trappe dodged into a dark overheated little store, bought her paper, and they continued on past the Quinsyburg post-office—the walls within painted over in flat WPA murals: frigid square-jawed men in overalls, holding trowels and staring off at horizons—and cut over by a semi-residential area toward the back of the college. The

houses, large and desolate, were all clapboarded egg-brown affairs
with sunken porches overcome with wisteria, an eruption of domicil-
iary pasteboards rising up in shingled capuches, far too close together,
and although the curtains were always pulled one could almost look
through them by way of imagination to see hooded furniture; engrav-
ings of stags in the hallways; perhaps an obsolete oil stove; a clawfoot
bathtub upstairs (with elongated orange stains under the faucets); a
single bookshelf, with copies of Law's *Serious Call,* Doddridge's *Rise
and Progress,* Orton's *Discourse on the Aged,* etc., and some poor
someone sitting in a calico apron, shelling peas, or all alone in the
darkness of a backroom, desperately praying for forgiveness.

The streets suddenly were then no longer paved. There were, in
fact, no streets at all, only stamped-out paths of red Virginia soil winding through low scrubby bushland into an outdistrict, poor, rundown,
aimless, that dropped away to an alfalfa field ballpark, where the trees
were the color of dirty money and the dust sifted into your shoes like
talc. Rusted old cars were humped on blocks in narrow driveways.
Tarpaper hatcheries were wired smack up to the tilted wooden shacks
that had either dirt or puncheon floors, no front doors, and through
the dim breezeways drifted the odors of frying bread, simmering
collards, and sweet potato pone. It was the black ghetto.

Most of the shacks had no indoor plumbing, and the listing
outhouses in the back of each yard had simply been clapped together
with dull, misshapen planks. There were pipe chimneys, makeshift
windows, covered in plasti-sheet, and broken stairs, a pauperization—
the direct result of racism in Quinsyburg—that kept the blacks, because poor, servile. It was a little world of fatigue, inanition, and
wasted minds. Quinsyburg, only a few years previous, had closed its
schools for half a decade rather than integrate, simultaneously building a private white academy, notwithstanding federal pressure, to
maintain racial purity. The blacks were forced into separate schools,
separate churches, and even a separate cemetery. The rents were
adjusted: if a black family aspired to fix up its house, that meant it
had money; if it had money, that meant not only a decrease in
servility—"uppityness"—but also that it could pay more rent. An
adjusted rent cured that. It was a "ceiling" theory, for people who
had no ceilings. Indeed, they hadn't much of anything. They lived
out their lives as they had for centuries, cutting up logs, washing toi-

lets, scrubbing doorways, and quietly knocking on white folks' back-doors with a nickel to ask if the noise of their old gear-hobbing lawn-mowers would disturb the peace of the nobles inside.

The afternoon sun began to turn coppery as Darconville and Miss Trappe crossed downhill toward the ring-road. Old sambos, with nap-kins on their heads, sat on their warped cane-chairs and waved, while out front little black girls—their hair braided in corn-row tight plaits, their legs ashen—either played with their pedaps or skipped barefoot, hand in hand, to the Piggly Wiggly for gumballs. A few young men sloped back from the A.B.C. liquor store with bottles of fruit wine in crinkled bags and joked as they passed doorways where buxom young mothers in bandanas, looking away as they smiled, rocked their car-riages with one foot and gave pieces of fatback to their children for pacifiers. There was a life here that would forever go on unchanged, immutable to pain, to policy, to the passing of pleasure, and there was perhaps in the constancy of it all, if finally in nothing else, at least something on which they could depend.

A loud chorus of "Lift Every Voice and Sing" could be heard from the small mal-shingled Negro church that suddenly came into view be-tween several live-oaks and beyond which, as Darconville and Miss Trappe turned, the two large dormitories of Quinsy College rose across a half mile or so of woodland. The bell in the church's squat steeple was bonging slowly, a mournful, solitary peal that seemed, echo upon echo, to get lost in the sunshine and become, ironically, the more forsaken. A group of phantom ladies in weepers, supporting each other, began to leave the church. They were crying, trying to stifle sobs with their handkerchiefs. What could have happened?

Detective, Miss Thelma Trappe stood stock-still in the middle of a hunch. She went suddenly skewbacked, unflapping her copy of the *Quinsyburg Herald,* and ran her eyes over the front page. She turned to page two. She turned to page three. She turned to page four, bent down, newt-eyed, and sighed. Looking over her shoulder, Darconville followed her finger—for she never said a word—to a simple photo-graph. It was the quizzical face of a spoon-headed black boy, about thirteen years old, and underneath were given brief reportorial facts: name, age, address, place of burial. He had been struck and instantly killed the day previous by a hit-and-run pickup truck at the corner of Main and High streets. The several witnesses from the Timberlake, dominoists by avocation, could give no description of the driver, so the sheriff closed the investigation. It was only God's way, he no doubt felt, of turning a leaf in the Book of Eternal Decrees.

"Precisely," said Miss Trappe.

Darconville heard the irony but kept counsel, feeling only the vibrations of her increased step in awkward silence as she stumped along homeward, pausing only to eye the sky at intervals from under her wide hat as if searching the heavens for any indication of justice or balance, a clue, of any degree, to the moderating power of the universe, some kind of proof of the stamp celestial. They were soon not far from the street where they'd first begun their walk when Darconville's companion decided to speak.

"I lost my stepmother in the same way," said Miss Trappe, her little mouth trembling. She tried, unsuccessfully, to shape her hands— carelessly hopping up—to an attitude of resignation. "She was coming home at dusk with several just-packed jars of autumn honey and was run down by a passing motorist, who simply drove on." Her eyes were filling up, her hat quivering. "She was not killed right away—the report from the hospital was that she kept feverishly repeating, 'My honey. My honey.' Just that. 'My honey.' I mustn't fail to tell you, Darconville," sobbed Miss Trappe, "I was neither the pretty nor the favored child, but how I ran—" She gasped to breathe out pain. "—ran to her." She smiled up through a runnel of tears. "Hearts," she said, "was Mrs. Battle's favorite suit." And wiping a tear from her pitted nose, she repeated, " 'My honey.' " She swallowed. "I wanted to believe, you know, that she was asking for me."

"She *was* calling you."

Miss Trappe lifted up two little gerbil eyes and simply shook her head. Her nose was dripping. And as Darconville took her hand, soft as bird's-eye, she heaved up the sorrow weltering in her heart. "No," she wept, "she said she never loved me, then *screamed* it, Darconville, laying there like dead metal, she scre—" Darconville's heart almost misgave. "I was s-so ashamed," she whispered into his chest with a tiny humiliated voice, shattering with sobs, *"I completely w-wet myself, all over."*

Weeping to her feet, she suddenly turned her face up defiantly toward the sky and looked with a hideous grimace into infinity, as if to say not balanced yet, O crafty universe, not balanced yet.

It became impossible to think. Darconville could say nothing: so overcome with pity, he could find no words adequate to consolation and knew beyond reason that any poor stuttering attempt on his own part must fall terribly short, for touching things sometimes can only be felt, and yet before he could make any show of what he felt, she kissed him on the neck, turned her little crabapple of a head toward the westering sun, and then disappeared over the hill like a dot.

V

Were There Reasons to Believe That in
Quinsyburg
Visionaries, Fabulists, Hilarodists, and
Hermeneuts Would Suffer the Dooms,
Chastisements, and Black Draughts of a
Depression They Otherwise Didn't Deserve
and Deteriorate Utterly?

Ample.

V I

President Greatracks Delivers

"He hath builded towers of superarrogation in his owne head."

—Gabriel Harvey, *Pierces Supererogation*

"College! There's a little word for you, dear girls, *college:* neatly pronounced, pronounced as spelt, and correctly spelt s-a-c-r-i-f-i-c-e—the battle cry of the United States of God Bless America! And who's telling y'all this, some up-spoutin' no account dingdong in a string tie pointing his head out in the direction of his face and looking for to impress you? Exactly wrong! It's a man who knows what sacrifice means, and costs! Now, button back your ears, little cousins, for I only aim to say it once—I know all the tricks, every last one of them, and unless someone out there can tell me how a brown cow can eat green grass, give white milk, and make yellow butter, she best just sit down tight and listen, OK? I been evywhere but the moon and seen evything but the wind. I been to the edge of the world and looked over. I mean, I can fight, shout, win, lose, draw, turn on a dime, and meet you coming back for change, you hear? Good, now you mark time on that and we gone get somewhere."

IT WAS PRESIDENT GREATRACKS, the college headmaster, a man fat as a Fugger: a bun, a ham, a burgher. He was a charming and resourceful academic illiterate, politically appointed, his brain a *pot-au-feu* of boomism, bad grammar, and prejudice, his face very like that of the legendary Leucrota whose mouth opened as far as its ears. The school auditorium was decked out for the opening assembly, with all eyes fixed on the keynote speaker. He showed the conviction of a roundhead, and, having traversed the dais with an oafish and peasant-like lumber that betrayed his grim-the-collier background, he bulked now over the lectern around which had been slung a banner lettered in blue and white

QUINSY
WELCOMES
YOU

and then hamfistedly fussbudgeted back and forth in a suit the color of sea-fowl guano, wagging a finger like Elijah the Tishbite and trooping out his dockets, posits, and quiddits like a costermonger his pippins.

"When I was a little wagpasty of a lad back in Free Union, Va. in them days of the De-pression, which you wouldn't know about, my tiny ol' mammy wore galoshes, used thorns for fishhooks, and buck-washed me in a hopper. We were so poor we couldn't even pay attention, and it was a dang holiday, nothin' else, just to go and play stoopball with the swivel-eyed halfwit next door or hop along down to the grocery to splurge on a box of penny chicle.

"I worked the nubs off my little fingers for wages the coloreds laughed at, trundled out of bed at dawn like a filthy sweep, blinking and looking for the life of me just as white and hairless as a egg, a little eyesore in my mussed overhalls and my sweater hind-side-to—so low I had to reach up to touch bottom—and not a soul, but for mammy, who had a good word to say to me. But you are what you are and you ain't what you ain't, right? We thanked the good Lord, and thanked Him and how! School-rooms? Who said anything about schoolrooms? Shoot, no one thought of them, sir! Only thing I knew was my 15¢ Dicky Deadlight picture book—that is, until mammy took me in tow to learn me my devotions and reading. And if I didn't oblige the dear thing? Why, she caned me scarlet in the attic and set me to kneel on peppercorns for punishment, and if you think that tickles! I want to tell you, many's the night—

O, it seems like yesterday!—I sat up into the wee hours in my ripped jim-jams, my eyes pinched tight from candlesmoke, going over and over again the sentences in my mustard-colored copy of Edward Clodd's *Tom, Tit, Tot*. But, dagnabbit, I got my sums, didn't I? I got my Bible, didn't I?"

Greatracks rose up like a huge fat glyptodont, capitalizing every word with his voice. He chop-gestured. He beckoned to the ceiling. He took oaths and blew air and circled his arms, all with a jumped-up and inquisitorious duncery that thumbfumbled truth and opened up a museum of bygone pictorial mediocrities which magnified puddles by rhetoric into blue fairy lakes and fobbed off hawks for handsaws.

"Now, I'm telling you all this for a mighty good reason, girls—and paying it no mind, you'll find me as unsociable a creature as ever chawed gum, I guarandamntee you! At Quinsy College here, it's either fish or cut bait. Ain't enough *insurance* in this here world better than perspiration, which means nothin' more than good ol' sweat to right-thinkin' folks, which is just what you better be aimin' to be, hear? Yes? Then stand on it! I mean, I want everybody—*evahbody!*—on automatic here! You mope. You get bounced. You get up to tomfoolery. You gone tom-foolerize yourself right out into the street, see?

"Why, only last year, now to mention it, one of those self-important lit-tle undergraduate cinderbritches with a cheek rubied like a dang poppy pads into my office fixin' to have at me, see, stands there wheel-high to a rubbish truck, and then comes out with, 'I'm fed up with college!' I remember standing there amazed, thinking *what* the sam hill? *What the tarnation hell?* O no. Said she was hangin' it up. Said, shoot, she couldn't care a straw for book-learnin', not me, no, I'm a big shot—failin' to real-ize, course, feelin' sorry for herself and walkin' around on her lip, that what she really wanted was a 7 × 9 patch over her mouth! The poor little trapes, obviously humble of brain, mistook college for the handball court or your Five County Fair. I about died—*dahd!* Well, I read her the dang riot act for starters and then helped her into tomorrow with a kick strong enough to knock a billygoat off a gut-wagon! She spelled college f-u-n, see, which is no kind of spelling at all. It's mis-spelling is what it is. *Mis*-dang-spelling! And if you yourself ain't wrapped too tight, I best remind you to prepare for the same kind of treatment, girls, or there ain't a hog in Georgia, 'cause it's only fifteen inches between a slap on the back and a swift kick on the place you wear no hat!"

Perspiring, President Greatracks—wailing like a preaching jebusite and orthonational—drove in with his industrio-protestant creedal for-mulations: a clattering windmill of cheerings up, pep tonics, across-the-fence chat, and general protrepticos, fanning, in crisis, all those who, in asking, seeking, or knocking would receive, find, or have it opened unto them. The volume of gas increased, according to physical principle, as his temperature did the same.

"At Quinsy, we have no truck whatsoever with those so-called Northern, well, *views* and, that being the case, aren't so all-fired anxious for revolution, evolution, devolution or any other damn lution y'all want to come up with! I've seen the lot of them, sneakin' around the campus at night with beards like Stalin had and sandwich-boards broadcastin' 'Freedom!' or 'Down with God and His Saints!'—all of them socialists, won't-work liberals, and bleedin' heart sombitches—high-steppin' like coons and tryin' to turn this place redder than a hawberry with their radical Commie bushwa! Sowin' discord! Havin' into the coop! Huh? Prit-near right, ain't I? You better know it. Shoot, I could quote you chapter and verse!"

His fat body shook like a balatron, as if his soul, biting for anger at a mouth inadequately circumferential, desired in vain to fret a passage through it. He blated. He blaterated. He blaterationed. Out blasted a flash of oratorical n-rays and impatient oons while the echoes of his voice, pitched high, strident, like the hellish sounds of Vergil's Alecto, drumbeat through the auditorium and went right to the pit of the stomach.

"You see that majestic piece of dry goods with the stars-and-stripes hanging yonder? That speak to you of revolution? The deuce, I say! And it aggravokes me like you wouldn't believe to see these pseudo-intellectual puddingheads—every one of them dumb as a felt boot—buddyin' up to Moscow! Well, put you in mind, we don't hold with this down South here. Eskimos eat the refuse out of their pipestems! Japs fry ice-cream! Them little puck-faced Zuñi Indians from Mexico drink their urine! Polish dogs bark like this: 'Peef! Peef!' And instead of sayin' hello in Tibet I'm told the poor jinglebrains just stick out their tongues and hold up their thumbs! That mean we do it? Huh? *Think!*

"The Southran way, cousins, is the way *we* aim to follow. Item: we study here. Item: we won't walk around here lookin' like boiled owls. Item: we'll be sticking it through until we ain't got enough strength to blow the fuzz off a peanut, and then we'll work some more! Thread and thrumme! *Don't* study and your chances of stayin' here are between slim and none—and slim is on a plane-ride to Tahiti, you got it? I see any of them irritating thimbleheads, house-proud pippins, and intellectual willopus-wallopuses around here with signboards and complaints, and it's goodbye Quinsy, hello world, and that's a promise, sisters, that is a *prom-*

ise! You have to get up early, remember, to get out of bed. Now, I always close with a quote from my favorite author of books, one Arthur de Gobineau, a European person who once said, '*Attaquez! Attaquez! Attaquez!*' which means attack, of course—in French. Gaze boldly into the past and put the future behind you. Don't let your brains go to your heads. You'll thank yourself someday—don't mind thanking me, I don't count. Now welcome to Quinsy College, hear?"

It was a rhetoric that would have taxed Quintilian himself: a few final admonitions, accompanied by several rumplestiltskinian stamps of anger—for the particular hardcore few who, he thought, could not understand an order unillumined by force—emphasized the need at the school of what his very manner contravened, but this was by the by, for he had clearly argued himself into a state of such broad magisterial cheek that he was virtually beyond not only the accusation of such vulgarity but also beyond its being adduced, in the same way that, philosophically, at the exact moment of offense defense is clearly immoment. Not Berosus with tongue of gold was he, neither silver-throated Solon, rather a moody-sankeyan yammerer from the old school who, finishing now, wound down to the conclusion that made up in volume what it lacked in finesse. He jerked his head forward with one last glare, beady as a vole's, then picked up his clatter of clenches, abstersives, and cephalalgics and thumped out into the wings on his monstrous feet.

One daring little beast in the back row frowned, held her nose, and said, *"Puke."*

VII

Quinsy College

A hen is only an egg's way of making another egg.

—SAMUEL BUTLER

QUINSY COLLEGE, est. 1839, was a quaint old respectable school for girls. It stood in the seminary tradition of the female academy: a chaste academic retreat, moral as peppermint, built in semi-colonial red brick and set back in a deep green delling where, alone—at least so felt the Board of Visitors (ten FFVs with swimming eyes, three names, and hands with liverspots)—one's daughter could be lessoned in character and virtue without the indecent distractions that elsewhere, everywhere else, wherever led to vicious intemperance, Bolshevism, and free thought. There were other girls' schools in the area —Falcon Hall, Longwood College, St. Bunn's—but none was quite so singular as Quinsy.

It had been strictly private years ago, one of those dame schools in the South, usually called something like Montfaucon or Thirlwood or Miss Tidy's Establishment for Young Ladies and run by a woman with a name like Miss Monflathers, a bun-haired duchess of malfeasance from the English-Speaking Union who was given to wearing sensflectum crinolines and horsehair jupon and whipping her girls at night. At the turn of the century, however, Quinsy came under state receivership and, although suffering the shocks of democracy, remained yet blind to change. It was an institution, still, whose expressed intention was to diminish in distance and time the dangers of creeping modernity and with prudes for proctors and dowagers for deans to produce girls tutored in matters not only academic but on subjects touching on the skillet, the needle, and, though strangers yet to pain, even the nursery, a matter, it was confidentially given out, not unrelated to that regrettable but thankfully fleeting moment during which they would simply have to bite on a bullet and endure.

A legendary respect for the Southern lady—doubt it who dares!— was all through the histories. The War Between the States proved it. Robbed they might have been, subjected to privation, yes, and burned out of hearth and home, but NEVER once had they been set upon by masked outlaws, howling and rapacious Negroes, or drunken Yankee soldiers who couldn't see straight anyway. And would you perchance like to know why? Their *manners* protected them. And those same standards of conduct would always prevail in the South.

The Quinsy handbook—a little bluebird-colored affair which bore on its cover the sphragistic of a dove rising through hymeneal clouds and carrying a banner with the college motto, "We Preach, You Teach"—codified behavior for the girls. They were not merely to have a type-and-file appearance. They were asked to wear white gloves pouring tea, to perfume the wrists, and to maintain custody of the eyes. They were advised to tithe, to avoid boisterous hats, and to use the neglected herb, cerfeuil. They were asked neither to lisp, squint, wink, talk loud, look fierce or foolish nor bite the lips, grind the teeth, speak through the nose, nor guffle their soup. They were encouraged, on the other hand, to sew turkeywork, to refer to their young men as "gentlemen callers," and to accumulate, with a view to future use, egg-frames, salvers, muffineers, and knife-rests. Above all, they were to familiarize themselves with the history of the school.

The Virginian's was a record of which to be proud. Tradition! Cus-

tom! History!—a meal of fresh heritables all to be washed down with
flagons of the fermented wine of the past. It was a living heritage.
There were no limits, furthermore, to the historicogeographical importance of Quinsyburg itself, and it had long been a matter of great
pride to the townsfolk there to reflect on the fact that Mr. Jefferson,
once stopping by overnight, had found the old Timberlake Hotel
"clubbable" and that, in 1865, General Robert E. Lee with his brave
soldiers, on the march from Saylor's Creek to fateful Appomattox,
straggled through this very town, at which time the little sisters of
mercy in the college dorms flew with unspeakable horror to the sides of
the wounded and selflessly gave of themselves, cradling their hurt
heads, applying cupping glasses, plasters, and bandages, and humming
strains of "The Bonnie Blue Flag." But today?

Today was another story. Few even bothered to put flowers on the
Confederate monument anymore. The historical society, its funds
dwindling, had been removed to a room over the theatre. And who
ever took time anymore to visit the rare-book room in Smethwick Library where Miss Pouce, not without effort, had carefully gathered in
a row of glass cases all that Quinsy memorabilia? It was primarily a
collection of old photographs, gum bichromate prints, and bent plat-
inotypes preserving the memory of so many dear girls, a thousand
blushing apparitions, who would later go on to make their mark in the
world, whether in the cause of society, Stopesism, or the suffragettes:
a group of languorous girls, sitting cross-legged with hockey sticks,
staring into the middle distance with eyes pale as air and jelly-soft
cheeks; one dear thing, oversized, rolling a hoop somewhere; two
husky tsarinas posed humorlessly on the old athletic field pointing in
mid-turn to a third with a faint mustache and a bewildered expression mis-gripping a croquet mallet, one high-buttoned shoe poised on
a small striped ball; a marvelous wide-angle shot, none the worse for
time, of forty or so students in bombazine—Quinsy girls all!—trooping like mallards in pious, if pointless, gyrovagation along the path of
a field called now, as then, "The Reproaches"; and many many
others. (Miss Pouce had secretly boxed three of the lot, offensive ones
which she kept down with the discards in the basement: one, a girl in
a droopy bag swimsuit à la Gertrude Ederle pitching off a diving
board, certain of her parts having been circled in neurotoxified purple
ink by some poor twisted Gomorrhite years ago; and two others,
shamelessly thumbed, showing (1) three girls in chemistry lab smirk-

ing into the camera while they held up a guttapercha object of unambiguous size and shape and (2) the same girls but one—and she, in
the distance, screaming with laughter, and the object gone.) Smethwick was open until 10 P.M. It would be 9 P.M. on Saturdays, the rare-
book room, of course, by appointment only. Miss Pouce would be ever
so pleased if you came by. Had no one such time for things anymore?

That was a fair question, for if Quinsyburg had a wealth of anything it was certainly time, and, beyond that—as the handbook so
sagely put it—didn't sloth, like rust, consume faster than labor wears,
with the key that's often used remaining always bright?

The girls in that little gradus, if they paid attention, had their rules
for life. The most trifling actions, they were reminded, if good, increased their credit but if bad became a matter, when done, no apology could rectify. They were not to fork for bread, dry their underpinnings by the fire, leave lip-prints on drinking glasses, touch the teeth
with the tines of a fork, use rampant witticism, stipple the shower
stalls, nor effect shadowgraphs with the fingers at the Saturday movie,
neither were they ever to thrust out the tongue, sigh aloud, gape, swap
underwear, eat fish with the knife, use French words as that is apt to
grow fatiguing, nor cultivate mimicry which was the favorite amusement of little minds. They must never strike out wantonly nor snip
their nails in public, neither hawk, spit, sniff, crack fleas nor drum
their fingers. They were asked not to jerk their hair out of their eyes
nor sip audibly nor effect the branch of a tree for walking purposes
nor indicate assent or dissent by motions of the head, as was the wont
of Northern girls. Neither must they spit on their irons, crunch on
cracknels, use primroses for floral decoration, say rude things like "Stir
your stumps!" or "Tarnation!" or mutter anything whatsoever disrespectful about the universe. In sharply turning a corner, coming suddenly in contact with another, they had already abused a right. They
were not to whistle, toast cheese in their rooms, make memorandum
knots in their handkerchiefs, wangle their fingers during conversation,
or indulge in parades of learning, for they would surely live to see
verified that a woman who is negligent at twenty will be a sloven at
forty, intolerable at fifty, and at sixty a hopeless mental case. To flee
affectation and to be circumspect that she offend no gentleman caller
in her jesting and taunting, to appear thereby of a ready wit, was,
above all, paramount.

There was, of course, this business of young men, a matter nearest

their hearts because most agreeable to their ambitions, for a Southern
girl without a man was like a pushwainling without wheels. Southern
boys, superintended parent and patron alike, must be polished at all
points and trained correctly lest they flag in those battles for which
they were now in the very preparation, whether against the enemy
agents of this country or in behalf of Southern ideals, of which the
girls at Quinsy College, and like schools, were the most charming
synecdoche, and while there was a generous plenty—an epidemic, in
fact—of prep schools and Presbyterian colleges all over Virginia, anti-
intellectual rest homes which taught overadvantaged quidnuncs how
to wear rep ties and smile, the closest parallel to the female academy,
juxtaposing chivalry with charm, was the military academy.

Virginia is famous for its many military academies. All, in point of
fact, are one. It is at best a technique mine of Prussian fanaticism, an
encampment of stibnite-colored barracks and halls sticking up dolefully in the middle of acres of castrate lawns, and, as advertised, usually in the rearward pages of national magazines—always showing either a little chevalier midway over a baffle or some lost, disappointed
boy, too old for his age, staring out in parade dress—it is invariably
named something like Stirrup-and-Halter Hall or St. Bugle's Academy
or Furlongville and run by a man called Colonel Forksplit, a vole-eyed
martinet with a back straight as a Hepplewhite chair and a mouthful
of sententious stories, all lies, about Stonewall Jackson's boyhood. His
charges—you can always see them standing alone, glum, in the Washington, D.C. bus terminals after holidays—must adhere to the regimental uniform which is nothing more than a bit of jerry jingle stolen
from the Yeomen of the Guard. But uniforms have plenty of buttons,
and Southern girls, whose adoration for uniforms must be listed, after
amour-propre, as the most pronounced regional hobble against the
First Commandment, *always* hold you by the button when they speak
to you.

Were Quinsy girls, then, familiarized with all the social graces,
schooled to realize that by a failure of either fashion or forthputfulness
it might very well cost them an M.R.S. degree?

The handbook, encouraging power without aggression, covered all
contingencies. The caveats were long and letter-perfect. They were
never to dip sippets, lap stamps, or chew gum, and upon the occasion
of being invited to dine out to wear dotted Swiss, eat little, and
remember that one variety of meat and one kind of vegetable was the

maximum. At least one half of the fare, a sop of grace to gluttony, must be left in the plate. They were told that game bones must never be lifted to the mouth nor strenuously attacked, scraped, or twirled. They were always to use palliatives when giving opinions of consequence and yet, at the same time, encouraged to shape the gentlemen callers who were over-saucy with them, or who had small respect in their talk, such an answer that they may well understand they were offended with them, not so sharply, however, that the escort be irrevocably turned away. They were asked not to crake or boast, not to use any fond sauciness or presumption but, if dancing, say, to dance well without over-nimble footings or too busy tricks—and it was advised they neither reverse in waltzing nor dip.

Curtseying was encouraged, as long as every girl remembered that there have been many women who have owed their ruin to an awkward attempt at such. She was counseled against shingling the hair, sipping audibly, effecting a need in public for toilet facilities, and always, in instance without number, to take heed that she give none the occasion to make ill report of her, whereupon, for example, if she went riding, she must never ride astride, whoop untowardly, or button the third button of the hacking jacket. The carriage of a young lady must, at all times, be respectful without meanness, easy without familiarity, genteel without affectation, and insinuating without design. Finally, they were asked not to speak of themselves, for nothing could ever be said to varnish one's defects nor add luster to one's virtues, whereas, on the contrary, it would only make the former more visible and the latter more obscure. She who lived upon talk would die fasting. Good manners will minister to the shop, and the shop will minister to thee. "Industry," as Stonewall Jackson once precociously lisped to his mother from his bassinet, "needs not wish."

Quinsy College would not only endure, but prevail. It had before in times of trial and would again. Its policies, fashioned out of an impatience with this new age of permissiveness, said it all, with this hope expressed, this continuity dearly wished, that in such schools—with the laws of both discipline and decorum meted out by the best teachers of *bienséance*—there would surely be an eventual return to the good old American Way. Had times changed? They had, yes, they had indeed, but if President Greatracks himself, as he so often said, had to patrol the campus by night in specially made sneakers snooping for socialists, so be it! Had customs changed? They had, yes, but if one

could no longer catch a glimpse, as in days of yore, of Southern belles
holding parasols, wearing frilled bonnets, and tripping across lawns in
fragile blue-and-white prints with handkerchief-pointed tiers of feminine chiffon and cascades of quivering ruffles, it didn't matter—they
were still worshipfully kept alive in the rotogravure section of every
true Virginian's heart. Had laxity set in? Yes, yes, yes, laxity, slackness,
looseness! It was the age. But if ideals were honored more in the
breach than in the observance nowadays, it took nothing more than a
quick look up at the college rotunda to have one's faith restored, for
there the flag still flew. The *American* flag, sir!

The flag, indeed, still flew. And yet a paradox presented itself, for
the democracy which that flag represented was somehow the same
democracy that the admission board, the administration, and the
alumni were under jurisdiction, sometimes, in fact, by federal writ, to
oblige—resulting in a perceptible latitudinarianism which included,
among other things, extended curfews, widening of student privileges,
faculty raises, the lowering of entrance requirements (two new high-
rise dorms had to be filled) and now a consideration for the actual
admission of *black* students!

The South was trying to rise again. But where was the yeast? "Freedom," as President Greatracks had said on many occasions, "is all
very well and good, but—"

VIII

Hypsipyle Poore

Do what thou wilt, thou shalt not so,
Dark Angel! triumph over me:
Lonely, unto the Lone I go;
Divine, to the Divinity.

—LIONEL JOHNSON, "The Dark Angel"

"I *NEED* IT!"

"That's a lot of pudding, miss."

"I'm signing up, anyway."

"The course, I told you yesterday, is *not* open to seniors," exclaimed Mrs. McAwaddle, the registrar, her mouth cemented shut against the possibility of further discourse.

"My daddy," the girl drawled, charging through in interruption and waving a slip of paper, "had the dean on the telephone last night. Now, y'all want to read this?"

The student, obviously used to exacting compliance, was an arresting young beauty in sunglasses with a soft pink sweater, raven-black hair cut to perfection, and a pout of wet lipstick that made her mouth look like a piece of candy. She stepped back, unvanquished, and seemed satisfied to wait, speaking to no one but admiring from a corner the indisposition of the other girls there who were trying to arrange their schedules during the first discouraging days of registration. They shuffled about in determined little squads with drop/add cards, course syllabi, and countless papers to have signed and stamped.

The room was warm, sticky, from the crowding bodies, but the girls, somehow, all smelled of fresh soap and mint-flavored gum. They were Southern girls, after all, and unlike their counterparts in other sections of the country whose morning beauty, from the normal wear-and-tear of a day, too easily faded only to be carelessly ignored, they tried to keep powder-room perfect and as presentable as possible. And, after all, this time there was a man present in the room.

"Some people can just whistle and wait," snapped Mrs. McAwaddle, going jimmy-jawed. A mite of a thing, resembling the perky little owl commonly depicted resting on the hand of Minerva, she was wearing a dress covered with hearts. She spindled a card angrily and looked up at the man who'd been standing there for some time. And now. His name? His business?

"Darconville," he said, smiling.

The girl with the black hair, waiting behind him, took a crystal vial out of her handbag (tooled in studs: "H.P.") and, closing her eyes, sprayed a musky lavender fragrance around her perfect, prematurely formed silhouette, waxen as a delicate shell.

"Ah, of course," beamed the owl of Minerva, "the new professor." They laughed together. "And I do believe I detect a Yankee accent?"

Darconville asked about his courses. He had met his freshmen already but hadn't yet been given the list.

"Your freshman class list? O dear," muttered Mrs. McAwaddle. Apparently, it had been forced into more revisions than a Dixiecrat caucus and so laid aside. She searched a tray, lifted up a snow water-ball of glass, and then shot open an acidgreen file-cabinet, finally rummaging up the sheets for English 100. He read the first few names on the list:

Muriel Ambler
Melody Blume
Ava Caelano
Wroberta Carter
Barbara Celarent
Analecta Cisterciana

"Would you let me," smiled Mrs. McAwaddle, her little head at a prayerful angle, "admire your coat?" Several girls nearby exchanged glances and winked. Darconville's coat people loved. Cut to princely lines, it was an English chesterfield as black as the black swan of Juvenal. "I do declare, if this isn't the most dashing—but here," she added, hunching up to the desk, "there's an ever-so-small tear here, by that button." She patted his hand. "Now you have your wife mend that and—"

Darconville leaned forward and, like Wotan consulting a weaving norn, whispered with a close smile, "I am not married."

Mrs. McAwaddle stared a moment—and then, with a conspiratorial wink, motioned him into a side-room off the registrar's office where under a portrait of Jefferson Davis a purple-stained mimeograph machine went *bwam-bwam-bwam,* spitting out single sheets of copy. Conventicle gave way to conclave. "Always remember," she said, gripping his wrist, "to a handsome boy like you—how old are you?"

"Twenty-nine."

She made the sound of a pip. "—to a handsome boy like you something wonderful will happen. You'll find a girl to love you as sure as wax candles have wicks." She had lost her own husband, she told him, eight years ago (tainted knockwurst, Jaycee picnic), and now it was just hell dipped in misery. To live alone? When the good Lord created someone for everybody? Ridiculous! "But now," she added, folding his hands in her own, "you be careful: these girls at Quinsy College can work the insides out of a boy without him having a clue and, simple yokums though they may seem, can be the untellinest little commodities on earth. You saw that child out front fussing at me? I could have spit nails. They have nerve to burn."

For the advice of this little hole-in-corner sibyl Darconville was grateful, though he couldn't help but attribute her suspicions to the exigencies of her job, and, excusing himself, he worked his way out of the office, looking up only once: but then to catch, above a blur of fluffy pink, a perfect face unblindfolding slowly from a pair of sunglasses the fire-flash of two beautiful but dangerous eyes in which, he thought, he detected a sly, premeditated smile. He paused in the outer corridor and once again looked at the names entered alphabetically on the list; it read like a spice chart:

> Ailsa Cragg
> Childrey Fawcett
> Galveston Foster
> Scarlet Foxwell
> Opal Garten
> Marsha Goforth
> LeHigh Hialeah
> Elsie Magoun
> Sheila Mangelwurzel

A single name there meant something more than it was: a *symbolum* —both a "sign" and a "confession." But which one was it? Which one was hers? It was curious, his preoccupation, for he'd seen her only once. Inexplicably, however, it mattered, if only for the hardly momentous irony that by knowing it he could then immediately dismiss it and put an end to it all. Her look had injured a silence in his life. The known name might somehow injure the look, and with the look gone the silence could continue, allowing him in consequence and inducing, for diversion, the equanimity to create out of the dormitive world the something out of nothing we call art. There was actually scant attention being paid to this unnamed girl in the upper part of his mind, but in the lower reaches she several times appeared, a thing, rather like the libration of the moon, alternately visible and invisible.

He flipped a sheet and read more names.

> Christie McCarkle
> Trinley Moss
> Glycera Pentlock
> Hallowe'ena Rampling
> Isabel Rawsthorne
> Cecilia Sketchley

Darconville couldn't help but smile. The names seemed absurd, but one didn't really have to spend very much time down South to realize the regional compulsion for this particular extravagance, daily coming upon such weird examples as: Cylvia, Olgalene, Marcelette, Scharlott, Coquetilla, Mavis, Latrina, Weeda and Needa, Mariedythe, Romiette, Coita, Vannelda, Moonean, Rhey, Flouzelle, Balpha, Erdix, Colice, Icel, and Juella, all desperate parental attempts to try to work some kind of sympathetic magic upon their daughters from the very start. And yet how was it that upon hearing them one saw only majorettes, waitresses, and roller-derby queens?

Darconville passed by the refectory (and the odor of mercilessly boiled brussels sprouts) and sat down in a circular room where in the center stood a sculpture of Chapu's Joan of Arc, the college patron. This was known as the Rotunda. The main building at Quinsy College, its egg-shaped interior was a respectable cream-and-green color, open, as it took one's attention higher and higher past two circular balustrades, to a voluminous inner dome covered with fake but sumptuous, over-elaborate, neo-biblical murals in rose and gold. On several walls at ground level, a series of past college presidents, bald and severe, glowered out of their frames. He was still reviewing the list, empty pier-glasses, and pronouncing names, all but hers hostile to him because not hers, but yet none hostile because to him any might be.

> Butone Slocum
> Millette Snipes
> April Springlove
> Lately Thompson
> DeDonda Umpton

The memory had persisted. On an otherwise unexceptional day, for the first time, he'd met that class of freshmen, silent little elves bunched-up and sitting terrible-eyed as they contemplated the four years of college to come. No one had spoken or said so much as a syllable, but all took down the assignment and then the name he'd chalked on the board by way of introduction as if they were borrowing it for some felonious purpose. And then, turning, he had seen the girl, a face out of Domenichino declaiming itself with the supremacy of a mere look that rose like an oriental sun not announced by dawn and setting left no twilight—only the persistent memory of two brown eyes, soft and fraught with soul, imparting a strange kind of consecration. Darconville, looking through the mist of his reverie, then turned from his own idle thoughts and read the last names on the list:

Shelby Uprightly
Martha Van Ramm
Poteet Wilson
Rachel Windt
Laurie Lee Zenker

"Yoo-hoo!" Halfway down the front stairs, Darconville turned back to the voice. It was Mrs. McAwaddle, scooting after him on her tiny slue feet. She was relieved she'd caught up with him, she said, puffing, her hand pressed to her heart. "I'm doing my level best to keep your classes down to a minimum, especially from those"—she handed him a piece of paper—"who have no business being there. The dean has decided to leave the matter up to you."

The particular piece of paper, the formal request of a senior to take his freshman course, was signed by the dean and countersigned in an affected paraph of lavender ink with the name: *Hypsipyle Poore.*

"You remember that child out front fussing at me?" Mrs. McAwaddle shook her head. "They have nerve to burn." And she squeezed Darconville's hand, turned, and trundled away toward her office, one shoulder lower than the other. "Yoo-hoo!" Darconville looked up again to see Mrs. McAwaddle standing on the landing. "Be careful."

Dear Mrs. McAwaddle, wise Mrs. McAwaddle, widowed Mrs. McAwaddle, owlish Mrs. McAwaddle, compassionate Mrs. McAwaddle, Mrs. McAwaddle in her dress of hearts! But how could she know, poor soul, that it was entirely someone else who was on his mind and to whom that stricture better applied: be careful. But of what? Of whom? For still, of the many names she could have, she had none.

Darconville, however, consigned her to the obscure and folding the class list into his pocket walked out into the lovely afternoon, the rarefactions in the air opposing, however pleasantly, his general conviction that the state of art should be in constant panic. The artistic nature, he knew, had an inborn proneness to side with the beauty that breaks hearts, to single out the aristocratic contours of what in human glory quickens the impulses of life to mystic proportions. He found himself, again, absent-mindedly thinking of the effect of that look in which everything that was most obscure in the relation between two people rose to the surface, and yet he could find no possible expression of it in words. But curiosity, he thought—the weakest form of solicitude, even if it was the beginning of it—was not love.

And crossing the lawn he only hoped that he'd gain somehow in veracity what he lost in mystery—a compromise, it also occurred to him, he wasn't always ready to make. But what *was* he ready for? He didn't know. And so laughing he headed home, walking without so much as a touch of regret up the street to his house, his book, and the supramundane.

IX

A Day of Writing

Exercise indeed we do, but that very forebackwardly, for where we should exercise to know, we exercise as having known.

—Sir PHILIP SIDNEY, *Defence of Poesy*

IT WAS TOO EARLY to rise. But Darconville, long before dawn, couldn't refrain from literally jumping out of bed, the excitement in the sense of well-being he felt serving as the best premonition possible for a full, uninterrupted day of writing, and when the sun bowled up over Quinsyburg—which Spellvexit, somersaulting, always greeted with a glossoepiglottic gurgle of joy, something like: "Gleep!"—he welcomed its appearance with three finished pages and an emphatic resolve to write a few more.

After his coffee, he smoked awhile, and then set to work again, his desk cluttered with notebooks, pens, and piles of paper. The skull, *norma frontalis,* was even smiling its approval this morning, for before long Darconville was fully re-engaged in that silent and solemn duel in which the mind sits concentrated in the most fearless of disciplines, the tidiness of which, he felt, life could never hope to emulate and the wonderful and deep delight of which nothing whatsoever else could hope to match. It was worth the loneliness. It was worth the time. And if the blazing rockets of his imagination came whistling down mere sticks, as occasionally they did, it was worth it still, for truth indeed was fabulous and man, he'd always thought, best knew himself by fable.

Was truth, however, discovered or constructed? Darconville, actually, was never really sure, and, of so-called "experience," well, when he thought of it he tended to believe that it had to be *avoided* in order to write—a matter, in fact, that couldn't have been given clearer focus than during these last few weeks in Quinsyburg when up in those rooms, conjugating the games of speech and light, writing pages racily colloquial, classically satirical, stinging and tender in robust and ardent sequence, he had been interrupted with a frequency that almost bordered on devotion: students-in-crisis; evangelists—two ruby-nosed Baptanodons, especially, whose particular theory of disputation was that one should aim, not to convince, but rather to silence one's opponent; and even several locals who knocked to inquire, alas in vain, about the possibility of buying his car, the black 1948 Mark VI Bentley in front of the house whose tires they invariably kicked, crying, "What a mochine!" So he had his telephone pulled out. He kept his shades pulled. He locked his door. And the Lords of Pleroma stood by.

When not teaching, Darconville worked very hard on his manuscript and, in doing so, was entirely free from any feeling of having committed sacrilege against the vow he had made with himself before coming there. His was a kind of asceticism. The writer was not a person, Darconville felt, rather an amanuensis of verity, who would only corrupt what he wrote to the extent, that he yielded to passion or shirked the discipline of objectivity.

The noon bell sounded from the library clock, work continued, and before too long it was midafternoon, reminding him quite poignantly of how slow the imaginative struggle was—for were not artists those few of us flung down from the heavens into mortal garments?—and how difficult it was to return. To do, however, was not necessarily to make, nor to shape, to shape correctly. A maniacal stylist, Darconville worked to *shape* what he wrote—contour of form with respect to beauty, coherence of matter with respect to blend—and to dig in matter the furrows of the mind, for in all creation matter sought form, form matter, and that was as profound an exhortation to the artist as any: form matter! The Greeks, he reminded himself, designated the world by a word that means ornament, κόσμος, and the Romans gave it the name of *mundus* for its finish, its grace, its elegance. And *caelum?* The word itself meant a tool to engrave!

The horizontal sun, shooting its rays through great dark banks of western clouds, sent a last coppery glow under the shade, the fiery reflection of what was left of a good day. Darconville closed his eyes, strained from concentration, and leaned back. With a furtive movement of his shoulders, he turned, feeling suddenly a girl's phantom presence in the room. But he ignored it and continued working on into the night, his face a shadow above the gooseneck lamp—the cat snoring—rewriting the pages he'd spent the day on. It was abundance, to be alone, in the solitude of night, watching what you fashioned and fashioning by the miracle of art what was nothing less than giving birth by parthenogenesis. At last, in the middle of the close and quiet night, he saw he was done. He looked up at the old watch hanging on the nail: late, late—the tortoise of the hour hand, the hare of the minute hand epiphanizing the ambivalence of time that both weighed on him and bore him up. But then there on the desk, completed, lay the finished pages, washed with silver, wiped with gold. And the phantom?

The light was out, and he was fast asleep, happier than anyone deserved to be, and the only phantoms he could see were the benevolent ones he found in the fleeting fancies of his dreams. And that was fine with him. Accident he would leave to life which specialized in it.

X

Bright Star

The unthrift sun shot vital gold, a thousand pieces.

—Henry Vaughan, *Silex Scintillans*

THE CLASSROOM was old. It seemed in dark and incongruous contrast to the delicate femininity it both isolated and yet protected with a fastness like that of some battlemented watchtower. On the wall hung a portrait of the Droeshout Shakespeare and a canvas map of Britain, pocked with red pins. This was English 100, a freshman section of girls who were almost all dressed *à la négligence* in the present-day fribble-frabble of fashion, mostly jeans and wee pannikins.

Darconville strode in and sat down. He placed his books on the desk, and, as he smiled, the girls straightened around to squeaks, the click of shoes, the scent of earth-flowers. The moment was immediately memorable, for instantly aware at the corner of his eye of a sparkle, the fluorescence, of a jewel, he looked up with sudden confusion, as if bewildered to discover art in nature's province. It was she: a faery's child, the nameless lady of the meads, full beautiful, sitting in the front-row seat at the far right with her eyes lowered to the desk in a kind of fragrant prayer, her chin resting gently on the snowy jabot of her blouse and her hair, tenting her face, golden as the Laconian's. Prepared for her, he saw he really wasn't. The heart in painful riot omitted roll-call.

"Shall we look at the Keats?" asked Darconville, quietly. It had been their first assignment: to analyze one poem. There was a marked self-consciousness in the straightening of shoulders, in the coughs, as the students settled down resolutely to consider the poem.

"As one must pronounce a Chinese ideograph in order to understand it," said Darconville, "so also must a poem be read aloud. Would anybody care to do so?" He waited.

Silence.

"Anyone?"

The girls remained earnestly hunched over their books, submissive to the idea that obscurity can be found in the solemnity of well-aimed concentration.

"Anyone at all?"

The linoleum snapped.

Darconville was amused. It seemed like vesper hour at the Shaker Rest Home for Invalid Ladies. The discomfort was palpable, with not an eye on him. Then a hand shot up.

"Miss—" Darconville looked at his roll-book.

"Windt," the student provided.

It was a girl in the third row who resembled Copernicus, the shape of her pageboy, its two *guiches* coming forward like tongs and swinging at the jawline, making her look small as a creepystool. She turned to one of her girlfriends for confidence, then stood up, and began.

> "Bright star! would I were steadfast as thou art—
> Not in lone splendor hung aloft the night,
> And watching, with eternal lids apart,
> Like Nature's patient, sleepless, *um*—"

"Eremite," said Darconville. "Hermit."

Rachel Windt, wrinkling her nose, squinted at the word. Darconville, repeating the word, prodded her.

"E-eree-ereem—"

"Just pronounce the consonants," Darconville said, laughing, trying to relax her, "and the vowels will fall into place." Two girls in the
back row exchanged cold glances; they didn't find that particularly
funny. Rachel Windt bewilderedly twisted up a noil of her hair,
shrugged, and continued.

> "The moving waters at their priestlike task
>   Of pure, *um,* ablution round earth's human shores,
>   Or gazing on the new soft fallen mask
>   Of snow upon the mountains and the moors—"

"Perfect. Let's stop there," said Darconville, "where the octave and
sestet hinge. This is a sonnet—composed, if you'll notice, in one sentence—in which the poet expresses a wish. And what, let's ask ourselves, is that wish?" He paused. "Anybody?"

"He's wishin' he was a star?"

Wishin'. Your thlipsis is showing, thought Darconville, looking in
the direction of the voice.

It was a long-nosed piece of presumption in the last row, wearing
an armory of Scandinavian nail-jewelry, who was less concerned with
a Romantic poet's tragic wishes than after-shampoo flyaways if the
comb she simultaneously shuttled through her hair to the repetitious
snaps of chewing gum meant anything. Darconville smiled and kindly
suggested that she was, even if a trifle so, somewhat wide of the mark.
Snap. Another hand? Anyone?

"Miss?"

This voice came from the direction of—but it was not hers. Darconville, with no small difficulty, fixedly tried to keep his eyes focused on
this student alone, a moon radiant only for the proximity of that adjacent sun whose beauty, even in a condition of reflected light, seemed
startling enough to destroy his sight on the instant.

"Trinley Moss," answered the girl, standing up, her six bracelets
jangling, in an opera blue turtleneck sweater and plaid wrap-around,
safety-pinned at the thigh. "Well, I believe he's right unhappy," she
said, "and that this star he mentions, symbolizin' brightness, is drivin'
this poor child here, I don't know, to wishin' he could either touch it
or, I don't know, just plain ol' flop down and become a"—she
shrugged—"a eremite?"

Darconville began to feel like St. Paul, watching errors creep in at
Colossae. It wasn't all that bad, hardly a matter for despair. He took

teaching to be a mission, not a trade, and sought to avoid the by-the-numbers *Drillschule* technique that, for one reason or another, had apparently long been held in vogue there by various pompous doodles and burgraves-of-fine-print on the Quinsy faculty, teachers, for whom students were the little limbs of Satan, who bored the girls to distraction repeating opinions seamed by cankerworm and reading from lecture notes long since parched by the Dog Star. He would be patient. At Quinsy it was an essential requirement, for although the state constitution laid claim to its being a school of higher learning, he from the very first day of arrival wondered just what level they were measuring from, and if they took salt tablets when doing so.

Darconville ranged the room with his eyes for a better answer—they couldn't as yet settle on *la femme d'intérieur*—and noticed a girl, her pencil poised above her notebook, a response in her eyes, an answer on her lips. He nodded to her.

"I am Shelby Uprightly," she said, neatly pressing her glasses to her zygomatic arch with one finger. "John Keats in his sonnet, 'Bright Star,' wishing to be steadfast, as he states, but not alone, is quite painfully expressing, as he often did, the particular tension of feeling he suffered when torn between a desire for the Ideal, the lovely star, in this case, and the Real, the girl mentioned in the last lines, someone he must have—"

"Excellent. You outdo yourself," exclaimed Darconville. "And would you read those lines?"

"I'm sorry, sir. I'm afraid I won't," she replied, confidentially lowering her voice. "I do not read well enough for declamation." She tilted her head. "Is that acceptable?"

Darconville was nodding but continued to listen intently long after the girl had finished speaking, as if struggling with an idea encountered, not in the classroom, but at the innermost of his being, one he was unable to comprehend—then, suddenly embarrassed, he looked up from the fanciful call of that mysterious girl in the right front row whose beautiful hair, like that of the Graces, enshrined the face he couldn't see. Who then, asked Darconville quickly, would like to read the lines? He found a girl sitting directly in front of him, bent down, and smiled into her eyes.

"You are—?"

She was speechless.

It was Millette Snipes, a girl whose comic little face, perfectly round, looked like a midway balloon. She blushed, tapping one of those pencils-with-funheads, and with a farm-bright smile looked up with huge oval eyes that told instantly just how deeply she'd been smitten with love for her teacher.

"Shall I thay the whole poem, thir?" she asked, brushing aside a cinnamon curl that had stuck to her nose.

A wave of giggles broke over the class, until Darconville, soberly, tapped the desk once with his pointer like Orbilius *plagosus*. Then Scarlet Foxwell, her eye inset with something of a humorful character, leaned over to show her where to begin, but not before glancing back at DeDonda Umpton and Elsie Magoun who were both pinching their noses to keep from exploding with laughter.

Then Millette Snipes, her elbows akimbo, her book high, spoke in a voice from the family Cricetidae.

> "No—yet thtill thteadfatht, thtill unchangeable,
> Pillowed upon my fair love'th ripening breatht,
> To feel forever itth thoft fall and thwell,
> Awake forever in a thweet unretht—"

"Crisper, child," said Darconville.
Inevitably, she spoke louder.

> "Thtill, thtill to hear her tender-taken breath,
> And tho live ever—or elthe thwoon to death."

The girl tenderly pressed the open book to her bosom and looked up soulfully, her wopsical eyes moist and glowing. Darconville thanked her.

"Very good. Now, the poet here, as Miss Uprightly earlier pointed out, aspires to the star's steadfastness but, you see, *not* at the cost of hermit-like loneliness. He is in a state of suspicion about what must be sacrificed in the pursuit of the Ideal. It is the problem, perhaps," said Darconville, "of the paradoxical man who wants to move, say, but not migrate. Fanny Brawne, a coquette of sorts, was the woman Keats loved, and while she was not specifically the subject of the poem—it could be anyone—the poet wanted to live forever with whomever it was, such was his passion, or else swoon to death."

"Thwoon in the thenthe of thuccumb?"

"Precisely, Miss—"

"Thnipeth."

"The Romantic, you see," said Darconville, "is a man of extremes."

"It'th tho thimple," said Millette Snipes, "a thad poem, but tho very very thimple."

"The greatest lines in English poetry," replied Darconville, "are always the simplest." He lifted a lectern onto his desk and leaned forward on it. "I have something for you—call it, if you will, 'The Principle of Trim.' The poet, you see, is rather like the seagull who has a perfect process for desalting water, although no one can explain how it works: he baffles *out* of a given line, if he's the enchanted metaphorsician we hope he is, that which otherwise would directly explain it."

Darconville wanted to make this clear.

"The simple line seeks to outwit, not merely resist, the complexity of thought it noncommittally grows out of and, by definition, filters out the ideas it must nevertheless, to be great, always raise, do you see?"

As he felt the presence of that one girl near him, he listened distractedly to the voice that didn't seem his. *Who are you?* thought Darconville. *Who are you?* He tried to concentrate his whole nature in one terrific effort to summon up, that he might dismiss it for once and all, the formidable magnetic mystery on his right that drew him so relentlessly off the subject.

"And therefore the greatest lines always imply the longest essays, discourses, metaphrases which the poet quite happily leaves to the agitation of critics, schoolmen, all those academic Morlocks who study the brain of a line after its face has come off in their hands." Darconville looked around. "Do you want me to repeat that?" (cries of "yes, yes")

Darconville thought for a moment. "The ring of a mighty bell," he explained, "implies, logically, a technical if less melodic success in the shift and whirr of its gudgeons, a secondary sound that can be muffled only in proportion to the genius of the campanologist."

Glycera Pentlock, throwing an exasperated glance at her neighbor, Martha Van Ramm, recklessly resumed scribbling away in her notebook. But Ailsa Cragg, chumbling the tip of her pen, gasped and blurted out, "What is a campanologist?"

"Use," said Darconville, "your definitionary. It's one of the last few pleasures left in life."

Poteet Wilson looked aggravated. Wroberta Carter spun her pencil. And Barbara Celarent whispered a slang word which, though unbeknownst to her, was once held in common usage by the daughters of joy in fifth-century Babylon.

"Language," continued Darconville, "often disguises thought. The successful poetic line, never discursive, is always thought extensively profound—and surely, upon the examination that is our burden, will be—but at its very essence it is the furthest thing from it. Beauty only implies truth, as *fuit* implies *est*. The poet doesn't say so, however; the factophile does. Poetry is the more imperfect when the less simple. The nature of great poetry—a perfect art attempted by imperfect people— prevents the direct concern with truth and can only suggest by singing what it secretly shields by showing. The greater the simplicity stated the greater the complexity implied, you see?" Several girls put up their hands. "And putting aside for now the implications this has in the human personality, in affairs of the heart, know only that the reader is left to assume whether or not what the poet stated in Beauty he knew as Truth."

A yawn was heard, followed by the jingling of some Scandinavian nail-jewelry.

"Bear with me? God alone is pure act, never in potency, whereas finite things are metaphysically composed of act and potentiality. But, in poetry, Beauty is act, you might say, Truth the potency involved by inference in that act, and of course there follow many attendant questions that can be raised: will Beauty wane as Truth waxes? Is one the synonym, or the antonym, of the other? And what of the old idea that Beauty, meeting Truth, must always corrupt it—the Beauty that turns Truth, as Hamlet said, into a bawd? What are the implications—the essential question must be asked—of the Ideal?" A heavy inert apathy settled over the class. "We must consider the final lines of another poem of Keats, 'Ode on a Grecian Urn.'"

The students, exhaling sighs, actually seemed to decompress. It didn't matter. Darconville, perhaps not even aware of it himself, was busy sorting out matters in the depths of his own mind.

"'Beauty is Truth, Truth Beauty': I call this Keats's Comfort—he is saying his prayers and, embarrassingly, is overheard. It is a correct epistemological utterance, you might say," continued Darconville, "made aesthetically incorrect at the very moment it is introduced into the poem. Beauty is Truth, Keats forgot, only if and when the didactician is there to say so by whatever means he can. Arguably, Beauty is Truth precisely when it does *not* say so, just as, turn about, a holy man disproves his holiness as soon as he asserts it. Ironically enough, then, this, the most famous line of Keats, while starkly simple—

58 DARCONVILLE'S CAT

indeed, it is generally accepted as the classic example of such—denies
exactly what a simple line must be valued for, asserting what should
be implied, attesting to what it can't. The line expresses what it does
not embody—or, better, embodies what it has no right to express: a
beautiful messenger appears delivering ugly news. It's a paradox in
the same way that—"

Darconville paused, turned to the blackboard, and chalked out a
wide rectangle. He wrote something and backed away for perspective.

> **This boxed sentence is false**

"The paradox here is clear," asserted Darconville, "is it not? If the
sentence is true, then it is false; if false, then it is true." Various eyes
roved in troubled scrutiny over the board. "Do you see? A liar says
that he lies: thus he lies and does not lie at the same time. The *jeu de
mots* is fun grammatically," warned Darconville with a smile, "but
imagine how vulnerable would be your philosophical calm if this
translated into the behavior of a human being? Careful," said Darconville, "with your boyfriends."

The girls tittered.

It was an academic matter, of course, and yet, incredibly, Darconville found *himself* thus preoccupied, searching to apprehend a figure
in the distance, an interval so wide, for a thousand reasons, it dulled
the edge of consequence but a distance nevertheless that also warned,
by its very remoteness, that no real exchange of feelings was possible, a
morbid underbreath, as if aloofness itself, whispering, told him to
desist from that which he must inevitably be excluded. And yet how
often, even from childhood, had this been the case in his life! And so
he listened to what he thought, serving to clarify a matter at the heart
of things and verify a falsehood. It formulated his final remarks.

"The artist," concluded Darconville, going to the window and staring out at a group of hardy catalpas, "when a logical paradox to himself becomes, I suppose, the most unpoetical of men." A cardinal went
snip-snip-snip in the trees. "I don't know, perhaps Keats had one glass
of claret too many, loitered palely, and was overcome with the necessity of writing a line that could acknowledge two simultaneous but incompatible forces within him: poet and priest. He becomes a pomol-
ogist"—Ailsa Cragg looked frostily at Darconville and sucked a

tooth—"trying to get fruit back to its paradisaical best. 'Beauty is Truth, Truth Beauty'? It's a *concio ad clerum:* a sermon to the clergy, wherein the poet is attempting to cheer himself up—in a fit of unsteadfastness, say?—and is at the same time begging us to accept not only what we should but also that which, poor poet, he more than sufficiently allowed us without special pleading. The poet's own voice has interrupted him. He is awakened by his own snore. The line, which I digressed to explain, is only a false bottom, collapsing an otherwise beautiful poem—and one which provides, perhaps, the best single commentary we have on the sonnet, 'Bright Star.' " Darconville was finished. "Are there any questions?"

There was silence.

"We're clearer then," asked Darconville, "on the meaning of the poem?"

"It hath to do with the thufferingth and thorrowth of life."

Everybody groaned.

"I believe that young boy," came a sudden voluptuous drawl from near the back of the room, a low magical level of loveliness which absorbed with a kind of absoluteness any rival utterance that might have been offered against it, "was just sayin' the most obvious thing in the whole wide world."

It was the kind of female voice that Juvenal somewhere naughtily describes as having fingers.

"He was talkin' "—she touched her tongue to her upper lip— "about love."

Most of the girls, in icy silence, stared straight ahead.

"I'm sorry," said Darconville who, although not taken in—he'd seen her back there at the beginning of class and almost with amusement had been waiting for her to speak—nevertheless feigned surprise, "but I can't seem to find you here in my roll-book. You are a senior, aren't you, Miss Poore?"

It was too much. Every head in the entire class—excepting one student's, whose head was lowered—abruptly shifted from the teacher to her, the *only* student's name he had known! And there she sat, confident and cool, wearing a nubby placket-front shirt trimmed in beige to match a black velvet dirndl.

Then, very slowly, Hypsipyle Poore lifted off her sunglasses and, with one lingering provocative glance, revealed eyes as limpid as the pools in Heshbon by the gate of Bathrabbim—and everyone there could have sworn she winked as with a cryptic smile she breathed softly, "Well, should I see you after class?"

"Love has been mentioned," said Darconville, who saw he had a minute or two. "And suffering, as well. The history of romantic disappointment, I don't doubt, often does nothing more than document the schism between Beauty and Truth or, better, proves that Beauty, when it becomes an end in itself, often yields no Truth. The simple line, in such cases, had no complexity within it—there can, of course, never be too much. A knowledge of many things is possible, it's been said, but one can never know everything about one thing, though, sadly, one perhaps tries. The relationship with a boy or girl you spontaneously took for perfection-in-beauty but didn't sequentially know by examination-in-truth can result in disaster. The implications of the Ideal? Who can really know? It is the chance one takes when one falls in love—the discussion of which," smiled Darconville, "is perhaps beyond the province of the classroom here, agreed?"

The girls laughed—and prepared to leave. But Darconville, alert to the chance, quickly took up his class roll and began to call attendance.

"Muriel Ambler"

"Here"

"Melody Blume"

"Here"

The students, by turn, acknowledged their names. But for the suspense it might have been interminable, the list seemed so long. Here. Here. Here. But which was hers? Was it there?

"Sheila Mangelwurzel"

"Here"

"Christie McCarkle"

A carrot-top put up her hand.

"Glycera Pentlock"

"Over here"

"Isabel Rawsthorne"

A thunderclap!—then a flashing light across his book. Dazed, almost unconsciously, Darconville called out the remaining non-names, reflecting on this alone: only love makes the pain of lifting a shy head a grace. It equally unlocks a silent throat with the knowledge in the plaintive soul of what must be done, and so was, in the tender-taken breath he suddenly heard, soft as a swoon, say: "Present."

And sculptured Aphrodite, in loose-flowing alb, stepping slow and fragile under the loops of dripping ring willows, puts a finger to her lips, shakes out tearshaped petals from her flasket, and then holds high her holy lights which silver and bewitch the common wood where two, long asleep, sweetly wake under the baldric of a new heaven to blush at the silence, pause, and faintly hear a goddess whisper in a voice lower than leaf-fall: *"Tomorrow shall be love for the loveless, and for the lover tomorrow shall be love."*

In short, Isabel Rawsthorne looked up and smiled.

XI

Chantepleure

Repetition is the essence of conjuration.

—St. Neot of Axholme

"ISABEL, Isabel, Isabel, Isabel, Isabel, Isabel, Isabel, Isabel, Isabel, Isabel, Isabel, Isabel, Isabel." Darconville repeated the name into the unintelligibility we call sleep—and dreamt of desperadoes.

XII

The Garden of Earthly Delights

There foamed rebellious Logic, gagged and bound,
There, stripped, fair Rhetoric languished on the ground.

—ALEXANDER POPE, *The Dunciad*

FACULTY MEETINGS are held whenever the need to show off is combined with the imperative of accomplishing nothing. It was the case at Quinsy College. There were five every year—a rump parliament of "educators," all bunged up with complaints and full of prefabricated particulars, who sat around on their buns for several hours trying to correct various problems, whether of school business or personal bagwash, and to confront problematical variables, every one of which was always greeted with a salvo of idle questions, nice distinctions, sophisms, obs and sols, and last-ditch stratagems. The presiding genius? Brizo, goddess of sleep. The style? Extemporaneous. The par-

ticipants? Teachers, who, like whetstones, would make others cut that
could not cut themselves.

There were some preliminary matters, first. President Greatracks,
sitting up front like Buddha in a bad mood with his hands clasped in
front of his belly as indifferently as tweezers, was being presented a gift
(an unidentifiable rhomboid of pewter)—for his "unswerving leader-
ship"—in the name of the senior class whose metonym, Miss Xystine
Chappelle, student body president and sweetheart-of-the-school, after
tweaking the tips of an organdy the color of an orange fruit-jumble,
curtseying, and delivering her message with cute little eye-rolls, breathlessly concluded:

". . . as a class we really couldn't think of a more deserving leader. The
real meaning of college, hopefully, will remain with us even when we
have to face the reality of the world after graduation, the realization of
which, I realize, is not very realistic now. Anyway, I'm really proud to bestow this gift in behalf of all of us who can never thank you enough for
helping us reach our realizable goals." [*Applause*]

The agenda was full: it was the first such meeting of the year, and
there was a great deal to do. Swinging his nose, President Greatracks
motioned to her feet his secretary, a blinking anablept with mis-mated
eyes and slingback shoes who read the minutes from the previous
spring and then handed out the updated "Faculty Profile" booklets,
after which Greatracks, his cheeks puffed out like a Switzer's breeches,
stepped forward on his huge drawbridge feet and said he wasn't going
to be wordy because where was the damfool percentage in it?
No, his only grouse, he said, was about the budget. Money, he pointed
out, didn't grow on trees, was the root of all evil, lost one friends, and
talked!—too damned much, he said. This year, he continued—it was
prolegomenon to every faculty meeting—money was going to keep its
little mouth shut, and they could all paste that in their hats, OK? Mr.
Schrecklichkeit, an assistant biology professor with a white squill of a
nose, leaned over to Darconville and snapped, "There goes my course
in Vegetable Staticks, that *son* of a bitch!"

The meeting, then, was called to order—with several raps of the
gavel by President Greatracks, appearing rather like the Turk of legend who, ready to drink a bottle of wine, first made loud noises and
screwed out filthy faces to warn his soul of the foul anti-Koranic act

he was about to commit. First, Dean Barathrum, a born remittance man and author of several out-of-date arithmetics, introduced the newest members of the faculty. They were received, Darconville and several others, with eye-watering yawns. One man was continuously tracing the sweephand of his watch with his fingers. Another, staring out a window, was actually sucking his thumb.

Darconville's attention, however, had been drawn to the shiny-paged faculty booklet, alphabetically listing everyone with photo and credentials. It looked like a medieval bestiary: skipjacks, groutnolls, hysterical-looking circumferentors, frumps and filiopietistic longheads, micelings, whipsnades, and many another whose eyes showed a very short limit of accommodation. Several had actually taken no college degrees. Others were part-time evangelists, ex-army colonels, and car salesmen. And the various titles of their scholarly publications—books, articles, monographs, etc.—were scarcely believable: "English Nose Literature"; *Stephen Duck: More Rhyme Than Reason;* "The American Disgrace: Overabuse of the Verb 'To Get' "; "Fundavit Stones in Crozet, Va."; *Much Ado About Mothing;* "The Psychopathological Connection Between Liquid Natural Gas and Agraphia"; *The Story of Windmill Technology;* "The Significance of Head Motions in Peking Ducks"; "Infusions as Drinks"; "Abraham Lincoln, Quadroon?" and several other inventions, thought Darconville, of which necessity was hardly the mother.

Finally, the Great Consult began. They discussed tenure procedure. They revised policy on sabbaticals. They rehearsed, to palsied lengths, curriculum changes, cross-registration, crises in enrollment. It suddenly became a great din of objections, fierce denials, and loud peevishness all expressed in noises like the farting of laurel in flames with everybody going at it head to head as if they were all trying right then and there to solve the problem of circular shot, perpetual motion, and abiogenesis!

Staring in disbelief, Darconville looked on in a kind of autoscopic hallucination as each of the faculty members rose in turn to make a point that never seemed to have an acute end. It was all queer, makeshift, and unpindownable, for all the cube-duplicators, angle-trisectors, and circle-squarers seemed to keep busy avoiding any question that hadn't sufficient strength to throw doubt on whatever answer couldn't have been offered anyway lest an inefficacious solution only prove to muddle a problem that couldn't be raised in the first place. The discussion, rarely deviating into sense, grew round with resolutions and amendments as they sacrificed the necessary to acquire the superfluous and did everything twice by halves, for, like Noah, they had two of everything—two, it might be said, they didn't need so much as one of: two policies, two excuses, two faces and, always, forty-eleven reasons to prop up both.

There was, for instance, Miss Shepe the witty, Miss Ghote the wise —educatresses both, departments sociology and art education respectively—who fell swiftly to reviewing the college motto: should it be "We Preach to Teach" or "We Teach to Preach"?—a rabid grace/ free-will discussion growing out of their sudden but sustained failure to settle on the primacy of one over the other. They squared off, adjusting their plackets and glaring into each other's pinched and penny-saving faces. "I'm for less grapes and more fox," exclaimed Miss Shepe, confusing everybody. Furious, Miss Ghote—*brekekek-ekek!*— snapped her pencil in two.

"So much for your deduction," said Miss Ghote.

"I deduce nothing," sniffed Miss Shepe. "You've simply induced that yourself."

"Induced, yes, what you'd implied."

"You dare," snapped Miss Shepe, twisting her cramp-ring, "you dare infer I've implied what you yourself have induced, Miss Ghote?"

"Put it this way," replied Miss Ghote with an icy-sweet smile, "you've only surmised I infer what you've implied I induced—and I do believe your bra strap's showing."

Miss Shepe banged down her heel. "Then you conclude wrongly, Miss Nothing-in-the-World-Could-Make-Me-Care-Less, that I surmised you infer what you think I've implied you've induced!"

"But you only assume that I conclude wrongly that you've surmised what—"

"Elephant balls!" howled President Greatracks, the fat in his eyeballs quivering. A group of old fishfags from the home economics department, dosed to sleep by their own heavy perfume, immediately woke to clap their mouths in horror.

"I'm not certain I heard what he said," whispered Miss Swint to someone behind her. It was a faint voice, some staring ghost suddenly exclaiming upon Rhadamanth. The world to Miss Swint, piano teacher, her face two subtle shades of oatmeal, backlit both by a monocle, consisted merely of music, her collection of wheat-sheaf pennies, and the responsibility of playing the organ every Sunday at the Presbyterian church, the very place in which, years ago, she'd long since become convinced that maidenhead and godhead were indivisible.

There were soon other matters on the docket: dining-hall duty, election to committees, chaperon assignments. And some few raised questions about general reform, and yet while only a mere fraction of the lot were actually concerned with change—it was a subject met by children, with reform as the wicked uncle—they all jumped up like minorites, jurisprudentes, and tub-thumping Sorbonnists to debate it, all reinforcing the "yo-he-ho" protoglottological theory that words initially began as shouts. No aspect was overlooked, no fine point ignored, no issue diminished. It was complete havoc once again as they stood in coalition or squatted in caucus, breaking down every proposition like reformational hairsplitters into partitions, sections, members, subsections, submembral sections, submembral subsections and denouncing each other with mouthfuls of rhetoric warped by quiddling, diddling, and undistributed middling. One third believed what another third invented what the other third laughed at. Quid the Cynic argued with Suction the Epicurean, Suction the Epicurean argued with Sipsop the Pythagorean, Sipsop the Pythagorean argued with Quid the Cynic, and the whole afternoon dwindled away with one saving at the spigot and another letting out at the bunghole.

It occurred to Darconville that the expression, "ignorance is bliss," was a perception curiously unavailable to the ignorant as he considered, with great misgivings, the sad and inarticulate desperviews there whose identities had gone soft on them and whose grasp of reality was so slight and so arbitrary and so grotesque that each could have easily stepped from there into the hot pornofornocacophagomaniacal set of Bosch's unmusical hell and fit, snugly.

The meeting, finally, adjourned. A partition was rolled back, revealing at another section of the long room several tables with bottles of soft drinks (no liquor) and plates of cookies, candy, and cake. Papers rattled, people coughed, and chairs shifted as everyone withdrew.

"Y'all ever see so dang much shuck for so little nubbin?" complained President Greatracks who—a fake giant among real pygmies —stomped toward the food in the company of several pipe-smoking lackeys, all dodging about in his circumference. No, no, they agreed, no, they hadn't. His arms upon the boobies' shoulders, you quickly saw the gudgeon bite. No, no, they repeated, not at all. "Sombitches," he said, picking up five thumbprinted marshmallows and stuffing them into his mouth. "I can hear their brains rolling about like B-B's in a boxcar."

The Quinsy faculty, during the refreshments, took the occasion to gossip, but faction didn't really constitute disunity. It was as if, somehow, they had all been destined by some temporal and spatial anti-miracle of history to come together at the same place and time and to know each other on the instant by some mystic subtlety for mates, perhaps in the paradox of peculiar faces which, while each was different, all looked as though God had smeared them when still wet. They didn't have to talk. They weren't speakers, really. But they were *experts* at malversation.

"I know about budgets," said Miss Throwswitch, the drama teacher, with a scrawl of mockery under the rims of her eyes as she poured a soda. "This year, you watch, we'll be doing Chekhov in clothesbags and clunkies."

"They are saying"—Prof. Fewstone's standard opening line, never without its veiled threat—"they are saying that over in Richmond the legislature is cutting us off without a dime unless we put some Mau-Maus on the faculty." A history professor, Fewstone always kept to that one note, like a finch; his sour doctrines, masquerading as brands of economics and politics, fit his reputation as a miser far better than the hackberry-colored jacket he never took off, perhaps for that elegant pin (compass, square) awarded him by some Brotherhood of Skinks or other who worshipped trowels and pyramids. "Now in my book, *The Rehoboths: Reform or Reglementation?* I put forth the theory—"

"Attitudinizing," murmured Miss Gibletts, the Latin teacher whose thin, dry, hectic, unperspirable habit of body made her somewhat saturnine. She looked like St. Colitis of the Sprung Chair. Turning away to find another conversation, she carefully managed to avoid the dark stranger with the French name who'd just been introduced and who was standing all alone.

Miss Dessicquint, the assistant dean, looked like Nosferatu—a huge mustachioed godforgone, inflexible as a Dutch shoe, who was given to lying about her age before anybody asked her. She closed her eyes and begun to hum. "Look," she sneered, nudging her secretary and sometime bowling partner, Miss Gupse, an unhealthy-looking little poltfoot with one of the longest noses on earth. "There, by the table, in harlequin shorts."

"Oh no. Floyce."

"The flower of fairybelle land."

"He irks me, that one."

"He?"

Miss Gupse, smiling, caught the irony and licked her nose. "She."

"*It!*" said Miss Dessicquint, wagging a tongue long as a biscuit-seller's shovel. Her secretary had to turn around to stop the smile glimmering down the flanks of her steep nose. "He looks like a Mexican banana-split."

"I wonder," swallowed little Miss Gupse, "how those people"—she looked up over a cookie—"well, *do* it."

"Have you ever had the occasion," asked Miss Dessicquint, pausing for dramatic effect, "to look at the east end of a westbound cow?"

Floyce R. Fulwider, reputedly a ferocious alcibiadean, was a balding, fastidious art teacher—he pronounced Titian, his favorite painter, for instance, to rhyme with Keatsian—who could often be seen skipping across the Quinsy campus holding by his fingertips the newly wet gouaches and undernourished para-menstrual creations of his students or, as he called them, his "popsies." The college teemed with stories about the felonious gender-switching parties he threw, when he'd paint his windows black, put on his Mabel Mercer records, and encourage everyone to don feather boas and run around naked. He couldn't have liked it more. But Miss Dessicquint didn't like it and told Miss Gupse, confidentially, that he was getting a terminal contract this year. "Rome," she whispered into her companion's ear, "wasn't burnt in a day."

Then, turning, they saw Darconville.

"I hope *he* isn't a bumbie."

"He looks normal to me," said Miss Gupse.

"Well, you know what they say. And it's true," said Miss Dessicquint, with eyes like frozen frass, "there's a thin line between madness and insanity."

Miss Gupse, never strong, secretly thought herself the object of this cut and that very evening would proceed to call her sister in Nashville to inquire tearfully about a job there. True, that particular afternoon she had been in the midst of her *mois*. But the memory of having a big nose from childhood is perhaps at the bottom of more havoc than one can ever know.

In one corner of the room, occupying much of it, stood Dr. Glibbery, a walrus-arsed microbiology professor with a face, spanned by a dirty ramiform mustache, that had the nasty whiteness of boiled veal. His body resembled the shape in microcosm and odor in fact of one of those nineteenth-century lamps, the kind with a reservoir that gurgled periodically, emitted a stench of oil, and often exploded. A fanatical right-wing at-once-ist, he bullied his students—calling them all "Dufus"—with incredible lies about the difficulty of taking a doctorate and how, in pursuit of his own, he'd lived on ketchup sandwiches, got hookworm from going barefoot, and had to study upsidedown to keep awake. In point of fact, he had taken his degree from one of those just-about-accredited polytechnical millhouses in Virginia, identified usually by its initials, where the only requirements for graduation were to belong to the DeMolay and have two thumbs and a reasonably erect posture.

"None of these here dufuses *work* anymore. Well," pontificated Dr. Glibbery, "I'm going to knock their tits right into their watch-pockets for them, OK? You won't spy no grade of A in my roll-book," he said, "for love nor money."

He mumped a fistful of horehound drops and winked.

"*Or* money," corrected Prof. Wratschewe, doyen of the English department and proud author of several monographs, still, alas, awaiting the recognition of an indifferent world: "Bed-Wetting Imagery in Chatterton"; "Packed Earth as Anti-Resurrection Symbol in Wordsworth"; "The Caesura: Rest Home of Rhetoric"; and one slim book, *Menus from Homer* (o.p.).

But Dr. Glibbery only farted and grinned.

Miss Pouce, standing there, almost died of embarrassment—and, turning quickly, banged into a wall. Great snorts of laughter accompanied this, then grew—the lackeys, going beetred, doubled over with hilarity—as Greatracks, mimicking her, waddled yoketoed into the same wall, went crosseyed, and grabbed his nose. Qwert Yui Op, a midget Tibetan-Chinese, and Miss Malducoit, of the dirigible hips, both in math, applauded—and she spilled her drink. Darconville went to pick up her cup. "Thank you very much," said Miss Malducoit coldly, stepping in front of him, "I can do it myself."

Darconville, unwittingly, backed into a group of old ladies. It was the delegation, each old enough to carbon-date, from home economics. In the midst of them, studiously arranged that way, loomed a huge unproliferative boffa with tied oviducts and blimp-like breasts which sagged according to the law of $S=\frac{1}{2}vt^2$ named Mrs. DeCrow, associate professor in American history and local U.D.C. chairwoman, who was blowing a loud *ranz des vaches* across the room, subject: her summer in Biloxi. She had a voice like a faulty drain. There was a cruel pin in her hat, and she wore an eighteenth-century brooch with a painting of a litter of pigs on it. Famously disagreeable, at least so Dr. Dodypol, a colleague, told Darconville, she harbored a monomaniacal loathing—something not a few Southerners shared—for Abraham Lincoln.

"I know you but you don't know me," Mrs. DeCrow announced to Darconville, hoping she was wrong.

An arrangement, thought Darconville, that suits me fine.

"Wait," she suddenly exclaimed, holding a finger to her nose and turning to the other ladies, "but now who does this boy remind me of?"

Everyone dutifully waited.

"Not that awful Edwin Albert Poe who wrote horror poetry?" asked a sagcheeked lady cretinously mis-shoving a wedge of cake into her face.

"No," said bossy Mrs. DeCrow, cocking a quick snook at the lady. "I know," she said, interrupting herself, "Sir Thomas More."

"Saint Thomas More," corrected Darconville, for whom such distinctions meant something. But he was smiling.

Mrs. DeCrow, arching an eyebrow, didn't care. That remark, though she smiled a hard smile, immediately cost him—and irrevocably—any invitation whatsoever to one of her Fridays, even if he lived to be a hundred. *She* knew where to stick the knife in.

Darconville submitted to his uneasiness and in the contending noise, the rambling incoherent flow of talk, found that the most delectable social delight there seemed to be the quarrel that stopped just short of violence, discussions ending in repeated barks and loud flat interrobangs. It was a tragedy of language. There was no dialogue, only monologue, wherein each of the thimbleriggers and pathologically self-defensive opsimaths gathered there, most of them educated on the fly at one of those narrow and sectarian chop-and-chance-it swot factories in that region which was named after some square-capped fifteenth-century Protestant joykiller, only kept to a mad and self-referent fixity of subject and blathered on to no consequence.

Suddenly, there was a buzz of intrigue by the doorway: someone reporting a car accident. Xystine Chappelle, calling from the Quinsyburg Hospital, had reported that, while driving them home, Miss Shepe and Miss Ghote, sitting in the back seat, had willfully resumed their "I-think-that-you-think-that-I-think" argument, whereupon Miss Ghote leaped in frustration from the moving car and broke her femur.

"Them ol' beangooses," muttered Dr. Glibbery, fingering through the candies, "I do believe they gone get married one day."

"Are you?" Darconville, surprised, looked behind him. "Are you married?" It was the German instructor, Miss Tavistock (a.k.a. "The Clawhammer"), a flat-chested girl with a cataleptic smile who had the curious habit of suggesting to perfect strangers that, frankly, she thought they were in love with her.

"No, I'm not," answered Darconville who, suddenly noticing Mrs. DeCrow empty-handed, offered her some cookies, but she would have none of it and walked past him in a snit—the snit that would last a lifetime.

"The writer," sighed Miss Sally Bull Sweetshrub, the tournure of her phrases as precise as cut glass, "has *no* time whatsoever for such things as marriage. No, I'm afraid she has not. The devotion which asks her to feel the deliberation of art asks also that she choose the single life." A senior member of the creative writing department, Miss Sweetshrub carefully lifted off her half-glasses and, patronizingly turning her head from person to person, lectured the few people nearby on the difficulty in question. She was—how to put it?—an "unclaimed blessing." "I am a novelist, you see," she said, "which is spelled d-e-v-o-t-i-o-n."

"I see," said Mrs. McAwaddle, the registrar, who passing by with a tidy of licorice-whips on a napkin and a paper cup of purple soda unintentionally got hooped into the conversation.

"But do you? Do you really?" asked Miss Sweetshrub.

Mrs. McAwaddle, to be kind, gave the mandatory sign of ignorance by pretending to reconsider and said, "Mmmmmmm." Long having been a fretful auditor to Miss Sweetshrub's explicit polysemantic chats, she knew the hopelessness of trying to extricate herself. "Well," she reflected, charitably, "I have no doubt but that I might not."

Prof. Wratschewe, ducking his head in, interjected. "Excuse me,

Mrs. McAwaddle? The word 'but,' I believe, is used unnecessarily after the verbs 'to doubt' and 'to help.' Strunk & White, Book Four, I think you'll find."

"I wouldn't have made that mistake," riposted Miss Sally Bull Sweetshrub, bowing her head and fluttering her eyelids with the advantage Prof. Wratschewe's old, but as yet inconsequential, crush on her allowed.

Miss Sally Bull Sweetshrub, *aet.* 50 or so, was classically affected and wore out-of-date dresses that looked like Morris wallpaper. She had a perched Jacobean nose, like a dogvane, a waltzing oversized bottom, and wore her pissburnt-colored hair in an outlandish bun at the back anchored by several severe combs that matched in horn her conversational brooches. A bottomless fund of clarifications and cruelly sharpened pencils, she was known for giving strawberry teas and answering all her mail on Featherweight Antique Wove, Double Royal 90 when she couldn't attend a function, which, of course, she always could—and, when so doing, always did in the company of her pet beagle, "Howlet," and a monstrous alligator friend who some years ago left its native land in the form of a handbag. She was *the* pillar of Quinsy College, a woman both impregnable and unbearable (what she might have borne were she pregnable would, indeed, be unimaginable!)—one of those starboard-leaning High Anglicans, famous and innumerable in the Old Dominion, whose factitious sense of vanity in a private conversation makes it frankly public: the raised and punishingly assertive voice of the insane queen which includes, willingly or not, everybody within earshot.

"You perhaps know my work?"

She was looking at Darconville with her eyes shut, her lavender gloves buttoned shut and crossed immaculately in her lap.

"Possibly. Could you name—?"

"My novels? Let me see. My first was *Answer Came There None,* then, respectively, *I, a Stranger; Also but Not Yet the Wombat Cries; The Big Regret; The Interrupted Woman; The Same, Only Different;* and *The Black Duchess.*" It was the genre of course of Hoodoo, Hackwork, and Hyperesthesia, the popular dustjacket for which always showed a crumbling old mansion-by-moonlight and a frightened beauty in gossamer standing before it, tresses down, never knowing which way to turn.

Darconville, listening in spite of himself, was trying to repress an image of the prattling angel, Glossopetra, who reputedly had fallen from heaven to spend his eternal punishment wagging like a human tongue.

"There was a volume of my early verse, *Naps Upon Parnassus*. I followed that," continued Miss Sweetshrub, "with a critical work on Robert Browning called *The Snail on the Thorn*." Miss Throwswitch, standing behind her, periscoped two little fingers over her head and wiggled them, while Mr. Schrecklichkeit and Qwert Yui Op smiled into their sleeves.

"Mmmmm," said Mrs. McAwaddle, breathing her hum back in, a sound more of fatigue than recognition.

"Thankfully nothing on Abraham Lincoln!" piped in Mrs. De-Crow, making a loud transition to the powder room.

Miss Sweetshrub chastely crossed her legs. "My most widely reviewed book? Difficult to say. I guess I'd have to say it was my *Tlot! Tlot! The Biography of Alfred Noyes*."

"My," said Mrs. McAwaddle, hooing low but wisely, like Minerva's owl, "you've sure written a lot."

"Permit me? A lot is a parcel of land. I have written"—she drew her little finger fastidiously across her eyebrow—"much." Then she smiled around sweetly at everyone, especially Prof. Wratschewe whose approval was never in doubt if the handful of tiny white valentine candies (inscribed "Skidoo," "Be Mine," "Kiss Me," etc.) he solicitously extended to her meant anything. For eleven years there had run the possibly not unfounded rumor they'd be married any weekend now—who knew, perhaps the five-hundred-and-seventy-third would be it?

"Good grief," cried Prof. Wratschewe over his pocket-watch. "It's late—and I've a lecture to prepare this weekend."

"Weekends few," sighed Miss Sally Bull Sweetshrub, recrossing her hands and anticipating, perhaps, only the title of another novel she'd one day write, one she saw somewhat wistfully that there'd be plenty of time for as she sat there silently, as if straining to hear the celesta of wedding bells she felt could now peal only across the landscape of her fiction.

And so it went.

The last rays of the afternoon sun brought a feeble light through the meeting-room, and Darconville, heading toward the doorway, found a last group of teachers to meet. He was introduced to Miss Ballhatchet, a muscular valkyrie from the physical ed department; Dr. Ex-cipuliform, a history professor with afflicted eyes and a Transylvanian hop in his speech who despised the left-wing American press ("Intel-lectschultz! Velfare! Gummonism! Rewolt! Neekroes!"); cheery Miss Skait, from physics, who, immune to paradox, bouncingly assured him that Quinsy College was actually one big family; the Weerds—Aldo and Dodo—a young Pekinese-faced couple in the English department who spoke only to each other, wore rucksacks, and had occasional bouts of *purpura haemorrhagica* which they insisted on calling poetry; a six-foot maliarda named Miss Porchmouth, chemistry, who had a handshake that felt like pebbledash-siding; a certain Mr. Bischthumb, head of anthropology, who, tucking into an enormous piece of cake, bit off half the doily which got stuck in his weasand—and, wheezing tearfully, had to be raised by four men and lifted out of the room kick-ing skyward cataleptically in one of the most indecent postures Dar-conville had ever seen.

There were others. Darconville met Mr. Thimm, government de-partment, who told him, several times, about his wife's egg-in-the-armpit deformity; Drs. Knipperdoling and Pindle, two sententious ballachers from economic geography, who in a little vaudeville skit of theirs constantly pitched back and forth various adages and truisms about life, invariably beginning, "Well, I've learned one thing from the rough-and-tumble . . ." or "Now, I've been shinnying up this old stick for forty some odd years, and . . ."; and, finally, Dr. Speetles from the general education department, an anti-intellectual gepid who claimed the study of Skakespeare to be completely worthless, prefer-ring instead the applied sciences and confessing wittily, "I teach all my classes, see, using only a toy fire-engine. It's a multi-concept factor, you know? With this as a point of departure," he said, sucking a candy-spangle from his thumb, "I can teach sociology, government, civics, visual and environmental studies—hell, you *name* it." He tapped the side of his nose and nudged Darconville, who at that point was seriously on the brink of calling upon the angel, Hodniel, who supposedly had the power of curing stupidity in men. Instead, he put on his coat.

Walking out, one of the unaligneds of the faculty who may have stood, perhaps, for the several Darconville hadn't yet managed to meet, confided to him, "You know, when ol' Greatracks bangs down the gavel in these meetings and says, 'Begin!' well, I always think, shoot, that's about the longest word in the damn books—and ain't *that* the truth."

The thought hadn't been uttered a second when Prof. Wratschewe, grammarian, suddenly jumping-jacked out of nowhere and said, "Actually, I think you'll find that the longest word found in literature, Aristophanic in origin, is: *Lopadotemachoselacogaleokranioleipsano-drimhypotrimmatosilphioparaomelitokatakechymenokichlepikossypho-phattoperisteralektryonoptekephalliokigklopeleiolagoisiraiobaphetrago-nopterygn.*"

Somehow, it summed up the day.

XIII

A Lethiferous Letter

And, behold, there came a great wind from the wilderness.

—Job 1:19

Dear President Greatracks,

I feel I have made a mistake in coming to teach at Quinsy College. My intention here is not to sit in judgment, but your failure in my opinion to recognize the true ends of academic life—a circumstance I can't yet believe you are disinclined to preserve—raises questions less to the extent than to the source of the trouble, and since I shall be foolish in saying more to this purpose, while trusting you to understand, may I trust with more reason to ask pardon for these remarks? We seem to have lost our way, becoming righteous rather than virtuous, rigid in form but lax in substance, and, not secondary but rather accessory to the urgency of my decision, reconciled to the old idea that vision is perilous where vision is profound, a fact leading not only to a singular want of refinement but to the kind of fatal ignorance, excusable only where it cannot be overcome, that has put us at variance with ourselves and advanced the cause of various griffon-like promoters and apparitors on the faculty whose names I would in all places esteem it an honor openly to abhor.

I have been forced by deliberation, therefore, to weigh advantage against loss in a matter touching not only my students and myself but also a book I am presently under obligation to complete, whence I here mean by conscience to advise you that, upon the firm setting of this persuasion, I believe it my duty to resign—

Thinking of Isabel, however, Darconville reconsidered and, running his great black pen over the words, registered a rainbow over the Universal Deluge.

XIV

The Witchery of Archery

All myths are attempts to explain contradictions in nature.

—Claude Levi-Strauss

"FIRE!" cried Miss Ballhatchet, the forty-nine-year-old physical education teacher—her body, in the vintner's phrase, orotund—and she waved her arms, megaphoning her way in a ballooning duck gym-suit through the front line of cherry-cheeked freshmen, their bows at the ready. Suddenly, she blew her whistle in a flutter of angry pips. *"Wait!"*

"Must I repeat? The cock feather," she fumed, her muscles tense, "must be at *right* angles to the nock and away from the bow! Miss Moss here must have thought I said left angles." She glowered at

Trinley Moss and pointed. "Is this what you mean by a left angle, or what?" The girl's bow was canted ridiculously.

"Your bow is canted ridiculously."

Miss Moss murmured.

Miss Ballhatchet again blew her whistle and closed her eyes. It had been broiling on the archery field earlier but the day had darkened by afternoon, a pewter-like sky settling in with full clouds. "Now, remember, a bow fully drawn is seven-eighths broken, hear?" She pointed, nose to nose, down the line. "This is a sport, I shouldn't have to remind you, in which women have excelled—far better," she snorted, "than men—for thousands of years, so shall we let up now, tell me? Well, we won't, pure and simple." She blew her whistle. "OK, go for your golds. Position! Aim! Draw!"—and, pausing dramatically, she pointed like a bellwether to the ten old targets (the broom-corn stuffing in each bulging out of the rips) which rose at one end of the long sward expanse like striped comic moons and boomed, "Fire!"

Snap! Twing! Whirr! And to squeaks and squawks a sluice of twenty or so arrows—apterous some, most snapping off in slices and hooks—were released, heftily, in a fluttering of novice-like bowshots. No more than two or three hit the targets. Some flew sideways. Several twirled right around the bowstrings. And one deposited in a lateral whistle not four inches from Miss Ballhatchet's manfully emplanted feet, whereupon, almost swallowing her whistle, she hopfrogged up with a piglike squeal.

"Beautiful!" she barked. "Oh, just beautiful!"

Each girl, her six shot, trooped out after her spent arrows, all of them waddling like dabchicks, stooping, wading around, hopping. The successful few dawdled at the targets, delaying the sweet necessity, for the benefit of all the others, and notably Miss Ballhatchet, of unplugging their shafts from the blue treble bed or the near-perfect red.

The archery class was almost finished, the grey light creeping slowly toward the west. A few more clouds bulled up in the northern sky, darkening, making it cooler.

From a distant knoll at the verge of the field, having strolled over after his classes, Darconville sat and watched the girls at play, trying at the same time to finish writing a letter, a deposition to the Venetian court, at least his tenth, in reply to various interrogatories touching on the litigation of his grandmother's palazzo. It felt good to be outside. He hummed quietly, content in his solitude. The ritual across the archery field, a kind of dumb-show being acted out wordlessly, he sporadically studied: especially hirsute Miss Ballhatchet marching amphitheatrically to and fro, like Lady Paramount, waving her special self-nocked lemonwood bow and bellowing outraged but indistinguishable commands that reverberated off the dormitory wall of Clitheroe and shook out croaks of crows. A thought, with one of them, flew across Darconville's head: *onto a shaft the bird's own feathers are grafted as fletches, and what must that bird think whose own quills, shafted and sped, strike it a fatal wound in mid-sky?*

The lesson down on the field continued. Miss Ballhatchet explained the technicalities of the Sioux Draw, the Mongolian Draw, the Pinch Draw. She fiddled out a timberhitch, dissertated on fletching glues, distinguished between various bow woods, and finally showed how to wax a string correctly, at which point—her breasts walloping up and down to the vigorous action—she told the girls they had damned well better stop laughing, stop immediately, she didn't mean maybe, or someone was going to find herself with a fat lip, did they understand? —good!

"Now together," clapped fit Miss Ballhatchet, "which eye do we sight with?" She placed her hand to her ear.

They shouted in unison: *"The right!"*

"And on which side of the bow is the arrow placed?"

"The left!"

So. Miss Ballhatchet marched down the landskip, turned, and blew her whistle; came the bellowed orders: "Position! Aim! Draw! Loose!—*Loose, for godsakes!*" But it was of a sudden a mis-exploded fireworks of tackle, shaft, feathers, and bows. Elsie Magoun overdrew. Martha Van Ramm didn't anchor and wobbled her arrow. Twosie Kelter closed her right eye instead of her left and then looked up, at the cost of a bulbous thumb, too soon. Sheila Mangelwurzel's shooting tab flew off. Grace Lerp's nose wasn't touching the string, her arrow spinning off like a pinwheel. One girl's string—it was Bertha Tinkle— unlooped from the nock, and she sprang forward onto her head, tripping in a ricochet over her ground-quiver to a burst of laughter and, clattering her arrows, just missing a fatal impalement on one of the several parallel-pile target points sticking up. Sarah Lou Huckpath, never very bright, moronically jerked out her bow with a bending-load of such vengeance that it immediately went *crackkk!*—and she just stood there, bewildered, holding it up like a poorly yerked wishbone. And fat little Millette Snipes, her abundant forearm unable to accommodate the conventional leather arm-guard, missed by seconds Miss Ballhatchet's initially sage, but belated, howl—"You, your arm is kinked too far into the arrow!"—screamed, bent over double (no mean feat in itself), and then zigzagged off the field with her mouth open and a flaming welt on her inner arm the shape of a nasty smile.

"O my God!" groaned Miss Ballhatchet who threw her bow spinning into the air like a boomerang. "O my God! O my God! Will you all *look* at you?"

From afar Darconville watched the girls: their youthful and soft-sinewed bodies warm from activity, perfect, shaped to full and nubile curves within the close-fitting white uniforms, like Greek maidens, heedless of time, sporting on the ancient plains of Lyrcea. They weren't all awkward. Several were quite efficient. They ingled their arrows into place, strained against their cinctures, and, leather-wristleted, with golden legs forming now to a wide stride, their valentine-shaped buttocks round and taut and full, they drew back their bowstrings slowly, the wings of their shoulder-blades peaking and tense in the sudden stasis, and then release—*thwink! thwink! thwink!* —and it rained arrows, some dudding in short arcs, many jiggery-pokery, but, again, those distinct few whizzing into the targets with firm, authoritative splats. Defter than the others, more consistent, was one lustrous bow, drawing, releasing, and whistling arrow after arrow into the bullseye as if she owned it.

The archer?

It was Isabel Rawsthorne, the chaste huntress, a golden Phrygian in white tunic, her hair knotted behind in a bun of attic beauty by an oxhide thong. The girl, plainly sought after, wooed, admired, seemed to breed idolatry among her classmates who consistently coupled up to her for conversation. She was the best in the field. Everyone knew it, the students, the teacher. Oh, certainly the teacher. The teacher, indeed! As stared the famished eagle from the Digentian rock on a choice lamb that bounds alone before Bandusia's flock Miss Ballhatchet stared on Isabel.

Darconville, even at that distance, isolated her and watched her graceful movements—she worked as dexterously as a Mede, a Scyth, a Lycian. He could almost feel the sweet perspiration on the glistening down of her cobnut-colored arms, flushed with each triumph, shot after shot. Splat! A gold. Splat! Splat! A red. A gold. Splat! A gold. So pleased was she that fit Miss Ballhatchet, otherwise aggressing from one to another to stay the trembling hand, to thread the wobbling shaft, to mutter an apt warning, never failed to circle this girl by the waist, take her to herself, and sapphonically whisper a soft word of praise into the belomant's golden hair, as if to say with Kalliphonos of Gadara: "O love, thy quiver holdeth no more wingèd shafts, for all thine arrows are into me."

The thought, however, was not Darconville's. It *couldn't* be: fate, as he took it, had long ago convinced him, if of the magic of earthly and mortal beauty, then also of its dangers. One, he knew, could not infer the existence of a reality which departed from the idea one had of it, and it was not enough to have the idea of a beautiful woman to conclude that it also existed. Gentle she seemed, breathtaking and mysterious, yes. A child of his daydreams, one glorious flower of many and glorious, a girl of fierce midnights and famishing morrows, no doubt, yes, yes, yes! But the artist's love of beauty, he also knew, should be totally separated from his desire, no? Yes! And between the soul and its abilities who, that would look into the heart of all vision, would admit a difference?

Darconville, smiling, signed his letter, stuck it into an envelope, and getting up—he noticed it was becoming overcast now, the sky above the color of claret—walked like a stag around the far edge of the field toward the Quinsy post-office, but glancing back once in the direction of the archers, he thought he saw one particular girl, standing off from the group, turn and look up long at him across the expanse of green— an irradiated countenance that now, for a month or more, had shone upon him at sudden, heart-stopping, and unlooked-for moments, like spirits meeting air in air.

It was all quite strange but, if a fantasy, nothing more than that. Darconville had no *intention* of anything more than that. They had never exchanged a word, and mightn't, and it didn't matter. Darconville felt a sacred thrift in the convenience of the Great Abstract, rather like Drayton who addressed his lady under the name of "Idea," fearing in relation to his dreams to lose wonder in losing faith. The aesthetician, thought Darconville, is mystical, his the mysticism which has no need to believe in objectivity, in the reality of the object: it was pure mysticism. And despite the fact that the distinguishable affections for her that came to him in the obscure of night gave him pause, when, at unsettling moments, he began to think of Earthly Paradise as a social possibility instead of a geographical dream, he piffled all away— because not accustomed to doing anything else—as a glorious if inviting nothing and ascribed all to that preternatural somnolence in which man, immanent with his earthly dreams, seeks for platonic support by unconscious melodious pleading in the equivalence of angels. Thus, thought Darconville, are *we* open to arrows. It is the nostalgic sigh of air that supports the whistling shaft, shooting at us precisely from nowhere; such, like a waiting target, is the pervious heart. And so not at first sight, nor with a dribbed shot, did Love give the wound. He saw and liked, he liked but did not love.

Crossing the street, Darconville heard the distant sounds from the archery field: the harsh voice still issued commands, the commands still echoed off the dormitory, the dormitory still echoed the crows.

The post-office was ready to close. The student union, the corridors, the rows of numbered mailboxes—all were empty. Darconville managed to shove his letter under the hatch just before the postmistress was ready to bring down the window-roller. He paid the lady, abruptly turned, and his heart quopped: Isabel Rawsthorne stood directly in front of him. She smiled faintly, lowering her eyes, and almost voicelessly asked past him for a stamp. Then the roller hurtled down for good. And in that empty corridor, they found themselves together, for the first time in history, alone.

Darconville swallowed: she was positively beautiful, her skin luminous, glowing with perspiration, her hair pure flax drawn back from her youthful temples showing slight blue veins, and her eyes as clear as the waters of the Dircaean spring. She was still wearing her archery clothes, wristlet, and arm-brace, and, while she seemed mortal enough, he might have been staring upon the angel Zagzagel, flaming above the burning bush.

It was whimsical and fatal, at once.

"Could you c-come to my house tomorrow, Isabel?"

The reply, positive, was almost inaudible.

"I live—"

Her eyes sparkled. "—in the old white house?"

And she was gone, and had been for five minutes—or a year— before Darconville, waking to fact, noticed she had forgotten her stamp.

The weather had fully turned. Darconville walked out of the building under the skirts of a promising thunderstorm, the sky britannia, the clouds ruined at the edges in black mist. A wind came up, cool, smelling of rain. As he passed along the street, heading toward his house, he looked down over the archery field, now empty, and thought: what will happen now? Curiously, he wondered if she were simply the result of his own curiosity about himself, as he might be for her. The trees shushed in the wind, as mist could be felt in the air, and he saw several crows squirt from a gigantic maple, one of which swung high over him like a half-born thought, squawking in loud cracks: *actaeon! actaeon!*

A line of poetry suddenly came to him from nowhere: "Therefore that he may raise, the Lord throws down." He recognized the line, thought for a minute, and closed his eyes.

"I am Donne," quoth he.

XV

Tertium Quid

Sir, say no more.
Within me 'tis as if
The green and climbing eyesight of a cat
Crawled near my mind's poor birds.

—Trumbull Stickney

THE OVERHANGING WOODS around campus were lovely, a shiny black-green in the fine mist blowing, swirling, in the warm wind that fluttered the poplars and swept yellow leaves from the tall maples across the dark wet walk of Fitts dormitory. A skyful of sullen clouds, piling out of each other, promised a glut of rain. The dorms, their hundred hundred windows lighted against nightfall, shed a fictitious glow over the landscape growing obscure now toward outlying Quinsyburg.

"Where all is Isabel?" asked her roommate, Trinley Moss, to several of her suitemates there who at the last minute were fitting on earrings, brushing out their hair, and touching on lipstick before running off to the dining-hall. It was dinnertime. "Out walking?" asked Glycera Pentlock. "Beats me," shrugged Childrey Fawcett, trying on a transparent rain hat. "Probably," said Sheila Mangelwurzel. "I haven't seen her since archery, have you?" Annabel Lee Jenks, who'd seen her coming out of the post-office earlier, said she mentioned she might not be going to Charlottesville with her this weekend.

Squinting through the dark window, her hands clapped to her temples as blinders, Trinley spied down three floors and suddenly exclaimed, "Now, if that don't beat all!"—for there was Isabel, still wearing archery tunic and wristlet, skipping heartfree through a cut-path and joyfully kicking up leaves and crunching acorns all the way up the front steps. Trinley shook her head, laughed, and left the window on a charge to join the others scampering out in slickers, raingear, and old trenchcoats faded to white and soiled to brown.

Suddenly, Isabel heard a shout—and, turning to the street, she felt her heart sink.

An old blue car, dented and of an indistinct make, was parked across the way. It was not so much the familiar eyes scowling over the driver's window, befogged and lowered halfway, that upset her so much. It was the crooking finger that beckoned her. It was the imperious crooking finger. It was the crooking finger.

The sky dissolved in heavy rain. Squealing, the Fitts girls scattered through the puddles in their galoshes, drenched for the farcical umbrellas that had blown inside-out. Winnie Pegue, Castoria Fletcher, Ghiselaine Martin, Shirley Lafoon, Lorinda and Lucinda Belltone, Hallowe'ena Rampling all ran ahead. Late, Childrey Fawcett and Trinley Moss, clutching their rubber hats to their ears for dear life, tore from the doorway and happily spatterdashed in high boots across the lawn toward the archway of the dining-hall. They ran past the mall, hardly looking up at the blue car where two people, sitting within, seemed ghostly silhouettes behind the steamed windows—one motionless, one gesturing wildly as if the entire world was hostile to him and he to the world, as if, as he talked, waging continuous warfare against everything around him.

"Was *that* the boy," yelled Childrey through the downpour, giggling, licking driblets from her face, and running as fast as she could, "who drove Isabel down here?"

"Yes," hooted Trinley.

"What is his name?"

They were running furiously, squelching in long hops across the grass.

"Govert."

"I said," gurgled Childrey, just out of earshot, "what is his *name,* stupid?"

The rain was hammering down in sheets. Trinley, running hard, turned exasperatedly, put her hands into a foghorn, and shouted, "I told you. Govert! *Govert van der Slang!*"

XVI

Quires

I met gnomes
In a garden with many-colored flowerbeds.

—Maria Leuberg

FRESHMAN PAPERS, phenotypically, leave something to be desired. The stack of them on Darconville's desk, a bundle of odd-cum-
shorts, seemed fathomless as he worked them over with a red pencil
long into the night. The work took his full attention: for some reason,
Isabel, leaving him a note, had postponed her visit to the following
night.

So on he read. It was dreary prose, indeed, a sententious parade of
marrow-pea wisdom, garbled quotation, and fractured syntax, the
more frightful, most of them, for having been written out in longhand.
Niggards separated words. Ideorealists upslanted. The morbid girls in-

tertwined lines; the vain whorled; the corkscrew hand seemed to indicate a kind of obstinacy. Everyone's handwriting had a physiognomy of its own. It was a revelation of sorts, those, of course, that could be read, for there were a few specimens of the hook-and-butt-joint variety which looked as though they'd been written with a spitsticker misgripped between two non-opposable toes.

But the subject matter—there was the fascination! The girls were Southerners, uncompetitive in terms of mind, and while each approached her topic, alien because academic, with buffleheaded equivocation and ineptitude, the papers almost all digressed into an autobiography of dreamy fancy, teasing indulgence, and orphic posturing: a high-souled but predatory tone of flirtation which reduced everything of intellection to a floating and eddying mistfall wherethrough each author's face could be found cutely peeking with batting eyelashes and that romantically illuminated look usually reserved for meeting one's lover.

Darconville sighed and looked, sighed and looked, sighed and looked, and sighed again—then finished. He entered the grades in his class book.

"Martha Washington, Hemstitcher" by Muriel Ambler	B—
"Sawmilling: Why It's Important to Us" by Melody Blume	C
"A Look at Tarot Packs" by Wroberta Carter	D
"My Summer in Chincoteague" by Ava Caelano	B—
"Freshman Worries!" by Barbara Celarent	C
"*Three Wogs:* My Favorite Novel" by Analecta Cisterciana	A
"How to Candy Shoups" by Ailsa Cragg	C
"Fidelity in Penguins" by Childrey Fawcett	B+
"The Legend of Kālī Pátnī" by Galveston Foster	B
"The Life and Works of Kate Douglas Wiggin" by Scarlet Foxwell	B
"Jesus Christ: My Personal Savior" by Opal Garten	B
"The Day We Lost Our Dog, Pee Wee—and Found Him Again!" by Marsha Goforth	C
"My Pet Peeve: Pet Peeves" by LeHigh Hialeah	C—
"My Life Eats Shit" by Elsie Magoun [nervous breakdown]	Inc.
"Quinsy College: That First (Gulp!) Glimpse" by Sheila Mangelwurzel	D

"Was Shakespeare Shakespeare?" by Christie McCarkle   C

"My First Batch of Potato Cookies" by Trinley Moss   B—

"Dating vs. Non-Dating" by Glycera Pentlock   D

"Love at First Sight" by Hypsipyle Poore   B

"*Areopagitica*" by Hallowe'ena Rampling [plagiarism!]   F

"An Embarrassing Occurrence at Zutphen Farm" by Isabel Rawsthorne

"My Prize Hen" by Cecilia Sketchley   B

"A Poetic Analysis of 'The Pig Lady'" by Butone Slocum   B

"Coiffures Through the Ages, 1936–1970" by Millette Snipes   B—

"Pellagra: Blight of the South" by April Springlove   C

[missing] by Lately Thompson   F

"4-Hing Can Be Fun" by DeDonda Umpton   D

"A Short Study on '*The Essay of Megalanthropogenesis,* or, the Art of Producing Intelligent Children Who Will Bear Great Men'" by Shelby Uprightly   A

"Quain's Fatty Heart: A New Disease?" by Martha Van Ramm   B+

"Dinky, My Favorite Rabbit" by Poteet Wilson   D

"Menopause: It's Closer Than You Think" by Rachel Windt   D

"'Traveler': General Lee's Loyal Steed" by Laurie Lee Zenker   D—

Darconville dropped in his drawer the thirty or so little maimed and undermedicated projects, roughly eight to fifteen pages in length each, stapled, bradded, corner-crimped, and of course those several gathered together feminologistically with a punched hole and a loop of yarn.

The one paper he'd set aside—after shooing Spellvexit away—he now had a chance to review in peace. The calligraphy was spidery, a thin arachnoid scrawl, but unique in its own way and, he thought, rather beautiful, with somewhat of a forward slant, long t-bars, and the overuse of hyphens, along with perpendicular ascending final sweeps and, well, the rather choleric preference for red ink. It wasn't, frankly, either a hand or a prose style comfortable with language, nor was it, upon the reflection of several re-readings, a person perhaps very comfortable with herself. The pity of it! He found himself—queerly, he was not certain why—loath to give it a grade. It was strange: a judgment of any kind seemed presumptuous. Nettled only in that, while logic told him the paper was flawed, truth told him it wasn't, Darconville delayed.

Although exhausted, he lit up another cigarette and went to the window. He wouldn't grade it: no one is equal to only one thing she does. He went to bed. But he *had* to grade it—so he got up, turned on the light, and read it again.

XVII

"An Embarrassing Occurrence
at Zutphen Farm"

We had but one interview, and that was formal, modest, and uninteresting

—OLIVER GOLDSMITH, *She Stoops to Conquer*

Précis: The Disquisition recounts how Isabel Rawsthorne, upon the Occasion of being invited to dine at the large farm of her Wealthy Neighbors—surstyled van der Slang—was overtaken with nerves, and, giving Further Particulars concerning that, is then wholly devoted to a Full and Faithful Report of what befell the subject in mid-meal when, twiddling her plate in a vigorous attempt to separate for consumption an obdurate chop, she embarrassingly jerked her portion of peas across the table, a Lapse in Elegance she begs leave to offer, while confessing no other motive which her heart had informed her of, as caused by finding herself in Unnatural Surroundings, after which the Narrative reverts to the High-Dutch pedigree of her Neighbors (q.v.), containing under Different Heads everything Illustrative and Explanatory of a social class disquiparant to her own, superadded to which is not only a Digression on the current value of the Angus cattle they owned but also an Episode, provided for comic relief, that treats of Diverse Little Matters anent the reactions of the Boys in that family, how they laughed, &c &c, appending then a Touching Moment when the adjudged *delectus personae,* though pulsing by secret oath to refuse it, is given an Open Invitation to return, this comprising a Final Exit concluded to the satisfaction of Practically Everybody, intended all, as so put, less as a rehearsal of the Scanty and Defective social graces of the author than an example of the Voluminous Essay, indeed Book, which she implied could but never would be written on same because of her insignificance. It was signed: Isabel Her Mark—and graded A.

Awkwardness is the prerogative of kaleidogyns.

XVIII

Isabel

Art thou that she than whom no fairer is?

—Christ Church ms.

THE NIGHT finally came. A porchlight was lit. Upstairs, Darconville sat at his desk, a single finger in cogitative support of his head, flinging arbitrarily between one thought and another and staring into space. It was Thursday.

He wasn't worried. He felt apprehensive, but he noticed: it wasn't his kind of apprehension. She was coming to visit him this night, and, although he tried to work, driven by the fact that for several nights he hadn't, he couldn't and, furthermore, perversely deemed it of no consequence. He had of course often written scribble before, but that wasn't it—now, nothing came.

There was, he supposed, a secret logic to it all, as there was to so much in his particular life thus far, but he suspected that the man who has faith in logic is always cuckolded by reality, and so his brow was drawn with this worry: that he wasn't worried—an apprehension neither diminished nor temporized during those long hours of silence that eventually passed and, after the faintest knock, brought Isabel Rawsthorne into his rooms with all her bravery on, and tackle trim, sails filled, and streamers waving. Instinctively, Darconville kissed her cheek (surprising even himself!), the only displacement activity he could manage for the hitch in his throat that kept him from speaking. He set out some candles. Silently, he went to pour some wine and, after standing in the kitchen with eyes closed for a moment, returned. Taking her glass, Isabel thanked him.

They both stood silent in obscure embarrassment, facing each other. No mood was ever more subdued in relation to what was felt, yet etched with those graceful and tiny observances that somehow connote aspiration and make every ferial act festal.

Darconville who couldn't speak tried.

"I've often wondered—whether you can see my light from Fitts."

"And I've often wondered," she whispered, "which of the lights I've seen from my window in Fitts were yours."

There was silence.

"We neither of us know."

"Neither of us," she echoed, looking up. Any look with so much in it never met his eyes before.

It was a face—*ecce, quam bonum! quam pulchritudinem!*—sweeter than Nature's itself, her soft eyes full of light. She was wearing a slight summery buff-pink dress, low cut in front, with a design of cherrysprigs and long sleeves flounced out at the shoulders, a fashion that did not adorn so much as it was adorned. A pink lutestring ribbon matched one wrapped in a bandeau around a weft at the back of her flowing hair. She was like a beautiful apparition of heather, white, pink, and rose.

There was a radiance in the unspoiled face which glowed, as Darconville looked at her through the clouds of golden hair, above the swip of the flickering candle. It was a flesh, sculpturally considered, whiter than new-sawn ivory. Her eyes, fawn's—clear and agatescent at the edges—were the gentle brown of woodsmoke (if a trifle too close) showing a light as if the heart within were sun to them, with the trace of a smile there, a sparkle, her lips in a second renewed, a sweet aristocratic curve which drew a faint line by the cheek at a perfect angle of incidence, creating on one side an ever-so-slight dimple. She had a positively perfect mouth, with yet a curious *concordia discors* to that face.

It was a scar—a slight pale dartle, once stitched, like an elongated teardrop coming down the left cheekbone, a small disfigurement as if a tiny, tiny dagger sat there, as if, perhaps, the Devil, his breath black as hellebore, had shadowed her birth-bed, stepped through the valance and, astonished for envy, leaned down and paid her the exaction of a poisoned kiss. But what awful conjectures it gave rise to! Had she been knived? Had someone thrown something at her? Had she been imped by a wicked family? And yet, Darconville recalled, hadn't Helen herself had a scar which her lover, Paris, called *Cos Amoris,* the whetstone of love?

"Are you—a writer?"

"Yes," said Darconville, turning from his thoughts.

She only smiled, her girlishly soft hands lying motionless in her lap. She seemed so different from other girls he'd known, her unmeretricious eyes, her face full of messages one had to read in a single flash. Intrigued, he felt he would never know her fully but that, somehow, she would always enjoy the compromise of exception—an exception that proved the rule of what beauty was and is and yet but once seemed a dream for us only for want of being seen. Standing up, she looked around Darconville's room with curiosity, pausing at certain objects she touched with fleeting taps—the skull, the fat pen, the watch on the nail—exclaiming over them with a kind of knowing sympathy for his strange, perhaps cracked romantic life. She bent over his manuscript.

"I was going to say," said Darconville quickly, a feeling of sudden embarrassment and undeniable discomfort emanating from what she in nature embodied compared to what he in art attempted, "that since I first saw you in class I've found myself—"

Ecstatic? Miserable? It would have sounded ridiculous, whatever he said. He poured some more wine with innocent confusion.

"—I don't know," he stammered, "I guess I found myself wondering if you were anymore at h-home here than I."

He wanted to tell her that he couldn't sleep or write, that there was, in spite of that, a lovely inevitableness to the suddenly unmeasurable

and reasonless order of his life now, a supernatural sort of coexistence
with angels who left him with no choice, somehow, only alternatives
and often confusing him to such a degree that he couldn't tell the evil
from the good, demons from daevas, satans from seraphim as they
crisscrossed through an imagination given over before now only to
fiction. And so he wondered who are you, Shekinah? Who are you,
Emanation? Who are you, Anima, who framed such another ideal?

"Here? You mean, in Quinsyburg?"

"Yes."

"It's lonesome at school. But," she said, pulling her thumb, "not—
here." She looked up, her color high. "In this room."

As Isabel paused at the mantelpiece, Darconville noticed more
clearly what before he'd but briefly noticed: a peasant-like thickness in
her legs, a flesh of babyfat (touched here and there by pink arborescent veins) which overloaded the lower body somewhat and forced
her into a kind of affrighted retention of movement, a defensive posture in which, so poised, she seemed always ready to back away, all to
contect what, by accepting, might have made her even more beautiful
because less self-conscious. Argive Helen with fat thighs? It didn't
matter: he prayed she could see for herself he *knew* it didn't matter at
all. Trees grew more out of the air than out of the ground, didn't
they?

There were long silences, the kind where everything seems to be
being said but nothing at all is uttered. She was faithful in her attention, but there wasn't a sound. Such a strange tenderness reached him,
but no one said a word.

"I haven't thanked you, Isabel," said Darconville suddenly, "for
your gift."

"My gift?"

"That."

"Ooooh, yes," Isabel laughed softly and gently picked up from the
mantel the pomander ball. He could see it pleased her to have done an
action by stealth only to have it found out by accident. Darconville
also noticed that she always picked up things delicately with the exclusive precision of only thumb and index-finger, a seraphically nimble
sleight-of-hand with all the other fingers (ringless, he saw) spread out
fan-wise and tapering to the flattest of fingertips.

"It has the scent of a fairy-forest," said Isabel, breathing in the orange and cloves and regarding Darconville, sideways, with a covertly

wistful smile. And then, foreshadowing a "changeling" fantasy he'd soon see was often hers, she quietly told him of a dream she'd with abiding continuity had from childhood: she was a solitary princess, wandering barefoot, lost in a desolate land whose perspective slid down into lonely valleys and empty meadows where people were cruel and no one understood her or who she was until one day she came to her fairy-forest, an enchanted world of flowers, castles, animals—

A knock at the door interrupted her. It was Miss Trappe, tiny under a huge straw hat, holding an armful of—but it triple-somer-saulted with a whine out of her hands, rucked up a rug, and went skidding beneath it only to the point of its blinking eyes and pink nose, parts all recognizably Spellvexit's. That, then, became the happy occa-sion for Darconville of introducing Isabel Rawsthorne to Miss Trappe who, excusing herself, mentioned she only wanted to be sure the cat got in (she swore he mewed "Why, *good* evening, madam!" from the front porch), but before she left—exclaiming upon Isabel's beauty—she invited her, anytime, to come visit a lonely old woman. And then she was off. Darconville told Isabel how much she would like Miss Trappe, as he himself did, and encouraged her to accept that invita-tion. "And this"—Darconville's lap was suddenly filled with an agi-tated creature, flumping its paws and eyeing Isabel suspiciously—"is Spellvexit, who walks by himself and all places are not alike to him. He talks."

Isabel, unsuccessfully, tried to touch him.

"I don't seem ever able to communicate with anybody," whispered Isabel as if she were breathing on glass, distractedly twicking her thumbnail, the cuticle of which, saw Darconville, was curiously wrin-kled. The words almost broke his heart.

"Surely your mother and father—"

"I have no father."

It was spoken so fast that Darconville, struck with it, could find nothing whatever to say. Isabel, it seemed, never said anything impor-tant to him except while making some physical movement to distract attention from her words, for simultaneously she held a cushion to her-self and something jumped in her eyes, now tense with search. He couldn't define it at once, but after watching her for a space, while his brain pressed for the right words to say, he thought perhaps suddenly he'd understood the meaning of her dream. But beyond that, his spirit extended outward, rising from stoical self-sufficiency and reaching, like

sweet miracle, to a conscious concern not to flout the souls of the lonely
on earth, and so Isabel went to Darconville's heart by the very nearest
road, which was the road of pity, smoothed by grace, and beauty, and
a gentleness that seemed, at last, the one ray of light in the darkness of
Quinsyburg.

Darconville sought a way to put her at ease, experiencing, however,
an intimation of helplessness in the face of what he guessed to be a
strange pride and almost exultant loneliness, for without a sigh, without a break, she pondered wildly, floating upon some inner sea of feeling while yet being frightened, it seemed, of suddenly drowning in it.
He attempted to reach her, carefully, without trying to contribute to
the invasion of forces that within her had clearly already begun. And
in someone so young! Come, asked Darconville, wasn't she only seven-
teen? No answer. Eighteen? She nodded. Where did she live? It was a
place called Fawx's Mt., about seventy miles north of Quinsyburg.
And hadn't she wanted to go to college?

"Isabel?"

"Everybody thought it best," she replied, her grave reflective calm
obviously masking an unsettled temperament in the matter. "My
uncle, who lives with us, didn't really care. My mother, I suppose, did.
But I told my mother, no, I really wasn't anxious to come. I
wanted—"

But Isabel hurried across the passage, silently, leaving in the stead
of whatever it was that slipped away simple resignation, and mechanically smiled at her hands. He looked for something to say.

"Did your mother drive you down to Quinsyburg?"

It was an ordinary question ordinarily asked, but she looked away,
smoothing the nap of her dress over and over again. The poignancy of
her shyness, or her hurt, or her fear—whatever—increased his
awareness of the suspense between them.

"No," whispered Isabel quickly, lowering her eyes, "a friend." She
glanced imperceptibly across her shoulder in a brief but distinct scrutiny. "Just a friend."

Smiling, Darconville hurriedly looked round for something to do or
say, anything to precipitate a change of subject and arrest not one, but
two minds beating against the unknown, for a counterpoise had lowered: a *friend*—the commonest dysphemism in an affair of the heart
—is always a member of the opposite sex. He saw the shadow of someone else cast across her life. It didn't matter, he thought; inevitable

things don't. And in spite of his anticipation of that very possibility, he leaned forward, his hands under his chin, and quoted humorously,

> "My maiden Isabel,
> Reflaring rosabel,
> The fragrant camomel."

Isabel paused, left off biting her underlip in concentrated thought, and pulled her thumb. "Oh, I ruin everything," she burst out. "I seem to ruin everything." (She pronounced it "ru-een.") "I do! I do!"

"No, not at all. No," Darconville heard himself insisting, shaking his head, mad to absolve her of anything, "you don't ruin everything." She seemed so lost, outside the world looking in, divided from him in some way not as yet understood, drawing away and revenging herself on her own magnificence as if trying to distance the perfection she, by embodying, couldn't know. She hunched down into herself, saddened, like a small batrachian in a hide-hole.

"I feel small, for some reason," she said. "I feel like a little thing."

Sympathetically, Darconville touched her chin and lifted her head. "Then I'll call you that," said he. " 'The Little Thing.' " Isabel couldn't stop the smile extracted from her, but at the words, automatically, she pulled her dress to cover her legs as best she could. *Can't you see it doesn't matter?* thought Darconville. *Can't you see that?*

"The curfew," said Isabel. "I must be getting back."

Darconville drank some wine. "Oh," he said, "but we haven't told you anything about us?"

Isabel looked startled, hearing the plurality of plural pronouns, and said almost below her breath, "I thought you—were all alone."

She pulled her thumb.

Suddenly, her eyes grew luminous with that special excitement of sympathy that can bring tears from something deeper than passion as Darconville lifted up Spellvexit—a twitching, bewhiskered explanation—from the top of the large trunk he then dragged from the corner of the room. And as he sketchily outlined the course of events that had brought him down South, filling in various facts of his past, both eccentric and ecclesiastical (she agreed, as he preferred it that way, to keep those religious adventures a secret between them: for privacy) he sorted through the trunk to show her what, over the years, he'd collected: a golden ikon; old flags and coins; a few of his own manuscripts; ancient books, several written by his ancestors; photographs of

Europe—many of Venice and, of course, his grandmother—and other romantic bits-and-pieces evoking a thousand distant places all more exciting than the little town of Quinsyburg from which, suggested Darconville, his eyes sparkling mischievously, they could both secretly escape that very night! Isabel's gay laughter rang like a peal of bells and, upon fleeting reflection, asked as if really to know, "Where will we go?"

Darconville was almost ready to pull out a map!

The assortment of odds-and-ends in the trunk, however, took Isabel's attention, and as she delicately lifted out each object, attracted especially to a carved Russian fife, she seemed for the first time truly animated and excited. She found confidence. She asked questions. And always she was full of exclamations, charming Darconville by the cadences of her voice, now rising, then dropping to a rich whisper of roguishness in which a slight rural monotony of speech disappeared and a soul resounded.

"At my house—how could I *forget?*—I have a real snakeskin *and* my grandmother's diamond ring *and* an actual tintype, really, of Lee on his horse, let me see," she continued breathlessly, "and a very old bracelet my grandfather found in China a long time ago."

Darconville, impishly, asked: "Was he Chinese?"

Isabel laughed into her hand.

"Silly," she said, clicking her tongue and tapping his nose with her finger, coming close enough for Darconville to feel the weblike softness of her hair and almost taste a breath like candy, Sweet William, golddrops. "He was in the navy."

Amused, she feigned to strike him. "He's been around the world, you know. Several times."

"It must be lonely sailing around the world"—quickly, Isabel looked at Darconville to see if somewhere in his consciousness by obstinate resistance he were opposed to such a thing—"unless, of course," shrugged Darconville, "you have nothing to keep you on land."

There fell an odd silence. Darconville looked at her. But Isabel was staring enigmatically past him, her brown eyes fixed upon vacancy as if she were scrutinizing some faraway image on a distant horizon, trying to divine, as it were, and perhaps overcome its limits by some studious, some private act of the will. Darconville, at last, thought that he had met someone as romantic, as full of dreams, as impractically and wondrously mad as himself. Then she looked up, her sad smile like the light of white candles shining from a quiet altar. Darconville reached for something in the trunk and asked her if she'd accept it as a small gift. It was the carved Russian fife.

Thanking him, Isabel folded it to her breast. She waited a moment, solemnly. "You—" She hesitated. "—you won't mind if I ask you something?"

With precise thumb-and-forefinger she carefully picked up the fat pen lying on his desk.

"Would you, sometime, write a poem for me?"

"I promise," said Darconville.

The piety of her expression, the peculiar intimacy of that mysterious girlishness anticipated in his imagination, nourished all his happiness. She exhaled so deeply that he was instantly reminded of the Elizabethan idea that each sigh costs the heart a drop of blood.

"Oh dear," whispered Isabel, "I feel so safe here now."

"Here? You mean, in Quinsyburg?"

The room grew strangely quiet as Isabel, coloring, bowed her head, her eyelashes sweeping down in a sedulously lowered glance. She paused.

"Near you."

The candles, swipping, took their attention for a moment, throwing shadows this way and that. As she watched the flames, there was a complicated wistfulness in her expression until, in the solitude, itself almost predatory for the spell it threw, she turned to him. "We won't meet again like this—for the first time. We won't meet again, will we," she asked, "when we're strangers? We know each other now?"

Was it a question? A statement?

There was not a flicker of a doubt, however, as to the summons he received from this girl who for so long, or so it seemed, had insinuated herself into his life as an almost spectral apparition. Gently, touching the small of her back, he drew her body with scarcely perceptible pressure against his own, as she leaned forward, her heart beating fast, a certain virginal detachment in her awkwardness, and she came forth, as if collapsing, towards him, her flowing hair scented with a fragrance of almost immortal influence. Fairest of mortals, thought Darconville, thou distinguished care of a thousand bright inhabitants of air! They looked into each other's eyes in an admixture of sudden beauty and confusion, and, in that pure light, Darconville clasped her almost to suffocation against his heart and kissed her until destiny, fulfilled, seemed no longer necessary. It is always the most beautiful moment in a love affair.

Isabel was already on the porch and down the steps when Darconville, in a hushed voice, called to her through the darkness, "What will you give me for a basket of hugs?"

And just before she disappeared into the night of fells and foxglove, silence and stars, Isabel turned and ran back several steps to lean forward and whisper with the inaudibility that is at the heart of joy itself, "I will give you a basket of kisses."

XIX

Effictio

How to name it, blessed it.

—GERARD MANLEY HOPKINS

HEAD: Stately

EYES: Brown demilunes (something too close together) proving Astrarche, Queen of Stars, a twin

NOSE: A nobility softening its slight acumination

MOUTH: Perfect, with the tremlet of a dimple at the edge. The tallest hyperboles cannot descry the beauty of its smile, which flashes, however, teeth too large.

LIPS: Full

EARS: A gynotikolobomassophile's delight

FACE: Simonetta Vespucci's, in the ecstasy of transverberation:

"A face made up
Out of no other shop
Than what nature's white hand sets ope."

The scar weeps once, forever.

HAIR: A beneplacit of God. Shode at the center, it falls in fine burnished gold either straight down or is worn, alternately, in a single bell-pull braid.

HEIGHT: Ca. 5'7"

BREASTS: Doe's noses

HANDS: Big-boned. The fingers, with flattened tips, are long and strong.

WAIST: Clipsome, sized to Love's wishes

ANKLES: Scaurous

LEGS: The one devenustation. What intrusive image will you have, swollen fetlock? Curb at the bank of the hock? Puffed gaskin? Thoroughpin? Stringhalt? They are "filled" legs, in the tradition of the round goblet which wanteth not liquor, an heap of wheat set about with lilies. There is nothing to forgive. The Venus de Milo wears a size 14 shoe.

XX

A Wandering in Brocéliande

Wrapt in my careless cloke, as I walke to and fro, I see love can shew what force there reigneth in his bow.

—HENRY HOWARD, Earl of Surrey

THERE WAS A MUSIC in the world that night never before heard, strains reaching Darconville alone across moor and highland, field and common, cliff and vale and watercourse and piercing his heart in a sweet, impossible ache. Unable to sleep, he'd dressed hastily, run down the stairs, and driven to an out-of-way spot miles outside Quinsyburg. At the edge of an open field, rising to a wooded height, he for no particular reason came to a stop and got out.

It was well past midnight. The vault of black sky, its clear stars so sublime and infinite above him, seemed in its immensity to speak of what it was in his power to become. Darconville walked and walked, directionless, across the night-dark grass of the meadow, perfumed by the musk of the earth, and his heart beat in his chest as if it would burst. He soon found himself across the field. It was wooded now, wonderfully gloomy, somehow steeped in legend, and he imagined that every clump of trees, every hollow, every vine was a part of Brocéliande where the enchanter Merlin dwelt and that every boulder was a menhir behind which, secretly, a druid hid, spying on his joy.

A cold mist haunted the fallows, with the odor of trees, stubble, and seeds; dampness and earthmusk; and the spotted plage of decaying leaves. An owl pitchpiped. The trees were loaded with mast, their boughs pendulous and brown, and piles of leaves gave way to his tread. What was there in forests, representing more of mystery than light, that now promised to illuminate just where he must go?

And now he was climbing up over the rocks, the branches and leaves in the moonlight throwing strange pelicasaurian figures everywhere about him. A wild wind gusted at his coat at several points, only blowing up his fever to climb up even higher as if resolved to discover in the spectral, astropoetic light of some clearing above—a height, perhaps, fashioned from what he felt—the tall presences of aeons and archons, peris and paracletes, mystic thrones and twelve-winged kalkydri beckoning him forward less from where he stood than closer toward where she was. It was fated: their souls must have been in love before they had been born and were dreaming this dream they were living, a promise of love, though blind and slow like all prophecies, that participated in and so would last an eternity.

The moon, bright, blackened shadows, gave every green thing a fivefold addition to its greenness, and whitened out a way. The wind swirled and looped his coat as he reached the very height of the hill, and the uprushing of enchantment he felt flooding his arms, making him almost delirious, seemed to send him soaring past the regions of the earth where, giving to the wind the kisses it returned—high in the cataracts of air, beyond the running clouds—he pointed to the world that formed her face and cried out in ecstasy, *"I love you!"*

XXI

"The Little Thing"

What a tyranny, what a penetration of bodies is this! Thou
drawest with violence, and swallowest me up, as Charydis doth
Sailors with thy rocky eyes.

—Philostratus Lemnius

FOR WEEKS THEREAFTER, Darconville found the small notes
left everywhere for him always infested with little one-dimensional sets
of peepers, like the two eyes of Horus; thus:

They were signed, "The Little Thing."

XXII

The Clitheroe Kids

Like moody beasts they lie along the sands.

—JOHN GRAY, *Femmes Damnées*

"'Rafe, throbbing, thought: I'll fix you, sweetheart—and, hitting that dame a good smack, he flung her onto the bed and prepared to throw his hot gooms into her,'"

read Jessie Lee Deal, licking her upper lip.

"'O brother, he thought, as she jiggled lasciviously in her scanties, this is some brawd! And not exactly overdressed! And then, hornmad, he drilled his lust-hungry tongue deep into Rhoda's ear and hissed, "O.K., boobsie, show me some of your tricks!" She arched her back and writhed about. O beautiful! thought Rafe, this kiddo is wide-open, no buts about it.'"

It was a cold winter night, and in one of the rooms on the fourth floor of Clitheroe, a senior dorm, the girls from several adjoining suites had gathered together, as was their habit, for a general bull-session of gab and gossip: sitting around in pajamas, swapping stories, and, on this occasion, listening to random installments being read from a currently popular and exhilarating fuel-burner called *I Knew Rhoda Rumpswab* by 16 People (Troilism Press, N.Y.)—a paperback, slightly damp and fungoid from overuse, that sprouted open if left on a table to several well-reviewed passages. The room was filled with an eye-watering canopy of cigarette smoke. A couple of girls were yawning. But it was better than studying.

"I declare," said Cookie Crumpacker, with a wimbling tongue, "I'm about to just plain boil over listening to that thing, honey, and you can *believe* it if you think you can't!" She rubbed her hand over her gluteus medius and whistled out in two beats the commonly understood flirtatious iamb: u —!

Anaphora Franck, sitting on the edge of the bed, grabbed the book. "I have fifty reasons I'd like to be Rhoda Rumpswab. Want to know one?"

"Hey, but isn't that a pseudonysm or something?" asked slew-eyed Celeste Skyler, the bulb of her head voodooed with bobby pins, pink rollers, and metal clips, and she pointed to the book cover (Woman, Leg up on Chair, Unhooking Fishnet Hose). The herb wisdom at Quinsy, let it be said, did not grow in everyone's garden.

It was a question, however, given small attention. No one was listening. No one ever listened. Added to that, it was just the very *worst* time of year. Christmas had come and gone, and even the picturesque dusting of light snow on campus gave short relief to the students, now facing exams. The night-to-morning processus during Finals Week rarely varied, obligations were unrelieved, and the faculties of concentration lagged. And then of course the girls all knew each other— usually by chummy diminutives like Muffie, Mopsy, Sissy, Missy, etc. —and any new habits, opinions, or quirks at this late date could only come as a surprise. So they just lazed about doing what girls together have been doing from time immemorial, primping, talking about boys, and raising, as only groups in dorms can, those neo-ethical, quasi-theological questions usually reserved for the wee hours, you know, famous old topoi like: Would You Confess Under Torture? Which of the Five Senses Would You Rather Lose? How Would You Commit

Suicide? Would You Ever Eat a Human Being? (And, of course, its ancillary: Which Part?) What Would Be Your One Wish If You Had Only One? What If You Were Alone at Night and a Weirdo Came into Your Room?

Mimsy Borogroves was ironing her hair. Sally Ann Sprouse, smoothing gouts of depilatory cream over her saber-shinned legs, wondered out loud if erections hurt boys. Glenda Barrow, visibly keratoconjunctivine, said she was going to sue the college linen service and asked if anybody wanted to take bets on it. One fat little puella, Thomasina Quod—a girl, reputed to be an ovarian dwarf, who was often disparagingly called "Buns"—lay back eating a poptart and reading a pamphlet of intimate advice with her feet up on the wall in tiny slippers trimmed with moth-eaten squirrel fur. Holly Sunday, a folksinger with a macrobiotic complexion and straight blond hair, was strumming a guitar and singing with exquisite purity to a darkened window. Aone Pitts, wimpled in a towel, sat in a corner tossing a beanbag frog up and down and claimed she once heard of an unmarried girl transvestite who fell in love with a married homosexual man! Well, interposed Donna Wynkoop, there was a guy on *her* street back home who was famous for stopping the interior opening of his nostrils with his tongue! And what, Robin Winglet wanted to know, did they think she found that morning on a wheat biscuit in the Quinsy dining-hall? No one asked. And so she tried, unsuccessfully, to tell lovely, spoiled, rich Pengwynne Custis who was not listening but who had been for some time confiding to everyone, while blowing her nails dry, that she had lost her virginity in the Zakopane Forest to a Polish officer with sideburns when she was fourteen—and she loved it, she said, she didn't regret it one bit, she'd do it again, and they could all eat their hearts out for all she cared, OK? But to care was, logically, to have listened. "*I* lost it the night of the sophomore prom, in a car," said Mona Lisa Drake, with a broad smile. "I just kicked my yellow satin pumps out the window, yanked up my organdy, and got tagged. It was called 'The Spring Bounce.'" She winked. "The prom, that is."

A spate of rape stories followed. Sex, of course, was by far the most popular subject in Clitheroe 403, but it was equally understood, in that particular room at least, that bragging about one's sexual adventures with any kind of conceit or competition was simply not done, and most of the girls there generally talked about sex as if to avoid it or exorcise it, as Eskimos, say, use refrigerators to keep food from freezing. The reason wasn't difficult to figure out. It was Hypsipyle Poore's room.

"A cockroach," said Robin Winglet, to no one.

A knock, an entry.

The room went silent. Loretta Boyco—tall, ill-complexioned, homely as a winter pear—stood in the doorway with her hair-dryer and, explaining that the hum was bothering her roommate, asked if she could plug it in in their outlet.

"Plug it in—right over there."

"You can plug it in *any*where," pitched in Cookie Crumpacker, smirking and stroking her tummy underneath the football jersey she wore which showed, to her advantage, a rather extreme case of bouncy overendowment. She crossed her legs and winked at Loretta, who glowered back. They weren't friends. Loretta, not one of the "regulars" there, was of a somewhat different stripe: secretary of the Tidy Lawn Club at Quinsy, proctor at Fitts, and ex-president of the Baptist Student Union at Consolidated High School in Chattanooga, she toed the mark. She used pink sponge-rubber breasts and kept a picture of God in her room. Her hobby was twirling. As she clicked on her dryer, sniffed serenely, and began to read the book she had brought with her—Caroline Lee Hentz's *Linda, or The Young Pilot of the Belle Creole*—several girls behind her raised their hands in claws.

Charity was scant. It was of course a critical time of the year and nerves were on edge. Day in, day out, there had been nothing but one long round of work for two weeks: getting up in the morning, walking through the grey dawn to a classroom, waiting with faces like piggy-banks for some fanatic to hand them an impossible exam, and then, what? Returning to the dorms for another night of study and sweat? Horrible! It was like prison! They murmured. They made faces. They moped about like the defiled Moabite women of Shittim and all the while suffered from things like bad bowel rotation, eyesquint, omphalocele, swelled hummocks, and pinworm! For a stupid degree? They didn't need? When they were all going to get married anyway?

Certain girls, however—the "scroops!"—loved it and the better to study hid themselves in out-of-the-way places like airshafts and broom closets making lists, writing out mnemonics, and underlining their textbooks in red with massive felt pens. But this was a rare group. Most of the girls at Quinsy, braless and indifferent, either sat around drinking coffee or just went simpling from room to room with a thousand stinks and curses about the impossibility of cramming an infinity of knowledge into the finity of mind in one single night!

Ah, but for the copesmates in Clitheroe 403? It was considered by most of *them* vulgar to worry. Tomorrow? A pother, a pox! A feather, a fig! For if for them the night grew short, the morning was a world away, that was that, and no amount of pressure could ever hope to lessen the conviction beating in their little hearts that had been established there for all time in the immortal words of Miss Scarlett O'Hara, the Belle of Tara, who, when bravely standing against the world, deathlessly pronounced, "I'll think of it all tomorrow . . . after all, tomorrow is another day." It was the true *materia poetica* of Dixiedom, a regional quintessential, the primal scream of the South.

"O gross!" cried Anaphora Franck. "Listen to this!"

" '. . . the diddling was hot, hot, hot. Rhoda, utterly enslaved, was sobbing, moaning, gasping and rolling her eyes. How hard, thought Rafe, can a dame press up to a guy, huh? Bro-ther! And why, he wondered, do a dame's tears taste so good? He squeezed her ninnies and humped in heaves, like a crazed rabbit, while the little sextress, groaning low in the throat, dug her enamelled nails into his hairy back. "O baby, this is positively maddening," squealed Rhoda, even though she felt like 2¢, "you're driving me crazy, you hear me, *crazy!*" The sexcapade continued. She had spunk. He liked that. And so Rafe took his huge lubricated engine and . . .' "

"I'm going to get wet," said Mimsy Borogroves, revolving her torso.

Sally Ann Sprouse made revving noises like an engine.

"Y'all *shush*, will you?" screamed Loretta Boyco who, dropping her book, leaped up and, nearly garroting herself on the cord, was yerked backwards like a yo-yo. Panfuriously unplugging her hair-dryer, she stomped out of the room bristling like a hedgehog. Mona Lisa Drake, cellotaping her wet-locked hairdo, simply fluttered her eyelids and stuck out her tongue at the door Loretta Boyco summarily slammed.

"Who's she, somethin' on a stick?"

"Straight arrow," said Donna Wynkoop.

"A wonk."

"I am the Queen of England," proscribed Hester Popkin, pointing a regal finger at the door, "and you are dismissed!"

"St. Loretta," said Jessie Lee Deal who took the book which,

giggling, Aone Pitts grabbed only to have it snatched from her by
Geraldine Oikle who read:

" '. . . like a wild stud, suctioning her tongue, gasped on a wave of ecstasy, "You ain't seen nothin' yet, sister," and he lunged at horny Rhoda
whose skin was foxing with lustful chills. They kissed ravishingly. The kiss
snapped. And then he made quick little feelies all over her body with his
expert tongue, ranging over her diamond-hard nipples, and down, down,
down to the fringed secrets below. "Oh yes, yes, Rafe, yesss," husked
Rhoda, "Touch me *there!*" Ho-ly bananas, thought Rafe. What a brawd!
What bliss! What a sextravaganza!' "

"She must be *killing* him," skreeked Celeste Skyler.
Donna Wynkoop clapped. "Ain't it the bees' knees!"
"Well, shoot," interjected lovely, spoiled rich Pengwynne Custis,
lighting a cigarette and blowing smoke at the lot of them. "I was fourteen when all that happened to *me,* fancy. Which gives y'all a considerable something to think about, doesn't it?" The sentence had been
arranged for distribution as periodic. "You better believe it does."
"Not really, honeychile," came a sudden reply, cool as camphor. It
was beautiful Hypsipyle Poore, stepping pink and fresh and stark-
naked out of the shower. She slowly walked to the mirror and, unem-
barrassed, began to towel off, dabbing, patting, and caressing each
limb, her perfect curves, like a luscious and legendary Narcissa. It was
a body as smooth and soft as nainsook. She stretched and stepped
lithely into a tight pair of silk pale-green panties which fit her too perfectly. "Why, Pengwynne honey," breathed Hypsipyle with an oversweet smile, "at fourteen I could have written me a damn ol' book *I'd*
have blushed to read."
Splashing on friction lotion, Hypsipyle Poore paused and looked
around at the other girls to see if anybody doubted it: even so much as
the hint of a raised eyebrow, a smile not softened by belief, would not
only have cost the transgressor—and immediately—her friendship but
would have launched a campaign of rumor, as if of itself, whereby
particular faults suddenly attributed to such a one would become,
within an afternoon, distinct *faits accomplis.* Hypsipyle was strong-
willed, did not like to be contradicted, and, if Xystine Chappelle, the
class brownie, had been singled out as most likely to succeed, *she* enjoyed the reputation of being the most beautiful girl on campus.
Teachers asked her out. She often made the claim, publicly, that she

could seduce any male in the state of Virginia, six to sixty. You didn't fool with her.

The room was her domain. It was, in fact, not remarkably unlike the others—save that, concomitant with a recent financial gift to the college from her daddy, Hypsipyle had no roommate. The décor, best described as eclectic, was a combination of toyshop, brothel parlor, and theatrical green room. A mobile of crotal bells, wired together, hung from the ceiling. A Mexican jar held several peacock feathers. Three silver fraternity mugs sat on the bookcase, half filled with texts and half with rat-romances, tepid glucose-and-water things like: *The Killer Wore Nylon; Color Me Shameless; Miss Juliette's Academy, or Variety Was Their Byword*, etc.—and, of course, a foot-high stack of *Bride's* magazines, the college favorite.

Collegiate banners hung everywhere. An orange-and-purple University of Virginia pennant (with two football ticket-stubs stapled to it) was pinned over her bed, next to which stood a table: a stiff gold postiche sat on a dummy head. Stuffed animals, beribboned, were scattered about the room. There was a box of billet-doux.

Coolly, Hypsipyle Poore sat down before her bureau, straightening out the photographs of several boyfriends at the edges of the mirror which was bright with cute, goofy decals. It was her favorite place in the whole wide world, an arsenal of cosmetic powers: toning sprays, hair lacquers, bath oils, body unguents and creams, gums, pomatums, flacons of rosewater, barbaric ceroborants, vaginal gels, creme rinses, perspiration arresters, rouge sticks, eyeliner pencils, lipsticks, cuticle oil and nipple blush, eyelash curlers, bone combs, tissue boxes, and pintrays. A jewel box, découpaged red, was filled with rings, neck-chains, and bracelets, all gold. Hypsipyle walked her fingers over the phalanx of bottles, lifted out a vial of perfume, and touched a drop to her neck and inner thigh. She then took up a comb and, with the tracelet of a lewd smile in her eyes, tapped the lurid novel Sally Ann Sprouse was holding and now—to oblige her—reading:

" 'Rhoda was no little chickerino. She knew the game, the little she-cat —and how! And when they—' "

Hypsipyle, interrupting, shook her head and told her *precisely* the page she wanted to hear. Sally Ann Sprouse flashed back the pages.

" 'Tantalizingly she pranced—'?"

Smiling, Hypsipyle nodded.

" 'Tantalizingly she pranced around on her mules in a filmy peignoir, her pendulous breasts swinging like bell-tongues. Rafe, part Turk, was sure going to get all he damned well wanted—and then some! He's a real heel, thought Rhoda, but he really grows on you: I've *got* something for this guy. Meanwhile, Rafe's plans had worked to perfection, no soft soap required, thank you: he knew he'd be throwing hot gooms into her all night. Swiftly he cornered her and, overcome by passion, Rafe tore her flouncies off in one rip and coaxed her into unspeakable acts, but she drank them in greedily, howling, *"Whip me! Nip me! Use me! Slap me! Bite me! Goose me!"* Rafe dove headlong—' "

"Gooms," said Cookie Crumpacker. She snapped the elastic of her panties. "I *love* that word."

But Sally Ann Sprouse held up her hand, a semaphore to command undivided attention for the fantastic bit about to follow. She rattled the book and, screaming kinkily, raced on.

" '—dove headlong into her, wallowing in her creamy flesh. He bounced up and down waggling his inflamed root. What Rhoda felt for the hot bulging muscles, the hairiness of this brainless, insatiable, gin-befunked seaman couldn't be described. What the merchant marine hadn't taught him hadn't been *taught!* He'd been in and out of every port from Libya to Hong Kong, running girls, white-slaving, putting the boots to every dame who hit the deck! The sweat poured down him in rills as he pounced, re-pounced, and re-pounced again with that throbbing, pulsating, jiving, expanding spark-plug of his—' "

"*Neat!*" screeched Aone Pitts, looking up lively from the letter she'd begun to write—on illustrated stationery, the kind graphed with doodads (dancing mice, kittens peering over floral baskets, etc.) and contrasting envelope liner.

Geraldine Oikle smiled secretively, a little amative fang sticking out. "He must have—" She held her hands two feet apart.

"I'm soaked!" giggled Mimsy Borogroves.

"*Readin' trash,*" came a sudden outraged voice from somewhere, "*ain't no better than bein' trash!*" It was Loretta Boyco, standing on a desk in the next room with her mouth to the heating vent.

"Hey, Boyco," shouted Hester Popkin, hoisting up to her side of the vent, "how would you like it if I grabbed your legs and made a wish?" She listened a moment. "Or broke you damn ah-glasses?"

Cookie Crumpacker said: "That child, I swear, don't menstruate. She defrosts."

"But I wonder," asked Robin Winglet, soberly, "if men like them Turks really do make the best lovers, you know?"

"Y'all know which men make the best lovers, honey?" asked Hypsipyle Poore, rabbeting her beautiful black hair in long strokes. She turned from the mirror, closed her eyes, and sucked a tooth. "The ones you have in bed with you."

The girls all exploded into smutty giggles.

The bells from the clock-bearing cupola of Smethwick struck three, but having long since settled back, inert, open-thighed, sleepy, no one showed any interest in going to bed. What could they do now? Misty-eyed, Holly Sunday continued to strum her guitar. Gladys Applegate, coiling an arm over her head, asked if anybody wanted to sniff glue. Thomasina Quod said she was dying for a ham-'n'-cheese on a bulkie. "O, butter a bun, will you!" said Glenda Barrow, quickly cupping her mouth for the blunder. *"Thanks!"* snapped little Thomasina Quod, wapperjawed, her voice snarping like a grig's. *"Really. Thanks a lot!"* Straddling a cuckoo-flowered white chair, Mona Lisa Drake asked the other girls what they would do if they were alone at night and a weirdo came into the room.

A mood of spookiness suddenly settled in. Voices went low and glances were exchanged in a ghostly hush. Someone lit a stick of incense. The girls grouped closer together on pillows, sag bags, and throw rugs, somewhat uneasy—poised at any moment to give in to the screaming meemies—and covertly began to speak about peeping toms, whispering idiolects of the midnight phonecall, and Breughel-like howbeits with things on their minds who crept about the late-night shrubbery. It wasn't funny. Hadn't they, any one of them, ever heard *noises* outside? They admitted they had and turned morbid and immediately began to rehearse for one another those self-ramifying and shuddersome myths, habitually passed down from class to class, from generation to generation, that recounted how in the distant past at Quinsy College maimed half-wits, gub-shites with pointed ears, and deranged creatures who left no shadow had actually been seen at night on the ramparts of the buildings and sometimes dragging a gimp leg down the corridors of the dorms, wheezing, cross-eyed, and *dripping!* And that wasn't all! They returned every single year, different ones, things with names—Grippo! Hoghead! The Four-Eyed Man of Cricklade!—and icy grips, bulbed heads, and pee-stains all over them!

It was then given out that many, many years ago a certain girl at Quinsy actually woke up in the middle of the night and saw standing right next to her bed a refulgent something with flippers for feet named "Thimbleballs" who clawed his way up the bricks, crept across the roof, de-pended in a crazy hang, and then dashed himself howling through a window—to try to bite off her head! The authorities then found her the next morning, a blithering idiot, with her hair gone completely white, and, according to common report, she was said to be still alive to this day but not moving a finger, just sitting with folded hands in a rooming-house somewhere down in the Tidewater and repeatedly muttering only a single word, *"Wurble! Wurble! Wurble!"*

"I'm having the creeps," said Geraldine Oikle.

Jessie Lee Deal held up her arm. "Look. Goose skin."

"O poo," said Hypsipyle Poore calmly, carefully tracing on some brown eyeliner—lurking with strange synthetic perfumes, she always went to bed as if the Chevalier Bayard were there awaiting her—and so her weary, decosmeticized visitors, partially because they were sapping with terminal fatigue, put away their fears. Hypsipyle clapped her eyeliner into her make-up box and with the emory board she picked up, for one last swynk at her nails, pointed toward the door. It was time for them to go. Yawping and yawning, the girls wobbled up on their feet. Some stretched and groaned.

Cookie Crumpacker, tweaking a slice of underwear from the moist rictus of her buttocks, picked up the paperback.

"I believe I'll take this and read me some more about big ol' Rafe here—just," Cookie added, looking about like a little sly-boots putting out feelers, "just for a bit of a titty-pull. You mind?"

Most of the Clitheroe kids, on their way out, were too tired to comment.

"Well, I'll tell you who *I'd* like to have a titty-pull with," said Donna Wynkoop, working her eyes over a wide smile.

The girls stopped in their tracks. And just before they went to their respective rooms, sent down like insubordinate nuns to their low crypts to meditate punitively on their sins among the bones of their predecessors, they turned.

"Who?"

"*Come* on!" prodded Celeste Skyler, she of the porpentine head.

"Yeah, who?"

Tenders, in a pause, for all? Tenders, in a pause, accepted.

"*Darconville*."

There was, for the first time that evening perhaps, universal agreement, and, although laughing, they fluked Donna Wynkoop mercilessly and told her not to hold her breath. She wasn't alone. Charlotte Bodwell, a junior psych major, for instance, sat outside of his office all day every day! Sabrina Halliburton over in Truesleeve, they all knew, claimed that he had asked her out twice. And Brenda Workitt supposedly told her whole sorority right out that she'd like to cover his whole body with honey and lick it off!

"I'd use hot fudge."

"I'd use syllabub," said Robin Winglet, who majored in home economics.

"And what about that person-thing over in Fitts—what's-her-face with the long hair?"

"The girl with the fat legs."

Nobody knew her name. But the better to hear, they all moved closer, coming together not to praise but to bury. She *couldn't* live in Fitts. That meant she was—

"*A freshman?*"

The cats perked their ears, ear-trumpeting in the direction of whatever noise anyone wanted to make. Beautiful Hypsipyle Poore, alone of all the others, didn't say a word. She simply sat there, silent, touching up her lips with a bullet of cherry-frost lipstick. Hypsipyle, of course, made it an art. Before putting on the lipstick, for instance, she blotted her lips with a tissue, powdered lightly, then used a lip pencil along the natural contours of her lips, and finally with a lipstick of a similar color filled in the lip area—exactly! But she was listening all the while, listening harder than usual, for Darconville and Isabel Rawsthorne—especially to those who gave attention to such things—had not gone unnoticed. They had been seen together more than once, constituting a thousand times. Eyebrows, questions, had been raised. And the gossip raced, *ab hoc et ab hac et ab illa.* . . .

"Well, y'all can go run around the hoo-hum-hah," moued lovely, spoiled, rich Pengwynne Custis, "because I'm invitin' that boy to my recital next week and—"

"And, you watch, he won't *come*," challenged Mona Lisa Drake, laughing and golfing Pengwynne on the knee. The girls all agreed and, with their pillows under their arms, turned to leave.

"Wait," ordered Hypsipyle Poore, suddenly breaking her long silence and turning her flashing black eyes upon lovely, spoiled, rich Pengwynne Custis. "Shall I tell you why he won't come?"

The silence was deafening. Everybody turned to her.

"Well," questioned Pengwynne, closing her eyes haughtily, "why?"

Hypsipyle Poore put off her mask of burning gold.

"Because, honeychile," said she, harder than usual, "you look like *batshit!*"

And, unsettled, Hypsipyle kicked everybody out of the room, crawled into bed, and snapped off the light—harder than usual.

XXIII

A Promise Fulfilled

It can not be, nor ever yet hath beene
That fire should burne, with perfect heate and flame,
Without some matter for to yeeld the same.

—EDWARD DYER

THERE WAS TIME during the suitable interval of Finals Week for
Darconville to write out the promised poem for Isabel. It went as follows:

Love, O what if in my dreaming wild
  I could for you another world arrange
Not known before, by waking undefiled,
  Daring out of common sleep adventure strange

And shape immortal joy of mortal pain?
   Art resembles that, you know—the kind of dare
Nestorians of old acknowledged vain:
   "No, what human is, godhead cannot share!"
But what if in this other world you grieve,
   Undone by what in glory is too bright,
Remembering of humankind you leave
   That which pleased you of earthly delight?
Out then on art! I'll sleep but to wake—
   Never to dream if never for your sake.

That night he ran over to the student union, slipped it into her mailbox—number 120—and walked home delighted with himself.

XXIV

Giacomo-lo-Squarciatore

It is the nature of women to be fond of carrying weights.

—FRANCIS GALTON

THE TELEPHONE CALL seemed urgent: some student named Betsy, the unromantic praenomen matching her disposition, asking if Darconville minded very much giving her and her girlfriends some advice, so would he? It was a voice of shrill little bleats warring against, but intervenient with, the background noise of a dormitory corridor that sounded like Mafeking. Sitting in his office, Darconville could almost see her, squinched over, one ear plugged with a finger, nervously rubbing her left instep against the gastrocnemius of her right calf: she was in a dither. The girls at Quinsy College had hearts like chocolate bars, scored to break easily. Come ahead, said Darconville, come over.

So Darconville waited for them long after his classes had ended, his feet propped up on his desk. He was reading an old novel from his grandmother's library—*Giacomo-lo-Squarciatore* (1888)—to pass the time.

"We're ripping mad!" puffed Betsy Stride, breathless from the stairs, appearing in the doorway like a rising moon. She turned out to be one of his sophomores, a pompion-shaped grouchbag in a brown dress A-lined and middle-kneed who, in happier moods, was given to entertaining her girlfriends in the back row of Darconville's class by ingeniously shooting elastic bands from the braces on her teeth. And then she motioned in four others—a group Darconville had seen together more than once slouching around campus like walking morts—who, obviously whelped together on a mission, one, Darconville saw, that would soon be his, stood before the desk. It looked as if they were going to group-step, kick, and burst into a Victorian music-hall number.

"Tell him, go ahead."

Betsy judiciously castled two of her friends and moved a pawn forward with an impatient shove.

"It's all right," exclaimed Betsy, "tell him what happened. Well, aren't you going to tell him? *Mary Jane?*"

They made a perfect quincunx, all standing in place, with faces like apostle spoons, all deferring to each other as to who should present their petition, for it was clearly one of those irredentist ventures to restore a right or rectify a wrong, something invariably to do with library privileges, curfew extension, or some breach of the student moral code which at Quinsy was stricter than the Rites of Vesta. Darconville, now six months into the year, was becoming familiar with it all. The girls, most of them, actually worried about these rules, an anxiety, in fact, that over the year caused a good many of them to become overweight, and not a few who had come in September as thinifers would leave hopeless fattypuffs in June. The starchy comestibles in the Quinsy refectory, however, better construed to account for the condition of Betsy Stride, a girl so fat that were she wearing a white dress one could have shown a home-movie on her. Briefly, she had a beef—and, again, poked Mary Jane in the ribs.

"Well, I was studyin' real late over at Smethwick last night," began Mary Jane Kelly, shifting feet, "working on my project on shade-pulls. You know? Anyway, I—"

Darconville blinked.

"Shade-pulls?"

"My term paper. For Dr. Speetles' education course. 'The Effect of Insufficiently Pulled Shades in Classrooms on 4th-Grade Underachievers.'"

"Continue."

"I finished up for the night, see, and started walking back to my room—"

"Alone," Betsy reminded her.

"Alone," agreed her friend.

"*All* alone."

"Yes," sighed Mary Jane, "*all* alone. I was right tired, I guess, and"—she shrugged—"I don't know, maybe I just imagined the whole thing."

"You didn't," sniffed Betsy, shifting and looking away hurt as if suddenly betrayed.

Darconville looked at his watch. "And you saw a man," he said, "following you."

The girls all looked amazed, confirmed in their fears but astounded at the sudden conjecture: how did *he* know? This was a constant: the fumblingly speculative association in girls' schools of any mysterious or unexplained mis-illumination with some foul and forbidden chthonian, male of course, wreaking havoc among them, and any apparition, whatever the circumstance, desperately cried out for immediate rehearsal, redressal, and report.

"Did he," asked Darconville, "touch you?"

"No, not exactly. But, um, he shone a"—she made a gesture—"a thing at me."

"A thing?" asked Darconville, as the three girls who hadn't yet spoken grabbed their mouths, snorting back laughter. It was the vaguest word in the language and so the most deceptive. "What do you mean, a *thing?*"

"It was a flashlight!" cried Betsy Stride, barging forward with a hieratic hip-roll. "And he held it up to this real creepy face, like he was mental or something!" She looked desperately around. "It's really great, huh, the protection we have? What are they waiting for, for cry-eye, a bunch," she said, a trifle optimistically, "of undecent rapings? We want more lights on campus!"

Strange, thought Darconville. How many tragedies in this chiaro-scuro world were related precisely to that: light when it was needed, darkness when it wasn't; darkness when it was needed, light when it wasn't. The same gardens that grow digitalis for heart patients also grow the devil's oatmeal. Vinegar is the corpse of wine. Thus spake Zarathustra.

"Well," confessed Mary Jane Kelly in a near-whisper, "he didn't actually hold it up to his *face*."

Betsy Stride covered her eyes. "O my God."

"It's just that passing that spooky glade by the old tennis courts I saw a foot behind a tree. It had a sneaker on it. Not the tree," clarified Mary Jane, "the foot." The three girls, giggling, were pinching their noses to stop. "And then, I swear, it moved. Not the foot—"

Bursting, the three girls quickly turned around and exploded in laughter.

"The tree?"

"Well, see, I saw two eyes peering out by a branch, sideways, like they was—I don't know, *burning* or something! So I started to run and *he* started to run."

"And to scream, right?" interjected Betsy. "Tell him, *tell* him!"

"He screamed? What did he scream?" asked Darconville. He prompted her, ready to hear the fiercest Asiatic curses, the vilest obscenities.

Mary Jane Kelly hesitated, surveying her feet, and then, resigned, put her hands to her mouth and tried as best she could to mimic in two hoots the *tuba horribilis* she'd heard with such alarm the previous night: *"Socialists! Socialists!"*

The three girls, doubled over and quacking, had gone purple.

There may indeed have been a lunatic running amok on campus, or possibly a prankster, no one could say—although the reign of terror, it might be said, had in fact coincidentally taken place with the letting out of a Chekhov dress rehearsal for which a number of girls, to comply with the wishes of Miss Throwswitch, had been required to wear fake beards.

The fat, however, was in the fire. Betsy Stride, flashing her metal teeth, told Darconville that Marsha D'amboni almost got blackjacked a month ago, that Weesie Ralph found a man standing once in her gym closet *bare as a baby,* and that Shirley Newbegin once got whistled at by coloreds! And who cared? Xystine Chappelle, the wimp? Dean Barathrum? President Greatracks who kicked them out of his office and called them "pee-oons"?

With lampoon-lit eyes, Darconville promised he'd mention it all to Someone Important and, asking for their names, slipped them a piece of paper. One of the girls sorted through her handbag, clumping on the desk pretzels, lip-balm, five jawbreakers, a ring of keys, a penny-in-an-aluminum-horseshoe, and a snap-wallet thick as a fist, and shook out a molar-dented pen. They all signed their names:

> Mary Ann Nichols
> Annie Chapman
> Elizabeth Stride
> Catherine Eddowes
> Mary Jane Kelly

Profuse in their thanks, one of the girls pushed back a twist of flocky hair and quickly kissed Darconville on the cheek.

At that very moment, Isabel Rawsthorne appeared at the office door. It had become her habit, often, to stop by with something, a bag of candy, a box of exotic tea, and if Darconville happened to be busy she usually left a whimsical little note in that delicate spidery penmanship of hers, always signed "The Little Thing." But on this occasion when he looked up—she was wearing, typically, a half-length fur coat, pink hush-puppies, and jeans with three mushrooms (multi-colored) sewn over the left knee—he saw only two sad basset eyes. "Oh, excuse me," she said with a face like sudden night—then disappeared.

O no, thought Darconville. He got up, stepped past the girls, and called down the stairwell. But she had gone, out of the light and into the darkness. By slow degrees it dawned on him what she must have felt, even if absurdly, for jealousy, lineament by lineament, feature by feature, needs no scene or sentence but actually creates itself from what it fears.

The male professor at Quinsy College, in fact, whether attached or not, symbolized a plenitude he hadn't but by his very presence precipitated a thousand desperate necessities, a particular situation, needless to say, that often put in ludicrous but privileged ascendance those who would be gentlemen that late were grooms. He could act like a churl, use his hands for purposes of locomotion, or look like the Expansible Pig, the girls didn't care—*instans instanter,* he became a combination of father confessor, confidant, marriage counselor, friend, adept, and phantom lover.

Anxious to see the girls out, Darconville asked if there was anything else. They didn't think so and shuffled out, dolefully trailing a length of reluctant gratefulness behind them as they waved.

"Oh yes," said Betsy Stride, turning back. The moon, setting, rose again. "My last exam, remember?" She popped a peppermint into her mouth. "It was a 78. I was close to a B, right?"

"Close," replied Darconville, looking at his watch nervously, "only counts in horseshoe-pitching and necking."

"Necking?" she asked salaciously—and, grinning, snapped off the light-switch with her elbow. Her teeth-braces gleamed in the darkness.

"As you say," Darconville said quietly, "we want more lights on campus."

Whereat Elizabeth Stride thrust out her underlip, turned, and slowly walked away, the undissolved peppermint still undissolved in her cheek.

The sound of Isabel's light-running footsteps had made Darconville's heart, echoing them, feel empty, ineffectual, and made equally futile the hurried explanation—of what?—he saw he had to give. He quickly dialed her number: 392-4682.

"Fitts!" came a voice on the other end like Stentor the Bellower's.

"May I please speak to Isabel Rawsthorne?"

"Canyouholdonjessaminuteplease?"

The telephone receiver, summarily dropped, bonked against the dorm wall several times—*clonk! clonk! clonk!*—but Darconville waited intently. Had he been lax, he wondered, or scrupulous, seeing those he shouldn't have or seeing those he should? What had he done? He didn't know. Who pre-plots with intelligence? Hazard, he thought, itself was creative.

Still waiting, Darconville looked down the corridor which ran straight from his office to a water bubbler at the far end. On the bulletin boards lining the walls of that corridor had been thumbtacked various grammatical projects which the education-majors there, being trained—as opposed to educated—to teach the lower grades, had prinked out; they were sort of visual rebuses, narrative cut-outs on oak-tag paper, with titles like: "Miss Question Mark has her Period"; "An Apostrophe takes Two Pees"; "Old Mr. Bracket falls on his Asterisk"; "Little Cedilla has a bout of Diaresis," and so on and so forth.

So much for the trivium, thought Darconville, so much for the quadrivium.

"Hello again, mister?"

"Yes."

"Did you say Isabel Rawsthorne was whom was wanted?"

"Yes," he said.

There was giggling on the other end, muffled by a hand. "Excuse me," asked the voice, "but is this Govert?"

Govert? It was a shadow that seemed stronger than the substance that threw it.

"No. No, it isn't."

"Oh," said Miss Blunder. "Well, I can't seem to find her."

Darconville stammered. He felt ridiculous. Govert: wasn't *he* the no-see-um she once mentioned who lived near her somewhere in Fawx's Mt.? At Zutphen Farm or some such thing? O Iax, thought Darconville, angel of thwarting demons, are you there? Quickly, he asked the girl to check again.

"She's definitely not in. Can y'all try again later?"

"But are you certain?"

The girl hung up.

Darconville lowered the receiver, thought a moment, then called her name down the corridor. The name echoed back. It was imperative he find her, but where now should he look? He felt an appalling lack of energy as he dragged on his black coat, shut the office door, and, turning to avoid the nearest poster—"Mr. Comma empties his Colon" or whatever—went out.

Fog, with the smell of February. The dampness, settling in with dusk over the patches of snow, could be sharply felt by an easterly wind. The sky was a slate slab. Darconville walked slowly across the grounds, catching his muffler to his neck, and—but who was that?

"Hello."

It almost seemed a question.

Isabel, huddled up, was sitting on the wooden bench under the magnolia tree in front of the English building, her brown eyes moist like beautiful Israfel's and other angels who carry misfortune in their wings. Darconville kissed and hugged her, and she handed him a packet of photographs of herself—long requested, longer postponed—which, she said, smiling wistfully, was why she'd come. Then they simply sat together, preferring to keep silent, their two hands clasped like lost children in a world only suddenly found.

He couldn't define it all at once, but the feeling of her there next to him, a grateful one, gave way to a strange, almost sensual spasm of sympathy for all she was. Isabel Rawsthorne's loyalty—he should have known she'd be there waiting for him—kept faith with her humanity. It was precisely what he had ignored all his life, the humanizing re-demption of someone else for whom *he* dearly cared. Her silence spoke volumes. He thought how little he'd written since meeting her. Very well, he thought, I haven't written. But darkness had become light. Love, he saw, manifested itself not so much in the desire as in the need, and, who knew, perhaps less in the learning than in the loyalty. For the sudden recollection of his banter with the five girls, he felt chastised, for his lack of sympathy, ashamed.

To keep away from humankind, he suddenly saw, was to be its murderer. Dehumanized man was capable of enormities indescribable, and he bethought himself of what, in the absence of this child whose radiance outshone a Della Robbia angel, he could become—what, some psychopath, caped in black, scuttling with a hook before his face like a soiled shadow through the fog of his imagination only to wound victims hatched from the disaffiliations of his cruel and selfish solitude? Horrifying! And although hatred was not so much beyond Darcon-ville's capabilities as beyond his comprehension, he trembled at the thought, as happens in nightmares, of what is left a heartless and in-human force pursuing pure illusion.

O Isabel, O love, thought Darconville, turning to her, his heart swollen with what, because too overpowering, he couldn't express. In-stead, they both held hands, fearing to say what each thought the other knew but hoping that each would feel what both of them knew the other might be afraid to say.

XXV

Miss Trappe's Gift

And how reliable can any truth be that is got
By observing myself and then just inserting a Not?

—W. H. AUDEN, "The Way"

THAT PARTICULAR DAY, Darconville found a surprise waiting
for him upon returning from classes, for just as he opened the porch-
door—with Spellvexit, as usual, in attendance on the upper landing
and crying out—the cat skittered over something that came bouncing
down the stairs. It was a cylinder, the contents of which he carefully
fingertwisted out to find a rare Masanobu pillar-print of the eighteenth century, entitled *Kuroi Kōshaku Fujin*—a black half-
woman/half-bird, all beak and talons, plummeting downward. There
was a note attached.

Dear Darconville,

> I'd like to be a could-be
> If I could not be an are,
> For a could-be is a may-be
> With a chance of reaching par;
> I'd rather be a has-been
> Than a might-have-been by far,
> For a might-have-been has never been
> But a has-been was an are.

THELMA TRAPPE

P.S. I wanted you to have this, being an artist (an "are"), not like me (a "might-have-been"). I have a cameo for Isabel. Maybe she can come visit me? But, oh, she must be busy.

Glad for the chance, Darconville underlined the postscript, put the note in an envelope, and posted it all to Isabel for her good attention. He stopped by Miss Trappe's at the top of the hill to thank her and then hurried home to the mysterious packet.

XXVI

The Nine Photographs

Yet to calculate is not in itself to analyze.

—EDGAR ALLAN POE

ISABEL *was* always mysterious. The prospect, then, that Darconville had of looking at the photographs she'd given him filled him with high expectation. The idea of formulating them, however, to the fancies he had of who she was only accentuated the premonition he had that he already knew, at least abstractly, for, although only a newly baptized considerant in her religion, he loved her. And yet it was with some misgivings that he prepared to pit the prosperous freedom of his partisan imagination against revelations already cross-examined by the facts and fingerprints of the past, a still world, while too small for her secret and his curiosity, belonging to quite another day.

Darconville locked the door. It had to be quiet. He had no idea what he was about to see but felt a sensuous pleasure as exciting as the intense rushing in his heart experienced whenever he met her. It may have seemed a packet of trifles, worth nothing, but it was a trifling part of the world where she lived, and that made the difference. He opened the envelope and out fell eight photographs—all different shapes and sizes—of Isabel at various ages. He bent forward under the light, extending his hands so that both stood against the coping of each picture, and studied them.

(1.) *Isabel as a little tweeny:* of the "adorable" genre, it shows her in a white hair-bow and frothy white pinafore, plump, clutching an ingot of chocolate and hopscotching over a manhole cover, twice the width of her size in height. Part sylphid, part crammed poultry, her legs even then are more Saxon than Norman.

(2.) *Isabel as a premenstrual:* her face, pigtails, and big milk-teeth show a comic sunniness and a kind of rubbernecking innocence, though there can be detected a sad fleer playing at the edge of her mouth. There is a noticeable birthmark beneath her eye (the answer to the question of her scar!). She doesn't know she misses the father she knows is missing. The sleep in her eyes might seem to reflect, unfairly, on her I.Q. At this age, she'd have had a favorite ring with a pyrite stone, an imaginary friend named something like "Mr. Koodle," and a tiny patent leather purse in which could be found five pennies, gum, and a skate-key.

(3.) *Isabel as a high-school cheerleader:* here she's waving from an open car, after an Albemarle High School football game, and showing herself, if artificial, abloom. The chenille "A" on her sweater is just detectable under her heavy fur coat. In Adam's fall we sinnèd all. The smile is forced, the drive for popularity uncharacteristic, the birthmark gone. ("I, without artifice, taught artifice." St. Augustine)

(4.) *Isabel as a blur:* an operator's giggle shook the camera. Was that blob in the lower right-hand corner a figure standing in a boat? This is the only photograph with writing on the reverse side, the connotative hieroglyphic: "G v d S."

(5.) *Isabel as a prom queen:* spruce Miss Darklips, an eyebrow slightly raised, her hair styled and sprayed, her face overpowdered white like a *femme entretenue,* is wearing a white short-sleeved evening gown of Holland silk with a single green stripe at the Plimsoll line of her breasts, long gloves, and lyre-like shoes. She poses before a stone fireplace (hers?) on the mantel of which stands a model of a red-sailed, black-hulled ship and the demotic penates of the owner, *not* a Medici: a duck-spout pitcher, gimcrack bottles, a pewter cup. The hearth is surrounded in blue and white mock-Delft tiles and the tacky, mass-produced print of a rainy marinescape-with-ship-in-distress hung in glass behind her is, thanks to the witless photographer, ludicrously given a sun by the reflection of his lightbulb. (*His* lightbulb?)

(6.) *Isabel as stout Cortez:* a white farmhouse with a hip-and-valley roof and hippic-related fence lies within view of the beautiful subject standing hind-side-foremost. The photo has a *Sinnbald* character, with the back, awful and mysterious thing, impossible to speak about—that part of us we know nothing about, like an outlying waste forgotten by God. The photographer's elongated and fractured shadow—he would be just abaft her port beam—covers her in part. The ear of the sphinx is 4½ feet long.

(7.) *Isabel as a party guest:* a candid shot of the subject sitting on the floor, a Nike amidst a group of yegg-faced teenagers, playfully mussing a blond boy's hair, which action effectively disprizes one from a consideration of his face—but not, by any means, his ears! Her eyes are animated. It is strange to see her beauty so incongruously annexed, even if momentarily, to some kind of affection for this dolt-headed pube, a cobbler, clearly, who got beyond his last.

N.B. Wrong. The photograph compendiates a *rapprochement* of note. She leans toward him with such contentment fond, as well the sweetheart sits, would well a wife. The only photograph of hers thumbed.

(8.) *Isabel as a non-acquaintance:* a wallet-size rendering, from the shoulders up, of vacant preoccupation. A study of Van Der Weyden's lady. The lips are too full. The turtleneck sweater misuses her delicacy of clavicle. The mouth is winterset. That is not benevolence in the eyes. They look beyond you, more toward vanity than vision. The photographer missed. He will be taken out at dawn, blindfolded, and shot.

A long, long insearch—then Darconville shuffled up all the photographs together, and, inevitably, the jack-of-knaves came up on top. It was, supervening all, the thumbed and creased one: number seven (this, no doubt, in some kind of social apposition to the intentions implied in number five). Darconville wished, as did Momus of Vulcan's created man, that every person had a window placed in his or her breast. Murmur, fallen angel and father of ill report, whispered, *"Govert is covert! Govert is covert!"*

Quickly, Darconville slapped his hand over it. It was as if it had become another photograph, creating a fear in him, by way of diseased imagination, as inconstant as the shadows he surveyed. Who *was* this fellow? A name too little mentioned to suspect yet mentioned just enough to heed or learn to disregard. He looked at the photograph again. Weren't these simply the facts of certain events? And weren't events always the same as their significance?

It was incredible for Darconville to see how swiftly he could fall to torturing, tormenting thoughts, to scribble a biting and incoherent tragedy out of the restive suppositions he poorly fought. It was only to conceive one of those sticky, ring-swapping high-school junkets for the clang of mistrust: he threw a faithless cipher of moon into the sky, put beneath it a fatherless girl craving affection, and then helpless before the doom of his own contrivances watched in his mind, possibly on that very prom night or in a car parked on an overlook up in the Blue Ridge mountains, the hideous pyroballogy of some vile teenager with a hanging lip, his suspenders disengaged, prying off her gown with his grice-fingered hands and then bucking away like a country stink-cat, whereupon she—

But cruel! Cruel! Darconville, clapping the photographs back into the envelope, instantly grew disgusted with himself. He was scandalized by thoughts transported into the very deeds he disbelieved. If I create loveliness, he determined, there *is* loveliness. If I create monstrosity, there *is* monstrosity. Away with it! To play the part of accuser, one had to be word-perfect in that of hypocrite as well!

XXVII

Master Snickup's Cloak

The routes of ideas in history were also the routes of contagion.

—G. M. TREVELYAN

THERE WERE MANY DISAPPOINTMENTS during these
months for Darconville but many, indeed, for Isabel herself, and not
one, somehow, that didn't compound another. She was only eighteen
—"the age of the duck," in his grandmother's phrase—a period of
diffidence and confusion, generally, but in her case somewhat exacerbated by her keeping to herself and refusing to share her problems
with anyone at Quinsy she wasn't scrupulously sure of, a situational
irony that only sent effects back to causes.

It was not much help, beyond that, to be suffering the vicissitudes
of freshman year. One of the deans, for instance, had several times

summoned Isabel to her office, inquiring after the propriety of her seeing too much of a certain professor, especially in view of the fact that
she had flunked almost all her courses for the first semester, with one
glaring exception: a grade of A in English. And then certain en-
terprising girls in the dorms, unspeakable in malice, had been making
her life miserable, a self-appointed group of spitesowers manufac-
turing stories, shaping hexes and false rumors, and blowing their green
cornets across her every hope. It was whispered that she was above her
station as Darconville was below his, and, as time passed the apocryphal, simply by repetition, became the apodictic.

Isabel, initially undecided, eventually chose to major in art. A singular disappointment with this as its source took place one particular
night when tapping on Darconville's door—her eyes swollen from
weeping and want of sleep—she appeared holding up between thumb
and forefinger two prints she had worked weeks on and on which, for
both, she'd been graded F. One showed a square of ribbed wheels in-
terlocking on foil. The other, also abstract, was a thinly proven and
just-about-detectable sunburst squashed into a background the color
of the jellied broth of a canned ham. No, they were not good—and
were, in fact, quite bad. But what did it matter? He looked from the
morbid prints to Isabel's own soulful beauty and to indicate without
ado the condition of true art asked her only to accept herself, a good
at once appropriated, a glory-in-itself by virtue of but a moment's
reflection. It is to judgment, he told her, that perception belongs: true
eloquence makes light of eloquence, to make light of philosophy was
to be a true philosopher! Why, to fail to accept her own originality,
not by force or exactness but by comprehension, she could never accept his own, could she? Ordinary persons, he said, smiling, found no
differences between men. The artist found them all.

Not to undercut his own argument, he continued.

But he thought: what was art next to *her?* It was a lie, he explained
(aware of this implication, however, that the book he was writing
would become, increasingly, a more difficult task), a contrivance to
find the mind's construction only where it looks and how it will. Darconville looked into her eyes, and beyond. In the selfish state of the
human heart, he thought, to consign to the exercise of the wayward
imagination those facts, correspondent at hand but held as contrary,
was possibly to lose everything. The imagination was, after all, only
that poor faculty that strived to make the ideal real, wasn't it? There

was once a medieval tournament, Darconville told her, where favors to the victors were bestowed by the Queen of Beauty: the third prize was a silver rose, the second gold, but the highest award—given to the best knight of all—was a genuine rose.

Thinking of his own response to the photographs, he began, uncharacteristically, to dwell on the possible havoc that resulted from facts fully falling prey to the imagination.

Darconville suddenly had an idea. He wiped her tears and, shutting off the lights, took Despondency's daughter, Much-Afraid, by the hand toward the bed where he cradled her head on a large pillow, loopholed her arm to his, and tried, for catharsis, to work the only witchcraft he knew: he would tell her a story. Isabel, closing her eyes and snuggling up to him, felt better already. "It's a sad, sad story."

Master Snickup's Cloak

One morning, it was the Middle Ages.

The sun shone down on the foundling home at the end of Duck's-foot Lane in the quiet little dorp of Sleutel in the Netherlands. The year was 1307 (by Pope Hilarius's corrected calendar, of course).

Master Snickup, a tiny ward there—wearing the black and red uniform of the home—gleefully played punchball against the cobbled wall beneath a yew tree near the town weigh-house.

It was a feast day: the Pardon of St. They. Cattle were blessed. Children processed. You heard litanies.

"Wat is Uw naam?" asked a new little orphan girl who suddenly appeared at his side, smiling, plumcheeked, and wearing a chaste wimple. Her beauty put to shame the roses of Paestum.

Superfecta—for this was the name of the flax-haired frokin—immediately stole Master Snickup's heart quite away.

The two children, thereafter, spent day after day playing games of noughts-and-crosses, ducking mummy, backy-o, all the winkles, stickjaw, egg-in-cup, stitch-away-tailor

And skiprope, when they frisked and jumped to the jingle

> *"Do you love me,*
> *Or do you not?*
> *You told me once,*
> *But I forgot."*

Happily, Master Snickup even did her chores for her, scowring cups, dipping tallow, and decoaling the squinches; he even did the washpots. She played the dulcimer.

A decade passed, just like that.

Superfecta, who'd bloomed into indescribable loveliness, now drew smiles from each and all. There is no potential for permanence, Master Snickup told his heart, without a fear of threat.

And so they were betrothed one day at the shrine of St. Puttock of Erpingham—and swapped gifts: he gave her two white pigeons and received from her a wonderful blue cloak.

Now, there lived on the verge of the village at that time one of the richest burghers in all Gelderland—the ill-living Mijnheer van Cats, an unctuous cheesegobbling fat pants who smoked a clay pipe and wanted sons.

But who'd be his wife? A purse of 2000 gulden was put up.

In vain, however, did the merchants of the guild offer up their daughters, a group of off-sorts who had pointed noses and pointed caps.

"Knapweed! Hake! Twisses!" screeched van Cats and hurled other unprintable names at them. Modest pious folk covered their eyes.

One winter dusk, it so turned out, the orphans were given a special dispensation to go to the Haymarket to watch the "illuminations." Mijnheer van Cats, in attendance, sat up high on the balustrade of the guildhall, whereupon his gaze fell—fatefully—upon Superfecta. That little boompjes, thought he, will soon be mine.

An ouch of heavy gold was hers the day following; his, a sealed envelope, which he slit open with his pipestem. What could be the decision?

"Yaw, yaw," guffawed the fat Dutchman.

A record of the wedding can be found to this day as a small entry in the old chronicle of Nuewenburgensis. You will do, as the diverb has it, what you are.

Master Snickup, disedged with grief, took up scrip and staff and, wearing only his blue cloak, set out to pick his way across Europe. He sought the antipodes.

Hither was yon, yon hither.

Mountains were climbed, mazes thrid. He crossed a sea that had no motion on the ship, "What is Pseudonymry?" and came to a desert

where he said penances and fed on caper buds, dormice, and lentils.
Still he pilgrimaged,

Reading the footprints of geese in the air,

To reach eventually the Black Sea where, living alone on an
uncharted shale island, he chastized himself with thongs and subsisted
only on air and dew. Rain fell on his blue cloak, which he sucked
supplying himself with vitamin B₁₂.

Swallows sang upon his wrists.

"Sero te amavi," whispered Master Snickup to God—and prayed
constantly with perfectly folded hands, a shape best fitted for that
motion. Small furious devils hated that

And visited him in a variety of shapes and torments: six-fingered
Anaks, freexes, nasicornous beetles, chain-shaking kobolds, Saúba ants,
red-eyed swads, sorcerers who could disconnect their legs and flap
about like bats, and pin-headed Hippopods, with reversed feet, who
leapt instead of walked.

Master Snickup soon fell ill. But who could help? For ships in sight
there were none.

The town of Sleutel, meanwhile, rang with news. Superfecta van
Cats was delivered of a son. "A witty child! Can it swear? The
father's dearling! Give it two plums!" boasted its sire, butterballing it
with his gouty feet.

But hear of more. Mijnheer van Cats, now fattened on perfidy
itself, had turned syphilitic and even more hateful than before. He
sang curses against his wife in the taproom and, roiling and hissing,
streeled home drunk. He locked her nights in the black windmill. He
chased her through town slashing her with timothies.

Sadism and farce are always inexplicably linked.

The orphanage, in the meantime, closed down—without so much
as two coppers snapped together to prevent it, despite the bulging
wallets of all the snap-boilers, razor-makers, brewers, and
guilder-grubbing rentiers who lived thereabouts. O events! God could
not believe man could be so cruel.

Winter settled hard over the Black Sea. The soul of Master Snickup
now grew pure—a hagiographical commonplace—as his body grew
diseased. He never washed his bed save with tears. The tattered blue
cloak had become infested with worms and rotifers,

Which also battened on his holy flesh.

It snew. And on that desolate shale island, since fabled, Master Snickup one day actually looked into the heart of silence, rose and—with a tweak-and-shake of finger and thumb toward the sky—died. Rats performed the exequies.

The moon, suddenly, was o'ercast blood-red in an eclipse. Thunder rumbled. Boding?

Ill.

A rat flea, black in wing and hackle, flittered out of the shred of blue cloak and flew inland—as if carried along by destiny—toward the Crimean trading port of Kaffa. The infamous date was 1346.

Stinks were soon smelt—in malt, barrels of sprats, chimney flues. Physicians lost patients in spates.

"The plague! The plague!" *squealed the chief magistrate, biting his thumb, his fauces black, the streaks of jet vivid along his wicks and nose, and then dropped dead as a stone. Fires were lighted. The harbor was sealed.*

But it was too late. Ships, laden with produce, had already set sail in the pestiferous winds and headed out along the trades to Constantinople, to Cyprus, to Sardinia, to Avignon, and points beyond—

Sleutel, among them: a town that, recently, had expanded and grown to the clink of gold in the guilds, the crackle of flames in the tile-kilns, and the mercantile sermons in the new protestant kerks.

Why, there was even entertainment.

The town brothel, formerly the orphanage, represented the major holding of a certain Mijnheer van Cats who lived alone with his son, a dissolute half-wit seen once a year moping into town to paint its shutters and touch up the wooden sign out front that read: De Zwarte Hertogin.

It became famous. Merchant sailors, visiting in droves, always wept with laughter at the idle boast of its madam, that she had once been the village beauty.

Or was Time, indeed, the archsatirist?

For the place was run by an ooidal-shaped sow with chin hairs, a venomous breath, and grit-colored hair who always carried a ladle and trounced her girls. They called her "Mother Spatula."

The legacies passed on by the sailors were worse than the legacies they received. It began with the "sweats."

The town of Sleutel was soon aflame with flews, black spots, boils, pink eye, and the stinking wind that broadcast one to another. Lost souls screamed aloud to be crimped with knives like codfish.

A whole Arabian pharmacy could do no good.

Nothing could stop the contagion, neither chanters nor flagellants. The townsfolk spun into dancing fits, cat-concerts, and fell to biting each other and frying jews. Men castrated themselves and flung their severed genitals into the hopeless sky to placate an angry God.

"The Black Death" struck, and struck, and struck. Bodies fell like the leaves of Vallombrosa. It beggared rhetoric: recorded only by historians as the worst disaster that had ever visited the world.

Mijnheer van Cats, staring upon his son's flapping tongue and hopeless insanity, waddled up high into the black windmill, took off his clogs, and—pinching his nose—stepped past the revolving vanes and cowardly made his quietus.

They both went to their accounts impenitent.

But more. Mother Spatula ran into her dank room, made mouths in a glass—and shrieked! Her drazels, horrified at the telltale nosebleed, held to her lips a little statue of St. Roch, the Plague Saint; but she went deaf as a beetle to their pleas, curled up into a fork and died, notwithstanding the fact that to her black feet—in order to draw the vapors from her head—they had applied two dead pigeons.

She didn't seem to attach a good deal of importance to them before she went.

Darconville whispered, "Isabel?"

But she was fast asleep in his arms, her face still smeared with dry tears, her complexion washed of its color and showing a slight antimonious tint. He noiselessly raised himself on one elbow and, watching over her in the darkness, first blew softly on her forehead and cheeks and then stanched with an ever-so-slight kiss a single tear that sparkled at the edge of one eye like a tiny drop of chalcedony. He felt the physical ache of love as he watched her perfect mouth, slightly open, exhaling the sighs of sleep. They had never made love, but the synecdoche of desire, he knew, waited crucially upon the larger understanding of love in whose fiefdom, until proven true, it always walked a stranger. And, then, he wasn't even certain she was in love with *him!* Or ever could be!

There was so much he wanted to tell her, and it seemed a perfect time to confess it, to hear matters spoken which up to that time he hadn't, but privately, dared even acknowledge, and yet he hesitated lest the tiniest utterance break the spell of that beautiful moment and, somehow, end it—like the angels called Ephemerae who lived merely for the twinkle of an instant, expiring upon the second they recited the *Te Deum*. Only let me live, prayed Darconville, as he watched Isabel there, no longer than I might love.

A sleepy voice, then, murmured something. It was inaudible. Isabel suddenly swirked up in alarm. "Oh, if I miss my curfew—"

Darconville placed a finger to her lips, assuring her he'd have her back to Fitts in plenty of time. She smiled, hugging him, and in a sleep-enthralled voice told him about the strange dream she'd had: she was a princess in a beautiful white dress, living all alone in a kind of fairy-forest where she was safe, and then one day—but Isabel clapped her mouth. How thoughtless of her, she said, to have missed *his* story! Darconville laughed.

Story, tale, book: what were these, he thought, next to the gentle creature whose waist he now took, whose eyes he now searched—and it shamed him to have held back the words of passion, born in his heart, that still beat against his consciousness for deliverance. But what, asked Isabel, could she do to make up for her thoughtlessness? *Tell me you love me.* Darconville, pushing her back, insisted the story he told was nonsense and that she didn't have to do anything.

"Oh please."

Tell me you love me.

"Well, let me see." Darconville paused. "All right," he said. "Have you visited Miss Trappe yet?"

"That's what I'll do!"

"Do you promise? She wanted to see you, you know."

Isabel took Darconville's face in her hands and kissed him, her eyes, sending out sparkles like a carcanet of jewels, brightening with resolution. She witched him in one set gaze, and they fell against each other, giving and taking kisses, with Isabel pausing only to add, by repetition, to the weight of her vow.

"I promise."

XXVIII

A Promise Unfulfilled

Ascend above the restrictions and conventions of the World, but not so high as to lose sight of them.

—Richard Garnett, *De Flagello Myrteo*

A WEEK LATER Darconville met Miss Trappe in the street. She mentioned in passing, again, that she had a special present she wanted to give to Isabel: the cameo. But, asked Darconville, hadn't she yet come by for a visit? Miss Trappe smiled sadly. That night when Darconville inquired of Isabel why she hadn't gone to see Miss Trappe, it was with some surprise that he heard her reply. "I don't want to dominate her," said Isabel.

That seemed very odd, indeed.

XXIX

"Sparks from My Anvil"

> Vain are the documents of men
> And vain the flourishes of the pen
> That keep the fool's conceit.
>
> —CHRISTOPHER SMART, "A Song to David"

Rumpopulorum, meanwhile, was going poorly. The manuscript had lost its kick, and Darconville, as late as March, flashing back through the accumulation of sheets, found only an unedited mess of junk and logomachies, a collection of pages pierced by arrows of afterthought, marginal loops, and harebrained squirts and scribbles twaddleized out of doubt and belated reflection: a penman's alibi. It was, he felt, as if his ability to write were now only a tiny, fitful flame, no, not a flame even, a scarcely visible vapor flickering over a chaos of conflicting wishes, purposes, and hopes that were so disorganized as utterly to cancel one another. A line here. A line there.

It was wounding not to be able to write easily, upgathering what of life seemed barren without the expression of it, but Darconville hadn't written well for months and recently had almost begun to grow ill when walking into the room to work, a dull nausea overcoming him at the prospect, troubling his mind as a touch of lust might trouble a soul only half-escaped from it. Write, wrote, written: it was the most painful verb in the language. He somehow couldn't believe in it anymore.

There was nothing to be done. He pulled out a cuesheet and randomly set to for half an hour with his pencil, tentative tool, but the words sat on the lines like disgusted birds forming and fulgurating in a cacophonous gamut along a washwire. Doodled mimicries pulled faces at him from the margins. Furious, Darconville x'ed out three trial pages, clicked off the light, and smoked in the dark thinking of Isabel's photographs and how, perhaps, he should never have seen them. Did he mean that? Maybe. Eurydice is impossible if Orpheus looks away. No, it was a stupid blasphemy. He wouldn't think of it again.

At best, Darconville now coped. He who once wrote with beauty and speed, who in the late hours of creation, even after those long walks in Venice from his home out to the Isola di San Pietro and back, could almost forgo any illumination as his fingers gave out the necessary light, now found himself in the grip of woeful indolence—not writing, nor organizing to do so, but waiting around idly leafing through lexicons and coming to resent the fat cast of characters alphabetically lined up there as if in some melodramatic pre-theatrical to defy his direction and so challenge his art.

Verrine, one of the evil Thrones, had begun to tempt him with long and unrelieved bouts of impatience: "the lyf so short, the craft so long to lern." Words! They seemed his *only* experience, his only sophistications. And yet what were they? Merciless little creatures, crowding about and eager for command, each with its own physical character, an ancestry, an expectation of life and a hope of posterity. And yet how he wanted to scream or stamp his foot and scatter them away, terrorizing them into disappearance letter by letter, all those clicks, bangs, buzzes called consonants and vowels that howled and ululated and cooed! It was frustrating, for he *believed* in the word-as-written, those sweet puncts, safe from the dangers of loss and paralalia, which alone rendered ideas clearly, and until words were written, formulated, he felt, they couldn't even be considered properly thought out. No, previous to the word, Darconville had always thought, one couldn't argue that even the most elementary relationships existed. But if they expressed, he wondered, did they communicate? He didn't know anymore. He put out his cigarette, stubbornly to go back to work, and clicked on the light. The skull on his desk was still smiling.

Darconville set out a bottle of ink and filled "The Black Disaster," the pen that had served him so long: it seemed labor in itself. He felt a sudden dread in the suck of the drawing nozzle—it sputtered "Govert"! He ignored it. And consulting the watch on the nail he resumed, with obsessive intensity, trying to write, with this insane fancy taking possession of him, however, that at that moment he knew something of what the lonely Power behind life must have known as it drove towards the purpose of a creation which then and thereupon, in the form of two humans, refused to ascribe any benevolence to the act. He hovered over his desk, the pen motionless. But nothing came. In an absurd kind of game he then systematically tried to force himself to believe he was *totally* incompetent to the task of writing, a methodic dialectic he used with himself on occasion taken from homeopathic therapy in which, to reverse a mood, he dosed himself with a relentless and pitiless exaggeration of it in order to reconstruct its opposite. For who is always what he is at any instant? And so, hopeful, he went profitably hopeless, to remind sickness of health, evil of good, and hunger of abundance, but for it all he made small headway and saw out the profitless forepart of the day with only a single ragged paragraph, one split in two by a particularly inexact image that reflected in the mirror of his craft exactly what he feared he had become—and so he drew his pen in a looping *circumlitio* over the page and walked out of the room.

The afternoon went poorly, as well. Darconville sat in another room, drinking, wishing to detach himself from the pressure of reflection, the better to mock memory and the misery it made in a mind to worry it to words. Parody of anticipation, parody of meditation: slouching on a sofa, he found the mindless darkness to be even more venal than his own disabilities, the room a Piranesian cell where he sat in demented soliloquy, an examination of his own self-disobedience which, even if it clarified the sense of order at the core of his worst outrages, still kept him from work. He drank more and smoked until his lungs, never strong, ached, thinking, for some reason, of the

strange people roaming the world called Coords who, though hating
the devil, worshipped him lest, unplacated, he destroy them utterly in
the fullness of his malice. Spellvexit, butting about between his legs,
was whining—a sound, terribly, like "Govert! Govert!" It was ridiculous. Darconville drank even more and, borne up like the duck who
floats on what he drinks, put back his head, concentrating on trying to
improve accident by meditation, and closed his eyes for what seemed
more hours than idleness warranted or despair ever deserved.

It was late when Darconville woke up, his head light, his body cold,
the colder, somehow, for the March winds blowing outside. He went
to the front window, gazed at the leafless hedges under the huge tree
that still retained a few withered leaves, and returned to his desk. He
took up his pen, which seemed to parch like a martyr in his hand. He
began to write, nevertheless, addressing the nine-and-ninety lies of the
moment he hoped to bargain with for a night of *saloperie* at the side
of the twisted strumpet, Fiction, who lasciviously rolled her eyes at
him, hised up her skirt, and beckoned him on. He had come to detest
every aspect of that chair and desk which began to assume the shape
of a scaffold and found now in the repetition of each failure there a
spirit of corruption and death which only confirmed that they were
the end of *all* endeavor, rendering effort itself absurd. The room with
its old-fashioned wallpaper seemed an illusion of life, a shadow-
scenery of disorganization. And the skull! The skull, making sardonic
commentary on his predicament, seemed to cry, "I am still alive, you
fool of folly, while you are dead! Hoodoo! Hoodoo! The most beautiful things in life blossom and fade, while only ugly things like ice-floes,
boulders, and the brainless ooze remain. *What* is to be preserved forever? The attributes of immortality are cruelty, greed, and the dogs of
war—the serpent with its deathless coil round the concept of Eden!"

But Darconville wrote, and wrote while he doubted to write, and as
he wreaked his harms on ink's poor loss, there was nothing for the
trouble in his head, and more, for always—scratch, scratch—the pen
went whispering across the page, "Govert! Govert! Govert!" He
wrote, erased, and wrote. A line here. A line there. He worked for an
hour and, weary, leaned back to look at the dead syntax and desuete
word-groupings. A face loomed up, grey. With angry joy, he erased its
filthy ears—and began again.

But it was impossible: he saw only an incomplete and unwieldy af-
tergrief in front of him. Sentences were pulling out of paragraphs,

phrases didn't fit, and words got lost, slip-sliding about in baffling arrangements all their own like those emanations of God we are doomed now to curse, now to bless, in eternal alternation, yet never fully to understand. The tragedy of writing was that its hiding place was its habitat, those secret and inaccessible desert places we seek to violate, like tombs, for miracles we'd have but can only blaspheme in the touching. It was hopeless to know and nowhere to be had. I have divided my life into pages and pilcrows, thought Darconville: a squid's brain is only one-sixth the size of his ink sack.

Refusing to abide the futility and fakery, the fear, of ritually waiting to write, trying in surviving the world to transfigure his survival, he resumed—until he thought he heard a noise. He listened a moment, then went back to work. But again there came a sudden knocking at the door. He went to the window, threw it up, and called, "Isabel?" The world, he thought, is always as near as my doorknocker is loud. "Isabel?"

There was no answer.

Darconville walked downstairs, wiping his eye, and opened the door. It was iniquitous: in the doorway—*tacita sudant praecordia culpa*—stood two pedantic ushers from the School of Anabaptism who nightly went trudging about Quinsyburg, house to house, looking for converts. He went to shut the door, impossible for an interposed foot.

"I have in my hand here," said one of them, "a personal love-letter from God, and—"

Darconville almost came at him. The speaker's face fell, seeing danger, and became a patch of wavering greyness against the blanket of night into which, the better to avoid this gothic adversary and his mood of incorrigible refusal, both suddenly fled. A pamphlet fluttered down in the vacuum of their sudden departure—reading "Sparks from My Anvil" by W. C. Cloogy, Evangelist.

Shutting the bolt to, returning upstairs, Darconville roamed the room in maniacal pursuit of what became only confused and scrambled thoughts that left only shadow within shadow, and, although his poor heart was beating at the time for quite another cause, he took a long hard look, one out of which all sentiment had fled, in the direction of his desk. No doom, thought Darconville, is ever executed in the world, whether of annihilation or any other pain, but the Destroying Angel is in the midst of that visitation, and, not ignorant, not blinded to supernatural horror, he could hear the overhead thrashing of evil

Exterminans and his bat-colored wings, on parole through the universe, sickening the air with his logocidal wails.

A vision rose up before him. It was Cacotopia, suddenly, all around him, a land of nightsoil swept over by aboriginal winds and lit by a dim moronic moon under which, songless and illiberal, the only tribe of humans left on earth sat around shouting and mocking all that language could, a cultureless people who, having looked back into the past, saw there was no future. Agitprop throttled fable, libraries had been torched, and in the rubble of what once was were enacted scenes better imagined than described, with words, no longer lovely magical influences on nature anymore but now bleats of perversion serving only as a means of evil report, slander, strife, and quarrel.

The final day of pollution had come, and everywhere crowds of the disaffected gathered together in an earsplitting din to smash printing-presses, incinerate books, and befoul manuscripts in an orgy of violence, with everyone spitting, shitting, and bouncing up and down on his heels. Impatience was upon them! Where can we go, they screamed, never to hear or read a word again? They clapped in chant to be led somewhere. But where, where?

Suddenly, political sucksters and realistic insectivores, shoving to the front, puffed up their stomachs and blew lies out of their fingers! A parade was formed! It was now an assembly on the march, an enthusiastic troop of dunces, pasquil-makers, populist scribblers and lick-penny poets, anti-intellectual hacks, modernistic rubbishmongers, anonymuncules of prose and anacreontic water-bibbers all screaming nonce-words and squealing filthy ditties. They shouted scurrilities! They pronounced words backwards! They tumbled along waggling codpieces, shaking hogs' bladders, and bugling from the fundament! Some sang, shrill, purposely mispronouncing words, snarping at the language to mock it while thumping each other with huge rubber phalluses and roaring out farts! They snapped pens in half and turned somersaults with quills in their ears to make each other laugh, lest they speak and then finally came to the lip of a monstrously large hole, a crater-like opening miles wide, which, pushing and shoving, they circled in an obscene dance while dressed in hoods with long ear-pieces and shaking firebrands, clackers, and discordant bells! A bonfire was then lit under a huge pole, and on that pole a huge banner, to hysterical applause, was suddenly unfurled and upon it, up-sidedown, were written the words: *"In the End Was Wordlessness."*

And as the night grew darker, the noise reached a more deafening level than ever, a thunderous earth-shaking explosion of curses, imprecations, and terricrepant screams which worked the crowd up to such a pitch of frenzy that, suddenly, everyone began leaping into the hole, plummeting into the yawning darkness, flying in feet first as if crazed by oblivion itself! And then it was over. A few harpies and birds of Psapho circled overhead. But not a word, not a note, not a sound was ever heard on earth again.

There was such hopelessness suddenly felt in the room that night that Darconville, who took anthropomorphic devils seriously, snatched up a page in a paroxysm of utter despair and ripped it in half; snatched up another and did the same; then with a spasm of savage relief, he swept the entire manuscript off his desk and without a pause violently kicked the wastebasket into the air. It bounced like a shot across the room—"Govert!"—and rebounded upsidedown—"Govert!"—and then rattled toward a single spot, foolishly spinning to the sound, again, of that enigma variation—"Govert!" And then unable to bear it anymore, Darconville cried out like some adenoidal moron in a gulf of high winds with a voice that collapsed all his grief at once into a blind lamentation that could have been the question he might have asked but, for fear of knowing, was afraid to: *"Why must one's double always be one's devil?"*

XXX

Examination of Conscience

From the suffering of the world you can hold back, you have permission to do so, and it is in accordance with your nature; but perhaps this holding back is the one suffering you could have avoided.

—FRANZ KAFKA

ST. TERESA'S, the small Catholic church in Quinsyburg, was the one place above all others where Darconville could always find peace. The following morning found him sitting alone in a back pew and, while regarding the crucifix hung over the altar with its battered, twisted corpus, feeling humiliated by the perfection of form he sought, ignoring life, in his art. Was it possible, had he taken his own personality merely as a debt to discharge that he might sublimate his humanity, seeking to acquire through the vanity of high aesthetic the power of becoming that which he felt threatened him in the beyond? It was a terrible mistake, to be seen as truth only by the gaslamp from which Gérard de Nerval hanged himself.

It had been for more than half a year now that Darconville, long beyond reconsidering the question as to whether language as such was capable of expressing *anything* of the meaning of life, actually wondered if he himself were. The particular gifts which he had formerly possessed seemed to vanish as he grew in consciousness, as though his very attempts to understand himself, to accept himself, in relation to Isabel, had dried up the springs of his creativity.

Writing, he'd come to see, was the spiritual disease of which it considered itself to be the cure. His "real" jealousy of this person called Govert he aligned, with increasing conviction, to the "ideal" coruscations of his writing, antipodal and, for that, curiously related extreme points of dehumanization, both, with each a fussiness that failed to comprehend that the most important thing for lovers, as for writers, was to know how love, how writing, can be kept vital, not what must exist without it. It was almost a revelation. He had been for so long increating, looking into his artistically nihilitic heart, or otherwise excreating, looking beyond the stars for further promises of the sky and demanding, with romantic arrogance, all suit him, that he had failed to see just what was in front of him—stretched out, as he was, in a hopeless parody of Vitruvian man, his arms unable to close in anything like an embrace. Thales had fallen into a well while gazing at the heavens, as Pliny had, into a volcano, while searching the fires. Was there a lesson here?

There was.

It wasn't that Darconville perceived the world and its meaning differently—he had, in fact, found *more* meaning—but he could no longer put that meaning into words, nor could he find reason to. The embellishments, the slippered voluptions of his prose? It was praying into a mirror, he saw, in which, reflecting only what was outside it, could be found only the mock and pockless life within the symmetry of its frame. The mirror reversed nature! He knew now why he couldn't write, for art, like jealousy—living upon what they must deny—considered a sphere of facts altogether distinct from a sphere of values. Darconville looked long at the terrible figure of Christ. Perfection of form, unpronounceable artifice was, he realized, insufficient, and concepts and images without any genuine relation to existence could never any longer for him convey what was most important in life. The Word was made *flesh!* And yet what had he made it?

Darconville considered his idolatry: the imagination peopling a vain theogony with creatures it is satisfied to stand back and watch bombinate in the vacuum of art. And so was it with jealousy. A photograph hadn't come alive, a fancy had. The artist, rarely emerging from himself, so deceives—a man who tries to bribe God with examples of what he means by that deception, offering to a coterie world what he has fashioned by staring at the universe through an eyecard and arranged in fussy selection of what life offers to avoid: an agglomeration of methodically ordered masterproductions in paint and plaster, marble and music, sheetpads and stagecraft which assume the bounds of the conceivable to be the limits of the actual. The more orderly the art, thought Darconville, the more dishonest. The more methodic? Then did it render less the complexities that hide in the causes of man, his love, his astonishment, the stunning shocks which await him in the savage forest of equivocations and inscrutabilities. The very nature of art—failures by which man sought to memorize his experience—spiritually underdeveloped the very disciples who most needed to know what it wasn't, could not be, able to do. The symbol of art is the tombstone, thought Darconville, an obelisk sticking up out of the earth with the inscription, "I count!"

It was blasphemy, concluded Darconville, who'd long been a student of meanings that stole out in subtle replies, a sacrilege to bang gold, hammer silverswirls, and fashion anti-vital faces with blank and pitiless eyes squinting out cold and one-dimensional from niches cozily recessed from the flux of the world where suffering, if inevitable, at least proved life real. The aesthetic mode, he saw, was that of anti-renunciation! And even as he sat there under that crucifix, before those flickering candles, in that silence, Darconville fully assumed this mandate, that the man who entered a church to get out of the heat or cold lived closer to the spirit of God than he who came there for reasons aesthetic. Darconville prayed. Shall I, he wondered, shall I become some ikonodule, tall and white as a paschal candle, its aesthetic feet folded in prayer? A simulacrum of Mme. de Maupin, that he-she-or-it draped in jumbles of jewels and flowrets, skirting out of the world and begging entrance of the doorman of the ideal? One of those anti-social geniuses of refusal, pteriopes wrapped in procinian cloaks, or pale spectres who, with a delicate extremity of leg put forward and wrists turned after the manner of Parmigianino, floods the world with perfect tears and sighs with pampered weariness, "O come to me, Death! Come, lovely wanton death, to me!"?

Away with drawn pentacles! Away with my pretty pages! Away with formed perfections, compounded electuaries, phoenixes raised out of hypocritical flames!

If he didn't write, Darconville determined, so be it. He was in love, and the lover who didn't prove selfless committed a solecism with his heart. And if his writing became poorer in image, it would become more human, he felt, in intent. Away with a prose squeezed free of the real! The shallow jealousies he'd felt low in his soul ate through to his conscience, shot through with self-indulgence and merciless egotism where the difficulty of writing—even the attempt—had its origins. He had committed, he saw, Durtal's sin of "Pygmalionism": corruptly falling in love with his own work while bearing a grudge against anything that went against it. Onanism! Onanism and incest! It *was* a new sin, the exclusive crime of artists, a vice reserved for priests of art and princes of gesture, the father violating his spiritual child, deflowering his dream, and polluting it with a vanity that was only a mimicry of love. Was that one not mad, thought Darconville, who draws lines with Archimedes whilst his house is ransacked and his city besieged? The slogan of the artist is *eritis sicut dii*. The Anatomy Lesson of Dr. Tulp is a dissection scene of the physicians.

Darconville prayed harder. He saw that jealousy was not the obverse of vanity, rather its ugly twin, the failure in full sumptuousness of one's private aesthetic, and that was what he suddenly came to loathe in the aesthetician—antagonism by exaggeration for what of nature he couldn't realize in himself. Jealousy! Jealousy! Was it the cause or the symptom of his madness? What did it matter, for mad it was, the madness that parodied love. A monster! Other's harm! Self-misery! Beauty's plague! Virtue's scourge! Succor of lies, which to one's own joys one's hurt applies! It proved a faithlessness, not a devotion, to the girl he loved—and fed on the solitary weaknesses and perverse images of those symbolist projecticians and chimerical madmen for whom language, immoderate, diseased, cabalistic, was an entity, not an activity. To love Isabel was to *live* for Isabel, for what sculpture casts a shadow that can be touched, what shadow, empty as

shade, thin as fraud, that doesn't recapitulate the static figure throwing it? Were his fictive characters then the servants who'd live for
him? Foolish in the conception, twice foolish in the extreme!

Sorrowfully, Darconville looked up at the beaten, traduced Christ,
crowned with thorns, stabbed and naked, omnivisual over all the
tragedies of mankind that were as real as sin and as heartless as betrayal.

I will polish no massebah with my kisses, vowed Darconville, nor
suffites will I light to myself. He rose and, walking to the front of the
church, lighted a votive candle. Reflected in the shiny obsidian foundation there he saw his face. It was sculpted to shape affectation and
to peddle vanity, like one of those hieratic or royal effigies in relief on
the antique medals of the Medes. He wished to pray as he watched
the asterisk of fire touch the wick aglow and so prayed more deeply for
simple selflessness than he had ever prayed before—and, feeling an
uprush of grace in the very intention, shed the night in his heart and
called it light. And walking out of the little church he felt confirmed
in not only the worth of his whispered prayer but in the realization, as
well, that Christ had become man and not some bell-shaped Corinthian column with volutes for veins and a mandala of stone foliage for a
heart.

XXXI

A Gnome

Hang up philosophy.

—WILLIAM SHAKESPEARE,
Romeo and Juliet

"I WANT TO BE what I was when I wanted to be what I am now,"
said Darconville to his cat after he got home. Spellvexit, with one eye
raised in a slight circumflex, rather wished his master might descend
into particulars, as aphorisms tended to be vague. But Darconville said
no more, locked his manuscript into the trunk, and went out for a long
walk in the bright sunshine, stopping several times to listen to the
nightingales, for spring was advancing rapidly, with multitudes of
primroses, a prevalence of crocuses, and on some trees, sycamores,
chestnuts, blackthorns, the lower buds were already opening into leaf.

XXXII

Fawx's Mt.

I slept and dreamt
That life was joy;
I awoke and saw
That life was duty;
I acted and beheld
Duty was joy.

—RABINDRANATH TAGORE

"MY UNCLE is deformed," said Isabel quietly and kept staring straight ahead. Although it was the first time she'd ever mentioned that, Darconville said nothing in reply. The Bentley wound through several verdant declivities, bumped over a small wooden bridge, and slowly took the hill when the loaftops of the Blue Ridge mountains came into view. It was pine country with faintly Augean smells, a rolling landscape running into lopsided barns, tiny sikes, and dark groves. This was only one of several trips that year along that familiar serpentine road through Scottsville, into Charlottesville, then north over the pummeled turns to where Isabel lived, but Darconville had, for some reason, never met the family. It seemed to be more of a consolation, somehow, for Isabel finally to have got shut of her news—how long she'd kept silent!—than suddenly to hear Darconville say it didn't matter. And then they arrived.

A tiny man in a queer peddler's hat was thrashing in the turnips down behind the house. The name on the mailbox read: *Shiftlett.*

"O Lord!" squealed Isabel's mother, snatching at her haircurlers and bouncing up from the sofa, the springs of which flexed with the noise of Homerican Mars, "why, welc—" she barked her shin "—come to Fawx's Mt." Rushing to snap off the television set (a buzzer show) and clapping a bottle (cheap gin) into an under cabinet, she revociferated her boisterous welcome. She took Darconville's hand and squeezed it damply. The striped housecoat she wore—of a croquet-ball pattern—billowed behind her. She explained to Isabel, while dumping an ashtray sprouting a bouquet of long butts, explicitly what she wanted Darconville to forgive and implicitly forgave Isabel what Darconville didn't really need explained. It was Saturday, she said. A good ol' reason, she said, just to take it easy. She said not to mind her one bit. "We've sure heard right much about you from Isabel, my," she exclaimed, straightening on the wall a dime-store painting (browsing horse ignoring sunset), "I declare we have. Now you make yourself right at home here, y'hear?"

Isabel seemed embarrassed. But Darconville was frankly relieved. The magic flute of his imagination had, previous to this visit, blown a few melancholy notes: the High Priest Sarastro caught out trying to rescue Pamina from her wicked mother, the Queen of Night. It was not perhaps to be overlooked, least of all by the subject, that he was a Northerner, older, a Catholic, an artist, and that he drove a foreign *car!* And he never wanted to put in a position of having to be civil to him anyone who'd have to be; it seemed discourteous. It would have been perfect simply to state that he loved Isabel right then and there, if not to justify his presence then at least to free his mind, but he knew Isabel felt awkward about expressing intimate words in front of anyone, especially, as she once confided to him, her mother.

"Call me Dot," smiled Isabel's mother, lighting a cigarette and covering with that commodious housecoat most of the kitchen chair upon which she perched. She was a comic but slightly nervous woman, a mudsill whose English was a queer gumbo of mispronounced words and faulty grammar. Suddenly, the filter of her cigarette, to her great amusement, burst into flames: she'd lit the wrong end. Her face lost its modest attractiveness when she laughed, less for the grin that was too wide than for the myocardial ischemia one heard at the height of risibility.

A tall long-footed woman, she had short perked hair and her eyes, too close together, almost oriental, hesitant enough at times to suggest an affrighted conscience, had a protuberant root-vegetable look which under certain conditions was more exaggerated than, but slightly resembled, her daughter's. Her cheekbones were pronounced. It was a kind enough face which, however, became queerly distressed and almost cootlike when she was drunk or made a stupid remark—the frutex and suffrutex, surely, of keeping herself too long to the strict boundaries of Fawx's Mt.—and she spoke, gesturing with secretarial hands which looked like tough bast fiber, in a slovenly Southern accent that refaned even the most regular words into small indistinguishable poverties. Her conversation consisted only, always, of misdistributed stresses, spoonerisms, and other ingenuities that extended to using the word "city" as an adjective and even to the founding of a new state, *"Massatoochits."* It was, nevertheless, the stupidity that endears. And she had suffered.

Mrs. Shiftlett loved to talk. Her surname—a not-royal one—had been legally reassumed following the dissolution of her marriage, an acidulous failure she hoped to forget in the process of lifting herself out of general disenfranchisement into local respectability. The axiom that has it that there is one good interview in everyone held true in this case. The story was, however, an old one. A Scotch-Irish trimmer who'd wandered out of Arkansas with only one change of socks and even less principle than education, Mrs. Shiftlett's husband—Isabel's father—decamped almost at the very moment she was born and then remarried soon after. ("He had no conscience," confessed his ex-wife, who added not only that she'd never marry again but vowed, somewhat cynically, that grand and mighty visions were sure as hell visions not of this world.) The hapless mother, sans wedbed and getting even further separated from her alphabet, scrooped about as best she could from Norfolk to Richmond to Petersburg trailing along her daughter through an inclement world of hunger, disappointment, and recession for more than a decade. They lived for periods with relatives, struggled and saved, and then rented a listing farmhouse on the edge of the woods adjoining Fawx's Mt. whereupon, it so fell out, her only brother, having initially come to the hospital in Charlottesville for a perilous operation—it was explained he'd been shot in the face during a card-game—eventually moved down from over the mountains, some three or four years previous, and settled in with them. They pooled what money they had for a somewhat better house. Life, such as it was, continued. And Isabel kept her father's name.

Mrs. Shiftlett bird-wittedly gaped through the window down to the turnip patch and gulped a drink from another bottle that suddenly appeared. "You know he's—"

"Yonder," interrupted Isabel, nervously. They hadn't been in the house ten minutes, but she turned to Darconville with pained, pleading eyes. "But let's go, anywhere," she whispered, "*please?*"

And so they did.

Fawx's Mt. was a jerkwater—a little rustic boosterville running in a crazy thalweg along the base of the Blue Ridge chain and hedged in by slonks and dark deciduous forests of rotting logs, leaf-mold, and eaten-away pines. The village consisted of a single street—a woodcart rut brimming with rainwater, wisps of fallen hay—where hunched together were a midget post-office, one general store-cum-gas-station, and two sad old churches of indeterminable denomination. It was a place sunk in blind ignavia, a chaos, a nulliverse of stifling monotony, little movement, and a zipcode of ee-i-ee-i-o. Nature itself, weirdly, seemed not to have existed there in any shape of health. A terrible seriousness breathed through the place, a grim deutero-canonical uneasiness in which, with suspicion their mood and subjection their lodestar, the townsfolk all trod the particular path that paradoxically led to isolated houses, to isolated lives, and to isolated fears. It was as if the people there felt preternatural powers spied down on them with evil intent, with each haunted, whether in the ghost of blight or the spectre of depression, by whatever dismal fantasy he chose as penalty for his puppet sins. There was a subtle mood of guilt there, of unproductive renunciation, of anger. People kept to themselves. And there was usually never a soul in sight. You might have heard the sound of a buzz-saw somewhere, a pigsqueal from a faraway farm, wind. But that was all.

On one particular day, however, the hamlet was all astir. This was *Saturday*—the day of exception in the South that can repel the heaviest stone melancholy can throw at a man and which alone among others, even in the hazy-mazy stillness of a Virginia heat that breeds flies, sloth, and humidity in the scuppernong vines, can relieve responsibility and somehow refer it to fun. And with what joy is it met! With what excitement! Suddenly, everybody appears. The tools and trials of the workaday week are put away, inhibitions are forgotten, and all tumble-belly together—in feed-hats and hickory-staved bonnets, chinos and calicos, crocheted shawls and cracked leather jerkins—for a bit of community: ice-cream socials, barbecues, country sings, quilting bees, barn dances, or, hell, just an afternoon of plain ol' hanging around. It was the one day in Fawx's Mt. when all the good ol' boys who worked their truck patches or humped pulpwood all week could put on their boots and boiled jeans—the original straight stovepipes—and come into town to suck beers, ogle girls, punch each other with mock sidewinders, and swap stories in terms generally borrowed from the category of human evacuations. But best of all they preferred just to sit around and gawp.

These were the "hearties" of Fawx's Mt., not a great deal different, truth to tell, from the other wonderful sapsuckers down South that might be classified under *ordo squamata:* yomp heads, mountain boomers, rackensacks, hoopies, haw-eaters, snags, pot-wallopers, buckras, goober goopers, scataways, pee-willies, wool hats, pukes, raggeds, boondockers, dug downs, tackies, crackers, and no-lobes. It's a kind of club—300-pound dipshits, always named something like "Hawg," Kincaid, or Harley—who drink flask bourbon, have chigger-bites on their arms, and wear their hair either short or slicked back (the comb tracks are always visible) to reveal faces like those reversible *trompe-l'oeil* funheads you snip from the Sunday paper to fool someone with. They have no chins, are inclined to be goitral, and are always chewing down a blade of grass fiercely and absentmindedly. They are given to wearing suntans, white socks, work boots, and cheap acetate shirts, the sleeves of which are always rolled up to a point higher than the triceps brachii in tight little knots. They like whiskey with good bead, respect Shriners, whistle a lot, drive with one hand, slide crotch-first onto barstools, and—just "funnin'"—love to hang around butt-slapping and goosing each other, punctuating certain remarks of course with that significant nudge just before they're going to fart. They like to wade into swamps and jacklight rats, are big lodge-joiners, and know everything about guns which they always handle, silently, with phallic reverence. They have hands like cowhorn, with nails bitten to the quick. They have spools of rusting cable in their backyards, nail coons to the walls, adore rodeos, and their execrable grammar is half informed by protective coloration, half by rank stupidity.

Chainsaws are their toys. They're given to sheep jokes, often engage in games with each other like "Squail the Pig" or rustic variations of *"Detur Tetriori:* or, The Ugliest Grinner Shall Be the Winner," and are fond of spitting contests. But the favorite redneck recreation is incest. They fear women, so hate them, but as most are latently homosexual they fear that even more, and so fifty times a day boastfully and loudly proclaim for each other's benefit that they'd hump a rockpile if they thought a snake were under it. They invariably refer to their penises as "Big Sid." They are usually married, but each willfully keeps confined to home his jittery gap-toothed wife, always either pronouncedly fat or thin—they all look as if they support nature on a diet of lucifer matches and gin—who, when not peeking half-wittedly around the doorframe of a dogtrot cabin, squats on her porch dandling a big thick-necked gosling of a child with a purple hairbow and an I.Q. that doesn't even register, repeatedly telling it, "Wave to the street!"

They loathe sentiment but thrive on sentimentality, violently beat their women with pony-leads on Saturday night but weep with guilt at Sunday-Go-to-Meeting during the singing of "The Old Rugged Cross," their favorite. In groups, they're dangerous; each, alone, is a simpleton. Fanatically patriotic, they're all knee-jerk defenders of state sovereignty and go blubbery at the mere sight of the Confederate Battle Flag. They're either whispering sideways about Jesus or bawling obscenities, georgic in imagery, with stentorophonic might. They're handy, can always tell one car from another, know the right weights of oil, love to use the word "ratchet," and always know when to use baling wire and when to use bagging wire. They know everything about loggerheads, trace-chains, and hames and can always be found driving the backroads in trucks, filled with wood, wedged with chocks, toward a sawmill shed in the mountains. They all smoke, snite from the nose with the forefinger, and suffer from very particular ailments: Basedow's Disease; gleet; fishskin itch; furunculosis; rodent ulcer;

pyorrhea of the gums; Walking Typhoid; mucous patches; and tic douloureux. They all know shortcuts through the woods. They lurk.

It was a Saturday, then, much like the others, and all the feebs-in-overalls and donkeyphuckers one saw pitching hay in meadows during the week—they stand stock-still, with upright pitchforks, and stare out of expressionless faces as you pass—were now in high report. They'd *met* to be. And the best place was the general store.

Darconville and Isabel pulled up in front. The big car resembled a hearse, with Darconville undertaking, this time, to buy some cigarettes: he looked out the car window and, although torn between feelings of suspicion and frank amusement, got out and shut the door. A crow rased out of the eaves of the store.

The Diet of Schmalkalden had convened: there sat the country gnoofes, Hob, Dick, Hick, and a few others all perched on palings, eating cheese with clasp knives and whittling and spitting in the direction of a battered expectoroon behind them. Darconville couldn't take it in all at once. It looked like a group of people—*quocumque modo* —who'd somehow just about managed to survive the Permian extinction: sowskins, ferox-faced oaves, hedge-creepers, pig-slopping curmudgeons, bungpegs and lickspittles, scummers-of-pots, and low venereals with red-nosed papier-mâché faces gumming chaws of Mail Pouch tobacco. But what seemed incredible was that each and every one of them—minds, clearly, unviolated by the slightest idea—all looked remarkably the *same,* wearing in their faces the fatal traces of degeneracy and the physiological signs of the consanguineous parentage that caused it. Not a word was spoken.

Custodially, Darconville walked by Isabel into the creepy low-lit store, a sheet-iron stove prominent, its half-filled shelves a wilderness of canned abominations and pioneeriana: fishing tackle, diuretic pills, jerked beef, tires, secondhand rifles, tractor parts, wholesale tins of peas, hoses, galvanized pails, tins of fish roe, flypaper, thistle seed, and a magazine rack—Darconville stepped closer to look—crammed with back-issues of *Midnight Cry; Watson's Magazine, The Christian Banner, American Opinion, Menace, The Searchlight* and, sanspareil of the lot, *The Fiery Cross.* Taking Isabel by the finger, Darconville nodded to that last magazine; she closed her eyes, smiled, and shrugged. How, Darconville wondered, could there be such innocence, such beauty, in the midst of such ugliness? She was a perfect lotus springing from a swamp. The greatest balsams, he'd heard, lie enveloped in the bodies of the most powerful corrosives; poisons contain within themselves their own antidote. He kissed her quickly, thinking *but pray, not the reverse,* and made his purchase.

The proprietor—someone, to Darconville's astonishment, addressed him as Mr. Shiftlett!—stood behind the counter, serving notice on him with an arsonist's eye, like the squint of one polyplectronic cock eyeing another; he was about three feet high and had the face of a barn-owl, angry, surprised, harelipped. He ignored Darconville's pleasantries and, turning away, ended them with a rude fnast of disgust down his nose. And so they left.

Out front, as Isabel got into the car, Darconville heard from behind him one of the peckerwoods make a snort, followed by a dry stercorous whistle—and he turned. No one moved. Darconville got into the car. Quickly, a young bumswink with hair the color of jackass stepped forward; it was a face full of mother-wit—the perfect redneck's—with a long nose and a voluted nostril, and, turning to grin at his partners, he revealed a mouthful of imperfect teeth, pegged and pumpkin-seed shaped. Thin, tattered, and lousy, he scarcely retained a human semblance; in his filthy face two minute glittering eyes squinted furiously inwards at his nose. He hitched up his trousers with his wrists, spat sideways, and nodded toward Isabel. "I like a good milk cow myself, Captain," he said, "don' mean, yowever, I got to sleep with one." Darconville kicked open the door but saw it was no good: he was suddenly looking down the barrels of two rusty shotguns, wagging impatiently up and down—and meaning *go.* He backed slowly into the car, where Isabel sat ashen, and then thundered away up a small road, driving as if behind them lay not a hilltown of twisted pines, broken fences, and scutch-grass but the Abomination of Desolation itself.

Without a word, Darconville drove on, cradling Isabel's head to his shoulder while she kept repeating through her tears, "It's unfair! It's unfair!"

They wound through country roads, a repetition of gimp fences, quirked barns, and fields with dead rusted machinery, for what seemed like hours, riding into and then around the low hills. Cattle, skewbald, roan, and dappled, drowsily munched tall grasses and meadow weeds as field upon field led past woodlands toward the mountains that, upon approach, seemed indefinitely prolonged. The mountains, however, surprising him, turned out to be more low hills, unimpressive and empty except for an occasional farmer or two who, never saluting, rolled by in old buckboards with sawn-oak wheels. Out of the hills now, they swung around returning by backroads eroded by spring branches and runs all bubbling along, an area at several points of which, Darconville noticed, stood small signs directing the way to: *Zutphen Farm.*

It was, Darconville remembered, the van der Slang property—Govert's house.

Silently, Darconville kept to those directions. They jounced onto a fairly good road and, heading straight west, soon got clear of the woods when a large farm came into view. Isabel crouched lower, her mood of oppression seeming to darken here even more. The farm was larger by far than any in Fawx's Mt., but grand, he thought, only by comparison, for on the mountain side of it were nothing but grim little shacks and hovels-with-tin-chimneys, whereas on the town side, though not much better, could be found a few normal but still insignificant spit-and-brick affairs of the modern stamp—the Shiftletts' house was an example—built soon to bury. A white wooden fence by the dirt road circled the grounds of the van der Slangs' where grazed some horses, goats, a herd of black cattle, and set back in a dim glade stood the main house, white and cold and silent. Surrounded by fat whin-blown meadowlands, it was one of those spacious farmhouses with high-ridged but sloping roofs and low projecting eaves under which hung flails, harnesses, various bits of husbandry. So, thought Darconville, there in that stronghold farm lived that broad-skirted and faceless Dutch urchin he feared; he saw himself as Ichabod Crane: a New England country schoolmaster and worthy-wight—in form and spirit like a supplejack (yielding but tough)—sojourning in that by-place of nature, in love, but somewhat out of his element and exposed to the commonness of rantipole heroes given to boorish practical jokes and rough country swains and bumpkins, standing back, envying his person, his address, and his girl.

A bowlegged woman in a bandanna and high rubber boots appeared in the near distance of that property feeding a goat. Darconville intended to say nothing but found he couldn't.

"Could that," he asked, driving past, "possibly have been Mrs. van der Slang?"

Slouched down, Isabel slowly peered up and then back in the direction of the receding figure. Are there silences, wondered Darconville at that moment, in which if one listens closely may be heard screams?

"Really?" she asked. "I didn't even notice."

"Maybe not."

"*Maybe*—" Isabel's eyes flashed in anger.

"Not maybe you didn't notice," said Darconville, surprised, "maybe it wasn't Mrs. van—"

"But," repeated Isabel, exasperated, almost as if wanting of him what she wouldn't of the figure, "I didn't even notice." Strange, thought Darconville, strange. And so there was nothing more said on the subject, which of course, he knew, was a good deal.

They spent much of the afternoon driving, exchanging small talk. Darconville would often ask innocent, almost childlike questions dealing with things Isabel might know and things she could never be expected to know, leading her through entire dialogues before arriving not at truth as such, but at some final irresolvable question of which, perhaps, they together—curiously—both loved to be ignorant. Actually, Isabel said rather little on such occasions, far less indeed on others, those predominantly of the social stamp. She never directly approached people: if she came upon people she wanted to know, she allowed herself only a smile to bridge the distance, and invariably they approached her, with Isabel feeling then the boon of sudden value she initially suspected neither of them had. Fair is not fair, he thought, but that which pleases. Helen was not, but whilst she was.

Darconville wanted badly to know her, her successive selves—why, in fact, he loved her. In a way, he wanted to *be* her, that much better to know. Perspective as seen, he thought, is never reality. Wasn't a stopped clock correct twice a day? In fact, perspective was anti-creative, for if we painted what we actually saw—reality, say—we'd literally have to paint double images. Compensating, compromising, we look toward dead center only to contect what we'd know, to scrutinize the inscrutable. Isabel *was* inscrutable. Was he, for instance, Darconville wondered, charmed only by the fact that she lived a life of which essentially he knew nothing? Where so little was given, he thought, much was left to the imagination. The man in love, he knew, often constructed his beloved from the compilation of small data he was insistently delighted was so small. On the other hand, perhaps, maybe she was simply the product of his own temperament, the image, the reversed projection and "negative" of his own sensibility, opposed *and* complementary? Did she lead a life unknown to him to which he could gain right of entry only by loving her? Was he merely unloading on her the state of himself, the worth of the girl not in question, but only the quiddity of that state? And did her silences simply feed his own vanity whereby, giving him the illusion of intelligence, he saw reflected only the worth he pompously assumed he himself had?

Well, Darconville didn't know, you see. He wanted only that she come to believe in the sublimity he felt, feel enough to believe the sublimity possible. Hope, after all, was as cheap as despair, and vision? Vision! It was perhaps nothing more than believing it could be arranged. Isabel was silent, yes, and mysterious beyond that. But those who saw in their loved one only what was obvious or actually present, concluded Darconville, were incapable of understanding the select activity of love and—fools curial! fools primipile!—addressed it with a solecism. The romance of imprecision is not the elision of the tired romance of the precise. Mint, in a glass of water, exhausts pounds of it. Whoso feels the meaning of eternity is in it. Q.E.D.

J'adoube, thought Darconville.

The sun fell behind the mountains, an income of cold breezes and blue dew now being felt along the high countryside of Fawx's Mt. The woodlands of pin-oaks, sour gums, and box elders darkened. Clutching his arm, Isabel moved closer to Darconville, sleep drawing her head toward his chest. He drove on a bit further through gloomy dimbles and boggy slades and little unnamed places with boondock courthouses, then circled around near the funny little airport, a red windsock over a barren tract, on the outskirts of Charlottesville, and passing back through Stanardsville under a sky filled with clouds like weasel tracks bounced over narrow, lonely roads along which bordered tumbled-down stone walls and desolate dray-horse farms sticking up out of moss and moor, holt and hill, and then came again to the edge of Fawx's Mt. where Darconville saw a roadhouse in a stand of pines —and pulled over.

It was a shabby place.

The hairy wabblefat at the grill—you couldn't see at the neck where the head adhered—had an acromegalic jaw and a five o'clock shadow; he took a toothpick from his mouth and half turned. One of his eyes was milky with trachoma. The close air, as Darconville and Isabel sat down, smelled of sawmill gravy and fried meat. A jukebox was playing a country song about adultery. The waitress, a slatternly blonde with orange lipstick and a severe case of underbite, came over to the booth and unhooked an order pad from her hip. Darconville, ordering a coffee for himself and a hot chocolate for Isabel, asked the time. The waitress scratched a tiny spot in the nest of her hair with the sharp fingernail of her medical finger and, with a pencil, stabbed behind her in the direction of the clock. It was with unexpressed disbelief but a suddenly profound sense of mis-wish that, finding the time, he also read in faded letters pericycloid with the clockface the name of the establishment: *Shiftlett's*—incontrovertible proof, thought Darconville, that demons were rife on earth. It was a Land of Submultiples!

The roadhouse was like all others in the South. The pattern never varies. A crusty exhaust-fan, wafting out the bacon smoke, whines in a high pigeon-flecked window. In a cubby-like pantry off at one end slouches the *plongeur*—a bindlestiff, working his way down to Chattanooga or Mobile, in a paper hat, ripped T-shirt, and apron tied gracelessly low—who has his mouth pursed to a perpetual whistle (nothing ever comes out) and is dunking in and out of the cold, soapless water thick white cups and bowls washed over the years almost to fossils. The owner, of course, works the grill, clarifying his drippings and juicing alive the comestibles—fat snaps, grease cracks, oil spats—but he's a windmill of efficiency, jackflipping burgers, whiffling batter, and sieving oil out of the fries, his ear professionally cocked to the laconic input of orders barked by the waitress, his perspiring eye on the dusty moon of the clock on the flame-scorched ceiling above him, next to that pair of antlers you love, and the calendar printed up by the local dairymen's association showing in front of a red barn a freckled girl-child in pigtails and overalls hugging a cow, its caption reading, "Let's Bring the Curtain Down on Mastitis."

That tone held here. There was one addition, however—an unpredictable variant—on a side-wall by the door. It was a framed photograph, frilled around in the crushed bunting of the Stars 'n' Bars, of a group of thirty or so country jakes in string ties, identified collectively on a plaque underneath as "Knights of the Great Forrest." Darconville, always curious, wondered who they were. The Prophets of Zwickau? Contra-Remonstrants of the Old Dominion? The Second Synod of Dort? "Bunkum," he demoted.

Darconville took Isabel's hands on the table and smiled, for he saw she was justifiably uneasy about the place. He wanted to avoid saying something from the it's-important-that-you-understand-that-you-must-trust-me-if-you-want-me-to-help-you school but, as she seemed distraught, he gave her full attention. *This,* she said, peeping her eyes sideways and lowering her head, was exactly what she wanted to avoid in her life. Please, said Darconville. No, she said, her eyes filming over, she meant it, really, she *meant* it. And then out of the blue, for the first time, she explained—her heart now a hotpond of regrets—how she'd grown up in the midst of such, such—she fought for words—

"Lower-class—*things!*" she whispered hoarsely. Isabel thrust out her underlip, blew up at her hair, and then told Darconville in language a shade too vehement how, how, how weak, really *weak,* her mother was, although she loved her, naturally, who wouldn't love their own mother? O, said Isabel, couldn't he *see?* She bemoaned the fact that her mother rattled dishes in the sink early in the morning, that she drank too much, that she mispronounced words, and on and on. Why, her uncle never even flushed the toilet after using it! They were poor, uneducated, didn't even *talk* right!

Darconville listened to her, who seemed now so out of charity with almost everything, as if all joy had suddenly passed out of the world, as if God, and simultaneously with Him all creation, had suddenly bowled up on the horizon, angry, revengeful, and cruel. Isabel had a woman's worries, but the child lingered on in her complexion and in the sweetness of her mouth. Apparently, for Isabel, her mother's failed marriage was a crushing blow—her thunderbolt, her Stotternheim—which dropped her into such darkness of soul that she saw herself doomed. No, she *didn't* hate her uncle; see, it was what he *represented.* And what was that? How, Isabel fell to an even lower whisper, how could she know where to begin?

Poor simple voice, thought Darconville, she fails, and failing grieves, and grieving dies; she dies—and leaves her life the victor's prize, falling upon his lute. O fit to have, that lived so sweetly, dead, so sweet a grave.

The confession was diffident, scrambled, and unclear. Darconville, however, pieced together what he could: Isabel's mother worked in Charlottesville, the source, she granted, along with her uncle's job in a local parts factory, of her college tuition, but on weekends, apparently, both of them were foolishly given to inviting pig-ignorant loons and locals over to their house for potlatches of excessive drinking, loud music, card playing, and—with Isabel sitting quietly in her bedroom absolutely mortified—frivolous and nearly insane displays of laughter and vulgarity that lasted into the wee hours of the morning. O yes, said Isabel ruefully, she owed a great deal to them, it was true, but nevertheless she still resented them and the desperateness in her they wouldn't, *couldn't,* even recognize! Why, her mother, added Isabel, the scar on her cheek whitening, her mother even considered her to be a snob for placing herself above the neighbors. Neighbors? asked Isabel with fire, metonym of war, in her eyes. *Neighbors?*

Silently, Darconville listened to her descriptions of them—I shall never have any trouble from her neighbors, he felt—and, looking around him, ironically discovered there in that very roadhouse the perfect illustrations of her running text.

On the long row of stools by the counter and in the booths sat old whiskerandos blowing their whit-flawed fingers; baleful giants with narrow eyes and unijugate ears; a cowboy out of nowhere; interstate truckers with pussle-bellied paunches and split shoes; tiny women wearing baseball caps; and in general an entire assortment of culex-ridden farmers, bust-hogs, and chawbacons, most banging in and out for coffee, some doped from stupidity into motionlessness, and others synoptically eyeing the waitress and making gawky, insinuative reverences whenever she bent over to flap away the pack of cats snooping the local accumulations on the floor and anybody's inflamed feet.

The patrons ranged over their plates like nimble spaniels, each using his primary utensil—an aggressive fork, pointed down—to cut, saw, shear, shape, and worry around his food. They buttered their bread in the air, folded it, and held it out, bitten in gouges. They shook salt onto the counter by their plates, dropped sops into their gravy, slurped soup from the front of their spoons. They masticated, smacking, with open mouths. They ate asparagus and celery by the fist, spat out the hulls of peanuts, and twitched bones onto the table or cracked them for marrow at the back of their teeth. They tongued ice-cubes, while talking and grunting, from glasses stippled white with lip-prints and drank with their spoons in their cups, elevating the vessels as if, rather than drinking, they were trying to stand them inverted on their noses. Finishing their meals, they tipped up their plates for any spilled chankings, fingered up any, and then, burping, banged down a few coins, shoved backwards from the counter—pausing maybe to catch on the jukebox the last clanging, twanging offerings about store-brought happiness, careless love, and women either living on the cheat-in' side of life and/or takin' their love to town—and went out. You were looking for the overture to *Xerxes?* This was the Vale of Tempé?

O Fawx's Mt., Fawx's Mt.! thought Darconville. Behold, your house is forsaken and desolate.

"You see? What it's like? I don't know what I'd *do,*" cried Isabel, her hands beseech-side up, "if I hadn't found you—be thrown to the wolves, I suspect, I really do. I don't think I can live here another day. I have nothing." Darconville heard in her words the locutions of her mother. He didn't know what to say in response, but he who at one clap would have summoned from above all the Angels of the Triplici-ties to help her knew it fell to him alone. The prospect frankly delighted him, for he loved her, although in that, he feared, perhaps he wasn't alone. "I have only the woods and fields," she said with a forlorn look. She pulled her thumb. "And animals."

Darconville saw his chance.

"At Zutphen Farm?"

Isabel looked away. There was nothing there for her, she promised. Yes, it was true she would walk over to visit when she had nothing else to do; the little farm-related chores there gave her pleasure, she said, but she didn't do it for money, even though they were wealthy. She never really liked that family, she added, nor respected them very much.

And as she talked, Darconville put together what fragments he could: Captain van der Slang, rarely at home, was a semi-diplomatic species of merchant profiteer-with-schemes who, thunderballing the watery world in his *blaue Schuyte* from Libya to Newport News and shifting barrels of oil, natural gas, and pig-iron hither and yon, nourished pretensions of great significance. They were of the rentier class, the van der Slangs, supposititious zee-drainers who'd recently moved from somewhere in Delaware to Fawx's Mt. and this particular farm the captain bought to keep his wife and family of idle boys busy. The mother, it was clear, was a hex-faced busybody who, while studiously avoiding the Shiftletts of low degree down the road, never-theless patronized Isabel not only to help her with the farmwork but also because she harbored secret hopes of moral advancement for her foolish sons, both roughly of Isabel's age, whose ambitions thus far, apparently, proved less than complete. (But Isabel gave no details on either of them.) The farm, in any case, was a going concern, and more, with great profits realized in selling livestock and breeding Black Angus cattle. The family, the richest in Fawx's Mt., was nevertheless somewhat unpopular with the common serfs and chapped hands who hired out to that farm; rumor had it, said Isabel, rather circumspectly, that they cheated on their taxes, arbitrarily manumitted the help, and were remorseless in the matter of buying up more and more land. Their niggardliness was legendary. "You did mention once," said Darconville quietly, wondering if, when a bullet traces a line, every point in that line sustains it, "that one of the sons—"

Isabel, watching his eyes, kissed him quickly and said, "I want you. I need *you.*"

Need, thought Darconville: the *quaestor* that sells indulgences love buys. It was true, however, that they hadn't yet confessed their love, which, under the circumstances, nevertheless, seemed only a formality. There was more need for time to know than pressure to convince, in any case, wasn't there? No, it was good that he'd come to Fawx's Mt. For no reason, Darconville thought of Hypsipyle Poore, whose beauty somehow always outran her grace, and he thought of Aeneas's passion for Dido, sudden and not sanctioned by the gods or favorable auspices, whereas the ultimate union with Lavinia, for whom he formed no such violent or hasty attachment, would have recommended itself to every noble Roman.

It was time to go, with Isabel yawning into her hand as Darconville got up to pay. The mesomorph turned from the grill and, wiping his hands on his pants-seat, took Darconville's money—but not before suddenly and suspiciously tracing that stranger's eye back to the photograph of the Knights of the Great Forrest, supplefaced in their framed repository. The proprietor never took his eyes off Darconville, not in ringing the cash register, not in returning the change.

Darconville said, "Thank you, Mr. Ayak."

The man munched in a bronchiospasm—then crouched up menacingly into Darconville's immediate vision, squinting like a mole through a musit. "Don' mention it, boy," he drawled cruelly, one eye coldly galvanizing into a hard marble, and then repeated slowly, "Don' *mention* it."

The night outside seemed fierce, inquisitive, with heavy masses of shapeless vapor working through the woods. The upper segment of the arch of the sky was all purple, blotched purple, and descending on all sides were bleak clouds thrusting their heads into the purple in mountain shapes. They drove away and weren't a mile up the road before Darconville turned to Isabel to put her curiosity at rest: that road-house, he told her, was a meeting place for the Ku Klux Klan. Isabel arched an eyebrow, dubiously. But Darconville's close friendship with a black minister in Quinsyburg, who'd once nearly been hoisted by them during the tense period when the public schools there had been closed (and a few hours of disbelief thereafter reading in the library), had some time ago put him in the picture. Not surprisingly, it was in just such small sheriffwicks and timber- and box-producing outbacks as Fawx's Mt.—the land of the piney-wood folk—that they set up their hate factories and bigotoriums. Darconville told her about the Klan's early playful pranks in Pulaski, Tennessee, and then recounted how that small group of unreconstructed bushwhackers, ill-concealed pop-ulists, and cut-rate anti-alienists who rode out hooded and nightied in the witchlight through lonely dingles and phantasmal swamps had grown into a nationwide klavern of "brothers-beneath-the-robe." Theirs was a perpetual hallowe'en. They paid the initiation fee—the klectoken—and then, whenever they spied anything whatever alien, Catholic, wet, black, nullificationist, or remotely anti-American, they officially klonvokated, paraded, and clashed. There were four stages of klankraft, explained Darconville and, after due deliberation there back at the roadhouse, he found he could name them: K uno, duo, trio, and quad, or ordinary Klansmen, Knights Kamelia, Knights— Darconville tapped Isabel on the knee—of the Great Forrest, and at the top of the pyramid Knights of the Midnight Mystery. Ooooo-eee-ooo! Darconville could picture them: the little hoodoos creeping through low brush toward the midnight lodge, listening for noises, and then, after a few gymnastic handshakes, sitting around in their pinheaded cowls pantomancing each other by candlelight with stories of Communist carpetbaggers, secret hatchet factories run by niggers, and disgusting Romish excesses, for the actual proof of which they thrillfully displayed to each other little gingham bags-with-drawstrings especially manufactured for conveying out of convents the fruits of priestly lust.

They passed in silence the little collapsed schoolhouse (The Brig. Gen. Cadmus Wilcox School) where Isabel, on a former visit, once mentioned she attended the early grades, a pentecostal church painted red, and, finally, on the road to her house, a wooden building set back in a foliage of evergreens in front of which, in plaid shirts and neckerchiefs, a handful of Fawx Mountaineers smoked pipes while fiddlers inside were playing a medley of square-dance tunes: "Rats in the Meal Barrel," "Frog Mouth," "Got a Chaw of 'Baccy from a Nigger," etc.

"Who knows," laughed Darconville, "that chap back there might have been a Kleagle, a Wizard, a Kligrapp, or a Kludd perhaps. Maybe even the Imperial Emperor himself!"

Isabel said, "You still haven't explained why he seemed so angry. Maybe it was because you called him, what was it?—that *name*."

"Ayak?"

"Yes."

"*Ayak*," said Darconville. " 'Are you a klansman?' The response to which is *Akia*: 'A klansman I am.' " Then Darconville dramatically swung out his arm and bowed. "*Kigy!* 'Klansman, I greet you!' "

Those words weren't out of his mouth a second when straightway he was up and into the gravel driveway of the Shiftletts (the ones who weren't the others) and shut off the motor. Suddenly a face—O brutafigura!—ballooned up at the car window out of the pitch-darkness. It was a fish-white pretext of eyes, nose, and mouth which, mis-aligned in God knows what tragic hypocaust of fate, instantly turned the roots of one's hair to ice-needles. Horror dorsifixed Darconville. Immediately he felt—why?—a stab of profound love for Isabel but in the grip of sudden shock only heard her spool down the window to ask her uncle, in a diffident whisper, if he would like to meet Darconville.

"Thnairsz," came a voice like a toy air-horn, with a hole in it.

It meant yes.

XXXIII

Gloss

I am bound to you beyond expression

—GEORGE LILLO, *The London Merchant*

DARCONVILLE would hear that man's tiny, thumbtongued voice—saying "thnaowr"—only one more time.
   And then it would mean no.

XXXIV

Hansel und Rätsel

If you were April's lady
And I were lord in May . . .

—ALGERNON SWINBURNE, "A Match"

Fortunati ambo: they fooled around most of the spring, wandering, in joyous twinship, with Isabel laughing always and Darconville feeling there wasn't a happier person than he, anywhere. They went on picnics, roamed through the woods, and drove in and around the countryside with Spellvexit perched regally in the back seat, whenever they could get away from the college. They went to movies, walloped tennis balls, swapped useless gifts, and in high spirits always chased down whatever curious fatamorganas could be found in the Quinsyburg

Darconville now, for Isabel's presence there, almost grew to love. How primal, thought Darconville, the secondary can become!

After classes, habitually, Darconville would wait on his porch for her: and how often, sitting there, had he worn out his eyes trying to grasp in the distance a certain, undeceitful form coming toward him, which by failing to come only became an uncertain figure going away! More often than not, they left each other notes before lunch, hailed each other on the run in midafternoon, and, leaving behind the little Pittenweem witches of the dorm, hand in hand escaped that deinspiring world to follow the endless caravan of fascinations their own delight, their love, daily afforded. The mind defining reality creates it. The sun was hot all spring. The world sang.

"O, you're going to leave me, *I* know," Isabel would cry, laughing, whenever he might be late, her arm flung, Camille-like, melodramatically across her brow—then she would burst into even wilder laughter, light silver peals flying up like a flash of swallows. It was a favorite joke, a riddle posed as a catharsis, documenting perhaps the early fears of their delicately exigible love but becoming a humorous catchphrase from then on, one never used without a lilt and a laugh.

"Never!" Darconville would reply with comic feverishness. "You're going to leave *me*."

It has been said by some and several that Desire wishes, Love enjoys, and that the end of one is the beginning of the other. That which we love is present; that which we desire is absent. But it was not so with smitten Darconville. He felt he would never know enough of her, present or absent, so little, in fact, he knew. His love only compounded his desire. And, as he wished to enjoy, he enjoyed this wish: his *love* to desire. And yet his wishes, even in her presence, were not misapplied, for there was so little of Isabel known in so much of Isabel seen: Queen Enigmatica of Quinsyburg. The Little Thing, indeed! She herself was a riddle.

There were matters, for instance, on which she was close as an oyster: her poor grades, her occasional disappearances on weekends, Govert (neither mentioned him: not him, not her), and the inexplicable secrecy she seemed to assume whenever they went to Fawx's Mt. —but part of her beauty was her mystery, thought Darconville, who went about his business in the face of such conditions, immortalizing her, like Surrey's Geraldine, in dew-besprent complaints she never heard. She was that ineffable factor whose precise definition—if one should avoid in definition the word of words one's trying to define—could maddeningly be put in no other terms. She was equal only to herself. It was her first glory. But there was no disclosure. She could not be found in the line of a palm or explained in conclusion to a series of formal donations. She was not in the tarot, untraceable through pounce paper, incommensurable—a flash like a flame in an opal. Nothing was really applicable. But if no name was put to their happiness, still it was abundance. They were both frankly in love.

Subrationally, they needed each other, with each making the other proud and worthwhile in the way lovers do when attention is freely given, when one is loved less because he or she deserves to be than because he or she creates, is created by, the other's grace and both become transfigured not as opposites but as reverse images of the same character. It was a pact, to save each other from trouble, to protect every consideration come to them in the inaudible glory of each other's trust, to find, miraculously, in the sudden emptiness of one heart the beautiful contents of another's filling the void.

They packed lunches and took trips, the sunroof of the Bentley thrown back, its radio playing, driving to Richmond, to Appomattox, to Charlottesville, telling stories, taking pictures, and always laughing, laughing from horizon to horizon, as if space were endless and they'd triumphed over time. They locked themselves in the music rooms of the college and danced, acted out scenes with the skeletons in the labs, and delivered funny speeches to each other in empty lecture halls. One night they were returning from the movies. Walking by a hydrant, Isabel found sitting on top of it a filthy old discarded seaman's cap, but feeling silly she picked it up (typically, with exaggerated thumb and forefinger), stuck it on her head and, with her face rubberized into a foolish grin, said, "I think I'll join the navy!" "O my God," exclaimed Darconville, "take it off—you may get cancer!" And Isabel was overcome with uncontrollable laughter, a rat-a-tat-tat of lovable, bubbable squeaks. It was Spellvexit's noise *exactly*. My wonderful cats, thought Darconville, my—

At that very moment, he happened to glance up: about ten feet ahead of him—near his house and in the *exact* pose of the cat from the curious drawing he'd done as a child—stood Spellvexit, looking sorrowfully at him. It was strange. It looked so much like a look of pity.

And then, together, they often crept at night into the Episcopal church in Quinsyburg where Darconville, under a pinlight—with Isabel, lusorious in a pew, giggling and clicking her tongue (always a colophon of her joy)—worked melodies on the organ out of its dusty wheezes. Still, Isabel was always apprehensive there. The pastor of that church had once invited both of them to a dinner party, their first social affair in Quinsyburg together, but Isabel, sitting on a central divan and wearing a dress insufficiently volumetric to cover her poundage of leg, self-consciously went the entire evening without saying a word and still thereafter sought to avoid him: she never wore a short skirt again.

They even made several films with Isabel's old 1940 plug of a camera, often spending days together walking around town and periscoping everywhere for subjects: smews in flight, misspelled signs, rosydactylate sunrises-and-sets. One of their films, a plotted four-or-five-minute comic drama shot on location among the bent stones in the wisteria-strewn Quinsyburg cemetery, was a masterpiece of creative irreverence. It was Isabel's *capolavoro,* shot in perfect sequence: Darconville, funebrist, motors slowly in his Bentley through the main gates; cuts to Darconville, memorialist, stepping from the car holding a myrtle wreath; cuts to Darconville, sobrietist, who halts before an odd gravestone hewn to the shape of a ship; cuts to Darconville, dadaist, suddenly clutching his heart and dropping down dead; cuts to Darconville, karcist, rising up creepily, slowly, from behind the stone with a gleam in his impish eyes. Blackout. They almost died from laughter every time it was shown.

But their most memorable film?

It was most certainly the Day of the Kite, one golden afternoon out on the Quinsyburg golf course over which, limitless, a perfect blue sky from mid-heaven down opened for the sun, heating its own shining light, to transfigure a rolling field to the Garden of Shiraz, the air holding the promise of dreams in it and blowing around the scent of flowers in washed wind.

"I'll let out slack, you tug the mainline," Darconville called out to her. The wind ghosted. She clicked her tongue and ran, tipping and toeing down the staircarpet of grass.

A jet-colored scalene affair, with little orange eyes and the contours of a bat, the kite staggered and upcut brainlessly across the air, then swooped in several tendentious circles, and suddenly shot straight up on tightening line. It shimmied out further and jiggered up to a tiny size. Isabel turned to Darconville, thirty yards or so behind her, and clapped her hands like a child, then suddenly racing after the floating string as he let go to pick up the camera. She leaped and got it, as Darconville whispered to himself:

> "Followe thy faire sunne, unhappy shaddowe,
> Though thou be blacke as night
> And she made all of light."

Quickly, he began to film her: gamboling, circulating, snudging the distant kite. Her shoulders jived with every puff and gust. Isabel wore a red jersey, white trousers, no shoes. The wanton air in twenty sweet forms danced after her fingers and flashed its transparent song about her golden hair, blowing as blond as once in the same light blew that of Helen, Polyxena, Guithera. The natural light, thought Darconville, that showed Socrates one God and disclosed to Democritus the atoms now epiphanized this dancing, peddling child whose laughter almost broke his heart. She skipped and ran and stretched up, actions revealing her more-than-a-moiety of thigh. It didn't matter what wasn't seen. Darconville had simply conceived light visible and found the girl he loved. He would have gone barefoot to Jerusalem, to the Great Khan's Court, to the Far Indies to fetch her a bird to wear on her finger. She never seemed more beautiful.

"Look! It's umpteen miles high!" cried Isabel, her untied hair drifting aerially behind her as she ran.

Darconville was now filming her shadow.

"That cloud, up there. Isn't it beautiful! It's shaped like a bird—a swan, look." She turned and came over to him. "Is that true, that the swan sings when it dies?"

"I don't know."

He brought the camera close and shot her nose.

"No, really. What do you think?"

"The swan," said Darconville, smiling, "remains silent all its life in order to sing well a single time." A parable of art, he thought—and a perfect excuse, it delighted him to think, for having put aside my writing for *you*. Good: there was more piety in being human than human in being pious.

"What does it sing about, anyway, if it's dying?"

Darconville happily replied, "It sings about, O, what of heaven it was always reminded of—but couldn't have—on earth. Glaciers: clouds. The sea," he said, "is the nightmare of the sky, you've heard that, haven't you?"

"The sea?"

It was unbelievable. She seemed to freeze in a reverie, blankly studying a spot of nothing in the far distance, as if all of a sudden, to solve a riddle imposed on her from without, she were waiting for the answer she was incapable of giving to come. It was undeniably like something of unhappiness moving in her spirit, the look of a person who had discovered, not something she hadn't known before, but something she had known before and didn't want to hear again. He came over next to her and, as she turned abruptly, almost kissed her on the lips: an *effleurage* suddenly reminding her of where she was. She lowered her head with a slight blush.

"I mean," said Darconville, taking her arm, "there is a sort of consolation in seeing that little thing squittering around up there, you know? It jigs, you could say, to synthesize worlds that have been separated, folding its wings and shooting upon its errand out of the Valley of Funnel and connecting even for a brief interval the five elements."

"Five elements?"

"Earth, air, fire, water—"

"And?"

You, thought Darconville.

"And ether," he said. "The quintessential."

The kite caromed in the faraway air. As if preoccupied with one of her thoughts, Isabel tweaked the line and silently watched the tiny vessel plaintively tossing in the vast and mighty ocean above her. Preoccupied himself now, Darconville took the conversation a bit further.

"Sometime, Isabel," he said, "open the Bible to the book of Genesis. There is a little fright there amid its exegetical thickets: the phrase, 'And God saw that it was good,' is for some reason omitted after the second day of Creation. You know what I mean?" Isabel wasn't sure. "I mean, no one has ever figured that out. I've often thought, however, that—"

A gust of wind sent the kite into a lunatic figure-eight, whereupon, looking up, Isabel opened her mouth expectantly.

"—well, that on that particular day came the first disuniting of what God had created. The elements, if now separate, were once all one, an unindividuated world become multiple only in that it might be comprehended, and, say, in one thunderclap that hitherto indivisible ur-world suddenly banged into a vast network of *intermundia:* gases, air, flame, and huge chunks of smoking telluric mole flew out into a gravity-locked exosphere!" He waved his arms up. "The One became the Many."

"What a pessimist you are," said Isabel.

Darconville said: "But can't you see that that is optimism? There," he said, pointing up past the kite, "is our exit, inspected from an ingressive angle, camouflaged only by our fear of taking it. Vision overwhelms us! I don't think vision is anything more than daring to seek unity, no matter the—"

Isabel put her hand on his mouth and said *shhhh* . . .

"You remind me of poetry," she said.

The black kite suddenly spiked out sideways, shivered, and then hooking started on a plummet to hell. Isabel cried out, her nates tightening. Reaching over, Darconville swiftly yanked the string. The kite swooped up, listed deferentially, and then nosedived almost on an aim down, downward, across the field into a tangled web of treelimbs, hanging upsidedown there as if brained. Isabel, disconsolate, her hands dropping, pulled her thumb. Tears sprang to her eyes.

Darconville, lifting her chin, hugged her close, a photogenic gold-blue mirage of that beautiful day. They walked slowly over toward the surrounding woods and silently inspected the ruined kite, dangling in pieces. A why sat in her eyes which he kissed, finding them grum, now gleaming with high-wrought inexpressibles. They stood silent, watching each other, listening to the real words of the imaginary dialogue being whispered from heart to heart, and a very special closeness was theirs that afternoon, an eternal bond shaping itself in the late sun, the flower-scents of Eden, the windsong. Still, no name was put to their happiness, although a new happiness was understood as Darconville and Isabel, associate sole, left the field together hand in hand. A low-flying bird, trailing its legs across the sky, pulled in its wake the sunset and all the heat of its fire. Dusk crept in.

They returned to Darconville's rooms, without a word.

It was so still: Darconville's thumping heart, as he opened the door, was interrupted by a whisper not to turn on the light. He kissed her quickly, turned, and then turned back again desperately as if at last all the words lost on the desk behind her might now be spoken; but Isabel would have no words and, giving up in his arms, leaned into him with a long kiss, the obscure surrounding them as the flesh enclosed the soul, as if simply to explain how, in the course of love, the body took part in its affections. They couldn't get close enough to each other, sucking out both breath and being as if to gain time for the merciful recognition between them both knew now they could never give up; and, needing suretyship no more, they together passed over questions like riddles not ignored but solved rather in the quiet but beseeching assurance of each other's promised faith: did love yield or was it conquered? Was to rule by love to dominate by emotion? Did love fulfilled cease then to be love? Was to remove the mystery to take away the wonder? May one love only what one knows, or was love that which made knowledge possible? Did love have to have a meaning?

No, no, not if it meant what it was.

"I love you," said Darconville.

"Oh, I love you, too."

And they made love in the naked darkness, two lost children looking for rebirth in the glory of each other, struggling upward, like their wayward kite, toward the cold particulates of one world where, joining sky and sea by song, they found another, and then reaching up higher still to behold in the frost and starlight the very beauty of very beauty, neither begotten nor made but being of the substance and essence which is beautiful unto all eternity, they made a wish, stretched forth and—poof!—blew out the birthday sun, and were blind at the climax of vision.

Coda

Those were the carefree, intimate days they shared together before the weird and fateful turn that wound its intricate way back to a certain letter—not even a letter, in fact. It was a questionnaire.

XXXV

A Questionnaire

Time's fatal wings doe ever forward flye,
Soe ev'ry day we live, a day wee dye.
—THOMAS CAMPION

THE QUESTIONNAIRE caused a lot of trouble. It was quite common, now, that Darconville often found little gifts left for him in his office, presents—it was typical at a girls' school—offered up during the course of the year by gentle giglots, maidens blushworthily abud, and softhearted flouts whose dear heads Love had turned, whose dear hearts Love had wrung, whose dear hands Love had moistened and who, most of the time, tripped in and out of his shadow as quietly as mice, walking by his house, watching him from windows, and generally bearing the agues, itches, stones, cramps, and colics of cruel and anonymous passion as best they could.

It was common enough, and harmless: at the oblique of a given hour, up to the second floor of the English building and into the silent corridor the little *pixiarda* would steal, arrange her gift—boxed, bottled, or bowed—and then according to the law of self-denying ordinance secretly hurry away to an outlying willow tree under which she sat, a bundle of regrets, listening to a bobolink in the branches above mocking the pity of human passion. It was indeed harmless and easily explained, the consequence, in most cases, of an infirm social calendar, the overabuse of spices in the college diet, or simply the love-philtre that is the muskrose season we know as spring.

And sometimes there were notes. And so it was on one particular Friday. Taking a brief respite before his four o'clock class, Darconville walked into his office and stepped on what he picked up. It was a lilac envelope. He slit it open, took out a sheet of matching stationery—out of which slipped, along with a heady lavender fragrance, a small red-green gem: a bloodstone—and read the following:

<blockquote>
Do you

1. hate me ☐ ?
2. like me ☐ ?
3. love me ☐ ?
4. feel indifferent to me (the worst) ☐ ?
       Yours forever,
              H.P.
</blockquote>

There would have been no doubt as to the identity of the pollster here, initialed or not. No, even if Darconville had not recognized the lush hue of paper, or breathed in its deep perfume, or identified the feminine slant of those semi-uncials, he knew the correspondent well. Of course, Hypsipyle Poore was not alone. There were other girls *de la faute fatale* during the year—quoits homesick for spikes—who also left behind little gifts and select remember-me-bys. These were not all shy. Neither were they all anonymous.

Sprightly, unforgettable Mercy Tattycoram once left him a robin's egg with her name signed on it in lemon juice. Tadzia di Lido sent to his house biweekly letters, of the saga genre, with envelopes coming three at a batch (marked ⚹1, ⚹2, ⚹3) and the stamps on each always arranged amorously *tête-bêche*. A senior English major, Iva Ironmonger Dane, was wont to leave tucked in the carriage of his typewriter intense little poems, each, usually, a one-sentence tranche

written in pedantic sentimeter, arbitrarily spaced, and given a title
something like "Mouse," "Rain," "Loneliness," or "Untitled," that
special one too ineffable in content to be named. For the monthly jar
of gooseberry preserves, all thanks to the annual-editor, popular
Pepper Milltown, who once snapped a photograph of Darconville in
his Bentley which, later, Isabel pointedly requested her to remove
from her dormitory mirror, but she wouldn't, she said, until she had
good reason to, which that afternoon, sitting in the infirmary with a
swollen foot, she had. Cygnet Throwt brought him a reproduction of
an eighteenth-century clay pipe from Williamsburg. Michelle Arcan-
giolo gave him a glass pistol filled with candy. Then Hazel Anne
Glover, whose paintings he once complimented, presented him her favorite osmiroid pen with its ancillaries, a box of titquills spilt on his
desk and so arranged to spell l-o-v-e. And Fanny Appleton's, one
couldn't forget, was the tie-clasp and the foot-high card at Easter.
Finally, Yancy Dragonwagon, offering *herself,* simply spent every day
of the week sitting loyally on the dimly lit stairwell outside his office.

The obliviscible on this day was, of course, like all the others in intention. It differed only in its effect, becoming swiftly the *protarchos
ate*—the crime that sets other crime in motion. No, there was no
question as to its author; no doubt as to the type of epistle, indited, as
an attorney might bonds, by leaving blanks; and no hesitation as to
what must be done. Smiling, Darconville put the bloodstone in his
pocket. He ripped up the letter, dropped the pieces into the wastebasket, and went off to class thinking no more about it. About such
matters—over protestation, over evasion, over repetition—Darconville
had long expressed a dear wish to have less ceremonial and more understanding. Or, at least more attempts at understanding. Or, better
still, more insistence at making understanding explicit and verbal. But
little had come of it. And so he began to take it all in stride. You see, it
was about the twentieth time that year he'd received such a note.

On the other hand, it was Isabel's first.

XXXVI

The Deipnosophists

What mighty Contests rise from trivial Things.

—ALEXANDER POPE, *The Rape of the Lock*

THE INCIDENT was memorable. It fell out this way. A party, thrown annually, was always held in late May—a retrospective at end of term—and the faculty, every year, generally took it to be the party "to end all parties," a mode of expression, of course, that had to be taken—along with so much else at Quinsy College, especially in matters of education—figuratively. Traditionally, it was held at the home of one of the faculty members, some professor or other chosen for it, one customarily hot for advancement in the royal court of deipotent Greatracks *le roi* who, let it be said, never disallowed his subjects any chance to screw themselves into whatever new little dignities they coveted and his grace-and-favor might allow. All vied for his wink, the mere wave of his sceptre, and a subsequent ho-ho-ho raised, it was common knowledge, many a low academic from vassal to knight to baronet to lord to viscount to earl and, with luck, even put him right next to the Higher Who.

College presidents love meacocks. So everyone tried to please President Greatracks in every way he could. He was wined and dined at every turn by little jellybones and psychobiological suckeggs who, never missing a chance, scraped, climbed, snatched, glozed, cozened, and collogued. Inside every faculty member beats the heart of a merry andrew. The word of kings is the queen of words. The ambitious there were captives.

The hosts were chosen. The many-called who were overlooked, disgruntled, nevertheless appeared on Friday night and found that no expense had been spared. There was music, dancing, and no end of delicious food. As darkness fell, long white candles were set out in every room, while in the capacious gardens out back a string of paper-lanterns rattled in the warm wind, to which later in the evening, if things went as usual, a good deal of caution would be thrown—at least so the bets went, for this particular year the host-couple, from the psychology department, was a stylish and exciting coprolaliac-écouterist two who'd come in September with Darconville named Felix and Felice Culpa.

> "When I take the plunge
> I drink like a sponge,
> No bladder holds liquor like mine—"

sang irrepressible Felice Culpa, flinging the door open, standing there in purple slacks and gold shoes, her wig ablaze with jewels, and continuing, much to the shock of the guests behind her, to round off in near-perfect numbers her romantic roulade:

> "So would you get hot
> For my sweet little twat
> If I peed the most excellent wine?"

It was Darconville, surprised, at the doorstep, and Felice, laughing mightily thereat, stroked down her thighs in a parody of mock-preparation, mock-lust, and yanked him in with a big and most felicitous kiss of welcome. Where was Isabel? she asked, taking his coat. He promised she would come.

Darconville rather liked the Culpas who, few among many, certainly could not be numbered at Quinsy in the taxonomy of academic mumpers, wirepullers, and bootlickers. The two of them, independent and carefree, were simply a *commedia dell'arte* of pranks, bog-jokes, and liberal thought, the kind of free-spirited teachers who for no particular reason came to these small towns, taught a spell, and then dropped out of sight for good. They were certainly not long for Quinsy College, less for holding specific views on the equality of races than teaching the virtue thereof. It didn't go down, and with it they were humming their recessional. President Greatracks, nevertheless, had once been a guest at one of their famous dinners, a copious and mouthwatering manicotti imbottiti à la Culpa, with homemade bread, cannoli, and bottles of sparkling asti spumante, a celebration, in fact, for Isabel's birthday (Dec. 30). They were both wonderful cooks, and lavish, and so on that occasion, though unbeknownst to them, they were earmarked as the host designate for the May bash. Pushing himself away from the table that particular evening, Greatracks had belched and with perfect seriousness declared, "Lordy, I love Hawaiian food!"

*   *   *   *   *

Friday 12:30 P.M.: The *débouchement* from the Quinsy dining hall is loud. "O, I *knew* there was something else. I won't be going up with you to Charlottesville," exclaims Isabel with a secret smile to her tablemate, Annabel Lee Jenks, who'd given her open invitations for weekend rides. In her excitement, she forgoes dessert: snowcones. She doesn't lag but scooping up a fardel of books rounds out of the doors (thewm, thewm) on a zip to the library: not, however, before dancing up the stairway to Darconville's office to try to catch him—catch? kiss!—and assure him that she will (a) hurry to finish her termpaper, (b) call for Miss Trappe who, as understood, would go with her, and (c) meet him, according to plan, at the Culpas' party the minute everything was done. Drat, the office is empty and—but, wait, what is here? How often the slip between objective cup and subjective lip! But what does it matter? Isabel's face drops, almost as if she had never in her life seen a letter, or at least one colored lavender.

*   *   *   *   *

Pouring a drink, Darconville shoehorned himself into a noisily buzzing crowd that reached to several rooms. It was a large omnium gatherum composed for the most part of the Quinsy administration, faculty, and staff, along with a handful of other *Lumpengesindel* from downtown Quinsyburg: town officials, local voivodes, and influential porkers from the mayoralty, all grouped together—hale-heartedly chattering, jingling the ice-cubes in their glasses, blinking at each other through a vast smokering—to concelebrate the end of the school year. People embraced each other like orchestra conductors. Allocutive jill-tipplers and firedrakes with tight permanents hissed salutes of sudden recognition, while gorbellied husbands-in-tow, wearing bright red faces and outlandish sport jackets, barrellassed across the room, flapping their hands, to announce themselves and yawp out greetings. A few businessmen in sudoriferous shoes snuffled and snorted, while their pert wives, all bowlegged, stood around with menacing smiles pricing the furniture. Jackdaw perched beside jackdaw. It was not unexpected, for this was not an age for the piety of hesitation, the which, alas, in Quinsyburg at least would have to wait another century or two to come from its ossuary and be recognized. It was the Age of Smirk. It was the Age of Intrusion.

"Hah, har *yew!*"

Good grief, thought Darconville, what language was that? Pushtu? Wolof? Gic-Goc? He turned.

"Over here."

Darconville turned again.

"Dang it, son, over here!"

It was President Greatracks, shinyjowled, hunkering low on his elbows and snickering through the funkhole of the bar. His face ballooned out comically. He stuffed a roll-mop herring into his mouth, then another, and another, and then with a loud thoop sucked a huge gobbet of sour cream from the fat of his wrist. "I saw y'all—" He swallowed hard and wiped his chin. "I say, I saw ya'll day or two ago, you ol' coon hunter, with just the prettiest little ol' gal *ever,* steppin' out of that big au-to of yours, huh?" He winked a wink of fat-bound comprehension, eased back, and swung his rumbling, drumbling body around the side of the nook. His tie was stuffed into his trousers, the belt of which, tight, squeezed him just above mid-point like a transvected sugar bag. "A mighty tall drink of water, and cute as pie. Mm, mmm, cute as *pah!*"

"Yes," said Darconville.

"Beautiful as a o-riole."

"Thank you."

"Shoot, you was grinnin'" he wheezed, "like a unwarshed mule eatin' briars—and then some." He fished for a crumb in his teeth. "Well, good. Longhair or no longhair, you still ain't one of them sad little bumboxes around here about to drive me crazy with damfool requests and extracurricular thises and thats, no you ain't, son, and I'll give you that!" Ironically enough, Greatracks liked his people soaped and regimented, a tour years back in the navy having taught him, he repeatedly pointed out, not only spiffiness—here, he always raised his voice in contribution to the betterment of the proximate world—but *discipline!* "These touchholes," said Greatracks, gloomily looking around, "they're all arse and pockets! Some of these bastards have been on their knees so long, they've forgot what it's like to have feet!"

He grabbed a bottle of bourbon, filled Darconville's glass, and tapping a toast hausted right from the bottle in one long suck. "We right in hopin' you find Quinsy here to your likin'?" He burped. "Hell, sure you do, we all do, right?" His tongue was resting on his lower lip in half-witted expectation. "Right?"

For confirmation, President Greatracks leaned over to grab Qwert Yui Op, but he was explaining to Miss Porchmouth and Dr. Excipuliform—unfortunately, in Tibetan-Chinese—about the method used for sowing soybeans in his country: they stored seeds in their ears, if his charade meant anything, and hopped through the fields at a 30° angle. So, reaching out, Greatracks hooped in the then passing Dodypols to reassure Darconville how happy they all were. Dr. Dodypol, a friend of Darconville's, was a short little fellow from the English department with a sad starched pallor and bloodless, nickel-sized ears and, upon seeing him, always waved at pocket level with a little flap and said, "Hello, Darconville. Fair grow the lilies on the riverbanks?" But on this occasion he said nothing, nothing at all. Twice his height, Mrs. Dodypol carelessly pushed her husband aside and, holding with exaggerated care a fuel-smelling drink at arm's length to protect a dress the color of winter cabbage, on long morbid feet moved leering up to President Greatracks with a face salacious and rouged to a Grock-like mask, her eyes smiling like moonfish. She playfully squibbled his cheek.

It was a blatant rudeness, not to Greatracks, of course, who loved it, but to her husband, for common report had it that she was Greatracks's mistress, that *he* had finagled her the managership of the Piggly Wiggly, and that on more than one Saturday night their twin, fully unambiguous shadows had been seen thrown against the indiscreet shades of the otherwise irreproachable Timberlake Hotel.

"Honey," exclaimed Mrs. Dodypol, slightly inebriated and turning to Darconville the countenance of a bummish down-and-out clown, the umbo of her nose scarlet and her general features flaking like an old moist Roman fresco, "think. No crime. Country air. Plup-pluppl," she hiccuped, "plain folks." Her eyes swam, crossed, reddened. She was all mops and brooms, and as the heat rose to her face, frazzling her hair, she seemed to reinforce Casanova's theory that any woman over fifty-six need no longer be considered among the living. "And then what about that shweet child," her tongue thickened, "you take out walkin'?" She tapped his heart. "Solid. Loyal. Faithful." It was the common, amplified anti-rhetoric of the drunk: brief, non-discursive, laconic.

"And cute as *pah*," pitched in Greatracks, putting her drink vertical.

"You stay on," breathed the Dodypol Better Half through her powder and fucus. "That right?"

"Sunshine," said Greatracks, beaming, "you as right as rain!"

Lowering her mottled face, Mrs. Dodypol took a thriftless slug of fruity domestic. "And so," she hiccuped, "will you will or won't you won't?" She waited with the drunk's fussy care, the ungainsayable doggedness. "Yes, sugar pie?"

"Now don't go crowdin' him, dumperling," said Greatracks, jogging Darconville in the ribs. "He be back, shinin' like a nigger's heel. Right?"

Deliberating, Darconville thought: *yes, I will be back.* It was suddenly strange, for of the many times he had heard the question this was the first time he had heard the answer. Was to agree to yield? he wondered. He didn't know. He had been fearful for so long that if he came to like Quinsyburg he might not hate it anymore, the fear faded: the act committed by not acting. He thought of a related question: precisely what of that freedom which, exercised, relinquished itself? And that led to still another: may one be consoled in the absolute that everything is relative? It immediately occurred to Darconville, then, that to allow for the absence of danger was somehow to acknowledge the possibility of slavery. And yet he was in love! He had opted forever, and for something to be entirely romantic, he thought, it had to be irrevocable. So choice itself had been made irrelevant. His freedom, paradoxically, was the deliverance from it: the choice, chosen, never to choose again.

Darconville, nodding, said he would be back.

"That is a *joy*," brayed Mrs. Dodypol, almost bleaching Darconville's hair in a spatter-spray of drunken yux and wet-cupping her mouth. She turned merrily and pronged President Greatracks in the bullseye of his navel with a fingernail the color of potassium permanganate. "Isn't it, skeezix? Just a ol' joy?" There was no response, however, other than that of a great dopplerian whoop of laughter, for having caught sight of a tray of ham slabs and a mess of wallop-sized buns Greatracks was now more than halfway across the room and moving fast. Without a pause, Mrs. Dodypol, part-time *grisette* and supremo of the Piggly Wiggly—spilling her drink—bounced into the air and sprang after him through the room with a scream like that of a crazed woodfreak.

Darconville just stood there. Colorless as an etching, resigned, Dr. Dodypol looked up at him. He blinked. Then he silently picked up several crackers from a plate and put them into the pygmean side-pocket of his graveclothes and walked aimlessly through the smoke of the noisy room, looking back only once: to smile sadly at Darconville, hold up a cracker over his head, and then, inexplicably, bite it in two in one ferocious turtle-like snap—after which he turned through the crowd and, solitary, followed himself out to the garden where the Chinese lanterns were. Darconville looked on until he disappeared. And then he looked at his watch.

*   *   *   *   *

Friday 4:03 P.M.: The Smethwick library, though open, is virtually empty, not a rare thing, alas, on weekends at Quinsy College. Isabel is there, however, sitting noiselessly and alone in the tomb of the reference room, surrounded by shelves of maroon encyclopedias, newspapers racked in binding-shafts, globes. (That is Miss Pouce rearranging the art oversizes in the next room by the window with the mixed bowl of maypop and bunchberry.) Isabel stares through a blank notebook to the face of mournful Ate rising in a page, faintly frowning back at her with expressionless lavender lips and profane eyes; her pencil waits in her fist, her fist on her cheek, her cheek pale. Thesis: apprehension is foreknowledge. Antithesis: what we see is what we sometimes by mistake think we foresee. Synthesis: Isabel, knocking on her head, subdues a wish to probe further and determinedly turns to her index cards, fact-filled with notes for her art termpaper on the subtle and artfully worked technique in Dutch potting of concealing dull earthen pottery in pretty white glaze and decoration: "Decoys in Delftware."

* * * * *

Soon, the party was in full swing. The flint was struck, a spark flew out, and the dry little birdnests that were the hearts of the participants, once ignited, now crackled, then spread. The crowd grew, as if the guests in some kind of ridiculous fission seemed to double at every turn. It was a *Wimmelbilder:* a teempool, now in high report, of party goons, noisome dowds and doodles, truffatores, pusspockets, stoopnagels, and a whole crazy retinue of hoopoes-in-fine-fettle.

Guests, being introduced, were rotated like tops. These were the Ho's, those were the Hum's. Those were the Go's, these were the Come's. The Snipps met the Snapps and the Snapps met the Snurrs. It was endless. But Felice Culpa, who had no end of energy, loved the combinations. Dr. Roget, Miss Carp; Miss Carp, Dr. Roget. "Delighted," said motograph-voiced Dr. Roget, one of the pawns on the Board of Visitors, "overjoyed, highly-pleased, gratified." "Peachy," replied ninety-year-old Miss Carp, her long cigarette wagging up and down on the two syllables. A former teacher at Quinsy, she was one of those outspoken choleric old sticks down South who smoked three packs a day, said anything she damned well pleased, and was given a wide berth—in this case, a wider one than most, ostracized as she'd been in the Quinsyburg community ever since casting that irreligious vote in 1928 for Al Smith. The Culpas, her neighbors, liked her and thought to do something about it, but not everyone approved, and Mrs. DeCrow, looking like Vrouw Bodolphe come alive, thought the invitation disgraceful, clacked her teeth, and turned her back to the room.

Others couldn't be introduced. Dr. Glibbery was searching for hot sauce in the kitchen. The Weerds, alone, were talking to each other in the backyard. And Dean Barathrum was in the bathroom. In two cane chairs on the porch, side by side, Misses Shepe and Ghote were sitting like pharaohs, their hands on their knees. They noticed Darconville. "Forget the black clothes," muttered Miss Ghote. "It's the long hair gives me the dreads." "Well, long hair," sniffed Miss Shepe, "*is* sanctioned in the Bible, Miss Ghote." She smiled. "Judges 13:5." Miss Ghote arranged her fingers into a reef knot. "I hate to disappoint you, Miss Shepe," said Miss Ghote, who hadn't the slightest intention of sitting passively by and allowing her neighbor the luxury of placing the teapot of her Episcopalian proclivities on *her* Baptist trivet, "but long hair is *not* sanctioned in the Bible." She shifted indignantly on her sapless buttocks. "You want to re-read I Corinthians 11:14, I'm afraid." It was only another one of those pull-devil, pull-baker affairs that would last long into the night, good old ecclesiastical counteravouchings, each felt, having both source and sanction in such great biblical priestesses of yore as Euodias, Syntyche, Priscilla, Phoebe the deacon, and all the other spoof-proof little charmers who traveled across the sacred pages of Scripture in numbers too big to ignore.

"And these," said host Felix Culpa, perspiring into his ascot, for though he was big of heart, his almost thrice three times thrice three feet in breadth sometimes got the better of it, "these are the Thisbites."

"I'm sure," smiled a few dears from the personnel office, gentle souls with shell-pink complexions, precise hairnets, and steel girdles, the type of women at parties who are always, for no particular reason, just leaving—and never, somehow, without a brown package tied with string under their arms and seventy-five goodbyes at the door.

Miss Thisbite, a Dixiebelle, was one of those girls of the beauty-pageant variety, with that typical Southern smile that is always just a bit too high. She had baby-blue eyes, a round face—piefacedness has always been the Southern ideal of feminine beauty—and had just come down from Richmond for the weekend, driven by her brother, a young blond ephebe with a perfect head and skin the color of moonlight who was also in attendance. She was being interviewed for an opening in the English department. "A real armful, huh? I know the type," Felice said, playfully tapping Darconville and nodding in the direction of the girl whose short skirt revealed long lithe legs and stockings worked like the marquisette of a butterfly net. "Shapelier than Isabel in the legs, OK. But I'll give you two to one she'd be harder to get into than the Reading Room of the British Museum." Then she tweaked his nose and pranced away on an arc, very like the smile she sent him on the way out.

Southern women, it occurred to Darconville, were a case-study in extremes. They were in fact like sausages: some—the minority—were so soft and pink and moist they could be spread with a pliable knife; the others were as hard and dry as corundum, a kind of thin indurate *Landjaeger*, its groats tied off tight and cold as marble in the bung of a fierce, almost unbreakable coil. There seemed to be no other kind. In any case, most of the men at the party, old dodders, young dudes, immediately honed in on Miss Thisbite. They lit up trick bowties. They puffed the college's reputation. They subjected her to rustic stories, pseudodoxies, tall tales.

"They are saying"—it was Prof. Fewstone, of course, sidling up to Miss Thisbite with his overfilled shirt and yogibogeybox-shaped head, the strange hairdressing of which gave him a big roach in front and a curled effect at the rear which he tucked under a roll—"they are saying you want to join the team, yes? First-rate! I tell you, we're thick as three in a bed here at Quinsy. Wonderful! But now tell me, have you been told about the cutbacks over at the legislature, the budget, all the—"

Miss Thisbite, kindly refusing his offer of a wheatcracker smeared with lobster pâté, circled the button of his jacket with her finger and softly asked if money was scarce.

"Scarce? Why, non-existent, gal, non-*existent!* Listen, I was around this place when they paid you through a bean-blower, shoot yes, and it ain't no better now. Thing is," he said, moving closer, "I happen to have my foot in the door with the governor, see, and—"

He suddenly felt cold and looked up.

Mrs. Fewstone, standing across the room in hard brown shoes and wearing a dress that looked as if it had been cut out of zinc, had him transfixed with her snake-like eyes in a cruel *fascinatio.*

At this juncture, Darconville worked his way to the front room to see if Isabel had come. Mrs. DeCrow, noticing him, continued the shabby game of studied indifference she had played for almost a year now and turning cock-a-hoop, her nose sharp in the air, whisked past him with a face like the Uffizi Medusa. Shaking his head, he lit a cigarette: the tinker, his dam. But as the Great Snibber looked back—she had snibs in her, and snibs, and more snibs!—she banged smack into a bureau, eliciting a snoot of glee from the for-the-moment uncharacteristically joyous Mr. Schrecklichkeit who, not that he could know it, immediately joined both Darconville and Abraham Lincoln as a funeral urn in the necropolis of her mind. Bristling, she shoved the bu-

reau with one swipe of her pipefitter-like arms. Schrecklichkeit was a
simp, everybody knew that. But Darconville? He tasked her, he
heaped her. She adjusted her breasts. She glowered around. She
stepped to the table. Correct her, would he? She stabbed into a bowl
of smoked oysters with a toothpick, spitted three, and, poor little
beasts, they were mollusks no longer but now part and parcel of Mrs.
DeCrow.

Meanwhile, Darconville looked around the dim front room, and
looked, and looked.   •

*   *   *   *   *

Friday 5:40 P.M.: The shaft of light from the overhead lamp
bleaches out a spot on the front steps of the library, where a figure is
standing. Are you going to dinner? No. Have you finished your termpaper? No, no. Isabel Rawsthorne is staring through a nightfall thick
as a fault to the outline of the tree in front of Darconville's house, only
a largeness of indifference—not good, not evil—the pendulous boughs
of which the wind jostles with the feverish excitement of a sacrilegious
thief. All are not abed that have ill rest, and one of them, lacking most
because longing most, begins to pace out notions. Of these notions one
lodges itself finally in her mind with cautious exactitude as the very
thing indicated by the occasion. It's a cat's walk, a little way up and
back. Then it's not a cat's walk. The figure is gone.

*   *   *   *   *

Darconville soon began to get restless. At sixes and sevens, he wandered through the hall and went into the library; he half-pulled a
book out of a shelf—*The Gnomes of Zeeland* by Rex Hout—and
uninspiredly pushed it back. He stepped out on the veranda and
looked at the sky. Strangely, an intuitional hindsight occurred to him,
but it passed as he strained to count the distant peal of bells coming
from the library. Nine o'clock. Thank God, Isabel would be coming
soon.

"Titbits?"

"Kickshaws?"

"Kitcats?"

It was three horae from the home economics department at the veranda doors offering the hors d'oeuvres they'd brought. Impossible to
avoid, these fructatory genii and inveterate tray-passers with fat

dimpled elbows, polished faces, and smelling of soap and starched linen had been shoggling through the party since they'd got there, the ball-like contours of their heads revolving as they bowed and dipped from guest to guest with plates of airfoods. One of them who'd flunked Isabel first semester for absenteeism thought the grade confirmed in not seeing her there. She went on about it with some concern, embarrassing Darconville, having become her father-by-proxy, his proxy-by-placement. An hour passed. He checked his watch. It was 9:04.

The guests, meanwhile, circulated, mooning from room to room, discovering each other again in a different place but under the same circumstances to resume their similar chat. Taken altogether, it was not unlike any other faculty party, archetypal, to be sure—if more pronounced at Quinsy—with its predictable cast of poltroons, gum-beating fibsters, and others whose brains were kept in jars above the moon; to wit: the Funster with the double-jointed thumb which also serves—to everybody's dismay—as a finger-puppet; the Trendy Wife (always from California) wearing hoop earrings and a bandanna who's found the most *fantastic* recipe for sharksfin soup; the Good Ol' Boy, a fox-snouted churl in a perpetual sulk who sits alone in the den misanthropically crunching pretzels and flipping through a five-year-old issue of *Knife Digest;* the Female Poet, smoking a cheroot, who has a cat named "Cat" and calls her poems "friends"; the Foreigner, coddled by all, who is perfectly willing to talk about agrarian reform in his country; the Chubby-in-Residence who, after twenty-seven visits to the dog-whelk dip, publicly—and virtuously—refuses her dessert at dinner; the Etymologist, thoroughly bottomed in his Skeat, who is silent in any given conversation until that crucial point when he interrupts with, "Actually, I think you'll find that—"; the Televisioniste, somebody's boyfriend, who with more confidence than brains deathlessly mis-recapitulates for everyone the interminable plot of last night's late movie; the Convenientologist who at some moment or other always comes striding out of the bathroom saying, "Why, Felice, you never told *us* you installed a bidet!" and then always, of course, the Favorite Child, the little towser with the cowlick dragged down from upstairs in his pajamas-with-feet, blinking and clutching a truck, who is called upon to sing in a voice like a puppetoon—and reluctantly—"Jesus Wants Me for a Sunbeam."

Darconville, who didn't want to, noticed everything. He *fought* not to notice. If the people there, however, could have known with what

punctilious accuracy their every movement and mannerism was recorded by him, not through viciousness, not smugness, nor any
premeditation, they'd have sued him on the spot. He couldn't *help* it.
Behavior is comment, the articulation of action, and these nopsters?
With their fipple-fluting tongues? Their pretentious piety? Any satirist
worth his salt would have banished them forthwith in a jingle, not as
victims but as *executioners:* an authorized punishment, seeking to cure
disease by remedies which produce effects similar to the symptoms of
the complaint, for what to correct as hangmen they'd have to know as
the hanged. There is not a bauble thrown by the silly hand of a dunce,
thought Darconville, that may not be caught with advantage by the
hand of art. Pausias, in painting a sacrifice, foreshortened the victim
and threw his shade on part of the surrounding crowd to show its
height and length, an offense that exaggerates a mood where defense,
sickened, lies and, stricken, dies, for are we not all implicated in what
we hate by what we otherwise might love? But I am no writer anymore, reasoned Darconville, so how would I know?

It was less for the observations he made, however, than the emotions he felt that gave Darconville an indication how extremely anxious he was that Isabel should come, so both of them could leave. The
party was ridiculous. It was one fantastical opinion after another, mad
fugitive theorizing-on-naught from bore to batman to boobie, and
behind everybody, everywhere, was somebody, somewhere, making
signs with his or her eyes which he or she meaningfully manipulated
for another, anywhere, to meet and mock.

Miss Malducoit—the kind of woman who always says she's going to
make a long story short but doesn't—stood in the middle of the dining-room, meanwhile, and not surprisingly de-edified her listeners as
she plucked from the *damnum fatale* of her new feminist consciousness
this remarkable theory, that, if women would become more like the
men who thought they were better than women, then those men
would become more like the women who thought they couldn't become men than those women who, thinking they could, already had—
a remark that Miss Ballhatchet, the college sapphonic, thought ironically aimed at her, whereupon she withdrew, reached into her pocket,
and furiously began squeezing a handball, an action, misinterpreted,
that took the attention of Drs. Knipperdoling and Pindle, who nudged
each other knowingly, long having learned, both, from no less a hal-
lowed shrine than their mothers' knees that the wages of refusing "to

make a decision for Christ" were clear, i.e., a faint mustache, an abridged haircut, and the penchant for wearing gym shorts with a zipper-fly.

"I wanna tell ya," said Pindle.

"Breaks your heart," agreed Knipperdoling, tossing some hazelnuts into his mouth.

"This mortal coil," said Pindle.

They exchanged glances.

"Life," they said in unison—and shook their heads.

Mr. Schrecklichkeit, blowing his huge white nose, heard the word. "That's my field, life," he muttered, "which is only another word for mortality."

"Maybe that's why"—everybody turned to this voice—"why everybody has an M on the palm of his hand?" faintly offered Miss Swint, peeking over her glasses, but the gentlemen to whom she was speaking all breezed past her and went to the foodtable.

Religion, of course, was the favorite staple of conversation at Quinsy College. Indeed, it has always been a subject that could touch off Southerners faster than anything else, creating a fellowship, however, that had less to do with binding them to a disposition to truth or Christian charity than with allowing them to turn with grateful relief to the one totally subjective, squibcrack-proof topic they could all pursue—every last self-ordained half-wit who wanted to—without the attendant personal humiliation of having to explain, clarify, or reconcile what the strict tests of either an informed intelligence or thinking heart, put into play, might serve to disprove and so disparage.

Miss Sally Bull Sweetshrub told everyone that art was religion. The Weerds, now upstairs in the attic, were each jointly confessing the other to be his and her religion. Crouching, Mr. Thimm was in the pantry being threatened by an infuriated Baptist minister with a raised fire-shovel for blasphemously having claimed that the greatest book on religion ever written was the privately printed (and, needless to say, dictated) edition worked out of his father's deathbed confession, called *Crows as Foreboders.* And by the rosy punchbowl, Prof. Wratschewe, syntactitian and local authority on the shall/will rules, visibly disturbed several in a circle of blue-haired ladies gathered around him by posing to them the question that also happened to be the subject of a monograph he was only that afternoon swotting up: "Where Is the Christian Homer?"

Include me out, thought Darconville, hearing the question. Resigned that his own book would never be completed, he kept silent. But that was all right, he felt, for next to him who can finish is he who has hid that he cannot. Still, he wondered how long it had been since he'd last sat down and finished a page, the answer to which speculation, if there was one, immediately destructed in an explosion of sudden dismay at his elbow.

"O poo, I don't believe it."

"I thought everybody knew."

"A fiction."

"A *fact,*" snapped Miss Gibletts, her neutral articulations rendered none the more fetching for the plain brown shift she wore that sagged from her like a punctured windsock.

"But, Lord," asked Mrs. McAwaddle, snatching nervously at her pearls, "how in the world could she have done that?"

Miss Gibletts, closing her eyes, simply shrugged. She knocked back a small tumbler of Southern Comfort, then one more, and another—respectively her eighth, ninth, and tenth that evening—rather annoyed that Mrs. McAwaddle didn't believe her. She set down the glass, audibly. "It is said, you know, that the poet Ovid—Publius Ovidius Naso —had the longest one in the world. It cast a shadow. It could accommodate pigeons."

"I simply can't believe it."

"Read your Roman history."

"No, I mean I can't believe"—Mrs. McAwaddle swallowed— "*that.*"

Darconville believed it when he'd heard it, however—and since he heard it everywhere he went, he walked to the far windows, leaving the subject of this conversation, along with the two ladies, behind. The topic was disturbing: fortuneless and dripstick-nosed Miss Gupse, the previous March having been asked to resign—the verdict was "overtired"—had been found apparently by the odor, stiff, on the business-end of a halter in the backroom of a Nashville doss house with a note safety-pinned to one of her anklesocks reading only "Because." The police later gave out the information that, tied round her head on a string, had been found an item crocheted by her own hand—a pointed nose bag.

Peering out expectantly, Darconville could not see Isabel through the darkness of the window. He saw only Miss Gupse, somewhere, now beyond anyone's poor power to add or detract, and bent over there, his hands on the panes like blinders, he thought: you can never love too early, you can only love too late.

* * * * *

Friday 8:58 P.M.: Tableau: Girl, With Door Ajar. Artist unknown. Round-eyed in fright, Isabel steps into Darconville's dark office and seems to feel the room *waiting* and aeroferic with suspicion, that strange disturbing noise which sits at the heart of utter silence: white noise. Closing her eyes, she hears wounds in the doleful sounds of the bell tolling out nine leaden bongs from the old Smethwick clock and pauses in her cold shoes: no candle gutters, no shutters bang, no suit of armor creaks. Swallowing, she steps quietly out of her footprints— and waits again. O interminable! She decides to leave. The wireworm that has crept into her ear now moves: *"Why then was this forbid? Why but to awe, why but to keep ye low and ignorant, His worshippers."* There is some shame and remorse, less for finding the letter removed from the desk than in pinching out the fragments from the bottom of the wastebasket; thereafter, not so—the moves of the operation are then all swift and precise: excogitating, a vein like an S raised on her forehead, Isabel oops piece to piece, piece to piece. She inhumes a hot sigh. A letter comes up in lavender. A low moan rises up through Isabel to echo in a shrill piercing cry of agony matched only by the proclamation of the angel Hadraniel, dropping from somewhere, his voice penetrating through a million firmaments to plead, "Come back, come back!" But the door of the English building is already slamming, slams.

* * * * *

"I've ate rook pie."

"Rook? Pie?"

"The ruddy duck, yessir!" deblaterated Dr. Glibbery with a smattering of mustard on his nose, his cheeks huge walletfuls of pork. "The most scabrous and torn-downest little ol' birds what am, let me tell you." He aimed the barrel of his fat finger into a wall-mirror. "I potted messes of 'em smack out of the air back in college just to keep alive. With prices skyhootin' like they was? In my day—matriculatin' and all?—christ, it was pronto dogs and blinky srimp from one day to the next, take it or leave it. We didn't have rubber assholes in my day,

jack. And nobody, excusin' God, can know to the number of them
rooks I ate to this day, nobody—and I mean, *no*damnbody!" Pork-
faced Glibbery then began sucking the pig grease from his fingers as
vigorously as the pig itself had ever sucked its parent. The whole mode
of piggery itself, in fact, applied to him—the very kind of face, arguably, that had turned Islam against pork. "What, these sophomore
dufuses backin' and forthin' around here going to tell me? Sowballs!"
he cried, ripping away half of another sandwich in one thyestean bite
and speaking through a smacking medley of loud champs and chews.
"Rooks, for chrissakes? They'd be havin' the living dorts scared out of
them, these people, they so much as *looked* at one!" He mowsed the
rest of the sandwich. "Sowballs!"

Everybody laughed.

"And sowballs again!" Dr. Glibbery repeated, through a mouthful
of food.

"Excellent," chuckled Mr. Roget, pulling his perspicacious nose.
"Perfect. First-rate. Flawless."

The dining-room looked magnificent. A long table, set off in the
center by a huge beef roast stabbed *entrecôte* with a miniature of the
Quinsy College flag, was spread out with bowls of conch gumbo,
cheese wheels, platters of Virginia ham, potato salad, buns. The guests
swarmed around, wolfing sandwiches, gobbling meats, drinking.

"As paprika is to a Hungarian so am I to esoterica," lisped Floyce
R. Fulwider. He plucked a twist of candied Metzelsuppe, ate it, and,
closing his eyes, delicately wiggled his fingers over the heavenly taste.
Miss Dessicquint, standing behind him, mimicklingly pursed her lips,
went limp in the wrists, and stuck her bum out like a poodle. Miss
Shepe and Miss Ghote, having their ginger-ales in lovely stemmed
glasses, both agreed that the highlight of the party had been the appearance of the little Culpa boy who'd been brought down to sing that
adorable song; unfortunately, twisting his pajama string in an initial
moment of nervousness, he'd managed to pull it out.

"It didn't seem to faze Mrs. Culpa, did you notice, that everybody
could see—" Miss Ghote paused and looked away.

"His bow-wow." Miss Shepe had a brother.

They sat silent momentarily.

"It was—"

"Yes."

"Flying expressly in the face of Galatians 5:2?" asked Miss Ghote, archly. "O my."

"Circumcision, Miss Ghote," said Miss Shepe, whispering, "was condoned in Genesis 17:10. Ask your Rev. Cloogy."

"Lapser!" cried Miss Ghote, with a muttlike snap.

Dr. Speetles, munching some rolled-sprat, cavalierly presented a plate of leafalia—winter-rocket, cress, endive—to his ample wife who, adding five slabs of roast beef, roundly told everybody she wouldn't be having dessert. Lately arrived, Miss Pouce took a jam roly-poly and tea. And Mrs. Fewstone, her unforgiving shoulders tense, was facing the wall nipping a cayenned egg, but when her husband offered to make her a drink she wheeled around, her mouth hardening into pliers, and bent him like cheap wire, hissing, "You—*pimp!*"

Miss Swint, sitting on the piano stool and eating spooms-in-a-cup, said she didn't think she heard anything.

"Actually, I think you'll find," pipped in Prof. Wratschewe, turning from the discussion he'd been having with a now thankful, now disappearing Darconville, "that the etymon of our word 'pimp' is taken from the Greek verb πέμπειν: to send." He beamed and bowed.

"I theash clatherx," said Miss Gibletts, listing.

"Yes, Miss Gibletts, I know. I know you teach classics," said Prof. Wratschewe, looking behind him. "I say, Darconville?"

But Darconville was in an upstairs bedroom, trying to telephone, with some apprehension, the third floor of Fitts. It rang and rang and rang. What could be wrong? Then he began to fear that she might have felt unwanted at the party, for it had been reported several times during the past year by a scandalized handful of faculty vestals—with Miss Sweetshrub i/c and a few other shades of Orcus in the rear— that the two of them had been spotted "marketing together" (*ipsissimus verbis*) at the local Piggly Wiggly with only *one* pushcart. Dean Dessicquint once nearly bit her head off for signing out on an "all-night," learning only afterwards of the anthropology class field-trip to Assateague—a coal-run to Newcastle—to study these people's dialect. And once at the movies with Trinley Moss Isabel overheard Miss Tavistock, sitting behind her, tell someone that a psychic had recently told her that she would soon be marrying "a dark handsome stranger" and then—mistakenly?—bumped Isabel with her umbrella. Guileless as she was, Isabel, a mere freshman, had managed to exercise just

about every bitch and barge-wife in the Quinsyburg locality. It is the
Cyclops' thumb, thought Darconville, by which the pigmy measures
its own littleness. Perhaps she was right in not coming to the party. He
hung up the phone.

Spotting Miss Pouce at the foot of the stairs, Darconville asked her
if, earlier, she'd seen Isabel Rawsthorne in the library. Miss Pouce
only sighed and said that, oh, no one had time for libraries anymore.
He pressed her no further, but his head was as filled with worry as his
heart was filled with love. How he missed her! He sat down momentarily on the stairs. Grand old Miss Carp was watching him.

"The apple of your eye, is it, dear?"

Darconville nodded, and then explained not only what was bothering him but what might have been the occasion of it, a matter she herself understood only too well.

"So the pair of you are currently dating? Good," said Miss Carp,
puffing her cigarette. "You have your reasons. I'm plumb fed up with
these old kumquats around here who want to throw lime in your eyes
for it. The policy on faculty/student dating—rules that should have
been pruned long ago—was a lemon even when I taught here. You
just give 'em the old raspberry, y'hear? Me?" She blew out a can-
nonade of smoke. "I couldn't give a fig for them." She tapped his nose
three times. "Not. One. Fig."

The dining-room table was in chaos. It looked as if the Harpies had
descended and flown, leaving a disorder of nutshells, slubbered glasses,
cherry stems, and half-bitten macaroons. Gastronomes blouted. Hip-
pophages belched. Fruitarians burped. And all the low candles, flickering, seemed to wink a final notice to all those guests who doggedly
remained and in whose eyes, now, sensitivity and sobriety were so
comfortably abed.

"They used to call me 'Temptation Eyes' in high-school," muttered
bedraggled Mrs. Dodypol who, in the obvious grip of Korsakoff's Psy-
chosis, rocked shakily past Darconville and walked straightway into a
linen closet. She might have spent the rest of her life there had not two
hundred pounds plus of lubberly self-assurance—with a stink-pot cigar
and a suit splurched with the orts of a cream bun—tiptoed by. It was
President Greatracks who, wheezing with laughter, hammered on the
door. There was no answer. He squatted, giggling behind his hand,
and began bouncing up and down and crooning in the manner of a

jump-rope song, "Your baby wants his *hap*py! Your baby wants his *hap*py! Your baby wants his *hap*py!"

"This is hilarious," said one of his lackeys.

"What fun."

"I'm about to split my si-hi-hi-hides," said another.

But the door tipped open—and Mrs. Dodypol pitched out backwards, her hair sticking out like a wig created by Klimt, and fell supple as a tobacco pouch into the outspread arms of President Greatracks, who wabbled backwards on his ill-smelling feet and angrily looked about him and wondered out loud just who the hell in the dang a-rea, goddamit, aimed to grow themselves enough backbone to get a poor child a drink of water? The pipe-smoking lickgolds, each cautious as a medieval guard watching over the king's *nef*, all hopped to. "I will," said one. "Leave it to me," said another. "No, me," said still another.

"I think I know what to do," said Miss Skait's date, appearing from nowhere. "I saw this here movie on television last night where someone got shot, see, and the victim's brother, no, his father from, I don't know, someplace where they wear those fur hats, what, Czechoslovania or something, the Orient anyway, said to elevate his feet, I mean head, and—"

Checking his watch, Darconville took advantage of the distraction and ran upstairs again to the telephone. He dialed several numbers. The ghost in Isabel's dormitory wouldn't answer. The infirmary nurse, doing her bedpans, rudely told him to call back. And the sheriff was out.

* * * * *

Friday 10:20 P.M.: Isabel *solus* is sobbing on a bed too real, covered with a quilt too narrow. She writhes, she twists, she toils, perspiring and spiked from within. The sleeping pill she took sustains but a periodic unconsciousness, easing neither the dying out of life nor the living out of pain. A black dream enacts itself in her fever: a telephone, locked on its rack, is screaming and screaming for help, as if being tortured alive. Isabel's shadow comes at her bellowing, *"She won't pick it up!"* Isabel cries in reply, "She can't pick it up!" *"She won't pick it up!"* But Isabel cries, "She can't pick it up with a hand that wants to!" *"She won't pick it up! She won't! She won't!"* The

screaming then stops, the telephone is dead. Trembling, Isabel wakes
and tries to call Annabel Lee Jenks, who has gone. Her puffed face
burns back at her from the night window in a foolish swollen reflection. Everyone has left her. Everyone hates her. Everyone has gone to
sea. In a sudden wingstroke of will, Isabel, standing on her shadow,
brutally shakes the telephone to life, dials another number, and—as
the Incidental leaps up to throttle the Essential—whispers low to the
party at the other end, "Govert?"

* * * * *

A painting of Mt. Vernon took pride of place in the living room.
Floyce had done it for the Culpas earlier in the year, and now as the
various members of the faculty sat around there, drinking, it came
under discussion, meeting with drunken abuse from the men and,
from the women, unfeminine swipes that in the eighteenth century,
the Virginian's favorite, would at least have been whispered behind
fans, an uncharitable belowting that ridiculed the beginnings of skill
and the ends of art. Miss Throwswitch called it untheatrical. Dr. Glibbery asked if a nigger done it. And Mrs. DeCrow, snickering, pretended to look at it sideways and yet still had to admit it honored a
great American, no, *not* Floyce, she added, putting an objurgatory
sibilance to his name—but George Washington. "First in war, first in
peace," she quoted pompously, "and first in the hearts of his coun-
trymen."
      "Still," said Felice, her eyes smiling, "he married a widow."
      Mrs. DeCrow, her eyes going ablaze with prosecutional bitchery,
turned cat-a-pan and marched out of the room. "Terribly earnest,"
murmured Felix Culpa, unwrapping another bottle of bourbon.
"Well, you know," said Felice to Darconville, "the poor old pelican
hasn't been the same since the operation. The cosmetic work, not the
tubes she had twisted. Her plastic surgeon grafted skin in the
damnedest way. I won't tell you where, but every time she gets tired,"
Felice winked, "her face wants to sit down." Felice wet her forefinger,
nicked the air, and, screaming with laughter, took Felix by his belt
and pulled him out into the garden.
      "You want to know what I think? I think these people are revolting
and disgusting, that's what I think," said Miss Malducoit to Miss
Porchmouth, who was with her enormous hands trying unsuccessfully
to worm a cherry out of a bud-vase she'd filled with gin. She looked

down censoriously at only half of stone-blind Qwert Yui Op who, rendered *hors de combat* from milk—a digestive indisposition characteristic of that race—was lying under the sofa, with only his little twig-like legs sticking out. But Miss Malducoit couldn't believe what was going on at the other side of the room.

For Miss Ballhatchet, her eyes wide as a lovesick potto, had wangled a place on the couch with Miss Thisbite and, chatting her up with a few choice misandrous asides, asked the girl—who politely overlooked the deltoid massage—if she didn't agree with her that one man made a market, two a mob? Meanwhile, Floyce R. Fulwider, equally zealous, excused himself to a group of old ladies wearing necklaces strung as if with the teeth of peccaries and gynandromorphosed past them in short, mincing steps, holding high a couple of overly befruited drinks and singing, "Coming through! Coming through!" He set one, gently, into the hands of the slim blond boy who was Miss Thisbite's brother and told him he looked like the young Louis XVII. The old ladies were not *quite* sure how they felt about it, and, closing into a circle, proceeded to commit several sins against the Eighth Commandment. Dr. and Mrs. Speetles, philoprogenetists, then began passing around to everybody there—saving, of course, the Weerds, who were down in the cellar talking to each other—several photographs of their hydrocephalic baby playing with a fire engine, a little meldrop of snot shining under its nose in every one. Dr. Glibbery said he looked like a dufus and handed them to Darconville who passed them to Miss Tavistock who thanked him, stared at him steadfastly a full minute, then asked, "Are you in love with me?" There was an awkward silence, broken by a whistle—Felice calling Darconville into the kitchen.

Darconville excused himself just as Dr. Knipperdoling, loaded to the scuppers, was remarking how good old Mr. Bischthumb of recent memory would have enjoyed the party, bringing to mind, with significant pauses, both the doily of his undoing and the irony of death-by-laughter. Touching on the odds and ends of life, he pointed out that life *was* odd and yet that, funnily enough, it would have only one end, you know? The profundity struck him, and he blew a long unmusical note of grief into his handkerchief. Dr. Pindle turned to his partner with an I-suppose-we-in-a-way-expected-it-but-how-horrible-just-the-same face, drawing an arrow out of his sententious quiver. "In one way," he philosophized, "life is pointless, but a needle isn't."

He paused. "You know?" His friend knew. Oh, his friend knew very well. And Dr. Knipperdoling burst into tears.

"Forgive me," Felice said to Darconville. "I saw you over there being pried by 'The Clawhammer' and couldn't bear to see you trapped." He smiled. "I wasn't really trapped, but—" Darconville stopped short. He snapped his fingers at the sudden idea. Miss Trappe!

Swiftly, Darconville got to the bedroom, shut the door, and made his call. Of course! Isabel, making that long-delayed visit, had *forgotten* all about the party. But Miss Trappe had been asleep. He could see her at the other end—it almost broke his heart—just wakened, confused in the dark, wearing an elfin nightcap and groping for an identifiable chair. Her voice sounded far away, as if it were underwater, old and tired as hope.

"And she didn't call you at all?"

"Not really," came the distant voice.

The palliative expressed her charity. Darconville, perspiring, shifted the receiver to his other ear.

"Wait. I think I know," said Miss Trappe, trying. The voice faded, returned, faded. "Perhaps she concentrated on *trying* to remember instead of concentrating on remembering—and forgot."

Apologizing, Darconville thanked her and said goodnight. Quickly, he dialed the infirmary again: the bark of discord on the other end identified Nurse Bedpan and both—the bark, the discord—disclaimed with the punctuation of a double-negative that it knew anything about anybody named Isabel Rawsthorne. She hung up. He sat by the telephone in the dark, thinking that the lover possessing a luxury with which merit had so little to do must perhaps stand a constant penitent to such arbitrarily dispensed grace. And anxious in the vitals, he felt an even more profound love for Isabel coming upon him, swift as a wish: the knowledge of good bought dear by fearing ill, the value of gain bought dear by feeling loss. But what ill? he wondered. How lost? He reviewed fifty inevitabilities and, selecting none, was now the owner of all.

The door moved.

Darconville looked up at the shadow.

"Hello, Dr. Dodypol."

"Hell-o, Darconville. Fair grow the lilies on the riverbank?" He paused, then came noiselessly into the room. "I'm just pecking on a cracker." He peered closer. "Are you—all right?"

"Yes. Yes, of course."

"I like a cracker now and again."

Darconville nodded.

"My wife isn't big for them, crackers. But she bakes them."

"Yes?"

"Mrs. Dodypol? O yes. She actually bakes them. Few wives, taking it all together, do nowadays. No, I can't complain."

A silence fell. Only the tight little crunches could be heard in the darkness. Then Dr. Dodypol, alone like Darconville, sat by him on the bed. He sighed and folded his hands, prayer-like, as if in supplication to Coquage, god of cuckolds.

"Drudgery? O boy, you wouldn't believe it. Harder by much than me making my verse. She first sets out her tins, whisks, cutters, the lot. You know how women are. Then she does her sifting, salts to taste, proofs the batter, does Mrs. Dodypol. Well, you want them natural, see. To get the benefit. It's all in the books, about nature, I mean. Isn't it? Wholesome, they say. They do say that, don't they? Oh yes, scrupulous about doughs, my wife, but the kneading gets her here, in the back, right"—he motioned—"here. Well, you can imagine. Anyway, she cooks them to paper-thin on preheated tiles, and, mmm, when offered up warm—" He looked at Darconville, who noticed tears rolling down his cheeks. "I'm sorry. I'm lying. I hate crackers. I hate nature. And I hate my wife. I'd like to take a pair of shears and snip off her cruel merciless tits. Well, goodnight." And he left.

* * * * *

Friday 11:43 P.M.: The light of the full moon, burglarious, steals through an eagre of dart-shaped clouds, shifting west. A blue car, dented, winds onto the ring-road that curves around to the front of Fitts dormitory. The mausoleum is not empty. There is a face at a third-floor window, watching out in the autarchy of an isolation no worse than dreams. A wistfulness awaits—Isabel, throatcramped, apprehensively twicking her thumbs over a thought: what does my sorrow matter if I can't be happy? Suddenly, she stirs up, pale, on her feet as the car pulls up out front, its headlights flashing on-and-off. Rapunzel, Rapunzel, let down your hair! Out of the building, into the car she runs, her odd cheerless expression transforming to resignation; gunned, the car backfires and races toward the Quinsyburg line, not *to* it, for turning off the main road, it bumps over a dirt drive into a glade, and stops. A fatidic stir of wind is blowing across several obsolete fields. A dog howls, somewhere. Matter-of-fact Govert van der Slang, chauffeur and *zielverkooper,* turns to Isabel. There is, he says, no alternative: he, Fawx's Mt., and the time is each, respectively, tired, far, and late. They sit there, coevals in the night. 'Tis not so much the gallant who woos as the gallant's way of wooing. He is walking now, flanked by a silent girl on one side and her robin's-egg-blue valise on the other, both safe in his omnivicarious hands. The glow above her is, she thinks, at least a personal glimmer in the impersonal darkness and, reaching to palpate a stray cat glowing eerily now red, now blue, she manages successfully to avoid a second look above her at the blinking neon-lights—mistakeproof in the night—of the Bide-A-Wee Motel. An agreement is made: "witness our hands." The goddesses of Greece became the goddesses of Rome.

* * * * *

Posthumia, mistress of revels, eventually brought most of the guests outdoors, and under the magic of the paper lanterns everyone's inhibitions gave way to a variety of feats and games and pranks: chairing the member, guessing-which-hand, and pulling faces in skits and foolish charades that looked as if they were trying to act out scenes taken from a series of Thraco-Pelasgian wall-paintings. Behavior became ridiculous. They cut capers, yelped at the moon, and chased each other around the hedges, shrimp-whistling and bum-goosing anything that moved.

Dr. Speetles, one over the eight, gave a vigorous if implicit endorsement for the necessity of laxatives by delivering—upsidedown on a picnic table—his own rendition of "The Lass That Loved a Sailor." Blissful Mr. Thimm danced blissom Miss Swint squealing over a ha-ha. Miss Porchmouth, her eyes red, white, and pinwheeling, screamed from a tree that a beaver she couldn't see was chasing her. Miss Pouce who'd got into the pokeberry wine was meanwhile wandering round the house in a circle, reciting the rules of the Dewey Decimal System —and every three or four minutes, as she passed, her exultant monologue would swell out and decrease again. An empty shandy glass had rolled just out of reach of Dr. Excipuliform who lay unconscious under the porch in a strange facioscapulohumeral cramp. Someone walked by with a wastebasket over his head. And then came a shriek to wake the very dead—Miss Gibletts, looking like the devil before daylight, tearing down the backstairs in her underpinnings and screeching at the top of her lungs, *"Flammeum video venire! Ite, concinite in modum 'Io Hymen Hymenaee, io Hymen Hymenaeeeeeeeee!'"*

"A u.f.o.!"

"It's only batwoman."

"She looks like Pharaoh's mother's mummy," said Felice.

Darconville only watched. At a window, he impassively sipped a drink, the velvet bite of vodka a small anodyne to lessen the pain of a truth foremost in his mind, that fortune alone is victorious. To know something was wrong was to argue, perhaps, that he didn't know something more important—just what, of course, he couldn't say; but speculate he could, and he began to understand that his love for Isabel, so new in the declaration, was bound to walk upon the tiniest hurts: the cards of a new deck, so judges the cartomant, have been insufficiently shuffled if two people immediately hold the Royal Flush. Cynical, he thought. *Un altro, un altro, gran' Dio, ma più forte?* Difficult, he thought, difficult.

Perversely, he felt rather glad he'd thrown up his writing. Not so much vanquished, he began to feel—this night more than ever—a gathering despair over the very nature of communication itself, a desolation growing out of hearing so much so remarkably unwritedownable: the gossip, the laborious stories, the twice-told tales, and the scrappet-like micromonologues, forbidding conversation, which assumed that to be frank was to be rude. Here sighed a jar, there a goose-pye talked. At every word a reputation died. And writing? The true writer, thought Darconville, must not only be a man whose Christ shows no discontinuity between Creator and Redeemer—a perfection, he knew, he failed—but a man with faith in that perfection. One couldn't write in a chimney with charcoal. But for Isabel, he thought, this would be my personal farewell party. Suddenly, the dragoman, Abactha, one of the genii of confusion, shook him and cat-whispered into his ear, *"But she isn't here! She isn't here!"*

The Culpas' backyard now looked like the Shevardino Redoubt. Here and there, bodies lay sprawled around the grounds like dead cuddies. Dr. Glibbery, his periodic guffaws echoing out of the dark-

ness, was creeping around the backwoods trying to siphon-bottle sleeping birds. Prof. Wratschewe, who'd earlier in the evening frankly told
Miss Sweetshrub to go marry her beagle, was now engaged in a game
of belly-blind with Mrs. McAwaddle, who dearly hoped it wouldn't
offend her husband, despite the fact that he'd been eight long years *in*
pectore Abraam. And Miss Gibletts was now handspringing naked
and discalced through the shrubbery, which Miss Ghote said—though
Miss Shepe disagreed—was the Unpardonable Sin and for that disa-
greement hit her with a pie, splat! the force of which knocked Miss
Shepe dumfounded and fenderless right over the picnic bench where
she sat in a pile and began to cry. To the loud music of the phonograph several couples—bartered brides, groping grooms—shifted back
and forth in the upright position of neo-copulative thrall. Back in the
dining-room, Mrs. DeCrow, ravenously cro-magnoning a last platter
of beef, saw no one about, shoved a ham into her handbag, and disappeared. The Weerds, ready to go home, together decided they'd col-
laborate on a poem about the party and call it "Party." And President
Greatracks, puffing his mugwumpist cheeks, fought exertion and tried
as best he could to get Mrs. Dodypol from under the table where she
was so often found to the top of it where she was so often left. He bent
over, his buttocks sticking out like two curious faces—or a single hideous one—and grabbed her by her skulled toes and pulled. It was impossible. She was stiff as a knout.

"A pity," said Darconville. He couldn't get Dr. Dodypol's words
out of his mind. Hell hath no fury like a husband horned. Standing
beside him at the window, Felice quietly stirred her drink with a
finger. "Does she always get carried away with herself?"

"Only," said Felice, "when there's no one else to do it for her."

Darconville wondered. He looked out across the garden past the
lanterns and saw Dr. Dodypol, to hide, presumably, his bereaved wits,
pacing up and down a path ignoring the flowers and struggling no
doubt to get out of his head a horned syllogism: the *syllogismus cor-*
nutus. He was waiting for his wife, of course. He would wait until the
crack of doom. Blind endurance, thought Darconville, was a kind of
faith, and in the bewildered souls of those cuckolds who, like water-
men, row one way and yet look another, was a strange bravery.
Dodypol had it—and yet against what odds? Darconville knew Dodypol's black view of nature both directly and in a little poem he'd once
read of his:

> Your eyes please keep
> Above the puppet man—and weep,
> For when he nods
> The operator's wrist is God's.

How many such caitiff-ridden husbands and traduced wives were there, walking around aimlessly, each carrying his or her metaphorical sandwich-board reading "wittol"—creatures who wrapped their cracked and heavy hearts in the disguise of jests and tiny poems? It was all odd, as if he, Darconville, were reflecting on himself who was so much luckier than they. Was it perhaps because Love itself cuckolds the man who, left alone, can't express it?

As often happened, Felice Culpa knew more or less what he was thinking. "Isabel is tired," she said, attempting to console him. The beautiful name, uttered, filled his heart. Why haven't you come, my chrysopoetic girl? Why haven't you called?

"What hurts, teaches." She paused. "Do you believe that?"

"I don't know."

"You will, my darling, you will."

Darconville couldn't smile. She kissed his cheek and repeated, "Isabel is tired."

Hearing that, Darconville wondered: and does that bode well? And does that bode ill? The present tense, he thought, overflows categories of past, present, and future and drifts into the unreal, timeless realm of ideation. The present tense argues, lexically, the habitual mode, reflects that which is essentially unlimited and a-substantial. Isabel is tired, Isabel is forever tired, Isabel is tired four hundred years ago, *per omnia saecula saeculorum, amen*. There was no time, for there was no creation, no movement, only the sepulchral mode. It did not designate a temporal coordinate as the "past" or "future" did and remained as vague and unassailable as a killer virus, a stasis, a settled vision unto itself. Vision? There was no vision, for in the present tense there could be no development. It thwarted change, revision, growth, alteration, rehabilitation, and hope. What, marching into its depths, could be made in the way of progress? And what, he wondered, might there be to change in her that he might be unable to change, ever? But time and change, he reasoned, were existential *proofs* of each other, weren't they? It was precisely, thought Darconville, what Dr. Dodypol banked on over there, walking with eyes askance through the midden of that dark garden of his life, asprout with caveats: poison poppies, dwarfed tulips, deathful lilies. Dr. Dodypol's faith was as rare as the horns on a rabbit—but faith it was. And Darconville knew he must learn from that.

Darconville chastised himself, for, cross-examining his fears about Isabel, he had willfully assumed the worst. The opposite of faith, he realized, was not believing in nothing but rather believing in *anything*. And so home through the night he walked, resolved any error whatsoever to contain lest by more truth he find in himself more pain.

XXXVII

Expostulation and Reply

None but himself can be his parallel.

—Lewis Theobald, *The Double Falsehood*

THE NOISE was unmistakable: *thissst*—something had been slipped under his door, and, not asleep, Darconville quickly rolled up and forward, bouncing Spellvexit in a high bumbershot from the top of his chest into a hollow of the blanket where he lay low and pouched for safety. A little vimbat of a face slowly appeared, with whiskers twitching. " 'Swowns!" squeaked the cat, who'd been brought up better than that. Ignoring him, Darconville grabbed his bathrobe, stumbled to the door—the noise from the party still in his head—and called Isabel's name several times. There was an envelope on the floor. Perhaps this explained—?

But it was a poem, written by Dr. Dodypol.

HAVES AND HOLES

Like a novel, like its sequel,
Marriage is *that* equal:
Halves, but one half previous;
The other, somewhat devious,
A counterpart, say, in the following way—
As a workweek equals a Friday's pay.
Two stones grind in an ancient quern,
One stays static, one will turn.
Nothing in nature is equal quite;
Jaws don't match in a single bite.
Your ear on the right, your ear on the left—
Some will say "reft," some will say "cleft":
The words to that queer inner-porch both apply.
The cave from the darkness who can descry?
The terms are the same, but not so the ears,
With shapes as different as smiles from tears.
A push, you say, is only a pull?
A glass half empty is a glass half full?
The riddle's the riddle of number two;
The one call me, the other you.
But a couple, alas, is not a pair.
Love's disappointment's precisely there!
If a simple kiss is what one wants
Turning the cheek is the other's response.
The vision you'd share can never be,
Not to another who cannot see.
For the singular act of one's creation
Absolves the other of obligation.
Love-letters sent, countless and grand,
Parch the pen in the other's hand.
The fair, they say, requires foul;
An owl is cognate to its howl.
And if with love you see your fate,
Why, be prepared to suffer hate!
In the duchess you woo at the midnight hour
Claws a black-faced bitch mad to devour.
You seek to select and select what you see,
But is what appears what then must be?
The nature of choice *itself* is sin,

Where one must lose and one must win!
One eye's inaccurate. Two we need
To watch, to learn, to know, to read.
One image is gotten of those two:
But is it real? And is it true?
Distinctions! Differences! All life long!
You can't do right if you can't do wrong.
The bride, the groom on a nuptial bed?
Spills one white, spills one red.
Yet each fulfills defect in each,
The epistemology of stone and peach.
(But when it comes to the hungry lip,
Are equally praised, the flesh, the pip?)
A paradox, say, that can never be:
The strange conundrum of lock and key.
Man's "too much" he boasts to show;
Woman's "too little" down below
Incorporates as best it can
The larger half of her messmate, Man.
A larger half? Yes, there's the catch!
It's the deathless quintessential,
The flint, the strike, the spark sequential
That fires every human match.

—D. I. Dodypol

Darconville put it on the desk—a mouse-colored paper with the thirty or so jumping jingles pecked out so hard that the typed letters, snap-riveted and bitten full into the page, made the verso side read like a lunatic cantrip in braille. He read it several times. What could he reply? Wasn't keeping faith a cause, not an effect? And the irony of love, who knew, perhaps it gave us the relative dimension we needed to experience it without being fully consumed by either the absolute or the agony of it, no?

Axioms, axioms. Darconville picked up his pen and spent most of the day writing to his friend an essay that had been growing within him for some time. It had a simple title.

XXXVIII

Love

—I pursued
And still pursue, the origin and course
Of love, but until now I never knew
That fluttering things have so distinct a shade.

—WALLACE STEVENS, *Le Monocle de Mon Oncle*

"LOVE," wrote Darconville, "is as rare as the emotion of hate. I pray your divided attention: they are the extreme antipodes of each other in temperament but never in endowment, and so bear a strange complementarity. Every time someone executes the action of one of them, the other, specifically, becomes the victim of not being executed. Each is of each a mirror-image, yet explicitly looking at each we implicitly look at both, as when looking in water face then answers to face. To be in the grip of one is to relish precisely not being in the grip of the other. A yes is valued only because it could have been a no, and vice-versa, for the philosophical upshot of freedom, shaped by choice, is that we would not be able to love in act if we were not also able to hate in potency. The lowest number is two which, lying down together in the sum it incorporates, pips the child, Relativity. The mirror is, indeed, the parable of love, but you will remember this also: what one sees in the mirror is not in the mirror at all. The anagram of 'Determination: thorough evil!' is 'I mean to rend it through love!'—the perfection of equation being the missing i that must necessarily be lost for salvation in another.

"Love is the thirst which vanishes as you drink. It is, however, always in a state of becoming, moving from one definiteness to another, a synthesis of both identity and otherness. Approaches solely rationalistic or empirical fail in the face of it. We fall through such formulae weightless, for love often declines as fast as reason grows: it is not a what but a that. To ask questions of love is to commit the sin of avarice, for it yields nothing of sense to those intellectual quackshites, daubers of logic, and gowned vultures and spies who, with rule, glass, and compass, surround it in some kind of official jingbang to try to finger out answers and prod it into comprehension. The emotion is not subject to the imperatives of Cartesianism nor is it kind to men of literal minds, but, on the other hand, see it only as figurative and you die starved on theories, impaled on promises. The colors of love are hues. And yet we will never cease to hear noises made, as they were of old, when in the white dust of the Agora, the philonoetic Greeks sat with legs crossed, feet decussated, and raised endless questions on "the unbridled delirium": does love love for love? Does love love to love? Does love lack what it loves? Does love like what it loves? Love loves to love love, it occurred to them, as hate hates to love love. 'Therefore,' exclaims Prometheus, 'hate loves to hate love!' 'Hate *loves?*' gasps Epimetheus. 'Why, 'tis impossible, sir!' 'Say you so?' replies Prometheus. 'Then hate, hating, cannot desire itself?' And so they grapple, and so they will.

"Knowledge is often used, mistakenly, in the sense of wisdom. Of such ideas let us soon hope to be rid, for no brainsick questions, mythical intricacies, or the froth of human wit can probe love—you cannot explain it. You point to it with a question exactly when it hasn't an answer for you. It mocks the academic efforts of men. Medicine talks mere folly. Theology must hold its peace. And Logic, that parody of human reasoning, must positively die of embarrassment in the face of it, for one cannot pound arithmetic like a drench of yew. Love is not simply what it is, for in this matter, strictly speaking, what it is implies also what it ought to be, and as it exists always in a state of becoming, when it exists at all, it is never fully in a state of being. You define it only by preventing its development and preventing its development you hazard its loss. You circumscribe it only by limiting it. Persecute the syllable, logical positivists! Shift it about your mechanic paws, polyhistors and polymaths! Does it lisp? Did it cry out? Pinch it, cuff it, tweak it, employ the bastinado, and squeeze it for moots and lessons! But come, come, I will see the barometer wherein, that it might be read, will squat a typhoon. Iago is more rational than Othello. And thereby hangs a tale.

"True love is the *dolce nemico* of daily life, for love deals not with what is happening but with what ought to happen. The L of love is not the L of logic. For how many centuries has the air of the earth been refrigerated by the tears and heated by the sighs of ruined suitors who failed to realize this? You cannot buy it, make it, fake it, steal it, or ever expect it to appear, for, like can over may, it is only a question of possibility, not permission. It is a grace all hear of, none deserve, few understand; it owes little to merit, less to honor, and, queerly, more often than not finds a home in those sad, shipwrecked, and unready hearts not proud for the expectation. You can only hope for it, which is to say you must shed tears and keep boxes of alexipharmics in your pocket to support you in your loss, for the very imagination that informs hope inflicts the horror, always, of alternative.

"A lover hopelessly in love is not only a lover impatiently in love but a lover impatiently hoping. There is no declaration of love which is completely true, true in the sense of complete; it is always a declaration of hope, with equation the paradigm—a phenomenon of projection that seeks to become a phenomenon of equation, the only settlement of which rests in the meaningless but mystical tautology: $A=A$. The proposition of identity translates 'I am' and 'I am' to 'we are.' The finding is in the seeking. But you are never fulfilled, satisfied only in that other satisfactions await and with an equable temperament content only by dint of approaching in mystery but not reaching in fact an equation that never is solved. A real gambler always returns the money he's won.

"Love, like flotsam, floats. It is proposal, not proposition. There is no doubt but that it is through the ineffability of its glory that men first feel the awakening of their own real nature, becoming convinced, with overpowering clarity, that they have a soul. Vision makes room for vision. Everything is transcendent in love. The little vatican of truths within us—even those stupid, inelegant fibs which, when told, at least give us an idea of what we're trying to become—whisper to us by hints of just how they may be confirmed, and confirmed, held, and held, maintained. Lovers move asymptotically toward the paradise the relative implies is to come in the absolute. Man loves in order to live in another a life missing in himself, for perhaps love does love what it lacks: we want to *be* what we love, even if what we love wants us to be, when we love, what we are. A couplet we may recall from the celebrated Welsh erotikon, *Duges Ddu,* goes:

> Our life? Our love. Or else indict us
> With merciless quotes from Heraclitus.

"In one way, the lover is the purest autobiographer, for he must attend to his personality for another beyond his own, all to shake out, shore up, and shape in an art that's ideal what he can in truth of his life that's real. Love, in any case, means union and what is not union is not love. You will either build a bridge or build a wall. In building a wall you remain the despicable crunchfist you always were, interested in neither projection nor equation but only in acquisition. You are priap. You will pray to St. Unicycle and use your nose for erotical labors and your unloving hands shall be avaricious as horns. You shall be called hard names: we shall call you Manchineel and perceive you more and otherwise than you think. In building a bridge, then what? Neither then, alas, can you be certain any will pass over. But you shall be called Chevalier, for you are brave.

"It is an emotion, love, the moral implications of which quicken out of time, passing the clouds, to touch the instant of Creation. Love murders the actual. (Reverse the sentence, it's still true, but terrifying.) You must be what you are, always, however, in the hope that what you can be is exactly what you pursue in love; and ideally, of course, you shouldn't be anything but what you should be, a difficulty which the thought itself raises. Loved, nevertheless, you find yourself favored with the greatest of all possibilities for transfiguration, assisted, paradoxically, by what you would attain, but failing that, a kind of devastation few can know. *Cave amantem!* It carries the full weight of your soul with it. Our ideals are our perils. The heart of the loved one is an autoclave in which you have placed your own. Ravens bleed from their eyes during coition.

"Love! Say the word: how the velarized tongue drops, astonished, to the sigh of a moanworthy O that comes from low in the throat and trembles into the frail half-bite that closes on it like a kiss! The word is not spoken, it is intoned, proselytizing both the one who breathes it and the one upon whom it is breathed. What indeed has this to do with mortals? Whose spoor is this tracked so inexorably and so repeatedly toward it—can it be mere man's? What supernatural flame leaps from the darkness of man's soul that it can not only conceive, not only imagine, but somehow attain to such beauty? The philosopher increases in wisdom as he grows old and rots. Oysters are generated in scummy foam, medlars savored only if eaten when decayed, and ambergris is taken from the whale's rectum. Ovid explains that the sweetest Roman cosmetics came from that part of the wool where sheep sweated most. The wolf-spider impairs her womb to furnish the material for its beautiful silk. The worst soil yields the best air. In the slopped and muddied palette of Botticelli patiently sat *The Birth of Venus*. Isn't there a metaphysics in the making here?

"Woman's beauty is the love of a man: they are not two things but one and the same thing, for love is the very shadow of the monument it creates. 'I am to each,' says Love, 'the face of his desire.' Now love creates beauty because love needs beauty—the symbol of this act of worship—and the greater the projected image of one's ideal the greater the glory that settles on the loved one. Love has to do with the comprehension of paragons; it tempts one forward, and that the object of love, in reality, serves only as the point of departure for incomparably greater vision, lambent, beyond our very nature, should come as no surprise, for the nature of the ideal is that it inspires what it isn't. Where it isn't, it suggests to those disposed to it, it can be. The actual desire for love, resident in so many hearts, is in fact only a tiny parody of the emotion it seeks and proves this as it tries to bridge the gap between what we have and what we want, what we are and what we want to become. The beauty that love creates is precisely the ideal it would realize. You receive—not the paradox it seems—what you have given, the colophon of which, perhaps, is best expressed in the matter of sexual congress. The beauty that love creates, the ideal you would realize: this can be the foundation of real union only when *two* people, irrevocably, find and maintain it in the face of all odds, which is principally why so few people successfully fall in love and live in it.

"A love affair, easily, can be doomed the moment it begins, due to a whole series of misconceptions, for of course one believes or wants to believe that the other person is the dream-complement of oneself; but, no, the other person mightn't be—the other person, after all, is only himself or herself. Only the *aspiration* in each to be the dream-complement of the other, effected always by sacrifice (the only way to prove one's love), can establish the basis upon which true love can be structured. The statistical probability of an equal, exactly mutual love existing is arguably next to impossible, and yet if both the conception of and the will to the ideal, as exerted by each with respect to the other, is jointly shared, then love, like death, makes all distinctions void. Real love, to be successful, must move each to each equally, an amphiclexis of souls wherein the giving by one generates, not taking, but a natural impulse by the other to give in return. It has been argued, nevertheless, that the individuals involved may be—and possibly will be, and possibly must be—unequal. All joy worth the name, some say, is in equal love between unequal persons, that the entire disclosure of love, even its necessity, becomes irrelevant when, for instance, equals meet. Real friendship, thought Bacon, is mostly between superior and inferior, where degrees are dissolved, willingly, in the sudden miracle of the emotion. But then what is predictable of this disease that, attacking the heart, the soul, the mind, and the spirit all at once, has no remedy but to love the more? It wants no cad or elf but is a perfect witchcraft of itself, promising nothing less than a new life, giving you the chance to lead another's and to multiply hers by your own.

"We have considered the projection of beauty and the pursuit of the ideal as indivisible. Beauty *in se* is kinetic; the *idea* of beauty is static, however, and to understand the distinctions and differences here is paramount. The only true paradise for us is the paradise we could lose—and the nature of all significant attachment is that, when that bond is broken, we are destroyed to that degree. The state of love, curiously, generates both the fear of such loss and destruction and yet simultaneously creates the only hope to prevent it. The song of love is always a cry for immortality: the permanence we'd have of love is only the perfection we would attain in the completion and utter fulfillment of ourselves and a projection of the idea of beauty. The *idea* of beauty is permanent, while every beautiful thing, every part of nature, such as it is, is perishable. Man has an upright face and advances his countenance toward the stars. Love looks seaward, outward, upward through the eyes of the kind of people in whom wonder never flickers down to a doubt, teaching the soul to dwell not where it lives but where it loves.

"We create what we love as we love what we want to become, our dreams, queerly, acting our temptations, for the higher men can raise their ideals the greater is the reflected glory which they feel at their devotions. Indeed, love, it might be said, is not directed toward beauty but toward the procreation of beauty, creating a *new* woman for man instead of a real woman and for woman a new, not a real, man. It does not solve, it contemplates; it does not examine itself, it awakens. We are reborn, as it were, in the mind of another, a perishable transubstantiated—in substance, not accidents—into an imperishable. This fully unattainable goal of all longing, love, cannot be totally realized in experience, in fact, and much of it must forever remain an idea, immaculate, which is why it is almost always associated with the awakening of the desire for purification and a disposition to inexpressible kindness. The idea forever beckons, tempts, ecstasizes, and the stargazer's toe is often stubbed. Whom the gods wish to render harmless they first afflict with love. A lover is utterly and totally defenseless.

"The strongest pulsation of the will towards the supreme good, directing the true being of man to a state between body and spirit, between the bald senses and the moral nature, between God and the beasts, is the direct result of loving. One can never directly experience the emotion without changing, and thus it comes about that only when they love do many men and women realize the existence of their own personality and of the personality of another, that 'I' and 'thou' become for them more than merely grammatical expressions. The greater a man is, the more he yearns for full identity, extending himself toward the reaches of the immortal where the experience of love, like the sounds of a city heard on the height of a skyscraper, is compressed into a single note. A man truly has just as much arrogance as he lacks self-realization, and true love always ends all arrogance alto-

gether, for the sacrifices it implicitly requires—it requires nothing else
—allow one to 'selve' for another and yet in doing so serve oneself.
Love is centrifugal, hate centripetal. Demons must hilarify as they
watch while we are drawn to someone unable, or unwilling, to love us.
It is easy to be cruel. One need only not love.

"*Caritas, agape, eros, amicitia:* love inspires us in the many ways
it's defined. And yet the whole apparat of formal understanding is foreign to it—in fact, a human being perhaps cannot love another whom
he fully understands or effectively comprehends because the very nature of the ideal discommends the empirical or rationalistic approach
to wisdom through analysis, always a felony in matters of love. (To
comprehend something fully is to be beyond or above it, no?) On the
other hand, one can project and pursue the idea of beauty relentlessly,
intuiting the possibility of it, this constantly renewed endeavor to embody the highest form of value, as a prisoner in the darkness of solitary
confinement might determine the season outside by seining through
the vegetables in his daily soup. And yet while union depends on
duality, the lover who does not seek his own soul in his loved one will
never find his own soul in himself, for the lover is a person whose
quaesitum desperately exists in, and indeed is—*is*—another. A transition beckons.

"Love is not contagious, only the idea of it is. And yet, again, is it
not fabled that for everyone there is someone, that, as in the epistolary
novel—its traditional subject, of course, always being love—we need
but post a letter to receive one, whereupon, then, is issued a sweet and
confident outlay of intimacy that documents the ratio of priority and
subsequence and so leads to the perfect ending we bank on? Who
can't want to believe it? Everybody aspires to fall in love. We look to
see the candidates and find multitudes, multitudes. But the chosen? A
minority. So overpowering is the emotion, however, so mighty the reputation, that it sends back, echoing down its hypostyle, sufficient
echoes of its living renown only for the shouting—and yet to what
good if no one is there to make it real?

"The mere postulate of love creates in its mythopoetic wake a
throng of pursuivants whose desire for it, if going no further, only par-
odies what lies tragically beyond its grasp. And yet how the world,
perversely to encourage our hopes that way, seeks to oblige us with its
suddenty and slubbering-over-with-whitewash conceits—the magic of
mood and music—that we all might upon an instant wake to find not

illusion but rather our heart's desire in the form of Venus Mandrag-
oritis holding out a love-apple. Look! There assembles a host of
would-be lovers and laplings who, seeing Cupid in a jar-owl and
sweetness in a colicinth, would have it gospel that one man's yawn
makes another yawn, one man's pissing makes another piss! They
fashion fancies and pull impressible faces and, smugging themselves up
in pomade and passion-flowers, step out into the moonlight poets write
of to project their disposition to desire upon another, as rich in the
confusion of intent as that person who judges a party a success because
he himself has been charming. There may be music with imposing
lyrics, wine, the tuition of promises. But then where is love? Make it.
But is it love? Fake it. But is not this a lip and that a lip? And can she
not shape her elbow to my arm? *O curas Chymicorum! O cuantum in
pulvere inane!* Faults are thick where love is thin. The sting of the
reproach is the truth of it.

"The passion of love is like a parable, by which men, often, still
mean something else. It is a step away from reality, conceived, among
other things, to improbabilize low aims and soar into a participation
with whatever divinity presents itself. The lover, however, is a person
never unaware of the frightful dualism of nature and spirit; desire,
characteristically, partakes of the former, love of the latter—and with
that recognition the morality play of Mutability and Constancy per-
forms a dress rehearsal in your head. Consider love and desire: are
they often not perfectly antagonistic? Man projects his soul onto
woman and she onto him with this hope, always, that the beauty of
bodily image embodies morality, only one of the variations of expectation having to do with love.

"But the kinesis of beauty (as opposed to the stasis of the idea of
beauty)—*res aptus studendo*—is, indeed, often nothing but a blocking
agent to the continuity of love, annulling it by either change or alteration. It is this that so often surprises and saddens a lover when it is
revealed that beauty does not necessarily imply morality in the object
of love; one, in fact, often feels that the nature of the offense is actually increased by the conjunction of beauty and depravity, unaware,
perhaps, that up to that time the woman in question only seemed
beautiful to him because he still loved her. All aesthetics are created by
ethics; and beauty, more often than not, is a bodily image in which
morality is archetypally felt to be represented. The less transcendental
the beauty is, the less permanent we are usually convinced it will be, in

direct proportion, for our faith resides here, that we love what we esteem, a usufruct of heaven beckoning us to the bettermost, and so to preserve in spirit what we've captured in nature it often falls out that love and desire are sometimes two unalike, mutually exclusive conditions. If love, for instance, is only true, as has been written, in proportion as it is pure, what then is the ideal?

"Thumb your histories. Xenocrates, passing nights with Lais of Corinth, never touched her. Socrates, who doted on Alcibiades, sent him away precisely at a moment when the opportunity to lie with him presented itself. And Petrarch, sempiternally burning for his Laura, did not take her to himself when she was offered to him and, even losing her, somehow possessed her more. If it be the case that there is no adoration utterly free from desire there is no reason why the two should be identified. What, in fact, are realities worth compared to the mirages we would know? Shall the true lover be satisfied to comprehend his intoxication only by sensation? The very rapture of one's love, surely, no longer limits him only to earth. 'Reality,' it's been written, 'is the only word in the language that has no meaning without quotation marks.'

"Have you then understood me to say to love only in the mind? I summon a thousand angels to disprove such a thing, charging you to love with your hands, your heart, your paper and poems, whistles and whispers, the light of your soul, its pathetical prayers, and the candle that sits in your head pointing its flames toward the goblin perched over your head called night. O, illustrious Trismegist, you who love, you *yourself* are the very miracle you seek to keep! You have been given the gift of love!

"Go and love! The exhortation must be shouted in twos, else for you shall the world be dark as Lycophron. Lovers, you move toward the completion thankfully never complete. You are the denial of denials. You would do all and dare outdo what, done, deems yet more to do. You would practice months of refusals and scoff in the teeth of exhaustion but to comfort her! You would, like Alexander, burn to the ground the entire city of Persepolis if it stood in the way of your love! You would pull down an entire sky only to present her with a supply of calliblepharies for her eyes! You would tremble in the night at the sound of far-off bells, fearing the merest implication of new events and change, for you have been given the gift of love. You would heal the pottage of Gilgal, suck up the Nile at a single haust yet still cry out for

thirst, and watch through tempests of provocation to see it snow eryn-
goes and shower down the sun! You would willingly die tomorrow
only that she might kill you with her own hands! You would be
drugged with Spanish licorice and let your bones be used for hell-dice
only to look into her eyes and see yourself reflected there! For you
have been given the gift of love!

"Proud would you be her phaeton, her gig, her shoe-latchet
snapped shut to walk her safely in the fittest steps toward paradise, to
the snows of Monte Rosa, to the heights of Horeb where each dream
dreamt is only yet another dream dreamt among dreams. You have
been given the gift of love. You believe it only when you realize it, and
yet at that very stroke you cannot but have removed its momentous secret far beyond the hollow formulae, abstract terms, and words such
as these that since the beginning of time have stammered after it, pitifully, in the desolation of vain human syllables."

XXXIX

The Cardinal's Crotchet

The lioness had torn some flesh away,
Which all this while had bled.

—WILLIAM SHAKESPEARE, *As You Like It*

DARCONVILLE that afternoon took the essay to Dr. Dodypol's house and turned by Fitts on his way back: Isabel, apparently, had gone to Charlottesville for the weekend. And so he returned to his rooms and, with nothing else to do, began sorting through his trunk. He found something at the bottom he'd long forgotten he'd put there: an old book.

It was a rectangular folio—soiled, plates missing, bisected at the spine—whose tight biscuity signatures and stiff pages, each a *pointillisme* of brown spotting, could hardly be turned, and the lower corner of each recto was polished to yellow horn from its many long-ago encounters with curious and inquisitive thumbs. A page was turned to a symphony of crepitations. It was a relic of the sixteenth century, something of a gradus then, but handed down through the centuries it bore, increasingly, the characteristic of a strange little joke within the family. What value, then, if any, might be assigned it? The question, somehow, always posed itself to Darconville on those few occasions when he'd ever bothered to look at it. What value? Historical, at least, he thought.

He puffed dust from the cover and smoothed his hand down the buckled vellum. He marveled at it. The book had been indited in the Year of Our Lord 1574 by that common ancestor of the illustrious "writing d'Arconvilles,"* the learned grammaticus and saintly but uncompromisingly tough old mumblecrust—whose blessed memory we recall, annually, in the glorious martyrology of the Church—named Pierre Christophe Cardinal Théroux-d'Arconville (1532–1601).

Born in Rouen, he entered the priesthood and, distinguishing himself in canon law at a quite young age, was raised to the cardinalate at thirty-three. An age of apostasy had set in. It was decided, so legend went, that he be sent with speed to England—so horribly crowtrodden

---

*Dame Marie Geneviève Charlotte d'Arlus Théroux-d'Arconville (1720–1805), author of *Vie de Marie de Médicis, princesse de Toscane, reine de France et de Navarre* (1774); *Des Passions* (1764); *Discours sur l'amour propre* (1770) and many notable others. The first French translator of Chaucer, Prior, and Pope, she also acted in a theatrical production of *Mérope*, directed by Voltaire himself. Jean Thiroux (1691–1740?) in his *Gallia Christiana in Provincias Ecclesiasticus Distributa* (1715) documented current monastic studies at that time. Louis Théroux de Crosne d'Arconville (1736–1789), lieutenant general of the Paris constabulary, wrote the classic monograph, still in use, called "Les Interprétations criminelles des oreilles" before losing his life to the Jacobins and their despicable peasant revolt. ("*Après la prise de la Bastille, il se démit de sa charge entre les mains de Bailly le 16 juil. 1789*," *La Grande Encyclopédie, trente et unième,* Paris.) Charles Victor Théroux-d'Arconville (1803–1862), captain of artillery and theoretical militarist at the École Militaire de Saint-Cyr, attacked in his polemic *La Flotte marchande* (1853), for abuses, all the parasitical birds-in-hand of the merchant marine who, educated at government expense, greedily sought to acquire private fortunes in civilian life in lieu of military service. It will be here pointed out, in discommendation of any such charge, that none of the above writers falls into the strict category of the professional, a vulgar correption to which true nobility need not, and must never, submit, especially those through whose veins pounds the blood of the heroic Valois.

there was the ancient faith—where, even before his arrival, a clandestine one (as nuncios from a hundred sees were being slain in their innocence on the very shores), he had become simply from reputation the scourge of several pernicious Tudors and more than one profligate, not to say schismatic, court, the most significant, for our record, being that of the mongrel queen, Elizabeth I, the essential tenet of whose religion proved to be little more than prestidigitation.

The facts are scant. It is known, however, that Cardinal Thérouxd'Arconville had at one period secretly worked with the holy pamphleteer, Robert Southwell, and had personally seen to the welfare of both the Jesuits, Campion and Parsons, upon their arrival in England in 1581. It was a dangerous time for Catholics. It was perfectly murderous for priests. Great bonfires, fed with roods, pyxes, and sacred images, were burning in the streets, and execrations were being heaped upon the names of those guilty of no crime but that of showing fidelity to what had been honored in England for a thousand years. The Grey Friars of Greenwich, the Black Friars of Smithfield, the priests and nuns of Syon and the Charterhouse, the abbot and monks of Westminster, all were deposed, and, with their sees confiscated, countless holy bishops—Watson of Lincoln, Thirlby of Ely, Bonner of London, Bourne of Bath and Wells, Turberville of Exeter, Scott of Chester, Pate of Worcester, Heath of York, and many loyal others—were thrown headlong into prison (most of them never to be delivered) so that Elizabeth, with her overriding ambition and underriding conscience, and all the exoletes, dunces, procumbents, and unpalteringly ugly bagmen she called her councillors could begin to carry out their scheme of relieving the emptiness of the Exchequer.

The cause of Catholicism in that lapsed country, of course, had long been closely bound up with the claim of Mary Queen of Scots to the English throne. If the illegitimacy of Elizabeth were granted—and there was no doubt whatsoever of that—Mary, as the granddaughter of Margaret Tudor, was the lawful sovereign. Consequently, the cardinal soon became a vigorous, but secret, friend of the Duke of Norfolk, whom he sought personally to wed to Mary, hoping that with the support of Spain and such prominent English Catholics as the Earl of Northumberland; the Throckmortons; the Stourtons; the Berkeleys; the Arundells; the Scropes; the Vauxes of Harrowden; and the deposed Suffragan Bishop of Hull, Robert Purseglove (who sheltered the cardinal for several years), he might restore the country to the

Mother Church, but then, with the uncovering of the Ridolfi plot by Burghley in 1571, Norfolk in due course was brought to the block, and Cardinal Théroux-d'Arconville was thereupon hunted throughout the country like a dog.

We hear of him wandering, starved and exhausted, through Yorkshire, Herefordshire, and Chester, which probably had the largest aggregation of ardent Catholics within the realm, and then, shortly after the harsh enactments of Elizabeth's sixth Parliament of 1586–1587, finally being captured in Lancashire, "the very sincke of Poperie," and sent with other recusants to the gloomy dungeon in the castle of Wisbeach on the Isle of Ely. The charges were clear: civil disobedience, disobedience to the statutes of Parliament regulating public worship, and deliberately undermining the Protestant orientation of the realm, the penalty for which was death.

One need go no further than the nearest non-sectarian history to read the facts of his brutal execution, the direct order for which was given by that stork-faced malphoebe, Betsy the Bawd, she of the thousand fright wigs, who—with a drop of the cruel blood of the Visconti in her veins—found nevertheless her hysterical proscriptions could do everything, apparently, but curb truth. She could stint the victuals of her hard-fighting soldiers. She could shop up in the Tower her caracoling courtiers. She could bumfondle any lackey in sight, sink her black teeth into thousand-year-old dogmas, and hound holy priests into ignominy, exile, and death. But she would never kill the spirit of one noble cardinal, who, although his pen was wrested from his hand and his tongue silenced, nevertheless glorified God and edified the Church by patient suffering and invincible constancy as the opponent of heresy and schism. His name will ever be in benediction in the Catholic Church in England as one of the last and not degenerate successors of St. Hugh and St. George.

Apologists, generally, believe Cardinal Théroux-d'Arconville to have written a good deal more than the two works of his extant, the less famous one—for which in his fifty-seventh year the then Holy Father, Sixtus V, presented him the cross of the Order of the Holy Spur with a diploma and patent bearing the great pontifical seal and declaring him in his quality of doctor of laws *pronotarius apostolicus extra urbem*—the exact but brief animadversion in flawless Latin, dated 1584, in defense of the assassination of that goofball in the orange helmet, mouthy William the Silent of Dutchland. The by-far-greater work, one rare copy of which Darconville now perused, was the uncompromisingly frank propaedeutics he had written, in English, for the students of the school he had secretly re-established at the plundered monastery at Wednesbury.

This book was called *The Shakeing of the Sheets: A Yare Treatise on yᵉ Englissh Tongue and Sage Counsel on Clinches, Flashes, Whimzies, and Prick-Songs with Regards to Stile; or, Put Not More Inke on thy Paper Than Thou Hast Brains in thy Head.* It was now witty, now rather heavily doctrinal, showing the rhetorical power of Gorgias but, often, the herpetical glower of the Gorgon. And how so? Its advice as to how to achieve an understanding of, and a respect for, language was indeed formidable—yes, and this was commendable—for the old cardinal saw, wisely, that correctness in language was the foundation of clear thinking, that clear thinking would lead to right reason, and that right reason would not only shed light on the quidditive perfections of Catholic dogma, proving the inexorability of the Roman persuasion, but also that, for once and all, it would put paid to all the lies and willful deceptions of the faithless clerical secundigravidicals thereabouts with long faces and square hats who, though living in England, were breathing the air of Geneva and Wittenberg.

Sitting there, turning the pages, Darconville nevertheless found one particular aspect of the treatise disagreeable—its misogyny. That bias rose like a poison fume from almost every paragraph, and Darconville, who, even in his early teens, had been somewhat scandalized the first time he read it, was no less so now—and, possibly for being in love, more. How, he wondered, could *anyone* hate women? What, he thought, had the contrivances of that nail-spitting abishag called the Virgin Queen wrought in this poor priest? And yet in spite of that what validity value could ever be given to such an unfair, out-of-hand denunciation of the most beautiful half of the human race? The fault was not larger than the fault was fine—but nevertheless a fault. It was foolish and sad, long having been the cause of Darconville's keeping silence, sensitively, on both the subject and the saint.

Darconville knew from his heart what to reject in the book, shut his thumb on a page, and then put it away, glad at bottom not only that no one ever bothered to read it nowadays but that no one had ever even heard of it anymore.

XL

Oudemian Street

We do not feel terror because we are threatened by the Gorgon;
we dream of the Gorgon in order to explain the terror we feel.

—Jorge Luis Borges

DARCONVILLE, meanwhile, was living solitary as a waldgrave. His
days seemed as empty as the window frame he often paused before,
staring out, intermittently, for almost two weeks now. Isabel seemed to
have vanished. Hopeful, he had waited for her to come, initially to
have it explained to him why she'd dropped out of his life, but then
simply to have her with him again, a secret, if not divulged, that at
least should have been understood. He either slept too much or stayed
awake too long, listening for the slightest noise and smoking, so much,
in fact, that when smoking one cigarette it became a strange source of
misery to him that he wasn't smoking another.

It seemed almost diabolical, her never appearing. *Oh, I know,* he thought, *you're going to leave me*—but he dared not laugh at the irony. God might misunderstand it.

One more day passed, then two again, and another. Darconville claimed to himself in the mirror that he was being haunted by a succubus who crept into his bed every night and that, though he flogged her, it was his own body every morning found full of welts, but the unshaven face in the mirror, showing havoc and rueful lines, spoke back to him: "A true lover doesn't mind being disappointed. But he cannot bear the thought of his loved one being disappointed, and it frustrates him beyond all else, for disappointment, worse than mere complaint, is blackmail." Spellvexit, who despised philosophy, showed an utter disregard for Darconville's neautontimoroumenotic pain and preferred to stay outside clacking his teeth at birds until all this blew over.

It was time to do something: graduation week, Darconville realized, meant time was running out. But the telephone calls were all the same: seven numbers dialed, a slight quietus in the swallowing phone, several expectant rings, and then the apology of each correspondent— pal, protectress, prothonotary of the Queen's bench—whereupon, opening the door of that close booth at the Timberlake, Darconville held out the receiver at arm's length, deliberating what to do and letting whatever little impotent voice it was squeak on and on. Forfex, commander of thirty legions of devils, had become a ventriloquist. The conspiracy seemed school-wide. It was a concert of deceit.

The alternative was search-and-seizure. Classes at Quinsy College, excluding those for seniors, were still in session, and Darconville hoped that, rather than be found waiting for her at some door, he might meet her in a casual encounter. He roamed out by the hockey and archery fields, looked into the old tennis courts, and then walked out along, and then back by, "The Reproaches." He stepped into the art building and went upstairs where in one classroom six narcoleptics, fast asleep on their notebooks, were missing the pointer-to-board lecture of Floyce R. Fulwider:

"This [tap] is a pot-walloper of the Flemish rubricator who called himself Pieter De Hooch, the grandfather of American gin. For his dates you'll want 1629 and 1677. You may or may not be disheartened to know that he wanted nothing heroic [tap] in his art. His dry, domestic, explicit-as-arithmetic masterpukes [tap] tend nevertheless to narrative.

Now let us look at this bit of scrumpy [tap]: *Courtyard of a Dutch House.* Notice the light archway with a woman in shadows staring off? Where is she facing? And why? The shading here is . . ."

Darconville left the building and crossed over to the music building. He checked all the piano rooms: nothing. The auditorium was locked. He wandered over to Smethwick, going floor to floor, aisle to aisle, and found no one but two girls, upstairs, flipping through old *Bride's* magazines and Miss Pouce, down in her office, pasting a concealing strip of paper over two blasphemous lines in the fourth stanza of *Atalanta in Corydon.* Where could she be? He cut across the street to the English building—opening doors, closing doors—and went through the history department to the Rotunda and then down to the dining hall. She was nowhere in sight. He was outside again, on the run now back around the ring-road by Gund and Truesleeve, heading toward the high-rise dorms which led, past the woods, toward the cemetery where in certain moods that had become all too characteristic of what in her frightened him Isabel was wont to go, to read, to think. But he saw only the memory of himself rising up creepily, slowly, from behind a gravestone with a gleam in his impish eyes—but this time of ridicule.

The seniors, during these days of grace, were sunbathing on dormitory steps, by the student union, across almost every lawn that Darconville crossed. They sprawled about in the sunshine like delicious confections in a sweetshop: tarts in wicked shorts; cupcakes in halters and cut-away jeans; and turnovers in swirl skirts up to the hips and brief shirts without so much as the hint of a bra. The main topic of conversation, of course, was the graduation dance to be held that night. It was *the* social event of the year.

"I'm about to blow up from excitement," exclaimed Tracy Upjohn.

"Me too," squeaked Berthalene Rhodie, catching her hands.

"Forget the dance," said "Pookie" Pumpgarten, rising an inch to unpinch her shorts grown moist from the dewy grass. She winked at Mehitabel Huntoon and Betty Ann Unglaub. "It's what's for *later!*"

"Well, it just dreads me to death," confessed Shirley Newbegin, unchambering a mouthful of bobby-pins and twirling out a set of pink, snailshaped rollers—"spoolies"—from her hair. Her fears, not to the dance, were rather being addressed to arrangements then being made for a midnight party at the Bide-A-Wee Motel.

"Dean Barathrum will shit feathers," said Shrimpie DeVein.

"Hush your mouth!" shouted Harriet Bowdler, prick-me-dainty and whilom Sunday-school teacher at the Wyanoid Baptist Church. Harriet's, alas, wasn't a lucky life: she had trout's eyes, a bad case of pimples, and an unfortunate walk—she toed in—which the girls constantly mimicked.

"O turn blue, Bowdler," muttered Divinity Jones, slipping on her sunglasses. "You want a little damn confidence is what you want."

"Exactly. Like this girl here," said Quandra Tour, who snapped back a page in the book she was reading and declaimed for everyone:

" '—to receive his instructions in psalmody was Katrina Van Tassel, the daughter and only child of a substantial Dutch farmer. She was a blooming lass of fresh eighteen; plump as a partridge; ripe and melting and rosy-cheeked as one of her father's peaches; and universally famed, not merely for her beauty but her vast expectations. She was, withal, a little of a coquette—' "

" 'Vast expectations'?" repeated Harriet Bowdler. "I believe that's dirty."

Everybody groaned.

"It means she's on the lookout for boys, for cry-eye," said Gerda Bean, "nothin' else."

Harriet, near tears, explained. " 'She was with all,' it says. You heard it, same as me."

"O, put a sock in it!" snapped Cookie Crumpacker.

"Confidence, that's all he means," said Quandra Tour, shrugging. She turned to the twins, Scarlett and Melanie Longstreet. "It's symbolism."

"Who means?"

Quandra Tour jerked the book to the opening page and showed Mehitabel Huntoon. The frontispiece pictured a man resting his cheek, authorially, on two fingers. "Irving," she replied. "One of America's greatest authors."

"Sounds like a little ol' jewboy to me," said Divinity Jones, cracking her gum.

Ravissa Deadlow, lying face down on a towel, muttered into her armpit, "And she sounds like a fat little *bitch* to me."

"With a whole lot of boyfriends," said Quandra Tour, tapping the page with a little plic-plac of authority, "so don't knock it."

"I want to *get* knocked," giggled Tracy Upjohn, reaching out insatiably with both hands and salaciously wadgeting the tips of her fingers in a charade of manic intemperance.

"An evening of sex!" screeched Betty Ann Unglaub.

"Kissy-poo! Huggy-poo! And—"

Harriet Bowdler, wincing, had her ears plugged.

"You name it," cried Cookie Crumpacker, joyfully shaking her moon-shaped earrings and proudly adjusting the maroon-striped jersey she wore to punctuate the comment, twice, with what natural increments were hers. "And if I die tonight, hey," she added with twinkling eyes, "they'll have to bury me in a Y-shaped coffin!"

The day was glorious, with honeysuckle dangling about in festoons, the syringas thickets of sweets, all perfuming the sunshine that elevated moods all over campus and increased the general excitement. The girls were all making careful preparations to look spontaneously beautiful, sampling scents, swapping pearls and purses, and chinning up to the shimmering rays as their skin turned from the airiest, fairiest tones of straw to the awfulest, tawniest fawns. The dance mattered deeply to the girls. No detail was too small to hold their interest, no project too large for them to entertain—and both, the detailed project and the interest they entertained, were keenly seen to by no less an *arbiter elegantiae* than Hypsipyle Poore who, though not now among the group, with slow love from her room looked at the scattered colors of the afternoon, pleased to lose herself in those intricate dreams of hers where desire and possession somehow became one. Hypsipyle exacted the very kind of personal adoration and attendance-dancing from her following that Isabel missed. She lived raptly in a play-world and could find romantic adventure every time she walked down the street. She softly taught her coterie the art of making drama from the most ordinary everyday events, and so with indescribable delectation her girls generally kept mental trysts, had revelations and premonitions, saw miracles flowering under their very eyes, and, ready to find mystic excitement in the most casual occurrence, always looked for magic in a mood. The motel idea was Hypsipyle's, and each of the four years she'd organized it. And so plans were afoot.

"What, you just register—for the *night?*"

"I haven't a clue."

"It's a no-tell motel."

"And what about Miss Dessicquint, huh? Huh?" asked sitting-up-correctly Harriet Bowdler, chastely buttoned up in spite of the sun in her school blazer of sober watchet which displayed on one pocket the disc of the college insignia. "What about her?"

"She can go suck a blanket!" said Gerda Bean.

"And stop squinchin' your eyes all up," said Ravissa Deadlow. "You do manage to get all bitey, Bowdler, don't you?"

"*I* manage to get all bitey?" Harriet Bowdler wailed. "You do, *you* manage to get all bitey!" She looked about her for support. Calmly, Ravissa Deadlow openhandedly appealed to the same group, asking everybody who in fact was the one who got all bitey? *"You get bitey!"* everyone screamed at Harriet, who burst into tears.

Berthalene Rhodie, meanwhile, was wondering if the authorities would *let* them all take rooms, offering for consideration the trouble they'd had in previous years when the townies and the boys from Hampden-Sydney College, all shoe-mouth deep in liquor, spent the night banging doors and running around the premises like whistlehogs.

The twins, Scarlett and Melanie Longstreet, agreed.

"Remember last year? Bambi Bargewell's boyfriend got himself all yopped up with bourbon," said Melanie, putting by her sun reflector, "and then flingin' free as you please into one of them cabins went and daddied her baby right there on the pile carpet."

Shrimpie DeVein gasped happily.

"I saw her all pooched up in Thalhimer's last fall," added Scarlett, rubbing an antbite on her calf with her left instep, "buyin' kimbies."

"While he ups and goes into the navy."

"I don't care," said Tracy Upjohn, "I'm for the Bidey-Bi!"

"Ditto," said Mehitabel Huntoon, with fluoroscopic eyes.

"Off the wall!" hooted Betty Ann Unglaub.

Shirley Newbegin, converted, carefully tied a fascinator over springing curls. Everybody looked at Harriet Bowdler. Was all settled? No, not yet, not quite.

"And if Quinsy revokes your degree, *then?*" asked the outraged girl whose hippocrepiform legs—to assure the position of sagacious fakir— she crossed with difficulty. *"Then?"*

"Why, then, I'll tell them to twist my diploma into a cone, Harriet dear," pronounced "Pookie" Pumpgarten, her arm falling languidly over her eyes against the glare of the sun, "and shove it where the moon don't shine."

"My *life!*" said Harriet Bowdler.

In the meantime, Darconville was having no success. From the

cemetery he went over to the Piggly Wiggly, bought some cigarettes—
he was smoking himself into a state of near etiolation—and returned
to campus by way of a gate that led to the indoor swimming pool. The
empty pool smelled like an empty terrarium. He cut through a corridor with the gnome Umbriel astride his back repairing to search the
gloomy cave of spleen that was the gym. It was also empty. He called
out, "Isabel?" The echo called out again. Nothing.

The laboratories were next. Classes in that building, however, had
been dismissed for the day, and the late afternoon rooms were
tomblike, the silence broken only by the hysterical coughing in the
main corridor of some blue-in-the-face squidgereen—all doubled-up
and being thumped on the back by clappermaclawed Miss Porchmouth—who had half-wittedly suctioned up through a retort, and
swallowed, a half-litre of phenolphthalein solution. The anthropology
department—where Mr. Bischthumb's classroom (they had not re-
hired) was commemoratively kept empty—showed the same end-of-
the-year inactivity, except for one particular classroom where some
swivel-chair tactician or other, back to view, was winding down a lecture on virvestitism in the Benelux countries to five girls: three fast
asleep, one, gongoozled by boredom, refrogging a silver chain, and the
last, in the front row, was the student body president, Xystine Chappelle, upholstering her 4.0 grade point average—and she was au-
diting.

Out a side door, across the mall, and Darconville was in the social
sciences building. He took the stairs three-at-a-go to the first, the second, the third floor and paused, searching faces, at a classroom where
a group of girls sat in the semi-darkness watching one of Dr. Knipperdoling's gripping geographical filmstrips; the pictures flashed to a
recorded voice:

"—Faletua Uliuli is still, of course, a poor Samoan village by our own
standards. The daub-and-wattle hut here has served them for centuries.
[beep] Irrigation methods, as used by their fathers and forefathers,
were far too primitive to keep up with modern production. Not so, now,
with the recently introduced flutter-wheel. [beep] American advisers, ex-
perimenting, have saved them an untold number of good harvests this
way which is why, when revisiting, these men are invariably greeted by
smiling peasants bearing armfuls of taro root. [beep] Miracles abound
here now. The great crane you see here scooping up earth can do the
work of fifty men. Pride and self-reliance have been restored. [beep] You

can witness the results on the face of young Emilio here who is just learning to work with leather—to grow up a useful and happy citizen in his own country, a proud people, in a strange land, far away."

The lights came up to long stretches and gulping yawns, and Darconville, peering skygodlin through the door window, searched intently from face to face as if he were candling eggs. He saw nothing—and no one—of consequence, left, and returned to the main building. It was getting late.

In the long lecture hall there some forty or so students, Darconville noticed, were slaving away on their final exam in American history under the eviscerating stare of peripatetic Mrs. DeCrow who, in expert fashion, managed not only to survey them all but monitor each at intervals of sudden command: "Eyes front, people!" "Sit around, Miss Nosy!" "Who in the second row in the white blouse wants her testpaper torn up?" Craning his neck under the half-pulled shade, Darconville saw no Isabel—only the shade snapped up and Mrs. DeCrow disgustedly glaring out. A turn by the registrar's office was equally futile: no Isabel Rawsthorne—only ubiquitous Hypsipyle Poore, there to badger Mrs. McAwaddle for an extended curfew that night, suddenly turning to him with pursed lips and an acknowledgement, effected from the knee, by a dipsy-doodling of her index finger. Dark Angel, ever on the wing, who never reaches me too late, thought Darconville. He dragged himself downstairs.

At the English department office, he asked the secretary if any messages had been left for him. There were none. He slipped into an empty classroom next door to gather his thoughts, his eye randomly falling on a map of Europe on the wall: he fixed Venice. Will I ever go back there, he wondered, and will I return with more vices than I went forth with pence? How remote those days were! The dreams he had had! The attempts in mind to travel *aux anges!* Was that perhaps a fault, the famous fall that infamous pride goes before? Original Sin, perhaps, was related not so much to the feeling that we must die but rather that we feel we can live too majestically. And what of the *via negativa* he had once chosen? Poustinia? The Empty Quarter? The subtle distinguo between loneliness and solitude? The remorse he began to feel came to suggest he hold himself back, purposely aloof from everything of implication, at bay in a lifelong quarantine of imagination —coopted by some unimposing anti-fate neither to write nor live but, chastened of all impulse, simply to stop. Nevertheless, he felt resources which buoyed him up in bewilderment. I could give her up, he felt, if necessary. But I love her, he thought, I love her so much.

Across the way, Darconville suddenly heard a recitation in progress. He leaned forward, looking, to find Miss Sally Bull Sweetshrub's four o'clock class—*Great Southern Writers*—now under way. With her eyeglasses low on her nose, she was giving a passionate rendition of Maria J. McIntosh's poem, "Frown Not," as a consolatory prelude to the final exam the girls were about to take. He went to check the class —Isabel, who should have been among that number, wasn't—but, before he left, sidestepping glum Howlet, who sat doggo by the door, took up a mimeographed copy of the exam from a stack of them on a chair outside. He read the following:

Great Southern Writers

(1.) Confute the charge that Almira Lincoln Phelps's "Southern Housekeepers" is narrowly regionalistic. (Be careful. Be honest.)

(2.) Develop my view that Emma D. E. N. Southworth's *Sybil Brotherton, or The Temptation* is "the most perfect plot in the American novel." (Illustrate by example.)

(3.) Identify: a. Samuel Minturn Peck
          b. Henry Lynden Flash
          c. Mirabeau Buonaparte Lamar
          d. Sallie Ada Reedy
          e. Stringfellow Barr
N. B. Hard part: which of the five is greatest?

(4.) How is Henry Timrod's brilliant poem *Ethnogenesis* in the same epic tradition as Milton's *Paradise Lost?*

(5.) I prefer a) Caroline Lee Hentz's "Aunt Patty's Scrap-Bag"; b) Rosa Vertner Johnson's *Hasheesh Visions;* c) Sally Bull Sweetshrub's *The Big Regret;* or d) Una Altera Hint's *The Black Duchess.* Dissertate amply.

(6.) Write a cogent essay (using only one side of the paper *please*) discounting the efforts of Mr. William Faulkner as contrasted to Jane T. H. Cross's *Wayside Flowerets;* Anna Peyre Dinnies' *Wedded Love;* and the prose-pieces of fascinating Octavia Walton LeVert, the "sweet rose of Florida."

(7.) Anna Cora Mowatt Ritchie's "Armand's Love" is/is not in the cavalier tradition. Why? Why not?

(8.) Compare and Contrast: Mary Windle and John Banister Tabb; Eleanor Percy Lee and St. George Tucker; William Byrd of Westover and Edward Coote Pinckney. How discouraged would you be to hear that they were all, at one time or another, tempted to rip up their manuscripts?

Name

Pledge

I am both low and down South, a redundancy, thought Darconville, if a poetic turn of phrase. South is down, isn't it? South *means* down. He shaped the exam sheet into a tiny futuristic airship and launched it, somewhere, on the breath that was the exhalation of his disgust—and walked dolefully up to his office.

"She's not good enough for you, sir."

Darconville, surprised, turned to see a figure step out of a shadow. It was Winnie Pegue, an overweight sophomore whom he had known for an F in his novel course the previous semester. She had hair both the shape and color of dulse and chubby legs, now quakebuttocking under her as she moved forward.

"I can imagine how it feels to be deserted," said Winnie Pegue, the words rushing out as if memorized. She stood before him, a little *mont-de-piété* nervously hugging her buldering armpits and perspiring frightfully. Then she asked him if he thought she had any right, being as she was nothing, to ask him if he had any right, seeing he was everything, to throw it all away. Staring at her saddle shoes, she snuffled up a sob and said, "If I were you, sir, I'd forget her. You're— you're too good for her, for *anybody!*" She scooped her handbag further up her arm and broke down completely. "All life," she wept, "all life is ahead of you! The sun, the stars—!" She couldn't go on for the tears, however, and, turning, flew pigeon-toed down the corridor, around the corner, and out of sight.

Philosophy major, thought Darconville.

He shut the office door. He sat down at his desk. A fact couldn't be ignored: he had been for some time now looking for signs—revelations, of a sort—to determine what direction he should take in the coming year. Perhaps, now, a sign had come. Or symptoms of a sign. He loved a girl much younger than he, for one thing, and what could one really expect of it? Obscure gestes, lost love, short commons in the midst of plenty. He had been jealous, intemperate, weak of faith, and,

suffering both in action and consequence, unproductive—doing everything but what, in fact, he'd come there for. That was the truth of the
thing, for sure, suiting the word to action, not action to the word.
Goodnight, sweet print.

And then what of Isabel? Was it one and the other? Or one in the
other? Was it one for, through, or against the other? *Against?* Was it
possible?

Darconville looked up on the office wall to see his favorite photograph of her. It was technically one of the poorest, a large black-and-
white blowup of her head and shoulders, the brown seeksorrow eyes,
the hair like clarified honey pulled back to a beautiful knot, and the
gentle mouth, almost happy, yet not quite ripening into a smile. (No
photograph ever quite caught her: each of the many taken spoke of
the one that got away—with El Dorado, maddeningly, waiting just
outside every frame.) He loved this one photograph, however. It had
absorbed more vows than he thought admissible to admit, and yet he
felt absolved, for he had come to believe, under that head, that he
couldn't live without her *morally,* that her faults, in fact, were both
what he himself must personally overcome for his *own* benefit and yet
not overcome at the risk of damnation. Almost literally, he was she.

What Chrysostom could explain, what Cassiodorus write, the story
of this love? It began, simply, with diffidence, followed by sudden devotion, and then the thought that he might ruin her life if he left her,
a pressure she transmitted by implying that his life might be ruined if
she stayed, for in the intensity of their deepening love the sweet confessions left unspoken were too often interpreted as hesitation and doubt.
She seemed to believe that passion overstated the love she didn't, for
some reason, deserve, while he believed her loving soul needed what
he could only give insufficiently. What, wondered Darconville, what if
he *had* held back? What if in dreaming we have actually entered another world, daring to commit all but our consciousness? Why, journeys and dreams went together like two people very much in love.

Overcome with weariness, Darconville laid his head on his folded
arms and shut his eyes. I love her, he thought, and yet I want to
leave: a plural I and a single gloom. Or was the gloom merely a plural I? Whatever, two antagonistic Darconvilles, smitten to death, had
fallen desperately in love with her. Duples imply choice. He was dou-
ble-damned. Park your *ka,* Egyptian. Yes, he thought: the possible
that did not become reality was impossible. No, he thought: it was

possible. *Cumaea Sibylla horrendas canit:* nothing which will not be in reality is possible. Let the ambiguity stand, concluded Darconville in a last sleepy reflection, for in the dungeon of our dreams images embody the sensations they can also cause.

He was soon fast asleep, when beating forward through the darkness to the front of his mind came the poisonous archlucifer, Satan himself, who, ready to kill what he wouldn't yet devour, squatted down by his ear like a foul gryllus and whispered:

"I am Gog's ghost, come alive, to pipe to you! Here, would you see it? My porphyritic hoof? I rode up in a dogboat now to boot your god. I pun to amuse you, poet. Pay attention to me! I talk unlike you want to hear, upsidedown and backwards, with a nice repetition of G's—the hump in them is the hump in your gunzel: tumorous, a gold cancer, the load you bear on your back. Isabel! There she is! Mistress Gummigutt! I know you are ashamed to feel this way about someone you love, but, look, the girl's legs are a proximate occasion of sin to a cannibal! And that's your ideal? Laugh with me at her, can't you? Yaw, yaw. No, with more conviction! O, how I hate her, her mammoth legs, her vanity about her hair which she has either just washed or is about to. I hate the back of her head as she rides in your car with her collar turned up. She eats a lot: snacks. She doesn't know whether her arsehole is punched or bored. She weeps in the most unconvincing way I've ever seen. She repeats what you say and rarely offers anything to a conversation. Your ideal? I hear you call an ideal what I take to be a personified inconceivability. A galeopsis is nothing but a thing with a cat's face! But, soft, she troops by with her mother! Parnels march by two and three saying, Sweetheart, come with me! Pay attention to me, or you shall not see all I see! I love you, Mahershalal-hash-baz. Too partial a piece of piety? I love you but I pity you, for is it not written: 'Before the child shall have knowledge to cry "My father and my mother," the riches of Damascus and the spoil of Samaria shall be taken away'? I will remind you of poetry if you let me, I promise. Not so she. She takes too much humoring and requires more attention than a rosebush with greenfly! Are you laughing? O yes, laugh! That is wonderful! Reverence to this! Stand beside me and watch. I knooow you have a conscience. Look! She is holding your book! She is reading! She is going to pronounce about it! 'Blap,' she says—can you hear her?—'that's a great verb!' O she is wise. Isn't she wise? Yaw, yaw. The father's chuckling! Give it two balls! But

trust her, whorepouncer? Touch pitch and be defiled, for isn't a vision
grim when a vision is great? She wants to be safe. I want you to hurt
her. Please, I love you! Accept her rejection, for he who won't when
he may, when he will he shall have nay! I talk unlike you hear, but
does one go to Greece by Rome, riddler? Pay attention to me! Leave
her! Hurt her! Dispatch her to the land of Ganabim! I used a G for
you just now, now you do something for me. A ruse. A sprat to catch
a mackerel. I won't put up a wall between us, I promise. Ask her
something I know about now but your face won't see! Ask her about
me! I will whisper it again for you. Ask her—"

A crash! Darconville shot up out of his chair, in a cold sweat, his
mouth open in terror. Wavering, he steadied himself on the desk to
watch the nightmare dissolve like water in water, having dreamt, he
felt, what he feared but feeling he caused what he dreamt. His hand
was trembling. How long had he slept?

The windowpanes were dark. Darconville went downstairs, his
mind stammering down to reality, and left the building. It felt good to
be outside. The sky, made exotic by a sickle of moon, was so clear and
black it seemed to fetch one toward it, and, looking up, he could almost feel the nutation of the earth, the swing of the universe. On the
other side of town a train rocketed through the night, leaving behind a
few spotballs of smoke and a disembodied wail. Essences were in the
spring wind. He could feel the warm breezes chuffing the leaves of the
magnolia tree which stood sentinel-like, an *Urpflanze,* over the lonely
bench that sat more than one memory in it. But it all saddened him.

The tall live-oaks and elms like black-cloaked prophets muttering
urgent warnings of the vanity of all flesh seemed to represent some
kind of extinct symbolism—with any interpretation made owed more,
perhaps, to the homiletic power of the mind observing it than anything else. But every focus of concentration, regardless, seemed only to
serve that mind for purposes of dejection, of apprehension: he looked
out dolefully across the grounds and, turning one way, then turning
another, set out again like a Rufa'iyah dervish in his black coat,
searching for a trace of his promised but lost and unadaptive child.

XLI

The Turner

As falcons to the lure, away she flies,
The grass stoops not, she treads on it so light.

—WILLIAM SHAKESPEARE, *Venus and Adonis*

THE CURTAINS BILLOWED SOFTLY in and out with the night breezes that also carried the music of the dance across campus into the front parlor of Fitts. Isabel Rawsthorne, waiting by herself, had her chair set up halfway between, and faced around from, the two open windows and the door which she had locked. She sat unobserved, wearing a smock-with-flowers, jeans, and pink canvas shoes and staring without reaction into the flame on the far wall she had studied for more than an hour now: a reproduction of one of those Turners where the ocean seems on fire. The proctors had disappeared, the girls had gone, and the room was perfectly dark, silvered to ghostliness, however, by the streetlights outside.

It was a complete solitudinarium. The *empressement* of the parlor's interior, old and distinctly Southern, was also the source of its gloom: the moquette carpets, sofas the color of asparagus rust, a grandmother clock severely ticking. There was a defeated grace to the room, somehow worse than the oppressive silence made by the sudden evacuation of the gentlemen callers who'd come, picked up their dates, and disappeared. Fixed to the flame growing out of the sea, Isabel was only waiting and listening to the slight flutter of the velivolent curtains behind her, thinking neither of gentlemen callers nor addressing with despair the feeling that time is too short. There's no end to nothing, she thought; there's always an end to something, but there's never an end to nothing. So if I can just be nothing, she thought, I can even be bigger than something. She twicked her thumbs. I *am* nothing.

Now she knew that without the shadow of a doubt: that afternoon she had been summoned to the registrar's office only to be told by Dean Barathrum, as Mrs. McAwaddle handed her her grades—with each one lower than those of the first semester—that, as probation no longer applied, she couldn't return to Quinsy College unless she took the fall semester off, reapplied, and hoped for the best, understanding, of course, that there would be no guarantee, without a full review by the admissions board, she could even be readmitted. Her reaction, strangely, was almost ceremonious, subdued, as she was, less by shame than by the simple ineluctability of fate. She remembered walking to her room, packing her clothes, and now—it was so sad and simple— she was waiting only to go home. What medium is the darkness, she wondered, that one can lean on it?

"Isabel?"

The voice, a familiar one, called through the window. Isabel's scar whitened: she froze in her chair and, motionless, shut her eyes only to feel tears roll down her cheeks. There's always an end to something, she thought.

"Hello? Isabel?"

She experienced a sudden sensation in her arms and legs of terrifying lightness, a suspension effected by the mind to feign invisibility, and immediately she felt she would disappear. She took refuge in interior mystery, a forest appeared to her, a magic world where as a princess she—

"Are you there, Isabel? Please?"

Determined, covered in the dark robe of her closed eyes, the night, the shadowed room, Isabel sat perfectly still until the voice called out no more, and she knew beyond all truth that there was never an end to nothing. And she never moved but only rested her head against the back of the chair, resigned in will, and continued to stare toward the wall at the impossible, paradoxical flame splitting up through the darkness of the canvas like some pale and lovely summoner beckoning her beyond her failures and broken dreams into the safety of nothingness, a place where there were no consequences, no grades, no plans, no expectations, nothing to live up to or long for or even love, for love was not only over but love was the worst something of all.

She was waiting, she remembered, and she was waiting, she knew, for someone. But who? she wondered. But who?

XLII

The Jejune Dance

A hall, a hall! give room! and foot it, girls.

—WILLIAM SHAKESPEARE, *Romeo and Juliet*

THE QUINSY DANCE—sound lutes! tabrets! bombardons!—had begun. The large ballroom of the student union, decorated with flowing blue-and-white bunting, was brightly lit, and a felt oriflamme proclaiming the year (apostrophe, two digits) of the graduating class rose in the shape of a Q behind the main table, where stood hundreds of paper cups filled with red punch. There was to be no tippling. The previous night, President Greatracks had delivered to the class his usual Levitical caveat on the subject, a flat denunciation for the most part, complete with anecdotes, of that prince of winepots, General Ulysses S. Grant, "a dang winebibbin' dipsofreek who couldn't wake up of a morning without walkin' sideways!"

"The girls are quiet as question marks now," said Mrs. McAwaddle to Prof. Wratschewe, the other chaperon, "but I fancy they'll all be running us jakeleg around here later on." She was dressed in a blue double-knit, a necklace of huge dead turquoises, and serviceable shoes. "I trust you'll prove, being the senior member here, to have the eyes of a potato?"

"Potato," observed Prof. Wratschewe, graciously bowing a cup of punch to his colleague. "Did you ever stop to think that if 'gh' stood for 'p' as in 'hiccough'; 'ough' for 'o' as in 'dough'; 'phth' for 't' as in 'phthisis'; 'eigh' for 'a' as in 'neighbor'; 'tte' for 't' as in 'gazette'; and 'eau' for 'o' as in 'beau' "—he snapped out his ball-point and scribbled on a flattened cup—"then the correct spelling of potato would be *ghoughphtheightteeau?*" He looked up smiling.

But Mrs. McAwaddle was already on the other side of the room.

The band—a blotch-complexioned group from Charlottesville named *The Uncalled Four*—ripped it all open with a muscular rendition of "Dixie," always so popular, always so malapropos, and then settled into its repertoire of out-of-date tunes and shopworn instrumentals, abuses made even more frightful by the almost parturifacient din coming from the direction of that one great guy with big ears in the schnitz-pie-colored tux (that's him on the electric guitar) who has a voice like a toad under a harrow. But his money paid for most of the instruments. And they travel in his car.

At first, no one would dance, some shy, some not yet ready, but eventually they moved: a general forth-issuing onto the floor, with all *le donne mobile e nubile* in their long white gloves and flouncing dresses looking like so many ortelans-in-papillotes, bell-flowered, orange-flowered, poppy-flowered, curl-flowered. Her eyes star-shining, Alphia Centauri sighed and whispered to Pengwynne Custis at the cloakroom that, gosh, everyone sure looked as fetching as fetching could be. "Bull," said lovely, spoiled, rich Pengwynne Custis, thrusting her wraps at the black attendant, "I've seen prettier faces on a damn ol' iodine bottle." "Why, I just *love* your gown," came a voice from behind Pengwynne. She turned. It was beautiful Hypsipyle Poore, mysterious, enveloped in black faille, with a blood-red rose at her waist and a Gainsborough hat framing her perfectly oval face. "But, tell me, where were you when they fitted it?" And, smiling, Hypsipyle tinkled her finger across the room at several boys.

The boys—young *beaux sabreurs* in the Southern tradition—were mostly overappareled little rakehells from nearby colleges, dashing bucks and guys with names like Reggie Deuceaces, S. Waverly Carter, Guggenheim Grant, Fern Hill, Sheraton Commander, Hampton Court, and Schuyler Colfax or, perhaps, Colfax Schuyler—it didn't matter. They idled about, smoking and chatting and, periodically, dancing their dates woodenly across the floor toward the outer balcony where they either fell abruptly into gourmandizing kiss sequences or produced flasks which appeared at the ends of their fingers, out of nowhere, like conjurers' doves. And some couples—some couples went out to their cars.

There was a general mood of excitement, waltzing and whirling, swinging and swirling. Behind, four years of work! Ahead, the future! But now, fun! Most of the girls conservatively kept to the punch, others didn't, but some, already flown with insolence and wine, were squealing and running niminy-piminy through the arcades, putting the come-hither on their boyfriends and scooting like little grunions into the side-rooms for fumbling but passionate embraces. Heather Tilt's date, his urgent hand rummaging hopefully toward her *drageoir*, got himself a good slap in the face for it. Mona Lisa Drake and her date were engaged in a long, deep kiss in the shadow of a column when she looked up soulfully and whispered, "Be careful, it's my heart." One yahoo with a juggler's face—her blind date from Washington and Lee—actually *proposed* to Charlotte Rumpelmeyer who, in spite of his altiloquence, thought it might be a happier marriage if they knew each other longer than five minutes. And in one dark room Poppy Mandragora ineffectually tried to struggle up, as her hot-blooded boyfriend nailed her down on the couch with kisses, sucked her sighs, and cannonaded her with dabs at the lower neck, and she just about managed to gasp through a space in his arm-hold, "Ashley, *please*, let's not spoil it."

It was a perfect night in Quinsyburg; warm and romantic, with the scent of honeysuckle, yarrow, and beebalm heavy in the air. Solitary as a substantive, Darconville crossed the campus, circling as unobtrusively as possible by Bryerly, Harrop, and Fitts dormitories—and noticing, in the latter, the darkness of one particular room. He stood awkwardly by the front walk outside the parlor of Fitts for a moment and called out Isabel's name several times, but his voice, hollow as the soul of an echo, came back and embarrassed him. He went round behind the building, emerged through a walkway by the greenhouse and saw the lights, heard the music, coming from the student union. All along the street, couples sat in their cars croodling, sipping from bottles, or shifting about with exasperated cries like "You're on my hair!" or "I'm hitting my head!" or "It's not a snap, for godsakes, it's a *hook!*"

As Darconville crossed the street, he heard from an adjacent car a little squeal, monarticulated and lubricious, which posited, by dint of accompanying coos and whuffs, a diabolicating two, exercitants, clearly, in the rites of Venus Pornokrate. Suddenly, the girl, coming up for air, looked out the car window and skreeked, *"O lord!"*

It was Robin Kreutznaer in high apostrophe, mussed, looking unavoidably at—and straight into—Darconville's face. Both were embarrassed. Her flowery anadem was askew, her long dress unambiguously bunched and disarranged. Beside her, buckling up his suspenders, sat some fat-witted bedmaster or other with a mouth like a cigar-fish and a plastic bowtie clipped to one side of his limp, open collar. Darconville's student was disconcerted, it turned out, less for having been nobbled not ten seconds previous than for another reason; she produced a rat-tail comb and spoke, apologetically, between shuttles.

"I sure am sorry," she said, "for not submittin' my poetry paper, sir. I *clean* forgot last week, layin' off, see, to bring it by this week, but then what hap—" Robin hiccuped "—pens? Right. Didn't I get to ailin' something awful, sir? Monthlies. You know? Oops!" Robin's date, snapping open an imperial-size can of beer, sucked in half the can, wheezed manfully and, grinning, lustfully climped her on the thigh, but she pulled away—a bobolink sitting beyond a cat's jump— and continued. "Point being, I gave out to Dean Barathrum that I'd finished up my work for graduation, see? And what with his notions, I mean, uptrippin' me tellin' a lie and all? See what I mean? God, I'm wicked embarrassed!" She groaned and slapped her head back onto the seat. "The question is, see, when *can* I hand it in, bein' as tomorrow is Sunday and we all around here"—she gestured backwards with her comb in the direction of Cagliostro—"well, we were plannin' to cut for Richmond, see, I mean, you do see, don't you? Like I say, last week, shoot, I was all intentions. Then Friday came and—"

"Have you seen Isabel Rawsthorne?" asked Darconville with tears in his eyes.

The dance, at a discreet interval, was called to a halt. It was time for some matters of great pith and moment. The student body presi-

dent, Miss Xystine Chappelle, wearing a honeysuckle-colored linsey
dress with puffed-out sleeves and a full-gathered skirt, appeared in a
trembling spotlight. Sweetly, she welcomed everybody with a prepared
speech, fashioning a metaphorical vase, as it were, into which poetess
Iva Ironmonger Dane, clearing her throat, placed a medita-
tive/descriptive flower for the whole class entitled "Where?"—a little
piece that ended with a bit of advice:

> "Do not follow where the
>   Path may lead.
> Go, instead, where
>   There is no path
> And leave a trail."

Commemorations followed. Miss Quinsy—Hypsipyle Poore herself,
escorted by two white-gloved young men (the others, all watching in
silence with thoughts uniform: no more than the delightful sporting of
the intellect with the flesh that is its master)—was called upon to do
the honors. First, she presented a set of two walleyed Staffordshire
dogs to the class adviser and assistant dean, Miss Dessicquint, and
then the belated retirement gift of a Jefferson Cup to Miss Thelma
Trappe, not in attendance, and who couldn't have been reached, certainly, if upon such a thing depended the volume of applause. All of
this was followed by the Longstreets *ambo* who, swaying, sang a duet
of "Carry Me Back to Old Virginny." The special sentimental finale
having concluded, the young people began to drift away for more
dancing, but wait—who was that puffing in through the fire-door,
shod in sneakers, a flashlight bulging out of his back pocket?
It was President Greatracks himself who, finger-popping the inside
of his acoustical cheek three or four times, recommended everyone's
attention for a sudden, impromptu speech:
"Here, y'all!" he clapped. "It's only me who clum up here, not to
preach, not to teach, but only to put in my jerp's worth about this
here dance, OK? Now, I don't want to be accused of bein' nar-ruh
but I'm in charge here at Quinsy for you outsiders who mayhap have
got another im-pression, your college president, the straw that stirs the
drink! These is facts, in horsetradin' lingo. I'm feelin' like a bull
moose tonight! And why? *Wha?* Well, I cain't hardly memorize,
lemme tell you, the last time I set my peepers on gals lookin' so mightily good appearanced, mmm-*mmm!* Glo-rious! We folks from the

upbrush, 'course, never had anything near as good a time as this, bein' poor as Job's turkey and all, but then, see, we don't count long as y'all in high fettle here at the graduation dance, hear? Delivered.

"But now pay me some mind: I naturally don't expect y'all to be in low cotton tonight, do I, and I want that put in capitals, see?—yowever, I hear tell been some liquor-tipplin' going on here, yes? That right? Look around, this kind of thing prelavent? Huh? That Southern quality? You been raised up—where, *Paree? Babylon, for cry-eye?* I only just now put my hand on one wimpbucket here in his dang shirttails, I want you to know, walkin' around slantindicular and actin' like a field-nigger at a weekend funeral! You can wipe off them phony Miss-Little-What-Me? faces, girls, 'cause, I can tell *you*, I been all the way there and back again! I took him a twist by his ear, that's right, and showed him into the middle of next week where that ol' boy goin' to be wakin' up famous with the collywobbles and a nice *pro*-nounced case of kitney trouble, bet on it! OK? Now you can set your foot down on this, people: *I ain't gonna buy this kind of thing! Not here, not there, not nowhere! You got it?*" He pulled his mouth. "Good, now keep it. I'm hot as a sunburnt sheep up here, them lights is in-tense and like to give me pinwheels in the eyeball, and I need me a Co'-Cola."

There were murmurs. President Greatracks, stepping down, gulped a cup of punch so quickly it splashed down his chin and squittered all over the paper tablecloth and then, making a battery of reluctant handshakes, he drew out his flashlight, waved it, and went charging back into battle. Whereupon Xystine Chappelle, as the applause died down, motioned everyone forward to hold hands and sing the school song, "Pledge We to You, Quinsy, All Our Troth." The lights dimmed, the band again flouted up a medley of slow uningenious waltzes, and in the semi-darkness couples once more closed in, groin to groin, clutching in tenacious spasms of ardor but showing now, at least it seemed to Mrs. McAwaddle, too much in vertical behavior of what seemed, clearly, horizontal intentions. After giving one couple the benefit of the doubt—had they caught *buttons?*—she stepped onto the floor, touched a boy who had his head buried in his partner's neck like a hatchet, and whispered too loudly, "Elbow room!"

Returning to her place, she sought a collaborative response in the face of the other chaperon, who merely blinked.

"Elbow room," repeated Prof. Wratschewe, interlacing his fingers. "Do you realize, Miz McAwaddle, that Shakespeare was the first person ever to use that expression?"

Mrs. McAwaddle was utterly adsorbed.

The clock bonged its lonesome numbers from the library. Darconville, a multitude of one, had positioned himself at some distance on a hill rising up toward Truesleeve dormitory and wished, as he watched the lights of the college and outlying Quinsyburg below, that they were the lights of Venice, a city that now seemed further away in time than in space. The palazzo, remaining under a writ of *quo warranto,* was still stuck in the courts and yet he didn't care—there was London, Paris, Rome—as he thought for the first time of going away, anywhere. The student union, noisy and aglow, stood below him on the phenomenal level, but what, he wondered, but where, my interdimensional love, shall I search for you on the noumenal level, down or up? What, he asked himself, could he want with such a *will* to want it? What, he thought, that I need it with such intensity?

Darconville ached, he believed, to know the ineffable thing-in-itself! I am in love, he thought, with the *Ding-an-Sich!* To postulate, yet not perceive: it was a doom that now began to ask too much of him. O artifactual game! O artificial pastime! He longed for her, for Isabel, for the prepredicative heart without which he felt, truthfully, he couldn't live, but his knowledge was conscious of its own insufficiency, a "learned ignorance" to which, even with the bribe of desperation, truth saw fit to supply little or nothing, suffering forth only a spate of murderous questions: what was the part of the subject, the object, in knowledge? Did man's limited ability to know necessarily deform objects according to his own subjective nature? Was truth the concordance of knowledge with itself or with that which is? Did we have in all domains of knowledge the same certitude? Darconville was not even convinced that the question, whether they were important questions, was *itself* an important question. They were questions, clearly, not to be solved without immortality, in which state all philosophy was once only one philosophy, and mortals had only a handful of fragments like puzzle-pieces to prove it true. Who knows what will happen? Do we know Who knows but not know what? Perhaps, thought Darconville, the doubter *was* the true savant—to prescind from judgment and know, by default, that which you wouldn't judge. There is no Doubt but Doubt, and Aenesidemus is his prophet!

The trees soughed in several rushes of night wind, blowing as if off an invisible sea upon which sailed only that which sailed, was meant to sail, and meaning nothing more, and Darconville, imagining himself, the while, at some point in the future recalling this particular moment, found it restful to think that somewhere some things existed without significance, without dreams, without memory. But that was memory, wasn't it? And what had memory wrought of joy? Memory wounded. We must free what we are in time, he thought, *from* memory and live toward the future which, second upon second, made memory irrelevant even if it increased its size!

It was well past midnight now, and the band, at a primordial pitch, challenged the Quinsy girls, the drumlike beating in their blood leading with incredible rapidity to various misadventures. Ariadne Naxos swirled toilet paper around her and, vamping from one boy to another, danced her smoldering "Veil of the Beguines." Trudy Lookingglass, having punted away her silk pumps, sat perched over the balcony dangling one of her garters and rotating her shoulder *à faire provoquer* while a dozen or so boys went scrambling—bookety-bookety!—through the doorway and up the stairs, howling with encouragement. Dancing a sexy shuffle on one of the tables to a clap-chant below, Sabrina Halliburton slowly hoisted her gown almost to her hips, revealing a pair of legs smooth and delicious as a pawpaw. And all the while, her beautiful eyes narrowed in black disapproval, Hypsipyle Poore watched from a distance, being made no happier, certainly, by finding her escort, a blond cavalier-in-uniform from V.M.I., staring at those legs. She puffed exasperatedly through her nose and shifted position. The young man, turning to her, asked if anything was wrong. Hypsipyle merely sighed, loath to establish another's credibility by a criticism that could only be misapplied, for Southern girls, actually, alarm each other quite easily: such is their homogeneity, in fact, that one's particular actions are always another's in potency, and so, with each a simulacrum of the next, they must all sustain in constant reflection what approving of themselves within they must hate in others without—while the concomitant virtue, paradoxically, of *admiring* in another for self-esteem what the burden should logically reverse is curiously absent. It is often common for them, in fact, to make friends in order to avoid enemies, a contradiction, in this instance, that could no more be eliminated by explanation than it could be diverted by disapproval or reversed by ruse.

"Are you sure nothing's wrong?"

Hypsipyle sighed again, looked searchingly into her escort's eyes, and leaned over to whisper softly—with a breath oversweet from pastilles—into the shell of his ear, *"My silk panties are too tight."*

The night grew more perilous as the night grew late, with passions being fueled by liquor and liquor being passed around now, openly, like love-philtres at a sabbat. Alicia Lutesinger, nimptopsical, was skipping in a circle and swinging by a loop half a six-pack of beer still attached to its polypropylene zeros. Rebecca Lemp, at her wit's end, was losing the grip she had on the shins of her boyfriend, a big-bellied snewf from Hampden-Sydney who, goaded on by the rebel yells of his fraternity brothers, was hanging upsidedown from a balcony in the Trendelenburg position and trying unsuccessfully to chug-a-lug the full bottle of grain alcohol that was splashing below like a fifty-foot waterfall in a loud clapotage. And of course there were casualties. Olivia Oona Osborne, going stone cold, suddenly dropped her jaw and her tenth cup of cheap bourbon and reeled over backwards at the top of the staircase, the egglike alliteration of her name matching the echoing wail as she bounced, bum over beezer, all the way downstairs with a loud dopplerian *"Oooooooooooooo!"* And then in perfect sequence came another crash. Nora Buncle's date, mousing her thigh, never knew what hit him—for, unprepared for it, she squealed and kicked up with a whoop of surprise catching him a desperate shot full in the *corpus spongiosum* and, instantly, he snapped shut into a fierce genupectoral vise, unflexioned, and then wheeled about and hit the floor where he lay stiff as a stoolball in the rising fumes of whiskey and friable bits of glass from the shattered hip-bottle underneath him.

"O my weak heart!" cried Mrs. McAwaddle, shrieking in owl-blasted anguish. "Is there a doctor in the house?"

"House," said Prof. Wratschewe, reflectively. "You hear yourself, Mrs. McAwaddle? The most curious pronunciation in the idiolect of the Virginian. I believe its phonemic transcription"—he drew signs in a dribble of spilled whiskey—"is best rendered /hɜəus/. Hoose: the voice hoots." He looked up. "Mrs. McAwaddle?"

But she was in the powder room, gulping a handful of strain-abaters.

Meanwhile, Darconville had decided he could wait no longer. And although he could not shake off the feeling that his soul had become a drifting multiplicity without any nucleus—indeed, he began furtively trying to annihilate with his imagination his very life there—he walked down the hill from Truesleeve and around to the front of the student union. Three pale *roreres* from the University of Virginia, all wearing varsity shirts and nothing else, stood on the landing outside chanting "Wahoo-Wa! Wahoo-Wa! Wahoo-Wa!" and then wended their spiflicated way, arm in arm, down the front steps beside which some poor child, pinching her nose clothespin-fashion and urging her sick self forward, doubled up like a foot-rule and passed out. The campus police were called in, and after searching the grounds, strewn everywhere with gartering, inkles, nonesopretties, and gloves, they marched the drunks they collared and the vandals they nabbed right over to the chaperons.

Mrs. McAwaddle, all in a dither, hadn't appeared on the steps ten seconds before Darconville stopped her short. Please, had she seen Isabel Rawsthorne? Anywhere? No, he knew she hadn't attended the —But Mrs. McAwaddle, her dead turquoises clicking, squeezed his hand, told him to be calm, and reassured him: Isabel wasn't ill, no, and in fact that very afternoon had been over to the registrar's office. Although Darconville had more questions, she stopped his lips with a finger and turned momentarily elsewhere.

The police, inquisitively shining flashlights at thirty or so college identity cards all at once, were trying to prevail on Mrs. McAwaddle to help them match owners to face. It must have been a frightful day for her, thought Darconville, as she seemed to have nothing left. It was only partially true, however, for in spite of the furor there, Mrs. McAwaddle, having excused herself to Darconville more to deliberate her response to him than anything else, had bad news—how could she tell him that the girl he loved had cashed in her three Fs, one D, and an Incomplete for a job in support of which she, Mrs. McAwaddle, had only that afternoon, begged for it, written a letter of recommendation? Isabel, going home, was to take a job as a telephone operator. She had flunked out. The ball was over.

And, somehow, Darconville knew it.

"The grades, why I couldn't half under*stand* them. But they weren't good, I'm afraid. They weren't"—Mrs. McAwaddle, closing her eyes, shock-absorbed his unbelief—"sufficient?"

The moonlight whitened the grounds. He crossed the dark street, the dead sound of his footsteps making his heart feel desolate and empty. Crickets stopped chirping as he passed. There was no one in sight as he left the area of the student union, where the dance had broken up. The long year, soon finished, was on his mind. At once he pitied Isabel, and then never had he felt less inquisitive, less concerned, for the hopelessness of it all and the questions asked that never seemed to have answers, adequate or enough. He was tempted to walk forward, past his house and past the town, and let the whole thing go, disposed to let the night fall about him in that place of memory and seal the dwelling shut.

The beech trees and maples whispered overhead. An owl hooted. And he began to feel that he himself shared those nocturnal movements and sounds, that he was no stranger among them but rather a secretive and lonely earth-life removed from self-respect, an incompetent at fostering hope in another, and a would-be lover open to the whimseys of what he'd never understand. He passed by the low brick wall in front of Fitts—how many times that day had he done so?—where over the doorway, set some thirty feet back, the front lamp was lit. Darconville stopped, and his leg jumped as he looked. He looked again. He dropped low and cocked his head to spy into a serendipity he wouldn't yet believe. A figure was standing in the morning-glory vines.

The night itself seemed to hold its breath. Darconville moved closer, not daring to turn salutation into irruption, drawn only toward the luminous darkness that revealed her golden hair and flesh as white as elder pith, and extending his hand he heard only a slight exhalation. Was it a sigh for a yes, a sigh for a no, or a sigh for an I-can't-bear-it? The figure stepped forward once, the moisture in her throat moving to her eyes, clear as the tears of a penitent. They did not demand, or plead, but simply said *understand me, please understand me?*

And they turned into the parlor, Darconville and the girl who, as she turned, left behind in the shadows her suitcase the color of the dented blue car (a guitar in the back seat) that suddenly roared up there and waited in front, waited for five minutes in front, then waited in front no longer but, blowing a sneer on its horn, disappeared on a furious curvet into the night.

"Forgive me?" asked Darconville to Isabel. "I know not what I did."

Adversity always made him epigrammatic.

XLIII

The Unfortunate Jilts

Little pitchers have wide ears.

—GEORGE HERBERT

LORETTA BOYCO pressed in another piece. Clapping her hands, Harriet Bowdler squealed in excitement and reached for another bottle of grape soda. The puzzle was half done. Left on the shelf, so to speak, while the others did the sprint, the two seniors, wearing quilted housecoats and scuffie-wuffies, had spent the evening of the graduation dance in a sitting room off the front parlor of Fitts. What fun!

The girls, earlier, had bathed, creamed their faces, twirled up their hair, and together gone to the front desk to sign out the puzzle—it had a hermeneutic theme, one of the many donated to the college by the Southern Baptist Outreach Association, and was entitled: *The Rivalry of the Brothers Absalom and Ammon.* They had worked on it all evening. And now they sat, cross-legged, first trying this, then trying that from the mess of little pieces left on the floor and nibbling from the bag of sweetchews they brought along for reinforcement. They'd done the edges, of course, the easiest part, and were just starting on the sky, always the hardest.

It was late, with Harriet and Loretta fingering a few last nookshot-ten pieces, when, alerted by a noise, Loretta quickly put her finger to her lips as a sign for silence. Closing their eyes, they listened: those were voices. Loretta, unable to control it, squelched juice from the candy in her mouth, when Harriet, midway across the room on tiptoe, turned and gritted her teeth to chastise her—and then continued in high exaggerated steps to the door of the front parlor where she peered through the keyhole.

There stood a couple facing each other, talking.

XLIV

Heroic Couplet

Much speche they ther expoun of druries greme and grace.

—*Sir Gawain and the Green Knight*

DARCONVILLE
Your hand is of a temperature, my love,
As to persuade me now against my hope
That you, indeed, must hate me always—
(*pause*)
If I hadn't but been promised otherwise
With what life and limb I still believe.
I love you. I can tell you that again.
ISABEL
You put it well, but then you always do.

DARCONVILLE

I shouldn't then, and always shouldn't?
Stammer no such words? Pouch up my mouth?
And stand away from love as best I can,
Mum like Mumphezard, hanged for saying nothing?
I have questions that outnumber themselves.

ISABEL

You can be as cold as winter light—

DARCONVILLE

A light, then, very like your hand.

ISABEL

—or mild and warm, exactly as you choose.

DARCONVILLE (*ironic bow*)

As my crippled heart wills, you mean.
That logical distinction serves more true
In choice or will (or is and seem!)
For, tell me, when is not, with both, one first
That mistakenly seems joint with the other?

(*pause*)

I fixed upon your hand just now with guile
And you addressed with passion, nothing less,
For can one better greet what turns a smile
From hot to cold than that which turns it so?
Who in sorrow speaks of choice? O cruel!
For you, to make your absence now a studied one?
For me, to take it so to win myself
What proverbs like to call a fonder heart?
I pray I'm less a blackguard than a fool,
Yet here I spy an artifice in art:
For on Love's sweetest arrow's tipped a dart.
But when with passion, please, had choice to do
Which, improvising, turns and turns and turns about
To disavow methodically that pleasure for this pain?
No matter now: my mind begins to shout.
So here, Necessity, allow what more weeks will.
I'll be resigned to play it well until
I'm told to shift about a mood again.
I see, if I'm to keep my love for you,

(*moves closer*)

I may, I must, I can, I will, I do.

ISABEL

You are more and more to me a stranger.

DARCONVILLE
"What a strange man is Chichikov," thought Tententikov.
"What a strange man is Tententikov," thought Chichikov.
ISABEL (*almost inaudibly*)
And sometimes you're—you're frightening.
DARCONVILLE
Yes? Is it so? Or does it simply seem?
Does passion invigorate expression, then, to grimace?
Why then surely here it greets itself—
Think, however, not so with surprise,
For passion passion meets with a rolling in the eyes.
It cues its own posture over nothing in fact,
And though a comrade it wants, a double in spleen,
It self-begets selves unnaturally
And worships what cannot be put in a creed,
Yet wants when it isn't what it wants to be.
The nature of passion's the nature of strife, as well,
Where in thinking a thought it makes it a deed;
Who can actually speak of its brutish routine?
When it is what it wants then it's also in hell.
Between passion and another way of life
There is no question of choice at all—
Only between passion sought and madness seen;
Its heights are high, from heights we fall.
True enough, indeed, but more truth worth.
Passion and madness are one regardless, quite:
The putting off of both, this desperate relation,
Is as much an accident as their birth.
But madness holds fast with no end in sight,
While passion's a mock, a spoof of duration.
The triumph of passion is found in its defeat;
And victory's won by honest love's retreat.
(*pause*)
The defeat of passion, just between us, is inevitable.
ISABEL (*archly*)
It seems we know what's between us, then.
DARCONVILLE
Or between you and anyone else.
ISABEL (*her scar whitening*)
Yes? Yes? Tell me more.
(*pause*)
You can make so much of what's never been done,
Raising up issues like raising the dead!

You can make a person feel ever so small!
You always never stop writing a book in your head!
I promise I've nothing to tell you at all.
You can make a trifling relation with anyone—
                    DARCONVILLE
Or someone.
                    ISABEL
Or *some*one, yes, if you insist on that.
                    DARCONVILLE
Although it could be anyone, yes?
This to clarify: for since no one is anyone,
Until of course he's someone, see,
Why then someone is equal to one and won
                    (*shrugs*)
And everyone else can anyone be.
                    ISABEL
What are you saying?
                    DARCONVILLE
I hear a footfall in my head, moving in circles.
                    ISABEL
I hear whispers that girls exchange in rooms,
Of jealousy, scorn, reproaches, and hate,
Injuries, words of deceit, matters of doom.
          DARCONVILLE (*to himself*)
And early believe what never comes too late?
                    ISABEL
I don't believe everything I hear.
                    DARCONVILLE
But judge, is it possible otherwise? I'd know
Of that wily mouse that breeds in a cat's ear.
I smell reformationists
                    (*pause*)
And betrayal.
                    (*pause*)
You weep at the word? It's that accurate?
                    ISABEL
There may be someone here. Outside.
          DARCONVILLE (*darkly*)
The devil.
                    ISABEL
You frighten me, you frighten me.

DARCONVILLE

The creature causes what affects you still.
I say I love; you stall.
Why are you troubled? Have you felt ill?

ISABEL

No.

DARCONVILLE

Not ill, is it, because not at all?

(*pause*)

There is something I must ask you now:
Has anything happened, intentionally or not,
Whereby you should suspect I do not love you?

ISABEL (*lowers eyes*)

No.

DARCONVILLE

Brief.

ISABEL

Too brief is what you mean, isn't it, and
You'll insist on that, won't you, forever and ever?
Just absolutely forever and ever, won't you!
A stupid victory is what you want.

DARCONVILLE

I want you
And would only ask the same of you for me.

ISABEL (*pleading*)

I want you to know I want what you want
When you may want to think I want what I don't.

DARCONVILLE

Dark. As a thief's pocket.

ISABEL (*twicking her thumbs*)

I want to be safe. I can't say it any better, I can't think anymore, I feel
something will happen to me, I failed my courses and now have to take a
terrible job, I have no friends but you, and you'll go away, I know you
will, I would want to go with you but couldn't, I know, what bothers me
is missing you and wanting to be with you, like everyone does, yes, I ap-
preciate you trying to find out what's wrong with me, most people
wouldn't do that, which is why I'm afraid of them, and, O, I know I'm
lucky about so many many things and shouldn't be sad, I know that, but
then I think of all the wasted opportunities in my life and begin to believe I actually deserve so much trouble for that and all the unhappiness
I've caused in the past—

DARCONVILLE (*swallowing*)

The past?

(*pause*)

I feel about me the presence of something
Not of this world, a bleak forbidden remnant
Standing in this room.

ISABEL (*stirs up*)

In this room?

DARCONVILLE

A shadow.

ISABEL (*frightened*)

A shadow?

DARCONVILLE

I hear a perfect echo, making dialogue a mock.
It now arises you must tell me what
Not asked would truly send me mad, in shock.
Please don't give to me an answer, though,
Born of a desire less than mine,
No answer of deliberation, nor answer fine,
I beg you neither from a page of fairy,
Fantasy, silly fescue, or of formal wit,
Your name below a paraph lovely writ
That might distract me from a truth you owe.
But only give to me an answer. So.

(*pause*)

Speak it plain. Are you in love with Govert?

(*shaking uncontrollably, Isabel cries out*)

I have named the name then? Govert.
The simple truth, miscalled simplicity.

ISABEL

You simply do not understand.

DARCONVILLE

I think I've not been asked to understand.

ISABEL

The person that you mentioned—

DARCONVILLE

Govert.

ISABEL

Govert, yes! Govert van der Slang! I do not love him!
I do not! I do not! I do not! I never did!

(*pause*)

A few years ago, that family moved down the road from us to a farm at the foot of the Blue Ridge mountains, in Fawx's Mt., as you know. It's hard to recollect how I—. I remember only seeing them at school, the boys, well, not all of them, I don't know. I would just visit Zutphen Farm, they were like a family to me, but what does it matter anyway? I guess I—pitied Govert, who was the outsider of the family and different; no one understood him or cared or took the time to listen to him, no, not his mother and his father was always somewhere else. They ridiculed his music, he plays the guitar, and so I tried to do what little I could, although I know what you're going to think, but it's not true and never was. So anyway he depended on me, I guess, and I grew closer to him and he to me because his brother, more successful supposedly, were never at home either but were always away at—

(*pause*)

sea.

DARCONVILLE

That would be the coast guard?

ISABEL

The navy.

DARCONVILLE

In which case, you didn't see any of them.

ISABEL

Not when they didn't visit.

DARCONVILLE

Which however they sometimes did and sometimes do?

(*pause*)

Come, any news nourishes the gnawer of himself.

ISABEL

Sometimes, yes.

DARCONVILLE

Whereupon you knew it. You are close to this family.

ISABEL (*softly*)

I would say—I don't know.

DARCONVILLE (*ruefully*)

Every division of a line produces another line.

(*pause*)

My God, will jealousy make questions of itself?
I'm deuce-eyed. I'm shillaber and shaman.
I never metamorphosis I didn't like.
Creeps in the dusk, it's true, before
One begins to look about for it.
I can imagine lovers trooping out
To you in afternoons of any weather,

Stealing as they did in Sparta old,
Legally, carelessly, and turning me, dumb,
Beruffianized, an out-fooled fool, sold,
The stupid, unpiperly make-bate I've become.
They come to kneel before you, penitential,
Or crouch in the spawl and wood and bits!
I flash a light and look to see lice—
Then look again and find their nits!
Look! Trillions of them, fawning and bowed!
The color of their eyes? Bice. Bice.
           (*pause, to himself savagely*)
Will many be burnt? Crowds. Crowds.

                    ISABEL
Dreams! Dreams! You talk like a book!

                  DARCONVILLE
I promise you, I am no dreamer,
For destiny will pass the dreamer by,
Because for nothing ever does he ask
But sits at peace within his very dream;
Whereas, you see, it must be more than clear
That even on a night as this one is
I would freely barter all my soul,
My body, mind, and disappointed hands
To free a mere smile in your lovely face.
But can't you see that? Can't you tell?
                  (*pause*)
What then, pray, has he to do with dreams
Who wakes away the night he wants to see
In sleep alone: but sleep alone so deems
The restful dreams I see it keeps from me.
I can report what takes the place of dreams:
Red magic, a witch that's howling a filthy cry,
Helldogs barking in contrapuntal,
A taloned pig that slits its throat to die!
I fear in the night what's always the same
And descry through the darkness, coming frontal,
Suddenly poising to squat on my chest,
Its eyes dirty gems, its sticky wings high,
A grinning monstrosity that's flown up from hell
To rasp in my ears one word, only "Govert!"
"Govert!" it rasps; it rasps again "Govert!"
It queaks. It spits. It chatters in fits.
The image will harden and then be dispelled.

I reach to throttle what disappears;
In midstroke, there, I swipe at its face
And there again, *again,* the same face sits!
It forks out a tongue it wimbles in hate—
In a rush of murder I behead only space.
(pause)
The noctambule? The thing doesn't stay.
It recedes of course like its antitype true
To some grey shoreline of fierce unrest
And out on the Straits of Lurking abides
Where, if a vow will bind in the modern world
And luck of design a residue, test
Me by holy relic and then by oath
If someday I don't contrive to meet both.
ISABEL
That "someday" has a cruel ring to it.
DARCONVILLE
Cruel to devildom, sweet frail?
(pause)
There is irony, the figure of speech
Which spits like a bivalve from its cackpipe.
I have an enemy, lady.
(pause)
Forgive me. That dissatisfacts.
ISABEL
He—
(pause)
—is not your enemy.
DARCONVILLE
He is not my enemy, and I am Jack Ketch:
And that is two lies, to tell the truth.
(pause)
But there is, I see, Dutch comfort either way.
It is you for safety, me for fright—
And yet a fear my rashness renders lax,
For with gimp-legged Vulcan I would limp tonight,
Hobble out on stilts like poor Amphionax,
Sit along the yawning edge of hell
Lest otherwise in safety's reasoned spell
Or in the bland assurances of tidiness
A sacrifice of limit be imposed on us.
But then do we then balance each other so well
That as one of us must love the more

One of us shall love the less?
Does here some existential burden sore—
Fidelity, it seems—frighten you so much?
That you must tempt me with a fruit
That I can never touch? But always need?
Shall love then die as dreams that die
With the very sleep they feed?
Shall I please to love you then
Just enough that I don't tell you so,
A mysterious veil concealing my face,
My hidden face concealing its thoughts,
With each of us destined so to live
As if the other, not won by love but caught,
Knew nothing whatsoever of its grace?
                    (*pause*)
This is this, then, and that is that.
It is as the unmanipulable moon to the fixed
Eye of my indivinable cat.

                    ISABEL
O this is—! I said nothing, I admit,
Because you'd seek what was no worth to know,
To rehearse each moment, to analyze all,
And inquire, inquire, and then inquire more!

                    DARCONVILLE
It was not that you didn't say anything;
You may have said two different things, you see,
Of unsimilar worth but at a similar time,
As astrologers will to kings and zanies
Mutter forth one horoscope for both.
The tragic fault, perhaps, is—what?
                    (*pause*)
Doubtless. That indeed they both inquired,
And more inquired, and inquired so again:
Cast our nativities, Chaldean!
Is it pleasure that awaits? Or pain?

                    ISABEL
I cannot answer everything you ask:
Who learns all of everything that's sought?

                    DARCONVILLE
But for me, sage, only this unmask:
Has anything happened, intentionally or not,
Whereby you should suspect I do not love you?

ISABEL

No.

DARCONVILLE

Considered, declared, exclaimed, indeed. But meant?
How so, if once again flits out at night
That sudden and unholy bat-eared pervert
Whose boisterous face out-blackens black itself
And caws at me repeatedly the curse of "Govert!"

ISABEL

You're raving, just as if it so fell out
You lost yourself and lost, as claimed, not me.

DARCONVILLE

I've watched madness too long untransfigured in face
And to you here confess that evil, defined,
Is more than that which so cruelly distorts;
Whoso *allows* distortion is evil in kind.
So to the transition that must follow suit:
How in method illogic a cruel fact can disport,
Where's found consolation in murdered grace
And fate is unshaped at the branch and the root.
For this I believe, that you wanted to find,
Or felt that finding was needful for you,
Some faithless transgression you feared in mind,
And, finding, confirmed what most you'd rue.
Thus knowledge is bought of a certain kind:
The suspension which kills is killed instead
And respite's achieved in the midst of dread.

(*pause*)

Our first desire is what will last.

ISABEL

And the future's only memory
If we don't overcome the past.

DARCONVILLE

Perhaps. And yet I must pause in reflection to ask
Whether me you consider as future or past
And how just continuance must keep me so
If on me the former you now do bestow.
And yet there's another who must feel the same:
A face I don't know, but a name I can name.

ISABEL

Why, *why* must you raise an issue that's dead,
Never really begun, and I've told you so!
Must you hate someone you don't even know?

DARCONVILLE

The countercheck quarrelsome won't save his head
(*pause*)
I could—

ISABEL

O say it! Whatever it is will please you, I think!

DARCONVILLE

If my delight be the cause of your wrath
Why is not, let me ask, this sorrow I feel
An equal occasion of your solace, pray?
(*pause*)
And counterpart Govert? I don't hate him, no,
Though not because my soul wouldn't try,
For seeing me here he surely would know
My own mirror-image at seeing him so;
And what here's said he too could simply say:
"There but for the grace of you go I."
And so this irony that irony compounds
As echoes will echo with the same resound.

ISABEL

It's foolish this—and only sorrow brings.
You were a monk? Then let me say right now,
Better that monks should analyze such things.

DARCONVILLE (*soberly*)

That's a secret no one knows but us,
To the keeping of which you gave your solemn vow.
And no one else will hear of it, I trust.

ISABEL

O how can this suffering come to an end?

DARCONVILLE

When not me, but Govert, is only a friend.

ISABEL

This rival, know, has sanction none from me.

DARCONVILLE

So from all rivals am I then set free?
(*pause*)
No, fairness, we'll see what waits in store,
To accept whatsoever fate will be ours.
If love, then love. There's need of no more.
But if to our lot a passion brief does fall
Where as rubies rare brought side to side
We gleam to the bad and each other do stain,

You and I will win experience unique,
Finding gain is loss and loss the only gain
And then to lose again what's found in pain
And for a lifetime merely seek to seek.
Passion's a bondage where's no planned release;
You will the pacific, until you've found peace.
A simulacrum of love, so from it estranged,
Passion's the madness that is not deranged.

ISABEL

I don't understand you so much of the time.
In all human actions are there reasons and rime?
Then why do my grandest hopes also impart
This fear in my soul which puts fear in my heart:
That vision is faulty when vision's sublime.

DARCONVILLE

If words were threads those very ones could weave
A perfect shroud for the corpse you've made, now leave.

(*pause*)

I will neither tilt with reason nor defend to you
The use to which are put to solve or appease
Matters too complex you say for minds to see,
But if you leave tonight with any reason true,
Please God, search for a reason other than me,
And if it's true you don't love me, then please
Don't hate me enough to tell me you do.

ISABEL (*with strange vagueness*)

My departure tonight I think is best for all,
To dream away what dreams cannot be seen
And live in sleep, in sleep to find my ease:
There heights are scaled, but one can never fall.
And this will sound foolish to you, I know,
To pretend I've found some fairy forest green
Where as a solitary princess, through the trees
I'd wander—

(*pause, embarrassed*)

O, I only want to be safe!

DARCONVILLE

Say no more to it then, if more you can.
You put in six words the epitaph of man.

XLV

Sounds of the Fundament

If any man among you seemeth to be wise in this world, let him become a fool, that he may be wise.

—I Corinthians 3:18

THE PARLOR DOOR suddenly flew open.

It was an errand of mercy, anybody could see that, as Mistresses Boyco and Bowdler, quillbristled in curlers, came pittypatting into the room and stood by Isabel, hovering over her like ministering angels. Homely, angular Loretta Boyco lapwinged down beside her and solicitously took her hand while Harriet Bowdler, smoothing the nap of her buffy white nightie, turned her trout's eyes toward Darconville with a lot less tenderness: talking was one thing, but this child had been weeping! Confusion gave way to consensus. The fellowshippers smiled at each other knowingly, and then Loretta said to Isabel, "Why don't you take up all your troubles, put them in a big ol' tow sack and give them over to Jesus?"

"*We* did," quacked Harriet, looking beatific.

"Amen," added Loretta.

Darconville asked: "Do you know this girl?"

"I've seen you in P.E., right?" said Harriet to Isabel who, bent over almost double, almost exanimate, didn't respond one way or the other. Harriet looked up at Darconville. "We've howdied, but we haven't shook." She closed her eyes. "I know the characteristics of the unconverted heart."

"It is prone to error," said Loretta.

"Idleness, tippling, profanity."

"And contention."

" 'My sin is ever before me, neither is there rest in my bones because of sin,' " quoted Harriet Bowdler.

Darconville sighed. He felt tired, unsplendid, and null, bewildered by this visitation and divided as to whether he should just apologize to everyone and leave or stay there and somehow try to give honorable and ethical form to something that had ended as abruptly as a page torn in half. Instead, he stepped back as the girls administered to Isabel—two Serbs, one beautiful Croat—with a vocabulary of Bible gems and the slightly dictatorial attitude that vigorous religious conviction curiously assumes, especially in the proving, preaching, and perfricative mind of the Pentecostal. Like fundamentalists, like poppies, thought Darconville: the more they are trodden on, the more they flourish.

I will not ridicule them, he determined, for he himself, he knew, had accomplished nothing in the way of helping Isabel and felt that nothing accomplished left everything therefore to be. Further, was it not said that God often wished His glory to appear in the dulling of the wise, in the fall of the mighty, in the bewilderment of the alert? And so he kept to the shadows, an outlaw, logiciannaire, the acute and distinct Arminius.

Although a crescent moon could still be seen through the window of Fitts, the pale traces of early morning just touched the lower sky on the eastern outskirts of Quinsyburg, out toward Richmond. Darconville went to the window, the mild breeze through the rapfull curtains cooling his brow and in a semi-arrested, inefficient state closed his eyes as he listened to Harriet Bowdler—Loretta had momentarily disappeared—supplicating with Isabel to accept Christ Jesus and be "born again" lest, unconverted, she die unredeemed and so caper about for eternity like the maroonest devils in hell, the particular area, Darconville knew, which the evangelical mind took to be God's chiefest handiwork.

As he listened, he wondered. Was it all so simplistic and dim? It was and it wasn't, thought the divided self. Darconville the rationalist: reality was not thinkable but in relation to an activity by means of which it becomes thinkable. Darconville the nominalist: but wasn't truth suprarational? Incommunicable in the language of reason? Analyze, analyze, analyze! Isabel was correct. Surely one must enter love with a degree of folly which he can deceive and so, by deceiving, make wise. That was wisdom. I must become a fool, thought Darconville, I who have been so vain to know.

Suddenly, Loretta Boyco came padding back into the parlor and, smiling (a bit manically), short-armed each of them with a pamphlet —copies of "Glints from My Mirror" by W. C. Cloogy, Evangelist. Harriet then quickly dink-toed over to whisper something to Loretta, whose eyes, as she listened, shut tightly in holy mirth. And then she clapped! Would they both come to church tomorrow, it being Sunday, asked Loretta, to *see* Rev. Cloogy? To *know* him? asked Harriet. To *hear* him? asked Loretta. An opportunity, Harriet breathlessly assured them—rising and shaking a finger like Jael wagging a tentnail —that may be given to them only once! The accusative/dative, thought Darconville: the Accusation that is a Gift.

But to the Baptist church? That was a kind of Accusative of Place to Which, thought Darconville, with himself the object, and he almost smiled, reflecting on how, formerly, it would have taken a miracle of the first rank for him even to acknowledge the existence of that steeple-hatted communion of nescients and nincompoops called Baptists, a religion, broadly, only by reason of numbers and the obfusc light of twentieth-century lamps. He looked at Isabel. But she sat silent: in fact, somehow removed from it all, she seemed, the *princesse lointaine,* to enjoy the efforts of those two dumbledores attentively buzzing around her. In any case, perhaps a miracle *was* necessary to bring them together. For where had facts got them? And in how many a holy synaxarion had he read as a youth of even greater wonders—of dearths forestalled, serpents extirpated, rods embudded, courtesans converted, fluxes cured, tyrants mortified, cadavers translated, and, yes, minds completely changed! Darconville didn't know what to say. He looked at Loretta, who stood with her hip sprung out. Well? He looked at Harriet, who folded her arms and asked again. Would they come? Ordinarily not given to habits of sudden adaption, Darconville nevertheless again heard sounded the depths of his own spiritual bankruptcy and intellectual obstinacy, and so just when one girl, again, was about to echo her coreligionist's question, he who had come within a finger-breadth of saying no turned thereupon and said, "Yes."

Struck like a duck in thunder, Loretta Boyco suddenly gooched Harriet Bowdler in the ribs and, shooting their hands up, both hysterically shrieked, *"Praise the Lord!"*

The town of Quinsyburg still slumbered. It was quite early yet, and, though on the horizon the edge of dawn promised to widen, the greyish darkness held. It had been one of the longest nights of his life, and that he'd survived it seemed to Darconville a miracle in its own right. He crossed the Quinsy lawns and, exhausted, came to his house. He entered and pulled the bolt; it syllabified a dactyl—*miĭ a. k'l!*

It was only then, dragging himself wearily up the flight of stairs that creaked with the pain that doubled them up in the middle, that Darconville realized the implications of his promise to go to the Wyanoid Baptist Church, a perturbation of spirit weighing on him not so much for the denomination as for another fact, suddenly remembered, that no miracle of Christ's ever took place in the Temple of Jerusalem.

XLVI

The Wyanoid Baptist Church

One can know what God is not; one cannot know what He is.

—St. Augustine

THE WYANOID BAPTIST CHURCH—a box-shaped affair surrounded by catbriars and scrubby, asymmetrical rows of chinaberry
trees—stood on the main street. There was a faint odor of mundungus
in the Sunday morning air, but the sun shone brightly. Southern
Baptists, who had separated from their Northern counterparts in
1845, were generally to be found a congregation of thin-lipped
believers in immersion, closed communion, and total teetotalism, and,
while it did not share his own ancient religion's boast eternal of
semper eadem—neither was it, at once, holy, catholic, and apostolic—
Darconville, standing on the front steps there, turned his back on the

history of sacrilege in its shingles and determined to try to be more al-
truistic.

The parishioners, stepping out of their old automobiles and dented
pickup trucks, all had something flat about them, and as they walked
into church, moved, each, perhaps by the thought of future glory
which he or she fought in himself as too worldly and so rechristened
duty, the mood was made manifest in the general soberness of appearance. It was all *flat*. They had flat heads, flat shoes, flat chests, flat
faces, flat clothes, and flat, very flat voices.

Darconville felt a bit guilty for such prejudgments and vowed, with
a smile, to discontinue "satirizing," the penance for which the great
medieval Church of Rome prescribed twelve genuflections at every
canonical hour, three hundred blows with a leather cat, and a cross-
vigil. At that very moment two black girls, wearing their Sunday best,
hesitated in front of the church, when suddenly a sanctimonious
busybody with pegged teeth came running down the front stairs, took
them by the shoulders, and, smacking through a hole of lipstick, told
them they shouldn't be there, *should* they, that they had their own
church, *hadn't* they, and that they knew that very well, *didn't* they,
mmm? The girls, wounded, looked past the woman to Darconville
and hurried away. The woman's face stank with virtue, he thought, as
his own inaction stank with vice, but what could he do? There was
nothing to be done, he reasoned, that would actually *do* anything, for
we are renegades all, he thought, unfair each, every one a fool. What
ever changed? The blacks are the invisibles of the whites. The poor are
the wealth of the rich—but the thought, swiftly addressed by some
words of St. Paul, only reflected the madness of all men: "For that
which I do, I allow not; for what I would, that do I not; but what I
hate, that do I." Slowly, it came to him that the enemy of Christ was
not the atheist but rather the bankrupt Christian, and with great disappointment he soon felt part of all he heard and what he saw, for he
himself was how it was, overwhelmed in the *the* of being there and
making not a jot of difference by the fact. And then, as recognition
caught hold of remorse, he suddenly realized that it had been on this
very spot not a year ago that, speaking to Miss Trappe, he had smugly
assured himself that the price for privacy was anonymity. And O, how
anonymous he had become! Buffoon of my own ruins, thought Darconville, miscalled Quinsyburg! I have become what I am!

Then, there was Isabel. The flower-de-luce looked pale from little sleep but no less beautiful than ever, her hair pulled back *à la vierge,* her fingers playing high in a little resigned wave. She managed a small smile. The sun seemed to be shining out of her rather than onto her, a fact confirmed now in the semi-darkness as they entered the church. Isabel remarked the dry, punkwoody, almost *tense* smell reaching throughout the place. "Schism," said Darconville.

There was no altar. It was a neo-funeral-home décor with faked stained-glass and buckets of ferns and tubs of cycads placed around the enormous stage up front in the middle of which was a high rostrum which held a gigantic red-leather Bible, its silk purple page-marker hanging out like a weary tongue. The two of them sat down immediately to find staring at them from the reserved seats at the side of the stage a group that looked less like the officials of a church synod than the botched supernumeraries from the Bosch *Bearing of the Cross:* a row of sour elders, civic schmalkaldics, and scowling proto-puritans swollen with the honor of wardenship. As the choir began its first hymn, "My Lord Our Pinkies Nice Can Tweak," Darconville hoped he didn't know what to expect but rather expected he did, only too well.

He recalled, for instance, one particular night the previous winter when, called upon for it, he had gone over to Dr. Dodypol's house to cheer him up but, when he arrived, found that little fellow reeling around drunk as a lord, his lower lip hanging so low it looked as if he were wearing a turtleneck sweater. The Piggly Wiggly had been closed six hours or so and his wife hadn't yet come home. It had grown later and later when Dr. Dodypol, fidimplicitary no more, burst into a crazy fit of laughter and with one low wheeple from the throat asked, "What does one need more than anything else in the world?" But when his visitor quite properly answered love, the poor poet, mur-derously squeezing his glass into a fist of bits, squawked, "For Mrs. Dodypol, I could make it *air!*"—and then passed out. Darconville had covered him with a blanket, he remembered, and, watching guard, turned on the television set. Network programming had just ended. At that instant, however, morning devotions—"Nitey Nite Necessities" or something like that—slotted in, a quiet organ *Schlummerlied* in the background supplying inspiration, when suddenly an aggrieved cleri-cal demivir dropped, ripe as a medlar, into the nasty little orchard that was everyone's life. Looking up from his busy ministerial desk, the evangelist swung off his glasses—candor—and immediately began gas-conading about this here being the free-est country on earth and, friend, the most decent, an assertion he underscored with the unu-sually colorful heresies, explicitly implied, that Christ had signed the Declaration of Independence, personally translated Robert E. Lee's horse, "Traveler," to the reaches of heaven, and was temporarily liv-ing in Crozet, Virginia (not uncoincidentally the preacher's home-town), where, carpentering a new church, He might be very, very pleased if one morning, you pick it, neighbor, He sauntered down the hill to find five dollars tucked into his R.F.D. mailbox just so's He could see to that new weatherproof siding! And tenpenny nails! And heating ducts! And ten dollars would buy twice as much! And twenty, why, four times that! An address for mailing was flashed on the screen, not before, however, those out there in televisionland were sent scurry-ing for a pencil. The preacher then flipped open his Bible, raced through a text, kissed the page, and then with his head lowered—caught looking up, his eyes custodiously emended—he slowly meta-morphosed into a flapping Old Glory upon which was superimposed a montage, in sequence, of cumulus clouds, a squadron of jets, grannies-at-prayer, the murmuring pines and the hemlocks, a towheaded tiny licking a raindrop from her nose, the fruited plains, and, finally, the Raising of the Flag at Iwo Jima, this accompanied all the while by the crescendo of an out-of-tune choir humming "I Love to Steal Awhile Away," after which a thunderclap and then the basso profundo voice of God the Father demoting from on high, *"I Am with You Always, Even Unto the End of the World!"* At which point, miraculously, Dr. Dodypol rose on a drunken elbow, claimed *that* was only the voice of a fat man bellowing into an empty keg, and then fell back again un-conscious.

"May the Lord love you *reeeeal* good!"

It was the heartfelt, if ungrammatical, wish of welcome boomed over a microphone—and suddenly waking Darconville to where he was—by a jug-eared rapscallion wearing a string-tie, a raspberry shirt, and a woefully carpentered hairstyle. Clamor flew with huge flapping wingclaps from wall to wall. The service was ready to begin.

"I come up here"—he wiped his nose on his sleeve and, snuffling, grinned—"I come up here in front of all you good folks and feller Christians to welcome you to our sixth-in-a-row doorbuster revival Sunday, is what it is, with the world-famous man, evangelist, and pastor of the Wyanoid Baptist Church, Dr. W. C. Cloogy, who you gonna see in jess a minute, but first—"

Doctor? *Doctor?* Darconville was surprised, but then understood: for what preacher, teacher, or sinister minister could ever course among his flock peddling his scriptural *exta* and exegetical guesswork without the security of some kind of honorific, unfurled over him like an umbrella? Doctor was the favorite. Reverend would do. Saint was too pretentious, Kalokagathiate not true. Arch-Rabbi was impossible. Misters just abound. And, finally, Metropolitan had a Euro*p*ean sound.

The interlocutor, meanwhile, asking for everyone's undivided attention, went straight into the preliminary segment of the program. Darconville looked around him to see people knuckling into their pews, snorting for excitement, ready to be entertained. Revival fires, burning, somehow recapitulated the klieg-lights of the Grand Ole Opry. It was a kind of *revue!*

Miss Gelda Lou Glikes, a girl of excessive beribbonment, blew out on her trumpet the old winner, "He Touched Me," blushed, and skipped into the wings. An ex-football star from the Cincinnati Bengals (30" neck, 5½" hat) mesomorphically loped to the podium and said that it may sound corny but he was lonesome for Jesus, a remarkable heresy, thought Darconville, contravening the orthodox argument that He is everywhere, but there was little time to reflect on this, what with the swift entrance of The Marvy Twins, male regulars, who swayed and harmonized to the favorite, "The Flame on My Wick Is Bright Tonight," the last chorus of which one hummed while the other narrated a poem about motherhood from an anniversary greeting card. Then a former dipsomaniac second-grade schoolteacher, choking back the tears—"witnessing"—told her story, God help her, about a spinfit she once threw after drinking only *one* highball, God forgive her, when she forced an unruly seven-year-old to eat a whole jar of mucilage and two pink erasers. And then a high-school boy in a wheelchair, waving the Confederate Battle Flag, was pushed out on stage to recite a snatchet from "The Conquered Banner":

> ". . . Keep it, widowed, sonless mothers,
> Keep it, sisters, mourning brothers,
> Furl it with an iron will,
> Furl it now, but—keep it still;
> Think not that its work is done . . ."

The showcase opened even wider. An octogenarian, garbed out in an American Legion uniform, was led out to wave just before what was clearly imminent cardiac arrest, one that would nevertheless proudly enroll him among the Army of Heaven. A dwarf named Larry appeared and spoke in tongues, the supernatural aspect of his delivery not untransvalued for strangeness by his harelip. And the last act belonged to one Roy LeRoy, billed as, and generally recognized to be, W. C. Cloogy's "best friend," for the evangelist, like the King of the Cowboys, always keeps such a foil: it implies a disposition to gregariousness, Roman *amicitia,* and cuts down for the ensainted preacher on the inevitable speculation the presence of wives causes. A kind of swagman, stooge, and jovial boy-friday, he sang in one of those parodically classical, out-of-fashion voices a medley of laxatives touching on the Jordan; chariots swinging low; Rolls Being Called Up Yonder; Loving Mysterious Strangers (age 33!); golden slippers; and Columbia, the Gem—as the famous mixed metaphor has it—of the Ocean, these being interspersed, narratively, with a didactic mess of "Why, Daddy?" stories; criminal-sons-and-saintly-moms stories; the Worm Turns stories; instant conversion stories; money-can-never-make-you-happy stories (always a signal for the collection), and, *testantibus actis,* a whole rosary of patriotic yarns.

The Americanistic pitch, of course, was old hat on the Bible circuit, as were subterranean virility fears common, the latter always animating the former in the extra-defensive and recurrent dream of the evangelist in which he sees himself, in full color and cinemascope, a lantern-jawed begrenaded U. S. Marine leaping out of a trench to beat the living shit out of the Devil who, widespread was the assumption, wore perfume, spoke Russian, and carried a purse.

"I must have your attention now, Lies and German"—it was the mannerbereft in the string-tie again, raising his eyes like Enoch Translated—"for to welcome the shepherd of you sheep, God's chosen minister and," he winked cutely, "the best li'l ol' buddy around—Dr. W. C. Cloogy!"

The star appeared in the east wing. And then he rumbled out, threw out his arms, and drew a bead directly on the ceiling overhead.

"The text for today, brothers and sisters, is: *'Why do you boast of your valleys, O faithless daughter?'* Jeremiah 49:4."

Everyone crouched.

"Sex! I'm puttin' in here today to talk to you about sex! Utter that blackest of words, neighbors, speak its two little syllables compared to which, dear, dear brethren, nothin'll give you the fantods quicker, hear? It's been the world's favorite word since time began, from Lot's wife to Pharaoh to the Queen of Sheeby, and yet as I speak I know full certain that half of you sorry pieces of plunder ain't in no more mood to give it up than to cross the Rivanna River in a hollow tooth! The Lord axin' you to be pure of flesh was axin' back small change on the dollar, see, but what? You smug as barncats, huh? Actin' like Nebuckadunsaw, right? Givin' in to your cravin's? Don't look around! I talkin' to you, not *someotherbody!* I talkin' to you out there, all stinking feathers and no hat, who say 'I'm mone live forever!' who say 'Not me!' who say 'Bull!' until you wake up one day to find the Devil hoppin' on you like a duck on a June bug, OK? Eyes closed, ears deef, lips silent, fanny stopped up, yes, yes, yes! O God, help! O God, rescue! O God, I seen it all before!"

The Rev. W. C. Cloogy, *Doctor Fundatus,* took his mumping cant right to the lip of the stage. There was about his face a more than passing resemblance to Ulrich Zwingli: a nose like a doorknob, round and brassy, poked out of an odd rutabaga-shaped head, while under his hooded eyelids two distrustful eyes constantly shifted back and forth black and snapping like a jackdaw's. Farcically he jigged in his smoldering clothes, flaring his nose, thrashing the language in accents penacute and rude, and, with deep and ominous wefts of breath, sidling up toward the congregation in jits. The Abbot of Unreason was loose.

"Mo-tels! Pa'back books! Sippin'-liquor! Goosedown pillows! *Supposed* hayrides! Men in bulgin' pants from magazines! Girlies with eyelashes like dang rakes! Profanity, that's how I pronounce it! But shall I put you in the picture, friend? Ain't never been a soul tumblin' through them Gates of Eternity but wadn't first a li'l heap of trash, born in shame, and set on magnetic north to grab at every pair of glands in sight, pawin' flesh and *doin' like hawgs!* You proud of it? You aim to be just another one of these crapmouses? That what I get for confabulatin' with y'all up here every Sunday of a morning? No? Well, you best *get saved,* boy, *Ephesians 2:2,* or don't come runnin' to me, 'cause ain't nobody nohow better plan on eatin' fish muddle n' shoe-fly pie forever, clear? You vaporin' with the Lord, you and you? And plannin' on gettin' away with it? Why, you gonna get jerked up, every last one of you! The wages of sin is death! The wages of sin, don't bet your chewing gum otherwise, is that you gonna die, die, die, die, you with me? Everything from figpecker to philosopher gonna *dah! Hosea 9:7.* Why, on the Day of the Great Dividin', Jack, you'll be pawnin' your crisping pins, big-city suits, mantles, fancy duded-up hats, and you name what-all from the Montgomery Ward, *Habakkuk 3:7,* and why, you ask? Go no farther'n here, I'll tell you, why just to buy your greedy profane little self one minute from Hell's black flames which can burn, sear, blister, spit, bubble, and boil, but too late, you dracs and sorcerers and fornicators, because by then the fahrenheit will have shot through the nipple of the thermometer like you wouldn't believe and be scorchin' out your spatchcock and gizzards, which'll be a thousand times worse if you took liquor 'cause that *catches!* And do you think the Lord is gonna care two diddlies if you fry—*frah!*—wipin' hellsmoke out of your eyes and dobbin' your body with ashes to dink the heat? Not if you ain't willin' to walk down Redemption Avenue! Not if you sloppy-kissin' the foot of Pharaoh! Not if you ain't right with *Him*—but that's either here or there, ain't it, 'cause if you was right with Him, you things of Gomorrah, you'd-a not been there in the first damn place!"

Darconville couldn't believe it. He looked about him. It was a *limbus fatuus* of devotees: old horsefaced ladies in absurd hats; various paralytici; hominids and monorhines; dishlicking Hutterites; tobacco farmers, their necks cracked and veneered by sun and wind; goosecaps with bowl haircuts; crofters and their wives, both with toothless Punch-and-Judy profiles; and, of course, the little foxes who spoil the vines, little teratogenic kids with wide mouths, round simpleton faces, and water-parted hair. And naturally there were those two bedizened women-in-orchids (there always are) sitting together and complaining they couldn't hear a thing. Most of the people, stiff as pipes, sat non-introspectively upright with the orthodox stares of faces on church windows, but others, perhaps reaffirming the idea that the human mind is more easily unhinged in matters of divinity than anything else, began jerking back and forth like woodpeckers. A few wept. And one or two tremebundi were knotted up in prayer, like frogs poised for a jump. There was the sprawler, the huncher, the croucher, the percher, the squatter, and one lady, either daft or in the "rapture" —the boundaries touch—was coiled around herself in a side-aisle and flapping in an *arc de cercle,* the characteristic posture of the hysteric.

Cloogy the concionator, meanwhile, saw he had them where he

wanted them, mustn't lose them, and so warmed to the task, a hot
scaldabanco now cuffing his assailant's shadow on the wall, wringing
his fingers, and verjuicing his sermon with every fright he could, he
spit his wrath and spanked the vices of his age without a break or
breath.

"I seen the end and the beginning! I seen fallen women, painted up
like baboons, who could sweet-talk a cat into a doghouse and, hopin'
to God never to see more, sportin' men in zoot suits shagging them at
the dance hall. But what really cracks my acorns is to see young folks
leavin' their little truck patches nowadays just to go mousin' around
the city with cigarettes like the ten-horned fiends of Revelations, and
for what?—*sexual monkeyshines!* Misfits, that's all! Misfits and
compost-sniffin' neathogs who don't give a pin's fee or a penny for the
Lord Jesus, born in the winter of the year 1, died in the spring of 33!
Joshua ben Joseph they called Him back then, bein' Jews of course
and too blamebusted ee-literate to ascertain He was callin' Hisself by
the name of Jesus, El Shaddai if you want to be fancy, which I don't!
'Course, I know nothin', you know it all, huh? So go ahead, smoke
yourself into fidgets! Coat your belly with the devil's drink! Fashion
yourself out as friends of pope-worshippers and *fai*-ries! Pinch up your
waist in calico, half nekkid, and take your love to town under them
bright city lights and honky-tonks, *Sirach 34:4!* But put you in mind,
you nasty little trapes, come the last trump of thunder—O mercy,
mercy on your souls!—you'll have no wheel to spin, no loom on which
to weave, no sickle to harvest with, no well-sweep to draw up precious
water! And then what a scouring! What an upturnin'! Lordy, what a
dee-molition!"

The brimstone rained down, but it didn't matter. Evangelism is to
Southerners what valerian is to a cat. The congregation whuffed ap-
preciatively, their Demosthenes, they felt, being as brilliant an orator
as ever the Pnyx had cheered. Not for them, if for Darconville—Isabel
was only bewildered—was it the trashiest piffle and most intolerable
bit of fustian since the days of thundering Whitfield, circulating
Summerfield, and weeping Payson. No, this for them was the Word,
and its speaker—with hewing arms, a face pot-liquor green, and a
mouthful of indicavits—might just as well have been preaching from
a fishing-smack dead center in the Sea of Galilee or sending the
Divine Message through the penal bars of the Mamertine dungeon.
Cloogy banked on that as he pointed a finger straight into their faces.

"I be takin' up a collection momentarily and will be axin' you to reach down deep in your pockets to pull out some *faith* which in this part of the Holy Land, for outreach work and general upkeep, is colored green and crackles, 'cause on your deathbed or, well, pallet, which is the same as a bed only narrower, you subscribers of sex and malfeasance, you ain't gonna own nothin', you ain't gonna take nothin', you ain't gonna *hear* nothin', not the thrum of a harp, not the carol of a bird, not the howl of a coon, not the whoooole doxology of congregations—doxology a big-city word for praise and glory, nothin' else—so be warned, you fleshpeddlin' spackies and shut-wallets and tithin' nigglers! 'You conceive chaff, you bring forth stubble!' *Isaiah 33:11*. But listen to me! Did I just say you gonna prance into heaven 'cause you e-void honky houses? Did I just say you gonna prance into heaven 'cause you ain't backslidin' but twicet a week? Did I just say you gonna prance into heaven, you rinsepitchin', fist-clinching, pennypinching dah-warves, 'cause you blow the horn in Gibeah and sound the trumpet in Ramah? I didn't say any such of a *thang!* No! No, no, no! You got to have *faith,* which means only trust—in God—a mot-to found on every dollar in the American mint! 'Put in the sickle, for the harvest is ripe!' *Joel 3:13*. Here now, do I hear you reachin' down now or is wickedness sweet in your mouth? O wheelbarrows, full of hates and hisses! O hard as stwones! I hear no jingle! I hear no jangle!"

Cloogy pulled no stops now as, before the congregation, he pumped and wheezed and bellowed. He hopped, capricornified, across the stage, glaring. When he put one foot down, he lifted the other up. He drove his fist down through the air as if knocking, peg-wise, every last metaphorical demon who dared lift his head. Barging up to the proscenium, he flung up his hands and with cheek-shaking fury let himself loose in bombs of rhetoric that hadn't been felt in that part of the world since Calhoun addressed himself to the doctrine of state sovereignty. It was all advertisement, no news: the theatrically "shattered" voice, moistened with sobs; the S's altered to Th's; the farm analogies; the birdperch finger, wagging; the faraway look on the radiant face on the glorious horizon; and, of course, the slow but efficient whining that built up like feeding in small-arms ammunition which culminated, suddenly, in the rapid-fire of machine-gun prooftexting.

"I can't *believe* it! The Lord can't believe it! You tryin' to abridge the Lord above, you bangdogs, you open compurgators of Satan, you

soupsnufflin' excuses of Og and Zedekiah and Tubal-Cain, whose face
was black as soot! 'Wail, O gate! Cry, O city! Melt in fear, O Philistia, all of you!' *Isaiah, 14:31.* There is your faith? Is Hell havin' a
banquet? Do I see you shootin' into your pocket for contribution?
Don't Jesus count? I want every man, woman, boy, and girl to lift their
hand high if they want Jesus to come hoppin' into their flinty hearts!
Lift them high! I ain't gone be up here all day, friends, having work
in the Holy Vineyard enough for a squad*roon* and outnumberin'
arithmetic itself! So hands up, c'mon, high—*hah, hah, haher!* I cain't
haft see them, widow-ladies! I cain't see them, poor ol' gentmin in
over-hauls! Or are you just a cootie? A stinkard? A inglorious piece of
fat ram-mutton? *Hah!* Wag your fingers! *Hah!* Shoggle your wrists or
somethin'! How many out there *cain't* lift his hand to Goddlemighty?
O how many! O! O! And now may we pray?"

Every hand, as if shot, suddenly fell as the organ began to swell. All
grabbed hands tightly in a display of tactile prayer. A symphrase of
indistinguishable nonsense ended up front punctuated with a burplike
"amen," and Rev. W. C. Cloogy, striding magnanimously forward—
just minutes, presumably, before his Bethany-like ascension—made
available to everyone there his pouchable goods, sundries, pigges'
bones, holy relikes. The purchases, came the assurance, were all in-
structible, indestructible, and tax-deductable. Gimme that Ol' Time
Revision!

While Cloogy piously knelt, the collection baskets were passed, and
Roy LeRoy sang, "If You Take Two Steps Toward Jesus, He'll Take
Three Steps Toward You." The interlocutor in the raspberry shirt
came forward and advised each and every soul—before the offers were
either suspended or depleted—that he or she could personally own in
his own home any one of the following: a glossy snapshot of Pastor
Cloogy riding a dromedary across The Plains of Sharon ($1.25); a
real pinion wrestled from an angel in the Land of Penuel ($6.00@);
The Marvy Twins' LP Album, *Hymns for Her,* featuring the much-
requested national hit, "My Dropsy Cured One Night It Was"
($7.95); cigarette lighters with a microdot of Mt. Vernon on the
strikeflint ($6.50@); a holy tablecloth showing Ishbosheth, King of Is-
rael, Being Assassinated ($16.00); an actual vessel of bottled darkness
from the plague visited by Moses upon Pharaoh ($12.75); stone
piecelettes nicked from the Rock of Ages, glued to a card underneath
the legend "America: Right or Wrong!" ($2.25); and, confirming,

perhaps, the idea, widely held, that the evangelical mind is obsessed much more with bowel irregularity than anything else, packets of lenitive powders ground from Palestinian pistachio shells for the diagnostically restringent ($5.45 for twelve).

There were free hams, a gift only to those, however, who made offerings of over $20 *or* whose contributions exceeded the mean of the per capita tally that day as certified by the public accountant who, at that very moment, was collecting the envelopes at the end of each pew. Certificates of honor would be awarded, of course, to special contributors: Soul Winners ($500); Prayer Warriors ($300); Scripture Seekers ($100); and Youth Year-Arounds ($50).

As the choir sang "Arphaxad from the Flood He Swam," the envelopes—a very small pile—were brought worshipfully forward and placed on the lip of the stage, where W. C. Cloogy, spying the size, had to bite his knuckles he was so angry, and then in one last fit of entheomania he came howling out at them in heat like the craven, great-gullied gastrolator he was, roaring horrisonously and, with nictating eyes, seeking for a final time to make mad mystery out of ignorance and inspiration out of dread. It was the high point of the show: the Decisions for Christ.

"Quail, O sinners! Cringe, O bedwarfed sons and daughters, and pray for dear life that the yield on the baskets will be bigger'n the envelopes 'cause these here are lookin' slimmer than a three-day fast! I don't know from the next who's holdin' back, I swear. But take the Lord—you fancy *He* don't know who tiddlywinkin' buttons and pewter pennies my way in the name of tithes? That *He* don't feel you weevilin' your checkbook around in the dungeon of your filthy pockets? That *He* don't see you peppin' up on nekkid pictures in the corncrib or cropin' down the backstairs at night like a red Commonist with your guilty little face all jellied up with lipstick and a dress on you tighter than a nigger's thumbprint? Shoot, He don't!—and the mercy is He don't snipe you right there in your socks! For what's He bound to think? Why, no evangel of Christ Jesus, you! No fellow-shipper of the Lord, Who died for your raggedy sins! No prophetess of adequate wardrobe, you! No advocate of Christian endeavor, you! No wise virgin with her range-oil lamp full, you! Well now, I'm about to give you one last chance to accept Christ Jesus as your personal savior, because, failing that, you poor bumblades, you lay whippin' straight into Hell where you gone be roasted into a snuff-stick the second you

arrive by flames cat-lappin' up to your chin and head! *Ezekiel 40:2.*
You ask is hell hot, and I'll ask is a bullfrog waterproof, OK? I tell
you, you gone be stir-fried! Barbecued! Whipsawed back and forth by
unnatural devils and squeezed 'til your pips squeak! But you don't
cotton to all this ruckin' and raisin' sand back there, do you? Gettin'
creepy-bumps all over your flesh, ain't you? Then stand up! Stand up,
you pathetic examples of homo dumbiens! Stand up, you insolent arrogant sharpies! Grasshopper down here to the front of this church
and in this year of Restored Salvation accept Christ Jesus into your
life or you be swallowed up in perdition quicker nor an alligator can
claw a puppy! Is there sin come between you and the Lord? Are you
man enough to kneel down here with me and pray? Then come on
down! O, come! Come!"

The organ swelled up in a chord and burst into that old staple,
"Just as I Am." And toward the front of the church came the inevitable parade of hobblers and tame villatic fowl: weeping girls; the semi-
cancroid; Malchians with severed ears; cured demoniacs; the now
thankfully upright hemorrhoidal; the luckless, with bad draughts of
fishes; the entrussed, the encrutched, and the enfeebled, all tapping,
jerking, and lurching altarwards in the owl-light like the Beggars
Come to Town.

Beaming, Dr. Cloogy stroked his huge nose. He greeted each soul
with a congratulatory handquake and then aimed them quickly on a
beeline into a backroom behind an ellipse there where each was given
a fistful of leaflets and brochures—not unlike those, in fact, commonly
distributed year round by Harriet Bowdler and Loretta Boyco—illustrated with pictures (lions nuzzling up to lambs, idealized couples-in-
profile staring into a nebula, etc.) and chronicled by various physeters-
of-lies who warned against the wicked system of things and generally
proscribed: two-tone shoes, beards, polysyllabic words, ecologists, ritual, enemies of the N.R.A., educated blacks, corn liquor, long hair,
the word *whom,* wayside shrines, uneducated blacks, actors, Harvard
University, stickpins, Bolsheviks, and pomeranians.

The recessional at the Wyanoid Baptist Church went off without a
hitch: Cloogy asked all ladies in the congregation who wished to engage in family-planning to please see him in his study, a last hysterical
hymn was sung so loud it rocked the floor, and bonking out of their
pews the little folks put on their sparrowbill caps and departed. Pastor

Cloogy decamped to someone's house for dinner. The doors were then locked tight.

And God? *Abiit, excessit, evasit, erupit.*

Darconville felt that Isabel—of no denomination herself and knowing nothing of religion—could never take it seriously again and so accepted the fact that, although he'd long fondly wished for her baptism, any commitment that way after this inefficacious Sunday must only be the first symptom of a great betrayal to which for her personal integrity she'd never consent to be party. That day would pass away, thought Darconville, with Isabel lost to the grace she deserved if only for showing that steadfastness so much less pronounced thousands of years ago when Mother Eve she span.

At the same time, the lapse of principle touching on his own failure to defend the black girls earlier caused him deep remorse. He tried to tell her what he felt, but before he could strangely she put a finger to his lips as if, expressing an impulse which exists only by opposition to the fear that ostensibly oppresses it, humbly to stifle the praise she wouldn't, couldn't, deserve.

"I will always love you," said Darconville, taking her by the finger. She simply smiled.

"Me too."

And they went to Darconville's rooms and made love.

XLVII

A Fallacy of the Consequent

Can reason untwine the line that nature twists?

—St. ALEXIS, the Vagabond of God

DARCONVILLE'S CAT peered from one to another in the darkened room, to Isabel asleep for her rhythmical breathing, to Darconville awake for his eyes moving down the rungs of a syllogism. It was
the end of the year, a time for reckoning, and in consequence of his
perhaps marvelous but certainly tenuous affair with a student it had
been judiciously pointed out to him—by certain colleagues, to intercept fate—that no Quinsy girl was able to love. Interesting, thought
Darconville, for because of her poor academic showing Isabel by
rights *was* no longer a Quinsy girl. And yet, having just made love,
wasn't she then a lover? And so what, he wondered, from that given

value were the values of other propositions immediately inferred by opposition and education?

1. No Quinsy girl is a lover. (**GIVEN**)
2. Some lover is a Quinsy girl. (False)
3. Some Quinsy girl is a lover. (False)
4. Some lover is not a non-Quinsy girl. (False)
5. Some Quinsy girl is not a non-lover. (False)
6. No lover is a Quinsy girl. (True)
7. Every Quinsy girl is a non-lover. (True)
8. Every lover is a Quinsy girl. (False)
9. No lover is a non-Quinsy girl. (False)
10. No non-Quinsy girl is a lover. (False)
11. Every non-Quinsy girl is a non-lover. (False)
12. Every Quinsy girl is a lover. (False)
13. Some lover is not a Quinsy girl. (True)
14. Some lover is a non-Quinsy girl. (True)
15. Some non-Quinsy girl is a lover. (True)
16. Some non-lover is a Quinsy girl. (True)
17. Some Quinsy girl is not a lover. (True)
18. Some non-lover is a non-Quinsy girl. (?)
19. Some Quinsy girl is a non-lover. (True)
20. Every lover is a non-Quinsy girl. (True)
    No!

A paw stopped Darconville, almost sitting up in panic; he'd tripped, unbalancing himself, over proposition ⚹18 and fell with a wild clutch at the question mark: the value was impossible to determine. It was the *one* proposition—her very age, at that—not available to formal inquiry. Words that cannot exceed where they cannot express enough cannot succeed when they try to learn too much. Yet mightn't that matter unillumined by, or contrary to, be above reason? He looked at Isabel. She sometimes smiled in her sleep like a cat whose upcurvital mouth showed perpetual joy. A non-lover? *Verbatim ac literatum.* Ridiculous, thought Darconville, for when with logic, he asked himself again, had love to do? If green is unripe, why then blackberries are red when they're green. And in that very same darkness that muddled his poor thoughts hadn't been consummated that sweet warfare having victors only? True enough, one needn't necessarily be in love in order to—

Darconville frowned.

No value could be inferred. Better count the pulses of Methuselah. Thank you, logic.

XLVIII

Charlottesville

Now are they come nigh to the
Bowre of blis,
Of her fond favorites
So nam'd amis.

—EDMUND SPENSER, *The Faërie Queene*

THE FIRST DAYS of June, fickle, were cooled and freshened by a touch of rain and then lapsed back again to a languorous warmth, the shivelights of bright sun teasing out of every throughway and thicket the pale first fruits; mead blew, feed grew, sounded the cuckoo, and summer, a-coming, came in.

The school year ended, forcing neither Darconville nor Isabel to any decision of consequence concerning the future. With his help she vacated her room at Quinsy and without any fanfare—save for the last-minute appearance of doting Miss Ballhatchet who, puffing across the lawn for a farewell, presented her with a gift (*The Poems of Sappho*)—they drove away, Isabel silent, her collar up, and Darconville feeling quite sad and empty.

Isabel took a job as a telephone operator in Charlottesville. And Darconville stayed on in Quinsyburg. He lived alone as usual, making occasional visits to Miss Trappe's house, and after some consideration took up writing his book again, not with the vigor he'd once known, rather with the comportment of the crane of legend who, to keep awake, gripped a stone in its footclaw. He felt vigor: it was not that he didn't: but his vigor was divided, a bilocation of spirit he felt necessary to support the half he loved more, and she was now sixty miles away.

Although the writer is a man who, paradoxically, must have nothing to do to do what nothing intimates he must do, Darconville felt he stole for art—*"You always never stop writing!"*—what life owned, hesitating too often before the thought of now trying to repay some fraction of his debt to her by offering her a book that was meant to be and then feeling she had nothing whatsoever to do with it at all. It was not so much a question of where commitment should lie in facing the divided self as to who should be the judge. It was with sadness, when he wrote, that he saw each page come up violent, with every loop a gallownoose, every period a bullethole, every break between sentences a crawlspace into which guilt crept home to hide; the words themselves sank down into the inkcrimped paper and perversely seemed to have an existence only on the other side of the page: a bebeloglyphics of revolt and refusal, backwards in dead black.

Isabel became his constant preoccupation. Strangely, he feared her loneliness, and, whenever he thought such a thing probable for her, he lived it himself, as lovers will, with twice the anguish. There were troubles—crises often coming simultaneous with letters from her, answers to the ones required of him to have hers (was this pride or humility?) which revealed, in attempts to hide her unhappiness, her unhappiness: family discord, the need for her own apartment, a roommate to share expenses, etc. How often we express what we can't, thought Darconville. A game is not won until it's also lost. The exclamation mark is always a digression. And so to assuage his own fears as much as her own, though moved more out of love than duty, Darconville would often put away his work and drive up to Charlottesville to visit.

The potholed road winding out of the seventh circle of Quinsyburg and its scrubpine forests takes a turn for the better just at that point where the James River debouches on a silly curve through low swampland and passes by the hog-soaping community of Scottsville. A swift change in tone is noticed: dirt-farms give way to orchards; farting pigs transform into sleek horses; and goose-faced peasants—lo!— are now sporting colonels in plus-fours banging away at birds. The grass of a sudden rolls away to smooth expanses of green, no longer anymore tall and shapeless twists of brome and creekthatch. Now in the air is the perfume of blooms, not tobacco, and one hears the content *weedio-weedio* of whistling quails instead of scraping whiffletrees and hens screeching through backyards draped over in hand-wrung laundry. There the northern part of Virginia begins to detach itself from the southern. Exit Calvin; enter Pelagius. Enthusiasm is out, neo-Stoicism in. The rod is put away, to be replaced by sweetmeats. You bank a wooden bridge some miles along and weave up and out of a last dingle to discover finally below you at the eastern foot of the Blue Ridge—always with surprise—the city of Mr. Jefferson.

Charlottesville was a city that loved prerogative. It was, in fact, one of those quaint places on earth where most of the inhabitants, emphasizing the value of ancestral origins, spent a lifetime zealously devoted to the cause of trying to correct the several mistakes, owing to their absence, committed during the events described in the first chapter of Genesis. This was the land of Wishes, Wirtses, and Weems, where every last ferblet in the county had the distinct impression he was a born gentleman and she a well-bred lady, and that was that. Theirs was that great legacy of the Southern elite, dames and colonels still, so it went, all in solid support of a proud slaveholding but benevolent republic—purified of Free-Soilers, locofocos, parlor pinks, realists, supporters of the Wilmot Proviso, and advocates of the League of Nations —which stretched majestically from Pontchartrain to the Potomac: not the United States, but the States United!

The Virginians in this particular area, briefly, had a marvelous idea of themselves. What was past was perfect! They doggedly held to a caste mentality. They kept a strict and incurable devotion to postures they felt couldn't be misinterpreted at Windsor or Schönbrunn. They still tried to register wills by regnal years, used seltzer bottles, and

habitually went on ancestor hunts (flatly refusing to accept the *lie* that
everybody had as many ancestors as anyone else) and while obsessed by
lineage many philoprogenitive parents in the South, to fix on a bygone
era by intra-family "arrangements," preferred to marry kin rather
than those unrelated by blood. It was of course inevitable some would
eventually have to take the bit between the teeth in relation to the occasional, slightly plumulaceous child who came along—a congenital
drooler, a nimfadoro in white boots, a little shovelmouthed surd whose
blood was so bad it was all he could do to keep from falling down. But
this too was sort of charming, see?—only one more touch of regional,
aristocratic cachet in that world of moonlight-and-magnolia which, in
a similar context, made every tree a dueling-oak, every house a planta-
tion, and every asshole in a string tie a colonel.

Myth, of course, flouted history. The tradition that all white men in
Virginia were "cavaliers"—a boast in Charlottesville put about by
even the lowest of dungcrunchers—was true only in that there had
been a general 17th-century disposition in that flyblown colony against
English parliamentarianism; at that time the humblest plowjogger in
the territory could be so identified, and was. Whenever a Southerner
dreamt of improving his lot, he kept "niggers"—stationed either on his
property or in a class, below him. Every owner of two Negroes, therefore, however dubious his own origin or squalid his existence, came to
be considered a cavalier. So was it then, such was it now. Facts, needless to say, didn't get in their way, and it was with enormous pride and
an almost martial zeal that the revisionist citizens of Charlottesville
cooperated to perpetuate the image of their forefathers as dashing,
emplumed gallants-with-mustaches out of Lord Rupert's dragoons
protecting women, daring battle, and running to hounds—when the
truth of it was they had been almost to a man nothing but a bunch of
lackeys, cacochymical scroyles, and middle-brow merchants who spoke
near-Gutnish and worked the head-right system, accumulated "seats,"
and lived out their whiggish lives pocketing quitrent, hustling slaves,
and selling snuff. But who cared? No one. Did it matter? Not a bit. It
was not in the image, never mind the interest, of the Old Dominion.
Thus the queer little mystery perpetually continued, for, blow high,
blow low, everytime a Southerner got *à vau-l'eau* he needed only
spread his sails to the winds of his own foolish fibs and flatulencies and
another start was made down-sun.

The fabulous traditions held firm in Charlottesville. The days of ye old carriage houses, stirrup cups, and bag-wigged royal governors shirted in frills and Mechlin lace were still commemoratively preserved in the hearts of the throwbacks there who, hunting foxes all day and tracing genealogies all night, were locked on the crotchets of Tory caricature: pinch-mouthed Federalists; titless Junior Leaguers from 20,000 Leagues Under the Sea; frigid bluestockings with matching hair; snudges with hip-gout; lords of rice-tierce and cotton bale, of sugar box and human cattle; civic bona-robas and bores; fatuous hippomants from country clubs; and incontrovertible bitches from the English-Speaking Union with saurian skin and faces that looked like they'd been cut on a catstick who—*suspendens omnia naso*—spoke to no one who wasn't someone and then only in the pluperfect. The men all had recurrent dreams of shooting each other for disrespectful remarks or having an affair with Sally Fairfax; the women, of being observed in the waxlight through frosty bowed windows dancing quadrilles or minuets in lovely eighteenth-century poses and saying things like, "It was simplytooshattering FOR words!" or "Why, Lord Cornwallis, you say such things!" or "O Macheath! Was it for this we parted? Taken! Imprisoned! Try'd! Hang'd—cruel Reflection! I'll stay with thee 'till Death!"

This was a species unto itself. They were the kind of people who sat around trying to imagine Patrick Henry, a close and familiar friend, stopping by for a visit and explaining between sips of Blind Pineaux what a *frightful* day he'd had with the burgesses! They hired amahs and black grooms. They gave cute toponyms to their houses like "Wit's End," "Ranelagh," or "Quivering Aspens." They didn't commit sins, of course, but only made faux pas and believed that creativity lay in things like arranging flowers and furniture or in knowing how much powdered sugar went into a mint julep. They talked constantly of hunting boxes and stables and gunrooms and went riding a lot–it was so inarguably aristocratic. They often made references to the game of cricket, without the remotest idea of how it was played. They imported English nannies to take care of their pinguid children who were always named something like Pruitt or Denison or Brawley. They loved to read—*nobiliaires,* especially; the most important books shelved in Charlottesville were, of course, Burke, Debrett, the Almanach de Gotha, Ruvigny, Fairbairn, and the Genealogisches Handbuch des Adels for such of those who, for whatever reason, couldn't pass muster in that Anglo-Saxon stronghold. The men were actually *too* gracious to women and the women too ingracious not to call it off, and so the summum bonum of their lives was to sit collectively in planters' chairs in front of columned porticos covered with creepers, drinking bourbon, watching a distant game of polo, and muttering down their chins, their general conversation being of the sort that's almost always wholly narrative (and, alas, autobiographical), coming at you in those over-pronounced declarative sentences which are usually reserved for out-and-out simpletons, nonagenarians, or myna birds and are filled with prejudices that are almost all ineradicable, being based on that kind of ignorance which is fully impenetrable to information coming from the real world. Every Charlottesvillian wanted to die in his own arms and conceived himself, upon the act, as entering Paradise by walking in genteel fashion down the Duke of Gloucester St. in Williamsburg. Each lived in a vacuum his nature positively adored. Each windowed well his head.

Good manners in Charlottesville had long ago degenerated into etiquette, which of course thrived on those social occasions when one had to have the right enthusiasms, the right prejudices, the right indignations. But that bogus aristocracy—feudal reactionaries, seigneurial landowners-in-rubber bowties, Dukes of Omnium, horse fanciers, Episcopocrats, paid-up-in-full members of the Colonial Order of the Acorn, University of Virginia trustees, the Dames of 1890, etc.—was in fact only a kind of club, a stuffy composite of thrusting attitudinarians who managed in a general and well-disguised parvenuism to throw for the *charming* people who dressed just too *divine* the *marvelous* parties they simply *adored!* They were nice without being nicer. Downward they climbed, backward they advanced. Venal, they were obsequious; obsequious, insecure; and insecure, they overstated themselves, out-anglicizing the English in that feeble mimicry which, born of inferiority, ironically made them even less secure. Dignity in the South became once again only a peculiar manifestation of gall.

Scenario: the Blacks invite you to their house, "Duchessa"; you accept and, appearing the following evening, are met under the portecochère by the small, sharplipped hostess herself—an overdressed grympen in peak shoes—who theatrically leads you by hand into the drawing room. There are paintings of celebrated race-horses on the wall, a Brown Bess over the hearth, its mantel a moonscape of old plate, and all of it surveyed from above by the glassy stare of a mounted buck's head, the huge beam-and-times sticking out in a stiff blessing. Two black maids—"reliable help"—offer you hors d'oeuvres. The host hands you a drink.

It's a fête worse than death. The room is full of people with faces like borzois, most of them drinking 8-to-1 ratio martinis and asserting one opinion after another with high-declarative candor, that subtlest form of deception. A group of over-perfumed fussocks, gossiping, and bilious old soldiers, chiming the gold in their crammed pockets, are standing around sipping—not just drinks—but the real Virginia possets: Col. Byrd's Capital Night Cap, King William's Toddy, and Daniel Parke Custis's Original Floster.

The introductions are made. It's the usual group of uniques and antiques. You meet the cheerful latitudinarian divine-cum-poacher and his young male friend. You meet the master of hounds who whispers a small salacity into your ear and wheezes good-naturedly into his cup. You meet the unsalvageable narcissist, a twenty-year-old blonde—her name is usually something like Grey Fauquier or Summer Bellerophon —who rides sidesaddle, infixes in every Southern male a compulsive desire to be flayed by her riding crop, and despises her mother for stealing her daddy with whom she is passionately in love. You meet the *agitateuse*-with-political-interests, wearing logie and fake jewels. You meet the Dear Ol' Thing, a fusty dowager who, decaying beneath piles of old-fashioned clothes, is chairwoman of projects like "Save the Peakferns" and dares say anything she damn well pleases between puffs of her tiny green cigar. They're all there, the blue-rinse set, city toparchs, university snobs, thorn-eyed starkadders with offensive orchids, gynecocrats from the hintermath of time, and all those overadvantaged rhetoricalists-in-ascots from Albemarle County who, gathered under one roof, would rather talk than breathe.

Then it's time for dinner. At the table of candles and wine, one experiences plenitude itself: the fruit-motif silver, the napkins folded tricesimosecundo, the plates heaped full, and the fat-rolls of the generous-waisted barguests bulging in expectation through the small spaces in the heartbacked Hepplewhite chairs. A black in a white jacket, answering the bell, dishes no meat but in silver: pies of carp's tongue, the carcasses of several ample wethers bruised for gravy, pig in sauce sage, and then flummery, jellies, and sweetmeats of twenty sorts, followed by cigars and cock-ale. The ladies and gentlemen then rise and retire to sit around the hearth and chat, your blissful if feigned half-sleep—a long vacation, no doubt, to Finibus Mundi—safeguard enough from having to have clarified for you, once again, the rubrics of dressage, the facts about racial inferiority, the virtues of Republicanism, and so forth and so on. It is only when they start—*again*—trotting out their parentals that you excuse yourself graciously and depart, not with any grudge or grievance, neither on the other hand with envy, but merely with the growing conviction, as you look back through the Charlottesville night, that there are some people in this world who are going to be gravely disappointed, indeed, on the Easter Sunday following their death.

But, oh, it went badly for Isabel and Darconville that summer. It wasn't so much the terrible meaninglessness of Charlottesville. Isabel seemed to be finding a charm in the very vanities Darconville had given up. She reacquainted herself, for instance, with a former high-school chum, the daughter of a crapulous woman novelist from Charlottesville. The girl's name was Lisa Gherardini, a dark-haired kakopyge with fat hands, an insipid smile, and the morals of a musk-cat. (Darconville suspected she was pregnant.) She had pretensions to art—of the craft-and-hobby sort—something Isabel both shared and admired, and when they took an apartment together Darconville tried as best he could to keep from bothering them, although it taxed him a bit, when he visited, to hear them giggling over secrets—of course there were secrets—from which he was excluded, only because good manners somehow forced him into the awkward position of having to inquire what they were. The taste for guessing puzzles he'd had enough of, God knows. But he was *involved*. St. Anthony, in the third century, offered the idea, Darconville knew further, that a seeker of God or any significant ideal, in spite of all his intentions, is doomed to community and in the end must intervene in the disputes of the world from which once he'd sought to flee. The commitment, in any case, had long been made.

The two girls were now working for the telephone company; for Lisa, with her gumball brain and strawberry-bright nails, a boon, indeed—but for Isabel? Why, her interests, as she'd often confided to Darconville, were wider by much. The possibilities—anything, she said, but a dull life in Fawx's Mt.!—were infinite; she'd shown a desire at different times to become an actress, a flautist, a veterinarian, an oceanographer, a harpsichordist, an artist, a biologist, a zookeeper, an archaeologist, a stone-jewelry artisan, a model, and a thousand other freaks that died in the thinking, notwithstanding—this, always with a knowing smile—a wife. And added to this random list might be that curious infantilism not forgot: a princess! But aspirations at that time were not very high for either, and so were high for neither. There was a good deal of aimlessness and inactivity. They were either washing their hair or were about to. They ate a lot: snacks.

The summer misresolved itself in a hundred ways. In spite of the countless efforts made to unify, splits took place. Darconville felt changes come upon them, divisions which, because they happened, seemed inevitable: he grave; she gamesome; he studious; she careless; he without mirth; she without measure. Despising himself for it, Darconville began to resent what seemed to him to be the effusive attention ("I dislike people," said Isabel, "who stare") the almost uniformly blond undergraduates ("I dislike blond guys," she added, "they seem to have no character in their faces") from the University of Virginia ("I dislike wealthy little snobs") paid to her in the street. The messages were welcome enough, thought Darconville, but the tone, the tone—and the values, if reversed, somehow would have been more agreeable. Isabel confused him. When she wasn't nervous, she seemed smug; when not happy, subdued; and when not gentle, sarcastic, the pain provoked in their various misunderstandings seeming to brace her up, as if to assent to the beauty of pearls she had to assent to the irritations that produced them. Each wanted to give, it was true, tried to give, tried desperately to give, but it seemed that as each gave the coordinate disposition to receive—how?—just vanished. I can prove on my fingers'-ends, thought Darconville, that *a dicto secundam quid ad dictum simpliciter*. They fit each other like two torn halves of a sheet of paper ripped from the book he couldn't write—belonging to each other, but unable to join. The same sensibility that brought her pleasure could always cause her pain, for being unhappy with what she was she couldn't then accept him for what he loved, or was it something else? He wasn't really sure, for often beyond each other's reach they sometimes perversely seemed less acquainted with each other now than when first they met. How exactly does that *happen* in love?

They tried nevertheless to see each other as often as they could, and when, for whatever reason, they couldn't meet at the apartment the two of them found a convenient rendezvous not far from the University of Virginia at the statue of George Rogers Clark—a public commemoration, perhaps, for his having by connivance obtained from the

Georgia legislature an immense personal land grant on the Mississippi near the mouth of the Yazoo?—but at such times there were often disagreements and, just as often, they seemed to have little to say. To her way of thinking he seemed preoccupied; she to him preoccupied his thoughts. Resentment succeeded bewilderment. Her withdrawals evoked his reproaches, and his reproaches her anger. Sometimes each found cutting words for the other. I love her, thought Darconville. And Isabel thought she loved him. But it was as if these were the very worst emotions to feel that summer.

The periodic visits to Fawx's Mt. were peculiar, as well; Isabel—Darconville had now come to notice it several times—grew nervous there, balked at being seen, avoided the street that crossed by the yard, looking only toward places where whatever she sought or sought to avoid was absent and catching herself up in the sudden half-turns by which, others notwithstanding, she even seemed to frighten herself, as if Tubriel, the unholy sefiroth of summer, shimmered towards her through the Virginia heat in waves of flame—but boding what? What was she afraid of? Or who? There was nothing to know, he found out, once meeting her on that head. Generally, they returned to Charlottesville that same day. And often in the bedroom of that low washed-out apartment—before Lisa returned, all thumbprints and reek, from visiting the hairy Idumean-from-UVa. she slept with—they made love, beautiful twins complected in the anonymous darkness they at once both needed and yet both feared.

But that was all by the way.

An event took place that put the entire affair on the shelf. It began with a party that was not significant and ended with a letter that was. But it was not really the party, not really the letter. Destiny, it might be said, simply opened its mouth to speak and, for reasons no one really knew, fambled to a halt.

It so happened that Lisa Gherardini, having suddenly decided to go to Hawaii, was given a farewell party (one made conspicuous notably by the absence of her boyfriend) on one of those flat-gold late summer evenings in Charlottesville when, shining down on things unlawfully begotten, the moon merely smiles and winks. Lisa's parents, of course, invited Isabel, and Isabel, importuning him, asked Darconville to come up from Quinsyburg to attend. File, which ever attends to Rank, obliged. It was of course one of those gatherings in the mode heretofore described, a kind of social vivisepulture with whole platoons of things-in-orchids coming youward with bourbons in hand and vicious, premeditated smiles. The guests on this occasion, people predominantly from the horse-latitudes, still proved to be less homogeneous than usual—Mrs. G (pitifully born that way) so wanted to be open-minded—and one had the redoubtable pleasure, this time, of meeting not only the ubiquitous gongster-voiced matron and mahogany-faced whipper-in but also several jimkwims from the University of Virginia, some fraternity boys and their brother bungs, two terminal poets, a few telephone operators, and a lot of other spunky nots-and-dots from the neighborhood who'd spoiled around at one time or other with the Pineapple-Princess-to-Be. This particular party was characterized by that mood of horrid democracy one so loathes; disparate factions didn't separate but actually tried to relate to each other—and while old farts, trying to dance, flapped about like wounded birds, self-assured teenagers—in whom confidence is such a vile characteristic—pontificated above the noise about politics, careers, and money-schemes. Here, a fifteen-year-old was revealing his plan for a nation-wide megalopolization of paper-routes; there, Mr. Gherardini, bald as a Dutch cheese, was twirling around like a buffoon and trying to learn the intricate steps of a dance being taught him by a high-school girl in short shorts. Mrs. Gherardini, weaseling through a network of balloons, came up to Darconville and said, "You're a writer." "No, I'm not," he replied and disappeared. It was a wonderful party.

As the evening wore on, Darconville noticed a man was flirting with Isabel across the room. Flirting perhaps was wrong: say *pluming*. The species was unmistakable, one of those over-pronounced middle-aged microlipets having some connection or other with the university—Charlottesville was full of them—who had never married, waved his hair in a fussy marcel, and had a handshake so ornate as to persuade you on the spot that you must hate him always: only another one in that grand group of prissy, theatrically erudite Episcopal hyperemians down South with his thousand-and-one stories about mother, Mozart, and miscegenation. He fit to type in his suit of rather ministerial cut, white shirt and black tie and kid slippers with soles as thin as dancing pumps, bold in the nose and given to whispering catty asides in little sibilants about everybody he met for the amusement of the maidenly young men from UVa. whom he loved to keep within a foot's-length of himself wherever he went. He isn't precisely homosexual—he is too passionless for that—but consistently worried about the size of his gib-

bals, he always drinks too much and, becoming sweetly nasty, affects
to offer his rudeness as a general defense of style and good taste of
which he invariably sees himself high-priest. He wears jewelry, keeps a
British blue cat, and simply *adores* the novels of Jane Austen.
Strangely, the type attracts women.

Fear is an eye. Darconville, nevertheless, stayed where he was,
striking up a casual conversation with a pale, somewhat avitaminotic
young man there whose ample ears jutted out of his long blond hair.
He was rather plain and not very intelligent but likable enough, and,
since both were alone, they quietly sipped their drinks and made small
talk, quickly coming to agree that neither of them belonged there.
Meanwhile, Isabel kept to her end, assiduously avoiding in her
byerespects and *bavarderie* that part of the room where Darconville
and friend waited; it was impossible to get her attention. The fop,
vaunting, would occasionally take her waist and, leaning over, whisper
whatever pretty-witted thing it was that caused her, just as occasionally, to lower her head and, biting her lip, stifle laughter. But she
seemed embarrassed. When a girl once began to be ashamed of what
she ought not to be, thought Darconville, was it not perhaps then possible that she might not one day be ashamed of what she ought? A
woman constantly blushing, thought Darconville, must be terribly well
informed. Growing disgusted, he looked away. Then everything took a
distinct turn for the worse.

Tapping on his glass for silence—clink! clink!—the fop stepped forward, calling for attention. "Here's glasses then to our Lisa," he sang,
smiling over at the party girl, "the namesake, I trust, of that best-
remembered of Elizabeths, the first so-named of English sovereignty
and patroness of the Old Dominion, mmmm?" He spoke in the key of
G-flat, like a mouse in cheese, and kissed her hand. "Bon voyage!"

Darconville gave out with a schwa of disgust.

Suddenly, the exquisite held up his hand, the poniards of his eyes
fast on Darconville; he had been waiting for the opportunity all evening.

"Aren't *you* drinking, handsome?" he called out, sarcastically. He
repeated the question again, louder.

Everyone slowly turned toward Darconville.

"I'm sorry, were you addressing me?"

"I believe I was. I do believe I was." He turned to Isabel, knowingly. "Wasn't I?"

"I can only disappoint you then," said Darconville. "It is not a practice of mine to toast the memory of dead, ambisinistrous queens, and should I ever choose to make an exception, whatever your name is, I hardly think I'd do so in deference to that illegitimately-crowned Welsh sprunt with a face like witch's butter named Bette Tudor." Murmurs could be heard. "Now go back to what you were doing and don't bother me again."

There was a perceptible chill in the room. Unconcerned, Darconville turned once more to his small conversation with the blond young man who told him, however, that he thought Isabel—he used her name—was encouraging his antagonist. (Can this fellow, wondered Darconville, have made her acquaintance, too?) The party had turned quiet, but the mood went outright morfound as the fop, giving no ground, made a kisslike inward whistle and spoke again across the room. "Someone should learn a bit of respect," he said, *"mister."*

This time there was no reply.

"You are *a* bore," he added.

Whatever good intentions Darconville had now disappeared for just as he turned he saw the man smiling priggishly into Isabel's eyes. His teeth were grey.

"And you are a self-satisfied, middle-class poofter," shot back Darconville, "masquerading as a Febroniast."

"What a lovely word!"

It was ridiculous. A theological *debate?* thought Darconville, unsettled in the extreme at the idea of it. But it wasn't in fact anything of the sort, rather only proof again, in the jealousy and insinuendo, that the world was early bad and the first sin, where reason was lost, the most deplorable of all, theological, perhaps, only in that all grief is. There should have been an end to it.

But Darconville's better judgment utterly failed him.

"It is a lovely word, for those who aren't. Unfortunately," he said coldly, "the antinomy which lies at the root of Protestantism, however denominated—namely, that there can be no earthly authority in matters of faith and that yet there must be such an authority—forces you to jerk your knee at the mere mention of that pelf-licking zook whom Pope Pius V's bull *Regnans in excelsis,* thankfully, allows me to abhor. I don't doubt I appear humorless on this subject, but, I am sorry, I do not count myself among those in the Church-of-England-as-by-Law-Established, I've always rather wished that Queen Elizabeth's dirty rebato had been a noose, and now I fondly hope the discussion is at an end."

The room had become a tomb. The guests, appearing foolish now in their party hats, stood in the middle of this strange distress—prerupting conversation—either by faking incognizance or silently striking attitudes of scandalized defense.

"So," came the inevitable reply, "the Pope has sent one of his papal boys encyclicaling down the streets of Charlottesville, has he?"

"I am not here by choice."

It was unfair. Darconville knew it.

"You'd prefer to be," asked the fop, drawing out the words with scorn, "—where, *Quinsy College?*"

"I'd prefer to be," said Darconville, "where the ancient traditions of Douay were still flourishing."

"And where might that be?"

The question hung there, as Darconville looked from the hatred in his face to the girl he loved. Heretofore, Isabel might in her actions have bred melancholy or momentary indignation, but not doubt; sad he may have been, but not, at bottom, worried. Now as she stood there across the room, he had to wonder, thinking *The shadow has the same outline as the body which, by obstructing the sunlight, casts the shade.*

"I *said,* where might that be?"

Darconville pitied her in his heart for the burden she bore, standing there, head down, caught in the ignominy of the sudden crossfire and unable to move in the fear of what she might have set into play. Again he ignored the question. Mutter away, cypress, he thought.

"*No!*" Darconville heard, and the fop, having become violent, was shrugging off all attempts to temper him. "I do *not* approve of dark foreign figures saying dark foreign things!" His face twitched. "Is that clear?"

Still, Darconville fought to keep calm, but contemplation can seem to the weary mind so much like despair. And, O, somehow all the failures of the summer, the disorder, the wasted days and enormous misunderstandings, all, all drew up into a single opponent, immediate and real. Then came a high whinnying laugh, full of contempt, from across the room.

"*Damn you! Damn your Romish opinions! And damn your Pope!*"

And Darconville wheeled around.

"I am not used to being spoken to by drunk, mannerless sanct-seemers with mouthfuls of bad teeth," he raged, "but enough: I will meet you here. This mediocre century, blasphemous as yourself, is apt to conceive of the Pope as some kind of remote, semi-diplomatic species of colporteur, petrified in outdated glory and nourishing pretensions the reformational skrellings and unholywater-swallowers who founded your own quaint faiths themselves embodied. You will do well to remember, however—and every other forty-faced Mason like you—that the Papacy is *not* the house of Orange-Nassau and that neither I nor any other coreligionist of mine sees anything whatever figurative, metaphorical, or extravagant in the exordium addressed to him at his investiture that he is, and always will be, the Successor to St. Peter, Bishop of Rome, Patriarch of the West, Spiritual Father of Kings and Nobles and Head of the Whole Church, Servant of the Servants of God, and the Sovereign Pontiff and Earthly Vicar of Jesus Christ, Our Lord, from Whom comes the power of his pontifical magisterium. I can expect neither you nor any advocate of some autofacient church for which false witness is the principle of propagation to understand such a thing, but you might have the grace, sententious pettifogging mediocrity that you are, to keep away from"—Darconville, pale, inhaled and pointed—"her."

The fop slowly parted his way through the gathering and, coming up to Darconville, smiled—looking once back at Isabel—then whispered, "But why? *I am no monk.*"

It happened in a second. Darconville helped him a savage blow across the face, walked out of the house, and drove away.

XLIX

Coup de Foudre

That same hideous nightmare thing
Talking, as it lapped my blood,
In a voice cruel and flat,
Saying forever, "Cat! Cat! Cat!"

—ROBERT GRAVES, "A Child's Nightmare"

SEVERAL WEEKS PASSED. There was no correspondence in that lapsed time, a period when Darconville, deliberating what he should do, where he should go, could imagine just about everything but a strong conception of God's mercy; he compared his attempts at love to the fruit of the paradisaical tree: in the same chapter God forbade eating it, the plants were not yet grown!

The rift, a fault, separated him from everything. He reflected on that and, at the mercy of another relationship, prayed only that the object which ignited the ardent flame in his heart—a terrifying dependence—was also capable of extinguishing it, and yet the love principle *inside* his heart showed no such alternative: he could no more emerge from it voluntarily and reasonably now than he could fit it into everyday life which, curiously, ceased to be everyday life in relation to the repeated crises of separation and reunion forced upon it. Isabel inhabited him completely and yet was at the same time a stranger to him. At the very moment when losing her would have made him suffer a thousand deaths, he found himself—or some self—considering her in everyday life with a sardonic eye but noting down simultaneously that what was missing in their lives was, indeed, what also could be: a "beyondness" outside everyday life which yet, perversely, needed it for support. Briefly, Isabel was both the only means of access to love and not the means. Darconville drew it all out to this paradox, that on the one hand there are temporary beings whom we love but who are ever changing, and beyond them there is the eternal object of love itself which is incorruptible, permanent, and ideal. And yet it is not only through the former that we can take cognizance of the latter, we would, without the former, actually have no *idea* of the latter, the imperfect relative giving us our only idea of the perfect absolute, and we advance by the dangers of delay, shipwrecked from a boat to know the sea, where mildness, glassed in the fragments of storm, must be discerned. Time is the evil, usurping the semblance of eternity. Your prayer, your disappointment, are the same.

One afternoon, however, Darconville chose to drive up to Charlottesville to apologize for everything. It was to be a momentous day. He picked Isabel up after work at the telephone company, and they went to her apartment and talked; perversely but inevitably raising thoughts they deeply wished to keep away, they scolded, contradicted, pished and pshawed, and tempered in a sentence of sweet mercy justice stern. But Isabel could always free his anger with a smile, and this time was no different. The pulled shades made that awful flat much less objectionable than it was when daylit, Lisa had since departed, and the place was now all their own. Darconville had come to see that privacy beyond privacy was necessary for Isabel to find any composure or, as she often put it, to "feel safe," and as her will was there, her will was met. She had remembered to lock the door. She had remembered to put her job out of her mind. And she had remembered, in spite of recent recollections, to make love with all the feeling she seemed to have before.

But she had forgotten the letter on her bureau.

Darconville mistakenly came by it while Isabel was asleep. Stepping out to buy some cigarettes, not to disturb her, he was himself about to leave her a note when the scrap-paper he picked up turned out to be an unposted letter covered with that familiar spidery penmanship. He should not have read it. He should not have thought of reading it. But he did read it and read what upon the glance—are things seen things as seen?—made talking a pitiful invention. His heart club-fisted. He froze and, following all esteem, sympathy, love, faith, and friendship out of the world—there was no more of love, no more of friendship here—took up Echo's ghostly part and gave back the discord of those still remembered sounds repeating on the page. Darconville read:

Dear Govert,

I'm so sorry I ignored you that night (!), but I'm like that I guess. What you must think of me! I don't seem ever to be able to communicate with anybody, especially, as I guess you know, when they're away (self-explanatory). I seem to ruin everything. It's just that I've been so confused these months which is what's behind it, I suppose, and which is why—as discussed—we were stopping. On Love's sweetest arrow is tipped a dart, I guess. (Forgive my poetry.) Everything will turn out alright, don't worry. I'll never forget—how could I?—that day in the middle of our fairy forest and that beautiful moment in the field.

Love, ISABEL

That moment? In the field? Darconville's spirit utterly sank. He read the letter again: the thing unseen became the thing seen. Why, thought he, all things that breed in the mud are not efts! There was in the *we were stopping* the syntax of terror; it wasn't the single photograph of the aorist of discontinued time (ἐπαύσαμεν: we stopped) but rather the successive motion picture of the imperfect of continued action (ἐπαύομεν: we were stopping)—continued, repeated, and customary. And how imperfect! How tense! Ah, sluiced in my absence, thought Darconville, and my pond fished by her neighbor, by Sir Smile, her neighbor! So this was love, opaque to probability, fractureproof, impermeable to death and disloyalty, immune to lies, an answer to the spoof of duration, content and holy peace, the twins of Eden, drawn round by the curtain between you and the world?

The observer infects the observed. Darconville read the letter again, holding it down with his cold shaking fingers, and it told him again that we are only deceived in what is not discerned and that to err is but to be blind; think not, it read, that always good which you think you can make good nor that concealed which the sun does not behold. He began to tremble, turning through the front room with his hands over his mouth, then, swept over with nausea, he found himself in the bathroom, and, whether whispering or shouting he couldn't say— whatever, it awoke Isabel—but an echo, interrupting him as echoes will, replied in a wail, "I am unjustified, serving to deduce conclusions from premises insufficient to imply me!" Thus the Devil played at chess with him, and yielding a pawn while thinking to gain a queen, did.

Quickly, Darconville began bathing his face from a sink filled with dead water, losing his breath only to look up to see his face in the mirror, a mask of disbelief shallow, bewildered, and unlovable. All is as St. John said on the path of Mt. Carmel, he thought, nothing, nothing, nothing—even on the mount was nothing! That which cannot be altered, he realized, must then be borne, not blamed—and if borne, then altered perhaps—and follies past should sooner be remembered, certainly, than be redressed. There was a grace that he could still feel that way, squeezing the last tear from poisonous sorrow. But what otherwise? Force someone to decide to love you and thereby, proscribing choice, make of a lover a slave? Then N'mosnikttiel, the angel of rage, suddenly appeared and mouthed mockingly in Darconville's ear: *so close to glory! But at the center of both sits a zero, see? Now, where is your damoyselle au joue tortue? And where are you? Oh yes, pray where are you?*

I am here now and then will be gone, thought Darconville, dispelling the grey dominion, and if I am robbed of a deep love I am spared at least a moderate one. A sign had been given. There was nothing more to say, he was determined on it.

Darconville was already telephoning the dean's office at Quinsy College when Isabel appeared in the doorway with contorted hands and begging-bowl eyes which seemed somehow to have surmised everything. She took a step forward in her shift, alarmed, no longer conscious of her heavy legs. She hadn't been listening a minute when, aware suddenly of the letter, the extremity of the moment, her metallic screams tore holes in his chest. But of course it was too late—Darconville immediately resigned from his teaching post. The following day he was packed. And before the week was out he departed for England, resolved now to believe he had been spared the duty but denied the pleasure of hearing her lie and yet wondering as the thousands of miles were being fast put behind him if in some century long past he and Spellvexit hadn't stopped one final time in a place called Fawx's Mt. and whether he and the girl he loved so much had actually gone into the woods across the street where, upon a tree, they carved the word "Remember" and how the loveliest pair that ever stood between heaven and earth begetting wonder—a figure all gold, a figure all black—could possibly have said goodbye in what had been a last Zoroastrian kiss.

L

Dialogue on a Dank October

Ah, *mon Dieu!* how is it I didn't think of it before? It's the gipsy girl with the goat.

VICTOR HUGO, *Notre Dame de Paris*

"I TELL YOU," exclaimed Mrs. van der Slang, rowing a spoon through her tea, "this could happen only in a *book!* I knew of course you were thick as thieves for a while in high-school, and of course that was then. But now, tell me, are you certain? Him?"

"Yes."

"And not—"

"No," said Isabel, "not really. Not anymore, I'm afraid." She looked away. "But I don't know if he will be."

"Will be?"

"Certain."

Mrs. van der Slang arched a brow and blew on her tea. "You mean *interested.*"

Isabel nodded.

"Well, I'm sorry to say, I don't know myself. We don't see him much, there's that. Then, he's young and frankly hasn't fulfilled our ambitions for him nor his own for us. Sugar?" It was one of Isabel's privileges to take sugar. Mrs. van der Slang moved closer and continued; it was a voice like dishwater gurgling through a sink. "Now I'm a practical woman. I'm a businesswoman. So I'll be frank. I must say, you seemed to drop the whole business last year, didn't you, when you went off to college—and, gracious me," added Mrs. van der Slang, crossing her bowed legs and making a slight bleat of nasal peevishness for the benefit of the responsible party, "we didn't do entirely well there, did we?"

Isabel fixed her eyes on the woman's feet.

"There you are, you see. And I do think," said Mrs. van der Slang, her forehead filling with centripetal furrows, "a young woman should maintain. Oh, schooling, general efficiency, what-not—I don't mean," she smiled coldly, "the telephone company, hm?" She smiled a great deal, smiled *angrily,* but her mouth was large and when she smiled she tried to hide her teeth, which were large and yellow. It wasn't scolding but innuendo: the scolding of innuendo. "I don't know, it could become a condition in this whole matter, not, Lord knows, because I want it that way, but, heavens, I've asked it of my own boys." Isabel nervously began twicking her thumbs. "I mean, wouldn't you? Want us to know you could, well, maintain? Of course you would. *He* would. I promise, he is not insensitive to things. He's realistic. His feet are on the ground. For instance, I remember—"

Squinting suddenly, Mrs. van der Slang rose to nudge out of an italic position the marinescape hung askew over the fireplace.

"It is lovely, isn't it. *Storm on the Zuider Zee,* it's called. Pricey though." She popped her eyes. "In the hundreds." Mrs. van der Slang, a woman with that loud persistent eloquence of an auctioneer in the slave-market, was the typical polder peasant; wealthy, humorless, clever in business, indifferent to the impatience or irony of those annoyed by her crafty reticence and facial games, she had perhaps sturdy visions of one day returning to live on the Heerengracht, pulling close the shutters, and locking herself in to count her gold. She was one of those women who in moving from room to room carried one hand floating in mid-air, limp off the wrist, in a charade of what for some wildly inexplicable reason is assumed by such people to indicate grace.

"Anyway, as I was saying, I remember he told me he put a wall up between you and him: didn't want to interfere, see? 'I put a wall up, Mother,' he said." She sniffed. "I'll say he did, don't believe he ever came home much afterwards—well, but that was mostly summers. All this, in any case, not without reason, my poor angel. Mind you, it's all the same to me, the mother in all this, but I mean, after all, you had been seeing—" Mrs. van der Slang made foolish eyes.

"Him," Isabel freely acknowledged.

"*Him,* yes. But not—"

"No."

"And he's the one you want now." Her malerect ears twitched. "You're convinced?"

"Yes," said Isabel. "But I don't know if he might be."

"Might be?"

"Convinced."

Mrs. van der Slang blew on her tea and arched a brow. "You mean *available.*"

"Yes."

"Now I understand. We women always do it; no one ever notices it, but we must always create a small flaw in every image—it's for safety, right?" And then came the ringing antistrophe. "Look, I told you I am a businesswoman, didn't I? Good. Then let's put the foot to the fire. You don't know if you can take the chance of assuming he cares for you enough to wait for him, do you?" She took a sip of tea, swallowed, and looked up. "Do you?"

The rain outside continued. Gusting around the chimney at Zutphen Farm, it seemed almost wild enough to blow down the pipe and launch from the mantelpiece the little model ship with red sails and black hull sitting there. A fire crackled in the fireplace and played glowingly in crimson reflection on the cute blue-and-white Dutch tiles surrounding it. It had been an awful day, and, feeling low and lonely, Isabel had dropped by—she found she'd done so more and more of late—to talk to Mrs. van der Slang who on this particular day, in spite of the weather, had just finished dropping her bulbs. ("I always try to get them in by Columbus Day," said the mud-spattered mevrouw, waving a graip in greeting. "It worked out, as you can see, to the very

day.") Having come inside, shrugging off the rain, they'd removed as
usual to the living room, not so much for the fire as for the endless opportunities afforded Mrs. van der Slang to fish out in succession, while
announcing their significance and price, the variety of objects she kept
there for that specific reason. The visits, initially, had been short.
They'd sit and converse on charming nullities, with Mrs. van der
Slang most of the time, though polite enough, essentially uninterested:
in a masquerade of attention she'd either put her nose out like a
projecting horn, the beak of a shoebill, pointing upward and simply
wait it out or, slumped down, raise single strands of grey hair,
vacantly draw them along her fingertips to their limp extremity, and
every once in a while mutter, "hmm, hmm." This continued for a
time. It wasn't long however, as things go, before Isabel eventually
raised a subject which not only cut its complex way across her own life
but reached into the lives of several others, specifically the *boys* of the
family van der Slang. Then—and thereafter—Mrs. van der Slang's
sharp ears, like a goat's, displayed their pointed conches high up
among the indiscreet tufts of grizzled hair. After all, there was the
good of the family. There were her sons. There was the farm. And so
tea was poured and patience employed against the comfortless and
reverie-inducing rain that the inquisitive might attend to the declarative and, by acquainting itself with the question at hand, come to solve
it—correctly.

"I said, you don't know if you can take the chance of assuming
he—"

"No."

Isabel's voice, low and embarrassed, actually seemed to consum-
mate itself. But Mrs. van der Slang felt much better. She maneuvered
Isabel's eyes back to her face.

"There, was that so difficult, hmmm? Ideal visions, you'll find in
this life of ours, are unreal visions. Fact, huh? What is. What happens.
What is the case. So let's be practical, but, at all costs, let us not be too
hasty, advice," said Mrs. van der Slang, affecting one of her large assortment of miniature faces and pouring more tea, "your own mother,
you'll forgive me, might have passed along to you with more authority
at several critical junctures of late. Sugar?"

Isabel shook her head.

The older woman, balancing her teacup, looked up with portentous concentration. Her gothic eyes locked on Isabel. Her ears seemed to arch backwards. Her ruminant jaw shifted.

"You see, we can't yet say there aren't others involved."

A color like a rosy infusion in medicine flooded Isabel's cheeks.

"He mentions—other people?"

"He mentions, my girl, nothing of the sort. He's not home enough to mention anything of the sort. And I wouldn't tell you anything of the sort," she pronounced with throaty complacency, "if I thought it would wound you so. I'm only obliged, I believe, to tell you frankly that this wait of yours may not"—Mrs. van der Slang's nose-tips flared—"pay off."

"I see."

"I so hate to be blunt. But girls aren't reluctant, you must know, to telephone him at all hours when he's home. Why, only this summer—"

Isabel turned to her with swan-necked alarm.

"—but why bother going into it."

"Does he ever mention—me?"

Mrs. van der Slang stood up, conspicuously turned for the machinery of effect to the grey weeping window, and sighed. " 'Mother,' he said, 'I've put up a wall.' You can almost hear him say it." Wistfully, she sipped her tea. She scrutinized Isabel, however, through half-closed eyes as though measuring the perspective in a painting with which she was not completely satisfied. "Can't you?"

Isabel closed her eyes.

"Well, can't you?"

"Yes."

"Listen, why hedge? He's realistic. Let us be. We both of us, you and I, each want to see what we can get out of this. Forget me—now I'll come frank—the captain would love grandchildren, by all our sons, oh positively, no matter who or which or when. Then of course you've always been a help around the farm here, I can't deny that. On the other hand, you know, I'm sure, you could do worse than, well, join the team here at Zutphen. Indeed, you seem to want that. You've as much as said it. Certainly you know we're—comfortable, taxes notwithstanding. This Libyan rug?" Mrs. van der Slang closed her eyes in artificial grief and held up five fingers. "Ah, but that's all for later, isn't it, now it seems we must settle on a plan whereby everyone concerned will be as content as possible. Some, we know, won't be. But some will. You of course and especially—"

"Him."

"Though not—"

"No."

Isabel's face strained. "But I don't know if he could be."

"Could be?"

"Content."

Mrs. van der Slang neither arched her brow nor blew on her tea this time but sat back autocratically, taking Isabel in with a sharp avizeful eye, and said, "You mean *married*."

Always frustration, thought Isabel, pulling her thumb, fffruuustrationnnn! Always struggle, always life.

"So where then does all this put us?"

"I don't know," Isabel whispered.

"Well, wouldn't you agree with me that time," said Mrs. van der Slang, speaking from the lofty pedestal of Age, "will solve it?"

Preoccupied, however, Isabel had dislocated her attention and had turned to listen dolefully to the percussion of the driving rain outside. The Graeae and Gorgons seemed to be hailing in from the sea to distress her alone of all others, threatening the very last vestige of security in her being—and she who had so little!

"I say, wouldn't you agree that—"

"Yes," replied Isabel, her eyes rimming with bitter tears, *"oh yes."*

Mrs. van der Slang felt good.

"I find I must be candid, child. I think we should return to college —why, say as a kind of proof of intentions—just to see what transpires." There was a long silence. "We must above all show we can maintain. Is that unfair?"

"And should I wait—and should I wait that long?"

Mrs. van der Slang's face went surprised in a pout. "Perhaps you wish to suggest that I am not being kind? Well, you must see at a time like this one can't stop to think of convenience. Especially other people's. I asked only a simple thing of you. And am I being unfair? I don't think I'm like that, really. And I mean, who knows, it may turn out perfect and this romance of yours may all work out fine, just like, I don't know"—Mrs. van der Slang groped for an apt simile and then, finding one, looked up with one eyebrow drawn high in a whimsical vertex and smiled—"just like in a book?"

Isabel was now desolate. She knew she was alone but knew as well she couldn't be, she hadn't the strength. Walking home aimlessly on that terrible October day, she only felt the cirrus clouds, harbinger of even more rain, mist down into her isolation from the Blue Ridge mountains and then enter the confines of her heart, filled once with a hope of some kind but, alas, a hope no longer, for hope itself to tell the truth had now quite petered out.

L I

Conspectus Temporum; or
Short Excerpts from a London Diary

All places are distant from heaven alike.

—ROBERT BURTON, *Anatomy of Melancholy*

September 5th. Blessed be God, near the end of this year, I am in very good stealth, without any sense of my old pain, but upon feeling sold. I live in hack's yard, having my strife, and servant, Disdain, and no other family than us three.

6th. When did we three meet before?

That's a fair question. It was neither before nor after the lost year in Quinsyburg—the Land of Ymagier, beyond the regions of who did it and why. Y: the forked path of Pythagoras. Crossroads. Free choice. Unity and division. Wasn't he, by the way, the philosopher who put to school the idea that the opposition of the definite and the indefinite, working in concert, creates the world? (Check on this.)

10th. I saw that girl again on the stairwell; she smiled. What a fund of galleries, playhouses, museums. London! Call it Pariniban or Droiland, I am still Darconville.

N.B. Buy pens, lightbulbs, wine.

11th. This morning I went to Mass in the chapel-of-ease at St. Ethelreda's in Ely Place, Holborn, and made thanksgiving I'd not have to teach for a while. Classes would just be starting.

12th. Of what day is this the anniversary? (Dissembler!) P.S. But let it be. A Friday still buries a Thursday, a quart still drowns a tierce, and a quint a quart. Every new year executes the privileges of the old. I was never engaged to her, anyway. She was perfectly free.

I've decided to write both morning and afternoon.

14th. I will finish *Rumpopulorum* this year or sink into hell like a sheet-anchor. Q. Can you? A. I can. The cultivated life existed first; uncultivated life came afterwards, with the blight of the serpent, Satan. So it is a consolation to have to get *back* to vision, not create it anew. (I like your mode, Mr. Bulstrode: when the mind is a hall in which thought is like a voice speaking, the voice is somehow always that of someone else. Diaries diarticulate. The parrot's amazed *you* can talk. Eurycles, the Athenian soothsayer, throwing his voice, placed many a jest on another's lips. The paradoxical phenomenon of ventriloquist and dummy who, speaking simultaneously, never interrupt, always agree. The death of one is that of the other. Have I stumbled upon a parable of love?)

Ah, but now see the fitful subjects this anti-self can raise!

15th. I picked up my cat from quarantine at Heathrow this afternoon. That I brought him along, presently disporting with his shadow, is a constant delight.

> Accept my gentle visionary, Spellvexit,
> Sublimely fanciful & kindly mild;
> Accept, and fondly keep for Friendship's sake,
> This favored vision, my poetic Child!

16th. Wrote.

17th. I met her again, holding the door for her. Viking hair, blue eyes, features carved out of the cliffs of Sarjektåcko. Must I remind myself not to get involved? The half, said Hesiod, is fuller than the whole. There is a perhaps cosmic strength in this otherwise vain truth: to have none is closer to having all than having one. Everything, perhaps, *is* the only thing. Late have I learned that. And there's enough of distraction in this city to help me forget. (Marvelous, when you read back your own diary it gives an advice of its own!)

The trees are turning. Mass at Farm St.

18th. My room, shaped like the move of a chessknight, is situated in Pont St. at the very top of an old building built around 1702, just about the time William of Orange pipped. From my single window I can see chimneys, the wimble of a church steeple, and a big maple tree —why, I wonder, are those on the south side always the first to shed? —reminding me daily of the necessity of both shade and paper, the objective-correlative wants of a writer.

Wrote poorly, however, all day.

19th. The same. Resignation, resignation; it will come. *Vulneratus non victus.* The d'Arconvilles are Venetians, and do Venetians give up? No, he who so shall, so shall he who.

But bored, I invented a new kind of riddle. A Dutchman had three sons. The first, named Sllaf, is a mountain-climber; the second, Snrub, is a firefighter. The third became a sailor. What was his name?

21st. Postcard from Thelma Trappe. (No, dear Miss Trappe, I have never heard of the English herb "death-come-quickly," and I suspect *you* shouldn't have either.)

24th. The sky is leaden. Went to Mass: the Feast of St. Gregory, whom I pictured kneeling by candlelight in a cold medieval tower praying lauds. At the Gloria I felt such a new sense of resolve I almost wept for joy and thought of the lines: "I Hafe set my hert so hye/Me likyt no love that lowere ys." They came to me in a more mystical than antihuman sense, as only, of course—except for misinformed worldlings and Wyclifficals—they should. It is not enough to quit sin, we must attain virtue.

But, O, better and better! I will hate no one. There will be forgetting, there must be forgiving. (Why, however, must these always go together?) Forgive me, Frater Clement. I remember you for what I should have not forgotten.

27th. Wrote poorly. When one is tired, one's sentences are always the first to suffer. Seven pages of bumph for one paragraph and a polysyllable. "Will I have to use a dictionary to read your book?" asked Mrs. Dodypol. "It depends," says I, "how much you used the dictionary before you read it." Witty. But cruel. We are all too cruel.

Long letter to Dodypol. Just gone twelve. And so to bed.

30th. My lungs hurt. Smoking. And the weather is up. I chose England arbitrarily, would have chosen Venice were I a freeholder—cold,
but better air—and yet, the courts, the courts! Slower than Quinsyburg justice. And this sad, old month.

October 1st. The girl's name is Svarta Furstinna, a Swede, and she
lives across the hall. She looks like the beautiful girl Ronsard once saw
in the Château of Blois, bending over her lute and singing the branle
de Bourgogne. Spellvexit himself was flirting. Shall I ask her over for a
glass of wine?

Later: the courage necessary for the execution killed the sentiment.
Wrote all night, so write this another day.

3rd. Spent the day in the Victoria and Albert Museum reading
room, farming through the stacks for books on angelology. Darconville
Pseudangelos, wanting to be one? I checked, for the record, for *The
Shakeing of the Sheets;* not a copy. I looked, however, into the
Pythagoras question; to sum up: the opposition of the limiting (odd
and perfect) and the limited (even and imperfect) organizes the
world. The categories one, right, male, at rest, straight, light, good,
and square belong to the sphere of the former; to the sphere of the
even and imperfect belong the opposites: many, left, female, moving,
bent, darkness, bad, oblong. The science of cutting pies! Art shouldn't
classify, but declassify. A misogynist's ontology. Boring. Meditabund.

The idea that limitation poses a definiteness, nevertheless, warrants
further study. I've survived for that, perhaps, because to know the
worst is still to know what, having never known, is worse than worst
by far—indeed, to know the worst is to know you'll never know the
worst again. When you know the worst, in short, you don't. So truth is
then fortified by wrongs?

N.B. I love the confusion of trichotomies. They turn me into
enough of a fool to confirm by embarrassment the rejection in which
she left nothing otherwise to understand. Furthermore, I think I'm insane.

4th. The imagination consumes some part of reality. That would be
the essential salvation of writing, wouldn't it? Bark is cinnamon: therapy.

5th. Today, I bought two tickets to the opera. Went across the hall
and redeemed the time. Wrote until late: *nulla dies sine linea.* (Cello-
tape that to the wall!)

6th. "Who can't say, I may be some part of your destiny?" Thus pretty Svarta, at one point in a general discussion of lost love over a post-and-rail tea in a tiny cellar of a Beauchamp Place restaurant. I'd sketched, prompted to it, an abstract of the past year, following of course the parliamentary custom of avoiding reference to any particular member by name. But the sublime intoxication of recovered divinity was in the conversation only; women can be too wonderful in their mystery to need to know as individuals. I want nothing to *matter* anymore, not even enjoyment, the mystical truth near but not next to the heresy that everything human in us is an obstacle in the way of holiness. Henceforth, in any case, like the Stuarts I will govern without a Parliament. ("In an uneven number heaven delights." *Eclogue* VIII.75)

We walked through Kensington Gardens, saw the statue of Peter Pan, then home.

7th. Wrote.

8th. We attended a performance of *The Flying Dutchman* at Sadler's Wells. Catharsis, I suppose. I wonder, is that grizzled Ahasuerus of the sea correct in thinking, since Senta is recreant to her former lover, that she'll be so to him? If so, death must be exacted to prove faithfulness unto death. Novel, isn't it? "Antilogy; or How I Relinquished What I Loved Because I Loved So Much." (A cutisbound edition, of course.)

> Whoso would love
> Must make headway
> On a ship ever windward
> Of Table Bay.

God bless us out of it! Excessive joy, I've read, has killed men. I kissed Svarta goodnight.

9th. Wrote.

10th. The leaden sky puts its very own weather into my sentences: "With the sun a reminding touch upon their frozen hair the winged phagones of evil flashed out of Heaven into the fumerole of empty space, screaming, '*No, no! Not now! Not yet!*'"

Not too bad. Not too good.

11th. Wrote. The book looms up. Spellvexit asleep by the shilling heater all day. Rain for four straight days.

12th. Spirit of the Pities! I woke tonight in the middle of a frightful nightmare, a profane vision with a girl, outbawling with *joy*, being dragged by her long hair to a high wall as a sacrifice where perched

the goat god, Pan, whose pointed ears wagged lasciviously in anticipation of—Drank until morning. Wine is poison to hemlock.

The question is, has part of me stayed behind to retrace what I
thought I should otherwise have missed? Puritanical! Learning may
be the enemy of thinking, and thinking, of learning. I have never
known which I wanted and so am left with oneirotic circuses: fiction
—the other barber in the mirror, shaving the other you.

Mem. Never drink in afternoon.

14th. Feel grey as a badger. Haven't been out of bed for two days.
It's been raining longer than Louis XIV. Cramps from overdepres-
sants of smoke, drink, malneirophrenia. I've begun to lose the habit of
attention that is strong and extreme because I can think only of things,
God forgive me, I hold in contempt. The thing that will fail me first
when I get old will be my patience, a malefaction of Verrine, one of
the Thrones.

I must up burtons and break out.

15th. Worse, pre-eminently so. And so slept.

16th. Dies notandus. This morning I found several letters for me
down in the foyer, one—how I, an inventory of every anxiety,
approached that little thing—a cablegram from Fawx's Mt., postmarked, to be Petrarchally exact, October 12 and reading: "I love
you."

I will not drag Pyrrho from Elis to figure on this page. Things belong to the past quite quickly, that's all. (Ridiculous. The present, the
past, the future are happening at once!) But I am thinking: to know
the truth one must start by not believing in anything. I am thinking:
and so I sit here, doubting everything. I am thinking: I think something, and then I think, 'I doubt that,' and so it is false. I am thinking: that means I am sitting here and thinking 'I don't think I am
doubting everything,' meaning there is something I don't doubt. O
God, don't disappoint me! Don't stop time! O angels, clap your wings
upon the skies, and give this virgin crystal plaudities! *I am loved!*

17th. How decisions aren't decisions at all! How we believe what
we don't quite realize! I've spent the day shaking ink over a dozen
unposted letters, read all, liked some, mailed none. Transatlantic
phone calls from the Cadogan Hotel (Charlottesville number: no
longer in service; Fawx's Mt. number: no one at home), but the place
triggers the mind to create the place. Sent telegram from Knights-
bridge, repeating hers to the word. Only abide, rich Penelope!

Noctuarial entry: I can't eat for happiness. I can't write. I am the masked Touareg, brigand from the desert; the Bishop of Fun, in wonder of tabret and chimer of solisequious gold; Zeus with effulgent forehead and attributes. The sparkle in the tail of my eye could light up the world!

18th. Fortune is never mentioned in Scripture. The girl loves me, and if the time was brief, the time was overcome. But I'd hear fortune. Be the devil's advocate, diary.

DIARY: It's thanks to the Romans we know the Greeks.

DARCONVILLE: So we know the Greeks. I can distinguish one from the other.

DIARY: But by the other.

DARCONVILLE: Who valued them.

DIARY: Say transvalued.

DARCONVILLE: Therefore, to the Romans they are no longer Greeks.

DIARY: Who couldn't have valued them.

DARCONVILLE: Then let Greeks be known by a Roman mistake.

DIARY: The Romans endure.

DARCONVILLE: But the Greeks prevail.

21st. God is sitting on my pen. The pages during these five days seem to have filled themselves. How I love her! Isabel, she by reason of which the world below again becomes the world above! As I scribble away, my hand flashes avian shadowgraphs on the wall, falcons Spellvexit counts, his bottom wagging, pouncing upon each and all. We are both chasing our imaginations across spaces open for them. Enjoin me, joy! I am beside myself, and I also belong!

23rd. In love, my spirit, utterance, and invention are better. Must I, therefore, love for my wit's sake? To conceive children of the word? Prophesy, some Melampus.

Worked all day in the V&A, no lunch, and on the way home mailed her letter (I mention the possibility of an engagement).

28th. Cold and windy. Two letters today. The important one, signed with the colophon of two familiar eyes—and a name as pure as morning prayer—a packet of sheets folded so tightly in the envelope that lateral incision is necessary and written on both sides in that spidery hand, dipped and backswept and full of question sparks and looped i's: passionate apology, apologetic passion, and a colored feather. I hear the simple tender words of an oath-worthy, a white candle in a white hand. Its small companion, a letter in a monogrammed envelope the color of angelica, a declaration of some and similar consequence—were it consequential—and a photograph of the correspondent, supine, last summer, on a dune at Virginia Beach: Hypsipyle Poore, peering over her sunglasses. Cough on, Lady Malehaut.

Thynke and thanke God.

30th. I bolted breakfast, took a bus to central London, and mailed Isabel some gifts: a book, a bracelet, and a black velvet Russian dress, embroidered with flowers. Visited the National Gallery. There was a Fuseli exhibition. I saw his painting *The Nightmare.* It is said that this was a portrait of Anna Landolt, whom he loved. (He'd written: "Last night I had her in bed with me . . . anyone who touches her now commits adultery.") She tossed him aside and married a Mr. Schinz, a businessman; an enraged and hateful Fuseli then painted this canvas, an attempt to use black magic to give her frightening dreams. Desperation crutched out on the stilps of art. Was his hatred, I wonder, a function of preserving his dignity or an attempt to deploy self-pity by confronting resentment lest, nursing it, greater psychological imbalance ensue?

Any explication of the thing is less than approximate: perhaps hate loves to hate. It must, first. On the other hand, a man, thinking himself in love, may only be trying to understand that which is most strange to him; so strange, opposed; opposed, then, never to be had. The lover too often doesn't realize he must make his contract with a degree of ease—*disinvoltura*—by which he can deceive himself, at least temporarily, of the real passion he feels and thus, that she may be free to choose, courteously allow the loved one to deny what of course he prays she won't. More people drown from the torrential rains in the desert than die of thirst.

Do I sound smug? I confess to you, dear diary, dear double, I could still let Isabel go. I do love her, and desperately. But where, after all, was the trothplight? The commitment? There is nothing in bad art that good art doesn't have; it's all in the making—and what was done in the past was done in the doing, not in the making, whereas now what is hoped for will be made, not done. Isabel has *decided!* Is it a miracle or a natural thing? Perhaps what we take sometimes for resurrections are only syntheses. The only way to come back is to go.

31st. Hallowe'en. I am still writing my grimoire of dark invocations, mystic runes, mantic spells. The Royal Library of Nineveh called my head is filled with books which are being read. I wonder, *is* some black-hatted Strix right now whistling on a pitchfork through the thick and thin of the world to put calamities and ligatures among men and women? (Thought of Mrs. DeCrow and her group of familiars! Quinsyburg=Thessaly. An uncharitable remark, I suppose. "Thou shalt not bear false witness against thy neighbor." I've always wondered in this commandment which word was supposed to be accented.) I put up Isabel's photograph on my bureau.

Later: I met Svarta at the Grove Pub where we drank and spoke of spooky things. Smiling, she swore, quoting Wierus, that the devil often married beautiful women by whom he had countless children—easily recognizable, as she'd have it, by their growing inexplicably fat, by their voracious appetites, and by some exceptional flaw.

November 1st. All Souls' Day. I have mine still and so thanked the Author of it at a High Mass at the Brompton Oratory. Worked all day. Close on two. And so to bed.

5th. A penny for the guy, more sinned against than sinning. Fawkes' Mountain, never built, perhaps should have been. I get around this anti-commemoration, not forgetting in the ruinous fires the increase of penalties against English Catholics thereafter as before, by contributing my coin to his memory. If a traitor betrays a trust, Guido's had been stolen outright. A prayer to Our Lady of Ransom, for the conversion of England. Wrote all night into morning. The cock craw. The day daw.

7th. Letter from Isabel, who in a postscript—somehow, always the substantific of a girl's letter—mentions she's decided to return to Quinsy College for the Spring semester. The Caudine Forks! Will they take her back? Could she be happy there alone? Should I return, associate sole, or spend my life wandering from place to place like some gormless Holy Roman emperor in the fifteenth century? I can't say what I think I mean.

8th. When the answer cannot be put into words, neither can the question. The use of language, however, compels me to measure my thoughts—so one's journal becomes an examination-of-conscience: I rub my fears and worries through a sieve of days and up comes a pile of biography, brief as Solomon Grundy's. Where will I be a year from now?

9th. Decided to find out.

Wind, cutting and visible. Ran down to the hotel to telephone
Isabel. An hour lost for a connection, two pints of Tennant's, then, lo!
so soft, so gentle a voice, faint over the hornslate sea, asking, please,
when she would see me again? I believe I printed my fingers into the
very instrument, telling her how hopelessly I loved her and straining to
hear over the quorks and quirks of an astonished cable the cento God
alone heard in full but I can only approximate: ". . . so lonesome for
(pause, crackles) ever at Christmastime before it's too (clicks, delay)
me especially, not worth anybody's (delay, crackles) believe it, and
that now Govert knows (clicks, pause) feel better. Can you hear what
(crackles, clicks) love you forever and ever and ever?"

Dies creta notandus! I've loved everyone and everything this day,
everyway and everywhere. I realized suddenly I could have her over
for Christmas for a fortnight but that, in doing so—after one last cele-
bratory drink and an inquiring visit to Barclay's—I might run out of
money to stay on very long thereafter finishing the book. The decision
made itself: I would both finish the book *and* invite her over. The second possibility was arranged on the spot. And the first? I invoke no
foliots, no genii, no figures of augrim. I will but call on the ancient
name of d'Arconville, heroic in the cause of altar, sword, and pen, and
have done.

10th. A ring from Isabel—her grandmother's—arrived in the mail
today: size 5. I have a target to size up now, Miss Ballhatchet.

11th. Martinmas. The beginning of winter. I went to a quiet restaurant for the traditional feastday goose, outlined my final chapters, and
on the way home mailed Isabel a check for her airfare. I have enough
money left for a ring, then it'll be near the knuckle.

Tonight, a knock on the door—the clandestine knock: once—it was
Svarta, with a bottle of cider and some Garibaldis. We talked. "Tut-
tut," she said, upon seeing Isabel's photograph with its somnolent eyes
but face of Pentelican marble, indirectly lit from inside. "You have
hypnotized her?" Then she told me, in that kind of low whisper that
always seems advice in itself, that the idea of hypnosis as sleepy unconsciousness is a myth, for it's really a state of alert awareness. We talked
awhile, sadly, then she kissed my cheek, and said goodnight.

18th. A week of writing, straight. No recreation. Punk and plaster
and cold tea. Spellvexit is half-crazed with boredom.

P.S. Dr. Dodypol sent me a postcard yesterday: "I remain here in

Quinsyburg where adders' tongues still seek to talk away that long-lost Eden vile Nature's since replaced."

21st. I've spent three days in every shop in Bond St. looking for a ring, avoiding Gaud and his taints.

23rd. Found out Svarta Furstinna left for Stockholm yesterday by means of a (sad) note thumbtacked to my door; she said she couldn't face goodbyes but that, who knew, she might one day catch up with me again. Feel curiously alone tonight. I think a final goodbye is more oppressive, because less natural, than a death and the universe in which it happens so frightening, that I don't even want to think about its cause. Is that a non-sequitur?

December 1st. Another week enclosed in the forcing-house of the spirit. The writing goes on, but even an army of jokes, one after the other, is a cheerless thing. Christmas already in the air. I must finish.

4th. Telegram from Isabel: she's arriving Dec. 18th, to leave Jan. 2nd. *N.B. Be at Heathrow Airport at 5:45* P.M.!

5th. Wrote, I find, some 2,000 words yesterday—and will have a reasonably complete foul copy under hand before the week is out. The last ten pages look ragged from the top of the clock. A boast of despair cancels itself out. I spent the day X-ing out sixteen pages, then rewriting four. X X X: thus the millers of yore set the vanes of the windmill when they were home for lunch, turning them cruciform when they were back at work. Now, *there's* an analogue to art for who'd accept the grind!

6th. Freezing cold. Laid in more tins, a half-gallon of scrumpy, and cat food. I worked the day through.

I wonder what I'll say to her. Maybe she's wondering what she'll say to me. "But the days of childhood they were fleet, and the blooming sweet-briar breathèd weather, when we were boy and girl together." Beddoes. O, the complicated and difficult dance of lovers crossing and recrossing the wire in a high empty hall, hung with tapestries and scutcheons, the moon through the lozenge-shaped windows showing how far they can fall!

7th. I found a ring I bought!

10th. Hectic preparations: theatre tickets, reservation for Christmas dinner at the Anchor Pub in Southwark, New Year's plans. I bought two blue mugs and had our names inscribed on them. Returning home, I stopped to listen to the carolers and bell-ringers, muffled up and top-hatted, in Trafalgar Square:

"Once in royal David's city
Stood a lowly cattle shed,
Where a mother laid her baby
In a manger for his bed . . ."

Tomorrow: order cake, piped: *"Welcome, Isabel"*
13th. Busy, as before.
14th. Ibid.
16th. The room's a godawful mess still. A quick dashover with the broom this morning for paperballs, dust, grewsome ghosts. I boxed the presents, set out mugs, made a drawing of greeting—two bright eyes, offset with a message of three little words. Everything must be just right. Shall I wear my black coat to the airport?

No. (Was it for nothing that Pompey wore a dark-colored garment at the Battle of Pharsalia?)

17th. "Tomorrow to fresh woods . . ."

Caetura desunt.

January 12th. Goodnight, dear diary, goodnight. I think it is good morrow, is it not? I have been remiss. You have been in love. I have, and turn away no more. So pray, then, turn to what? Two old monks were speaking of a flag. One said, "The flag is moving." The other said, "The wind is moving." An abbot who happened to be passing by told them, "Not the wind, not the flag. The mind is moving." Wind, flag, mind—we move in concert toward that fortune which gives, it's said, much to many but less by far to more. Is life then in the loom? I don't know. I only know I accept my fortune and, with my cat and partial step, leave tomorrow not to unlearn what I've learned here, rather to seek a face remembered from another world which has been longed-for, though how I can't explain, which has been found and lost and then refound again. I seek to survive by means of a miracle I can't believe in yet but on which I must rely, for as my heart returns to my love, my love returns to Quinsyburg, where I have been before and, blind for love, now will be again.

And so I betake myself to that course, which is almost as much to see myself go into my grave; for which, and all the discomforts that will accompany my being blind, the good God prepare me!

L I I

A Table Alphabeticall of Thinges Passynge

It's not in Nursery Rhymes? And yet I almost think it is—

—Lewis Carroll, *Hys Nouryture*

A is for Arrivals, which came—and, coming, passed.
B is for Back, to Quinsy, yes, but each other at last.
C is for Contrectation. Their love-play lasted long.
D is for Diagenesis: bless change—whatever was, was wrong!
E is for Engagement, a mutual act of will.
F is for Faculty, who physicked the masses still.
G is for Greatracks, his knickers no less in a twist.
H is for Hypocrisy, still shrouding the college like mist.
I is for Isabel, the pure, the loyal, the good.
J is for *Je Maintiendrai,* the motto by which she stood.
K is for Kalopsia, when a town, not the best, seems better.

L is for Love, the sweet debt to which they were debtor.
M is for Misgivings: O, the normal wherefores and hows.
N is for Nonillionth, the times they repeated their vows.
O is for Ouphes, the dear elphin girls in their classes.
P is for Poore, who still, though in letters, made passes.
Q is for Quinsyburg, less the plug in the sink than the drain.
R is for Rivals, who were never mentioned again.
S is for Strictures: the Shiftletts, the sameness, the South.
T is for Trappe, still down, alas, in the mouth.
U is for Unfortunately: her sorrows were never few.
V is for Velocity, the speed with which time flew.
W is for Wedding, a hope in that strange place sought.
X is for Xenium, the gift that strangeness wrought.
Y is for Years, two passed as if but a day.
Z is for Zutphen, no longer a threat in the way.

LIII

The Old Arcadia

"Beyond the Wild Wood comes the Wide World," said the Rat.
"And that's something that doesn't matter, either to you or me.
I've never been there, and I'm never going, nor you either, if
you've got any sense at all. Don't ever refer to it again, please."

—KENNETH GRAHAME, *The Wind in the Willows*

QUINSYBURG was pretty much the same old place after two more
years, but so very much in love were Darconville and Isabel that, despite the confines of the town—and possibly because of it—they lost
cognizance of both temporal and spatial radii and remained fixed in
their chosen quadrant, the spirit level brought to bear on which measured but the verticals of dreams, the horizontals of passion. There
were tribulations, of course, but they were overcome, and when in

difficulty the two of them seemed, as if for it, to grow closer, heedless of setback or sorrow and inured to any trouble blowing their way, as on the rugged surface of the earth the daily revolution of the air encounters so many obstacles that it is not felt. They'd turned with the rolling years into a second cycle, like numbers in a periodic fraction, and called it resurrection. Tomorrow keeps its promise merely by coming today, and for them there were days time out of number, to be counted no more, but lived.

It was still a part of the South that constantly grew away from the rest of the country—or, if you will, was left behind by it—yet if its deadbright sun still raised up trees, solisequious if somewhat stunted, and shrubs, blighted but bearable, they had seen it all before and so the better could cope with it now. Mrs. DeCrow still crew. Dr. Glibbery galumphed, and pixilated Miss Pouce still pleaded from her library for patronage. There was the full complement: Floyce flouncing, Wratschewe writing, Shrecklichkeit scheming. Miss Sweetshrub had not married. Miss Ballhatchet had put on weight and put off depilatories. Miss Shepe and Miss Ghote weren't speaking to each other anymore. And dear old Dodypol still greeted everyone as he always had. Greatracks remained *imperator*. Gone were the Culpas, however, along with the Weerds, sometime since having decided to leave together and sail to Byzantium where presumably, under that very head, they'd proceed to write a poem with that very title. Ol' Hinge-and-Bracket hadn't changed—when Knipperdoling hyped, Pindle still became chondriac. Miss Trappe still tended her garden, troweling past her bushes of wind-tortured thorns. And Miss Dessicquint still gave striking proof to the fact that, previous to the time at which departed souls must be assigned final location, there was a middle state after death when the spirit was still allowed to wander the earth with a mouthful of admonitions for everyone in sight. Excipuliform, Thimm, Porchmouth, Fewstone, even the peculiar little Qwert Yui Op: these, thought Darconville, became the faces that for so long now had lived and died next to his own, in chaos, in celebration, in triumph, in tragedy—the old academical fun-show of incompetents and ventripotents, crop-haired goons and beghards with boring stories, monophthongs-in-bowties who got up committees, the bunty women, wearers of camei, and obtuse dowds with headmistress untouchability still flourishing their mimic and pseudoethopoetical gestures, and all those parched and juiceless prats with supercalendered skin and voices like tonks who went panking up and down the corridors like quail-hawks making sure the students were behaving.

The students, ah yes!—the soft, lazy, unchangeable, gracilescent, sweet-scented nixies-from-Dixie with their half-vowels, Dolly Vardens, and cheeks like cupid's buttocks, no, the students, the students could not be discounted. Darconville met them daily, teaching his classes, adapting as best he could, and kindly, to their indigenous inattentiveness and far-too-casual interest in matters alien because academic. He did his job, his brain running now less to analysis than to good will, and he tried his best, as if living in a museum, to walk softly and not trench upon with applied logic or severe scrutation whatever came into view; the galleries seemed straight—but in fact they ran in secret mysterious circles, curving furtively out, around, and then always back through all pantochromatic creation to that one work of art he valued most.

Clio Cliusque sorores: Isabel Rawsthorne—eighteen no more, neither nineteen, but now close to her majority—gladsomely fell in with her classmates, seniors now, and with vigor applied herself to the pursuit of her degree. She'd majored in biology and, without any real native gifts for its rigors, seemed forever perusing her chemistry textbook which she carried about the way a Pakhtoon holds his Koran. Of grades, beauty often assumes more perquisites than it should, very like the attitude Southerners generally show toward the black waiter. ("Shines? We always considered them *part* of a damned julep!" Dr. Glibbery once boasted to Darconville.)

Isabel did well enough. Miss Gibletts, not Tyrannus, gave her an A in classics. Her oceanography course she loved, as she did a few throwaway electives in printmaking. But the possibility of a few good credits in piano went west, disappointing Miss Swint, who mistakenly thought she could make something of Isabel's handspread. And microbiology gave her fits, and a dirty pass. Math she flagged once, and then again, a related scandal ensuing that very afternoon when Darconville cornered her teacher—Miss Malducoit, unmarried, neither oblivious of Isabel's diamond, had dared to suggest *some* of us were doing all right in life, weren't we?—and, in Isabel's defense, not only decried the injustice but came within a hair of forgetting the Fifth Commandment and throppling her on the spot. Oh, Darconville was biased, but then wasn't she his responsibility? And how could her own folks intervene in such matters, living as they did way up there in the pines and peesashes? Reason enough, thought he—if less than justly—to have given her the highest grades possible in all her English courses, which she naturally enrolled in with an eye to the professor, the source of whose unspoken remorse lay less in his situational ethics (a perioptometry heretofore uncharacteristic of him) than in the fact that she'd promised repeatedly to write for him, sometime, anytime, the termpapers she subsequently never did. But he knew she loved him as he her, you see, and, what do they say?—a February snowfall is as good as manure. A failed promise is nothing to a lover if to him or her it is not the thing-to-be-ascertained. A loved one's every shape is an attitude of prayer.

Darconville's book, *Rumpopulorum*, was eventually published— and well received and discussed more or less everywhere but in Quinsyburg, where to no one's surprise, least of all its author's, it was met with a most aristarchean silence. Every Homer has his Zoilists. He couldn't have cared less.

Speed contracts time. In the rarefied heights of love Isabel and Darconville experienced over the short and quickening years of plenitude impossible, but for the time-dilation factor only travel in space sanctions, to explain. They both felt they would live forever and ever—in manner, in mind, in mood—and striding in Seven League Boots strode, before they looked, past time itself. Is the infinitive strictly to be called a mood? No, perhaps not, but so it seemed with them. Darconville didn't question it. During those years he often wondered, in fact, whether thought *ever* really helped a man in any of the critical ways of life; there seemed as little need to discern patterns as there seemed use for them, for life seemed its own justification, and he came to see the warp and woof contriving patterns made difficult, often impossible designs not only outside one's choosing but also beyond one's understanding, intricate elaborations in which, although unknown to one, one was being inextricably and fatefully bound but of which, even if known, one hadn't the power to reckon the significance. It was true, to seem to stand above the accidents of existence was simply to enjoy in an uprush of fancy the illusion that if you didn't accept them they didn't exist. Hoping only that what would happen to him would happen on *their* behalf, he merely decided to allow what would, for, well he knew, what would, will—and when it wished. And so Darconville relinquished complications of thought that he might better act and,

acting, love, and as loving told him that thought was a laziness that
prevented action, he accepted what was said, said what he felt, and
gratefully found himself soon equal to the fate encouraging him—it
didn't matter where—to complete participation.

They went on trips to Richmond, Charlottesville, and, in contrast to
a strangely uneasy visit several years before to the same spot—they'd
hardly known each other!—to Appomattox Court House where in the
green meadows that were fenced along with old white palings they
laughed and talked and had memorable picnics of quiche and wine.
Once they went to Williamsburg, driving back after a weekend into a
beautiful sunset that matched in richness the gold of their young, un-
complicated hearts, beating, as if to speak: "You are my doneé, I give
you my will. You are too my devisee, I give you all the estate of my
soul."

It might be mentioned that Darconville and Isabel never lived together, formally, that is—which, of course, prevented nothing save her
summary expulsion from school—yet it was with undisguised pride
and even wider statement that they still shopped together at the Piggly
Wiggly, rarely, however, without the feeling (for such were the super-
visional stares) of both the legal and local vulnerability of their con-
sortium. They were, nevertheless, inseparable. Not an odd day, it was
an odd minute when they weren't together, both the objects and ob-
servers of love. They packed the Bentley and often traveled to Washington, roaming around the museums and monuments, and several
summers even drove up to Cape Cod where they hiked, took photographs, and often made love in the ocean, but whenever school was in
session, confining them somewhat, they ranged the nearby countryside
and enfiladed the small neighboring towns around Quinsyburg for
whatever turned their eyes to chance marvels or any new adventure.
What fimble on what gate didn't they unlatch? What side road not
pass down?

Few ever saw Darconville and Isabel together without wanting to
be in love with somebody. They were thick as thistles: two distincts,
division none. They joyed one joy, one grief they grieved, one love
they loved. They rose with the wonderful ductile inflections of the seasons, school schedules, but most of all the irrepressible *superlatio* of
their twin spirits, for either was the other's, single nature's double
name, neither two nor one was called—yet either neither, the simple
was so well compounded. Original, they escaped repetition and yet,

free and imprescriptible, learned to find the best of old emotions the most beautiful. They went anywhen and manywhere, called the world nicknames, and sang glorias at the very top of their voices. No, not at the beginning of imagination because at the end of fact, they simply renewed just by a glance what they looked upon and wishing for nothing they didn't have lived intently only for what they did, for a while it truly might be said that never passed a minute when that sublime and prevenient grace arresting their young hearts to love didn't assure them that to watch the morning star one's eyes must always be a little brighter, neither did it fail to whisper low that once upon a time never comes again.

And, as time passed, they soon came to know how very serious they had become.

It became a matter of course, then, for them to spend their weekends in Fawx's Mt. Darconville didn't really mind. The farming community remained as misenunciated as ever, and one rarely drove through those depressing doles and secluded ravines without a sudden feeling of subjugation, an inexplicable sadness, but as the years passed he'd found, surprisingly, he'd adapted not only to the folks in those parts who looked like itinerant blackthorn sellers, what with their low-vaulted brows and cluttoned joints, but also to the land they worked and its parquetry of odd, misallotted fields where stupid large-bodied cattle with shiny red hides and massive horns ambled about. How often he'd heard the sounds of reapers skitching near a hedge or fence by the road! Slash, rustle, slash! Slash, rustle, slash. And, in fact, he actually came to measure the frequency of his trips up there—along with the parallel lapses of time—by alterations in the fields he passed: the tedding after the swathe of the scythes, then rowing, then the footcocks, then breaking, then the hubrows gathered into hubs, sometimes another break, then turning again, to the rickles, the biggest of all the cocks, which were eventually run together into placks, shapeless heaps from which the harvesters carted their hay away. Autumns it rained, the stubble soon took the snow, and before long spring had come again. But what distributions—irrotational, solenoidal, lunar—really mattered? Where was that in a world of mutability that must apply to him? The plug-uglies of Fawx's Mt., the eupatrids of Charlottesville, the quidnuncs of Quinsyburg? They were of no consequence anymore, for behind what people on this earth, thought Darconville, were shadows cast not black?

The weekends rarely varied. They talked. They took occasional drives. They often walked through the woods across the way and once or twice to their initially slight embarrassment but secret understanding found the tree where, the day before Darconville left for London several years ago, they'd in a far less assured mood carved the word "Remember." Generally, however, Darconville sat in the backyard reading—he didn't write, he never wrote when he was with her —while Isabel, either washing her hair or listening to records, waited to fix dinner. Mr. Shiftlett, who never said a word, seemed to have no end of work—Darconville never figured this out—down in the cellar. And his imperseverant and preposterous sister, her hair pinched into rollers, was always puttering about in the pseudo-carbuncular excrescence out front she called a flowerbed—it was less expensive than a psychiatrist—leaving off at successive intervals either for a stiff drink or the by now familiar roundelay-like exchange with her prospective son-in-law on the subject of noble intentions: for her daughter, now at her accidence, the fond illiterate mother wished only, if querimoniously, that she be thinking "aboot the footure." Darconville, of course, agreed. But as he felt that Isabel, for her *own* benefit, should finish her education and avoid, at the same time, any inordinate pressure attendant on future speculation, he preferred not to harry her in any way whatsoever. The flying arrow, at a given moment in a given place, is also at rest. They were content.

There was, nevertheless, the habitual Saturday night party when the Shiftletts and their neighbors (*minus:* the van der Slangs) put their workaday worries into a blender and shook out the concoctions of Lethe—a group of country skimpleplexes on dress parade whose ardor from low squeals rose eventually to the din of an Abyssinian thunderstorm. Darconville, by retiring early, avoided it. But in the next room, Isabel, with all that thumping, hooting, and laughter, lay face-up in the darkness most of the night, burning with shame. Morning, then, never broke in Fawx's Mt. without Darconville being suddenly awakened by the explosion of the 6 A.M. farm report coming over the clock-radio next to his bed; it was all agri-business: a rustic gaffoon with the diction of a guinea-hen, full of voiceless consonants and twangs, grackling his information out with such spitting, blowing, and hawking it sounded like a five-minute repetition of something like *mustaherttuatarmustaherttuatar*—in fact, it was the price-per-bushel rundown on red winter wheat, soybeans, and yellow shell corn which was then always followed by a familiar essay on the problems of pinkeye, parasite control, bull cross comparison, and hog-spraying.

There were other country matters, as well. Sundays, for instance, usually found Darconville and Isabel alone. No one there went to church. The Shiftletts, a somber two in low-crowned black hats, always set that day aside as a ticket-of-leave for a spin in the family truck to replenish themselves with the aimless but prolonged mouse-hunt that is the Sunday drive. Little varied thereafter in the wave goodbye, the locked door, the silence. Transcendental prolepses, or anticipations of thought: under the color of sudden opportunity then, interwished, they would turn like aimcriers to behold their chance, not with spoken words, but simply eyes that meet to seek what seeking always find. Mumbudget is the slogan. Isabel steps quietly to her room; a shirt's unbuttoned, off comes an umbeclip, and down flows her hair; and then a girl with tresses shining like that of a faxed star and a figure bioluminescent beneath a black diaphanous gown sprinkled with flowers turns with a gentle smile to the doorway and leads her lover, under a slowly twirling mobile, toward the familiar red-and-cream bed. There are kisses short as one, one long as twenty, and they make love, recapitulating with considerable skill what they'd done a thousand times in a passion now as restless and urgent as that need which into words no vertue could ever digest. Fire makes gold shine. In the swelter, Isabel is proof of it, always in the same way—she pushes herself forward in blind suspension, her arms lowered behind her, her hands locked tightly under the bed panel, her breath catching in soft aromatic yoops as if astonished, inexpressibly, at the wonder now of other impossibilities ever being found as true as that. And Darconville? Now in the floods, now panting in the meads, Darconville could not be found to ask, so lost for joy was he in those always indelible, compellable, but untellable hours of drury which nevertheless the stupid quack of a clock, set against invasion, always served to end.

"O, you're going to leave me one day, I know it," Isabel, raised on an elbow, habitually teased.

For they talked, often—yes, and hoped, and dreamed, and planned. Indeed, it had been one such chance remark on one such occasion, sometime during that first year after he'd returned from London, that one particular quodvultdiabolus was fully, and finally, put to rest; the topic of infidelity having been raised in the whimsical way that had become typical of her, Darconville would thereafter never forget how

Isabel, cajoled, suddenly laughed out that Govert van der Slang, not only someone now to whom she never gave a passing thought, had also been all along none other than Darconville's unprepossessing and inoffensive conversant at the nefarious Gherardini party the previous year! It was, if a belated confession, a disclosure at once explaining why, fearful at the prospect of suddenly finding two rivals side by side, she had kept to the other side of the room and how, in fact, she'd suffered so, a matter thereby encouraging her shocked, then relieved listener to try to effect greater efforts at a truce with him whenever they met, which they did, and a mutual understanding developed as the years passed to the degree that they might even have broached old subjects, which they didn't. Govert van der Slang was harmless. The name, Ignaro, did his nature right ahead even if once he'd loved her. "I never loved him, I don't love him now," said Isabel Rawsthorne, "and I will never love him."

Fawx's Mt. however, unlike that problem, never quite lost its inscrutability, nor had Isabel her mystic fancies. (What was it about that place, for instance, that made her so nervous and always looking about from port to stern?) Smitten, nevertheless, Darconville found her a child of the sun, to be faulted less in what she lacked than for all he could never know of her or ever have enough of: the incautious afternoons of love, her secret kisses pressed upon his hand, the closeness she felt sleeping in his shirts, and of course her many childlike exaggerations—"I know you're going to leave me." "Are we being 'lascivious'?" "I must go back to my kingdom one day, you know, because I'm really a princess." "If we ever parted I'd come back one day and you'd recognize me by—"

O, could one write her paralipomena!

It would be incorrectly given out, however, to call Isabel perfect. Loyal? That she was, and that for Darconville mitigated matters otherwise not always positive. She often took a great deal of humoring. She never sent thank-you notes, never read enough, and never visited Miss Trappe. She *lagged* a lot. She had a monstrous vanity about her hair, the combing of which became a particular hobble of hers exercised to death. Young, she was disinclined to keep promises, take chances, or, except in the woes of antipaternal lament, ever really be frank—and, even when driven to it, her responses were often too understated to match Darconville's enthusiasms which tended less to stifle them, often to her consternation, than to fan. She often said things out loud that most people generally preferred to think ("I know what I'm going to do—" or "I'm decided now—") but was just as often a talker to no purpose. The talker, by definition, is not a listener, but wasn't listening, deliberating, the key to the thought understanding requires? Then, she always said her worst fault was that she was always trying to please people, and yet she somehow failed to understand that, in doing so, she inevitably came to resent them, a fault that had its worst ramifications in the matter of jealousy.

Isabel loved Darconville, he was certain of it, but through her behavior often proved to need him even more—and suspicion is often an ugly, if habitual, facet of need. There were at times hysterical telephone calls. Several times, she read his mail—"I just looked, I didn't *see* anything!"—which upset him terribly only because it threatened him with implications of a disloyalty he never felt, quite the reverse, in fact, and so he would end up paradoxically insisting on his loyalty with wrath and on his love with anger. At such times, she wept in the most unconvincing way—she never hid herself to weep—but when Darconville, appalled at the vulgarity of such groundless suspicion yet terrified at the same moment that his presence far exceeded her need of him or underrepresented what need of hers he could meet, then made the suggestion he always swore within himself he'd honor ("Would you like to date anyone else?"), she always refused, always firmly and always finally. Stubbornness, one of the worst manifestations of weakness, here made him grateful. Yes, she was loyal.

But our virtues, indeed, are our vices. She never entertained a single thought about the mysteries of God, man, or the universe yet for that seemed innocent. If she had few convictions, kept her opinions at half-mast, and simply repeated what Darconville said, easy acceptance replenished serenity. Threatened by mediocrities much closer to her than to others—or at least she so feared—she effortfully aspired to graces others of her age ignored, and yet when she acquired them she too often failed, in terms of sympathy, those who *hadn't* acquired them—and far too often, in the light of those requirements where the social demands of Quinsy College, such as they were, refracted off the relatively advanced status her association with Darconville gave her, Isabel more and more began to feel her participation in them less a favor received than one conferred. That people with atrocious manners should now have to be polite and considerate in their dealings with her, that people whose habit was to stand aloof should now have

to be at her service, that the priggish and self-assured should have to
defer to her, all of this pleased her just a little too much—and yet,
while sometimes it cankered him, Darconville could no more by un-
conscionable criticism be disloyal to her than St. Paul who, ready to
anathematize even an angel if it preached another gospel, proved a
model of steadfastness.

There was not a lot to forgive, really, for while what she was exacerbated what she wasn't—the fairer the paper, the fouler the blot—
her faults were few. Isabel could be amusing, as well. Hers was a sweet
wiseacreishness. She made claims: that she never had a headache,
never drank a cup of coffee, and never—a howler of Southern
etiquette—went to the bathroom. She boasted she could tell by smell if
it were going to snow and that she knew jiujitsu. She suffered an acute
haptodysphoria in relation to peaches. She carried French sweets loose
in her pocket, stuck together with lint more often than not. She wore
a cheap perfume called "Figment" which was much less attractive
than her particular way of lowering her eyes in a smile when he flat-
teringly acknowledged it. The girl was difficult in the extreme to know,
a fact brought home to Darconville many times in the process, lately
begun, of recording for fun what she said, and did, and felt, memos,
then notes and random observations, and finally long reflective essays
that eventually grew into a box of papers on a subject whose wonderful inconsistencies he hoped never to resolve only if they led her to the
larger, deeper self he knew she had it in her power to become.

In Isabel's senior year, it so happened that Darconville encouraged
her, as a confidence boost, to enter the Miss Quinsy contest. Now, despite petty annoyances, there was no question but that over the few
short years they'd grown closer and closer. Difficulties attend upon adjustment. Perennials, unlike annuals, seem less attractive perhaps only
because open to longer scrutiny, but they endure, they do endure, and
if the splendor of their lives was occasionally overcast by shadow, neither of them was so confused as either to accede to the mundane or assume happiness was habit. And so every day they spent together, and
every day, no matter the cast, was too short—morning leaped high-
noon, bounded on a step to mid-overnoon, and always night came far
too fast. She stopped by his house every day, confided in him when she
needed that, and even if poorly read—she found allusions to Darconville's book, not having read it, disconcerting—nevertheless remained
for him a refreshing alternative to the dire extremes of academic dull-

ness. He still invented and told her little fables. She still slept in his shirts, still left notes at his office, and always of course exclaimed in her childlike way of princesses, fairy forests, and supernatural intercepts. They still played with Spellvexit, went on picnics, and flew kites out in the meadow, where, still, her tresses broke free in the wind which absorbed into its length her trailing ribbons and in a special wayward way, as always, seemed to claim her for its own by means of an adoption no more complex than simply taking her away. What was Darconville's surprise, then, when in the face of all that joy and seasoned understanding the Miss Quinsy affair exploded—a crisis, reaching to proportions he hadn't thought possible, that touched upon that one point of delicacy long unspoken of and which now ran arrow-straight to a single, unavoidable confrontation. It had to do with the size of Isabel's legs.

Isabel loved to eat. It was an expression of joy, a mode less of glut than of celebration. The weight she put on, however, unfortunately sank—to drop hopelessly, perversely, relentlessly into the crural sheath where eventually began to slumber, with little to be done that could reverse it, a fatty deposit of incipient cellulite, touched in places with arborescent naeves daintily penciled blue. Volumes, alas, grow faster than surfaces. The birth-control pills she took only worsened the condition. She was extraordinarily beautiful but low slung: not the Marquesse of Pantagruel, not Assumpta Corpuscularia, neither did her legs reach to the fabled size of a Samoan's, but she was frankly supracoxal and whatever counterefforts she employed to diminish the problem failed. An inceptive gammer was ever pushing from within to get out and create havoc. Each of her legs rather recalled the condition of Dr. Johnson's goose—too much for one, not enough for two! Cute, below, became cunning.

The long dresses and bell-bottoms she habitually wore—obsessively, as if her thighs were an approximate occasion of sin to a cannibal—she saw as a defense not so much advantageous perhaps as appropriate. Mind bifurcates: and often, with jaw muscles tensing, she suffered the torments of the damned from the observations she self-defeatingly ascribed to any onlooker in sight, coming to resent not only the observer but, sadly, the observed. Sometimes, her response was self-mocking laughter, the ironic kind, which, having to do with nothing, only makes the face lose its attractiveness in a paralytic ache, ossifying natural feelings in a ritualistic grimace, feigning fun, and so flatly refusing anyone who cares the reason he must have graciously to show compassion. Darconville was such a one. He loved her *precisely* for everything she was and wasn't, and, if sometimes he worried her worries, he simply assumed the compositional view, like that of the Japanese print, by favoring the pictorial elements gathered in the upper part of the picture and leaving the rest either empty or out of view. But nothing could diminish his love. There was too much else for which to be grateful. One crow didn't make a winter.

So the Miss Quinsy subject had been raised and, raised, dealt with, and Isabel's self-disappointment, running headlong from the challenge —misinterpreted mock—led to the humiliation she swore, she adjured, she insisted lay bound up with the mere mention of that public event she so came to abhor. She became convinced, utterly, that she had to meet "standards" for Darconville, in spite of his repeatedly denying it. "I'm *not* Hypsipyle Poore!" she cried, a terrible *chaudfroid* in her heart. She wept. "It's impossible! I just can't be what you want!" And several times she turned pridefully on her heel, her eyes flashing, with : "You watch! I know what I'm going to do, I'm going to lose thirty pounds and become a model!"

It was bewildering. Her tempestuous emotions merely burst into occasional flame that consumed but could not illumine. And it was ridiculous. Darconville wished he'd never mentioned the foolish pageant but having done so mistakenly tried to outface her fears and suspicions by further pleading—maximum efforts to minimize—and so only compounded the problem, stretching consequent hours of debate and clarification to limits beyond the powers of even Arabic notation to express. Finally, like so much else during those years, it sputtered, wound down to a whimper, and was heard again no more.

Darconville, the lover, put the matter behind him. But Darconville, the writer, lingered on awhile, remaining behind to retrace for some reason what otherwise he should have missed. And what he found he filed, for the better to know her impressions, her preferences, her remarks, her joys, even her outrages, the better to understand, he felt, and so better love. With lovers: with enemies—how strange!—there, in each, can one always find both a stimulus and a lesson.

And what exactly were they? The stimulus? Oh, the stimulus he knew. But of all the many lessons over the many years, Darconville came to learn, above all, that love mightn't be easy and yet still be love, that love might fade or fall or stumble or stoop yet still be love, that love might have to dodge and pivot through every scarp, counter-scarp, demi-bastion, pinfold or covered way, glacis, ravelin, half-moon, ditch, sap, mine, and palisado *yet still be love!* And he learned even more, and was glad for that, for too easily we come to love love first and not initially love that from which it comes.

And so aware of that Darconville came to learn about his lover.

LIV

Odi et Amo

A quirked vessel never falls from the hand.

—ANONYMOUS

Her Likes: ballet-slippers; salt; purple ink; abstract prints; mushrooms; jiujitsu; fairy tales; the novel, *Wuthering Heights;* herring roe for breakfast; combing her hair; movies; scented candles; découpage; spinach; unattractive girls; jeeps; tiny candies; the pronunciation of the word "lascivious"; gin-and-tonics; all animals, especially lions and ti-

Her Dislikes: mathematics; sand on the bottom of her feet; country music; peach fuzz; children; long tunnels; her relatives; coffee; poodles; the appellation "Honey"; reading; frankness; Quinsyburg; films; blond guys; poverty; beer; intellectual discussion; cities; writing letters; religious devotions; nakedness; feigners; the thought of deer being

gers; straw hats; illusion; getting mail; rings; the consolation following failure; halter-type dresses; rock music; flattery; seed catalogues; the endearment "Doo Doo"; Rima, the Bird Girl; wickerwork; clam chowder; the South; cookies; stories of waifs; the flute; nudity; solitude; plucking her eyebrows manually; money; the color blue; mobiles; hope; thick shoes; pomander balls; snakes; long dresses; antiques; stone jewelry; exotic shampoos; princesses; heat; security; herb gardens; fine-point pens; her first name; ice-cream; batiks; illustrated books; fields; venison; hoop earrings; feigning; horses; fossils; root beer; safety; movies; to be looked at; the known; photos of herself; things cute; balloons and kites; fiddler crabs; ginger ale; Charlottesville summers (?); Darconville.

killed; her legs; tomatoes; exercise; literature; hard peas; loneliness; having her nostrils pinched; shorts; men with long fingernails; cigarette smoke; rednecks; study; things cunning; Mrs. van der Slang's lack of ethics; cold; farmers; the unknown; the responsibility following success; chemistry; to be stared at; scholars; her real father; expectation; geraniums; her thumbnails; card-playing; Fawx's Mt.; eccentrics; the South; diners; Hypsipyle Poore; declarations of love in anyone's presence; college; attractive girls; analytical talks; Dr. Glibbery; standing up; references to storge; maternal inaniloquence; the past; the future; sailors; insecurity; words; square dances; running; beauty pageants; the name Shiftlett; Charlottesville summers (?); Govert van der Slang.

L V

The Timberlake Hotel

Sweet boadments, good!

—WILLIAM SHAKESPEARE, *Macbeth*

THERE WAS A LOT TO KNOW, more to remember, but remembering to forget became the significant self-protective feature for each of them that last year. It became policy, for Isabel's graduation—and its afterwending consequences—loomed up for them as an abrupt question as to what, then and thereafter, they would do. Characteristically, both lived with the piepondering but unexpressed hope that nothing for them would change, and yet while they postponed whatever decision it was the continued silence on that subject insured against their raising, hoping, perversely, became an obstacle to hope, for each and every fulfillment of theirs, no matter how small, seemed to contain in itself an impulse to further commitment, which somehow instantly ruined the purity of fact by theory. It was as if, while Darconville was waiting for something to happen, Isabel was waiting for something not to. Queerly, it came to the same thing.

Whatness translated into wlatness. It wasn't working, for both of them came to feel, painfully, that the avoidance of pressure recapitulated with considerable skill, analytic and mimetic, precisely the pressure they both sought to avoid. Graver by far than the problem became the solution. How answers, like effects, become the consequence of questions, like causes! It was baleful. Would they go? Where would they go? And would they go together? One decision, of course, hinged on another, then that to another, and so on, serving, eventually, to hasp the door so tight that, if once neither of them quite dared open it, they couldn't work it now at all.

It all came to an end—or a beginning—rather suddenly one morning very much like any other when the risk of Darconville's having given up everything for the sake of his love, *for* that love, seemed as inconsequential as ever. From class Darconville was called down to the English office to take a long-distance telephone call. The office secretary couldn't quite distinguish, at least at that moment, the difference between a groan of pleasure and a groan of pain—isn't more than inflection involved?—as she searched his face for a clue. Though having forsaken much—a humiliating charge he privately leveled against himself for abrogating, during the Quinsyburg years, so many former ideals—Darconville nevertheless held fast to what he still felt the best attribute of character: the power to refrain. The telephone call was brief. He said only one word: *yes.*

Darconville checked his watch, left the office, and quickly headed toward the dining-hall. The door of the classics department suddenly opened as he passed, and Miss Gibletts, interposing herself, tried to stop him. "A curious schoolprint," she said, "how would you translate the Greek phrase σούκισσα μέλαινα?" She sniffed. "I'm working up an article." Darconville, in mid-stride, said he was sorry, he was rushed, he really was. Miss Gibletts, stamping her foot, honked tearfully at him as he hastened down the corridor, "Don't mind me, nobody does, *I'm* just a snirt!" Darconville turned to explain but heard only, "Go back from wherever you came from and your ugly cat!"—and a door slammed. We just may, thought Darconville, smiling, we just may.

Now he was running, down the buckling linoleum, past the framed row of Quinsy presidents, and into the Rotunda where the odor of brussels sprouts still hung in the air. A student was standing in front of the statue of Joan of Arc. Darconville, almost out of breath, asked her if perchance she knew Isabel Rawsthorne and, as she did, requested that she go into the dining-hall and get her. When Isabel appeared, somewhat surprised, he took her by the hand to a far corner.

"We're going to dinner at the Timberlake Hotel tonight—to celebrate!"

"We are?" Isabel blinked. "Why are we?"

Darconville seemed to remember everything he'd ever forgotten at that moment, and, with his eyes positively gleaming, he quickly explored her face to see exactly where her joy, matching his, would express itself. The sun, elamping wide, streamed into the Rotunda.

"We can say goodbye to Quinsyburg," he said. "If I'm not going to leave you, you see, I'm afraid you'll have to come with me."

"To the Timberlake?"

"Guess again."

The Timberlake Hotel, through some error or other of inadvertence, had never been torn down. It perched over a walk-up, behind high trees, off the main street and wanted paint badly. The shades in the upper rooms, most of which hadn't been used for years, were always pulled. The old-fangled shutters slanted. There was an old, ghostly character to the place, its suffering points at immediate evidence to the eye and as close as the gloom in the main foyer—one stood in the middle of the worn carpet and heard only the sound of waits—which was dark, weird, and smelled like long-used prayer-books. Behind the massive front desk hung a keyrack, always full, and along the back-wall were replicated rows of mail-hutches, always empty. Sometimes someone was behind the desk, sometimes someone wasn't. It didn't matter. You hung up your wraps, waited in vain by the dining-room to be seated, and then eventually walked in.

"It's a miracle—a wonderful secret just between you and I," said Isabel, giggling and sipping more champagne. She looked up. "Or should it be me?"

"Should what be me?"

"Should I be me?" Isabel twirled a finger in her drink and laughed. "*You* know."

Darconville smiled. "Could you possibly be anyone else?"

The secret had been divulged, and they were both in high spirits, an exuberance fully as bright and as antic as the candleflames that lighted up the table and sparkled out of the silver and twinkled in the wine. Darconville refilled the glasses, and again they toasted the future that had just been offered them. But there was Doubt in the Mind of Royalty. "Harvard! *Harvard University!* But it's you," she added, playfully pushing his arm, her diamond ring spurtling with tiny lights, "it's you they want. Me, whatever would I do there? You know me, I don't seem to be able to communicate with anybody." She paused, reflectively. "I seem to ruin everything"—always, that quaint pronunciation—"but to ruin your career? To disappoint you? To not measure up?"

It was absurd, such talk. Loyalty? The virtue, going to such lengths, only turned upon itself, making faith as fickle as a lee tide trying to run against the wind. Oh, could she only have seen herself, for she sat as for a portrait, her honeycolored hair falling around a face as exquisite as noonshine and her long black dress leaving her shoulders bare and whiter than purity. Praise praises. Thanksgiving gives thanks. Couldn't she *see* that?

"What," asked Darconville, "could you possibly ruin?"

The smile died. For a minute Isabel seemed not to know, struck as if she'd somehow forgotten on opening night the dialogue that had gone too long assumed or unquestioned in her monologous lines of rehearsal. She grew silent, thinking she didn't want to remember what she, in fact, had forgotten. Darconville, watching her for a response, remembered all of a sudden a queer dream he'd once had: a couple, standing on each side of a dead beast, were bid to live together 'til death did them part and so, shaking hands, the wedding was ended. Who was that couple? What was that beast? Isabel, meanwhile, seemed for no apparent reason utterly shent and powerless, staring at, then into, and now through Darconville to the reaches of blackest orphny. It frightened him, that mood-change, and he touched a shiver in her arm. She looked up and around as if looking for something to do.

"How much they must have loved your book! Look!" She nervously pulled from her handbag a copy of *Rumpopulorum,* the formal cause of his being asked to teach at Harvard and so brought along as a guest, flipped it open, and read: "*'With the sun a reminding touch upon their frozen hair the winged,* um, *phagones of evil flashed out of heaven—'*" She looked up. "'Flashed,'" she said, "that's a great verb." The voice was happy but it wasn't her voice. It seemed a terrible echo of something even worse than false cheer: terror.

Darconville wasn't fooled.

"Please," he asked softly, "what's the matter?"

Isabel's face collapsed as if she'd just been stabbed—then, clutching his two hands, she pulled herself to his face and sobbed desperately, *"My God, do you really love me?"*

The dining-room itself seemed to fall away, the shadows thrown across it becoming now more ominous, its huge radiators like headstones and the faded perse drapes like shrouds over the windows effectively providing a last funereal touch. It seemed to transform back to the sepulchre it always was, not that the owner, were he ever brought that complaint, would have given a damn—and he'd damned well tell you so, too; but he spoke to no one, least of all strangers: he only stood around, tut-mouthed in his baseball cap, listening to his swine-toned radio, reading the paper, or maybe slouching out to that dad-docky veranda, knotted with grey wisteria, to play checkers with a few other old smouchers and layabouts who seemed to have spent a life-time devoted to smoking bags of filthy shag and patching grief with proverbs out front. That was the way it was. You didn't like it, you could goddamn well go down the road, OK?

The Timberlake did no business to speak of. The students never went there, the faculty rarely, and Negroes weren't welcome. It was a place for Quinsyburg's old people—veiled like outdated fabrics and wrapped in woolen stuffs—who stopped in, wordlessly hung up their coats, and then took their plates of boiled fish and glasses of water alone. On this particular evening, the dining-room was empty as usual but for one black waiter, several old ladies crunching breadsticks, and the unmistakable figure, hunched in a bib, of President Greatracks alone in a corner gulching a mound of meat. He had seen Darconville come in but only winked, wiped his oily chin, and fell again upon his meats and puddings as if to defeat them. Ordinarily, he would have come over and talked the runners off a pung. He obviously had other plans. But congeniality, even at the best of times, was not a big number at the Timberlake Hotel. Nor had Darconville chosen the place by chance. You see, it was absolutely impossible to have a celebration there, so it was the perfect place to have a celebration if you were never coming back. For Darconville, incidentally, there was no question whatsoever about that. But unfortunately he was now facing another.

"I'm sorry."

"You must be tired," said Darconville. Was it a joke? If so, it was a joke that hurt him badly. But he smiled.

"I'm sorry."

"You've been overexcited by it all."

"I'm so sorry."

"Please," asked Darconville, leaning forward, "what is the matter with you?"

"You."

"What's the matter with me?"

"Me," she whispered.

Darconville touched her hand and frowned, feeling clownish and homely and old. He was embarrassed. He didn't know what to say. *Do you really love me?* When love isn't proof of itself, it is suddenly impossible to prove—and words, which fit to fill the mouths of myst and mummer alike, cheapen on the tongue. And how many of them, to mock about meaning with mendaciloquence! No, if weeds were orchids, thought Darconville, people would come to hate orchids rather than cultivate weeds. But words were weeds, weren't they? They can mean their opposite! If I should cleave, must I then embrace this girl or be let to cut her into twigs? Let? Choose, it can mean both hinder and allow. Avaunt beckons and banishes, both, and *hostis,* why, it indicates a guest and indicates an enemy! Foundlings are lostlings! *Do you really love me?* I do, and so must loathe her, he thought, fashioning thus the truth that grows expedient, becoming Cato's lie. Question: Are you faithful to your husband? Answer: I wouldn't be with you—*there,* for manifold ambiguity to say that one deserved condign punishment is tautological; to say that one does not deserve it is a contradiction in terms. What of language, then, when opposites pip each other into life as faith will doubt and love will hate? If Moses was the son of Pharaoh's daughter, then he must have been the daughter of Pharaoh's son. Why, pluck out words that mean what they are, and language shan't have a tooth left to mump on beans! *Do you really love me?* It was a question, thought Darconville, that fully deserved the wrong answer—but, what, making it then, if language interpreted as it did, the right one? O wonderful world, when we can't mean what

we say! But wait, perhaps she asks what she too well knows and therefore doesn't know at all, as a person goes blind to the riddle of familiar
landscapes or sits deaf as a post listening in the depths of that infirmity
to try to hear more of the promiscuous roar she can't see has caused
and now prevents it. Good! I will outparadox paradox, thought Darconville, juggle intentions like balls, and make foundlings of lostlings
all over again! Opportunity is being ready for it! Checkmate!

"I want to marry you," said Darconville.

The statement was simple. It didn't subdichotomize. It didn't subdi-
vide. It seemed to Isabel as far from danger as she was from reason
and as near to love as she was now from folly. She felt strangely calm,
almost in the swoon of satisfaction that is at the last stage of penance
fully made. It was a moment to cherish, there in that ghastly hotel,
when perhaps for the first time in her entire life that vision which she
feared waited for her forked and misanointed in the middle distance
now came to the fore an angel of deliverance, its open hand gentle to
the possibility of it. It was so easy. There was suddenly confusion in
neither concern nor context: here was a person who loved her, a
friend to console her, a protector to keep her safe from the close world
of mouse-fretting worries and major disappointments she'd lived with
so long but could no more. If one *did* something, she saw, one didn't
have to wait anymore. She wouldn't—she couldn't—wait anymore.
There was nothing to remember. The statement was simple. There
was nothing to forget.

"Wait," said Darconville, swiftly interrupting himself to comply
with apprehension before it rose to overwhelm him, "if you want to.
You may want to spend some time alone, you may want more
schooling, your parents—"

Isabel's head was lowered, shadowed in a slant of candleshade. It
has been said that the happiest conversation is that of which nothing is
remembered, and, if so, whether a longer reply led up to what he
heard, Darconville couldn't say, but he would never forget that moment when she looked up suddenly with moist brown eyes, paused,
and whispered softly, "I want—what you want."

"When?"

"September."

"Where?"

Isabel fixed her eyes on him tenderly, her bosom upwelling with the tears she tried in vain, by swallowing, to absorb. "Where we were engaged."

A stone suddenly rolled away from his heart.

"I have to confess something," she said, smiling through the tears that fell and pressing the back of her fingers against his cheek. "I've always wanted since I was little to make my own wedding dress."

The driving rain outside—a sudden gowkstorm had blown up during the evening—turned the lobby of the Timberlake even darker than usual, the heavy curtains over the windows flapping about now in the room like the huge wings of angry birds. They had stayed on rather late, and Darconville, concerned about Isabel's curfew, was wondering how they'd get to the car. Hugging two empty champagne bottles, Isabel laughed that she didn't care and that she didn't mind getting wet and that, having claimed earlier at Fitts that she planned to go to Fawx's Mt., she'd signed out for an "overnight" anyway.

They waited on in some merriment, with Isabel gladdened to the heart and Darconville feeling a certain continual power, a sense of being attentive enough to a minute survey of the worth of real life that he might have been perpetually a poet. At that moment he looked through the window and saw a woman outside in the midst of the downpour. She was running up the front steps holding up a pink umbrella and an overnight bag. It was Mrs. Dodypol! Whether Isabel recognized her he couldn't say, but as the poor woman stumbled through the front door of the hotel with an alcoholic lurch and a fright of hairloops stuck messily to a face the color of margarine he saw how very much she evoked Isabel's sympathy—Isabel pressed close to Darconville.

"I love you for that. You care," he said, thinking of his own general indifference to that faculty wife, "sometimes far more, I'm sorry to say, than I."

Mrs. Dodypol, signing the register, quickly disappeared upstairs when Isabel turned to Darconville and, winking, whispered playfully, "Or is it me?"

LVI

The Wedding Is Banned

And all is done that ye lookèd for before.

—JOHN SKELTON, "Though Ye Suppose
All Jeopardies Are Passed"

THE SUMMER began with much to do. It was June already, and Isabel had passed her courses, was graduated, and had been driven back to spend an unemphatic summer—her last—in Fawx's Mt., not Arcady, no, but home. There had been a happy coincidence in her graduation gifts: her parents gave her a sewing machine, Darconville several hundred dollars for the nuptial silks-and-satins they together chose in Charlottesville for her gown and a blanket chest in which, with sprigs of rosemary, to fold it when finished. She also bought a small, blue used car. Now, as they'd determined to be married in London come September, time was pressing. When the particular discrimination called hesitation long exists, the reverse discrimination of haste must offset it, and so with that in mind Darconville returned to teach two five-week sessions of summer school at Quinsy and to organize as best he could what promised to be a frantic few months.

It was imperative, right off, to secure living quarters at Harvard and to find out when in the fall they were required to be there. There were other letters of inquiry, as well, one immediately to Westminster Cathedral to set a wedding day and another, also to London, to ascertain from the General Registry Office at Somerset House what procedures were required on the civil side. They would need reservations, licenses, certificates of a hundred kinds—and above all luck. (A less pactitious consideration—one no less, however, involving Isabel—was squaring away the matter of faith: he began to think about her baptism.) The hope, of course, was that all would go smoothly. His was to do, then report, and it became his habit to dodge down to the Timberlake at night to telephone any news of consequence. Sometimes Isabel wasn't at home.

The comfort, he knew, was that every effort in Quinsyburg that summer would be an effort finally put to rest and the occasion, finally, of putting that place behind him. Who'd have believed he would have stayed so long? Constancy was a word too hollowpampered to express so extraordinary a behavior; it wasn't patience; it wasn't longanimity. It was love—a wooing, leading only to one end, that had followed the same time-honored steps, the shared laughter, the wantsum misunderstandings, fearful and explorative, and all the other fits of uncommon passion for so many centuries displayed in the tempests between Father Weather and Mother Earth.

Struggle, of course—what else?—informs success, and there were those of Darconville's friends who, hearing now of his marriage plans, left him that summer somewhat in the dark less as to the wisdom of his new venture than as to the interpretation they placed on it. Quinsyburg was a lonely place, and loneliness often becomes the sole source of protection against the comparatively worse desolation *passing* friendship causes. Lonely they lived—why, wondered Darconville, do people have to have no money to spend less?—and lonely they would die; but pitifully he could find no words of consolation for such as those who, meeting him in the streets or at school during those final months, stopped forlorn as if to ask, not so much from him as of themselves, why bother to marry and beget when the search for union is doomed by implication in the very act? Why part a whole heart into halves if it is required to break it? Why not acknowledge, finally, that union is one and disappointment the alternative?

No, it wasn't that the remarks were put in such direct terms; Quinsyburgisms seldom were. There were hesitant glances, often, silly nods, comments odd and elliptical. For instance, one day Mrs. McAwaddle stopped him on the front steps of the library, sighed lugubriously, and —what byzantine warning was *this* in aid of?—tapped the side of her nose. Another incident as inexplicable occurred one afternoon in the college post-office. "Hello, Darconville," came a voice, "fair grow the lilies on the riverbanks?" It was of course Dr. Dodypol who, banging a stamp on a letter, then pointed at him with a quote:

> "If Nature's a vision, Art's a re-
> How can you write what you cannot see?"

Then he popped his letter in the slot and said good-day.

But Miss Trappe's, perhaps, was the queerest. Walking up the street one day under one of her boisterous hats, she suddenly reversed direction and on a detour came up to knock on Darconville's door. Disheartened to hear that Isabel hadn't stopped by to say goodbye to her—the old cameo lay still unclaimed—he was only confounded by what followed. "I was reading your book," she said cryptically, "and on page sixty-five I suddenly remembered, though I couldn't recall where, something I wanted to re-read." A worried smile quickened up to her temples as with a run of light. "Now, tell me, what page did I turn to?" Darconville didn't know what to say. "Why, page fifty-six," exclaimed Miss Trappe, her pitted nose pushing forward. "Page fifty-six!" And quickly kissing his cheek, she turned, and walked away. There wasn't in any of these encounters, either by word or gesture, that which raised so much as a hint of disapproval about his marriage and yet each referred, he was convinced, to nothing else.

It was that kind of summer.

Darconville soon found, with Isabel still unbaptized, he needed a dispensation from "disparity of worship" which had to be obtained from the Bishop of Richmond and then forwarded to the Chancellor at the Archbishop's House in London to have it cleared for execution in that diocese. Harvard University, meanwhile, notified him he was to be in Cambridge by September 10. So he busily set to coordinating matters. But in late June he was informed that he was required to obtain a special license for the dispensation of the residency requirements in England, and to that end he immediately wrote, as directed, to the Registrar of the Court of Faculties. He was busy as a piper: teaching, boxing books and clothes, writing letters, and preparing in the interim —he'd have no time later—his courses for the fall. The prospects were exciting. Would that he'd the time to dwell on them!

There were still to be obtained serologic tests, birth certificates, and letters of permission as well, and another matter involved the telephone calls to Fawx's Mt. where Isabel, presumably, was working away in as much of a dither, measuring patterns, cutting, and sewing away like the Three Fates all at once. By midsummer her letters fell off in frequency, but Darconville gamefully placed upon those that did come an even greater value, reserving in his heart only the spirited longing that such accidents might happen again and again. Contact with her kept him vital. And when the Adams House secretary at Harvard notified him of a vacancy there (a suite at $250 per month) his acceptance brought home just how crucial contact in whatever form would now become, for, as money now was critical, he was forced to sell his car. The trips up to Fawx's Mt. were over.

Ah, dear Bentley, thought Darconville, such a deed as from the body of contraction plucks the very soul!

It wasn't a week before another car appeared—a sleek foreign racer, chrome and plumcolored, screeching up to Darconville's house with a triple blast of its horn. The door opened, and then, wearing a lavender tube-top and demoniacally tight jeans, out stepped Hypsipyle Poore! "It's a Hulksaek Kongjak Puin! A present from daddy!" she called up to his window, snapping off her driving gloves and pointing to her initials printed on the fender. She blew him a kiss, stepped under the big tree, and said in a low breathy voice, "Only one thing faster 'n' better than this au-to, baby boy. Hint, hint." Laughing, Darconville came downstairs and explained for her, again, the situation she'd long known, only too well. "Good *lord,*" exclaimed undaunted Hypsipyle Poore, scribbling her telephone number on a napkin and tucking it firmly into his pocket, "but don't mean, surely, you can't promise to call me sometime by and by, now, does it?" Darconville said nothing. She smiled into his eyes. "You promise. I can tell."

Darconville that same day (almost as if to counteract that assumption) went down to Main St. and bought Isabel a pretty ring.

The whole plan, then, was struck a terrible blow sometime around the middle of July. Darconville uttered a round, mouth-filling oath at the post-office and left trailing in the air behind him a language which burnt it coppery all the way to the bench under the magnolia tree where he sat down to re-read, again in disbelief, the special delivery letter from London he'd just received.

The residency requirement couldn't be waived. The qualification for an English marriage registration meant either (a) a seven-day residence in Westminster before notification of marriage, plus a further clear twenty-one days before a marriage certificate could be issued—a total of thirty days including the day of arrival and the day of collecting the certificate, or (b) a fifteen-day residence plus one full day before a marriage license could be issued—a total of eighteen days, including, again, days of arrival and collecting the license. For the certificate, both parties had to put in the residency, for the license only one—but the other party had to be in England on the day notification was to be given to the Registrar.

As if that weren't enough, when later Darconville called Isabel to explain she wasn't home. He tried again, several times, and finally reached Mrs. Shiftlett who, outpacing herself in mutters and non-sentences, explained to Darconville how, that morning negotiating a curve on the road to Charlottesville, Isabel had skipped out of control —she always drove too fast—and rolled her car into a verge. She had been taken to the hospital. Yes, she thought the car was wrecked; no, she thought Isabel wasn't hurt. *Thought?* Darconville made five telephone calls to the University of Virginia hospital, only to find she had been released. *Thought?* That night he telephoned Fawx's Mt. Isabel answered and lightheartedly assured him she had been unharmed; he sagged, but fearful, worried, overwrought—in the knitting of himself so fast, himself he had undone—he cried out fitfully against all the tergiversations of love he could think of, which of course were only the tergiversations that stood in the *way* of love. But the telephone went dead. Isabel had hung up. He called back: no answer. An hour later there was no answer. There was no answer the following morning.

There was no public transportation north from Quinsyburg. The buslines in the Piedmont area, through either subterfuge or evasion, skirted completely around the poor but direct road that ran up to Charlottesville. For a simple trip north, then, this meant—in twice the time—the double, double toil and trouble of an hour busride east to Richmond and then back again west, another hour to Charlottesville.

But Darconville was desperate. He jumped the Richmond bus which, stopping for passengers at every snab and dole-house along the way, gave him his connection in that city, the return run shuddering along at about ten miles per hour into Charlottesville where, luckily, he hitchhiked a ride and followed the late afternoon sun into the fluecolored hills of Fawx's Mt. He appeared, dusty, at the front door. Isabel hurried him inside, not shutting the door, however, before taking several of those by now familiar half-turns, apprehensively looking toward places where the object she seemed to seek had turned into a ghost, disappeared in a puff of smeech, or flew into a tree. Darconville never knew which.

A television set was blaring in the small dark living-room, where the Shiftletts, submersed into the sofa, sat snoring upright and holding cans of beer in their respective laps. Darconville quickly looked at Isabel: she hadn't been hurt—and her car out front, dented somewhat, was still operable. In her bedroom, they sat on her red-and-cream bed where he tried to apologize for his thoughtlessness the day before by reading her what he felt was the cause of it—the bad news from London.

Isabel, curiously undistracted, listened calmly enough, but Darconville turned to the arithmetic of it all: the Quinsy summer courses ended on August 22 and yet the faculty were required to be at Harvard on September 10. The residency requirement—the shortest one—was eighteen days in London. The return flight back to the States canceled the ninth, which meant, if he could find someone to administer his final exams, they could leave on August 21. It was the only alternative. The tunnel of possibilities had narrowed to that. Darconville kissed her. It would be wonderful! It would be madness! What did she think? Isabel, twicking her thumbs, froze. She *couldn't*, she said: she hadn't finished making her dress! He laughed. And what, she asked, about all the other matters? Why, packing, invitations, and, and—she raised her eyes suddenly—she had decided she wanted to be baptized. Into the Catholic Church? Yes, that was what she wanted! Deliberating, Darconville wiped his forehead. He took her arm. He paused.

Then he asked her if they really shouldn't be married in Fawx's Mt. after all.

"No," said Isabel, disconcertedly wringing her hands. She looked out searchingly through her window, across the turnip patch, and past the old fences which the falling of dusk made nearly indistinguishable, creating an illusion of unbroken access even to that farthest house hunched under the aeviternal mountains whose ridges, Darconville saw for the first time, were inaptly called blue. They were in fact quite grey.

"It would be easier."

"It seems so."

"It is so," said Darconville.

"Yes," said Isabel, "it does seem so, doesn't it."

The following week in Quinsyburg Isabel stood holding a candle in the chancel of St. Teresa's Church, and, with Darconville as witness, was washed, oiled, and salted at the baptismal font. He felt very proud of her. He hadn't either encouraged or discouraged her but was happy, nevertheless, she stuck to her plans with deliberate speed and firm resolution; the process, to hasten it, took a bit of doing—Darconville had instructed her—and, while the emphases of time weighed no less heavy on them, he still managed to counterconvert the obstructions, delays, and postponements on other fronts to final satisfaction. It was only after the ceremony that he gave her the surprise that became her baptismal present. Kissing her, he mentioned the invitations could now be engraved. She looked at him, eyes questioning. (What blushing notes did he in the margin see? What sighs stolen out?) Then he told her: the wedding day was set for two o'clock on September 8—almost the exact date on which, four years before, they had first laid eyes on each other.

It wasn't easy for either of them. The strain told. In late July, in fact, Isabel wrote that she was too rushed with it all—the reasons, not given, she said were various—and thought they should call it off. Not to worry, thought Darconville.

August obliterated. The first few weeks sped by with temperatures soaring and Darconville rushing around in a feverish *va-et-vient* struggle with last-minute things: he had to register officially at Caxton Hall, reserve rooms at the Eaton Court Hotel in Belgravia, and, having changed plans, reserve his airline ticket from Boston a day earlier, the flight he'd now be taking alone. It was hairline procedure to observe, chaos to watch. It would pass, thought Darconville. Bread was made from panic, wasn't it? Sometimes the speed of it all almost exhilarated him. The gallop is a pace in which the sequence of steps, supposing the off fore to lead, is near hind, off hind, near fore, off fore, with a period of suspension—and *there* Darconville rested, content, pondering the joys that were to come in a race at the finish. And then one day that happened. And it was all over. It was done.

Darconville climbed in his rented van and left Quinsyburg as inconspicuously as he'd come. It was goodbye! Goodbye to Quinsyburg and its sapsuckers with feedhats and teardrop heads! Goodbye to its dacryopyostic onion patches and citizens with faces like leeks! Goodbye to its buckish slang and pickpocket eloquence! Goodbye to its vaticides, its dunces, its trelapsers of gossip! Goodbye to the farms on that Bebrycian coast and its water-tower! Goodbye, Your Foxship! Goodbye, Your Wormship! Goodbye, Your Gibship!

The winds were brisk off the mountains. A strange calenture came over Darconville, banking the wooden bridge into Fawx's Mt., and as he looked the cilicious weedgrasses and cowquake seemed to turn to waving water, a wisping in the meadows of sea-sounds as if blowing from some beautiful but lonely marinaresca. It made him long for the haven, that harbor he wanted, but knew still wasn't his; no, not yet; not even now.

Isabel and her mother, sitting at the back of the house, both waved. Parking the van, Darconville crossed the short lawn and came over to them. Without a word, Isabel handed him a card; it was one of the wedding invitations. She pointed to it twin-fingeredly—there were two flagrant errors: a misspelling and a botched date. Darconville looked at Isabel who looked at her mother who said, "And the whole job-lot's the same way. Fotched."

"We can do without them," said Darconville, looking from one to the other. "It's a formality, for friends. We can do without them."

Isabel, turning away, looked back at him with one eye, as if peering round a corner.

"Can't we?"

"I don't know what to say." She sheered away with what seemed utter indecision, tears rippling down her cheeks. "I *do* love you, do you know that?"

"Invitations?" laughed Darconville.

"It ain't only that. Sit down," said Mrs. Shiftlett.

Suddenly Darconville was given a turn. "Something is wrong."

"Oh," cried Isabel, sobbing and bearhugging Darconville as if she'd squeeze out his very life. "My wedding dress, I've gone and *ruined* it, I've *ruined* my car, I've *ruined* the invitations—and all your hard work, gone! Gone up in smoke, just like it never was!"

Darconville, bewildered, could make no immediate sense of what now prevented their going ahead with plans any more than he could explain what mother and daughter had already accepted as accomplished fact. He cradled her head to his neck, breathing her libanophorous hair and looking off miserably and inarticulately beyond her only to see Mrs. Shiftlett wink with risible eyes and mouth something —apologetic, if those convecting bowlips meant to indicate a pout of shared disappointment. Trembling in fright, Isabel almost killed Darconville on the spot with the innocence of the question that followed: would the wedding now be off for good? Off? For *good?* The sky went dull, lowering like a metal dishcover. Darconville was beneaped.

The two figures just waited there, unmoving, as confused as if each stood at the opposite ends of eternity itself. Mrs. Shiftlett had disappeared. Darconville's throat constricted: it was hopeless and he knew it. Bowled! The whole summer! The wedding had comperendinated. The end was now in the middle.

Speechless with disappointment, he couldn't rehearse what he wanted to say, for questions kept intruding: what had happened to the dress? Was she frightened at the prospect of marriage? Why had she let him know at the last minute? And then Mrs. Shiftlett reappeared and, beaming, bumped them both with a large cardboard box —it was filled with a crazy array of five-and-dime forks, knives, and spatulas—which she proceeded ostentatiously to place in the van, as Spellvexit dodged out; she winked on her way back, "Householdry." He interproximated a word of thanks. Hand in hand, then, he and Isabel walked across the backyard and looked away over the cowfield to the woods.

There is an unhappiness so awful that the very fear of it becomes an alloy to happiness. Darconville whispered that he loved her; Isabel whispered the same. Isabel whispered that she wanted to marry him but needed more time. More time, Darconville whispered, to think about it? More time, Isabel whispered, to prepare for it. He whispered one more question. She looked up at him and kissed him, and he felt her tongue on his lips, swift and cold, an infrigidation that perhaps reminded her, as she answered, of what to say. Isabel then—with conviction—whispered, "December."

It was with simple gratitude that Darconville accepted the facts as they were—it didn't matter, truth seemed thievish for a prize so dear —and that night he was only strengthened in his resolve to hold on, finding constant vigilance perhaps the part of vision that most was love, for just before sleep overtook him he caught in the bedroom a faint glimpse of Isabel silently sitting by him in the darkness, stroking his cat, and watching sentinel lest anything creep in from the dark ambisinistrous night to discover him there in that room.

LVII

Where Will We Go?

Why should the mistress of the vales of Har utter a sigh?

—WILLIAM BLAKE, *The Book of Thel*

IT WAS THE DAY of departure. The van, loaded to the doors, was ready to go, and after breakfast there seemed nothing else to do for Darconville and Isabel but make their farewells. Before the morning sun peeped over the mountains, the Shiftletts had gone off to work: that made the goodbyes less troublesome but somehow more awkward, for nothing could dissemble, nothing displace, nothing divert what by accepting they had to seem to condone. Isabel, in actions quick and acute, moved about with dispatch as if, in trying to bury in the camouflage of time the fact of pain, to say goodbye was not necessarily to see him go, and she preferred to leave it there like the maiden Marpessa who, choosing Idas over Apollo for her fear of immortality, was willing to renounce the sun as long as she didn't have to think about the consequences.

Darconville felt her uneasiness. And yet the intervening months, he saw, if keeping her yet in durance vile would at least modify the bad luck impetuosity had caused them and simultaneously increase the delight of sweet premeditation. It pained him to see her troubled, busy with the efficiency of preoccupation, but he sat her down—wasn't Genius the clerk of Venus?—and told her a hundred tales of the wonderful life they'd have, no matter where! But sometimes, she confessed, that very *thing* made her afraid, she didn't know why: where would they go? Trying to dispel her worry, he became playful. He asked where she'd like to go, Mt. Woodwose, Catland, the Island of Poke Pudding?—wherever, whereverever, she'd be *loved!*

Isabel tried to smile. Lifting her chin, he asked if he could see her wedding dress; that would be a bad omen, she said, and blushed nervously. Would she like to take a walk? No, she shook her head, no. It was a difficult hour. Omissions relating to his departure became more oppressive than any reference to it, and yet, apprehensively, she kept glancing at the clock. They took time to make love in her bedroom: it was cold and compensatory, faisonless, a sequence of tenses; usually, he loved the way she loved the way he loved her, but now, it seemed, she was worried the way she loved he didn't—and he could tell. It was clear, not quilts filled high with gossamer and roses, neither poppies nor mandragora, could have put Isabel at rest. The time had come to go.

At the door, Darconville turned, took from his pocket the gold ring he'd bought in Quinsyburg—two birds interclasped on a moonstone— and slipped it on her right hand. She handed him a box she'd pulled from under a chair: a gift of a blue shirt. He wished he hadn't had, that she hadn't bought, a going-away gift—it seemed too formal in the preparation. No one, he felt, should ever be ready for such things. They hugged each other for a full minute, silently.

"There will be times when you might be afraid."

"Yes," she admitted.

"Don't give up," said Darconville. "I'll call you. I'll write you. But you won't give up, will you?"

"Shhhh," whispered Isabel. She looked around through the dark inconvenient house. Darconville followed her eyes to a clock. "I'll think of it—I'll think of it all tomorrow."

After all, thought Darconville, *tomorrow is another day.*

"The main thing is not to be alone." The dark figure of Darconville, moving closer, shadowed her. "You aren't, you know."

Isabel swallowed her voice.

A sensation of the intensity of that thought curiously seemed to catch hold of her in an inexplicable way, his words, Darconville saw, sharply perforating her sensibility. She brought her thumb and index finger together, with the other fingers curved, and touched her lips.

"What—what do you mean?" Pale, Isabel traveled back on a foot. "I'm not, do you mean, alone with you? Without you I wouldn't be alone? Say what, please?"

"I mean," smiled Darconville calmly, carrying her identity so close to him that he couldn't see a single expression of it, "that I'll be with you always. I only ask you to trust me."

"Whatever happens, you'll—"

"Be with you, yes."

Of such a compensatory philosophy was the ideal justice of his dream certainly compounded; they were the premises, not the conclusions, of his life. And then with what improportionate joy did she then knot his arms! "O, do you mean you'll always understand, do you?" It was as if, quite suddenly, a gust of wind had swept up a mass of dead leaves, uncovering the verdure beneath: her whole face relaxed into a smile of disarming sweetness. "Do you? I'll love you for that," she pleaded.

"Understand what?" He was baffled. "I love you."

There was a sudden silence.

"Sometimes—I'm afraid." She pulled her thumb. "That's all."

"To take the step?" asked Darconville. Fright somehow came to stay with him as he talked it away from her. "Would you be afraid, perhaps, of coming?"

Isabel closed her eyes.

"It's not that," she said, voice unreliable. A kind of shutter fell as if she had returned again to some basic but incommunicable anxiety. "I—I only always sometimes wonder—" She turned completely away from him as if, by shifting, she sought to reduce the deliberate value of questions she felt only a lifetime could marshal to answer. "—what we will do. Where will we go?" Darconville turned her by the shoulders to comfort her, to answer, but he hadn't the chance for as he lifted her chin it was suddenly the agonized face of post-lapsarian Eve he stared upon, only asking again with the accents of futility and despair, *"Where will we go?"*

Was there a response?

No; never. It was as if, not wanting one, Isabel swiftly acted to stop it, suddenly crowding upon him with a kiss heated with every last force of passion and sweetened by the tears now streaming down her face: it was a kiss that sobbed from the soul, never yielding, unrestrained, almost an immolation, a kiss imploring itself to the opportunity it feared but sought, needed but had long deterred, as if all at once it simultaneously tried to beg for forgiveness, impart a blessing, and resolutely attempt in one single moment to convey something beyond the powers of all explanation—and its ache piteously sang to Darconville's heart all the goodbyes that could ever be and more by far than he knew he ever could bear. Goodbye! *Goodbye!*

It was with all deliberate speed that Darconville swung the van back down the driveway, shifted out of reverse—could that figure in the distance wearing a bandanna and gumboots and staring into his rear-view mirror possibly have been the cryptarch of Zutphen Farm?—and then bouncing over the Fawx's Mt. road he headed out of the mountains, raced toward Charlottesville, and, after smiling down at Spellvexit, his cat, and up at God, his palinure, he turned north and drove into the world.

LVIII

Over the Hills and Far Away

Let there be pie.
Why else a sky?

—D. J. ENRIGHT

IT WAS STRAIGHT OUT, all highway, a perfect shaft toward the sunpolished horizon. Whistling along at a good clip, Darconville listened to the clattering rattles and backfiring of the van, a music uplifting him as mile after mile fell away in a momentum that seemed to gather up once more the impetus of his life. Already he felt Isabel's absence and dearly wished her there with him if for no other reason than to toss her cares to the rushing wind and leave them all behind. *Where will we go?* He knew. It would be his gift to her, for with the ecstasy of knowing they'd never outrun the mystery and majesty of that question, he also knew the answer lay hidden in the most varied,

the most wondrous, the most divine harmonies possible, for no journey, he thought, is so delightful as that which leads no one knows
whither nor whither why—and what journey ever ends when, waiting
at the other end, one waits for love?

Where would they go!

Darconville, with the wind abaft his beam and the needle into red,
flew across the Virginia border and was sailing free! The melodious
racket of his conveyance somehow echoed the melodious racket in his
head—everywhere, the Rising of the North! To live, to work, to love
was the same thing! His heart exploded in joy and he cried out to
Isabel! Come away and marry me under a skyblue tent in Coroman-
del, dance a week and a day with the boggarts and bogles, and we'll
away on a moonbeam to the Isles of the Blest where winter all in
flower humbles the spring! Where would you like to go? To see the
white jaguars of Mustaghata? The petrified village in the Cyrenaica?
The buried cities of Turkestan? The spectres glimmering on the
Hörselberg? Or the Mongolian land of Bielovodye where there is
peace and plenty and never a soul has been? Or would you live a
strange remote life in the gold-encrusted valleys of Ophir, the spice-
land of Punt, the pepper forests of Malabar, the City of Mansa, or
Cambalu, where in the treetops funny-faced ghosts sit twittering all
the night? Come, hurry away with me to Quippishland, Mt. Yoop,
and the secret City of Blinking! To Goshen, the far Moluccas, and
Aspramont! To the porcelain abodes of Almansor, the Vale of
Rephaim, the Land of Juba, Bean Island, and the Cataracts of
Downcrash! Let us visit the weird towers of Klingsor, the excavations
of Transoxania, and the deserted city of Fatephur Sikri! Drop what
you're doing and travel with me to Holy Mulberry, the Eden of
Granusion, and climb to the top of Inchcape Rock where the abbot of
Aberbrothock once fixed a bell or visit the Magdeburg Spheres where
the pressure without makes a vacuum within and no one ever can tell!

Darconville bowled out of the Baltimore Harbor Tunnel just past
noon and soon raised Wilmington.

Come, we'll visit the sparkling Electrides and the Bitch's Tomb at
Capo Helles, the Cathedral of Quimper, the rubbish-mounds of
Krokodopolis, and the magic goldfields of Nimis Sollicitaris! We'll
wrestle an angel in Penuel, chase hippocentaurs to the ends of
Pluvalia, burrow into the vole holes of Mt. Radio, and sail into the
strange Cirknickzersky Lake in Carniola whose waters gush so fast out

of the ground its speed can overtake light! Or would you prefer to
visit Mohenjo-Daro in Sind and Harappa in the Punjab, ride into the
mists of Pellucidar, or follow the nomadic Hurrians into the sandcones
of Mesopotamia? Done! Done! Or shall it be the Nonestic Ocean?
The twin cities of Hieraconopolis? Or Castle Graveolent? The caves of
Aber Cleddyf? The Court of the Boy King, the windswept plateau of
Leng, or the rose-red lands of Araby, almost as old as time? Come,
heart of my heart, take my hand, and we'll trip through the firestorms
of Mount Chimaera, the sandstorms of Yazd, the lost colony of
Aphrodisium, Hither Spain, the promontory of the Cimbri, and into
the haunts of coot and hern to watch old Mrs. Hickabout kick bold
Mrs. Kickabout cold through the thickabout!

He left route 95, rumbled over the Delaware Memorial Bridge, and
swung onto the New Jersey turnpike.

Cry ahoy! Open scuttles! Our rendezvous are appointed! We'll
journey to Smyrna, Cyme, the Land of Pount, the Sepulchres of Zenu,
and the foggy forests of Ermenonville! We'll go hand in hand to
Quadling Country, the Oracle of Trophonius, the River of January,
the Shapeless Magma of Nun, and then to the Dark Mere of Loc-
mariaquer which vouches antiquities no body can know! And then to
the State of Swat! Walvis Bay! The Land of Dictionopolis! The black
pagodas of Kanarak! Come, we'll disappear in the Hills of the Rubber
Pig, the hidden islands of Tarquinium, Fairytown, and the pit called
Because! We'll look at the crocodiles of Arabastrae, the white elves of
Alfheim, the detestable Orc of Ebuda, the guebers of the Kerman Desert, and the Glumms of Nosmnbdsgrsutt who use their wings for both
flying and for clothes! We'll go to Great Blasket, Nantasket, and the
Valley of Casket, run through the Polyglot Garden, stroll about Suma-
tra under the manchineel trees, and listen to the clashing of holy ket-
tles at Jupiter's brazen oracle at Dodona!

During the long stretch of highway Spellvexit complained of the
heat, and, after setting him on a box to ride shotgun by the window,
Darconville put his foot to the floor passing Bordentown and was out
front and flying.

The earth does not withhold! Delve! Mold! Listen to the words of
the world! Come, come, return with me in time to the Kingdom of
Rimsin, Quatna, the bejeweled land of Palaikastro, the shaft-graves
of Argolid, the underwater remains of Nora, the Panionion of Mt.
Mycale, the bazaar of Dioscurias, the medieval thorp of Joiry, the De-

partment of Tarragon, and the Isle of Apedefts! We'll row over Atlantis in triremes, splash into the Gulf of Dews, drop wishing pennies into the sacred Zem-Zem, and watch the palms wave in Hispaniola and the bird-headed Zwings of the African deserts who make geometry of sunshine and peck words in the air with their beaks! We'll dance little rigadoons with the water-sorcerers of Vitziputzli, play bowls with the gnomes of Lint, march off to Dipsody, and chase flashes of light all the way from the seven-fold Nile to far Taprobany! Come, let's pitch our tents in Sechem, in the emerald meadows of Thuringia, at the reaches of Scrabster, on the Island of Usedom, above the high plateaux of Cundinamarca and Mount Two Breasts and the sky-ypointing rocks of mystical Wak-Wak which are transfigured by dawn into huge gem-bright amethysts! Run along with me to the land of Whimzies and Phantasms, the Points of Chance, the Closed City of Thera, ancient Regulbium and Rutupiae, Xuntain, Zawi Chemi Shanidar, and the duckmarshes of weird little Quailalia where trees bear fruit in the form of tiny geese who drop full-grown from the branches and proceed to waddle away!

Darconville wheeled into New York City, following the rays of the late afternoon sun.

Penetrate us, minstrelsy! Unfold our hands! Let us sojourn together in Mesach and dwell a spell in the tents of Kedar or on the man-made mountains of Cholula and ride submersibles down to the sunken harbors of Caesarea, Apollonia, Chersonesos! Come, we'll fly through muspel-light to the planet Tormance and somersault over the stars into the Bay of Rainbows, then paddle in a silly fat all the way to the Mare Frigoris, out to the Oceanus Procellarum and squeak tiny horns, and dunk in a puddle the Man-in-the-Moon who carries a bundle of thorns! Let's take the secret highway to Mezzoramia, pay our chiminage and visit the Eatalls in Ethiopia, the noseless tribes of Aetheria, the magic sheat-fish of Baggade and the pea-headed people of Particuous, and then trace the high coasts along the lands of the Strap-foots who have feet like leather thongs and the Blackcloaks that do live in the curves of the Caucasus! Courage, now, and we'll strike a match and peek at the poison hayfields of Crustimium, the Green Sea of Gloom, the toxic trees of Macassar, the bone-strewn cemeteries of Megatherium, the piggeries of Sljeme, dogless Sygaros, the dank-venom-dripping hall of Nastrand, the smoke-holes of Sittacene, and Jotunheim, the abode of giants, then tiptoe round the tower of the deceitful Witch of Sokótska Dama, avoid the naked night-traveling troglodytes of Moppinland who put away their dead amid laughter, tightropewalk the circular precipice that encloses Malebolge, and then pondering that put a hole in our hat and take a trip through our mind on a hunchback's back or a jampot smack or a walloping window-blind!

Night fell as Darconville crossed the Bronx and speeding into the New England Thruway he thought: O rising stars! O Isabel! Perhaps the one I want so much will rise, will rise with some of you!

Unravel the maps! Raise your eyes! Point! Where was your finger, on the tropical island of Samburan? The Palace of the Kyabazinga of Busoga? Heliopolis? East Harptree, Thrapston, Much Wenlock? The Seven Cities of Cíbola? Wherever! To the endless announcements! Wherever! Come with me to the Bridge of Whangpoo, the Land of Shinar, the Valley of Jehosaphat, the Isle of Robbers, the vast chaotic gulf of perpetual twilight at Ginungagap, the wilds of Barbagia, Weenieville, or Quintana Roo or Jamberoo or Timbuctoo or Waterloo or Fernando Poo! Let's poke into the jungles of the Ptoemphani who have a dog for a king, stare upon the headless Blemmyae, race the ostriches of Numidia, sample the delicious hotcakes of Naraka, sing riddles to each other in the Lantern language spoken only in the Isles of Nowhere, skip along to the Promontory of Figs and converse with the twenty philosophical recluses of Ulubrae, eat the fossil meats of Diplodocus, and sit in the briarpatch at teatime in West Barnstable with Old Mother West Wind and the Merry Little Breezes! Come, we'll watch the doltheads playing at skittles on the top of the Land of Magog, the dragons on the plains of Lop, the white sheep of Cephisus, and the alligators of distant Thorax who have pouches for eyes and snap their jaws when they sing! Will you come to visit the Gillygaloo who lays square eggs? Or question the Eternal Man who reclines on the Couches of Beulah? Tickle under their chins microscopical djinns or tease geloscopical dwales who live in The Tree That Can Never Be and fish for chocolate whales?

The lights of Bridgeport and New Haven flashed by, the sea air freshening Darconville but putting Spellvexit to sleep. Don't sleep, cat, he thought—live with me to love!

Welcome, space! Speed, time! Our fancies scheme for aspiration! Would you live with me in the Grotto of Sybils, Aleppo, Bantam, Laguna de los Xarayes, the darklands of Cabul or the blade of

Laurasia or the Thousand Isles of Spicery? What matter where? Wish but with a wink and enter the wheels of the Mundane Egg, ride in a dirigible over Rippleland, pass through the green Cimmerian Forest where things pushed into the ground can never come out again, or enter the Land of Brass, the untamed parts of Tzucox, Mosquitia, the Monastery of Altamura, east Griqualand, Ingatestone, the Kingdom of Stern, the Temple of Dobayba, and then watch pigmies battle the cranes in Upper Egypt, perch on the Siege Perilous at Camelot, visit the Knights Templars of Warpsgrove and the Crutched Friars of Whaplode, swim in Lake Chogagogmanchegegagogchbunagunga-maug, listen to stories of the Qarlugs and the Ghuzz and the Fatimids, make love under a Javanese thunderstorm in the ramparts of Bogor, summon carps with a clap in Kyoto, and then hand in hand we'll kick up the sand and travel to see the woman and man who killed the blue spider in Blanchepowder Land!

Halfway through Connecticut, Darconville pipped on his flashlight and looked at his watch: 10:30 P.M.

Advancing, let us tramp for what, undreamed of, has long awaited us in shapes, horizons, passages! Come, wander with me to the capital of Amaurote, Obulcula, the Continent of Mu, the campestral landscapes of Montfontaine and Loisy, the regal seat of Abdalazis, the horse boxes of Megiddo, the temple of Nisroch at Nineveh, the Island of Chaneph, the sparkling fountains of Mnemosyne, and the Mouse Tower near Bingen where cruel Archbishop Hatto was devoured by mice! We'll visit the Tartar shamans who can summon snow, the fools of Aegipotami, Queen Zixi of Ix, Og of the Iron Scales, the Great Lew Chew, the suppository traders from the Kingdom of Zuy, and the ornithocratic world of the Madonna of Goldfinches! All of them! The malevolent Octodecemajiences, the black Fungs of Baghdad, the faceless pirates of Strongolo, and the Ninox Owls who wear gaiters and live above the land that loses its shadow! Come, we'll splash down in Alienville, Concupium, and the sea of Sugar Cane Juice, question the Sick King in Bokhara, gather cat-thyme in Cilicia and attar of roses in Phaselis, take a sail in a ship with Jack Sixpip and Tom Bunyip and Dick Wishlip, then go and see old Pillicock sit on Pillicock Hill and sing "Hallo, Hallo!"

Darconville drove into Massachusetts.

We shall rise forever and drift over quintillions of things and thrust our beautiful faces into dawn after dawn! We'll go on long mysterious

quests to see the magnetic rock on the Klebermeer, the black knulps of
Shantung, Mt. Nebo where Moses is buried, the City of Humpbacked
Women in India, and the three trees of Hudimesnil! And then to Tyde
Castle, Fumeland, the Valley of Cheviot, the underworld Garden of
Deduit, the land of Nod, the savannahs of Blodd, and the faraway,
faraway extra-faraway all out-glittering stairwells of God! We shall
clasp hands and walk the dizzy heights of Wenchwan and Aucan-
guilca, then cross down the fried roads of Al 'Aziziyah and Dallol,
wrun around in Wroxeter, slide down the falls of the Sabbatic River
in the Kingdom of Agrippa that runs only on Saturdays and call upon
the Choromandacians who have no speech but only can scream or the
one-eyed Arimaspians or the Keakles who teach rabbits their prayers!
And on and on to Kurdistan, the lost Lyonesse, the monastery of
Disembodenburg, Winkie Country, the wooden palace of the King of
Tonga in Nukualofa, Opis, and the Shalimar Gardens, and if the
wind is up and the evening clear coast in a blue-sailed shell down the
Guadalquivir to hop on the Harpasian Rock a mere finger can twid-
dle, then stop by Yedo, the Thymbran temple, and hide in the
Riphaean mountains right in the middle! And then to Klang and the
secret abodes of the blessed in Twat and if you're not tired I'll tell you
what, we'll creep out at night with one and all and when the moon is
shining and bright trip out to trot and trot to dance and dance a jig at
the Jellicle Ball!

It was then into Boston, and Darconville soon caught the lights of
Cambridge, reflecting like drops of gold in the river Charles.

Welcome, fate! The future shall be greater than all the past! It
shines with prophecies, unborn deeds, liberty and love! Come, finally,
with me to the Land of Cinnamon, the olive yards by the river
Alpheus, the Isles of Orcades and the promontory of the Cimbri,
Aneroid and Gravelburg, the medieval castle of Broglio, the empire of
Lugalzaggisi and the masses of Negropont, Maleventum, and Ori-
noco! Come away with me and wander through the Upper Valley of
Greater Zap, eat the ten-pound peaches of Chinaland, climb the spires
of the foursquare city of Golgonooza, wave to the gold-guarding
griffins in the Deserts of Gobi, pray with the holy apocalypts in the ancient monasteries of St. Neot, Pill, Axholme, Stixwould, Drax, Tip-
tree, and Burnham-on-Crouch, then watch the Plow of Jehovah and
the Harrow of Shaddai pass over the dead, and then maybe sit on a
dune in the month of June by the amber waters of the Syllabub Sea

where the tide comes in in an opal mist, splashing in sweetly like the sound of a kiss, and we'll trip upon trenches and dance upon dishes and see whither the hither of yon, but if without reason you should find me gone, I won't be buried among the dead—no, go instead and look for me where eternity goes, in another world where the rain makes bows, for there'll be restored by the hand of art whatever's lost in the human heart, for something of us will always be, and forevermore I'll live for you if forevermore you'll live for me.

It was long past midnight and very dark when, awakening the night-porter at Harvard, Darconville was let into his rooms, and, exhausted, he fell down on his bed and went immediately to sleep.

LIX

The Doorcard on F-21

Well, who in his own backyard
Has not opened his heart to the smiling
Secret he cannot quote?

—W. H. AUDEN, "Preface"

HAD HE DREAMT IT? Darconville prayed not, and very early the next morning—it was still pitch-black outside—he went, still fully clothed from the previous night, into the dark living-room, opened the door, and by match read the doorcard over the knocker: *"Dr. and Mrs. Darconville."* And a flock of birds flew out of his heart.

L X

Harvard

> Fair Harvard! Thy sons to thy Jubilee throng,
> And with blessings surrender thee o'er,
> By these festival rites, from the age that is past,
> To the age that is waiting before.
>
> —SAMUEL GILMAN, *Ode*

THE BELLS in the tower of St. Paul's struck the hour: bong-bong*bang*bong, bong*bing*bang bong, bingbbang*bong*bong, bong-bingbang*bong*. It was noon. This particular morning, Darconville had awakened and gone back to sleep several times, but now he rose and followed a procession of sunlight into the living-room which suddenly seemed, like the great college to its founder, a "pocket of godliness in a profane world," for it was surely one of the most beautiful suites in Adams House. The rooms were paneled in old and elegant wood, the oak bookcases and rubbed leather furniture impressively set off at one end with a large fireplace by which stood a rack of blackened fire-tools. There was a sturdy Plymouth table in the center of the room and several Windsor chairs, each stamped on the back with the college insignia that was also replicated on the wall over the. hearth in a large, magnificent shield: giles three open books argent, edges covers and clasps gold, on the books the letters *Ve Ri Tas* sable.

Harvard! The oldest college in America. Darconville simply stood there, considering the wonder of where he was.

There were low windowseats into which one could comfortably sit and look down, on one side, over the streetlamps to the narrows of Plympton St. and on the other across the slate-beveled roof and curious metal ibis atop that queer Dutch castle on Mt. Auburn St. known as the "Lampoon" building, beyond which one had a faint glimpse of the far river. Darconville threw open a window, and Spellvexit leaped onto a seat. The traffic, the various noises of Cambridge, braced him up, and everyone and everything seemed at play in the bright air outside. Darconville ranged the immediate area below on Bow St.—his van was still parked there—and surveyed with a smile all the tiny intersecting streets, the few quaint shops, and the vines of English ivy twining around colonial buildings of deep red brick and white-trimmed windows which evoked in simple, unpretentious glory the spirit of Good Old Colony Times. They were extremely old houses, some of them, with little winking windows, oeil-de-boeuf windows, and strange lunettes, the low-arched doors, in some of the narrower ways, quite overhanging the pavement.

Darconville listened. Above him, some woodpeckers were hammering on the slate-and-lead rooftop, and he wondered, resolving to check later, about the exact shape of Adams House, for it had seemed, as he stumbled through the darkness the previous night, a Gothic maze of angles, bays, and strange alcoves. The sky was as blue as eyebright, with just a hint of mellow smokedrift in the air, prognostic, always, of the rich New England autumn soon to follow. Sunshine caught the fickling leaves on some nearby poplars, under which a group of children in knee-socks and caps passed swinging satchels of books. The trees, with some leaves falling, were just beginning to shed. The days were drawing in.

The building was empty. In any case, Darconville had seen no one about. What with the changed plans, it turned out he'd come up a bit early, earlier, apparently, than anyone else, but it gave him some added time and he took advantage of the quiet afternoon to unload his clothes and books. He was, all at once, happy, busy, and yet to be sure a trifle lonesome—a photograph of Isabel immediately went up on the mantelpiece. Darconville delighted in the fastness of privacy and warmth circumcluding the little study he arranged by the kitchen, having already developed a nice scheme of checks and balances on the facility of not only writing there but of being able to eat quickly and, most important of all, of maintaining a perpetual and unremitting vigil by the telephone—which had yet to be connected.

Several times, in fact, Darconville during that day slipped out to a telephone booth, dialing and listening expectantly, but the current, each time, hummed wastefully through Connecticut, New York, Maryland, Washington, and Virginia bearing only its own dullness. The other end rang on. No harm done; he could wait.

Later, he sat down and wrote Isabel a funny and multifarious letter about his long trip, heading off an awkward temptation to beg her to come up immediately—she needed the time for herself, of course—by losing himself in long and colorful description of their splendid rooms at Harvard. Then downstairs over in C-entry, the superintendent directed him to the telephone service, where minutes later the installation for his room was arranged, and, after writing down his telephone number on a postcard and posting both pieces off to Fawx's Mt., he took his dinner alone, contentedly watching the sun go down over the river. It was a fairly humid night, and for cross-ventilation he opened a front window and his apartment door. And to waste no time that very evening in a battery of letters addressed to various English authorities, civil and clerical, he reconfirmed their marriage intentions, asking that they be revised according to the newer plan he outlined and that a date be held open for late December for a nuptial Mass. These letters had to be done well, and in sequence, an orderly arrangement he knew he should have used before. But, in spite of himself, he fell asleep over the typewriter. At some point, however, in the middle of the night he was awakened by the city noise, hoits, yells, traffic below. He shut the window and went for the door—strange, he thought, he had been told he was the only one in the building. He strained to listen.

Could that have been a key chuckling in a lock upstairs?

The following days were spent by Darconville acquainting himself with the layout of Harvard. He got a map. He cut through the traffic on Massachusetts Ave., crossed down Quinsy St., and went to the English department office in Warren House to make himself known to the man who had hired him, but the secretary (handing him his faculty card, class schedule, and a catalogue) told him that Prof. McGentsroom hadn't yet returned from his summer vacation. She told him there was some mail for him. Darconville almost misgave from expectation as she rooted around in a series of letterboxes, all tabbed with professors' names: McGoldrick, Schreiner, Waxman, Stuart, Millar, Treadgold, etc., and then handed him a postcard: a lavendulate "Miss ya!"—the dot an extravagant circle—signed by Hypsipyle Poore. Well, well, thought Darconville, tearing it in two and dropping it into a goody's pail on the way out. He spent an hour or so in the Fogg Museum, walked around the commons in front of the law school, and circled back by Memorial Hall, a huge Victorian Gothic vault with large windows of colored glass stiffened dark with metalwork and stone tracery and memorializing the Union dead in what, in another part of the country—already thankfully forgotten—was generally considered to be the last of romantic wars.

Across the way, he entered the vine-webbed gates of the Harvard Yard, an old commons of skinnybranched elms and walkways surrounded by venerable red-brick college halls, quadrangular in form, cloistral in intent, an enclosure as neat and strict as a bowling green and isolating in time and space traditions of an intellectual and spiritual probity, uncluttered as a puritan psalmody.

The figure of John Harvard sat, dignified and aloof, staring across the Yard in a mood of piety and godliness. Darconville walked back through several centuries under the pleasant trees and had the strange feeling that, in peering up a dim stairway or through an old window or into some dark chamber-and-study, one just might happen to catch an anachronistic glimpse of some students reading *The Tatler* by candlelight instead of working their sophemes or construing their Demosthenes or perhaps a group of lads, with wigs a-flap, skipping up out of the buttery—the steam of hasty-pudding in the air—and balancing tankards and sizings of bread and beer or maybe several young blades drinking rumbullion and gowling against the excessive measures of Lord North, Grenville, and Townsend until one of them might leap up to shout, "Step outside and repeat that asseveration, Villiers, you damned Tory!" He stepped over to look at Widener Library, the beautiful white steeple of Memorial Church, and came out again, under an old archway adorned above with crowned lanterns, into the square.

The congestion in Harvard Square, a maze of stoplights and ringing commerce—almost island-contained—became a singular source of delight, especially to someone pointedly tired of the High and Main streets of Quinsyburg as the avenues of sophistication. Darconville crossed the street, the kiosk of the central subway entrance exhaling brakedust and stale air, and went shopping: he mailed Isabel some jewelry and a Harvard T-shirt. In the plaza of the Holyoke Center, he observed, were gathered all manner of people: bearded fellows selling flutes and sandals; drownbottles with split shoes sharing slugs of whiskey with each other; wagoneers selling books and records; three or four pale mystical girls offering bunches of dried-flowers from their trugs; a dinger holding on a leash a capuchin monkey in a red bellboy's hat, snatching dimes; and everywhere, in the crowds, professors and lawcats and transcorporating philosophers and other remnants of academe who for the way they talked, gestured, and dressed might have flown out of Baffin Land. It seemed one of the few places on the earth where one could stand on a street corner for five minutes and see and hear the world go by in a thousand fashions and in fifty languages.

When Darconville had time on his hands—there was a great deal to share but no one to share it with—he'd several afternoons left the square for Boston, aimlessly, meditatively, circuitously riding the underground transit in and then back out, with the seats crammed and the aisles crowded, and when the train pulled into Harvard Station, always, the conductors, thumbpunching buttons, called out, "End of the line, all change!"—the doors leaped hissing open, dust rose, and tired sober-eyed commuters with rolled newspapers hurried out in a rush, pushed up the ramps, and left the subway to lose themselves in the larger crowds on the street above. Darconville noticed the girls of greater Boston were lovely, lithe, and elegant—one, however, always gleamed in their ranks, her unassuming innocent self-withdrawal being brighter than the lights that danced over the cities he explored. And she wasn't even there.

The dewy sweet smell from the gardens of Brattle St. drifted through the fencepickets. Darconville put his map into his pocket and cut down Hawthorn St. where, walking along, he listened to the sad, quiet rustle up in the red and golden beeches and noticed the first decaying leaves, tawny and rusted, sprinkling like the bridal colors of autumn from the chestnut trees, always among the first to shed. He came out to the banks of the peaceful river and slowly headed east along a pathway.

The sun was beginning to go down, and a faint ring of blue autumnal smokehaze could be seen over the playing fields and boathouses across the Charles. He crossed the Larz Anderson Bridge and then cut down a grassy slope to sit by the water and consider the beauty of the college from another angle, a view sweeping and magnificent. Again, he looked at his map and named to identify the elegant brick houses he traced from left to right: Eliot, Winthrop, Leverett, Dunster, all stately and knitted over with withers and strands of ivy. Theirs was a spectacular fenestration, the jigsaw cornices and windowed front-doors facing across the courtyards and crowned above in a little parade, beyond the gates, of chimneys, turrets, and domed towers of green, gold, and crimson.

Trying to locate Adams House, Darconville found he couldn't. He tried to match map to terrain, following his finger through one courtyard, out of an archway, and into a second court at another distance. He lost his way and followed his finger back, to pause. It waited. He checked the map. He moved his finger now to count past turrets and a forest of chimneypots and mansards, but dusk, falling, either doubled them or truncated or made indistinct those that rose behind others. It was useless, for once again one was back at an angle that couldn't do anything but lead in a direction that discouraged the logic of the whole enterprise. He smiled. This person, he thought, is divided against himself: one part overlooks the whole, knows that he is sitting there and that the way is clear; but another part notices nothing, has at most a divination that the first part *thinks* it sees all. Darconville reflected, at that point, that these two could sit waiting for years, pondering the parable. Then one part said: if you know that, you have found your way. While another replied: but unfortunately only in parable. Would that be a comment on art?

Darconville almost laughed.

He walked back then through the narrow streets and turned into the iron gate on Linden St. that led into the courtyard of Adams House, where the master's residence, Apthorp House—a white colonial dwelling—sat surrounded by the high wine-black brick of what looked like an old deserted gashouse or Victorian railway station, the roof edge of which, sloping down to gimmaled windows, was interrupted at intervals by a series of beetle-browed gables jutting out in sooty-stained façades that diminished in width after the fashion of steps and seemed in the gloom of sudden dusk a perfect perch for rooks and cormorants. There were perpendicular rows of apertures crossed here and there by cantilever fire-escapes. The shades were all drawn. He went in.

There wasn't a sound inside of Adams House. One corridor led to another, communicating to ever more and more shadowy rooms, and, all in all, it seemed to be one of those places that had been kept, swept, and oiled, but locked up for ages and never to be used again. Gothic-shafted windows let in grey light. There were more exits and entrances, unexpected turnings and angles, than Darconville had ever seen—including the many Venetian palazzi he'd known famous for them. He was intrigued. He looked down—and listened—into stone stairwells that wound down and around as if into sunken, desolate dungeons. He started up the stairs, turning from landing to landing, higher and higher, and he came out of the surprising changes of level to the top floor of F staircase. It *appeared* to be the top floor. At the end of the staith there, however, just out of conventional view, a glimpse of some nearly hidden balusters invited further inspection; it was obviously a bam—the corners white with the striggles of spiders—of the stairbuilders of yore.

Curious, Darconville kept on up, entering a gallery that seemed contained in the thickness of the wall, an interior space which consisted of another winding ascent, not quite an inclined plane, yet not by any means a regular stair, the edges of stones, neat but primitive, having been suffered to project irregularly to serve for rude steps or a kind of assistance. Through this narrow stairwell Darconville crept to the top of the house, which was partly ruinous and full of nooks. There was a good deal of hooded furniture and old stuffed chairs, upsidedown and shrouded with linen antimacassars turned inside out, all blocking spare rooms reserved for lumber and empty portmanteaux. The dust was formidable. There, branching off at irregular intervals, horizontal galleries—full man height, but narrow—went round the whole building, or so it appeared, and received air from circular holes, wheel-windows that fell open from their peaks and were held by a chain. There were—rooms up there! *Inhabited* rooms!

Then came the sound of a sudden step. Darconville's heart squeezed in fright as, turning, he found himself staring at a delicate, slack-twisted boy of indeterminate age—fourteen or forty, it was impossible to say—whose complexion was the color of a slug. He had one of those faces, ellipsoidal and cricket-like, which resembled one's reflection when looking closely into a shiny spoon or doorknob. Blowing up fitfully at a wisp of his ashy-blond hair, he shifted, the better to grip the box of books and bottles he tightly held with nailbitten hands, and pointing from the wrist to a nearby door stammered in angry panic, "I'm *t-telling* Dr. Crucifer about this, y-you wait!"

LXI

A Telephone Call

If love should call, and you were I
And I were you, and love should call,
How happy I could be with I
And you with you, if love should call.

—S. J. PERELMAN

—ISABEL?

—This is Dot. Good lord!—*hush up, y'hear!*—some folks here neighborin' a spell but carryin' on like they was clappin' their feet in the air. Hello?

—This is Darconville.

—*Darconville!*

—I'm sorry to be calling so late. It's midnight.

—Midnight? Shoot, I didn't *think* it was 5:30. My watch was upsidedown, for cry-eye. But listen to you: too late don't count on Satur-day night, not here. (*pause*) *Will somebody turn that damfool thang down?* (*pause*) You still up yonder in Massatoochits?

—Yes. Yes, I am.

—Isn't that nice? That's right nice.

—Sort of. I wonder, may I speak to Isabel?

—What in the *world?* O law, here I am holdin' a glass in one hand and, fool that I am, nearly proceeded to try to drink out of the *tele-phone receiver!* (*pause*) Hello?

—Isabel. May I speak to her, please?

—Is she here?

—Um, don't you—know?

—Funny, you know, I don't *know* if I don't know. Here, you hold on, I'll be back in a breath. (*long pause*) Out, wouldn't you know it. Fickle, fidgety thing.

—Fickle?

—Well, fidgety, really. (*sigh*) I bleeve she got her a part-time job. Days, that child been ugly as homemade soap to me. I mostly let her be, Darconville, plain out. I'm at my end of the rope, I'm telling you. We *habm't* seen a sign of her much lately. She's been takin' to goin' on long walks night and day. All that. You know? In the woods. Off down the path. Hands deep in her pockets. All that kind of—*quiet!*—thing.

—Hands deep?

—All that.

—At night? Alone?

—Or maybe with someone else.

—Someone else? No.

—Well, I mean with someone else if she ain't alone, see? Hello? Your voice sounds s'small.

—Was she alone tonight?

—I haven't a clue. That's the point. It's difficult to say.

—When she's alone?

—When it's too dark to see. Hello? (*pause*) Wait, this is going to kill you—I was just talkin' into my beer glass!

—You mentioned that.

        (*pause*)

—Did I call you?

—I called you, Mrs. Shiftlett.

—Please, call me Dot? Besides I have a small headache.

—Listen, perhaps I should give you my telephone number so Isabel can call me. All right? Now, I'm giving you my telephone number: 1-617-495-3612.

—A mess of numbers? Lordy! I can cold out tell you, Darconville, they're sure to come out, whaddyacallit, *added* wrong me takin' them down now. (*pause*) *Was that a a-tomic bomb out there?* (*sigh*) A few folks is by, is all, turnin' some sweet potato vines. Sound like a bunch of aborgirines, though, don't it? I bleeve I cain't hear m'self think.

—I'm sure it's fun.

—Tyin' on favors? Steppin' on big ol' balloons? Puttin' up the RCA? O.

—You're enjoying yourself.

—Enormously. (*pause*) Enormously.

—Please. How is Isabel getting along?

—So well.

—Would you tell her I called?

—I will. I pointedly will—to use one of your big writin' words.

—I called all last week. I rang and rang.

—Pet.

—I miss her.

—We all do.

—

—You'll have to speak up louder.

—I—love her.

—You cain't bleeve how much that'll mean to you when I tell her.

—I'm sorry?

—Don't be. Maybe it's female trouble, this mopin' about. That's my p'effunce. Thrums or something, that kind of thing. The thrums come on me, I take a drink—

—Mrs. Shiftlett? Hello?

—Did you ring off? I thought you rang off, until I saw myself, what, fussin' with my glass where the receiver was. Hello?

—(*sigh*) I'm right here.

—Isn't it wonderful.

—What?

—Bein' there. Harvard? I just say the name.

—You couldn't look again, Mrs. Shiftlett, for Isabel, perhaps again in her bedroom? (*pause*) Are you there?

—Oh yes, but I'm afraid I cain't talk to you now, Darconville, I'm on the phone.

—So—so am I.

—Why, of course, don't mind me. I'm a-sloppin' and a-sloshin' about here like a rubber pig in a winter suit. But hold on, let me first put down this fool drink. (*dial tone*)

LXII

A Judgment in Italy

I don't envy your happiness very much if the lady can afford no other sort of favors but what she has bestowed upon you.

—George Farquhar, *The Recruiting Officer*

A LITIGATION, in the meantime, had been resolved in the province of Veneto. The attorney-in-fact, appointed by a magistrate of the Court of Appeal, conducted an investigation by locating not without difficulty and eventually obtaining the most recent judgments rendered in a dispute between the alleged heir of a small estate located in the City of Venice and the State of Italy and then sent the results ahead which from Quinsyburg were forwarded to Cambridge, Mass.

The affair began long ago, at the outset of the eighteenth century, when in 1718 and within that republic a certain *"benefizio semplice di patronato laicale"* dedicated to San Marco, patron saint of Venice,

had been created. In essence, the so-called benefit (*benefizio*) was established by one or more owners of certain lands (*patroni*) by execution of a deed assigning forever their income from said lands to an ecclesiastical entity, such as a church, in return for the perpetual
obligation of the priests, as designate by the *patroni* and from time to
time in charge of said church, to say Masses for the souls of the
owners, their families, and successors. The church (*capellano*) was entitled to receive from the cultivation of the owners, fishermen in this
case, a share of the produce (normally ⅕) and to administer the land
for this purpose; the *pescatori,* i.e., the fishermen, were entitled to retain the residual ⅘ths share of the produce. An inspection of this
benefizio by ecclesiastical authorities ascertained that, with the seizure
of the city in 1797 by the French, destroying its independence, it
ceded to the state. The *patroni* were sent down that judgment, the
deed was dissolved, and their names faded into oblivion.

At the union of the republic of Venezia with the Kingdom of Italy,
several new laws were then enacted, principally aimed at suppressing
the old ecclesiastical entities and transferring their rights to the state
demesne. Soon thereafter, law No. 1464 of August 17, 1873, established, in the absence of any notarial deeds, owners, or assignees,
various civic tenancies in the *benefizio* in question—a piece of land
with dwellings located, as it was, off the Canale della Misericordia.
The particular palazzo on the Corte del Gatto, one division, was declared by favor of the above law, and in suppression of the full
benefizio, an *orfanotrofio di stato*—an orphanage—in settlement. A
Venetian notary fixed its yearly allocation at Lir. 200.000 (about
$230). The foundlings taken in were given uniforms and arbitrarily
assigned surnames that were taken from herbs.

A corrupt official during those years, channeling the annual appor-
tionment of the orphanage to his own ends—engaging, all the while,
in a scandalous liaison with one of the young girls there—arranged to
close the home with the claim that the lost (read: stolen) assets
disallowed by default any settlement pursuant to the 1873 law, and
not only for the sudden eviction of its charges but also in view of the
brisk maritime trade through the Adriatic, he schemed a graft, attributed the grantorship to his own office, and proceeded to open a
house of assignation off the large canal. It flourished.

In the meantime, a certain Alessandro Dittami, a boy randomly
named from an aromatic plant which grows in the area of Mount

Dicte, found his way to the United States, specifically to New York City, where, in his teens and insolvent, he slept in what Italian immigrants there called the "Hotel Pepino" (i.e., beneath the stars under Garibaldi's statue in Washington Sq. Park) and assumed the trade of a tailor. He taught himself English, worked hard, and saved his money. With the passing years he came to learn the dark fate of the orphanage in which he had once lived—the child of a romantic and illegitimate love between a local senator there and a girl in service— and to which, after his own small success abroad, he had in the best of faith sent back charitable sums. The monies, unknown to him, were being converted of course to foul ends, still, however, under the guise of state control. Alerted, eventually, to the misappropriation of his gifts, Dittami worked desperately to re-establish the orphanage to the proper powers, less in the name of justice than as a simple act of compassion growing out of his childhood memories, and yet, while he learned that there was no way to effect this other than by looking back into the original *benefizio,* it was brought to his attention that, as the initial claim of anyone to the benefit had long ago dissolved, the state had every right to continue to assert title to the realty, unless, of course, a *patrono* could be proved to exist as to matters of letters-patent, grant, lease, custodiam, or recognizance.

Vigorously, he cast around to find ways to vindicate a claim, to free the estate of scandal and taint, and to accede now to full ownership which he sought to do not only by dint of his contributions but also because, as the benefit was essentially of a lay nature (*laicale*), it could not legally have been appropriated by the state in the first place under whatever jurisdiction or for any reason whatsoever. The issue was debated for the following half-century in several suits brought before different courts which rendered conflicting judgments, until the dispute was temporarily settled by the Court of Appeal at Veneto in a decision which gave full force and effect to the original compact between clergy and laity—but not before Dittami passed away. But what, in fact, had been decided? His widow—Darconville's maternal grandmother—was judicially prevented from the satisfactory conclusion of her husband's dream, for while it was adjudged that the state demesne had wrongly subrogated the *patroni* years back and taken possession of their rights, an unlawful abridgment of the formal *laicale,* there could be given no final resolution of tenancy and/or ownership for want of evidence as to legal continuance. An irony of a

legal nature followed: the appellant was awarded temporary jurisdiction, but it was over little more than a financially exhausted, debt-
ridden, overspoliated palazzo, a large account duty—substantial
charges and assessments—falling upon it coincident with the enormously devaluated lire of several terrible wars. She returned nevertheless to Venice upon her husband's death where, for the memory of
her husband and in the interest of Darconville, her sole heir, she reac-
tivated the dispute on her own, both as to claim and cadastre. Continuance followed continuance.

Finally, the Supreme Court of Italy (*Corte di Cassazione*), determining to resolve the controversy and dispose of the case in judgment
once and for all, suddenly disregarded the form of the transaction in
favor of its substance and confirmed the decision rendered pro tem by
the Court of Appeal of Veneto, and the matter became *res adjuticata*,
a conclusion reached in respect of centuries of litigation. The documents evidencing the decision were duly recorded, barring any other
claimants in the light of this last decision, exact copies thereof bearing
the proper seal were forwarded, and Darconville became the owner of
a Venetian palazzo.

LXIII

Figures in the Carpet

But while my lids remained thus shut, I ran over in my mind my reason for so shutting them.

—Edgar Allan Poe, *The Oval Portrait*

DARCONVILLE took out his black coat. A spell of bad weather, cold hard rains, set in about the middle of September. There was a torn and anxious quality to the sky. Days noticeably foreshortened: the season when warmth lay low upon the land, smothering it, was gone. The coolness in the air gave more than a hint that the last rose of summer, tired of blowing alone, had put on its hat and gone home. Cambridge now seemed small, dark, and strepitous.

It seemed a bleak, haunted Congregational world these days, and Darconville came to descry in the black-hooded clouds overhead the lofty pulpits of the Mathers, in the drizzle their gloomy and irritable prophecies. Fall classes had now begun at the university.

The first week there had been interviews to give: a long procession of ponderously uncertain students making application for his courses. Darconville's office was on the second floor of a secluded, rickety house on Kirkland St., and there he sat listening to their concerns, the usual olla-podrida of undergraduate worries and boasts, hoping no one noticed how hard he found it to concentrate. No, not hoping. Hoping allowed the possibility of hindrance, resistance, opposition—prophecies he refused to allow as the principal cause of events foretold, for we hope, so pray, only to lose our comfort in the marshaled expectation that creates a guilt, in which, feeling ashamed, we fall afoul of hope and populate a hell. Darconville could no longer, in fact, be numbered among those men whom obstacles attract. All experience now seemed vanquished by one that had already taken place—and he withdrew to *her,* now a refuge in all things; he waited; he sat still in the sweet paralysis of the past. The temptation to change or fully abide by new adjustments, of whatever sort, seemed only a closely reasoned paraphrase of rashness, and he didn't dare do what, in the doing, might be undone. He refused to acknowledge sorrow and at the same time tried to blunt his eagerness, lest eagerness sharpen the condition of that hope he now superstitiously held to be antithetical to faith: don't we hope for what we also fear we mightn't have? And *that,* of course, was unimaginable.

No, Darconville was only rational—and grateful. Without Isabel, however, his happiest moments became his saddest because he could not share them with her, and yet, while he kept it all to himself, he still saw fit—as he had for some time now—to record his every feeling for her in a notebook, adding, as well now, what he could remember of themselves, as far back as he could remember. It seemed a way of keeping in touch. At the end of each day at Kirkland St., he waited until the corridors were deserted and then walked home alone, usually by way of the Yard, sometimes so late that the wickets had been swung shut for the night, with the lights in the old halls long extinguished and only the striking of a lonely clock somewhere far away a reminder that beyond the black and impenetrable shadows was someone very close to him. And then he would whisper to her every single secret in his heart.

Prof. McGentsroom, an old scholar at Harvard, proved to be indispensable in those early weeks, becoming for Darconville not so much the person who'd hired him but rather instead a good friend who eased the transition, explained the rubrics of the university, and suggested—always kindly and usually in language that referred itself to the middle of the last century—how to go about things. At their first meeting, he'd presented to his young friend a volume of his own poetry, expressing only gracious regrets, as he inscribed the book to both of them, to hear that Isabel wouldn't be coming up until December. They still, of course, intended to marry? Darconville smiled. "The faith of man," said the kindly scholar, taking Darconville's arm, "is itself the greatest miracle of all the miracles that faith engenders." It was true, and, for strengthening him in his resolve, truer than ever. Only endure, thought Darconville, endure, rich Penelope.

A Harvard classic, McGentsroom—almost old enough to carbon-date—looked like a real pottle-fiend (at times, in fact, he did rather moisten his clay, as the phrase goes, somewhat copiously): he was thready, wore salt-and-pepper suits, and was always stuffing filthy old shag—the genuine Bull Durham—into his pipe. His ties were stained. There was awn sticking out of his ears and nose. He looked as though he couldn't find the holes in a bowling ball, but in point of fact he was a great polyglot and was currently being considered for another Pulitzer Prize, not so much for his masterful biography, rendering others obsolete, of Weef VI, as for his brilliant translation of a recently discovered tenth-century Russian manuscript called *Chornaya Gertzoginia*. He couldn't remember the carfare to Boston from Cambridge but could quote chapter and verse from the works of Defensorius, Synodite of Ligugé, and Baudonivia, the Nun of Poitiers. Darconville often took Prof. McGentsroom to lunch. He always got sauce on his nose.

Despite the fact that he was getting on—the previous year he had yawned and dislocated his hip—Prof. McGentsroom was widely held to be a wonder in the classroom. In he bumped, replete with umbrella and beret, looking as if he'd shaved with a scarificator, and without so much as a note began to lecture. He taught courses in comparative literature, but Homer was his love, and several generations were often given to regale each other with stories of how he always chuffed on fumicable feet across the front of the classroom, the standard opening since 1915 to his famous classics course in which he demonstrated that Homer sang in the rhythm of a choo-choo train! Classics: a course which teaches you how to live without the job it prevents you from getting. But to such complaints McGentsroom was oblivious. Lecturing, he was liable to nod off or perhaps reach into his pocket and take out something like a telephone-pole insulator, stare at it, then put it back. As he talked, he pulled on his pipe, slurped it, chewed the stem in deliberation. Of course he was a bit bunty, but the students loved him, especially those who, answering a question correctly, earned his ritualistic praise: he would step out from behind the lectern, extend his hands cardinalationally, and clap them down upon the fellow's shoulders, saying, "Oh, it *is* grand to be young." It was reported that he got angry only once—this was years and years ago—when he simply walked out of the classroom, shouted "Suffering Columbus, *no!*" and then returned, smiling and composed. Female students worshipped him and on the last day of each semester always brought him a balloon. McGentsroom was one of those people rare today who adored his wife, whom he invariably called "Little Mother." You always saw him leave Widener Library at 9:10, when he walked home —often the wrong way—for a small glass of scrumpy, the late news on his overheating old Philco cathedral, and then to bed.

At the beginning of the second week, Prof. McGentsroom invited Darconville over on Saturday night for drinks. It was something to look forward to, for the young teacher had been spending his nights alone working on a piece of satiric fiction which showed the ironic contradictions between the characters' confidence in themselves and what the reader knew about them, a kind of writing at which recently he'd became extremely adept. Writing he could manage; nothing else much interested him. There was in F-21 only the whisper of his pen, a familiar silence broken only occasionally down in the street by roaring students addicted to asserting in chorus that they wouldn't go home 'til morning, a needless vaunt in that, more often than not, it had usually arrived. As time passed, the pointless spaciousness of his rooms came to oppress Darconville, and he proceeded to move his bed, his desk, and his lamp into one room. He began to talk to himself, avoid the dining-hall, feel a fatigue he could only ascribe to—what? His apprehension to know suddenly explained it: apprehension. He wished Isabel would write. He tried to ignore that she hadn't.

But as night followed night it turned out the same: when darkness fell he always found himself facing auspiciously south, gazing through the windows of his room, yet observing nothing, only reaching with one hand to clasp the opposite shoulder, drawing it inward and sitting, as it were, cupped within himself. And it was quaint, for when the windowpane misted over with his breathing, he would wipe it with a handkerchief as if prepared, for some reason, to find in a breathless moment something terrifying looking in, very like the child who displaces fright and apprehension onto monsters and other imaginary creatures in order to preserve the indispensable belief, deep in his heart, that someone loving will then intercede.

His classes provided some diversion. The lecture room assigned to Darconville was located over in Sever, an old smutted brickbat-with-turrets in the quad—its main entrance a black gaping mouth—whose twists and coils of ivy, running down from its slateshell roof to the whispering Norman arch out front, were now turning the colors of autumn. The building enclosed within it ages of stifled air, musty, overoiled, dead, and when one opened the windows, wobbling on corbels, it was only to smell the rot in the stone outside.

The students, most of them, were confident, wellborn, and poised, and their determined eyes, straight Yankee mouths, and Back Bay inflections told the story of what it was within their power to become —indeed, several of them made no pretense at hiding either the fact that they bore the very same names that once made George III tremble or could trace their gametal descent from the lines of Dolgoruky, Edward the Pacemaker, or Pepin the Short. They were quick, forthright, and generally studious—and bore a refreshing dissimilarity to their preterimposterous counterfoils down South who for reasons known only to them took great pride in having enrolled in such schools as Sewanee, Vanderbilt, Baylor, and other sectarian wateringholes where the teachers were all history-whipped alcoholics who calculated the date of the End of the World to have been April 9, 1865, and whose intellectual concerns had less to do with the study of Shakespeare than as to why Longstreet delayed at Gettysburg or how in the subsequent surrender the infamous result for the Union had much less to do with a new birth of freedom than with several generations of piebald babies.

Darconville's seminars usually went well—they'd only met a couple of times—and all the students, crowded together in heaps of bookbags and bunched-up coats, seemed attentive. He would walk in, wheel out a perambulant blackboard, and deliver his lecture with dispatch, pausing only to answer questions or perhaps look out at the leaves fluttering from the trees across the Yard. Unlike most of the Quinsy girls, the students here worked with determination and results, studiously rack-and-snailing over their assignments with the precision of a clock, their ambitions, high, extending simply to honors or, in some cases, to the even higher aspiration of making the punching lists for A.D. or Porcellian, felicity supreme for many of those stouthearted leptorrhins with triple names and disposable incomes who leaned that way.

During those first classes, Darconville managed to establish a decent sort of rapport with most of them—owlish overachievers, bearded scholars, manic-depressive divinity students, sun-streaked blondes in parkas—and many a discussion, full of quibbles and amphibologies, vigorously continued outside on the steps, along through the Yard, and right on up to the brick sidewalks of Plympton St. where, late though it might be, he patiently stood talking to whatever concerned group was there until such time as he had to excuse himself for dinner. But invariably he wouldn't go to dinner. Nor, for interruptions, would he go to his room. He would wait until he was alone and then, for privacy, hurry over to a walkway in the Lowell House courtyard where there was a telephone box.

On the evening of September 20, he connected. It was a brief conversation, for all that depended on it, at least so he felt, after three silent weeks. It seemed that it took Isabel forever to answer the telephone, the explanation for which, when given, being that she'd been outside sitting under a tree, thinking. About? Nothing, everything. Darconville thought: *say all, and all well said, still say the same.* She asked him if he missed her or had he, well, met someone else in Cambridge smarter and prettier than she? She gave credibility to the question that, with a hollow laugh, she repeated, but he refused to accept the callowness it seemed he was being forced, that he might understand, to assume, and though more hurt than indignant he pretended to be neither—and went on, as he swallowed his emotion, asking her if she'd received his gifts, which she had, and if she'd write to him, which she promised she would, that very night. There followed an awkward silence. "I love you," said Darconville. He listened, hard, and heard a low, indistinguishable something, but whether of ardor or alarm or aphilophrenia he couldn't say.

Clearly, her mother was still in the room.

The following days Darconville spent writing, leaving his desk only sporadically either to eat or to check the mailbox—which still remained empty—and the time dragged, for after the telephone call he missed Isabel more than ever, wealth breeding want, the more blessed, the more wretched having grown. The woodpeckers rapping relent-lessly on the lead roof of Adams House, mocking his routine, demoral-ized him; it was ridiculous. Then the weather cleared, and he began to take walks, sit whole afternoons dreaming by the river, or perhaps take the train to Boston where he spent hours going about the streets until he was satisfied that a sufficient amount of time had passed to justify the mail delivery he ludicrously, illogically, came to expect as being somehow causally aligned to his absence: he would return, find the box empty, and then sit in his room in an agony of remorse at the thought of the day wasted. Such accidents with Darconville became weirdly consistent, and, more demoralized than ever, he'd read in his guilt an obligation to redeem the time and then proceed with murder-ous efficiency to write until long after the three o'clock bells tolled pages he'd throw away, for they somehow always curiously transessen-tiated into letters to Isabel—of love, of grief, of passion, of worry— sometimes in words as beautiful and enchanted as prayers but too often as remote and frenzied dispensations, bungled by lovesickness, which gibbered unmentionably outside the ordered universe where no dreams reach, no hearts touch, no love takes place. And then with yet another night almost gone, he would place another sheet before him and take up his pen. He'd lean to the right and then to the left. He'd sit forward. He'd sit backward. He'd sit *tête baissée,* bowing his head to the page, blank as silence, and then mercifully nod off to sleep in the holiness of his ignorance, fatigue becoming at last the very narcotic needed to cure itself.

The lively bustle in the streets outside eventually became a tempta-tion Darconville couldn't bear to ignore. Distinction, implying a difference, only meant isolation, and while he still felt a general indifference to the suffrage of the public he took again to roaming about, often observing in the streets a face, or a fraction of a face, which seemed to reveal to a hairsbreadth in mutable flesh what at that time he yearned to find in durable shape. Strangely, he felt so bad about Isabel's silence and her absence that it became almost like hav-ing her there! And yet he tried not always to think about her. There were, at first, small conversations with the yardcops. Then he accepted the invitations of several students to visit their final clubs, affairs called "rum sociables," during which he sat uncomfortably by himself

in discreet paneled rooms watching beautiful arrogant children—
golden-haired phaeacians with perfect heads and supercilious preppies
in striped ties—as they smoked bulldog pipes, sang ribald songs, and
played poker for exorbitant stakes.

There were also faculty parties at Harvard, a pinched hour or so
once a week in some upper room or other where vile little caphtorim
for whom ideology, like science, put a ring around the world and professors of both sexes, working their rubber faces, stood around in the
pavisade of closed circles, sipping sherry and earnestly trying to solve
the *vexata quaestio* of who shouldn't be given tenure, while their
voices, a blend of the servile and the congratulatory, the deferential
and the condescending, rose at moments of histrionic laughter or
dropped at moments for serious inquiry—conversations, in fact, that
proved to be little more than the gossip of swivel-chair tacticians and
the less-than-witty exaugurations of academical women hardfaced as
execution, crafty little critics, and anxiety-ridden sculptresses from
Radcliffe with complexions like drakonite who taught art and somehow all specialized in phallic and mammary bronzes. The men stut-
tered; the women mimped; and the cumulative effect, often rising to a
pitch of sensibility hardly to be distinguished from madness, only
seemed to recapitulate in the babble what tragic consequences lay in
store for those who would build towers to the heights of their Goddamned ambitions. Most of them had reputations, not for any particular wisdom, but for having authored with indefatigable manufacture
books of eighth-rate criticism which they approached like cutting
serge, getting their thruppence ha'penny change, and writing "settled"
at the bottom of their manifests with the pencil that had blacked their
teeth.

There was for instance the head of the English department, a show-
boat-fat idler in American Lit.—a salesman disguised as a catalogue—
who, with his hands in his pockets, rocked back and forth on the balls
of his feet and upon being introduced to Darconville said, "Ah, the
scrivener." Another one, expert on Wordsworth, simply snorfled sherry
and talked about His Book. A group of men, introduced collectively as
the Personnel Committee, tidily kept themselves to the rule of proportion and excluded anyone else from their charmed circle. It was all in
all a gathering of self-important and inaccessible fame-suckers who ate
too much, rarely taught classes, and had more sabbaticals in their lives
than Saturdays—copyright pirates, purveyors of secondhand sunshine,

and empiriocritical yahoos all ferreting and rummaging in the quis-
quiliae of time, making books out of a judicious mixture of other
books, and carrying owls to Athens. They were all at once silly, unimportant, and ambitious, minds which were logical and positive without
breadth, without suppleness, and without imagination and their scholarship was nothing but a school of peculation which suffered less in
the lack than in the excess of attention. The laurels about which one
dreamt wouldn't let the other sleep; another dreamt that his laurels
wouldn't let yet another sleep; and *that* one couldn't sleep because
only another dreamt of the very laurels he himself was disallowed.

Darconville would remember one particular afternoon at such a
party: a colleague in his department happened, *dared,* to introduce
herself as Isabel, and he was suddenly astonished to see how immeas-
urably sad he grew—excusing himself, in haste, to run immediately
over to Adams House for a look into his mailbox, with no luck.

There was, of course, an outer edge of vanity and pretension to
these occasions, these people, but the distractions were welcome. Anything that came to his mind became a preoccupation. A rough sea, he
thought, leaves a smooth beach. And one morning that idea seemed
confirmed in a wonderful way. A letter arrived: the wedding date was
set in London at Westminster Cathedral for December 23! He called
that night to tell Isabel. There was no answer. Quickly, he wrote her a
letter asking her if he could come down to see her.

The master of Adams House, meanwhile, had noticed that Darconville not only kept aloof at the faculty parties but also took his meals
alone in the dining-hall and so encouraged him to come to the
Wednesday open-houses up in the Senior Common Room—a weekly
get-together for associates, tutors, and affiliated professors where one
had the opportunity to meet other members, chat, and have a drink.
It was enjoyable, a versatile group of scholars, musicians, and lovely
intelligent girls who, brimming with laughter and smelling of hot puffs
of hairwash, effortlessly stood in to discuss their studies, vivisect the
worth of a movie, or explain what they wanted to achieve in their careers. Several—the master among them—had read Darconville's book,
which even became the subject of some discussion there. He began to
look forward to these occasions, the congeniality and quiet civility in
that room, with its noble bust of John Adams, keeping his spirits up.
By happenstance, one afternoon, Darconville noticed a person who
looked like a pale slug crossing furtively along the wall to the exit of

that room, walking with a kind of hop in his gait and frowning at the floor. It was none other than the blond shabrag of a lad who had so nervously accosted him in the dark that night on the top floor of Adams House.

"Excuse me," asked Darconville, interrupting someone, "who is that?"

A few people turned: then they all knowingly exchanged glances. There were raised eyebrows, excipient whistles of sarcasm, and one or two exaggerated reviews of the ceiling. One girl, sucking her tongue in disgust, looked away. The senior tutor smiled and shook his head.

"That," he replied, "is part of the caricaturama of Harvard. His name is Lampblack."

And he ran errands. But no one knew much of anything else about him, whether he was a graduate student or how long he'd lived in Adams House or in fact where he'd come from. Nobody could guess his age. The only incontrovertible fact, it seemed, common knowledge apparently, was that he was a lackey, a little aide-de-camp of sorts whose services at some time or other had been secretly (and, it was suggested, diabolically) given over—if one could believe the report— to one of the strangest human beings on the face of the earth: some mad apple, a creature few had ever really seen, they said, in fact, a professor emeritus at Harvard who lived his life out alone on the interdicted reaches of the top floor of Adams House. As those in the common room spoke of him, it was as if of ruin or disgrace, as if some diseased and unpentecostal wind had suddenly blown up in that room to scandalize their young tongues and yet somehow force them to pronounce, not without an uneasy, almost disbelieving hitch in the throat, the discreditable confession that was his name: Dr. Crucifer.

It was whispered that this remote figure held an absolute and malevolent jurisdiction at Harvard and, to Darconville's skeptical amusement, that he not only controlled everything there but that a good many members of the faculty, about whom he supposedly knew everything, had been brought to the university on the strength of nothing less mysterious than the power of his own secret command. "I take it he's a wizard?" asked Darconville, smiling. But no one laughed—in fact, as he spoke, he happened to notice the senior tutor, closely watching him, suddenly look away.

There were legends. It seemed that this Crucifer was the organizer of every last deviltry. Stories, passed along down the years, were many-handed, many-wintered, many-stemmed. He was evidently a genius, for which, of course, at Harvard nothing wasn't forgiven. Actually, there was small firsthand information: students, who conspicuously avoided that stairway on their own initiative, had in fact been strictly prohibited by house rules from all suites beyond the fourth floor of F-entry. That didn't, however, stem rumors. Dr. Crucifer's courses, no longer being given, had apparently been quite famous—it was said, among other things, that in the heat of a *rabidus furor* the ingenious method he once took for conveying to a lax and ill-prepared student the importance of discipline was to administer stripes to the fellow while having him repeat the "Miserere" on his knees in front of the whole class—but that upon Radcliffe's co-educational merger with Harvard he had immediately resigned. It wasn't explained why. Afterwards, however, he supposedly never appeared in the community again, although the word was that sometimes he'd been seen walking the downstairs corridors of Adams House late at night. Alone. Slowly. That sort of thing. Some said he shot at targets in his living-room with an air pistol, others that he worked in the lofts upstairs on demonic experiments, and several that he was writing a history of Harvard.

It was offered one to select any of a thousand dubious reports: he dressed only in red; he owned a library of cutisbound books; he was never visible to mortal sight for twenty-four hours running; he was an ex-priest; he'd once caned Kittredge; he smoked only Sherman's cork-tipped 100's and drank only imported Pharaon liquor; he was Lampblack's real father; and so on and so forth. His reputation reached everywhere. It was sworn that, once, he had been heard screaming from his upper window for a full ten minutes, that he purposely humiliated Jewish students in his classes, and that, with the remark "My bread, I think?" once dug his fork into the white hand of a lady who sat beside him at a faculty dinner. On another occasion he supposedly called to his table the patron of a local restaurant and ordered him to remove a consumptive from the doorway so that he could enjoy his meal without disgust. And a last flight of someone's fancy actually had it that this creature, in order to elevate himself above the weakness of humankind, once traveled—this was unbelievable—to a remote place called Zawyel-Dyr where in the dead of night he willingly knelt on a mat, lit by stars and a lantern, while some byzantine with a shanked and serrated clamp, fitted to an oval ring, illegally performed a surgical peotomy on him and—

Excusing himself with a smile, Darconville left the room. It was preposterous.

The oaks in New England had now turned. Winds piled every gutter and dark doorway full of scraps of red, amber, and yellow leaves. The passing days were as empty to him as his mailbox, and now even his writing couldn't take his whole attention. He developed headaches but managed to get hold of some amphetamines which temporarily cleared them up. It was not magical: the cure itself was a symptom, only confirmed what his headaches hinted at—his mind had become rigid in its preoccupations, and soon it seemed he was concentrating on concentration alone. Thought became a drama as an end in itself, with his mind both stage and audience. The packs of cigarettes he smoked left his lungs absolutely raw.

At the end of the week, he had his evening with Prof. McGentsroom, philosophical chat over wine in his sitting-room, a sensible and spontaneous amicability that built up in Darconville defenses against his weakness and took his mind off the intentionally brief letter, posing several distinct questions, he that morning mailed to Virginia. It had grown late and was soon time to start for home, the full harvest moon whitening the front porch where he thanked his host who accompanied him out.

"You've been very kind, the whole month. I can't thank you enough."

Prof. McGentsroom's eyes twinkled.

"It's true."

"My dear child," smiled the old scholar, gently bowing his white head, "we surely can't do enough for the princely relative of Cardinal Théroux-d'Arconville now, can we?"

Darconville was astounded. It wasn't important perhaps but it was something he thought no one knew, and yet, if known, it somehow bespoke an uncanny, even relentless investigation of him, a shadowing that, taking such a curious turn, now unsettled him.

"Please," he swiftly asked, "who told you about that?"

"Oh dear," cried McGentsroom, biting his thumb in embarrassment over the apparent blunder. "Does that bother you?"

"Who—could have known? And whoever it is," asked Darconville, upset at his own stammering, "w-what has he to do with me? My goodness, is that why I've been brought to Harvard?"

There was an awkward silence.

"I'm sorry, I'm afraid I must know."

Prof. McGentsroom blinked sadly, bewildered as to what he could now possibly do to explain what, for the reaction, he couldn't understand. He became confused. Then he fumbled out a piece of paper and without a word—strangely, it seemed the best of the worst possibilities—wrote down the title of a book, waited, with trepidation added the author's name, and then gave it over. It was as if he had written the names of sixty devils. He gravely, compassionately, took Darconville's hand and, pausing to add something, found he couldn't. A goodnight at that juncture, he felt, could only have sounded insolent.

LXIV

September 26

That strain once more; it bids remembrance rise.

—Oliver Goldsmith, *The Captivity*

LATER THAT NIGHT when Darconville returned to his rooms he found Spellvexit sitting on a telegram. He tore open the envelope and read:

SEPT. 26
YOU NEEDN'T COME I LOVE YOU LETTER FOLLOWS

ISABEL

He was still awake in his chair holding the message long after dawn had crept up Bow St. and pressed its haggard face against the window, and shortly thereafter the morning bells from the steeple of St. Paul's pealed and promised a new day. But that morning at Mass he distractedly wondered why he wasn't yet at peace. What was it?

Then he remembered.

LXV

Odor of Corruption

I shall teach thee terrible things.

—WILLIAM HALLGARTH

WIDENER LIBRARY is closed on Sundays. The following morning, however, Darconville was waiting on the front steps, a coverlet of morning dew blanketing the Yard, and when the doors opened he went straight to the card-catalogue and began to thumb through the listings, his fingers still cold from the vigil outside. He wrote down a number but in the stacks, when he couldn't find the particular title he wanted among several linguistic works by the same author, was told by a librarian that it was a special section book (an XR number), kept on the ground floor in a cage. Showing his faculty card, he was led downstairs, asked to wait, and eventually given the book: *Christi-*

anity and the Ages Which It Darkened by Dr. Abel Crucifer. He took a seat, opened randomly to a chapter, and read:

The Socratic manner is not a game at which two people can play. I suggest he wanted it that way, transmogrifying, way back when, an aesthetic into a pseudo-ethical world and leaving as a legacy to western man the total betrayal of all degree, priority, and place. In this chapter, *"Womanity,"* let us consider how in the ultimate demonetization of old values he established a platform for radical feminism: the topsyturvification of the sexual order which has subsequently set in motion a growing regiment of Bluestockings, trousered females, and other freaks of nature who happened to be born of a sex of which they failed to be the ornament. In the failed marriage of Socrates was man betrayed. Madame Defarge didn't want justice, she wanted testosterone. Hello, Medusa, here are my stones.

It is no secret that this low-bred male concubine of Archelaus named Socrates (469–399 B.C.) had an extreme influence on philosophy. That is the central miracle of the man. Born on the 6th of Thargelion of the sculptor, Sophroniscus, and midwife, Phaenarete, he was ill-shaped, ridiculous in carriage, and habitually dressed like a craptoad, his general appearance, no doubt, best put somewhere between a wishnik and a Jewish candy-store proprietor. He was almost certainly a pedicator. Juvenal refers to "the foulest sewer of Socratic sodomy." Firmicus speaks of "Socratic buggery." It is of course the modern fashion to doubt the pederasty of the master of Hellenic sophrosyne, the "Christian before Christianity," but even if we are overapt to apply our twentieth-century prejudices and prepossessions to the morality of ancient Greeks who would have specimened such squeamishness in Attic salt such a world-wide term as Socratic love can hardly be explained by the *lucus-a-non-lucendo* theory.

The man had no special education. He was an autodidact—and was very probably unable to read. A pedant, nevertheless, he knew that he knew nothing (Ap. *23 AB,* Symp. *216 D*) which did not prevent him, however, from seeking the reaches of an Atopia that actually was never there. His dissatisfaction with natural philosophy is well-known, less so, perhaps, his utter rejection of natural science (*Xen.* Mem. *I, i, llff.,* *Arist.* Met. *XIII, 4*). He claimed he heard voices—the classical smoke-screen—and, with imperturbable serenity, explained he took his mission in life from a reply of the Delphic oracle: to set in man an inner unrest and bring him into embarrassment (ἀπορειν, *Theaet. 149A*), his attempt to recoin current values developing into a kind of barren and allocritical eristic that took pleasure in the invention of clever but worthless fallacies,

berced, every one of them, by his own vile insecurity and then sent out on
a spin to brain the human race like a disselboom!

Poor in fortune, unlucky with women, hopelessly unfit for any office in
the Republic, he spent most of his days working his trade (making
claypots), bumsucking about for friends, and drinking neck to neck with
anybody who'd listen to him. He craved the acceptance of society—
especially women—and would go to any lengths to insinuate himself with
them, even if the transvaluation of current thinking itself was required to
do so. What then, specifically, did he transvalue? Pay attention, I will be-
queath you a funny story if you prove to misunderstand the following argument. It is offered less for your edification than for my own sense of
well-being. Say survival. I see your brain jailed by a Skuld.

Darconville laughed. It was iconoclastic, comic, absurd.

The philosophy of the West owes its origin chiefly to the Greeks of the
late Hellenic period. Your average schoolboy will testify, correctly, to the
fact that although a slight state of decline was evident in fifth-century
Athens—the City That Loved Beauty—a wonderfully simple view of man
still held: he was taken to be *whole,* with no distinction made between
his visible and invisible aspects. The traditional Greek view would never
have conceded that men and women could be valued on the strength of
their so-called invisible or "psychological" characteristics as considered
separate, say, from visible or bodily ones. (The classical Greek dramatists
never brought into the amphitheatre characters with inexplicable psychological problems: aprioristic madness never went unexplained, and critical mental states, always given with sufficient evidence as to how they
came about, were related to demonstrable tragedy.)

The general pre-Socratic view of life as they knew it, therefore, was
monistic, unitarian, whole. There is no dispute whatsoever about that.
And although the handwashing, departmentalized little scientists and
seers of today now regard man as a psycho-physical twin of himself, a
psychosome—some kind of metaphysical chest-of-drawers composed of
soul, mind, and body—the early wholesome Greeks made no such arbitrary divisions. The "wholeness" of man! Can anyone disagree that it was
a healthy and fully salvific view of what he aspired to be, shoring up
identity and mocking the currently fashionable bit of legerdemain which
condones and excuses, almost automatically, a score of revolting human
excesses committed in the name of lofty intentions? The brainless incompetence we forgive! The philosophical idealism we cite lest we censure!
To the pre-Socratics those tidy distinctions would have been dismissed as
a counterproductive fragmentation which could only lead to the kind of
society we have today, where, thanks to that little ill-born, thrusting Fa-

ther of Abstract Definitions, forcible-feebles can now accede to high political office, the poor are twigged of their money in the name of religion,
and screeching amazonians-in-pantsuits, shitfitsresses, and children-hating
ballockscourers can legitimately go larking about the world with more
complaints than Job and a bellyful of abortifacients all in pursuit of a
freedom they can't temper with responsibility and as an excuse for a
higher liberation they've never deserved! Blindfolded, you can at least see
the blindfold, can't you? It's only to witness what your wit won't see.

A librarian walked by rolling a bookcarrier. Darconville looked up
and, turning a page, went back to the mad polemic in front of him,
amused and fascinated and disgusted.

The Greek expression for a good man—καλὸς κάγαθὸς—explied both
good-looking and morally good, a notion at once attic, simple, and
undevious, with the body and soul fully integrated, valued as one, un-
separated in wholeness: boul or, say, sody. There were no pea-and-thim-
ble tricks effected to propagate the careers of incompetents, liars, or
faith-thumping dwales who spoke of what perversely they either couldn't
or wouldn't do. Man's integrity, as we use the term, is not unrelated to
the etymological denotation it more strictly conveys. You work out the
syllogism yourself. I've a philosopher to kill.

During the fifth century, under Pericles, the Greeks reached an order
of highest perfection—in art, poetry, sculpture, architecture, medicine,
history, drama, and science; it was plenitude, a paradise in terms of
man's effort that was the closest thing to the eye of God where the expression τὸ καλὸν κάγαθὸν served: the union of the beautiful and the
wise (so one translation might be), which gives birth to the good. Then
sometime about 428 B.C. Socrates, patron saint of equivokes, fartwhooshed
onto the scene with his little grab-bag of famous questions, the type
of which, when asked, perversely became answers (ἰεξετάξειν ἑαυτὸν καὶ
τοὺς ἄλλους *Ap. 28E, 38A*). I look back to Maieuticville and see a self-
absolving bore, an inkle-beggar with his pockets full of Crito's money,
a farting whaw-drover with ears like a question mark and more gall
than bladder. The problem now was to ingratiate himself, advance,
become accepted. He stole his method from Zeno of Elea. He hung
around young and impressionable people. And he claimed that he had
supernatural monitors and was open to some kind of divine pipeline,
the source of which inspiration history might better trace to the dark
den of his occasional companion-in-arms, the hetaira Diotema of Man-
tinea, to whose symposia, one imagines, everyone was invited save other
women and wives, possibly making of them—*termagants?*

The silly revisionism bewildered Darconville. He shook his head over the compounded lunacies, wondering just where all this went. What nonsense! What nothings!

Socrates began to preach duality, and except for several contemporary quacks of disapproval—Aristophanes, among others, and now mine, thank you very much—he got away with it for *two thousand years!* Think of it! He turned philosophical contemplation into enigma, called ignorance real wisdom, sabotaged tradition, ended no dialogue but in disillusionment, and yet all the while actually claimed that he knew nothing, taught nothing, learned nothing! Curiously, this didn't stop him—or others. Unhappily, he had two apprentices—you know them as Xenophon and Plato, the Hellenic Mutt and Jeff—both of whom ingeniously saw fit to transmit to following generations the quintessence of what that misinformed little bum-biter [*in the near margin someone had written the word "blasphemous"*] left behind, the which may be put in five philosophical headings:

    1. The soul's independence of the body
    2. The soul's superiority over the body
    3. The worthlessness of the body
    4. The immortality of the soul
    5. The duality of man, i.e., the two-sided existence of body and soul (σῶμα, ψυχή)

And what precisely have these tenets wrought? Stop up your mouth if you'd say little and say little if you'd say much. They raised everyone to indiscriminate equality. They effeminized society, leveled excellence, diluted the Greek ideal, and—our immediate concern in this chapter— put a megaphone into the hands of certain women whose hysterical neesings have deafened the ears of logic ever since in spite of the fact that the difference between the sexes happens to be a little matter Nature, I suggest, will never be so obliging as to alter.

Enter the feminists, however, gravid with this thesis, that if the body could be considered negligible, if physiological differences didn't really matter, if men and women were equal where it really counted—*inside,* you see—why, clearly it was the sudden solution to their persistently gnawing feeling of inferiority! And how swiftly women snatched at the idea! Witchwives, whores, all womanity! For if the body was negligible, equality was assured and the struggle for domination and sovereignty was theirs to win! The logic was as simple as sophistry, for if woman, essentially and chiefly of the body, could now ignore her bodily role in society —and with lofty philosophical reasons!—she would be that much more elevated to the very positions to which she aspired but from which, by every other standard, she'd been judiciously and legitimately prevented from holding, the remarkable first step, this, in allowing them to disassociate themselves from the unilaterally despicable and patently unfair obligation, reactionary and patrivincialistic in intent, of bearing children, suckling them, and dutifully standing by them in trial and trouble. Thus do they act as acted Mother Eve whose unnatural and vaulting ambition for equality took her to the fruit and bade her eat, destroying every one of us in the sudden committing at once of *all* sin: disobedience, covetousness, pride, unbelief, mistrust of divine veracity, gluttony, vainglory, parricide, jealousy, theft, invasion, sacrilege, deceit, presumption to godly attributes, fraud, arrogance, and sloth of thought. Nothing is less different from a woman than the very woman herself. There is only one woman, though there are a million versions of her. Ask my mother.

Darconville read on in disbelief, quite wondering as he turned the profane pages whether the author of this thing were actually human!

Socrates' philosophy at its very conception bore the seeds of its own corruption for it immediately gave birth to those whose existence rendered it worthless: he himself created his termagant wife—and in his pathetic defense of that marriage with his late espousèd saint (*Xen.* Symp. *II, 10*) proceeded to make of the married philosopher a music-hall joke. The little catosopher created millions of catosophresses who went on to catosophrize: the soul is the only *essential* part of a human being, the soul can have no sex, so the body shall no longer discriminate against the soul! Does a woman betray you, murder, deceive? Her excuses sit in the soul, pure, inviolate, a law unto itself. Her excuse *is* the soul, the one you had no reason to enjoin to that body you mistakenly assumed it animates.

Feminism inevitably arises out of a body-despising doctrine. To the envious, the bitchy, the grasping, the iniquitous, and the congenitally dissatisfied, Socraticism was a philosophy cut to measure. Indeed, in almost every example of the vile sisterhood, Goody Rickby and her noisy forges, the flight from domesticity and motherhood—never mind from one's very self—is always aligned to the flight to a "higher sphere." The Socratic doctrine, animating the impulse to emancipation which of course animates the mood to androphobia, becomes a free-ticket to Cloud Cuckoo Land where the mind/soul nexus relegates the distinguishing body to a pile of excess baggage.

The feminist of the radical stamp, however, is moved not by a concern for her own sex, public spirit, or female self-identity but rather, ironically, by the very grudge she bears against herself—the male element in her, perhaps, that lies at the actual *source* of her craving for emancipation— and yet if self-belittlement can be reduced by belittling what we compare ourselves to, it is not surprising to see to just what extent women act to belittle men. A nowt to catch a naught: it is advanced that to be anti-male is to be pro-ideal; sex becomes either the enemy of female virtue or, in war-like fashion, is used manipulatively to subject the weakest males to the female point of view which with the feminist, as it was with Socrates, turns out to be nothing more than self-loathing, the refusal to accept themselves as philosophically one, whole, complete—a calumny against themselves I find myself too ill-disposed to modern terminology to investigate here. A divided woman, simply, is a tautology.

Madness, thought Darconville, madness!

Socrates, often asked to absent himself from duplicity awhile, was soon accused by citizens Lycon, Meletus, and Anytus of corrupting youth; tried; and then sentenced to death by a majority far greater than that by which he had been pronounced guilty—and this during a period of time when, sadly, almost as a sop to the contemporary mood, female statues were curiously becoming altered: the leg-torso ratio grew to resemble that of the male! Indeed, the whole of Greek art progressively began to reveal a gradual increase in the length of the female leg relative to the torso and the modification of the female form. Or was it satire? A sudden decadence? A last vigorous outcry for the old stability and order that became revenge? Or was it simply a general acquiescence to the upheaval that soon put paid to the glory that was Greece? Conjectures are welcome. The philosopher, in any case, was given his cup of hemlock, died, and three days later there wasn't so much as a peep heard from the tomb!

But what of that hemlock on the skirt you paw at, reader? Beneath it a body, within it a soul, above it a head that titters? It is a Socratic labyrinth you have the choice of either entering or refusing to enter. I leave you this Pantagruelian advice, in any case, if enter you must:

> *When you dwell in Satan's arms,*
> *Should his wife prefer your charms*
> *Taking it into her noodle*
> *To enjoy your great whangdoodle*
> *And accept a few fell stitches*
> *From the awl inside your breeches,*
> *Pluto surely will not wrangle*
> *While you and his lady brangle.*
> *So, live happy and fare well*
> *In your marriage bed in hell.*

On the other hand, you can escape that hell and manifest in a terrible freedom what you'd save yourself from, lest otherwise you become determined by the very value you are not indifferent to! To be attached is to depend on, and to depend on something is to have one's freedom restricted. If women are the force that figuratively deny the body, perhaps he who literally denies it denies them and in so doing finds the freedom he'd seek. As in all ages of luxury, women usurp the functions of men and men take on the offices of women. Ours is a poor, weak age, with the sexes nearly assimilate and neither known by the knowledge of what they were. The epoch of viragoes was ever the epoch of eunuchs.

Irony, finally, used to interest me when I was younger and more impressed by the hollowness of the thing it castigates, but perhaps it should be pointed out that to become whole again man must take up a part: what depends, de-pend; what is attached, disattach. *"I hunted the beaver who, giving up, got away,"* once riddled a Skopt. (You see, I'm much more fun, may I say, than I seem?) The scriptural commonplace that has it that to find oneself one must lose oneself is true. I vouch for it myself. But I can go further. I can personally testify—*O castigat ridendo mores!*—to what you surely must see is the only essential lesson Socrates ever left us: sacrifice is self-interest. Sacrifice *must* be self-interest!

The air outside felt good to Darconville who left the library with a particular sense of grief he'd not quite felt before, and, too melancholy after attending to the reading to make an accurate report of his reflections, he found himself walking out along the granolithic walk by the football stadium, the huge emptiness of which he entered to spend most of the afternoon sorting out the many questions in his mind. What, he wondered, had this haughty and disordered malefactor named Crucifer to do with him? Had the rumors been true of his extensive power there? Why in fact had he himself been asked to come to Harvard?

And the perverse book? It was spawl, a piece of violent deception, fatally fixed like a grotesque ornament that had been gradually molded in the cavern of someone's head by the drip of calcareous water and hardened into a single point: the hatred of women. It was an introduction, oh yes. But to whom? To *what?* A spectre waiting upon his past and fathering forth whispers, orders, commands? But why? Darconville smoked and walked, walked and smoked, circling round and round the upper ramparts of the arcaded Coliseum like a pale, deliberating renunciant high above the abyss that beckons him down. What was he supposed to know now? And what of what he knew was he then to apply to what he wanted to know? He didn't know. There were only silences, echoes, detached voices on every front, and so he spent the day, brooding to no consequence, until it grew dark and he left the stadium, pitching a last cigarette through the dusk and crossing the Weeks bridge toward Adams House.

When he opened the door to his room, Darconville saw a note on the floor. He took it to the window and by the ghostly light of a streetlamp read what suddenly made him wonder whether there weren't more efficients in nature than causes. What interanimates what, he wondered, in what is foreordained? It was sinister, all of it, coming for some reason, yet, as no surprise—the mind, defining reality, creates it! We bless to appear what to avoid we curse: to loathe too much in the mind is only to rehearse or ten times twice *affirm* in an act of wild denial a hated fact. Greetings, conscience! I shall make from fear, thought Darconville, a rendezvous with dread.

And so he could do nothing but accept the terrible sequence of ironies he believed, in compounding, he'd caused—as if, in having been more willful to learn than willing to abhor, he'd but burned one candle to seek another. Solon made no law for parricides because he feared he should put men in mind to commit such an offense! Chance was only the fool's name for fate, thought Darconville, and by the eerie light coming in through the window of his lonely room once again read the words of the note:

> Sir, this to entreat you to step up
> to my study for a word. My occupations
> are all indoor so that I am always at
> home.
>   So I rest yours to serve,
>
> CRUCIFER

LXVI

Accident or Incident?

I would know whether she did sit or walke,
How cloth'd, how waited on, sighed she or smiled,
Whereof, with whom, how often did she talke.

—Sir PHILIP SIDNEY

THE LETTER Isabel promised never came. So Darconville, again, tried to contact her. He called the house at Fawx's Mt.: there was no answer. He called the telephone company in Charlottesville, re-checked the number, again called the house in vain, and then thought that he might try the van der Slangs. He called that number and, identifying himself, expressed his worry but Mrs. van der Slang said she was sure everything was alright. He called Annabel Lee Jenks who hadn't heard a word from her since graduation and Lisa Gherardini who wasn't there herself. He called Miss Trappe who told him about a bad dream she'd had. He even called the general store in Fawx's Mt.: they hung up. Later in the day he finally reached the Shiftlett house again and asked if Isabel were there, but the reply was only a single diaphonic mutter: *"thnaowr."* It meant no.

It can't therefore be fully charged against Darconville for turning where he did—nor perhaps explained, on the other hand, how in setting out for nowhere in particular he proceeded straightway out to F-entry and then up the forbidden stairs.

LXVII

Dr. Crucifer

It is a point of cunning to borrow the name of the world.

—Francis Bacon

THE ROOM UPSTAIRS looked forbidding. The door was solid, coopered to a great weight and blind-hinged. Its mullions stifled the sound of Darconville's repeated knocks; he paused to listen, then knocked again harder—*dmf, dmf, dmf*—but there were only echoes down the atrocious passageway. On the other side, footsteps ran past back and forth. Again, he struck the panels smartly. Suddenly, a key sprung in the lock and, slowly, the door opened an inch: a pair of little eyes glared out. Crossly, Lampblack whispered that Dr. Crucifer was asleep. But Darconville, with his foot fast on the bottom stile, told the boy to wake him. Stuttering angrily, Lampblack tried to shove the door shut, unsuccessfully, for Darconville forcefully stepped it open and repeated with a cold voice, "Get him."

Lampblack spat: he recoiled as if to strike, but Darconville, seizing his wrist, bounced him on a hop backwards into the room, whereupon, snarling, he disappeared through an inner door.

The living-room looked like a medieval oratory, communicating, apparently, with a bedroom behind it and running into a long narrow walkway to the right, embellished on both sides with framed atlases and prints, which led to more rooms. A cloister lamp hung in this main room. The royal purple plush of the walls descended four or five feet all around the room to old carved wainscoting, finely penciled wood waved and variegated with peculiar dramatic scenes and tetra-stichs in middle English. The ceiling was beamed. The furniture was of black oak, a great sideboard answering strangely well to the monstrous elbow-chairs in each corner that rose to ornamental knobs and rounded around to the front in leonine fistclaws. An Egyptian dagger hung in the liripipe of the hood of an academic gown (Jesus College, Oxford) draped over one of them. There was a touch of blasphemy in the antique prie-dieu which had been cannibalized round the kneeler to hold a chamberpot, inscribed: *"Mingere cum bombis res est saluberrima lumbis."*

It was the room of a person whose taste was luxurious to the verge of effeminacy, a person, thought Darconville, utterly and absolutely selfishly solicitous about his own wants, some mad decretalist or Sardanapalian whose caprices ran simultaneously to both lust and asceticism, which, for all anyone knew, were perhaps both part of the same destitution. There were rich labels under the heavy cornices of the walls, recessed for curiosities and antiquities from old châteaux and abbeys, and a plan of shelves were set off, directly across from the door, by a fireplace flanked by a pair of imp-faced terms and above that, framed in dark box, hung the bizarre painting of Delville's *La Fin d'un règne*. A Chinese screen stood against a wall. Between the two windows on the left stood a sofa of eupatorium purple, fitted at one end with a cellaret for decantered wines and liquors. The large old desk intrigued Darconville, for on its center panel, under a built-in lamp, it bore the carved face of Osiris, and there on a pulled compartment—where a cigarette box held a portion of tailor-mades (with blind and foil stamping on the marque of each paper in the extravagant form of his initial)—lay an air pistol. At the top of the desk rested a blue ball inside of which a knight was strangling a nymph.

Darconville had gone but a few steps into the walkway and was peering at the series of lugubrious prints on the walls there—Gotch, Stuck, Degas, Cranach, Baldung, and others—when he heard the paroxysmal scream. It was a woman with a man's voice and a hyena in her womb. The prevalent note was impossible to comprehend—it struck high C—for its thin wire-drawn pitch of *ee-ee-ee* somehow appropriated the shrillness of exasperation, pain, terror, and disgust all at once. Was it anger? Impatience? A protracted yowl of dismissal? Possibly. For all of a sudden a disarranged Lampblack flew through the living room, sucking his fist and sobbing for breath, and flung through the front door as if cast forever into the infinite leagues of black air. In his surprise, Darconville had turned in astonishment to follow the theatrical disorder of it all when behind him, suddenly, the tapestry curtains were drawn with a clash of rings over the windows. He wheeled around and through the comparative darkness saw himself under the surveillance of a figure standing across the room, someone whose footfall had attained the highest perfection of noiselessness.

"Welcome to Mother Sulphur's bagnio," said a tall and unattenuated shadow. It was Dr. Crucifer.

The form of the man, gradually, in little minor details, shaped to an outline in the emphatic darkness which immediately had something indecent about it.

"What do you want with me?"

"Will you sit down?" asked the voice in the darkness. The figure didn't stir. "You won't sit down? That's as it is."

"*Tell* me."

"Your visit is really most opportune, for I wanted badly to have a few minutes' chat with you." It was a voice unlike any other on earth. "You know I know you're a Darconville. But hold thumbs on that. I admire your beautiful face." Darconville could hear him smile. "I want to put on your coat. I believe Abelard had you in mind when he composed his *Pari pulchritudine representans.*"

Darconville gesticulated disgust.

"You'll have heard that countless times, of course. But you haven't heard it from me. I'm giving you a plain answer to a plain question, Al Amin."

The voice was a soprano's, with a little glub-glub sound in the throat like coffee boiling in a percolator, but there was a piping up higher in his birdlike syrinx, as if in a dry whistle it were fluting through a beak. It had no timbre, not at all what one would expect from such a big man, a hovering, elongated man. And, what, was that an accent? Mere phrasing? A glottal defect? As Dr. Crucifer continued speaking, the words in the darkness seemed disembodied, hanging in the air. "I have imagined us together having tea on dark afternoons with oatcakes and double Gloucester and then a late stroll on the misty common to give our swordsticks an airing." He added a word. "Alone."

Darconville said nothing.

"Now, what may I offer you? Some tobacco or tuck? Shall I chill a Muscadet? A glass of brown October?"

There was no reply.

"Sincerely yours?" asked Crucifer, earnestly. "Please. Let it fit gravity if it can't friendliness?"

Still Darconville said nothing.

"I admire your work, *mon fifils.*"

"Do you."

"I'll try again: I believe you're troubled." Darconville moved toward the door, but Crucifer, stepping forward, made a swift vibratiuncle with his left hand. "Permit me, it takes two to tell the truth—one to speak, one to listen." A wheeze of satisfaction followed. "How I should love to be your confessor! There, but enough. May I only hope to see you often?"

"You may hope," said Darconville, "whenever you please."

"Contentious," muttered Crucifer.

Again, Darconville went to leave.

"Wait," said Crucifer, his voice glimmering in fun. "I adore that. Why shouldn't Stromboli dispute with Vesuvius? A mountain and a mountain cannot meet, of course—but individuals can. Your style is like mine. We are co-supremes."

"Your flattery disgusts me."

"I assure you," said the voice, lowering significantly, "I don't want to bother you, only advise. It is not in my interest to persuade men to virtue nor to compel men to truth—in that, I'm typical. You forget, I am a teacher in America. I have a faculty, that's all, of seeing what I feel you should share. Call me a philosopher of error prevented if not

of progress facilitated—you're a writer, aren't you curious about it?—
and that being the case I am prompted only to wonder whether you
believe that the true liberation of the spirit is to empty it of the
thought of liberation, that one can legitimately espouse the destruction
of nature, that your personality and its worldly obligations are no
more than the sins you must absolve yourself from if you would
remain an artist. I am compelled to declare that anyone—no, we
don't need the light just yet—that anyone who shall dissent must either be very foolish or very dishonest and will make me quite uncom-
fortable about the state of his mind." Glub-glub: an attempt at laughter. "I'm like the Boeotian lynx. I can see under the skin."

"What are you talking about?"

"Everything."

"Everything," said Darconville, "is a subject on which there is not
much to be said."

Dr. Crucifer took a step forward. "I mean by 'everything' the essential mistake you must avoid. A glorious love is created in the artist by
the least sign of respect." His dry lips smacked. *"Breviloquentem,"* he
said, "I believe you intend to marry."

So that was it.

"You know so much," smiled Darconville ruefully, "who lives up
here in obscurity."

"I love cross-wits," the creature whispered gleefully. "Pray sit
down. You won't sit down? That's as it is, dear Darconville. Am I too
solicitous? Yours to hand? *Embrasse ta maman?* Forgive me, mothers
and those without balls bleat with similar voices. But then would you
understand that? I wonder, you see, for the more manly a man, the
less, I'm afraid, he will understand women—whether beautiful or
not."

"She *is* beautiful," shot back Darconville.

"You can't admire what is beautiful," said the grotesque voice,
"without becoming indifferent to what is wrong."

"And you confirm as you speak what I see I needn't fear as I listen."

"Blister upon heat!" said Crucifer, laughing. "Reverence to this.
You have the gift of impudence. Enjoy it. Every man has not the like
talent."

Solid line played against stipple. Standing there in the darkness,
Darconville at first scolded himself at putting up with this sudden fa-

miliarity, the forward remarks, but then thought if he bowed to the vexation he might somehow divert the force of it, so faint was the image of the implication of this passing visit upon his still as yet uninformed imagination.

"I must admit, I have always found it easier to understand women, frankly, than those who are interested in them. The which brings the meeting to order: why, may I ask, do you need a woman in your life? Give it over, Darconville, please. Women slacken the combustion of pure thought—they are analogous to nitrogen in pure air. Thinking and feeling are identical for them, whereas for men they are in opposition. I don't mean to offend you. You must only emerge from an illusion," he said, his tongue rasping around the word. "I am afraid for you."

"Your sympathy touches me."

"Sympathy? Sympathy is a non-logical sensation and has no claim to respect. It is a thing at the center of feminine ethics, a quasi-ethical phenomenon built on feelings like shame and pride. It's ready-made. Don't trust it. Surely you've read your great and revered ancestor on the subject?"

"Ah yes! Thus drops the other shoe!"

It was as if a veil had suddenly been torn away from a foolishness he'd called mystery: some perverse fealty owed to an ancient in his family was being paid to him in some kind of insane transferral or reciprocity centuries old.

"A Prince of the Church, murdered in the red of his robes," said Crucifer, adding a reverence intercalated with an Italian phrase while in the same breath sniping at the woman who in killing that old man could kill again—such was the madness up there—in the proxy of Darconville's bride-to-be.

"Be careful," said Darconville coldly.

"I can see in the dark," replied Crucifer.

"You don't see enough, and you assume more than you see." The foulness of it was indescribable but frightening. "You know nothing about her."

"*Her*," echoed Crucifer. "That word again. I haven't heard it for a long time. The possessive case of she, you mean. Not 'hirr! hirr!'—the international order urging a dog forward to attack."

Darconville's eyes blazed. "You—"

"—are mad?" He drew a breath, his voice whistling like a teal's.

"No, *mon gogosse,* I would say that I'm different than most only in that I'm simply ashamed to be human. I know the jollification of indifference. I am indifference. I have cheekfuls of words. I talk. They come out." The strange body of Dr. Crucifer was meanwhile becoming more distinct, still overshadowed, but the concealed, the unseen, slowly metamorphosed to contours discernible as human and yet oddly globoidal and unnatural. " 'I am a man and everything that deals with women disgusts me,' might have said Terence," said Crucifer.

And then suddenly came a pronouncement spent as though merely to exercise a long-held fetish of abuse and falsity and perversion, a dark extravagance, however, that seemed to excite in the person of the speaker an hilarity that belied its intended worth.

"I despise the sex!" he exclaimed. "Bedswervers! Painted trulls! Dupes of limericks! The tragedy of having to waste uncounted priceless hours in chasing what, according to Frater Ψ^2, ought to have been brought to the back door every morning with the milk! The word woman, my friend, is a lipogram of the letter E, and he who marries one commits the philosophical stupidity of trying to subsume the Many in the One. Marriage is cannibalism! Pauciplicate vanity! Men hunting for bargains in chastity and triumphantly marrying a waistline!" Crucifer's voice was whining like a twanged wire—and he moved to the center of the room in high giraffe-like steps in the most awkward simulacrum of motion Darconville had ever seen. But there was no noise! And then he reached up—he was wearing red slippers and a billowing red robe tied at the middle with a cincture of silk—and lighted the cloister lamp.

My God, thought Darconville, souls are on the *outside* of things, not within!

"Marriage is for inchlings, stinkards with mops, cats and mice! It is a reluctant concession to human frailty where the efficacy of ignorance in the experiment has not produced the consequence expected except for the single lesson of its history, collateral or appendant, that proves only once again that blackest midnight succeeds meridian sunshine. You'd dedicate yourself to this? To one, of one, still such, and ever so? Matrimony is matronymry! And if it gave you the smile which you, in contempt of your conscience, haven't used, reflecting on the ludicrous means by which two people have become five billion, then for godsake put the filthy thought out of your mind! My God, can't you hear me? Can't you tell?"

"It's true," said Darconville calmly, "what they say about you, isn't it?"

"What do they say?"

"They say you believe in nothing."

"It is true," answered Crucifer, his hands fluttering like spiders in their lairs within the voluminous folds of his robe. A green jade ring worn on the left thumb suggested a great scarab held captive by one of the spiders. "I believe nothing to know everything, to anti-crusade, to accept the fact that wisdom must bow down to necessity." He paused. " 'Ay, ay, Antipholus, look strange and frown.' " Then he turned his head madly to the side and whispered, "I believe love is what people don't mean by it."

"I believe," replied Darconville, "that love is better than what you believe."

And with a mocking whoop of execration, Dr. Crucifer, stepping under the lamp, spat with glee and threw back his head, which with an involuntary stir of horror Darconville saw for the first time was as pale and round and little as a dirty *boule-de-gomme*.

Dr. Crucifer could have come from another planet. His was a face of grue, a little balloon of dead-white cheeks and jowls with eyes, ringed in black, which seemed to have fixed the features they no longer animated: two windows, shades drawn. It was a head that Darconville perhaps had seen only once before—the bust of Niccolò Strozzi in the Dahlem Museum. There was no beard or bodily hair, only a parchmentlike, pasty skin which wasn't mat-white, neither the Chinese white of oil pigment, nor of that hue which leprosy had bleached out, but a sleek shiny fat with the tint of gambroon.

He was tall and cold and white, showing the same peculiar mis-configuration of body that was George Washington's, a pinball-sized head in striking contrast to the tall elongated trunk of the obesus which suggested a kind of blown-out gigantism and ran into swollen breasts, fat pads, and affluent buttocks that seemed to be pinguefying on their own steaks. The thyroid cartilage was inconspicuous. He had tits. He had a buffalo hump in his shoulders. His hands were pudgy, with dimpled knuckles, and his fingers were long and groomed like a woman's, the nails left sharp and cut almost to a triangle. The hair on his head was black, shiny, and hard, belying an advanced age that could be seen only in his teeth. The effect was that of seeing a great lubberly boy who resembled—forgive the unpicturable image—a giant dwarf: the pendulous belly, a low abdomen big as a budget, a draffsack with short ineffectual arms that implied poor muscular development, demineralized bones, and extreme fatigability. A malodorous perspiration could be detected as he came closer.

He smiled uncannily, glowered suddenly in a fit: there was no easy passage in his face from one mood to another. When he spoke he whistled through his nose, his ogival head moving slowly from side to side, and yet the expression on his face was generally blank, mobile only in so much as speaking demanded it. His mouth looked like a baby's, puckered out like a file-fish, and incredibly there was no salivation associated with it, for his tongue, mouth, and lips were *dry*—with no moisture in evidence at all—and the sounds of his speech, like cornshucks rustling, came out in rasps. It was a creature from the moonlight world.

"Love?" he screeched. "Love?" He looked as if he had been whipped in the face. "The impatient disease? The poor man's grand opera? That desert of loneliness and recrimination? The stinkingest word, you mean, in the *Schimpflexicon* of song and sentiment?" Crucifer banged the table furiously, the sudden and violent response turning his eyes white in an ophthalmic roll. "That thing which boys and girls spin tops at? The mood that can comment on every woe? The delusion, you mean, that one woman differs from another? That set of alcove manners, the demand for which hatred owes all its meaning, is this what you have in mind? That thing of dark imaginings that shapes by chance the perils it by choice can escape? The emotion that makes you leer like a sheepbiter, fawn like a spaniel, crouch like a Jew?" Crucifer swallowed. "Love—pronounced, I believe, *looove*," he mocked, "in the southern part of this country—is a state of mind sustained by a variety of imbecile distractions, the divisor of two solitudes shoved into the dividend of desperation for a quotient of what? Division! The inverse of multiplication!

"Can you eat love?" Crucifer spat air and waltzed vulgarly forward. "Can you cook love? Can you sit on love? Can you crawl under love when it's raining? Can you drive love to the Leucadian groves? Can you wear love when it's cold out? Can you taste it? Touch it? Feel it? Smell? Or depend on it? Can you do anything besides *breed* with it? Can you? *Well, tell me, can you?*"

For a moment, Darconville was actually frightened.

"Desire," whispered Crucifer, "is a sad thing, and love is all the foolish know to lighten the burden. You can alter a cat, perhaps, but not the stupidities of mankind. No, there is no authority but Milton's for Adam and Eve having left the Garden of Paradise hand in hand. I suspect he beat the living shit out of her"—as he laughed he covered his face with his hand—"and was left alone."

There was a long silence.

"Who—are you?"

Dr. Crucifer heard the question with one eyebrow raised in a whimsical vertex. He paused, as if about to take measures almost fatal to himself, then suddenly his face changed to an expression that bespoke the obvious pleasure of perhaps adding a welcome touch of understanding between them.

"I am a man of principles, and one of my principles is expediency. But what did you come out to see?" he asked. Darconville only looked at him. "It's not that I'm what nobody else in the world ever was," he continued, "for you could say the same. Sit down, won't you? You won't sit down? That's as it is, my dear."

Darconville made to leave.

"Wait," interjected Crucifer. "I shall be as cogent, to use the rhetoric of college examinations, as is reconcilable with completeness. But let's have everybody christened before we begin, shall we?" He closed his eyes, and like some prehistoric fish, quite white from the aboriginal darkness, of enormous size, and stone blind, he pipped his lips. "I am, I'm told, of the ancient Egyptian family named Quirtassi, englished Crucifer. I am male. I am a dark article. I am a human truffle which springs up and exists without any root, unstrengthened by fibers or filaments. (No one, incidentally, can actually tell whether truffles are alive or not, did you know that?) I am the Wanderer in the Wilderness, the solar glyph, a design on a Gnostic gem. I have huge great breeches full of sin and air and a face like a cutwaist: it buzzes. I sing hells. I fuck around with the black arts." He smiled. His smile was the dimmest thing in nature. "I wants to make your flesh creep. But what did you come out to see? I am a gynophagite, a dragontamer, a simple fatiloquent. I sin doubly because I sin exemplarily and have never read a description of any heaven I would not have left upon the very instant of my arrival. I pray to Nodina, goddess of knots.

My laughter is deceptive. I can bite wires. I have no goatstones, no sweetstones, no peepstones. I live in Middlesex. I am betwixt and between. But what did you come out to see? I am a pigment of your imagination, a lucifer to light your fag, a scream with breasts. I am a wicked pack of cards," he hissed. "But, please, won't you come into the library?" He waited.

Darconville didn't move.

"There's more to know, I'm afraid."

LXVIII

The Misogynist's Library

This is the place must yield account for him.

—MIDDLETON and ROWLEY, *The Changeling*

Burton on Infidelity: Speeches in the Star Chamber (1637); Juvenal, *Satire VI*; Rozanov's *Solitario*; *Der Krebs: A Study of Invertebrates and Monstrous Women* by Dr. Crouch; André Gide's *Et Nunc Manet in Te*; The Works of Aeneas Silvius; Angus Wilson's "Mother's Sense of Fun"; *The Pilgrim's Scrip*; Sir John Suckling's *The Tragedy of Brennoralt*; Ploss and Bartels, *Woman*; a pamphlet in boards called "Dr. Rondibilis on Cuckoldry, Wittols, and Gulls"; Kipling's *The Betrothed*; Görres's *Mystique naturelle et diabolique* (Vol. V); *The Influence of Women—and Its Cure* by John Erskine; The Very Revs. Kraemer and Sprenger's *Malleus maleficarum*; Hans Baldung's *Hexenbilder*; *The Merry-Thought, or, the Glass-Window and Bog-House Miscellany* (1731); *The Gnomes of Zeeland* by Rex Hout; Quevedo's *Pintura de la mujer de un abogado, abogado ella del demonio* (1608); Tertullian's *De cultu feminarum;* St. Augustine's *Soliloquies;* Wedekind's *Death and the Devil;* The Ascetic Works of St. Basil.

Andrew the Chaplain's *De reprobatione amoris;* the fragment, *Interludium de clerico et puella;* W. C. Brann's *Woman as Hypnotist;* The *Epistulae* of Pope Pius II; Esther Vilar's *The Manipulated Man;* Schopenhauer's *Parerga und Paralipomena* (1851); Sherlock Holmes's *Practical Handbook of Bee Culture, With Some Observations Upon the Segregation of the Queen* (privately printed, Sussex Downs, 1912); Oliver Brachfeld's *Die Furcht vor der Frau* (1928); Pierre du Moulin's *Anatomie de la messe* (1624); *The Ribald Rib;* the fourteenth-century "Pucelle Venimeuse"; *How to Tell Your Mother from a Wolf* by Roland X. Trueheaxe; *Talmudic She-Things;* George Shorb's *Mental Nuts to Crack; The Deceyte of Women* (1490); The Works of Alexander Neckham; Calderon's "El Mágico prodigioso"; Thomas Dekker's *The Raven's Almanac;* "La Légende des eaux sans fond" by A Gynakophobe; Max Beerbohm's *The Pervasion of Rouge;* Psellus's *De operatione daemonum;* the tracts of *La Société des Ré-Théurigistes Optimates;* The Bannatyne Ms.; N. M. Penzer's *Poison-Damsels;* John of Salisbury's "Frivolities of Courtiers and Footprints of Philosophers" from the twelfth-century *Policraticus; The Agenbite of Inwit* (ca. 1340); Noel Coward's *The Kindness of Mrs. Radcliffe;* Xenophon's *Memorabilia* and *Oeconomicus;* Ovid's *Remedies of Love;* St. Paul's Epistles; Sir Richard Burton's *Abeokuta and the Cameroons;* Gregory of Nyssa's "On the Making of Man" (*Nicene Fathers,* Sermon 2, V); *De nugis curialium* (1200) by Walter Map; Adrian Beverland's *A Discovery of Three Imposters, Turd-sellers, Slanderers, and Piss-sellers* (1709).

Bernard de Moraix's *De contemptu mundi;* the Sermons of Bishop Golias; Sigmund Freud's *Das Medusenhaupt;* the monkish chronicle *Gesta romanorum;* "Das nervöse Weib" by Albert Moll; William H. Smyth's *Did Man and Woman Descend from Different Animals?* (1927); the *Etymologiae* of Isidore of Seville; *The Jilts: or, Female Fortune Hunters* (1756); Somerset Maugham's *The Moon and Sixpence;* "I Shall Teach Thee Terrible Things" by William Hallgarth; the Pseudo-Cyprian's *De disciplina et bono pudicitiae;* H. X. Route's *The Cliteroid Ladies; The Chinese Book of Odes;* "Alice, An Adultery" by Alistair Crowley; Djuna Barnes's *The Book of Repulsive Women;* The Opera of Pietro Aretino; *Secretum secretorum: The*

Letters of Aristotle to Alexander the Great; I Own a Vagina Dentata by L. A. Burton; Arthur Schopenhauer's *Aphorismer zur Lebensweisheit; The Harlot's Ledger* by Kshemendra; Rev. Cotton Mather's *Memorable Providences;* Edward De Vere, Earl of Oxford's "Fair Fools"; Frederick Rolfe (Baron Corvo), *Women of a Woman Hater;* Wolfgang Lederer's *The Fear of Women; An Almond for a Parrat* by Thomas Nashe; The Works of Cillactor; M. Titfist's *White and Pink Tyranny;* "Handlyng Synne" (1303) by Robert of Brunne; Erasmus's *Senatulus;* Hugh Walpole's *The Old Ladies;* the Songs of the Carmina Burana; Thorstein Veblen's *The Place of Women and Pets in the Economic System;* Thomas O'Brien's, *The Tarts of Medford.*

Grimmelshausen's *Die Landstörzerin Courasche* (1670); Saki's "The Sex That Doesn't Shop"; Crashaw, *On Marriage;* The Decretals of Pope Soter (175–179 A.D.); Arabella Kenneally's *Feminism and Sex Extinction* (1920); Platina's *Fire Is Not Sated with Wood;* the Gaelic poem "An Fear Brónach d'éis a Phosda; *Die Schlüsselgewalt der Hausfrau* (Diss. zur Erlangung der Doctorwürde, Jena); Wallace Rayburn's *The Inferior Sex; Fiancées Financed* by Lex and Xoe Heartrue, Ph.D.s; E. Belfort Bax's *The Fraud of Feminism;* The Works of Simonides; John Milton's *The Doctrine and Discipline of Divorce;* Hans Christian Andersen's "The Swineherd"; Dr. Jacobus X's *Célibat et célibataires;* Mahieu le Bigame's *Lamentations;* Baudelaire's "Mon Coeur Mis A Nu"; *The Chastisement of Mansour* by Hector France; Thomas Middleton's *Blurt, Master Constable;* Fra Domenico Cavalca's *Specchio de peccati* (1340).

Boccaccio's *Corbaccio;* the Marquis de Sade's *Oxtiern, ou les malheurs de libertinage; The Withered Punk* by Joseph Addison; Νοῦσος Θήλεια; Tertullian's "On the Veiling of Virgins"; John Lydgate's "Bycorne and Chichevache"; Montherlant's *Sur les femmes;* the Jewish apocryphal *Testament of the Twelve Patriarchs;* Durtal's History of the Maréchal Gilles de Rais; John Knox's *The First Blast of the Trumpet Against the Monstrous Regiment of Women* (1558); Henry Howard, Earl of Surrey's "The Frailtie and Hurtfulnes of Beautie" (1535); Jacques Le Clercq's *The Case of Aristide de Saint Hemme;* Pere Torrellas's "Coplas de las Calidades de las Donnas" (1458); Aristotle's *Master Piece;* William Acton's *The Functions and Disorders of the Reproductive Organs;* the sixteenth-century sermon, "Slovo Zlykh Zhenach"; Alistair Crowley's *Confessions;* Martino

Schurigio's *Muliebra Historico-Medica;* Odo of Cluny's *Collations;* K. Dalton's *Menstruation and Crime.*

Antoine de la Sale's *Les Quinze Joyes de mariage;* Sâr Peladen's *How to Become a Fairy;* the Works of Gazeus; Ronald Firbank's *The Wavering Disciple;* The Poems of Sir Edward Sherburne; Franco Sacchetti's *Il Trecento Novelle;* Max Funke's *Are Women Human?;* *Der Misogyne, oder Der Feind des weiblichen Geschlechts* by Gotthold Lessing; William Blake's "My Spectre"; *The Koran;* E. J. Dingwall's *The American Woman;* The Monographs of the Pseudo-Clementine; The Cluniac Manifestos; A. Audollent's *Defixionum Tabellae* (1904); Strato's "Musa Puerilis"; C. L. Moore's *Shambleau; The Alexicacon* (1668); Li Yü's *J'ou Pou Tuan* (1705); *Livre des manières* by Henry II's Chaplain; *The Most Delectable Nights of Straparola* ("Piacevolissime Notte"); *Shponka's Dream* by Nikolai Gogol.

Ercole Tasso's *Of Mariage and Wiving;* The Analects of Confucius; John Bremer's *Asexualization;* Hugh of St. Victor's *De bestiis et aliis rebus;* Rev. R. Polwhele's *The Unsex'd Females* (1798); *Solomon's Proverbs;* the sixth-century poem, "Bandiúc Dubh"; *The Neurotic Choice of Mate* by L. Eidelberg; Orientus, the Bishop of Auch's *Monitoria;* Samuel Rowland's "Tis Merrie When Gossips Meete" (1602); Richard Steele's *Spectator* ⚡510; P. J. Möbius's *Ausgewählte werke;* Pierre Christophe Cardinal Théroux-d'Arconville's *The Shakeing of the Sheets* (1574); John Skelton's "The Tunnyng of Elynour Rummying"; Sir Comyn Berkely's *Ten Teachers;* Joseph Swetnam's *The Arraignment of Lewde, Idle, Froward, and Unconstant Women* (1615); St. John Chrysostom's "Homily 26 on I Corinthians," "Homily 15 Concerning the Statutes," and "An Exhortation to Theodore After His Fall" (*Nicene Fathers*, 2, v); Robert Herrick's *Waste;* Bruno's *De gli eroici furori* (1585); Martial d'Auvergne's *Arrests d'Amour;* J. P. Jacobsen's *Marie Grubbe* (1876); August Strindberg's *En häxa* (1890); Alexander Pushkin's *Gavriliada.*

John Cordy Jeaffreson's *A Woman in Spite of Herself* (1872); The Fairy Tales of Fouqué; Paracelsus's *Werke;* Mach's "Anti-Metaphysical Remarks"; George Chapman's *Bussy d'Ambois* (1607); Lorenzo Veniero's *La Puttana errante; Tom Tyler and His Wife;* St. Clement of Rome's "Two Epistles Concerning Virginity"; John Mar-ston's *The Insatiate Countess;* a chaplet of Weddirburne's "My Love Was False and Full of Flattery"; John Heywood's *A Merry Play Between Johan Johan, the Husband, Tyb, his Wife, and Sir Johan, the Priest* (1533); Richard de Bury's *Philobiblion;* Quevedo's *Mujer puntiaguda con enaguas* (1608); Otto Weininger's *Geschlecht und Charakter* (1903); Jean de Meung's *Roman de la Rose* (ca. 1300); Andrew Peto's "The Demonic Mother Imago in the Jewish Religion"; Stobaeus's *Florilegium; He?* by Guy De Maupassant; Richard Baxter's *A Just and Seasonable Reprehension of Naked Breasts and Shoulders* (1675).

Jacopo Passavanti's "The Mirror of True Penance"; *The Precepts of Alfred;* Henry of Saxony's *De secretis mulierum;* Sir Philip Sidney's "Fifth Song"; Aristophanes's *Thesmophoriazusae;* Dr. John Gregory's *A Father's Legacy to His Daughters* (1774); Alberti's *Satires;* The Contagious Diseases Act of 1869; Ouida's *Held in Bondage;* Anton Chekhov's *The Grasshopper; The Female Parson, or Beau in the Sudds* (1730); Machiavelli's *Clizia;* The Works of Nicolas Edme Rétif de la Bretonne; Tolstoy's *The Kreutzer Sonata;* Alexander Pope's *Epistle to a Lady;* Pietro Aretino's *I Ragionamenti;* Villiers de L'Isle-Adam's *The Unknown Woman;* S. Purchas's *Microcosmus* (1619); "Sadism in Women" by R. Allendy; The Complete Works of Guibert of Nogent; Jorge Luis Borges' *The Intruder; De ventre inspiciendo, or, Of the Right to Determine the Pregnancy of Widows;* Roald Dahl's *Someone Like You.*

Peter Abelard's *The Story of My Misfortunes;* Waverly Root's "Women Are Intellectually Inferior"; *Erin Catharine: A Pornographic Novel* by the Duke of Promesse; Edward Gosynhill's *The Schole House of Women* (1541); Gustav Theodor Fechner's *Nanna;* Ned Ward's *Female Policy Detected* (1716); Rudyard Kipling's "The Female of the Species"; Boussuet's *Elévations sur les mystères; Politeuphia* (1597); Gratien Dupont's "Controversy between the Masculine and Feminine Sex" (1534); John Donne's *Juvenilia;* Géza Roheim's "Psychoanalysis of Primitive Cultural Types"; P. M. Kaberry's *Aboriginal Women Sacred and Profane;* Heinrich von Kleist's *Kätchen von Heilbronn; The Happy Ascetic* (1693) by Anthony Horneck; *A Satyr Against Wooing* (1698); Jonathan Swift's "The Furniture of a Woman's Mind"; Diogenes Laertius's *Life of Thales Milesius;* Charles Bansley's *Treatyse Shewing and Declaring the*

Pryde and Abuse of Women Now a Dayes; Say It with Oil by Ring Lardner; Robert W. Service's *The Ballad of the Brand*.

St. Jerome's "Against Helvidius"; *Reliquiae antiquae;* Theophrastus's *On the Disadvantage of Marriage;* Edmund Goncourt's *La Fille;* Ludovico Sinistrari's *De la démonalité et des animaux incubes et succubes* (1688); Sir Thomas Overbury's "A Very, Very Woman"; *Golias de conjuge non ducenda;* Everard Guilpin's *Skialethia* (1598); *The Rabbinical Origin of Women* by Thomas Moore; William Dunbar's "The Tretis of the Tua Mariit Wemen and the Wedo"; Pierre de l'Ancre's *Le Livre des princes* and *L'Incrédulité et mescreance du sortilège* (1622); David Lindsay's *A Voyage to Arcturus;* Thomas Cooke's *Love and Revenge, or the Vintner Outwitted* (1729); the Works of Wilma Meikle; A. Memmi's *L'Homme dominie;* the medieval ms. "Fraus, Fraude"; Crowne's *Sir Courtly Nice* (1685); Joannes Henricus Pott's *Specimen juridicum de nefando lamiarum cum diabolo coitu* (1689).

Cyril Tourneur's *The Revenger's Tragedy; The Inevitability of Patriarchy* by Steven Goldberg; Friedrich Nietzsche's *Beyond Good and Evil;* The Works of the Honorable Henry Cavendish; Philippe von Hartmann's *Philosophie der ein Bewusten;* "Cackle of the Confined Women" (1663); Dr. Abel Crucifer's *Christianity and the Ages Which It Darkened**; Hipponax's *On the Things We Must Pass Over in Silence;* Wieth-Knudsen's *Feminism; Juris canonici compendium;* Tippu, the Sultan of Mysore's "Letters to Burohau-Ud-Din"; Robert Burton's *The Anatomy of Melancholy;* Jacques Loubert's *La Femme devant la science; Anti-Suffrage Essays by Massachusetts Women* by Ernest Bernbaum; the Albanian epic, *Dukeshë e Zezë;* H. T. Finck's *Romantic Love and Personal Beauty; Patrologiae Cursus Completus;* Compton Mackenzie's *Extraordinary Women;* St. Jerome's *Book Against Jovinian; The Masque of Queen Bersabe;* the Holy Bible; Horace Walpole's *The Mysterious Mother; Grausame Frauen* by Leopold von Sacher-Masoch.

Algernon Swinburne's "The Triumph of Time"; J. J. Bachofen's *Das Mutterrecht; The Book of a Thousand and One Nights;* The Works of André Tiraqueau; Clement of Alexandria's *Paedagogus;*

---

* Darconville lifted down this volume and, as he did so, a sheet of paper fluttered out of it—one he quickly saw was covered with a curious language. Unobserved, he put it in his pocket.

Coventry Patmore's *Religio Poetae; The Women Who Bark* by A Cynophobe; Le Solitaire's *La Femme ne doit pas travailler;* Wester-marck's *History of Human Marriage;* Nathaniel Ward's *The Simple Cobbler of Aggawam* (1647); *The Dutch Courtezan* by John Mar-ston; Tuteur and Glatzes's "Murdering Mothers"; E. Jacobson's *The Wish for a Child in Boys;* E. J. Dingwall's *The American Woman;* Thomas Campion's *The Third and Fourth Book of Ayres; Les Prières des Picards;* The Works of Andreas Salernitanus; *Hieroglyphic Tales* by Horace Walpole; *Modern Woman: The Lost Sex* by Lundberg and Farnham; *Women Beware Women* by Thomas Middleton; Hans Magnus Enzensberger's "Misogynie."

Apollinaire's *The Debauched Hospodar;* F. Lee Utley's *The Crooked Rib;* The Lyrics of Archilochus; Gelett Burgess's *The Maxims of Noah* and *The Maxims of Methuselah; The School for Reform* by Thomas Morton; Gascoigne's *The Steele Glas* (1576); Dr. Magnus Hirschfield's *Welt als Wille und Vorstellung* and *Geschlechtskunde; Reveries of a Bachelor* by Ik. Marvel; François Villon's "La Belle Heaulmière aux filles de joie"; Karen Horney's *The Dread of Women; Sex Antagonism* by Walter Heape; *The Difference Between a Man and a Woman* by Theodore Lang; Lord Berners's *Six Require-ments for a Happy Marriage;* Théodore Joran's *La Trouvée Féministe;* John Webster's *The White Devvil; The Chinese Book of Odes;* J. D. Unwin's *Sex and Culture;* Thomas Gisbourne's *An Enquiry into the Duties of the Female Sex* (1797); Walter Besant's *The Revolt of Man;* H. Fuseli's *Aphorisms; Religio Medici* by Thomas Browne; Correa M. Walsh's *Feminism;* John Betjeman's *An Oxford University Chest;* Dr. Heilborn's *The Opposite Sexes;* James Corin's *Mating, Marriage, and the Status of Women;* P. J. Proud-hon's *La Pornocratie, ou Les Femmes.*

Philip Wylie's *A Generation of Vipers;* John Lyly's *Euphues, the Anatomy of Wit;* Tertullian's *On Monogamy* and *On Pudicity; Why She Wouldn't Marry* (1948) by C. Linda; Thomas Otway's *The Orphan;* Rudyard Kipling's *Mary Postgate; The Enemies of Women* by Vicente Ibañez; "Men and Women Speak Different Languages" by Col. Thomas Stott; George Farquhar's *Sir Harry Wildair* (1701); *L'Homme-femme* by Alexandre Dumas, fils; Theodor Reik's *The Cre-ation of Women; The Fundamental Error of Woman Suffrage* by William Parker; Euripides's *Hippolytus;* L. Ron Hubbard's *Dianet-ics;* William Blake's "How Sweet I Roam'd"; *The Female Offender* by Prof. Caesar Lombroso; Ford Madox Ford's *No More Parades; The Fear of Being a Woman* by Joseph Rheingold; Dr. Fritz's *Wittels die sexuelle Not; The Seven Sages of Rome;* Karl Krause's *Werke* (14 vols.); Remy de Gourmont's *L'Histoire tragique de la princesse Phénissa.*

Thomas Dekker's *The Batchelars Banquet* (1603); Stephen Gosson's *Quippes for Upstart Newfangled Gentlemen* (1595); The Works of Barbey d'Aurevilly; W. S. Gilbert's *Gentle Alice Brown;* Heinrich Schurtz's *Urgeschichte der Kultur;* William Shakespeare's *King Lear;* Paul Theroux's *Girls at Play; Life with Women and How to Survive It* by Joseph Peck, M.D.; Pierre Janet's *L'Automatisme psychologique;* William Prynne's *The Unlovelinesse of Love-Lockes* (1628); Ben Jonson's "Epigram on the Court Pucell"; Benjamin Constant's *Adolphe;* Plato's *Apology;* Oskar Vogt's *Altindische Dichtung und Weisheit;* John Fletcher's *Monsieur Thomas* (1639); Alexis, the Attic Comedian's "On the Numerous Beauty Aids Used to Fit Young Ladies Out as Shiny Snakes"; *Rumplestiltskin;* The Complete Strindberg; Massinger's *The Duke of Milan;* Anonymous, *The Praise and Dispraise of Women;* John Fowles's *The French Lieutenant's Woman;* Ulrich Molitor's *De lamiis et phitonicis muliebribus* (1489); J. S. Redfield's *Modern Women and What Is Said of Them;* Aeschylus's *Eumenides;* T. X. Hoeur's *Die schwarze Herzogin;* Thomas Otway's *The Orphan;* The Works of the Knight of La Tour Landry; the *Topica Legalia* of Claude Chansonnette.

Augustus Wolff's *Die Frauenfeindleichen Literatur; Some of the Reasons Against Women's Suffrage* by Francis Parkman; James McGrigor Allan's "On the Real Differences in the Minds of Men and Women" (1869) and *The Intellectual Severance of Men and Women;* T. W. H. Crosland's *Lovely Woman* (1903); The Works of Chrysippus; Charles Reade's *The Woman-Hater; On Wives and Wiving* by Alexander Nicchols; George Gilder's *Sexual Suicide; A Briefe Anatomie of Women* (1653); "Viraginity and Effemination" by James Weir, Jr., M.D.; Edward Young's *The Universal Passion* (1725); Adnil Notrub's *The Kept Woman Who Didn't Keep Long;* Montherlant's *Les Jeunes Filles;* Aristotle's *Generation of Animals;* Douglas Jerrold's *Mrs. Caudle's Curtain Lectures;* Washington Irving's *Rip Van Winkle;* The Works of Nevisanus; Sigmund Freud's *Civilization and Its Discontents.*

P. J. Möbius's "L'Inferiorità mentala della donna"; *Wolf Solent* by

John Cowper Powys; The Works of Jean Weir; James Thurber's *Men, Women, and Dogs;* The Works of Procopius; John Donne's "Loves Alchymie"; Tolstoy's *Father Sergius;* Thomas Middleton's *Micro-Cynicon* (1599); Aristophanes's *Ecclesiazusae; Her Royal Highness Woman* by Max O'Rell; P. J. Proudhon's *Amour et Mariage;* G. J. Romanes's *Mental Differences Between Men and Women;* The Works of St. Bonaventure; *Matrimony: A Novel Containing a Series of Interesting Adventures* by John Shebbeare; Ben Jonson's *Epicoene, or The Silent Woman* (1609); Alistair Crowley's *White Stains; The Corridors of Time* by Poul Anderson; A. Conan Doyle's *John Barrington Cowles;* Ernest Dowson's *The Pierrot of the Minute;* Richard Sibbes's *Bowels Opened* (1641). Francis Bacon's "On Marriage and the Single Life."

St. Bernardino of Siena's *Prediche Volgari;* Darwin's *The Descent of Man;* The Poems of William Cartwright; *On Sleeping with Women* by Roger Lawson; *The Epic of Gilgamesh; The Embattled Male in the Garden, or Why Women Are Queer in the Country* by Dwight Farnham; G. E. Moore's *Celibates;* Philipp Mainländer's *Philosophie der Erlösing* (1876); the thirteenth-century *Coutumes du Beauvoisis;* Bronislaw Malinowski's *Sexual Life Among the Melanesians;* Semonides Amorgos's *Elegy and Iambus;* Axel, Thane O'Droxeur's *Love and Hate;* Francesco Barbaro's *De re uxoria;* The Works of Paraeus; August Strindberg's *Giftas;* the Tomes of La Croix; *De legibus connubialibus;* Les Opères de Cretin; the Doulaq Papyrus of 1400 B.C.; The Works of Palladis of Alexandria; *Miroir de Mariage* by Eustace Deschamps; the *Speculum* of Vincent de Beauvois.

Bram Stoker's *The Squaw;* The Works of St. Louis; *The Sullens Sisters* by A. E. Coppard; *Feminine Frailty* by Horace Wyndham; *Smith* by W. Somerset Maugham; *The Widow That Keeps the Cock Inn;* John Wilkes's *An Essay on Women* (1763); the *Divinae Institutiones* of Lactantius (c. A.D. 250–c.317); Johannes Adelphus Muling's *Margarita Facetiarum;* Henri Brieux's *Damaged Goods; Manon Lescaut* by L'Abbé Prévost; *The Samayamatrika* of Kashmiri Kshmendra; François-Charles-Nicholas Racot de Grandval's *Agathe, ou les deux biscuits;* William King's *The Toast* (1732); Gilbert and Sullivan's *The Sod's Opera* (ms. only); *Portrait of Crispa* by Ausonius (4th c. A.D.); Robert Frost's *A Masque of Reason; The Orestautocleides* of Timocles; Prosper Mérimée's *La Vénus d'Ille; The Whore's Rhetorick* (1683) by Ferrante Pallavicino; the Works of

Asopodorus of Phlius; *Songs Compleat, Pleasant, and Divertive* (1719) by Mr. D'Urfey; Francisco Gomez de Quevedo's *From One Horned Man to Another;* Alberto Moravia's *Bitter Honeymoon and Other Stories;* the works of Simonides; Henry James's *Longstaff's Marriage* and *The Story of a Masterpiece; Kara Düşes* by A Turk; *The Eroticon* of Paul the Silentiary.

LXIX

Biography of a Eunuch

And Jehu lifted up his face to the window, and said, "Who is on my side? Who?"

—II Kings 9:32

"I AM A SPADO. I am gibbed. I am only a part of myself, a maenad, a gelding. I live without heat or light," continued Dr. Crucifer, shutting the library door. "I am to the animal kingdom what good celery is to the vegetable, white and succulent. I have vowed myself to chastity, like the Jesuits or the Samurai. I don't speak to women, look them in the face, eat with, shake hands, or tolerate. I prefer ducats to daughters. I am like a Bosch painting: my secret is told in a single spot at the bottom. Will you look?" he asked, his fat white tongue, with its fissures and hypertrophied papillae, protruding and withdrawing into his open mouth. "I have no vagina. I have no penis. *Auf der Gräntze,*" he smirked, munching the German, *"liegen immer die seltsamsten Geschöpfe, nein?* But does that shock you?" There followed a whining involuntary sound under his chewing, a weird noise like that of a spring peeper or pinkletink whose flatulence vibrates its wiry tail, and with hands fluttering madly at his throat, he cacked in exaltation, "I am a eunuch!"

Darconville had been prepared for anything up in those rooms, and no outrage, he felt, couldn't have been perpetrated there, no excess lessened, no profanity unexplored. But this he couldn't quite believe.

The library was elegant. At the center of one wall hung an original Palma Vecchio. There was one stained-glass window, and a woodcut in a wall space showed a Maori carving of the Great Daughter of Night, eating her son. The rest of the room was taken over by long oak shelves filled with books on all sides that went right to the ceiling, and a wooden ladder attached to runners on the top could be slid on bearings right around to reach specific heights. The one small table between two leather chairs held a large fishbowl, filled with tiny, eerie transparent things moving in rounds of weak-finned and aimless nosing of the dirty glass.

"Blind cave tetras," said Crucifer, meticulously seeing to them with pinchfuls of tetron squidflakes. "I prefer them to houseplants—the queers of nature, don't you agree?" He hissed in laughter. "That *is* what they say I am, all the little worms and protists out there, don't they, a homosexual? A tiptoe? *Un entrouducuter?* A dash of lavender?" He rolled open the diamond-paned window and peered with disgust into the darkness outside. "No, I am not queer, my dear Darconville, although I do hail from the sotadic zone—you know, Mediterra, North Africa, the Middle East, that area. But I do not collect ephebai or cabana boys, neither do I engage in what Lord Alfred Douglas referred to as 'the familiarities.' Lampblack?" asked Crucifer, yanking a bell-pull by the curtain. "He is my servant, for pay. I kick him, and he does my bidding," he smiled cruelly, "to show that what he knew, he knows. No," he added, "I am an anorchid, an autotome, an androcrat. Pedicating is not my line. *Je marche à la voile et à la vapeur.*" He pulled shut the window and meditatively drew a finger down the mullion-panes of armorial glass. "I am indifferent to both sexes, for to love man is possibly to love women by sentimental transfer. The essential trouble with sex, you see, is that it brings one close to people. And I personally find people irritating."

Dr. Crucifer sprinkled in some more fishfood.

"The asexual male, of course, is the original sex. Adam and Eve had first been created sexless, according to Gregory of Nyssa, and the phrase 'male and female created He them,' I believe, referred to a subsequent act necessitated by Eve's disobedience," explained Crucifer, his eyes narrowing into pouches of flesh and making him look like an elderly cretin. "Had not that taken place the human race might have been propagated, I don't doubt, by some harmless mode of vegetation—and far more happily. Sex? I am not empressed. After a meal, tell me, who remembers the spoon?" He raised his little arms questioningly. "But here, how do you find Harvard?"

"I must be careful with my answer," said Darconville, "mustn't I? After all, it was you who brought me here."

" 'O world, world, world!' " mocked Crucifer, holding his hand across his face—a gesture without which he never laughed—" 'thus is the poor agent despised!' "

"You're mad," said Darconville.

"That's a bit hearty, isn't it?"

"I'm sorry, I can't help you."

"I can save you."

"From what?"

"From a wasted life, from misery, from error. Try those." He moved closer. "The subjugation of the Amazons was one of the labors of Hercules. Why it should have become one of yours I can't pretend to fathom," said Crucifer. "I heard you were living down South, teaching a school of ribbon-wearing slawbunks their grammar—the local mechanical college of Laputa, I gather."

"And at Harvard, what had you in mind for me?"

Dr. Crucifer slapped his moist palms together. "In all the books of etiquette I have read," he said, "it is explained that the tactful host does not map out the day too precisely for his guest in advance. Please, there will be time for everything, *insh'allah bukra mumkin.*" He paused. "I must tell you right off, however, I have one weakness: I am a kalokaitaphe—I admire the upper ten, the bonton, the real elite, see? You are royalty. I wish only to serve you."

"Not if I know it."

There was no motion in the strange creature's face: neither hurt, nor surprise. "My heart is as cold as the northside of a gravestone," continued Crucifer, running a finger horizontally along a row of books, and he selected one. "But for you—?"

Bowing, he handed it to Darconville, who turned past the bookplate (a dike-faced Aphrodite thumbing a snub-nose at a crouched aspirant to her favors) and read on the frisket-printed title page of the sixteenth-century folio in sixes the name in black letter he knew: Pierre Christophe Cardinal Théroux-d'Arconville.

"You honor me in bearing the name you see there. It wasn't his Church won me. I am part of his point of view, that's all. But here, the eggs are teaching the hen! Have you no ancestral memory? I would have him you and seeing you revise a world that killed what once I might have been."

"And that was?"

He looked meaningfully at Darconville for a few seconds.

"A saint."

It was as if that had been the most obvious answer in the world. Again, petulantly, he yanked the bell-pull and looked toward the door. And then, insinuating himself into a chair, Dr. Crucifer lolled back like an Eastern pasha, and as his low slouching stomach ran into his lap out slorbed three balconies of flesh over which, as he closed his eyes, he porrected his fingers and, so satisfied, began.

"The village of Girga lies at a bend on the Nile. I was born there one tedious and diaphoretic afternoon too long ago—the inauspicious child *d'un autre lit*—and directly given over by my father, a famous actor at the Khedivial Opera House who wouldn't publicly acknowledge me, to his brother for an undisclosed sum of money. I never saw him again. My mother was buried alive: the local penalty for adultery. Good day, goodbye. So much for gaps in pedigree," said Dr. Crucifer, his eyes remaining shut. He was talking. He was listening. "Understand, right away, we were not Mohammedans but Christians. I am a Nasrani, of Lower Egyptian Copts, the most civilized people on earth—with the exceptions just named—and the direct descendants of the ancient Egyptians. The rancor which we have so long cherished has generally embittered our character while the persecutions of the Mohammedan and the Byzantine Supremacy have taught us to be at one time cringing and at another arrogant and overbearing.

"We're both acid and alkaline." He humped his back to smirk

behind his hand. "I can fart rainbows—but would just as happily give a scalding-hot penny to an organ grinder's monkey or stub out my black cigar on the forehead of a street urchin. I can both howl out a rat's hole or cower like a priest." He tried to smile. "The power's in my tits."

Then his eyes went cold.

"My vicious uncle, a Copt whose hereditary aptitude for mathematics manifested itself in his personally counting out my barley, had a wife—dear aunt, dear stepmother—whose cruelty could take the polish out of a mirror. It was an acquaintanceship at best that had nothing but the sterility of mutually exclusive interests. I remember them for very little, her for the vanity of ever having to punctuate her face with rouge, him for beating her for it and forever screeching, '*Sitt al-ṣawad! Sitt al-ṣawad!*' And so into this marriage, wherein they perhaps still founder as I speak this sentence, was I dragged—a mere child. Mere," he breathed. "What else is a child? In any case, heaven, as they put it, having denied them offspring of their own, they fell against me with an unnatural virulence. I remember the Caramanian *fallāh* habitually brought in to bathe me often looking at my genitals and muttering, 'How ugly, how ugly!'" He shook his head. "Darconville, we are ruled by hags from birth: nurses, mothers, teachers. 'Behave, you little phalloggle, or you'll get no love from me!' 'Buy me a hoop, runt, to put in my ears, and I'll promise you anything!' Our almae matres, my friend? A figment. Life comes at us in her creaking shoes, with a cruel birch hidden in the folds of her skirt." Darconville looked at Crucifer's hands. They were knotted.

"This family, in any event, showed little interest in my doings, *exceptis excipiendis*—for it wasn't long before I started to wet the bed. What a disgusting crime, don't you agree? Oh, evil! It was a case of eternal recurrence: I was the more incontinent the more they screamed which caused it in the first place. I couldn't stop. Volition? It had nothing to do with it. I soon saw it was impossible to avoid committing a sin—that, in fact, sin *happened* to you without your wanting to commit it, without knowing you committed it, and whether you were contrite in committing it or not had small bearing on the fact. I thought I could forget about it. But I was wrong. I had reckoned without any idea of the commercialization of Lethe water. I had reckoned without acknowledging the array of goats which, in every letter and article and speech, butted into my life during that terrible period of sheepish ignorance. That was not all. I felt it was my fault I had lost my parents and could not choose but weep to have back that which, still hoping for, I always feared again to lose," he said with trembling voice, "but they never came back, they never came back, they never came back, they never came back to me." He looked across at Darconville, his face sick with memory. "I came to see I was guilty of not resisting illegitimacies, guilty of possessing a will bereft of the usual resources by which it can justify itself, guilty of not having done anything wrong. I was guilty of innocence.

"Briefly, I loved, wasn't loved in return, and so was shunted off again—this time to be raised in a burnt-brick convent outside the village under the Arabian mountains. It was a Roman Catholic holding, the oldest but one in Egypt, for let it be parenthesized here that we had been converted in those parts by Franciscan missionaries at the end of the seventeenth century.

"It was the custom of the monks, now, to take in wayward boys—yes, there were others, most born o.w. and unwanted, some insane, all with the grave disposition of the pharaohs. There were specimens of every kind of child, fellahin, captive Dervishes, Dinkas and Shilluks, Cushites, Abbasides, Bisharin, Ruwenzori dwarves, nilotics and niggers of a thousand tints. I wanted to be the flower of the playground, O Darconville, the glory of the palaestra! What didn't I dream, love, hope for! I took readily to certain subjects and acquired a precocious proficiency in languages, ponying for others and able to do Greek Unseen better than the form-master himself. I could have done my Collections, Determining in Lent, and proceeded to the Great Go at Oxford at fourteen years old, there's my hand on it, there is my hand. But the extreme of joy is the beginning of sorrow, isn't it? And Arcadia"—he looked away—"is brief." He closed his eyes for a minute. "Brief.

"My chief delight as a boy, however, was to go down to the west bank to watch the tourist-steamers pull in or to run around in the ancient rock-tombs which once belonged to the high-priest of This." A smile disinterred from the stern grave of Crucifer's face. "Not That." He took his hand down from his mouth. "Even then I was struck by the fact that Egyptian art hardly ever essayed to represent a woman, save with her legs pressed together as in a sheath. I particularly remember one time running back from a day rummaging over the walls of those tombs, meeting a monk, and asking him right then and there about the mysteries of generation—sex. He sat down and answered my question; it seemed to pique his interest. His reply, I shall never forget, involved the most revolting and disgusting tale I'd ever heard." Crucifer looked up, his eyes like caves.

"What," asked Darconville, almost surprised at the croaking sound of his own voice, "what did he tell you?"

"The truth."

Dr. Crucifer hissed. It was his way of smiling. It was his way of saying yes. It was his way of saying *see?*

"I wasn't a featous boy. I was a fat boy. Disciples not elephantine can't know the pain of it. They used to call me 'Bum Cheeks' in school, spill my bowls of milk, whip me across the legs with their *nâbuts*. They made up rude songs about me and pilfered from my tuckbox. They would thieve my rusks. They drew saucy pictures of me and chevied me out of my battels and conduct money and ridiculed me about my size and left me behind when they went tubbing or playing at bats, taws, or ducking-stones. They threw balls of camel dung at me in games of kherubgeh. To take me seriously became for others a form of insanity. The genius at school—not a gasconade, Darconville, I was —is usually a disappointing and often ignored figure, for as a rule one must be commonplace to be a successful boy. In that preposterous world, however, to be remarkable was not to be overlooked. The barber, as they say, learns to shave on the orphan's face. And although I cried out to them the pitiful error they were making, I saw with horror I'd become the visual quotation of the bad dreams I feared and so felt I was being treated as the vile scoundrel whom I represented deserved to be!

"For Christ's sake," he hooted through the library, "I only wanted an excuse in the eyes of the world for *existing!* I was a weakling, a trembling mouse of a boy with dirty hands and eyespots and yet growing in me was this readiness to substitute the hand of God for any whim of my persecutors. I gorged myself with sticky sweets. My schoolmates, broadcasting it, avoided touching the books I'd been using and spat upon my very shadow. Fat? Awkward? *Seine Figur lacht ihn aus?* That kind of thing, exactly. I escaped a good deal of painful attention, I confess, by the periodic *aegrotat* of the school physician, but then I was always released, wasn't I? And, always, there they were waiting for me. They put me in the middle of circles and pulled down my pants—I was so frightened I could have killed them

—and taunted me with archabominational threats and heaped up such obscenities upon this subhuman body you see here, even then as white and plump as that of some fat woodboring larva, that in that dreadful macédoine at the heart of all adolescent confusion I found I myself came to *agree* with them! But did I complain? Would I run to the Prior to weep, to peach, to accuse? I did not, I would not. My altruism, inversely proportionate to my low esteem of myself, knew no bounds.

"It had come to this pass, you see, that I began to love my neighbor *more* than myself. Now what theology, may I ask, supports that, what paradosis, what transmission of spirit? *To love your neighbor more than yourself? Can you understand? I saw no fault in others that I might not have committed myself and forgave in them for doing what I for causing couldn't absolve in myself!*"

Crucifer's mouth was distended terribly, stretching as if it would separate. The severe grip he had on the arms of the chair gradually loosened then, and he paused for composure.

"I slept in fear, woke in terror, lived in anxiety. I spent every night of my childhood *listening*. Yes, Darconville, all the spiteful, vile, stupid, cruel, vulgar, petty, errant human acts I'd seen from the day I was born taxed me for the explanation I saw I myself simultaneously provided in the question the vanity in my very own mind was asking! I knew it was committing a sin if I continued to think I had sinned, but I thought, at the risk of presumption of course, I could only not despair by failing to think, the which paradoxically preoccupied my every waking hour. A guilty conscience is the mother of invention. So I took another refuge. I became ashamed. I wanted not to be human, to be non-human, to be unhuman! I wanted to repudiate myself to the degree that in that self-repudiation I would necessarily repudiate the very self repudiating me! The you that is seeing yourself, you see, is the you that is seen. But one would be all," he said, leaning back, "and, in that one cannot be, here is loneliness. I'd done nothing actually to be ashamed of—except it made me ashamed to have had to think so. When I tried to become ashamed to be ashamed to be human, I then felt the ultimate shame—and became stationary. And, pray, in all this what age do you suppose this boy to be, Darconville? Name it now before I tell you. Why, twelve or fourteen. Or say eleven. No such thing: *he is not quite nine years old!*"

Dr. Crucifer drew his hands, pausing in a grim clench at the eyes, down his face.

"I craved release from the world—was it from pride or from humility?—and found it. I soon fell under the influence of a Nubian hieromonk named Fâdi, the very same holy man who had once answered my prurient question. (The name is Arabic for empty.) His austere and ruthless intelligence was allied, I noticed even then, to a certain melancholy. Living alone on an eremitic dependency on the river brink, though still on cloistered ground, he was a Christian, as we all were, but with a secret: a subtle dogmatic difference from the orthodoxy of the neighboring monastic community who, in countenancing, ignoring, really, what seemed to them to be the traditional isolation and excesses of the anchorite, bothered never to learn more— unlike me, who did. But I'm ahead of myself. I worried about Fâdi, always. He lived on bean-flour bread, onions and water, and long hesychastic vigils, intervals of prayer he several times a night imposed on himself, despite broken sleep. Fâdi alone understood my sorrow; correctly, he saw that the twentieth-century crisis was the worship of *life;* and one day he revealed to me how all could be overcome— briefly, simply, by the rigors of self-denial which I came to call 'The Naught One Can't Untie.' He told me that the highest spiritual knowledge led to the union of the knower, the known, and knowledge itself. How, I wondered, might that be achieved? 'By privation,' said Fâdi, 'for no spirit can rest until it is naughted of all things that are made.' A mystical commonplace? Perhaps. But with what joy did I receive his words, I who felt in sequent toil all sorrow did contend, I who had long known it was impossible to seize life without violating it, I who held humanity to be so spotted, so tragic a failure. I wanted to be nothing. A circle. A round straight line with a whole in the middle. I wanted to hear the inner sound which perforce kills the outer. I wanted to be eyeless and thouless—to reach *le point vierge:* the inmost center of the soul, the diamond essence, an absolute poverty. The Funklein!

"The existence of a perfect being, you know," said Crucifer, admonishingly tapping the side of his nose with his ring-finger, "is comprised in the idea of it alone. It became for me, somehow, the one universal element in a world of unsatisfying particulars.

"I abrogated humanity, then. I realized that everything human in us is an obstacle in the way of holiness. You turn away, do you? You sneer at me? But are you aware of Ibn Roshd's double truth wherein something may be theologically untrue but philosophically true at the same time? I found proof of my hope, comfort in my decision. Will you hear how? Good. Now, realize here that few nations in the East embraced the Gospel more zealously than the dwellers on the Nile. Accustomed as they had long been to regard life as a pilgrimage to death, as a school of preparation for another world, and weary of their motley and confused pantheon of divinities, whose self-seeking priesthood designedly disguised the truth, they eagerly welcomed the simple doctrines of Christianity. But, like Eutyches, they revered the divine nature of the Savior *only,* in which they held that every human element was absorbed; and when the Council of Chalcedon in 451 sanctioned the doctrine that Christ combined a human with a divine nature, the Egyptians, with their characteristic tenacity, adhered to their old views and formed a sect termed Eutychians, or Monophysites, to which the Copts of the present day still belong. Such a one was Fâdi.

"I learned his Gospel by heart—and *lived* it, emptying myself of values generally identified as worldly. Salacities, during my post-adolescent years, occurred to me. I fought them, violently. I abounded in youthful cupidity of every sort in my mind, and as I imagined my wickedness, wailed over what mentally I wallowed in, I wished I had wilted in my cradle! I was nightly fitted out at my own pious request with an *Onaniebandagen*—a little suit of armor fitted over my genitals and attached as a prophylaxis for masturbation to a locked belt, for the body, as time passed, was the only part of the world, I felt, which my thoughts alone could alter. A virtue cannot be said to exist, they say, until it is expressed in nature, correct? I thought about nothing else: wouldn't the ultimate action, I wondered, lead then to the ultimate virtue? But what *was* ultimate action? Ultimate virtue? Was it wrong to believe that being is not and that non-being must be? That to die out is distinguished? *Absterben ist vornehm!* Between volition and nolition there is a middle thing: non-volition. O, the sweet nothings I whispered in my ears! I desired in the strangest way to elevate myself above human weakness—from jealousy, voluptuousness, even the need for *joy!* I craved to emerge from the illusion and instincts of the universe, a pretense, a mask, I knew, of the secret beyond it. And Fâdi knew it—who, finally urged by the impulse of grace to approximate in me the divinity of his Lord, no longer withheld his final sacramental, and in a cave one night at the age of sixteen, while mor-

phiated with an admixture of yagé, hyascin, and anti-convulsant
sedatives, I willingly submitted to the mutilation of my 'precious.' Annihilation obtained a foothold on a living body in one rapid knife-
slash. The keys to hell dropped off the lock. I lost my stones."

Darconville gasped.

"There, there," responded Dr. Crucifer, wagging a chubby finger at
his guest. "We are pussycats. We are little slubs. We are only people
whose sense of fun has fed on queer food—and not a one of us who
isn't supple as a pair of Italian shoes and harmless as the wing of a
chicken in the pip. We're round and open as wells. I can push my
thumb into myself. You really mustn't wince, my friend."

Struggling up out of his chair, Dr. Crucifer went to the desk for a
cigarette, walking, without free and vigorous use of those long malign
limbs, as if he were being carried along by a balloon. Darconville
waved away the proffered box of them, and Crucifer again sat down.

"Angels are all alike," he said, leering horribly, "but devils are various, huh? Nevertheless, to place the eunuch in a category of real perverts is to share the ignorance of ancient times." He sucked on the cigarette. "Because I 'left the family'—as the Chinese euphemistically
describe my condition—doesn't mean therefore I'm some kind of incomprehensible bonze and consequently emotionless. In how many far
more terrible ways has figurative eunuchry in the sexes ruined the
world! Faugh! The *Kastrationskomplex* has fathered forth more pain
than all the spiders in Christendom, has peopled the very fucking university in which you now sit, has—!" He swallowed smoke in the apo-
plexy of wrath and fought, with swimming arms, for breath. "And *romantic love?*" He spat. "It has been responsible for more human
misery than any other notion on the face of this pocked earth. Anything lower, more obscene, or feculent the manifold heavings of history have not cast up! And that is why in one blow"—he snapped his
fingers in a fillip between his legs—"I have murdered my own posterity!

"I have dared the supreme ordeal!" he cried, grinning through
teeth that looked like a crossword-puzzle. "I despise purposivism! I
have sneaked out of an exit Mother Nature hadn't quite planned on!
I vail my hat to the Third Sex—Essenes, Valesians, Skoptsy, Rappites,
Gynaecomasts, Tribades, Semivirs, Thlibs, Clisti, the Priests of Attis,
and any other participles you wish to name neither split nor dangling!"

The creature seemed too fantastic to believe for Darconville seriously to acknowledge, a puzzle-headed caricature of spite with a large share of scholarship but with little geometry or logic in his head and yet a figure of method and merciless egotism, possessing a sinister genius.

"Proudly, I wear the imperial seal: 'the mounting of the spotted horse.' Tell me, have you ever looked closely at the pontil mark on the bottom of a hand-blown bottle? There! That's the badge of my lost, my crushed cremasters! I am a gold pencil, tipped with lead. And, O, but haven't we been colorful as eringoes? Tricky as thixotrops? Saturn was gelded, Origen became a human abstraction to save his soul, and Xerxes, King of Persia, would never act without the advice of his chief eunuch, Hermotinus. The proud tribe of eunuchs almost single-handedly brought down the Ming emperors of China—my God, I think of the magnificent Li Lien-ying in his dragon robes standing on the foredeck of his barge and addressing under a flying black flag twelve full cohorts of neuters! Farinelli, the famous castrato of the eighteenth century who frequently aroused such enthsuiastic admiration that of him it was often exclaimed 'One God and one Farinelli!' sang four songs to the Spanish King Philip V every night and was given his portrait set in diamonds by Louis XV of France. And Heliogabalus himself so loved his eunuch, Jeroles, that he nightly bowed and kissed his groin, swearing that he was celebrating the sacred festival of Flora." He pulled on the cigarette one last time and ground it out. "On the accession of Pope Leo XIII, in 1878, the practice of castrating small boys for church choirs, alas, came to an end. More's the pity, I suppose. We *can* still be found, however. We're international in a kind of silly secret way and will occasionally sprout up —look closely—in every place from Harvard to Chihli to Ho-chienfu. But the fact is to most of the world we are now obsolete as buggies.

"We've multiplied in palaces, ruthlessly acquired the knowledge of secret councils, and instigated the direst court intrigues, often by having been privy to the foulest secrets of women, which is of course a matter not unrelated to our traditional profession. We are, you understand, authorized in the New Testament—in fact, Pope Siricius (385–398 A.D.) actually advocated self-mutilation. Are you scandalized? And gay old Galen in his book, *Of Sperm,* roundly avers that to possess no heart would be a lesser evil than to be destitute of genitories. I've managed both, you say?" asked Crucifer, his arms bent the wrong way, almost tortue, as he leaned forward with a malicious wink. "Too true. No gimlet to drill, no beatlet to beat." His eyes were now glittering like a basilisk's. "I've always considered it the Devil's greatest feat to have succeeded in getting himself denied.

"Now, I am asexuated. I can neither enter the Crooked Gate of the female nor"—he cacked—"can I Make Fire Behind the Mountain. But, you see, there are those of us—some with kit and no kaboodle, others with kaboodle and no kit—who *can* practice the manifold *plaisirs de la petite oie* (masturbation, irrumation, feuille-de-rose, etc.). Me, I keep a traditional discretion about that which may best be left unsaid. I am docked utterly. I suffered the cut. I am pegless, shaven and shorn—entirely *rasé*. I answer the call of nature with a silver quill I keep in my pocket. But I once knew of a woman who lived near the Crocodile Grotto at Ma'abdeh who had a eunuch for a husband; he'd dry-bob her and at the point of orgasm—this would be a secondary discharge from the urethra—the great bitch'd wisely hold up a little pillow for her husband to bite lest he tear apart her cheeks and breasts with his teeth! When I was a university student in Cairo? A slovenly berber girl in an imperfectly lighted hall once grabbed my yardless body and leaping back in disbelief screamed, '*Mâ fîsh! Mâ fîsh!*' She was looking for a clinch. But what did she find?" Crucifer, his voice whistling in laughter, put his hand along his mouth. "Pudding!" He leaned forward. "But then why not? I was snapt. I had out-Potiphar'd Potiphar. I am as smooth as the front of your knee. I am a hollow stoutness, a human abstraction, a contralto. I am empty as Vanity Fair."

Crucifer suddenly stormed up and, fumbling for the bell-pull by the curtain, jerked it several times. He shook his head in disgust.

"There are minuses," he continued, sitting down again. "Don't misunderstand me, it's not all fun. We are easily susceptible to infection. We for no reason break into hot flushes and sweats and often, though we don't fly, suffer airplane earache for weeks on end, although under this head I can tell you our bodies are at the same time unfailing barometers, thermometers, manometers, and hygrometers. We prematurely wrinkle, the origin of what years ago became our vulgar nickname, '*Lao koun*'—impotent old roosters. We have the pale complexion of pederasts, so obviously the sun can't be good for us. Eunuchs, like children, often can't pronounce the letter R. It is often required of certain of us to insert india-rubber *sardes* or zinc or lead nails to prevent us from leaking. We are fanatical gamblers. We are inclined to have oedematous feet, and we despise Jews to such a degree that it actually affects our health. An intolerable Jew is, for us, intolerable twice. My penishole aches in the damp and the rain. My anus is lost in my weight. Unfortunately, it has fallen to our lot to have had repeatedly to see women at their least readiness—it sickens me to fix on an image—and this doubtless explains the eunuch's long-standing reputation for having a capricious and nasty temperament. We can be peevish as barn-cats. But the malevolence? Ah, malevolence keeps one alive. It's a preservative, like alcohol!" Crucifer saw the look of pity, bewilderment, and great sadness on his guest's face. He leaned forward to intercept that glance and said wistfully, "Here, but is it not the vice of distinctiveness to become queer?"

As Darconville did not reply, Crucifer pulled himself forward, awkwardly, by his toes and reaching out to touch him in a friendly way whispered, *"La ilaha illa anta subhanaka inni kuntu mizzalimin!"*—but his visitor pulled away in horror at the familiarity.

"On the other hand," continued Crucifer, refusing the insult, unsurprised, his ambition for momentary equality testing affection in a gesture that would be, he knew, either endured by clemency or condescension or, more probably, repelled by custom, breeding, and restraint, "there are pluses—more visible," he laughed, "than what isn't, may I add?" It was the humor of the embarrassed man. "We are seldom bald. We sing with voices sweeter than the music of Pachelbel. We look adorable in pants. And then castration, by extending the period of adolescence, prolongs the springtime of beauty. We are skilled to perfection in the art of flattery, I admit it. Languages, for us, are cake. I have not only Arabic but the Berber group, Kabyle, Shilha, Zenaga, Tamashek, plus Amharic, Ethiopian, Cushitic, including Agao, Beja, Bilin—are you impressed?—*and* inscriptive Numidian, he said humbly. Harvard values this sort of thing, you see? Chat, chat, mumble, mumble. Please," said Crucifer, looking up suddenly, "you mustn't think ill of me." He waited. "Darconville?"

But Darconville said nothing. And so there was nothing to do but keep on talking.

"The eunuch, as well, is marvelously cut out for employment; for the cash register, as for the harem, he is the perfect guardian—in all embezzlements, Darconville, and in all irregularities of accounts, a woman will have influenced a man—but we are also masters at organ-

izing squeezes and *douceurs* as perquisites for what we do. We are
geniuses in the science of observation, accumulators of gossip, and authorities on the art of poisoning. I am, like all of us, a gourmand." He
jostled his belly with both hands. "It's a fat bird who bastes itself, isn't
it? I love white truffles, shellfish, and pedroximenes wines. Finally, we
don't futter anything, the source, I needn't have to tell you, of more
buboes and bacteria than bad butter. In any case, my dear, I do not
conduct sultanas to their baths. But then you didn't think I did, did
you?"

Dr. Crucifer grinned horribly and pointed toward the void between
his hamlike thighs. "When you do this, it is not only men who become
eunuchs"—a clucking laughter, interrupting him, sounded as though
his trachea were rapidly opening and shutting—"but women also!"
His thin shoulders collapsed. "Revolting, isn't it? When the terrible
mutilations of one sex are necessary to keep the other pure?"

"The exigencies, of course," said Darconville, "of your Christianity."

The big protruding joints, the long bones, stirred, and Crucifer, in
two efforts, rose out of his incomprehensible belly like a drommeler,
his face a wax mask framed to a somber shape. He twisted close his
robe and began to advance on tiptoe with outstretched neck and listening ears.

"Priestianity, you say?" He touched a finger to his nose, meditatively. "But of course!" his voice glubbed. "I see I've omitted the best
part of my story, digressing as a man with a grievance always does.
Shall I pronounce about it?

"My life in Girga continued without occurrence. I loved God. I
worked, read, and maintained a singular fidelity, as I said, to the
promises I'd made to Fâdi, seeking but to patrizate myself in his holy
shadow." His lips parted, inhaled. "Then in the eighth year of my devotion and donkeyboyhood—my twentieth in life—I suffered the
reversal of faith, which, to be brief, after the completion of my education at Cairo and Oxford, haphazardly enjoined me to the secular
profession you know me by today: Eunuch-in-Residence, *Collegium
Harvardiensis*, at the sign of the motto, 'Va-Ni-Tas.'

"But that's as it is, isn't it? You want to know what happened to
me, of course, back in Girga, and because I want to save you from the
same disappointment, I will tell you." The eyes of most persons con-
verged when they looked at you, but Dr. Crucifer's, by some habit he

had acquired for effect, remained parallel. It gave the impression that he was looking straight through you to a wall beyond. "As I said, I wanted nothing from life but to strive for distinguished inconspicuousness and to live to the letter the lessons of saintly Fâdi. O, but Nature knows terrible and dire ways, doesn't it? I won't elaborate. It was, I remember, Holy Week in Lent—Crucover, when Christ was pacified—and I one afternoon on an inconsequential visit happened by Fâdi's closure"—he took a few steps toward Darconville and paused dramatically—"and in that ultra-violet doorway before I died saw the vidame of all my soul—a civet-cat bent on a stealthy errand of flesh—scumming around on the floor on top of *a naked woman!*" Crucifer's fingers knotted angrily. He was staring blankly before him into a distant point. "It was as if the Archangel Gabriel had suddenly visited earth and married a ravening cuckquean. I withdrew, weeping, by a tree, when later the two of them appeared in the darkness—for night is the paradise of cowards—and crept away hand in hand, hers in his, and his the left which even in Egypt couldn't have been used for a less honorable function." He leaned over his chair, almost gagging. "My *dégringolade* from grace can be charted from that day. No human being has ever lived up to the ideal my imagination created out of what I wasn't for what they should be." Crucifer's eyes, as he looked up, were savage. "I hate them all."

There had never been such silence in that room, with Darconville now bewildered to the soul as to whether that remark were proof of a defect in his understanding or the depravity in his heart. Crucifer twirled in the fishbowl with his finger.

"What's there to add? Faitery throttled faith. I had seen in an instant of cerebral death what I'd sought from birth and as that magic-muttering, instinct-bound piece of pawkery called Christianity vanished I knew I had learned Fâdi's lesson with a vengeance: I had reached the no-number, the root of the monad, a light-robe. *I was naughted!* There is a limit of ignominy in the consciousness of one's own nothingness and impotence beyond which a certain kind of man can go," said Crucifer, the roundels of colored light from the stained glass playing on his face as he crossed by the window, "and beyond which he begins to feel immense satisfaction in his very degradation. I arrived there! I saw Christianity for what it was, a religion expressing its piety in bows, fawnings, and prostrations of servility that went no deeper than themselves! I saw *through* God!" Darconville went mute, his tongue clave to his throat. "Mysticism, you see, and hoaxes go well together. I can't tell you how frightful a longing I have to revile God aloud," whispered Crucifer, *"always."*

" 'Woe unto him,' " said Darconville, his mouth smacking from dryness and gone completely hoarse, " 'that striveth with his Maker.' "

"I hear you call a Maker what I take to be a Personified Inconceivability," cried Crucifer, his voice like the sound of wind through a patch of dead cat-o'-nine-heads. "God, Zeus, Iddio, Bog, Dieu, Jubmal, Utixo, Bott, Bung, Zung, Gudib, Zenc, Jee, or the Great Kazoo, call him whatever you will—everything suggestive of metaphysical unity disgusts me. Mine is a world essentially manifold! In every man there is a vacuum in the shape of God, but where is he? *What* is he? That which is not sense! Exactly. Non-sensical. Literally, nonsense! I just *adore* the clemency he exacts that wears so flatly commercial an aspect, don't you? The fruit of actual purchase? The literal and cogent *quid pro quo* duly in hand paid? I tell you, all Christian victuals stink of fish, and his glory depends upon the antagonism of his creature's shame, degrading all of us whom he owns absolutely—we who re-create him of whom we are creatures—with every one of us, Mnogouvazheamyi Darconville, bound to him by every last goddamned tenure on earth but spontaneous affection! I tell you, the best proof for the tragedy of existence is the proof that is derived from the contemplation of what is said to be its *glories!* You will see!" The odd lines by Crucifer's cheeks drew out like isobars. "God being all things is contrary unto nothing out of which were made all things, and so nothing became something and omneity informed nullity into an existence: now I call that a nice trick, don't you? And then was he even acquainted with himself? All he could utter was 'I Am Who Am'—a tautology, excuse me, I take to be the essence of deceit."

"Your soul," whispered Darconville.

"What's the good of having a soul," asked Crucifer, grinding his teeth, "if you have a mind? And what need is there in heaven of my humility? No, you must listen to me! Can't I simply be devoured without being expected to praise what devours me? I am no French poet. I mean, does a creator necessarily become a master? And what about a creator not in right but only in might? Then, is a creator necessarily superior? Does a world that has a beginning, in fact, necessarily have a creator? And is a creating God necessarily an authorized God? Can a judging God be an object of love? What kind of diabolical God can create cats with dreams of satanic mice and simultaneously by some royal *exequatur* and *placet* give mice dreams of like cats? No, He Who smites without sword and scourges without rod I shall always remember, my friend, with an ingenuity worthy of a better cause—and forever revile! God, I tell you, is the center of the pathetic fallacy." Crucifer pushed his head out of his robe with a little twist and twitched it. "Thus, did Fâdi teach me well—and still of what he wouldn't did."

Standing close to Darconville, Crucifer gave off a foul odor.

"The fact of betrayal, finally, also abolished woman for me. It eliminated her utterly. She disappeared from the face of the world, for through Fâdi hadn't been revealed to me in the simplicity that is at the heart of all mystical truth the one and only lesson to be extracted from the doctrine of Original Sin?" Crucifer's fat arms shot victoriously out of the red robe, an almost aposematic coloration, it seemed, warning of a frightful attack, and he whistled through his nose. *"World loathing,"* spat Crucifer, *"is woman loathing!"*

The cry echoed throughout the room.

"The shadow of the deformed," said Darconville in a low voice, "is deformed also."

Crucifer's mouth twisted. He couldn't abide being told that. He was that terrible figure now whose tyranny did not consist in trying to make himself bigger than his surroundings but in shrinking the surroundings. He claimed εἰσπνοή—divine afflatus, inspiration. Humanly speaking, he was out of his mind.

"Be warned, my chevalier," Crucifer answered. "Disanthropize chance, I tell you. It is your own goodness that is the ideal you imagine. 'To fall in love is to worship at the shrine of a fallible god.' "

"You mistake yourself for a prophet."

"I keep abreast," he grinned. "I told you, I can see in the darkness." He pointed to his eyes. "It's a special gift, the reward in part of a pact I once made with myself"—he paused—"and someone else."

"Someone else?"

"Those were my words. It is a story, I'm afraid, over which the Muse of History must draw a veil. Inquire no further."

For the last time, Dr. Crucifer fell onto the curtain and jerked the bell-pull so hard it snapped out of the orlo. As quickly, the library door flew open and in ran Lampblack, out of breath. He looked up, pitifully, with that little nasolabial funhouse-mirror of a face. Completely out of control, Crucifer went flashing at him like a fire-zouave, thumping him mercilessly on the ears and kicking him for failing to appear earlier to make drinks for them, himself and the guest Lampblack was forced to acknowledge as Crucifer held him fast by the hair, twigging him backwards. Lampblack cowered, his open hands fluttering before his eyes to ward off further blows. Crucifer smiled up at Darconville. "My tapster," he said, "my turnspit, my child o' the bottles."

"I see hate comes easily enough to you," said Darconville, who, paradoxically, could have killed Crucifer on the spot.

"But they're related, of course," mocked Crucifer, "love and hate, aren't they?" He bent down over Lampblack and peered into his face. "Aren't they, millstones?" His eyes shifted to Darconville. "As I've said, hate owes all its meaning to the demand for love—got of themselves, I don't doubt, but far better got of a tutor."

He shoved Lampblack away.

"There nevertheless remains, of course, the argument—it's gone on for thousands of years—that one alone of the two perhaps adhibits more naturally to human nature." As Crucifer's rapid changes of front were incredible, Darconville for a moment wondered which of the emotions in Crucifer's perverse mind benefited more by the reservation. "The question, however, is which. Love," asked Crucifer, putting his tiny head sideways in a mockery of riddling, "or hate?"

There was no answer.

"*Voilà, mon candidat. Entre deux selles le cul à terre, n'est-ce pas?*"

Then Darconville said, "Love."

"Catshit. Duckshit. Birdshit," said Dr. Crucifer. "Dogshit."

LXX

Sic et Non

Suddenly ghosts walked
And four doors were five.

—MARK VAN DOREN, *The Story Teller*

YES, SAID ISABEL, everything was fine. No, no one had given her any message. Yes, she had been busy. No, honestly. Yes, she knew she hadn't written. No, nor called. Yes, she did realize it was October 2. No, it seemed to her to have passed quickly. Yes, there were some problems, to tell the truth. No, not over the telephone. Yes, they were complicated. No, what did he mean did she mean? Yes, she did think of him. No, she didn't need him to come down. Yes, she could come up to Cambridge. No, it would be easier. Yes, she'd received his gifts.

No, she wasn't ill. Yes, she knew he loved her. No, she'd come up there if she could. Yes, he could call back later if he wanted to. No, she'd be home for sure. Yes, she promised this time she would. No, she'd wait right by the telephone. Yes, at 7 P.M. then.

LXXI

The Deorsumversion

The best way to make your dreams come true is to wake up.

—Bishop QUODVULTDEUS

DARCONVILLE immediately called the airport. The next flight to Washington, D.C. from Boston would be leaving at 2:30 P.M., and he booked it, hoping to connect with one of the Piedmont flights continuing on to Charlottesville. There wasn't much time. He called Prof. McGentsroom and, explaining that he had to go to Virginia, asked him if he'd take his Tuesday afternoon class. Then he telephoned for a cab, packed a few things, and, putting his cat under his arm, went flying downstairs to leave him with the superintendent.

Suddenly, on the way down, Spellvexit slipped from his grip and skirted out of the inner door that let out into the courtyard of Adams House! Darconville called him, in vain. Dropping his suitcase, he ran

around after him, with increasing desperation as he heard the repeated blast of the taxi out on Bow St. It was hopeless. He watched
sadly as the little form disappeared around the corner of Apthorp
House. A cat never says goodbye. It just walks away.

The plane finally lifted off—and none too soon, for Darconville
hoped, instead of calling at seven, to be actually *in* Fawx's Mt. proper
at that very hour. It wasn't that there had been small effort made in
behalf of his appearing, rather too much in behalf of his *not*. What
would he find? The facts at his disposal, maddeningly, couldn't be
hammered into truth. Concept wrestled with data. Could one so solicitous not have written, so loyal not have kept faith? And what, he wondered, had it to do with those strange and apprehensive glances she
stole—from what? for what?—especially last summer? Was gravita-
tional pull inversely proportionate to the square of the distance that, as
the distance increased, the pull decreased? Why hadn't Isabel explained anything? He didn't know, he didn't know, and he sought to
stifle several aprioristic frights that occurred to him. Lawyers, he decided, could never be jurors—and thought *itself,* in fact, is the product
of a kind of paranoia. His own mind repelled him, a sort of auto-
immune reaction in which he categorically rejected his own thoughts,
for matter, he felt, only comes to life, life becomes thought, thought
will, and will goes back to matter. I love you, was his only thought. So
he settled back into contradictionlessness, resigned to this conviction,
however, that their wedding again might be postponed—he had no
idea why but knew she reasonlessly feared telling him so—and before
long he was fast asleep, as if taking refuge from what, by simply accepting, he then needn't seek to avoid: the awful struggle to deny that
anything beautiful is nothing else but dream. And there on the plane
he slept back a full three years in time to what was suddenly London,
dreamlit by memory.

* * * * *

Bis repetita placent: it had been one of the worst cold snaps in England, that Christmas. Nothing, however, would ever match it for the
happiness he felt, especially during those hours at Heathrow airport
waiting for Isabel's plane to arrive—then there she was, breathless,
snug in a short fur coat, her face shining! His throat filled, he loved
her so much. It had been five long months since they'd last seen each
other, and in this new, sudden context, for all her excitement, she'd

grown silent, even shy. The bus-ride into London, a cab to Pont St., the walkup of four floors, it all tired her out, and in her exhaustion she but barely acknowledged the cake, the inscribed cups, and the welcoming trappings before she was soon asleep. Undaunted, Darconville sat by her in the dark almost all night, feeling himself to be the luckiest person alive.

The following week was a glorious round of dinners, plays, and sight-seeing, and, as Isabel had never been abroad before, Darconville took the occasion to rediscover all the places and things he loved through her young and happy eyes. It was blowing cold, and in boots, mufflers, and tightly buttoned coats they walked everywhere, down old crooked lanes, through quaint side-streets, and into off-beat lamplit passageways lined with bookshops and antique-and-junk stalls, galumphing home later in the darkness with all kinds of jumble. They visited museums, boated up to Greenwich and down to Hampton Court, and went on long strolls through parks strung around with sparkling lights where carolers-with-cherry-cheeks, gathered together, intoned white puffs of air which turned, magically, into the sweet songs of Christmas. They often went to the zoo—Isabel's favorite!—and fed the tigers bits and pieces of cookies from the bag of them Isabel bought every morning in a special shop of hers on Beauchamp Place, and everywhere Darconville snapped pictures of her: not there, wait, over a bit, *grand!* And then at nightfall, alone at last, always, they'd light the gas-heater, bury themselves in each other's arms under a huge pile of blankets, and shiver in the close darkness until they met in each other's eyes enough warmth to heat all the cold rooms in the British Isles and then some. "When you become a famous writer," asked Isabel, "will you mention a night like this in your book?" They were children. It was paradise. "Yes," he said.

The first snow fell on Christmas Eve. The city of London took it beautifully, becoming in the pure white snow a panstereorama of powdered buildings, glistening streets, frosted windows, and not a light shining anywhere without its attendant corona. They went out in the afternoon, with Isabel wearing positively huge mittens, and attended a lovely festival service at St. Giles Cripplegate, singing Christmas carols, with each of them holding a candle, and in the beauty of each and every moment they grew even closer and more in love. At dusk they had drinks at the Cadogan Hotel where, happier than Darconville had ever seen her, Isabel wore her golden hair down and the black velvet Russian dress he'd once given her, with multicolored flowers sewn in panels down the front. She was beauty appurtenant to grace itself, and for a moment he feared that a mortal such as she might, upon a thunderbolt, be suddenly spirited away from him and enviously taken up to the laps of the bosky gods.

And then they set off through the snow in the direction of South-wark for their Christmas dinner at the old Anchor Tavern, situated on an obscure but romantic waterside lane by the dark-working Thames. It was a night like nothing else on earth, not so much for the crackling fire and candles, nor the traditional rejoicing, nor the delicious fare of roast beef, Yorkshire, and Christmas pudding, but rather because it all touched to the heart of symbol itself, foreordained somehow by fate as if to assure at least two small insignificant people that the possibility of a supreme incomprehensible peace had not gone from the world and so perhaps never would: it was one with the other, one through the other, one in the other, one for the other, always. It wasn't only love. God had visited them.

It was very cold and late when Darconville and Isabel left the inn and stepped into a blowing snowy wind that glanced even colder off the river. Inexplicably, he suggested that they walk up to London Bridge, but Isabel, as her feet were freezing, suggested they could post-pone *that* and laughingly pulled him in the opposite direction; urging her, however, he somehow prevailed—and so up they went and, once there, looked over the water toward the reflecting lights of the dark city across the way. Without a word, he placed a small box in her hand. Her eyes filled with tears as she opened it: it was a diamond-ring. "I love you," she whispered, her face outshining it by far, as he slipped it on her finger. "I will always love you." And flushed with ardor, she kissed him, wrapping herself around him in an embrace, as ivy does an oak, so long it seemed she might get the heart out of him, and there they remained, hovering forever, holding each other so close no one could have known they lived, unmoving in the past perfect tense until the bells of Southwark pealed midnight to wake them to a new birth, whereupon, walking slowly across the bridge in a snowfall of fable, they went home together in silence hand in hand.

The time inevitably came a week or so later for Isabel to leave, a prospect that both of them, characteristically, preferred not only not to mention but to ignore entirely during the course of her stay. Darcon-ville, however, could bear the thought of her absence no more, no longer; he needed her; and as long as he lived he would never forget how simply the fact of her needing him manifested itself and confirmed in him the decision he'd come so resolutely to make, for in the airport, as he watched Isabel from a distance walk through the crowds to embark, he saw almost despairingly, until he pointed, that she had turned the wrong way.

* * * * *

Darconville woke up with the roar of the plane taxiing into Washington, D.C. It was just past five, with the sun westering. There was no time to lose if he was to keep his appointment in Fawx's Mt., and he went quickly to the Piedmont terminal, where he found out, luckily, a flight south—stopping at Charlottesville—would be leaving at 6:05 P.M. He waited at the departure door, grip in hand: not thinking of Spellvexit, not thinking of Harvard or his class, not thinking at all. And then he was aboard again, airborne, and after a short flight was soon coasting down over the Blue Ridge mountain range into the tiny airport on the outskirts of Charlottesville, Virginia. As he disembarked, Sol went dead on the horizon and sputtered angrily out, leaving a dirty light behind in the sky. At dusk, the trees, transfixed, stiffened. His hot heart hurt, so intensely did he want to see Isabel, and that she was suddenly near him caused a flood of indrawn, inwinding, inseverable emotions he couldn't quite sort out. He forgot his suitcase and only because there had been so few passengers on the flight was that noticed. An attendant ran it out to the cabdriver who was asking double-the-fee to take him into Fawx's Mt., but, thrusting a handful of bills through the window, Darconville banged the door shut—and the taxi shot off.

There was always a nameless air of desolation on that backroad to Fawx's Mt. It was a stretch of gloomy, uninhabited land where life in whatever form seemed long ago to have become extinct, and yet if one looked closely—up the fire-roads, beyond the pamets, into the woods —certain wretched dwellings could be spied: shotgun shacks; axmortised cabins with flour-sacking in the windows; rabbit-box houses with wooden wings sticking out and draped over with old blankets and faded clothes. And *there,* Darconville noticed, was the infamous roadside diner: Klansman, I greet you! They passed into a semi-populated area where some fiddleheaded horses were cropping the mowburnt fields, stubbled with straw and bits of corn-nubbin. Shikepokes flew across the sky which was growing ever greyer. The lowering October twilight silhouetted the ravines of rampikes, corruption, and bog, making a derisive comment, somehow, on the idea that the force that guided nature was benign. In the west, the very last of the tender light disappeared and was replaced by a misty belt of grey-green. Darconville was somehow only able to discern in the spooky hillsides and clawing branches styxes, birds of ill-omen, alastors. It could have been a rookery of pterodactyls or humpbacked, be-shawled creatures with red eyes, spined wings, and torturous cries, a world of agelasts and executioners and cannibals who sat ready to spring. If God created nature, thought Darconville, perhaps He Himself is not *in* nature, that depraved place, for want of another, wherein are foolishly fumbled up the apports of that bleak séance over which perhaps we credulously preside only to know Him. Another landmark. They were close now. Darconville rolled down the window. "Hurry," he said, when over the hill a dusty little village came into view.

It was Fawx's Mt.

A few hambacked townies in swamper hats, looking like Chalcolithic forerunners, were sitting on nailkegs in front of the general store, eating moon-pies and drinking cups of parched-corn coffee. But Darconville kept to his directions: left at the fork, first right—stop. He got out. The moon was auriform, in its first quarter. A spreading pool of nightwind wet the air. The blue dusk chilled Darconville's sweatdamp ears as he wondered, for the first time now, whether Isabel would take this appearance to be an expression of his passion, a compromise with it, or a violation against it: whatever, it was too late. He saw lights in the house and checked his watch—seven o'clock, exactly. There was a woodsmoke aroma down by the hollows, and the croak of frogs, a variable plunk, clung, or jug-a-rum, could be heard across the street in the glades where old hickory pines and dark stands of junipers sent a terebrinthic musk out of the shadows. He picked up his suitcase and started to walk toward the house.

Suddenly, Darconville stopped short. He peered forward. Isabel's blue car was parked in the driveway, slightly dented as before, but with an uncharacteristic addition on the back fender: it was a bumper-sticker. His mouth went dry as a limebasket as he read the words on it—*"Sailors Have More Fun."*

Then night fell like a guillotine blade.

LXXII

Who?

The nightingale and the cuckoo sing both in one mouth.

—Old Proverb

THE RURAL CLOAK of blackness slowly dwindled down to a single figure stepping out of the shadows. Swallowing, Isabel Rawsthorne staggered back from the door and clapped both hands over her mouth, her face pale as if paralyzed by the flash of a lightbulb: a ghost wearing a body. All her life seemed to have taken refuge in her eyes. She couldn't speak but with a gesture suggestive of caution, the alarmed maneuver he'd so often seen before, quickly saw him inside to shut the door as fast as possible. Who are you with, thought Darconville, from whom you turn away, at whom you dare not look? She shut her mouth tightly, her face flushing with heat, the enhanced beauty which this warmth might have brought being killed by the rectilinear sternness of countenance that came therewith.

It was a bewilderment that became awkwardness: somehow every move and motion of hers made her legs, even more over-essex'd in the thigh now than he'd remembered, a perverse caricature of what once she feared, waterbulge, keech, a symmelian effect as if the lower limbs had literally fused from rumprowl to root. Her hair had lost its gloss. There are no faults, however, in something we want badly, and Darconville hugged her desperately, closing his eyes only to avoid seeing again what had immediately come to his attention.

Isabel was not wearing her ring.

Instinctively, Darconville wanted to tell her he loved her, but her face had changed—there was now a force of irony in it, the almost malignant joy of some sudden but unshared surprise, yet there was still that dreadful pallor, like some kind of psychic face in a photograph. He followed her into the kitchen where, greeting him with a note of hollow but booming effusiveness, her mother clapped her ironing board shut and discreetly withdrew to another room, the complicated significance of the look that passed between the two people, however, not being lost on him. They were alone now. Isabel did not speak. Darconville tried to smile. They both seemed to be judiciously waiting out the hesitation of some mutually pre-accepted worry or doubt or embarrassment that perhaps it might somehow vanish to ease the historical import the moment seemed to hold.

It wasn't the fatigue of the long trip down, it wasn't that he hadn't eaten all day, it wasn't the studied formality he felt all about him, no, it was nothing he could actually name—but Darconville began to experience a melancholy that drained his bones to vacuums. He smiled lovingly at her nevertheless and gently tried to lift her chin; it wouldn't lift. The note of the note of a thing is a note of the thing itself: he mentioned the bumper-sticker on the car. It seemed ludicrous. The air in the kitchen, however, loaded with the phlogiston of unspoken words, seemed about to explode. Had someone, he asked, given it to her?

Isabel's profoundly lowered head suddenly came up fast with an almost diabolical half-smile in its eyes—a look of hers he'd never seen before. She's a complete stranger to me, he thought. She seemed to be trying to control a happiness within her, despite the fact that he was suffering, despite the fact that she *saw* that, and, more, it seemed to confess with a kind of premeditated felicity to her own lack of power to please him with whatever reply he became increasingly more desperate to know, confirming the face to be its own fault's book. Darconville began to hear devils crisscrossing over his head. He experienced a sensation of starting to fall.

The dizziness began to overtake him. And all of a sudden the angel, Rikbiel, in the company of his Holy Wheels descended to try to minister to him, saying: *You will struggle up from green valleys into the mountains. You will recognize another valley on the other side, when suddenly the mountain whereupon you stand shall melt away under you. Then the two valleys will become just one wider lowland with you standing there in the middle of it. You shall travel thence to mountains far away to discover them likewise into disappearing, suddenly find that there is no end to the mountains, and realize that all the leveling of mountains outside yourself has caused a leveling within. You don't know where you are any longer, but you mustn't fall, my child. No, you mustn't fall, can you hear us?* But Darconville knew he was falling. He could feel himself falling into a monstrous vortex, reverberant with noise, loud with light. He couldn't stop.

He remembered falling a million miles away. He remembered as he fell slowly through the air how the known strangely became the unknown. He remembered trying to fix his falling attention on Isabel's lips to catch her words quicker than his ears might as he asked her a direct question. He was smiling, reaching out for her—but suddenly something was wrong with her face, a hardness in the eyes, a coarseness of expression flickering over her lips. Her scar whitened. And then a bubble burst, and then a world. Isabel said, "I love someone else."

Darconville went pale as a dishclout. His head detonated, like Goliath who took the stone—*thud!*—flat in the sinciput, and perspiration, like lace, broke upon his face. His hands began to tremble uncontrollably as blindly he reached for the table to steady himself. But he was falling slowly, slowly falling, and, as he fell, he felt his soul fly out of his mouth making a sound like, "W-who?"

Isabel turned to him the three-quarter profile the Dutch invented. Her lips curved into a sharp, foxlike smile as if under the pressure of some inner merriment or delight remorselessly beyond her power to suppress, for its triumph, for the force in the authenticity of its abusive truth, for the opportunity at last of its unexpected release, and then calmly spoke the words of his execution.

"Gilbert van der Slang," she said.

LXXIII

The Supreme Ordeal

And if I loved you Wednesday,
    Well, what is that to you?
I do not love you Thursday—
    So much is true.
And why you come complaining
    Is more than I can see.
I loved you Wednesday, yes,
    But what is that to me?

—EDNA ST. VINCENT MILLAY

"IT ALL BEGAN a long time ago," said Isabel, smiling wistfully at Darconville, "before I met you. I guess it was just fate." She seemed to turn his body into the frame of a doorway through which, though speaking of the past, she gazed out into the future. "I was first attracted to his brother, Govert, you know all that, in my classes in high school, but with him inviting me over to Zutphen Farm and all, well, it wasn't long before I eventually met"—she looked at Darconville who was obmuted into a shocked and fearful silence, his eyes frozen onto her—"Gil."

She paused. "Don't just *look* at me, please? It doesn't help." She waited, then shrugged exasperatedly and continued speaking with an increasing urge of mounting indiscretion and the kind of monotony in her voice which assumed that he, like herself, had rehearsed it all before. The tongue and the taste had memorized it for her.

"We dated a few times, not much. Then he went away to school," she smiled. "The Naval Academy? You know? I didn't break off with Govert, and, although I always liked his brother more, I tried to put him out of my mind. See? I had to, to survive." She was not speaking to him, she was speaking to people who were not there, approving people, people who understood her and liked her and would believe her. "Summers, he returned to visit with his family at Fawx's Mt., I knew that, but even though it turned out that he secretly cared, he intentionally stayed away from me," she said with an admiring rale in her voice, "because of—well, us. He didn't want to interfere, you could say," she beamed, "he's like that. And neither did his mother who didn't know how I felt anyway, though I'm sure *you* think she did, don't you?" Knowing herself to be a traitor, she read the accusation in Darconville's eyes. "Well, you wanted to hear this. You wanted to *know*."

A horrible noise, like that of something breaking, issued from Darconville's mouth. It flashed suddenly into his head: My God, theologians know something they can't tell us—*Adam and Eve chose knowledge over life!* And instantly he knew where, in those nervous halts in Fawx's Mt., she'd been staring all those years!

"Last summer, he told me later, he'd built a wall between us. Me," she clarified, "and him. I'd always sensed that, I think. Somehow"— Isabel's eyes flowered into a smile—"you just know. Anyway, I saw him around Labor Day, he was in uniform, when I was helping out at the farm—" She stopped short. "I see what you're thinking, that all this had been planned way back during the summer and that like my real father I have no conscience! Well, it wasn't in July! Or June!" A tragic contralto note came into her voice. "How *could* it have been those months," she asked illogically, "I spent them trying to make my wedding dress! Oh, it doesn't matter now, anyway. The point is, he could understand my doubts like no one else ever could, including—"

Darconville closed his eyes.

It all seemed like some resistless, inexorable evil, with the contrast in Isabel of what she once was as pronounced as the front of a portrait is from the back. Darconville's skin was stone cold as she continued her explanation in a tone of concentrated resolution.

"He told me about a friend of his who'd just recently gotten married but was miserable. Miserable! Don't you see, inevitably I had doubts about us? We talked. We talked a lot, about simple things: in plain language, no big visions, no big words—just walking around the farm, I don't know, under the trees, with a few little animals around." She lowered her head to contain a smile. "I'm just a country girl, I guess." An expression of foolish diffidence and utter relief struggled for mastery in her face as she looked up. "I felt a kind of security I've wanted all my life. I felt safe," she said with a supple-mouthed smile. "I guess I should have told you all this before, shouldn't I?"

Darconville uttered a long sentence but no words were produced. As she spoke, she seemed by leaps to ruin the words that plodded in bewilderment out of his heart.

There was an exaggerated eloquence in her confession, as if it were necessary to focus in her mind, with indisputable fixity, on those satisfactions, adulterated by her own proofs, she spoke to savor—a story made the more incontrovertible, at least so she felt, by the very fact of its being recounted and yet one somehow bootless in the telling, so closely knit was it all with instincts of which, in having been accepted as so irrevocably true, her brain had in fact long ceased to take account. It was as if the facts became such only in collusion with their being told, reaching, nevertheless, to a greater degree of importance as they were, with an exactness forced upon each and every detail by nothing more than the formal decision that not only informed them but indeed had given them birth. She prepared what could have been to serve what should have been, so was.

"O my G-God," whispered Darconville, from whose face every vestige of color had been drained. He was hunched in place, motionless, his fingers held so tightly they were but splints of pain. Struggling for words, trying to formulate a proposition, he began to stammer. She asked him what he was saying.

She sighed. "I don't understand what you're trying to say."

Darconville felt ashamed, almost invisible. "I'm a-afraid." He sank his face into his thin hands.

"That would be silly," she said, frostily.

"But you're my life," he said in a strangled voice. "You're all I have in the world."

Isabel pulled her thumb—and without closing her mouth, which with the droop of her underlip took on an almost vacant look, she frowned a little as she fixed her steady gaze full open on him.

"Not you! Not you!" He looked up. "I can't believe it. It's not *true,* I know it isn't."

"I'm afraid it is."

"Don't," pleaded Darconville, searching her eyes desperately. "Please d-don't?"

She looked deedily into his face.

"I heard you were seeing another girl in Quinsyburg this summer."

"No," he said with low parentilism, "no, d-don't say that."

With full composure, Isabel got up and placed a glass of water and a blue pill in front of him. "You won't say that again?" he pleaded.

"Drink that."

Darconville took the pill with hands trembling. He wanted to, but couldn't, ask exactly who Gilbert was, how in all these years she never *once* mentioned him; he was trying to shake free, literally extricate himself, from the horror of what was happening to him. With half-shut, malignant eyes, full of strange inward unction, she weighed him. As she removed the glass, he saw with utter disbelief that her face had been fully dispossessed of its natural sweetness by that mask of intransigence which, with the arrest of desire, horrifyingly implies a secret *point de repère* to a world forbidden to him and so reserved for another. It hadn't been a choice between, but of. She turned sideways in her chair, waiting.

"Will you l-look at me, Isabel? Please?"

"This just isn't the end of the world," she said, the contours of her countenance as imperturbable to his emotions as dark, slippery rocks to the wash of the sea. "Why can't you *see* that?"

"I'll leave Harvard." She held her head very high at this, and her eyes grew defiant. "I'll do anything for you. I'll move down here, if you'd like, to live." Coldly, she said that she was no longer living at home, that, in fact, he was lucky to have found her there when he did.

The Watsons, down the street, had offered her a small house behind theirs to live in. He asked if he could live there with her. Isabel closed her eyes and exasperatedly whistled air. *When will he go,* she wondered, *when will he go?*

It all seemed to Darconville like some weird, stupefying story that had been told to him long, long ago—a tale, ignored as fiction, so fashioned to be lived: the revenge of real dreams upon fake sleep. We can actually cause to exist, in the very act, what irrationally we fear, as perhaps we write less to get a second chance in life than to exorcise the demons peopling our minds. There was no real person named Dr. Crucifer, thought Darconville, I have created him!

The knowledge for Darconville that it was too late to offer apologies to Isabel suddenly became a haunting penance for him that exceeded the sin itself. But what sin? *What had he done?* Surely something! Or was this happening to someone else? Again, he thought of Crucifer: was this guilt by innocence? Oversight? Presumption? It has long been observed that men do not suspect faults which they themselves would not commit; so it was with Darconville, who nevertheless, too wracked with guilt to disallow the possibility of his personal hand in this, too deeply in love to want to discern it elsewhere, assailed himself in a fit of remorse and self-accusation that he mightn't absolve in himself what he wouldn't accuse in another. He spoke in a daze of baseless, unanswerable self-reproach, admitting his faults, proclaiming his regrets, but all to no avail—for she looked away—and even the joys in their lives he rehearsed suddenly seemed never to have happened as he recalled them. There was nothing to say he could manage, with but one exception.

"I love you," he said.

She deigned not to answer.

"Yet you wanted me. Didn't you? Why, you *must* have wanted me to be with me so long." She assumed a lethargic sulkiness. "I know you love me." He spoke into the hands that covered his face, a stammerer, literally afraid of what he might say. "I b-beg you to love me. Please?"

"Don't lose your pride. Lord."

Darconville looked up ashen and startled, for he suddenly saw that two personalities coming together can create a third, with each becoming different yet together making up one they are both surprised at separately.

"What have I got left?"

"Your genius." She shrugged. "Everything."

"I don't want everything that's nothing. I want anything that's something." His head was splitting. "I love you."

"None of that matters now."

"By the truth of your right hand," asked Darconville, searching her mind through her eyes, "do you mean that?" She nodded. Her eyes were clear and well-opened.

Was there no history? No memory? No continuity or meaning to love? They were questions the weight of which Darconville, weakened to the heart, hadn't now the strength to bear asking. He had grown yellow and pasty with fatigue, his face perspiring so much it looked as though it had just been raised from a basin, and his swollen eyes seemed to have taken their moisture directly from his lips which were now dry to smacking.

"After four years? You mean"—his throat stuck shut—"everything's g-gone?"

Isabel was unmoved. She turned away, exhaling in irritation and thinking to herself: is this to go on forever? Her hands were ice-cold. She touched the back of her left hand with the fingers of her right: gelid. *Confecta res est:* it was hopeless, for as she could no longer see in him what by the new dispensation she could not understand, she could consequently feel no sympathy for what she could not imagine. Where there is no imagination, there can be no horror. There was nothing to be done. The girl was gone.

"May I," asked Darconville, like a statue whose fixed stare corresponds to a once genuine reality but reflects in its cold and empty sockets no understanding at all, "may I sleep here tonight?"

"I don't think that would be right."

Reasoning, Isabel scrutinized him. She looked disgustedly at his trembling hands, then sighed, and relented—with the stipulation, however, that he understood it would only be this *one* night. It seemed a kindness to Darconville whose complete exhaustion, coupled with the sedative she'd given him, almost prevented him from walking. She proceeded with him to an empty bedroom where, overcome with shock, bewilderment, and grief, he fell onto the bed and let the darkness roll over him. Something rose out of him and actually looked down at himself from the ceiling, from the sky, and then from beyond the universe, making him feel smaller than anything that ever was in the world.

The exigencies of life quickly resumed control of Isabel. Excusing herself, she assured him she'd be right back; she shut the bedroom door, listened a moment, and quickly disappeared into the kitchen. And then with an efficiency that seemed a distorted echo, an ironic recurrence, of a previous but now long forgotten dénouement—one characterized as much by opportunity as desire—she acted with dispatch. She looked apprehensively back to the bedroom and then picked up the telephone to share with the only person that mattered now the sudden good-fortune she could only express in breathless, disconnected whispers which, while the consequence of her elation, nevertheless seemed to recapitulate in composition what only the most skillfully malignant and exitial of changelings could have transformed into a rhetoric of joy from the fragments of another's broken heart. She had not forgotten her stamp this time. The die was cast. It was over.

The *facies hippocratica:* Darconville's face, as he lay there semiconscious, had lost its subjective expression; it did not reflect his thoughts, he had none, but only the objective fact of the approach of death-in-sleep. It belonged to the supraindividual sphere of the ancestral life of the body, and had Isabel returned to him, which she didn't, she would have seen, in his sunken eyes, taut forehead, and leaden skin color, how that face in no longer resembling itself had but vacated the premises, going blank, in a gape of sudden fatality: the shroud in which, mercifully, one lies down to relax the heart. He spiraled down into unconsciousness. There was slowly no end of agony, the dance of unutterable sorrow and pain within causing him to writhe and twist in ceaseless turmoil as he wondered over and over again how Divine Providence could allow for such a cruel absurdity as God. The suffering grew unbearable, the sensations too ungraspable, too immense to handle, and in an instant, helpless, he sank to the terrible depths of what night really means, descending far, far below the reaches of mere sleep to perpetual delirium where flocks of ravaged, scissor-winged angelbats with pointed ears thrashed each other in turn to perch upon his toes, suck his blood, and fan him into further unconsciousness in order to continue the profanity of complete possession in a darkness that would never disembogue. Darconville suddenly screamed—and sat bolt upright!

He was alone in a room.

It was early morning, about six o'clock by the fading darkness out-side the window. Reflecting on the events of the previous night, he wasn't certain of what to do. His first impulse was to wake Isabel with a kiss, or had what happened really happened? Reality, he thought, was too varied, too abundant, to be mirrored in anything smaller, nar-rower, less varied than itself, but comprehension on any plane, of any size, was impossible. It was all he could do to keep in mind who he was at that moment, for dialogues within him were stumbling doubles out in a profusion that by reminding him he was no one suggested he be all.

Darconville dressed and walked outside to the fence in back of the house where mists hung over the distant cowfields and the air smelled of deep pools of rain. Some stars were still shining coldly in the sky. Should he leave? He deliberated, rubbing his eyes which were dry and inflamed. Should he try to stay? He walked around to the outside of her bedroom window and softly called to her. There was no answer. He thought

> Only the false are falsely true,
> Only the true are truly false;
> You are false and you are true,
>   Sweet child. Sweet song.

He decided, to urge her to the moment, to prepare to leave and so re-turned to his room, packed his suitcase, and let himself—not noise-lessly—out the front door. It was a vapor-smoked morning, and al-though the lethal dark still sat full on the uparching hills the east was gradually whitening. There was no one in sight and not a sound as he headed some ways up the lonely road. Surely, thought Darconville, this is a dream. This road? The silence? Miles away from where I'm supposed to be? He turned, hesitantly, and waited. The light in Isabel's room came on for a moment—and his heart leapt. He hadn't returned a few steps when the light went off, when the room, significantly, was dark again. He began to write sentences with his tongue on the top of his mouth. The panic he felt literally immobilized him. And she? She didn't want to know he was leaving, only that he was gone.

In an instant, Darconville was suddenly standing in her room—and then desperately shaking her with pleas repeated to convince her of her mistake. Please, he begged. Please, he ordered: did she really love someone else? Wasn't it all a mistake? Was she going to marry him? Had he touched her? Did she believe that one could love two people at the same time? Could he still hope? Had she ever worked on a wedding dress? Would she let him see it? Could he stay with her, talk to her, just be with her?

"*No, no, no,*" cried Isabel, pounding the bed, "*no, no, no, no!*" And in spite of the fact that blind belief in one thing is often founded upon disbelief in another, Darconville at last could see in her face how much an object of detestation he had become for her, how constrained and oppressed he made her. She fell sobbing onto the blanket, trying to convince him now she wasn't worth it, while of course, in spite of this piece of formal theater, believing she was, and when she looked up—for he'd grown silent from humiliation—her eyes were dry. She stood up and told him she would drive him to the airport. That was *it.*

"You said you'd be understanding," said Isabel, wheeling her car back out of the driveway, stopping, and screeching forward in a lurch.

"Don't call me you," said Darconville.

She stared straight ahead, her eyes small and malignant now like bullets, close-set, with that protuberant root-vegetable look of her mother's.

"Sometimes," she said, "I think you're the worst person in the world."

"I doubt it," he replied. "That would be too much of a coincidence."

The fingers of her left hand spread on the wheel and tightened into a fist. Her eyes glittered cruelly.

"No," interjected Darconville, fear vibrating in his voice, "I didn't mean that. I'm sorry. I'm so sorry. I love you more than my own life, more than life itself. Please listen to me?" The car careened out of Fawx's Mt. and turned north by way of the backroad. "But you don't want to listen, do you? You want to be safe," he said, "the bourgeois need to get through life with the least unpleasantness, is that it? That's it, isn't it? Even though you know you love me?" He turned to her, but there was a solitude within her now inaccessible to praise or blame, affection or accusation, a justice of her own devising completely beyond appeal.

"Please don't. Don't do this," he implored, rocking forward to claim her attention. He fell back. "How could you have just met some-

one else, Isabel? I should like to know how, you know? Even if you
convinced me, I wouldn't believe it." Isabel kept her eyes trained to
the road. "Do you think I can live? Seriously. I will not live. I have
been given another man's life and cannot use it. I *cannot* live. Speak
to me!"

Darconville was frustratedly clasping and unclasping his hands.
"What can I say? What can I do? There's no time left!"

They were speeding now.

"I've been trying to call you for a month, you, your parents, that
nightmare down the road named Mrs. van der Slang, and where were
you? Betraying me?" cried Darconville, his tear-blinded eyes blurring
the landscape. "You said you loved me. Was that an explanation? An
excuse? I think you should offer that bit of logic to the Museum of
Human Imbecility." He paused. "Look, I know love can be confusing.
I know that. But it doesn't matter, why should—"

Isabel banked a corner, swiftly, rushing the car dangerously off a
shoulder and quickly into the road. Darconville saw how recklessly determined she was to be free of him.

"I should denounce you to the world, you"—he almost choked on
the emotional throat-note—"you hypocrite." He turned to her. "Your
adrift-in-a-world-I-never-made pose disgusts me."

One of Isabel's eyebrows rose humorously, twitched a little, but, always, she gazed ahead with an expression of both relief and satisfaction on her face, and she seemed more like a professor of the equiv-
ocal sciences than anything else, showing an impassive, almost
contemptuous air as she listened to the last of his desperate entreaties
with an absent-minded smile.

"Isabel, forgive me," cried Darconville, "I-I love you so much, I
love you so much!" They turned into the airport road. He reached
over and pulled her arm. "Do you believe me? When I say that, do
you believe me?" He gripped her arm. She looked at him. Had he
gone mad? He was praying, but it was a hopeless sort of thing—words
spoken but without any sense or understanding. "Tell me, tell me you
love me!" But they had reached the front of the terminal and stopped.
Isabel, dreading this moment, wasn't sure what to do; she didn't
move. He fumbled for her hand and took the white, spatulate, always
slightly cold fingers. He waited in agony, but he had no more words,
and overcome with the pity of it all, he kissed her with what almost
seemed a question—one she alone, in returning, might have answered.

But she did nothing. They false and fearful did their hands undo. And he was out of the car.

Isabel turned her head away, paused a moment, and drove away. With his throat constricted, Darconville stood staring after her into the blank and pitiless morning. The loss of love loured overhead. He was abandoned.

LXXIV

The Empty Egg

The nothing experienced in anguish reveals eventually also the being.

—Barsanaphius, the Recluse of Gaza

THERE WAS A DESERT PLACE in Isabel, he saw for the first time, an emptiness smaller than Nauru and more lethal than the steady application of artifice or fraud: a cimmeria, a coomb, a cess. It sat below intuition in a theoretical sphere of fundamental brainlessness where nothing ever grew, ever existed, was ever felt, and no sally of genius or wit could be conveyed to the mind of whatever by it might be understood for its fatality lay precisely in its vacancy and ghastly implenitude. When she spoke from there or listened from there, she could agree with anything or not, say anything or deny it—it didn't matter. Its residues of ashes and cinders had nothing in common with fire but lay slaglike in the deep of its pure apophatica, a not-something excommunicating both pleasure and pain from the zone of its utter barrenness. No awe gripped her there, and no grief—no emotion, no concern, no plaints, no wheedlings, no needlings; it had no reticule of tricks; it devoured every variable by its own abiogenetic instincts and lived on the unlimited possibilities of inconstancy and contradiction. It was a deathmouth, mortally neuter, with killing its ceremonial, meaninglessness its motive. It was an empty egg. And *there* he was betrayed.

LXXV

Lacerations

Nature is negative because it negates the Idea.

—FRIEDRICH HEGEL

THE QUINSYBURG ROAD always left one with the distinct impression he had taken the wrong direction, a suspicion, even for habitual travelers, impossible to allay. A feeling of uneasiness sharpened at every curve of that lonely tract, a sense of oppression in no way commuted along the straight stretches that ran between russet slopes patched with twisted pines and stunted oaks into even wilder and bleaker downlands. The absolute stillness always seemed a preliminary, a shadowy presentiment, to some perilous undertaking of which one was unaware, and nothing perhaps better corroborated the threat than at that one point down the road where, blundering up in a kind of meretricious finale, was the wooden sign of the town which, instead of welcoming you, seemed to warn you off.

"Nature," sighed Dr. Dodypol, peering out of his car window, "you know—to me, it's evil." He turned to Darconville, whose head lay fallen back, his eyes open but lifeless. It almost broke Dodypol's heart.

"It frightens me just to say the word. Look," he waved his hand, simultaneously downshifting to urge his old car up a hill, "trees wormed out, sloked ponds, ravaged groves and dark and forbidding swales. Do you realize that the real name of Treasure Island was Skeleton Island? Nature is at constant war—something fails as something prevails. And then half of the species that have survived the long ceaseless stupid struggle are parasitic in their habits, lower and insentient forms of life feasting on higher sentient forms; we find teeth and talons whetted for slaughter, hooks and suckers molded for torment, claws and cusps sculptured all for death—everywhere a reign of terror, hunger, and sickness, with oozing blood and quivering limbs, with gasping breath and eyes of innocence that dimly close in agonies of brutal torture. Take these woods. I never drive this road when I don't think of the deeds of hellish cruelty, the secret wickedness, that goes on in there, year in, year out, and none the wiser. I mean, think of all the men whose bones have been bleached by the relentless blue of that cynically smiling sky. How manifold the dooms of earth! How singular that of the sea! A burst of gunfire—have you ever thought of this?—has all the colors of the rainbow. Nature? It's grotesque, with confusion its intent and accident its specialty, a constant reminder—remember, Eve bore no children in Paradise—of what, having once, we had and yet having had we lost." He paused. "There, lean back. Get the benefit. Are you all right?"

Darconville merely closed his eyes.

"It's in the tilt of the planet," continued Dr. Dodypol, a man with one of those special natures whose inner processes take place in that holy land of sensibility the border of which so often touches the marches of the kingdom of insanity. He was talking to himself. He didn't mind. He was worried about his friend. "Figure, with no tilt, there'd be no seasons: no seasons, so no migrations, no color lines, no language differential, no land grabbing—no war!" He shrugged. "It's all in the books. I mean, we're all arse over tip, aren't we? Swinish? Mechanically and sinfully dogged? Knitting guilty wool into the night?" Suddenly, Dr. Dodypol began waving crazily to the country-side. "Hello, Hobbes!" he shouted through the window. "Hello, La Rochefoucauld! Hello, Mandeville, fair grow the lilies on the river-bank? Hello, Vauvenargues! Hello, Schopenhauer! Christ, Darcon-ville, they all said it. Jansen, Bayle, Buffon, all of them. Emeric de Crucé? St. Augustine? Dr. Foster of Gloster? The whole shooting match said it. I myself said it.

> Nothing in nature is equal quite:
> Jaws don't match in a single bite.

My line. Doggerel, no doubt. Still, I suppose, it shows imagination of some sort.

"No, there's no route back to the Garden of Eden, Darconville, ex-cept by the imagination. That's why I believe in *you*"—Darconville felt Dodypol's hand steal into his to give it a reassuring shake—"and why I set off for Charlottesville the very minute you called. I may be speaking out of turn, but you weren't the only one she let down, my friend, not by half. It wasn't as long as two or three weeks ago that Thelma Trappe was asking the very same question: 'Why didn't Isabel ever visit me?' She doted on her, for some reason. You'd know. Parents, wasn't there something peculiar that way with both of them?" He shook his head and sighed. "A goosegirl ermined is a goosegirl still." He touched his friend's knee. "It's too late now any-way, I should say." Dodypol glanced over at Darconville and picked up speed. "Point taken?"

This further recognition of Isabel Rawsthorne's disregard com-pounded his hurt, and yet, strangely, as one report followed another in such detestable proportion, it only seemed a cruel attempt by spiteful and fathomless rumor to effect a revision of her which was sham and not her at all; one day trying to lynch four years? It was not going to happen.

"I don't think you understand what I'm talking about," said Dr. Dodypol, staring straight on.

Darconville looked up.   •

"Last night Miss Trappe committed suicide."

It was late afternoon when they pulled into Quinsyburg, with the last red streaks fading away in the western sky. Darconville never bothered to ask himself why he had returned, although he began to

feel he found the recollection of her to be more pleasing than her presence; something he remembered of her seemed to be missing when
he'd encountered her again, not only yesterday, he reflected, but over
the last months back to June. But here he was in this bizarre world,
again. Perhaps he hoped to experience again the feelings associated
with a happiness he'd known there in time past? It was possible, but
he began to realize, passing the countryside which bore so clearly the
mark of the waning year, that the nature of time is loss, to be reviewed
in memory, perhaps, but never to be regained, and suddenly he
couldn't put himself to review those memories that conspired for attention on every street, at every corner, for the past, once taken to be
so immutable, had instantly been transmogrified by the present to the
point of disfigurement—and what memory could now be singled out
that didn't lead in a single inflexible line straight toward the dissolution of it? The exertions of trying to probe into the purposeless series
of tragedies so weighed on him that, to escape them and to avoid the
bald amiabilities and questions which were sure to follow hard upon
meeting anybody from the college, he asked Dodypol to put him up in
a room at his house, where, after writing a swift retaliatory letter to
Gilbert van der Slang—declaring with what industry he would fight
for Isabel—he fell exhausted from thinking onto the bed and slept.

Later that night, there wasn't a sound when Dr. Dodypol peeked
into the bedroom. Darconville was so still he might have been dead,
but as his friend was concerned that he hadn't eaten for days he
touched him awake. It was too late, whispered Dodypol, as Darconville immediately rose to telephone Isabel—but when he cried out in
agony, Dodypol said no, no, he only meant it was midnight.

It was intolerable, this waking into facts, and Dodypol suggested a
walk. The night air was heavy with the odors of fall, with rifts in the
racing clouds that showed watery patches of color in the dark sky.
Darconville mailed his letter, and they set off, Darconville walking
swiftly, Dodypol trying to keep pace with his companion who was
speaking now with a euphoria which revealed itself in unjustified
optimism and grandiose plans, a compulsive chatter switching from one
subject to another so rapidly that his listener couldn't follow, and then
slowing down in spells of ominous reflection. He would halt, deliberating. Then he would suffer a kind of hypomania, his thought
processes, like film, running along at incredible speed: did she love
him, not want marriage, or not love me? Or love me, fear marriage, so

love him? Perhaps hate me, love him, and so want marriage? Did she love one more as she loved another less? If she loved me, he wondered, how could she love him? Then did she ever love me if she always knew him? If he didn't love her, would she then have loved me still?

Half-truth is a despot. By entering into the arena of argument and counterargument, of technical feasibility and tactics, by accepting the presumption of the legitimacy of debate, Darconville felt he was only foundering more.

But why had she agreed to marry him? When exactly did she meet this other person and with what disposition informed by what cause? How was it he had never once seen her wedding dress? And what was behind those ridiculous errors in the wedding invitations? The paucity of her visits, when she had the only car, last summer? The months of unbearable silence when she could have simply told him the truth? But what was the truth? Why, for instance, had she bothered to be baptized? Engaged? And why that recent telegram expressing her love? *Elle m'aime, un peu, beaucoup, passionnément, à la folie, pas du tout?* It was impossible. The torch casts no light upon its base.

They circled around the outer side of Quinsy College, walking down the empty streets in silence. The copses moaned and swung in the rising wind, and it wasn't long before, up on that small hill overlooking the train tracks, Darconville stopped in front of the dead dark bulk of a house outlined against the sky and looking ghostly and barren under the leafless trees that stretched out their black fingers over its roof. It was Miss Trappe's place. They paused by her garden patch where in the crooked drills lay the brown and lifelessly twisted stalks of her plants. Without a word, despite Dodypol's pleas, Darconville was up on the porch and inside. He wanted to say goodbye.

The rooms were plain, with a stillness in them that bespoke the probity and simplicity of its lost tenant: an old bureau, faded rag rugs, and bargain-net curtains. There was always a painful temperance about the place, but now, in a way, it seemed overfurnished and musty with the absence of human life. Darconville clicked the switch: the electricity had been shut off. He lighted a candle. There in the back room was a tiny bed next to which stood a table holding a vaporizer, a sinus mask, and a snore-ball. A print of *Latoney's Funeral* hung on the wall, and by either side of a window were shelves of books, most of which held leaves between the pages, or little round rings of dried larkspur blossoms pressed within. In the cramped kitchen quarters were rows of empty bottles, pincushions, tidies, and a pair of grape-scissors hooked to a little chart detailing frost dates and shrinkage ranges. The doorknobs were woolen with dust. He opened a closet: a bag of inactive shoes and piles of huge hats. And there on a bureau was a photograph of Isabel he had given her several years ago; by it lay the cameo—uncollected, unseen—she had promised the girl who had never come by, who had not kept faith, who perhaps in concentrating on trying to remember instead of remembering forgot. His sadness, as was often the case with Darconville, made him feel suddenly cold.

The last days of Miss Trappe, according to Dr. Dodypol, had been as lonely as ever. He said she simply went wandering about town in larger and larger hats meeting no one and stopping in the street only to look up at the sun and repeat, "Let me suffer, just keep shining! Let me suffer, just keep shining!" And then it happened. As no one had seen her for weeks, eventually they checked. They apparently found her, her old-fashioned nightgown with its high neck covering her slight frame with decent circumspection, buttoned to the full and sitting on a chair in a flexion of resignation, her skin in rigor and her grey lips buttered with light flecks; one of her thrawn hands was clutching a straight razor while the other, nearly severed, rested on the open Bible in her lap where a twiglike finger was *still* pointing to the text of Ephesians 6:12—

For our contention is not with the flesh and blood, but with dominion and authority, with the world-ruling powers of this dark age, with the spirit of evil in things heavenly.

The shadows, as he blew out the candle, closed in upon Darconville like a caress that killed. That night he crawled into a bed that seemed hot-forged in the furnaces of the lost angels. Eternity went by in an instant, and a second lasted forever. He looked for faces and saw masks. He sought nepenthe and found nitriol. The universe expanded and his heart contracted. Light utterly disappeared. And then all the heavens crashed headlong into hell, displacing sheets of flame that burnt him down into the unconsciousness of sleep for three whole days. It was time completely lost.

Darconville, upon awakening, found a revelation in the very act: time didn't stop; it continued; and so what he lost, mightn't then another? Stupor, which benignant fate sends by the side of extreme pain, conditioned him—and possibly deceived—but it cut through the hesitation of reason: it let him act. Defensively, his conception of self became consciously enormous. How? Why? To borrow some time from a part of the eternity to which it tends? To convince desperation, perhaps, that love is its reward? It was hard to say. But he became inspired with the absolute necessity for instant action. Miss Trappe was only Isabel who hadn't been loved! He was no longer restrained by any sense whatever of modesty or decorum. He knew it; in one way, he needed it; and he was suddenly wakened to deal with the distress he could once but now no longer *not* deal with, for a blast blown to the hounds is no less a blast blown to the fox. He prepared for violent activity, to snatch out of the formal malfeasance that had taken place behind him what in refusing to see as treachery committed he could only see as innocence withheld.

It seemed a monomania, the fact becoming almost more important than its significance. He loved her! And all the gods, aerial and aquatic, would never prevent him from loving her! He rose quickly and once again asked Dr. Dodypol to drive him—this time, *back* to Fawx's Mt.—and so away they went, racing once more up the road to Charlottesville and over those ragged hills where no phenomena, however uncanny, however evil, could now prevent him from reaching out to the one he loved. The morning dew, before settling, left rainbows shimmering in the tender light within various glades they passed. Dr. Dodypol, who'd have none of it, explained them away as nothing but concentric arcs with the common center on the line connecting the eye of the observer and the light source. Dr. Dodypol said, "A person cannot really stand at the rainbow's end. Not at all." It was a strange remark, perhaps, but no stranger a remark than the fact that no one else in the car would yet believe it.

They banked the wooden bridge and turned onto the road leading into the Blue Ridge mountains, but when they got to the Shiftlett house they found it empty—then Darconville remembered Isabel's new lodgings down the road. There they proceeded, with one voice hushed and one spirit subdued, until Dr. Dodypol at some distance from the Watsons' house stopped the car.

There was Isabel. She was wearing sneakers, jeans, and a green-and-white striped jersey and was carrying some articles into the small back house there when she happened to look up: she gave a violent start. Darconville crossed the lawn. He looked ghastly. From his gaunt wasted face his eyes showed the brightness of fever, and when he spoke to her his voice was crackling and spasmodic. He stepped to her; she bridled—the only time he had ever seen that verb. It was a deplorable spectacle, for she clearly wished he were a thousand miles away and conveyed it in her cold attendance to the few duties she refused to set aside (throwing unusables into a wastebasket: old letters, school note-books, a carved Russian fife, etc.) while studiedly moving around him and, with a civility more deadly than violence, answering his questions with a poisonous gentleness of speech. There was an intensity of hatred in her white, set face. She took a handful of books—on nauti-cal subjects, he saw—into the small house; he went to follow; she abruptly stepped out. She flung back her hair. What did he want? No, she would tell him *nothing* about Gilbert van der Slang! Darconville mentioned he'd written to him. Isabel pushed her face at him like a dark, blue thumbtack and said if he ever dared hurt him she'd—! The muscles of her mouth contracted, making her ugly. She lost her breath for a moment, but then self-contained and inflexible once again she showed the ethereal other-worldly face of the fanatic whose distant thoughts become the more remote as they become the more intran-sigent and replied nothing, did he hear, *nothing* was going to change! Let him do his worst, it was too late.

Her face lost its attractiveness in a smile of triumph that he saw no love, no pleading, no words, no *peine forte et dure* would ever change, and, although he loved her, a condition that might formerly have ab-solved in her personality whatever lessened it, he suddenly saw himself in the light of her aversion and actually began to share it. His lungs began to ache in the apprehension. An explanation, asked Darconville, would she give him that? For an instant, a convincing animation came into her countenance that prevented him from realizing how far away her thoughts had flown. He tried to take her arm, but, groaning, she waved his hand away—not touching him. She continued to regard him, beginning to feel that the moment was not only tense now but possibly dangerous. Yes, she answered, *if* he left she would send him an explanation. But, she added in a voice like wind from an iceberg, he must go! How extremes call to each other! It was flame and ice face to face. She went to step into the house. Darconville intercepted her. He took her waist, asking for one more minute, when Isabel tore away from him with cold cutting contempt, her eyes like a glass snake's.

"*I promised to go riding with Col. Watson,*" she said in a spitting whisper.

As the car sped away, Darconville turned back one final time and watched her disappear into the blurred, discolored distance that receded so fast into the blighted world it seemed literally gone even before it could say: I am the last picture of your life.

LXXVI

Abomination of Desolation

A great horror and darkness fell upon Christian.

—JOHN BUNYAN

THE LAST SIGHT of Fawx's Mt. became too much to bear, and Darconville cried out terribly upon it. May it be cursed forever! May it wither into the grin of the dead! May flowers and children die in its shadow! May the birds of the air refuse to fly over it! May it henceforth stand a desert of recrimination, spawning hunchbacks to eat ashes for bread and to mingle tears with drink! May Satan pinch into the faces of its inhabitants the pain of hell that by them it be sown with salt and continue ever an abomination to sight! May the maiden that passes it become barren and the pregnant woman that beholds it abort! May its crops be given to the caterpillar and the fruits of its labor to the locust! May the winged monsters be reaved out of the in-

fernal pit to dwell therein and demons sit high forever in its rebar-
bative trees to scourge it in satire and song! May the light of the sun
be withheld therefrom and the light of the moon be hidden from it
forevermore, with accursedness its perpetual condition and doom its
eternal reward!

LXXVII

The Nowt of Cambridge

Deux fois deux quatre, c'est un mur.

DOSTOEVSKY, *Voix souterraine*

ADAMS HOUSE: the one accommodation with its shades drawn night and day had a melancholy fixedness about it, an aura of prohibition as if something terrible, having once taken place there, must now never be disclosed. There was neither light nor movement nor noise from within, and if the rooms were inhabited it was as though someone, in trying to acquire the power of invisibility, had lost sight of himself as he disappeared from the sight of others. It was like an impatible vacancy in the building, a statement of the saddest isolation, intimacy without commitment.

The rooms, in fact, were not empty. Someone still lived there who, keeping to the darkness all day, was waiting—he couldn't explain it—

for waiting to end. And when night fell it was always the same. Darconville rose and went out alone to wander through the deserted streets of Cambridge looking for his cat.

The search became an obsession, a desperate compulsion, only one of several he experienced after he returned to Harvard. At first, he looked by day, the search no less real for the parallel quest of which he was unaware, a desperate attempt at invalescence—an objective, however, separated totally from the consciousness of the subject who in the passing days was no longer sure what he was seeking, a cat, lost love, or himself. It became hardly bearable. He found himself walking mile after mile, astonished and saddened, wandering in a state of mind that seemed a parody of all value between two worlds, one dead, the other powerless to be born; worth disappeared. He would aimlessly pass his students in the street, leave his change behind in stores, and in the most unlikely situations actually begin to pray out loud. He often stopped before shopwindows he didn't look into. Careless and sloven, he started to attract the attention of boys in the neighborhood. It soon became not only unbearable but frightening. He began to look for cars trailing him and to tremble suddenly for no reason and then he began to be afraid he'd start screaming in public places: often in the middle of crowded sidewalks he'd start to weep, biting his hands to stop. So time reversed: he disappeared from view, completely, leaving his room now only at night to roam through the Yard, wander along the banks of the Charles, or go miles out into old factory yards and back alleys and outlying areas of Cambridge. Several times, he sat up all night in Longfellow Park, and one morning in a puddle, rising in a mist, he saw Isabel's face, now flushed with excitement, now mournful and pensive, but when he looked again it was gone.

Isabel Rawsthorne's face haunted him. He put a vigil light in front of her picture in his room, slept by it during the day, sat by it when he returned in the morning.

There were periods of delirium—from eating nothing, smoking too much, walking hour upon hour—when he dreamt he was moving through time into eternity, but in lucid moments, then, he saw he was going nowhere wherever he went, for just as eternity is not prolonged time, rather its negation, he realized in wandering he might extend his area but never abolish space, and the efforts, he saw, only became foolish failures. But the persecutory delusions haunted him, the morbid wariness, the unspeakable forebodings. The night seemed to distend reality even more. Streets sped under him, cars went motionless, bridges stretched out and broke in the middle of their arches—even noises began to become removed from their sources. Things seemed not to live but to exist all the same. He began to pore over Isabel's letters and photographs, hundreds of them, trying to close out the actuality of time and change which he saw, however, simultaneously destroyed the possibility of expectation. Rapture without hope: it led either to desolation or a frightening kind of credulity; he experienced little fugues now—one in particular that touched a ghostly world whose symbols represented potentiality rather than reality: somehow, somewhere, he felt, his cat lived; somewhere, somehow he was loved— a superposition he repeatedly, self-hypnotically, began to construct for himself by projecting a hypothetical world where all possible outcomes could exist! He tried to *will* the fulfillment of his every desire by supreme efforts of concentration and at such moments would quickly hurry back to his rooms to see if his cat had returned, if the vigil light was still burning, if his telephone might ring, but it hadn't, it wasn't, it didn't.

There was never any change—only the photograph of Isabel on the shelf, his enemy twin looking in cold penetrance through his emptiness toward someone else. Gilbert van der Slang, the merchant semen. But who was he? A great fly of Beelzebub's, the bee of hearts, which mortals name Cupid, Love, and Fie for shame! And weren't brothers, having carnal knowledge of the same woman, damned by Scripture? What found King Henry VIII but Arthur drowned in the depths of Catherine's well, forcing him to spawn a dying nephew on his aunt and then sire in the belly of a six-fingered whore a most unnatural daughter as an excuse? A most unnatural act, then! But then what response? There but for the grace of God go I? But wasn't the grace of God, thought Darconville, available to all? *It wasn't! It wasn't!*

The long days passed, each instant hideously widening the fact of separation, multiplying its significance, leaving him more and more isolated. He rehearsed everything over and over again in his mind—a mind that whatever its sorties into the world of experience always returned to sleep only with its dreams. He was literally sick with love. Obscurely, it had never really occurred to Darconville that Isabel would leave him, the purity of which assumption, with the passing

days, he sadly came to reinterpret—for he began to borrow from the
delights of love its implements of torture—as being motivated less by
love or any medieval sense of courtesy than by the promptings of his
own self-esteem. He hoped for what he needed to believe, aspiring to
the measure of what he believed from the very measure of where he
was, almost as if to prove to himself that one can see stars during the
day from the bottom of a well. Still he would not abide a single thought
against her but continued to wait, convinced somehow that waiting *itself*—as though to obtain love we need but confess our own, as though
to perpetuate love we need only strangle jealousy—would bring her
back. Bring her back! Bring—! He tried to set his face against emotion but broke down and wept bitterly, his tears blinding him not only
for his own vanity and presumption but for the terrifying reoccurrences
now of sudden, irrational behavior: he began to speak to whoever it
was that lived in the same body with him, for there were two of them
now talking to one another, a dual form paradoxically shaping to an
individual he didn't know!

Darconville declined to be seen anymore—for real abnormalities,
seriously convincing him he was losing his mind, began to appear—
and he locked himself in his rooms. During the first few days he had
tried to write, savagely, but didn't, coming to welcome interruptions
and obstacles because they could be held responsible for his crude failures, then the delay, and finally his mercilessness; now, he fully refused to see anyone, to leave the rooms, or to answer any of the knocks
on his door, delicately holding his breath under such circumstances
until whoever it was went away. An appalling disorder soon prevailed
up there, and school papers became misplaced, communications went
unanswered, as he fell into more prolonged fits of mental and physical
torpor. The atmosphere of the rooms was now like a little self-
contained and closed universe, a kind of ambiguous gloom in which almost immediately it became hard to distinguish with certainty between the menacing and the merely ludicrous. Nothing was real or of
any significance except that which went on in his mind, and over everything hovered a subdued air not only of constant expectancy but
also of sibylline disappointment, of promises kept to the ear but broken
to the hope.

Whole days blotted out. He would sit in the darkness feeling a
weird urethral chill, frozen in silence, or go maundering up and down

for hours whispering to himself and trying to follow his torturous thoughts over every incident of the long four years as if in thinking, like surpassing the speed of light, he might move backward in time, but time is a curve, and, rounding around on him, it only brought him back once more to the immediacy of his own great grief. The coexistence of his despair with her joy became a hideous paradox. Did she feel nothing for him? Could there be nothing between two people? On the one hand, he reasoned, if there is strictly not anything between two things, then they are together! Or adjacent, perhaps—so joined? But what that is joined can then be two? A distinction thus emerged for Darconville between nothing and *a* nothing—and yet can you "have" a nothing? My God, he thought, there's proof of the thing in my very own heart!

One night he tried, unsuccessfully, to telephone Isabel sixteen times. He spoke, several times, into the dead receiver.

The terrible sin of *tristitia* set in. Darconville felt guilty now about his intellectual aspirations to probe, and, although in his heart he knew the conspiracy in Fawx's Mt. had been long in the making, he prayed: let me only understand, not judge. But why had it happened? What, he wondered, did losing a father mean to a girl? What immeasurable insecurity, what anxieties, had to be relieved? What unknowns did she fear she'd face in leaving that small town? What kind of love could instantly become so brutal, mocking him with his own words that once so loosely prophesied that one emotion by the other might be read? What had she feared in him, then? It occurred to him suddenly that perhaps Isabel inspired in him a desire for *much more than herself!* What if she knew, somehow, that she was only that inspiration and nothing more—even to herself—an insubstantial creature empty as the light by which someone else sought to find the very meanings she herself, merely hinting at, never embodied and never possessed and never would? Could that be? The beloved object not a beloved object but only a *means* of loving? The thought stabbed him. He sagged, driven and derided by the ridiculous and incompetent creature he'd become, by the derangement erotic passion had caused in him. It had been more than a week since he'd eaten, and if physical movement had become difficult now even the simplest reasoning seemed to require enormous effort. The persistently gnawing feeling of inferiority he felt, living as he now was between insignificance and silence, might itself be a clue, he thought, for perhaps she saw she couldn't be all that he loved, coming to hate in herself what he expected and yet needing at the same time to destroy the possibility of what she felt she could never achieve. Expectation is temptation. Where there's a won't there's a way. And yet could such things *be?*

Darconville looked at her photograph, faintly lit by the flickering candle: had that face, he wondered, been an inspiration or a challenge to his love? The composition of beauty could not have been more classical; it reflected what it had promised, yet in what had been shown was the utter moral defeat of its form. Content and form were at loggerheads. There were two simultaneous but incompatible forces within her—a classical love, embodied, and the disruptive insight, expressed, that that was precisely what she couldn't bear. Were both equally real and yet each unaware of the other? Was it possible? Can the mind prod itself into deciding which value it will observe in a universe where those unobserved, but equally real, have also actually happened? Could she hate the very legs she used to walk away and wish in the ones she never had to have come? The picture reflected exactly what it wasn't, as if framed in a paradox that seemed to ask "Who speaks of the failure of vision?" and implicitly answering "I."

The close reasoning somewhat deranged Darconville, and it became the point of departure for another one of his fugues, a theory whereby, in trying to re-establish his hope, he formulated an approach to experience in which radically opposed and yet equally total commitments to whatever event might be able to coexist in a single harmonious vision, and with painstaking exactitude he tried to make an existence assertion out of exhibitive but seemingly irresolvable paradoxes and contrarieties: *a realibus ad reliora.* Every negation, he concluded, is also a determination! And in that dismal set of rooms he resumed again that strange and willful attempt at psychokinesis—trying to move something by the power of the mind—and as if convinced that miracles must exist and didn't only for want of someone around to be amazed by them (for wasn't opportunity but chance favoring the prepared mind?) he this time began to reason that there must be an alternate universe that constructs the opposite decision points of those made in *this* universe, for if what doesn't happen could have, so somewhere, indeterminism says, it must! Desperately he tried to reason logical necessity into his love, for reality, he decided, was not thinkable but in relation to an activity by means of which it becomes thinkable: nothing that couldn't come to happen is unthinkable; nothing could come to happen that won't; nothing that could come to happen doesn't. I am who am not, thought Darconville, walking in circles and mounting fertile and despairing explanations for his own barrenness, for who can affirm, he concluded, that meaning does not exist in terms which don't also imply it does? Am I ignored, he wondered then, only that I might love the more, to savor in the breach what I can't in the observance? How else could Laura have been Petrarch's when she married someone else?

It was insane, Darconville suddenly saw, all of it! To try to divine exactly and scientifically the ultimate reality *which is not?* With a raw glare of grief into these monstrous distortions, he saw the tangle of logic for what it was, a confusion which pointed only toward itself as an example of the silence it feared and the truth it cowered before. The humiliation of not-knowing: it was a black fast of the mind, for what he knew was little, and worthless in the face of what he tried to believe without knowing, and still less in respect of that which he had been prevented from finding out. There was no light. There was no noise. There was nowhere to turn. He felt only the ceaseless thumping of his heart under the bedclothes, the rigid stillness of what passed for repose, and, occasionally, the absurd begging whisper in the darkness, *"Un altro, un altro, gran' Dio, ma meno forte."*

He soon began to go to the sheds. It was a condition of one anorectic day after another, exacerbated by furious smoking—and then drinking. He was now afraid to call Isabel, fearing in an irrational way the grief of fact more than the nothing of fantasy, wishing as he fell to remembering recollected visions of her face—laughing, sad, consenting, surprised, indifferent, affectionate, etc.—for a suspension of that mindless oblivion, if at all, then quickly, the waiting somehow for the worst news of all, the news that does not kill hope because there is none to kill, but merely ends suspense. It was a terrifying freedom, where to be free was to be alone, to be alone to be imprisoned and so to be imprisoned *not* to be free. The smirking folds in the curtains, the bedsheets, a coat thrown over a chair seemed at moments to leer at him. He sometimes thought he heard whispers, that someone was standing beside him in the darkness there. He would confuse one event with another, beginning to think of one thing as a consequence of something else which had in fact occurred only in his imagination, often the product of nightmares that were followed by an overwhelm-

ing apathy which formed, so to speak, the reverse side of his previous
terror, all leaving him in utter bewilderment with neither spirit to
spend nor resolution to spare. He began to suffer severe attacks of diarrhea for days on end and to experience the illusion of *water*
everywhere—on his bed, on his arms, on the floor. One night he unexpectedly caught his reflection in the bathroom mirror—frightening
himself—a matter that gave way to supernatural fears and speculations, the worst of which was that he began to think by performing
various acts in combination, no matter how banal, he might, by inadvertence, summon up the Devil. He lost all track of time. Once, when
the secretary of the English department telephoned to ask if he knew
he had a class waiting for him he hung up on her. He only prayed for
day to end, for night to fall, drinking heavily now to stem the tortures
of insomnia which he actually began to believe someone was *doing* to
him, and dawn never broke that he didn't awake—*lassatus sed non sa-
tiatus*—with a weltering grief at the very first start of consciousness.
He was in Cambridge no more. He was in the depths of Malebolge,
where the pains are not felt if you're half-dead unless you're also half-
alive.

The agony came to him in tenfold terror one night when, after
downing half a bottle of liquor and howling a repetition of wild, importunate cries to heaven—prayers only in the broadest sense, for they
grew increasingly more isolated from anything touching on need or
belief—he fell upon the bed into a haphazard heap like a dust-devil. It
was then that he had the nightmare: he was alone and threading
through the weeds of an old graveyard, past half-veiled urns, when he
saw an angelic stone figure with flowing hair averting her eyes with a
regretful hand and gesturing in pain as she stooped for eternity to lay
a stone-wreath on a barely traceable tumulus, woven over with wild
witch-grass, in front of which a lichen-covered cross leaned desolately
off-true; a crone, her face like an old tin peck-measure, with smears of
dough left sticking to its sides, inexplicably appeared nearby and
pointing to the angel cackled, *"Is it me? Or is it I?"* He shrank from
her and approached the stone figure slowly on dread feet and suddenly
froze in fright, for upon closer inspection he saw the angel's face fixed
in a hateful smile, its cruelty sharpened by a livid scar down the cheek
just below the eye! And then, underneath a hathi-grey sculpture of
himself, he read the legend on the tomb—

Darconville
Le Rival Donc

And then he was sitting up, breathless, his eyes loops of fright. The bedpost assumed the face of a Dutch sooterkin!

Welcome, Sir Diomed!

And, leaping at it, Darconville would have effected the brutal elimination of Gilbert van der Slang right on the spot had not the spectre within his throttling grasp dwindled back just as suddenly into a bedpost. The rage he felt! He had thought he'd heard enough of this shadowy creature in the ostensive reduction Isabel favored him with back in Fawx's Mt., an ill-concealed protext lisped as if she were wooing a cat and yet revealing what?—a little baggy-trousered midshipmite with his thumb plugged into his nether land and a mouth shaped like Flanders, the land that traded in many tongues! It was impossible to ignore this creature, as he had his brother, and Darconville now absolutely *thirsted* for information about him. But the regrets! During all those years when it would have been of capital importance to pay attention, everything conspired to the opposite, with both of them, lover and cuckolder, flying flags of convenience until it was too late. To know him, nevertheless, would surely be to know her! It wasn't enough that what had happened was true; it had to be explained! And yet only to hear a banal commentary on this thing which was incomprehensible—what was to be learned by that? What would he be told, falsehoods told against one suitor only to be reversed for another, that both might come to believe with a strength proportionate to the inaccuracy or even the unlikeliness of the information what Isabel provided? Come, tell a pin! And then what would he learn? Deceptions pried out of a score of shattering discoveries only to create, in the unchecked bluntness of a nimble investigation, a sudden new value for them they never had and so bring the two closer together in the fierce protection of it? No, strike not a stroke, he thought, for dexterity will obey appetite when the time is right. Govert! Gilbert! The princes orgulous! Newts and blindworms! Jackanapes with scarves! What didn't they deserve? Thank pity, thought he, if you would keep your ears!

Darconville's mind, however, now became his eye. He felt as love seemed to die, hate seemed to come alive, as if the very emotions fed on each other for proof, but still determined to it he refused to accept what had taken place and strove, almost superstitiously, to dedicate himself to an ideal of patient clearheadedness lest the demands of fanaticism, coming headlong and malicious, kill the sweetness he saw he needed for Isabel to come back to him. He prayed his pathetic prayers, staying up late and engaging in rigorous nights of exomologesis and palm-thumpings, and then one night found that waiting was no longer enough. It was finished. Had he not tarried? Aye, the grinding, but one must tarry the bolting. Had he not tarried? Aye, the bolting, but one must tarry the leavening. Had he not tarried? Aye, aye, the kneading, the making, the heating, the baking, and the cooling, aye, the cooling, for one may chance to burn one's lips, but tarry he could no more. Shivering, he felt a sensation of physical cold coming upon him, the kind strangely associated with, and coincident to, either sadness or amorous expectation, and so he picked up the telephone. The time had come.

He dialed: closing his eyes, he clasped the receiver with both hands. When suddenly he heard Isabel's voice he literally couldn't speak—the long days gone by, the pointless suffering, the awful love for this girl misassembled in thought's astonishment all he wanted to say. He could only see her gentle eyes, her mouth, her sun-shot hair. She asked who it was; he whispered her name. The silence that followed reached to forbidding degrees, an incalculable suspension like that moment of unknown consequence that comes when time, by a stare, seems to drop away in the intensity of trance. What, she asked with an overtaxed edge in her voice, what was it he wanted?—a question that became the sudden rectification fact imposes on memory, transforming his desire now into the terrible obsession he expressed and then forcing the answer she used, in a kind of grace, to slay with speed: *"It's too late— you'd better face it now! You're mad as a hatter!"* And she banged down the phone.

And then suddenly a hideous scream filled the room—the most dreadful and abject sound Darconville had ever heard: he sat white with terror, quivering, as it rang in his ears with inflexible steadiness until a silence, like denial, fell about him telling him what he could not feel and still could not believe. It had been his very own voice.

He sat there, in the darkness, shivering in the dreadful chill of his diarrhea. Then he stumbled over to the mantel, blew out the vigil light, and took a bottle over to his desk where he slowly prepared the moment—he artfully composed a letter to the Naval Academy on official Harvard stationery requesting a photograph of Gilbert van der Slang on the pretext of his having been selected by the college for some special award of merit: a sprat to catch a mackerel. He drank from the bottle in long pulls, gulping more, then finished it all, wishing he would die—not that he faced death with fortitude, he merely faced life without any. Laboriously, he proceeded to dress and for the first time in weeks went out of his room, the effort in simply descending the stairs—where he called and called and called his cat—leaving him weak to the bones and whiter than a corpse.

He made his way to the corner of Mt. Auburn St. and mailed the letter: *extinctus pudor.* It was a very cold night, making the simple act of walking—a struggle in illness and fatigue and drunkenness— next to impossible. Crossing back to Adams House, he looked up toward the morbid rooms with the pulled shades and tears of bitterness sprang to his eyes. You are crueler, you that we love, he thought looking toward the sky, than hatred, hunger, or death. He reeled. "You have eyes and breasts like a dove, and you kill men's hearts with a breath." A group of students stood in the Adams doorway on Bow St., and the gaunt unkempt figure pushed past them.

"You could say excuse me," exclaimed one of them with disdain. Darconville turned slowly.

"I would have," he said, seriously, "if I didn't have to speak to you."

The door closed, and he was no sooner inside before the hallway suddenly moved; the floor seemed to buckle. A strange black light leapt in front of his eyes. Darconville reached for the nearest wall to steady himself but fell to the floor, his face a greyslick, and lay there in a state of obdormition, more dead than alive, but alive still, alive nevertheless, relentlessly alive to the mysterious and deathless reality in which for no known reason he was living.

LXXVIII

The Prodigal Son

But now experience, purchased with grief, has made me see the difference of things.

—CHRISTOPHER MARLOWE, *The Jew of Malta*

IT WAS with Darconville now as with wastrels, left with thoughts such as sue and send, and send and sue again, but to no purpose, the evil of policy and plot having rained down like a plague upon everything of value he'd once owned. His was the compunction of one fallen from grace, whose wounds were of a nature to be cured no longer with balms but corrosives.

The folly! The sacrilege! The loss! The inheritance he'd squandered when, forsaking his father's house, he came down from Galilee and wandered south toward Moab, over to Edom, and then into Goshen itself! The wasted dreams! The pens, inkcakes, and writing palettes sold for a fistful of silver to buy rings and baubles and toys on night-walks through the shadowy *sûks* of Rephidim! Cheated at Damascus! Burnt with fire at Shushan! Robbed in the leaping-houses of Al-dūqa as-sawda! The pagan idols and teraphim on whom he threw away whole fortunes in rubies and gold! The self-satisfaction in the face of fate! The feasts and banquets given over to whole cities, the drinking out of full bowls, the dancing in silver-soled sandals to obscene flutes and timbrels! What truth hadn't been forfeited, what trust not mislaid? Beaten in Jezreel! Drugged in Bubastis! The excesses in the abiding places of Babylon, attainted of outrages on morals and perfumed with calamus and onycha, where to amuse herself one night a whore swallowed his richest pearl and, to flatter her, he wallowed in her flesh as if there to find it! The emptiness! The trivialities! The turmoils of weeping before the ghosts of what he couldn't have! All, all had profited him nothing! The profane songs sung to unkempt shepherds in the Wilderness of Zin, the dice-throwing with the soldiers of Porcius Festus, the wasted years dabbling in Gnosticism! Ridiculed in Gath! Corrupted in Philistia! The dissipation in the brothels of Megiddo where fops smeared themselves with malobathrum and ate pomegranates watered with silphium and collop-bellied tarts danced naked before the graven images of Baal! The fools and Marduk-faced losels and malefactors on whom he gambled away entire fleets of Cilician horses! The recklessness! The presumption that he deserved to be loved! The love he foreswore while, ignoring his faith, he sucked up to thralls and hirelings and read in counterfeit books and riddled wit with the high-priests and intellectuals of Ecbatana and Zebulun! The silences he took for adoration! The extravagance! Perverted in Admah! Condemned in Zeboim! The chances he had thrown away! Who hadn't loved enough could now not love at all! All, all lay dead upon his hands!

Crying out, Darconville struggled to get up—then fell back flat onto the floor, totally unconscious. It was late at night, gone quiet now, and there was no one around to help him who might have for who could have been found in the hallways at such an hour? That night God and Satan fought long hours for his soul. And God conquered. It was only left to be determined which of the two was God.

LXXIX

Keeper of the Bed

A brave scholar, sirrah; they say . . . he can make women of devils, and he can juggle cats into costermongers.

—ROBERT GREENE, *Friar Bacon and Friar Bungay*

"UNE NUIT BLANCHE, VIEUX?"

Darconville opened his eyes.

"It's cognac. 1884," said Dr. Crucifer, solicitously hovering over the bed and holding out a round goblet. "Please, won't you allow me to lead you beside distilled waters?"

They were in a bedroom of a portentous size, with a barreled ceiling crisscrossed with oak slats in a pattern something like a cat's cradle. A rich Burgundian tapestry hung on a far wall: two medieval figures hurrying out of a garden at the behest of a stern pointing angel. Below it stood a phonograph. There were silver sconces by the door, ginger jars, mirrors. A beautifully quilted counterpane heavily worked with a design of gold fishbones and anthropolatric-faced pentagrams had been neatly folded on a Jacobean cross-legged chair next to the four-poster bed in which, inexplicably, Darconville now found himself. It was a cumbrous load of oak—the sheets yellow silk sprigged in black—so tall to reach from floor to ceiling and wide enough that it appeared to be designed for three.

"What is this? Where am I?" asked Darconville, trying to sit up.

"You were found—drunk enough to piss through your shirt collar. Ill. Delirious. I don't doubt you've had a bad experience. I see you went down South, the Albania of America, mmm?"

"What—?"

"Lie back, my dear. Don't misunderstand me: the airplane ticket in your room—I went to fetch your pajamas—spoke volumes. It's irrelevant, anyway. You've been raving out loud about little else since last night, so I shan't pretend not to know what's happened. Fawx's Mt.," pronounced Crucifer with a snort. "Village life and peasants with water-buckets? Flown over by a bird of paradise? Heading towards the sun? How goes it down there—are men still men, women women, and the sheep glad of it?"

"I don't have to listen to this," said Darconville, attempting to rise but falling back, weakly.

"I should tell you," explained Crucifer, his babylike mouth puckering and making little glub-glubs, "there is a doctor's order involved. Your lungs, I'm told, aren't as they should be. And it's left for me to see that you eat and rest. Trust me, now, won't you?" Darconville waved aside the drink. "There is a bottle of tablets next to your bed: benperidol. It will relax you," he smiled, "—to say nothing of completely eliminating sexual desire. Take two." He waited. "No? Then keep them handy. You've been hurt, Al Amin. You went down there to the outreaches, like Alexander the Great, to find yourself surrounded by enemies on all sides: the licentious members of the Confederacy of Corinth; the tributary splacknucks of the province of Thrace; the inveterately hostile Illyrians with their steeple-hats and peaked shoes and dental preterites—and what happened to you? *Futuata!*" Dr. Crucifer removed the counterpane from the chair and in one belswaggering move sat down, awkwardly. It looked as though he could have taken up the slag of his belly and wiped his eyes with it. "Like a wood tick," he smirked, covering his mouth, "I grow big when I sit down. Now, tell me everything. The true riddle, remember, always asks a question that can be answered. I'm yours to the rattle, my child. Give me your hand."

"That," answered Darconville in an exhausted voice, "is a favor, I'm afraid, you must grieve to be denied."

"What are you *think*ing?" giggled Crucifer coyly, lilting the phrase musically and wagging a finger. "I wish but to console you. I am chaste, you forget. I have no feelings below the waist, although to that," he added, crudely grabbing his empty crotch, "I cannot testify. Gone are my ding-dongs," he said, laughing until his ears grew quite red, "my pair of dear indentures, king of clubs, dainty duckers, rose-nobles, myrmidons. I experience the *Hang zum Tiefen* in mind alone. I am as hollow as a chicken's vent. My temptations exist only in dreams."

"The reality is otherwise for me. Leave me alone."

Then Crucifer's face dropped as if the smile had been struck from his mouth by some invisible hand. His diminutive fingers twisted, whitening the dimpled knuckles. "Reality is *never* otherwise!" he screamed. "And the attempt to realize one's ideal in a woman—the expression is as unfortunate as the undertaking—instead of the woman herself, is a necessary destruction of the empirical personality of the thing. Love is murder," he said, blinking furiously. "As for the higher platonic love of man, women do not want it; it flatters them and pleases them, but it has no significance for them, and if your sweet little homage on bended knee to some doxy o'er the dale lasts too long, as it apparently has, Beatrice will transmogrify into a Medusa, as she apparently did." He smiled cruelly, his ordinary discourse as grave and sententious as ever abounding with those aphorisms and apologues so popular among the Arabs. "One signature, as they say in the book trade, is sprung. Call yourself a departee. You have been deserted."

Darconville peered sorrowfully over the coverlet.

"She is gone."

Crucifer passed him the glass again, and this time Darconville drank, greedily. He held it out for a refill, drank that, and then in a monotone characterized more by lassitude than sorrow or distress—his lips dry, his head back on the pillow—he took the whole confused story, almost as if he were trying to clarify it for himself, from the previous summer down to the present. But when he had finished, he wondered why he'd even bothered to tell it, for the abdominous creature beside him only fleered and nodded, dumbly and arrogantly, and it seemed more a blasphemy of the sacrament of confession than a shared confidence. Crucifer sat meditatively, blind as his fish, being urged on, or so Darconville now feared, to the lunacy of one of his enantiopathic remedies and the consideration, as a response, of perhaps trying to obtain an effect opposite to the symptoms of the disease. And yet a disease it was. Darconville was dying for love.

"I see it all now," muttered Dr. Crucifer. "The frame gives the picture perspective. She had a divided uterus, like a seal, ready to carry a pup in one horn one year and in the other the following year." He leaned back. "It was too late, of course, to grab her by the hypogaster and clap on a chastity belt. The Unfaithful Foul! She may not be the best girl in the world, but at least she's the worst, mmm?"

Crucifer went to the étagère by the window and took a cigarette from a box.

"She did not believe her own belief, from what you tell me, had doubts even as to her own doubts. She was never absorbed by her own joy or engrossed by her own silly sorrow. Casual, she pretended to be intimate, like all the smouch-faced Hebrews and Ibrim and Terachites from o'er the Euphrates with whom in guile she bears more than a passing resemblance." He lighted his cigarette, spat out a ball of smoke, and shook his fist at the ceiling. *"Le-Al-tahrir filistin!* With that selective memory, I think she was half-Jew! You know, forget the Palestinian diaspora, but remember the Holocaust, right? O Christ yes, Darconville, women in mischief are wiser than men. She never took herself in earnest and so never took anyone else in earnest—was neither enthusiastic nor indifferent, neither ecstatic nor cold, reached neither the heights nor the depths. Her restraint became meagerness, her copiousness bombast, don't tell me, I know, and I trust when trying to reach into the boundless realms of inspired thought—for her enjoyed no sooner, like sex, than despised straight—she seldom reached beyond pathos, right? No, she couldn't embrace the whole world but was forever covetous of it, correct? Believing in nothing, however, she took refuge in materialism, an avarice put on to convince herself, leaving you to die, that something had permanent value, and what value, what wonderful wonderful value! The Southpaw! And yet how many tales *the while* to please you had she coined, dreading your love, the loss whereof still fearing? But when she chose another—assured, of course, that whom she chose chose her—chose as well to rob you of your choice!" He drew on his cigarette. "'I, Helen, holding Paris by the lips,'" he puffed smoke at Darconville, "'smote Hector through the head!' And you won't call it hateful? Why, not all the suburbicarian churches of Latium, Campania, Apulia, and Bruttium could send enough prayer through the sky to forgive the most harmless act of this smiling psychocorrupter whom you call a woman but I call cat whore! Do you hear me? Cat whore!"

Darconville closed his eyes in anguish.

"I can see her now. Can't you see her?" he asked as if trying to show the speakable by clearly displaying the unspeakable. "Walking with stretched-forth neck, and wanton eyes, and mincing as she goes to Maître Gilbert Grippeminaud, making a tinkling with her feet, anticipating his every move, and then coming out with a little moue—the hypocrite! the glozer!—'O, I am mithunderthtood!' And while you are spending a month up here suffering the tortures of the damned for her, what is *she* doing?" Dr. Crucifer, grinding out his cigarette, smiled angrily at his friend—then bounced at him and in a lewd *geste à l'appui* drove his thumb into the well of his fist. "Hardly the work of a lady, my friend, but I suppose one should always applaud initiative." He turned to the tapestry. "No, Darconville, I take it to be axiomatic, a matter of breviary, that Eve, being a mere woman, was less like Adam than a serpent with a woman's face was like Eve."

Crucifer sat down again.

"But why," he asked, folding his hands over his layers of puppyfat and hunching into himself, "why did she wait for you to come up to Harvard to end it?"

"I don't know."

"You waited. You rejected immediate satisfactions with a view to obtaining subtler. Marriage."

"She told me she needed more time."

"Her presumption, yes. Your reply?"

"I told her to take that time. I loved her. I love her," whispered Darconville.

"A proposition you'll think she took the liberty of doubting—but you'd be gravely mistaken. Right there, that was the camel's nose under the tent. There was a plan in the making, can't you see? She knew what she wanted and only wanted to keep her promise abreast of reality until such time as she could with impunity do a quick

hundred-and-eighty in the other direction! She always wanted to insinuate herself into that family, it would appear, and to that end always kept her alternatives dry, you see, so as to be able to follow in future what you might call the Golden Rule: she who has the gold,
rules! The father's footling! Give it two thralls!" He laughed. "Amaz-
ing, isn't it, how but farting can engender little men? But this brother,
that," shrugged Crucifer, "strange all this difference should be 'twixt
Tweedledum and Tweedledee. As one was in the navy it's evident he
did everything on the double—o'erleaping his brother, yes? But
whether Ferrex or Porrex, Hengist or Horsa, or any other unphiladel-
phian two you wish to name or number she had best watch out: the
wrath of lovers is much less the wrath of devils than is the wrath of
brothers!" He winked. "Point taken? In any case, it was all as
reasoned as geometry for them, with no sudden passionate expeditions
on a stormy night to a waiting boat and then by muffled oarlocks to
Calais, oh no, don't fall for that." He paused. "But the plot—"

"I don't think she ever planned to come."

"You focus on details only to miss the whole," said Crucifer, blowing out his tongue to remove a flake of tobacco. "It's simple. She
hoped you'd find enough distraction in Cambridge to decide for both
of you to end it—and, ironically, like you she was waiting for nothing
but the very result *your* waiting explicitly forbade. It's hardly a matter
of Minoan complexity. She thought that you whose soul she stole to
break would get over what she herself never got involved in in the first
place—and never understood—a relationship that was an ideal she
was vain enough to flirt with, cunning enough to acknowledge, but too
small-souled to pursue, except, of course, in terms of this relatively
brief and temporary romantic lavolta—a light bounding kind of
waltz? In which the woman is assisted by her partner? To make fre-
quent high springs? Oh yes! She was the deed's creature, I tell you,
and by her female parent you lost your first condition.

"I can see her, can't you? No sooner a fornicator than a whore,
giddy for the mere exchange of arms, with all expenses paid? It was a
mind, Darconville, that could hold only one idea at a time, never proceeding to consequences felt in others and doing nothing in relation to
anyone but itself. It made a promise to stay and in a winky-winky it
was gone—once a pawn has moved, remember"—he leaned forward
and snapped the words out—"it can never turn back. She hasn't fallen
in love: it was a realistic decision she made, after straightening her

seems, to live without the vision she feared because of her shallowness would make her even more common than she is." Crucifer sucked a knuckle. "Have you ever noticed that women who abuse men are always those whom men have found unattractive? They confess to their own lack of power to please."

"She is beautiful," said Darconville, almost inaudibly.

"O, the very queen of curds and cream," replied Dr. Crucifer, mockingly clearing his throat with a rapid rumble. "I so happened"— he paused, making a comic glime sideways—"to see her photograph, several of them, in fact, when I stopped by your room." His breasts wobbled as he leaned forward. "Frankly, she has a low frontotemporal hairline, close-set eyes—with a marked trace of lubricity, I might add —a slight case of oxycephaly, tits like griggles, and a scar on a face, I'm sorry, that over-goes my blunt invention to say more. Lascivious grace in whom all ill well shows! You claim to love her. I smell the fallacy of *praemissis particularibus nihil probatur.*"

Delighted, Crucifer cocked his little head forward questioningly. It twitched.

"You defend her because you love her—'tis a pity you can't do so because she deserves it," he breathed, drowning his suspirations in the long draw of another cigarette. "Love is too partial a piece of piety, you see, for just as a man carrying a heavy bucket of water compensates to walk by cantilevering a leg, so you must alter your posture in order to keep your own balance, no, my friend? And speaking of legs!" He held his hand in front of his mouth, hideously, to laugh. "Darconville, Darconville, Darconville. Honeysuckle is a weed. We are deceived in what is not discerned, and to err is but to be blind. I saw nothing but a pudgy self-preening angel of banality with ankles like bottles, scarce twenty-odd years above the girdle, some fifty beneath. Hodgepudding! Globuliferous pig's-trotters! A pippin grown upon a crab! My God, it could diminish venery in a Turk! And I was going to tell you to keep a contemplative distance from beauty?" Smoke sifted through his teeth. "I looked at those lubberlegs and it made me wish birth-control were retroactive."

"You don't know what you sound like," cried Darconville. "You don't know the girl. You don't know anything."

"I know something," said Crucifer forcefully. "And of that something, much."

"You know much of little then."

"Let's just say, I don't know enough." He leaned forward. "Yet."
Crucifer smiled in his face.

"I do know she was as deficient in good looks as she was in intelligence and, yes, all right, dexterous enough to realize her own inferiority, I'll give her that, but ten ducats to a dime she went and left you precisely because she felt you'd one day leave *her,* having concluded in a final assessment of what she really was that she lived closer to her deficiencies than to her dreams. I know more. I know she is a woman and that all women walk in the sandals of Theramenes. And, finally, I know that if she had been brought up as—but whist, whist! You say she had no father?"

"Her father left her when she was a child."

"Interesting."

"She never knew him."

"Fascinating," said Crucifer, his voice squeaking. Then his face underwent one of its sudden alterations. "And I suppose I should now grow soft who with the same piece of luck years ago was packed off in the direction of my face to the Monastery of Monte Cretini? Do not hope it, Al Amin: my heart was broken, I broke none." He paused. "But it's curious, isn't it? Elizabeth I, bynempt Isabel—a woman who had more pricks in her than a secondhand dartboard—killed a lover because of her father." He spat in disgust. "I remember the riotous superlatives inscribed under her picture in the hall of the post-Reformation Jesus College, Oxford. The Virgin Queen, laughable soubriquet! The woman was the devil's quilted anvil, fashioning sins on herself and yet the blows were never heard! King Harry the Fat's murder of her polydactylic mother-cum-whore, however, was not forgot but flourished again in her daughter's anti-paternal slaughter of Essex. It was not only a revenge but a repetition, the murdered mother finally emerging in her to overthrow manhood in that dark inevitability and ghastly satisfaction by no means unrelated to her father's cruelty which, in a kind of bizarre chiasmus, was repeated in her own: it was no marvelous coincidence that Robert Devereux—or the cardinal who bore your glorious name—followed Anne Boleyn to the block. There was no husband. Belphoebe had her *own* balls! And there was no macBeth, although the entire realm cried out for one, but in any case she'd have strangled the boy in his crib, not so much that he might have grown up to kill a sovereign as that he'd have been pricked out in the sex she'd so proficiently come to hate. I've always thought it a pity," sneered Dr. Crucifer, "that the Massacre of St. Bartholomew didn't cross the channel to scour out a throne and turn that red-haired bitch back into the whibling she always was, ripping away that tallith of local religion she used to hide under and crushing underfoot that box of fortune-cookies called phylacteries she called her laws!"

Suddenly, he rang a bell by the side of the bed. "And yet how like sits upon like. Isabel: Elizabeth—one's a wonder, the other's a Tudor! Virginians two and two less than a deuce. When they meet in hell they can shout 'Snap!' How things come round at last."

Lampblack, tugging his forelock, appeared in the doorway. "Lunch, Master Numps," ordered Dr. Crucifer, who before the boy went out explained with sharp directives that he was first to pour him an apéritif and to bring Darconville anything he wanted over the next few days. "My bum-boy," said Crucifer, smiling at Darconville, "my clerk of the hanaper, my *exécuteur des hautes oeuvres.*" The boy quickly obliged. Crucifer took his glass and, standing, held it aloft to intone:

> "A lexical man came to marry
> And erred for the trull's mood did vary;
> The rosy cheeked bride, feared a
> Uxoricide.
> Prevail, worthy man, but be wary."

"Get my clothes."

"You aren't well."

"I have no intention of staying here."

"Tut-tut," warned Crucifer.

Darconville struggled to move up in the bed. "I do not like you," he said. "I do not acquiesce. I will never like you. I will never acquiesce. Now I'll say it once more: my clothes, get them." But he felt tired, disoriented, and, troubled by an elusive interdiction there, couldn't help but sense that everything for which he'd ever hoped or striven had somehow been relinquished in the confines of that room. His chest ached, and even in the dimmest light his eyes consistently hurt.

"You're not going to be ungrateful, now, are you?" asked Crucifer. He screamed for Lampblack. "You mustn't stir, in any case, not certainly until you've eaten and—"

Crucifer's eyes smiled, sheepishly.

"And?"

"—well, until the chlorpromazine wears off."

Smiling, Dr. Crucifer held up the empty cognac inhaler from which Darconville had drunk, twirled it between his clubbed fingers, and set it down.

"And so, you see, we can continue without fear of having to choose between other courses." Darconville slowly rolled over onto his face and breathed out in deep agony as the keeper of the bed took the occasion, swiftly, to refill the empty goblet from a special decanter he was keeping under the table. "Now, we were discussing motives, not ours, rather Mistress Commodity's. It would seem—"

But Lampblack suddenly appeared in the doorway balancing a tray at eye-level; it held two steaming bowls, some glasses, and a litre of wine. The boy carried it to the table by the bed. Darconville, however, refused to eat even as Dr. Crucifer, humped forward in hunger, told the fare: bush of crayfish in Viking herbs and frog cream, fingers of toast, and a sturdy Côtes de Montravel. Lampblack—it was his habit —waited, biting his nails, until Crucifer, waggling a bit of delicacy out of the bowl with his fingers, held out the trifle to the boy which he snapped up, and then he disappeared. Crucifer poured the wine and raised his glass: "Confusion to ladies!"—and he began to eat.

"I was saying," he continued, abrodietically licking his fingers, "it would seem to be impossible to consider this new mésalliance except in reference to you—the simple logistics of a ladder: touching points. It was a relationship, yes, but one of those relationships of contradiction whereby the error of illogical distribution—and of course," he paused, "in love," he sneered, "there is never enough equality to go around— prevented any logical conclusion. Why, even the proposition that hides in her name—I-A-E—serves no logical mood.

"We're agreed," said Crucifer, sucking in two fish from the spoon and waving some toast, "there was a plot. But why. See? How. She either came to look at herself through your eyes, in my opinion, and, flattering herself by what she saw in them, while at the same time not uncoincidentally making you indispensable, was driven to have that adoration confirmed elsewhere—a woman is repeatedly compelled to call herself a reward—or, as I say, your vision of the world frightened her to this point, that she came to take a realistic view of things and, reverting to type, capitulated for *security!* Money! Jews' butter! Fric! A fellaheen habit, I've seen it before. Semele, remember, prayed for a visit from Jupiter in all his splendor, but when he came his lightning killed her." He smiled gruesomely and grugeoned at the food. "I love that story." He wiped away the smile. "You of course asked very little of her, but hers, you mustn't forget, was a quest-in-reverse, an attempt to shed the meaning of her life rather than find it, see? Emptiness is the female form of perdition." He squelched, chewing his food, and breathed laboriously through his nose as he did so; the cult of the belly as an ethic appeared to him as perfectly natural, and it was obvious as he ate that he retained a predilection for such celibates who displayed the good sense of preferring gluttony to love. "Put a light load on a donkey, you see, and it thinks it can lie down, literally, in this instance —for women, like Egyptians, well know the principle of the inclined plane—and so she gilt up her eyebrows with arsedine, put on a tight sweater, and trotted off down the road."

"No."

"And notice when she acted: precisely when it would *pay off*. Good and evil in a woman's mind, I tell you, mean simply money and no money. Forgive me, but I suspect unless one promised her marriage it'd have been harder to plug her than to sneak daybreak past a rooster! What, you don't think he fucked her?" Crucifer grolched noisily. "This is embarrassing." He pressed his cheeks. "I'm not being wrong enough. I'm too *correct*."

"No!" insisted Darconville into the pillow.

"Very likely," replied Crucifer, "exceedingly likely. Very exceedingly likely."

He calmly lapped some cream off the spoon.

"And for a Dutchman! The Pilgrims, remember, left Leyden for America *not* for religious reasons—simply, their children were becoming Flemings! I've been to Holland. What, a sail down the Amstel, a box of sugar cookies, and an afternoon listening to the horrible rhythms of the Froth-Blowers' anthem?" Crucifer poured more wine and drained the glass. "Have you ever met this rival?"

Darconville said nothing.

"No answer."

He leaned forward.

"Did you ever try?" He waited. "No answer.

"The Dutch dog, tell me, is he—wealthy? His family?"

"Yes."

"A color card! I tell you," said Crucifer, fussing through some green sprigs to pull out another crayfish which he devoured like a borborygmite, "a woman's virtue is always in greater danger from opportunity than desire. Ambition has an intellect that runs like a rat through all the scrutinous possibilities here—and, I think, has snouted a hole! She wouldn't have been—"

Darconville turned questioningly to Crucifer.

"—promiscuous?"

"No."

"No," snapped Crucifer, sourly. *"Pride!* It is the very one that will tolerate none of the other Deadly Sins—not stinking, neither faltering, nor loosening its grip. It is self-contained, protectively secretive, and so poised between envy and antipathy, passions irreconcilable to reason, that as one monster seeks to predominate the personality the other cries it back, and wantonness is mitigated in the vain pursuit of self-esteem." Crucifer clacked through his bowl with a spoon for the last traces of cream. "Its disguises are not pretense but fact, revealing not sanity but concealing folly. Arrogance exacts seeming perfection! It acts a lawyer to the will, which, while appearing outwardly harmless," said he, looking suddenly strange, "conceals a most genuine depravity. I know about depravity," he whispered, never taking his cold eyes off Darconville as he rang the bell. "I can see in the dark, haven't I told you? When most I wink, then do mine eyes best see." He rang the bell again. "I have told you that, haven't I?"

Lampblack, breathless, hopped into the room.

"The tray, whetstone." Crucifer smiled at Darconville. "My amah, my sizar, my *valet de chambre.*"

The table was cleared quickly. Crucifer lighted another cigarette and, behind the smoke, watched Darconville carefully.

"Now, talk to me. Learn to confide. I shan't say a dicky-bird, I promise. Did she ever tell you she ever wanted to go out with other men? Once even?"

"Never. No."

"Exactly, you see?" Dr. Crucifer spat out a ball of smoke and offhandedly held out another glass of cognac to Darconville, which he took and drank. "The kleptophobe is cousin to the kleptomaniac! When any message is preached by a lover that makes its major claim to virtue the assertion that she wants to go out with no one else, it bears the poison of its essential destruction within its own breath. She only knew that, when she acted, she would act for good. There is always some brutish nether fault in starved vanity, deep and gleaming like the eyes of a shrew, almost hidden in its fur, yet when that shrew *decides* to move, no matter in which direction it goes, its hair will never muss. You would perfume, it appears, what stinks like a hoatzin. The thing is now Greek and now Roman. But during this four-year contrectation, tell me, was she ever given the freedom to choose other than you?"

"Often. Many times."

"Specifically."

"I went to London," said Darconville. "Then."

"You came back."

"Encouraged to it. We were engaged to be married."

"When precisely?"

"Three years ago."

"Why didn't you marry her then?"

"She wanted to finish school. We agreed on it. She was—" Crucifer nodded, saying, "Inexperienced. Say it. But gentle and kind, right? She was kind in the beginning, of course she was. The tare in its early stages looks exactly like wheat. Inexperienced, gentle, kind—yes, and young. But of canonical age," Crucifer winked, "right? But, tell me," he whispered salaciously, "was she of imperforate sex?" He leaned forward. "I mean, when you first—"

Darconville's eyes lowered sorrowfully.

"Dot dot dot," said Crucifer, smiling. He folded his arms. "This engagement, whose idea was it?"

Darconville looked piteously across the room, confused in the salvo of questions that made reflection impossible. "I can tell you this: I very much desired it, but when I was in London she wrote not only that she loved me but mailed me her grandmother's ring—unasked for, freely sent, yet happily received—to size another ring, another finger of the same dimension."

"A nimble finger."

Dr. Crucifer stood up, a belly-dance contortion that took three or four distinct moves, and poured some more wine. "A nimble finger, a thimble brain, and a fimble for a mouth. But did she talk much?" He arranged a few pieces of toast left there. "Conversation?"

Darconville shook his head.

"Precisely," said Crucifer. "And when she did?"

"It was—not always—"

"Remarkable? Of course not. On the contrary. *Distinguo.* Like all silent people when she opened her mouth she was a nag, thinking nothing of course but all the while speaking like Bumbastis. A woman's conversation is always an anaphrodisiac, and no one knows it better than they." He swirled toast around in his wine to remove the bubbles which gave him a headache and set his neutral groin on fire. "I know that silence from years in the classroom. *Pigritia:* plain slackness. But was it silence? I wonder. Dumbness, perhaps–a situation as regards women when they are at their most dangerous: men are only too apt to take their silence as quiescence or inactivity. But what an error in the estimate! The bitch had moves and countermoves. No one *ever* leaves somebody for nobody. She was the very Vicar of Bray."

He glubbed more wine. "She told you she loved you. To the last?"

Darconville nodded.

"Stories to delight your ears, favors to allure your eyes? She touched you here and there? Oh yes. The adverse party, with a suitable amount of proleptic irony, was your advocate. But the time that went by! Is it any wonder that Vulcan fashioned creaking shoes for Venus that he might hear her when she stirred?" Crucifer swept his arm from him. "She loved you—pish! She was loyal—bubble! Fair proportioned—mew! Gentle of heart—wind!"

Dr. Crucifer, meditatively, then began to walk, watching the unsteady outthrow of his feet in front of him as he paced the room with that awkward gait of his, left, right, left.

"Yet digged the mole," he murmured, "and lest its ways be found worked underground. Fickle, false, and full of fraud, this breeding jennet, in which with its pluming and fakery the South is apparently rich, ill-annexed opportunity and yet was still the owner of her face! It's astounding! My God, I am almost with child to get to the bottom of this. She was a speaking cat. The girl was a veritable Guicciardini." He moved back and forth on those premeditated feet. "To question is the answer. *Quaere:* why did her relationship with you coincide exactly with the years she spent as a student? *Quaere:* how could she chance to confirm your replacement almost on the very day you departed and not before? *Quaere:* what was her original resolve in having decided to tell you absolutely nothing of him while at the same time hazarding his disaffection in the cultivation of your love? *Quaere:* when exactly did she decide she needed you for leverage? *Quaere:* where had she spent all those days, weeks, months in your absence? Lies! Abominable lies! The adulteress's tenth muse!" hooted

Crucifer. "Fornication, spying, trespassing, lying, duplicity, bribery, procuring, and conspiracy! She munched vacuity and excreted fibs. Why, it's a whore deep as a ditch! And then take the dike-louper," he asked, "—this nautical neighbor—had she ever once mentioned him, even at the outset, years ago, or referred to him in your presence? During a row, say? After some balls-up or other?"

Darconville's closed eyelids trembled, his nostrils quivered, and he shook his head.

"And why?" asked Crucifer. *"Why, but to keep you ignorant!"* He was standing in front of the tapestry with his misshapen back towards Darconville, and then he turned, that ghostly unnatural face working hopelessly to try to animate itself with conviction, desperate, it seemed, to try to reach, to shape, to appoint the life in another he'd come to lose in his own but one, it was clear, he'd retrieve not for the purpose of remorse but for the purpose of rage.

"A fact, it appears," said Crucifer, "never went in partnership with the miracle you saw as her."

He took the remark across the room to Darconville and lowered over the bed, arranging the sheet to his feverish shoulders. He looked at the tender concave temple and would have kissed it but instead whispered, "Did it?"

Dr. Crucifer stared into his eyes.

"The number of vibrations," he breathed, "varies inversely as to the length of a string; thus half the length gives twice the vibrations, don't you see? The less she gave, Darconville, the more you imagined—and she couldn't leap an inch from a slut." He sat down and moved closer. "To live without facts, you felt, was to be at the beginning of imagination. The artist, I don't doubt, may learn a wealth of lessons in this connection but," he glubbed, "the lover?—O dear me!"

Crucifer minimized nothing. A chronic oppositionist, he had to depart every majority and to attack every authority. When in argument he often refused to allow his antagonist the chance to state his own case but would do it for him, suddenly, and perhaps even fairly—and then *demolish* it, gravely and frequently with an expression of sympathetic regret. Curiously, he tried carefully to conceal the way he secretly demanded things be understood, so that swiftly, inexplicably, he could become upset upon instantly being offended, and yet somehow, with a tongue laced with proverb and sermon, strap and ferrule, he never gave up one element of a problem for the sake of coming to a comfortable solution. He railed by precept and detracted by rule, seeking not to contemplate truth but rather to subjugate it. He made precedence out of example, underaccommodated, and wheedled. He entered every hole.

"That's not all. The robbery of one age becomes the chivalry of the next. She'll be seen a heroine for what she did."

"Do you believe that?" asked Darconville, astonished.

"As you come from the holy land of Walsingham."

It was insupportable: but there was more.

"I can see her. Can't you see her?" asked Crucifer, wiggling his fingers in front of his eyes and stutterstepping again forward. "There's a gathering of shagpats and semi-imbeciles in Fawx's Mt. in the midst of which, all smothered up in shade, she and her Dutch dunt sit with juggling eyes, and when called upon to explain the *bravery* of her decision, to keep it affronted, unassailed, she blushes as if a fulgence had gone into her womb, but when asked how they met, she curiously forgets all her scheming, plotting, and dissembling—for whatever guilt soever years should afford her is of course all prevented in her select and aboriginal ignorance—and putting her whorish hand on Gilbert Gooseboot's knee this object of common licitation lowers her eyes and sweetly replies, 'O, just fate.' " Crucifer squeezed his hands and squatted a bit. "You see, she aspires, she ascends. She's attentive, she's—"

An unnatural heat shot to Darconville's heart.

"Ambitious," he said.

"A grievous fault!"

Crucifer was almost beside himself.

"I can almost hear her: even *now* the turtle pants! She spreads and mounts like arithmetic! Sex upon victory! When cedars are shaken where shrubs do feel no bruise?" asked Crucifer. "The delight she must feel! The she-hippo! How she must have shrieked to see it done! She thinks you'll do nothing, of course—what, steal off to one of the square states of Middle America? Join the Carthusians to apply the cat, eat black radishes, and dig your own grave? Lose your wits in some peaceful province in Acrostic Land? Good, let her be right; it will console her for being nothing else," he said, "and yet—"

A *subintelligitur* crouched in the pause. Secretly he took Darconville in from the corner of his eye.

"Yes?"

"It was only a foolish idea."

"An idea?"

"An irrelevant idea," he replied. He waited. "But you do know I care infinitely for you, don't you? That I brought you here for no other reason? That the sheikh's tent is always pitched on that side from which the enemy is expected?"

"What is it?" asked Darconville wearily.

"Nothing."

"Tell me."

"No, it's none of my business. God alone knows what you'd find if you started turning over stones—though you can be sure he'd hold it against you if you did."

Darconville rolled his head back.

"But since you ask," said Crucifer, catapulting quickly on his hunkers by Darconville's ear. "We can change the meaning of a thing by seeing it in a different aspect. Do you understand? What I'm saying?" Darconville's fever-weakened eyes registered nothing. "As one object becomes warmer, an adjacent object must necessarily become cooler," Crucifer pointed out, "isn't that a law?" He began to look suddenly wild, and his ears, bemedaled with heavy lobes, actually shook. "I assure you, it is! There is a doing of right out of wrong, is what I'm saying, *if*"—he winked and touched a finger to his nose— "the way be found. I mean, if nothing is to be attempted in which there is danger, we must all sink into hopeless inactivity. You must look at my face: my explanations are bound up with the way I put them. Listen to me," he hissed excitedly, looking behind him as if to be certain they were there alone, "next to truth, confirmed error may serve as well, and if a wrong must be made right, why so it must even if the logic of it should lead you," he looked grave, then whispered under his breath, "to *do* something."

Crucifer fixed him with a knowing look.

"Do something," asked Darconville, swallowing, "to her?"

"You infer with acumen."

He hadn't a second to react before Dr. Crucifer suddenly placed a hand over his mouth. It was jelly-cold. "Wait. I say, *if* a wrong must be made right, *if* a way be found, *if* it should lead you to, could you? Do something? If," repeated Crucifer who, constrained by the fullness of his robe, clumsily bent to listen for the answer. "Say yes."

Darconville lay motionless, looking up as if everything had gone out of his eyes. Everything he looked at, in fact, out of the cursed necessity of looking at something, seemed subject to the relentlessly unfolding and cruel paraphrase of what had once been his life.

"It's hypothetical," pleaded Crucifer, his voice trembling in a little flutelike whistle. He stared at Darconville with a jesting challenge— something deep within his eyes seemed indulgently to flicker. "Just say yes. No one need know. Only yes." Slowly, he lifted his hand, his lips pursed to a careful kiss: the impress of his fingers lay across Darconville's mouth.

"Yes," sobbed Darconville.

"*My child*," whispered Dr. Crucifer.

LXXX

The Fox Uncas'd

Who hath the power to struggle with an intelligible flame, not in Paradise to be resisted, become now more ardent by being failed of what in reason it looked for?

—John Milton

"THE QUESTION NOW," declared Dr. Crucifer, "is what to do. You are bitten, you are not all eaten. But it will be so preached—I can hear the crabbèd textuists and paraphrasts now—that if you loved her once, you'll therefore love her always and by acting to ignore justice for peace so shall it be proved. The method of custom is so glib and easy though, isn't it? To prove you loved her, though she doesn't care a fig for you, you're supposed to spend a lifetime in silence with only a handful of glorious memories to keep you from madness? To feast, to fart, to finally forget?"

He turned toward Darconville with a condescending, slightly ironic indulgence but saw in that pale and chartaceous face (which made him seem more ill-shaven) only two uncaring eyes polished in grey staring indifferently, remotely, somewhere beyond the room. There was a sudden diffidence about him that Crucifer couldn't bear.

"What, shall you spare her? Let her spread among us until with her shadow all your dignity and honor, all the glory of your name, be darkened and obscured? Resist by what resistance would surely kill you? *Simply ignore it?*" he asked in a succlamation of outrage, "as if to say that if one were ill all one's life getting well might then be taken for another illness? Can it be? You'd allow them, the most loathsome example of twinning since Sodom and Gomorrah, to go scot free? Sit like a fool at home, Don Pimp, and eye your rashers while open-eyed conspiracy is all and everywhere about? I'd pray to Lucifuge Rofocale to set an edge upon my pipes and chase the dusk of conscience back across her face! I'd crack sixty axletrees to get at her! I'd be on her like white on rice!" Crucifer's angry face was in a torque. "And you?"

"I don't know."

"Φλυαρία!" screamed Dr. Crucifer.

He swung through the bedroom, reaching up furiously over his head as if he were going to pull down lightning, his lips quivering like rubber-bands, and then became stationary. He swallowed in embarrassment.

"Look at me." He tried to laugh and fumbled up a cigarette. "The future—you shake your head in advance, I see, but wait, *wait*—the future is memory, I was only going to say, if we don't overcome the past." Where, Darconville wondered, had he heard those words before? "The injury I insist you mustn't fail to dismiss without recompense, because you haven't, is not therefore entirely done away with, for to live still and not be able to love—you don't want that, do you? —is only to heap up more injury. The woodcock is near the gin," he prompted, puffing his cigarette, "and, what, shall it now skip away? O hell, perhaps it should," quillwheeled Crucifer, feigning loss of interest and eyeing Darconville surreptitiously, "perhaps it should."

Inhaling, Darconville pushed his head back into the pillow.

Dr. Crucifer studied his cigarette, looked at Darconville, shook his head, and continued staring at the cigarette. "You're gentle," he said, puffing. "Gentleness is nice—the very mood fair Isabel, I don't doubt, is this minute showing Captain Poop of the Yankee Frigate." He

puffed. "And courteous, though it won you no hearts. Obedient, but
blindly. And then, it seems, proud. Reverence to this! But of course
when pride rides, shame lackeys. Or," asked Crucifer, now drawing
closer, "are you simply fearful? Darconville?"

What Darconville desired at that moment as he had never desired
anything before was a place in which he could have lost himself forever. He drew a deep breath through his nose and tearfully turned
away. "Darconville?

"Ah, it's the justice, of course, the *ethics* of it, that's it, isn't it? The
law. You are still in blind servitude to the inquisiturient bishops and
shaven reverences of the Church! Come, Bocardo," he snapped impatiently, "save your tears for the fumes that live in an onion! Law," exclaimed Crucifer, "what is it if it can force itself against the faultless
properties of nature? Laws? My word, no. Laws do not indicate what
a people value but rather what seems to them foreign, strange, and
outlandish. You mustn't show them undue respect: they're but exceptions to the morality of custom, that's all—why, in another country
my seinsembling and scrotiform-faced stepmother would have thrown
off her bombazines-with-the-black-leg-of-mutton-sleeves for the scanties of a common tart." He crushed out his cigarette. "There are, however, a few points of law to be gotten of your bitch's falsehoods, in
spite of her—forgive the oxymoron—genuine hypocrisy. I will remind
you of poetry, if you let me. Will you listen?"

Crucifer rubbed his hands.

"The state, it could be argued, must be called to account as to one
of its highest functions, that of law—the hubris of human ingenuity—
and even possibly condemned by the standards implied in the utopian
idea of primal innocence, for hasn't it taken upon itself one form of
dominion after another," asked Crucifer, crossing the room with his
forefinger in the air, "and lorded it over all the others, pretending, as
though it were the daughter of the gods, to a privilege beyond all
other disciplines? Primal innocence?" He winked. "Dwale and delusion! So laws were grafted. Lawcraft? Sheepcraft! I won't bore you
with a history of all its agathokakological claptrap, Darconville, but
simply point out that, at bottom, it owes its essential existence to the
depraved and fallen nature of mankind—which it can never riddle,
which it can never rectify—and in my considered opinion is styled,
when at its most efficient, only to jingle at justice and to twill at truth,
especially in matters touching on that curious but primal antagonism:

the just thing versus the legal thing. The law and the gospel," he glubbed with obvious delight, "are hereby made liable to more than one contradiction, and if a mooching and piety-faced forgiveness is all you know of either, where punishment you take to be a crime, I must then reinstruct you that all law has its beginning in that first crime of our first mother and her low tongue—Johannes Goropius Becanus (1519–1572) in his *Origines Antuerpianae,* Antwerp, 1569, maintained that the original language of Adam and Eve, and so the tongue of primal betrayal, was Dutch!—and thereby cry out that you might let your severe and impartial doom imitate divine vengeance and rain down your punishing force upon this temerarious strumpet, this mistress of the adroit lie, until like that fen-born serpent she resembles at the root of all our woe she eat the dust of her penalty for the rest of her life!"

Crucifer wiped his mouth and, walking like Agag with a mounting gait, stepped toward the bed where Darconville lay; coming closer and closer it seemed to him that the creature became more and more insubstantial. He backed away and Crucifer made a mimicry of tentative assistance but he was far too anxious to make a point to waste a motion.

"I sniff the air and find something wrong here yet. There's an odor of virtue in this room. Could it be *forgiveness?* But please," asked Crucifer, "how serve virtues, tell me, other than merely to weaken? What in fact *are* they, my man? Old ladies' litations? The desiderata used by saints to engender self-contempt in anyone who must witness them? Nasty little abstentions put about by society and religion for individuals with a fortress mentality to live by, always to their disadvantage, for the promotion and sales of the general good? My God, how one is always privately victim to the virtues the public sends down! It disgusts me!" said Crucifer in a shrill piping hoon. "No, the strength of knowledge does not depend on its degree of truth but on its value to serve the nature truth, as we know it, molests. *Stricte dicte,* there's a stinking partisanship at the heart of *all* definition! I am stocky, you are short and stout, he's a fat little turd, isn't that how it goes? Why do we have to die? Because we have to live. What the hell is life, then?—a long death! It's all grimgribbing, Darconville! Good and evil are only the prejudices of God," he continued, with a species of mad hilarity in his eye, "and the dreadful conclusion is that the ancient deadly sins, seven in number, are in fact, all of them, very close to virtues, just as the guilt you feel after committing a few of them is arguably nothing less than responsibility in a funny mask! And then if these so-called sins never existed, why, what great authors, tell me, could have written their masterpieces of humanity? Or whereby that they might be corrected could we otherwise discern another's faults? And howso then maintain? Your enemy by any other standard, can't you see, would be an ephydriad. But, wait, here's latitude! It is precisely as *tame* animals that we show ourselves a shameful sight. I tell you, people need open enemies if they are to rise to the level of their own virtue, virility, and cheerfulness. I mean, if the end doesn't justify the means, then what the hell does?"

Exulting in his intellectual power and dexterity he seemed to be one of the greatest sophists that had ever contended in the lists of declamation, his spirit of contradiction and perverse delight in presuming to be able in argument to maintain and even defend the wrong side of things with equal aggression and ingenuity somehow making error itself rich, permanent, and distinguished.

"The whole conception of man really sinning against God is intolerably puerile. Call it sin? Sin is no sin when virtue is forgot. Call it evil? Why, evil is only a freedom exercised by one and invidiously disapproved of by another, done as effortlessly and as naturally as time passing. Dirty oil in a car means it's doing its job! Every great fortune is based on a crime, and fortunate crimes make heroes. Successful crime ceases to be crime. Success constitutes or absolves the guilty at its will. You have been thrust into this part, do not forget, and must remember of what you must contribute to it that if the scene, not the act, is the unit of construction of this Jacobean play, scenes *lead* to acts! If they call the reaper, whet thy scythe. No, I favor any skepsis to which one may reply, '*I am revenged!*' You needn't put an unnecessarily personal significance to it," said Crucifer, smiling in his eyes. "The rationality of the universe itself suggests survival, and, my God, I'd rather live in any loathsome dungeon than in any paradise at her entreaty! Be only thorough! Fill the unforgiving minute! You can't cure a personality. Teach the thing manners! Split her—how I adore the language that can tell you this—from coon-slit to cap!"

Darconville blanched, closing his eyes and trying to expel a terrifying picture from his imagination. The words literally seemed insane. He had finally come across a person, he realized, who, in that mysterious mythopoetic world in which his own imagination for so many years had insisted on moving, was a serious antagonist, a madman butting at him through a baffle of antilogic and embodying a depth of actual evil, the most terrifying aspect of which seemed to be that his opponents were selected with a sardonic delight in their incompatibilities.

"I can read your face, Darconville. You'd abstain from such action as you know it, there's no doubt, out of mercy, out of temperance, out of truth, indeed, out of love. Mercy's all very well, but what of holy cruelty, to disallow life for the misshapen, the ill-begotten, the gormless? Temperance"—he spit a pip sound—"is for nuns! If one continually forbids oneself the expression of the passions as being rude and bourgeois, the result can only bring about precisely what is not desired: the weakening of them, the degeneration of power into shallow and hypocritical etiquette! Truth? A logical or mathematical proposition such as $1+1=2$ we say is true not because of prior 'meanings' or rules, conventional or otherwise, much less because of some necessary correspondence with reality. Such a proposition we take to be true simply because, and in so far as, we choose to *regard* it as true and merely select signs to suit the terms. Figure like the Dutch: they have shaped their religion in the shape of their heads, which explains why there are three hundred different forms of worship over there, all supposedly Christian! True and false are but a blind turned upon a pivot. In combat every man fights his own war. There is no such thing as a rule.

"But love?" Crucifer's tongue seemed to sour on the word. "What is this bit of jackasserie from the goliardic corpus of pothouse verse other than lust for possession? The lover desires sole and unremitting possession of the person for whom he longs, seeking unconditional dominion over the soul and body of his paramour, demanding it exclusively. But if one considers that this in fact means nothing less than *excluding* the whole world, my dear, from the so-called precious good, if one considers that the lover aims at the impoverishment and deprivation of all competitors—a wild and uncompromising avarice that has been deified over the ages—then love is nothing more than the vilest expression of egoism and greed! This is the good you'd preserve to love, presume to lure, pretend to like?" His voice took on a tone of expostulation. "Why, admit this silliness a virtue and, by Christ, *you'll be but advocate to her crime!*" He joined his hands and shook them with blurring speed. "Shall I reckon for you in the law? Shall I? Then I shall tell you that the law is a blank to be filled in by circumstance!

To torture in Holland, for instance, is considered as a favor to an accused person! Haven't you read Dr. Johnson on the subject? No man was put to the torture there, he explained, unless there was as much evidence against him as would amount to a conviction in England and therefore an accused person among them had one chance more to escape punishment than those who were tried in England. No, there is not one thing with another, but Evil saith to Good, 'My brother, my brother, I am one with thee.' " Then his eyes became as hollow as the unboweled winds and he spoke low. "The concepts of good and evil merely address the idea of the expedient and the inexpedient! One holds, so it goes, that what is called evil harms the species, that what is good preserves. In truth, evil instincts are expedient, species-preserving, and indispensable to as high a degree as good ones—their function is merely different. Abandon all thought of consequence, says Krishna, for good and evil are essentially the same in a world which is an emanation of a unitary spirit." He quoted

> "The dart of Izdabel prevails!
> 'Twas dipt in double poison."

"Then think: in a world where penitence is boastfulness—is this virtue?—and giving an expression of hostility whereby, the cruelest form of bondage, a person is incapable of repayment—is this virtue? I smell only cadaver in a living body. Is this the zeal you'd have surround your cause? Think on 'quietism'—the gift of virtue she'd have you get. The slave accepts the kindness: it dulls the edge of rebellion and wins the donor a lifetime of subservience. The virtue that violates, the kindness that kills!" He shook his head. "Is it any wonder, my God, that the gospel of Laodicea urges people to be temperate in what they call *goodness* as in everything else?"

Dr. Crucifer took a breath, folding his tongue in the mouth that constricted in an ugly munch.

"I tell you, hard cases make bad law and where the law is so broad as to be applicable to all circumstances there is no obligation to obey it in any circumstance. A man must sometimes rise *above* principle!" he said with an angry smile. "Law, as I say, is ultimately the consequence of man's fallen nature. Hence came first the law of corrupted nature, which they call *jus naturale* or natural law, and among its excellent principles and rules—hope, ye miserable; ye happy, take heed—can be found these: *vim vi repellere licet,* violence may be driven out with

violence; *frangentem fidem fides frangatur eidem,* there is no need to
keep trust with one who does not keep trust; *falsa causa non nocet,* an
error in motive does not effect the validity of an injury in those who
deserve it for another just reason; *fallere fallentem non est fraus,* swin-
dling a swindler is no swindle; *volenti non fit injuria,* to one who asks
for it, there can be no injury; *si te vel me confundi opporteat potius
eligam te confundi quam me,* if one of the two of us must come to
harm, you or I—this, of course, to be applied," said Crucifer, his eyes
taking on a lurid look as if lit by the fires of hell, "to whom it fits—
then rather you than I. Oh yes, and much more of the same kind
which must be reckoned among the laws. Why, tongues I could hang
on every tree that might civil sayings show, but that's as it is, isn't it? I
don't think you have to hear more, Al Amin." Crucifer touched Darconville's arm, confidentially, as if to bring him further under his
influence and with slippery eyes moved even closer. "You know what
I'm asking for, don't you?" He looked over his shoulder like a conspir-
ator in a play and with sudden evaporating cheerfulness directly asked
in a low, low whisper, "tell me, have you no rasp in your farrier's kit?"

Darconville looked up at him.

"You smell."

Crucifer's rigid eyes shot contempt, and he stumbled up, caught by
reason of its bunchiness, on the hem of his robe and almost sprang to
the far side of the room where as if seized convulsively he sought to
expel, and expel again, and expel once again his sudden breath which,
rattling, seemed to indicate a valvular disease of the heart. The in-
durated pause that followed did not last long. He made a forlorn show
of jauntiness, and, as he turned, his face became more insinuatingly
piggy.

"I told you," he smirked, walking to the étagère, "we 'leaked'—an
inadvertence causative to my operation. Repellent, you're thinking."
He took up a Stiegel-type bottle and, unstoppering it, quickly perfumed various parts of his body. "But you wouldn't intentionally insult me, would you? Because I have no dowsets? Have a care, Sir Formal. I am inexact, I told you. I have no will. I have no tail. I am like
the *New England Primer,*" he said, "'adorn'd with Cuts.' I'm—incomplete." Amused, he held the stopper between his legs and dropped
it. "Here," he pointed, "I do not stand; I cannot do otherwise. It's a
wound, you see, I cannot help. But yours," he said, "you can."

Vainly, Crucifer waited for Darconville to say something.

"Ducdame, ducdame, ducdame," he whispered, coming forward in a hunch and depressing himself into a third of his normal displacement. "I must say this, and I wish I might underline it. A nullity and an entity, with like eliminands, yield an entity in which the nullity-retinend changes its sign. Shall I put it flatly? Clip the bitch, Darconville! Send her to hell with the lie in her teeth! Lap her in lead!"

"Never."

"Never say that," said Crucifer, his hands coquettishly demential, held high and apart. He pleaded, "You are complete. You don't need her. You do not *need* her!" He turned his head sideways to listen. "All right?" Appeased, he tapped the bed three times and rose smiling to himself.

"I do," Darconville then said softly. "I do need her."

Dr. Crucifer wheeled around, his face spinach-blue and reptilian, and huffing as if in his rage he would blow a monstrous bubble out of his mouth like the soul which the old artists painted flying from the mouths of the dying he screamed at the top of his lungs, *"You liar! You liar!"*

LXXXI

Oratio Contra Feminas

I'll set her on the stove and then she'll melt.

—HANS C. ANDERSEN, *The Snow Queen*

RISING to his full height, Dr. Crucifer split the air with a kind of anonymous shriek and jerked his head with a nervous tic as if he were trying to pull it off his shoulders, and then gasping backed away almost comically on those little pherecratian feet to shake out of his pocket a tiny bottle from which he took a pill. He stumbled agitatedly to the semisecurity of a dark corner where, composing himself, he raised his robed arms like angular fulvous wings and spoke:

"The time is come, Darconville, to the confusion I hope of the propagators of this slanderous imputation, that women are necessary, when I find I must address you in a more ceremonious form of speech and submit to your judgment this deliberate exhortation—for what avails the best intentions with the worst administration?

Exordium   —that you may weigh the nearly inexpressible baseness into which, but for this selfsame persuasion, *exigi facias,* you shall otherwise surely sink. I shall make no commands. I shall ask nothing of you I myself, in celebrating, do not believe and you cannot give, in spite of the fact that with Egyptians the obtaining of victory is a point of honor, for where would be the wisdom in giving such a command to an honorable young man, of illustrious birth, of an ancient family, or to try to interpose a jurisdictive power over the inward and irremediable judgments which in this, as in most cases, must fall to your choosing alone? I shall be witness for the prosecution. I shall plead and squeeze. I sense even now that I am about to come out with violent declarations, but to regulate, to rule? That would, indeed, be righteous overmuch, for forced virtue is as a bolt overshot, going neither forward nor backward and doing no good as it stands. No, I beg you only to *think,* which like the act of diving is simply to fight the natural tendency towards the surface and to make an exertion to get to the bottom. Pay attention then! Empanel a jury! Prorogue a parliament! I come to prove a crabbèd cudgel fits a froward whore!

"I have heard enough of this serpent who made you eat the apple of your heart! I have felt the Decian persecution of her silence! I have tasted of her inconstant, concocted, and venial sighs and smelt on her a stink of bitchery that not opopanax, nor jasmin d'Espagne, nor all the multi-toned scents on Carmel's flowery top could perfume. I have seen, finally, more than polite and attentive gravity should require of anyone, what is, I shall not much waver to affirm, far less in appearance a girl than a bass-fiddle of adipose, a steatopygous bulk, a contentious self-conjugating dirigible swollen with its own piety and blown with an appetite that, more greatly to be satisfied, might better betake itself to share in the fate of the dicteriads in the ancient Potters' Quarter or those shameless courtesans soliciting in the sinks and stews of Desvergonia!

"I see you before me *free!* Give me the liberty to say what I must ask you to learn not to question to believe. You are unrestricted, unrestrained, unreserved! Can you be blamed for this recent piece of inconvenience thrown at you as if a gift anymore than you should be

Propositio   praised, allured by the need to feed the pistrix of a carnal heart, for overvaluing another and pursuing in her the mortal incapacities and shifting but all-too-human flaws of your own personality? Rhetoric asks what logic must answer. No. No, you cannot be blamed! Two notes an octave apart can sound like the same note! You were not in love with her, only with the desire to win her, for colluctation grows out of concupiscence as quickly as the stricken hydra of old did sprout another head. I would not medicine your eyes, Darconville, for what's to gain there? But, reason, it is by acknowledging his own sexuality that man denies the absolute in himself, turns to the lowers, and proceeds to give woman existence. When man became sexual he formed woman—that woman is at all, in fact, has happened simply because man has accepted his sexuality, her very creation being the result of that terrible affirmation. Man has a sex; woman is a sex. Woman is only sexual; Man is also sexual. The *lares* and *penates* of a woman reside below the navel—she is sexuality itself, the objective correlative of your weakness. They arrogate to themselves, padlocking upon your neck their multipartitioned grip, the honor you give them and flagitiously conspire to transpose into a deferential treatment toward themselves the weakness usurped from you in the first place in that shameless, false-dealing, thumb-on-the-scale bit of joint-stockery involving only tummies, tushies, and thighs! Bottomry and respondentia!

"There are two sexes, yes, but the perhaps-for-you unpalatable truth of it must be faced: one's attempt at a merger can only end in heartbreak. When God saw how lonely man was, he tried again and made woman; as to why he gave up there are two opinions—one of them is woman's. No, the difference between the sexes is a little matter which nature will never be so obliging as to alter. But bless it! You're free of her! There is no longer an owl perching in your sunshine! *Ya, imshi imta, ya bint al-gatt?* O, if only one could be without the things that one should have convinced oneself one could *do* without, don't you see? There indeed is the hope, but if her weakness and stupidity should prove to bias you in her favor in spite of my words, I shall gain this point, nevertheless, to have made it apparent to whatever lords of shouting preside over our miserable lives that what was wanting in this case was not a criminal, nor a prosecutor, but only the terrible swift sword of a just and condign punishment to see it through! I shall rise and plead the case, then, and not restrained by the limits of your comprehension, nor aware of any of mine, my friend, I shall kick open the gates—stand aside!—and lose the gynaikopoinarian dogs, for a woman always respects a word she cannot spell.

"I am overwhelmed by the dire need to take immediate steps and of
the many proposals attendant upon, and coincident to, your renewed
health and benediction would press upon your attention and energet-
ically prosecute several of greater value, urging myself to the necessity
of these several causes: (1) to counsel you on the
Partitio   inefficacy of worldly love; (2) to admonish you against
the sin of mulierosity and the sorrow of marriage; (3)
to prove that malice and lechery were ever indigenous to the second
sex; (4) to define the nature of this apex predator; (5) to encourage
you to live the single life and to avoid women who, although made for
man, upon him yet were never thrust; and, finally, (6) to advocate
that you draw from her lurking hole this skulking neutral behind
whose every virtuous act lay only voracious self-interest and pay the
crime a punishment!

"Woman is the sin of man. He tries to pay the debt by love. It
should come as no surprise that woman was nothing before the Fall
and yet she cannot be understood without it: man does not rob her of
anything she had before. The tragedy man has committed in creating
woman, and still commits in assenting to her purpose,
Narratio   he excuses to woman by his eroticism, for of all the
paths that lead to a woman's love guilt is the
straightest! (Whence comes it, by the way, that a child cannot love
until love coincides with sexuality, the stage of puberty?) Figuratively,
woman is nothing but man's expression and projection of his own sexuality; man merely creates himself a woman in which he embodies
that disposition to carnality and guilt at being incomplete she initially
caused. The woman who resembles us is always antipathetic—what
we seek in the opposite sex is indeed the opposite of ourselves, a quasi-
electrical phenomenon in which to find satisfaction we're attracted by
resistance, driving away, at the same time, the things we truly need.
And thus remorse follows. The vagina is a human denunciation box, I
tell you, into which men drop their grief, their complaints, their guilt.

"You say you love. Let that stand, momentarily. First, however, tell
me, in relation to that falsehood iterated succinctly in the famous
Eclogue X of Vergil's—'*Omnia vincit amor*'—what has ever worked,
won, conquered, or in your behalf called up recompense that you'd
still swear it true? Or shall you let it serve a Dutchman just to keep
that oath? And yet, wooh!—the thing *does* conquer, for there you lie
to copartner the assault where's suborned your very own defeat! Feign

love, would you? It's all very well if you've a mate to feign co-equally. But where is she? I'll tell you, Al Amin, that hybrid, ambiguous, and scheming shape—strutting in the vizard of the very Queen of Sorrows —is wedding her perishable breath to another's and making overpolitic fetches with her tongue at the very minute you see fit to chafe and pine over her with your beggarly love! Whispering impudence! And paddling in his hands! You speak as if forsooth you knew not the facts! A woman is like your shadow: follow her, she flies; fly from her, she follows. Resistance, man? Why, resistance is proof of her *experience,* not proof of her virtue, and the pity of it all shall never be otherwise despite whatever despicable little frauenlobs you may hale in to shake their heads and mutter, 'Jub, jub!' You need only look under this head at the Homeric epics behind the action of which in both, notice, is to be found the question of fidelity: what are the women doing —it's implicitly asked—while we're here? And all the fighting, adventure, and sex with goddesses in distant lands is pitted against the potential betrayal by women of the male world. (All religion, I suspect, is created to minimize the fear men have of being betrayed.) When Odysseus and Penelope go to bed—Book XXIII, line 296—it's the real end of the song. Give the woman no credit, however. The loyalty got lax. Penelope was only Helen hounded by a son.

"Love strives to cover guilt, instead of conquering it; it elevates woman instead of nullifying her. In women love becomes an importunate superstition that will not hearken to the fact that they have no comprehension of paragons, and with no sense of a man's love as a superior phenomenon they only perceive that side of him which unceasingly desires and appropriates—the more brutally, I've heard, the better they like it: an instinct, nevertheless, I can't hope to think you'd share. The pathetic creatures are always happier in the love they inspire than in that which they feel—that is if they feel anything at all! But, oh my yes, women do often imagine that they love, and with all that faded and pettifogulizing ammunition of theirs—lipstick, rouge, pomade, and no end of swabbings from the stybian pot—pointedly set out to do so. But what? I can't think of a more desperate attempt, funerary sculpture excepted, at the gratification of vanity! The joke lies in what they are, doesn't it, in the very act of what they'd cover up? Why, at the very minute a woman vows she'll never flirt, she's flirting not only in the mention of it but with the very painted mouth by which simultaneously she denies it—only another one of

those so-called 'secrets,' miracle only to the ignorant, on which they
pride themselves and to which, although they don't know it themselves, they must give the alluring impression it's possible to discover
the key! And yet how these creatures, built strongest where the strain
is greatest, wish to appear to give unwillingly what in fact they're rav-
enous to give! The occupation of an intrigue, the emotional charge
gallantry gives them, the natural bent for needing affection and the
fear of its refusal, all persuade these sectaries of the god Wünsch that
they have passion, when really they have only coquetry, a sexual
hyperaesthesia that wanders singly up and down the town without
pale or partition like a biologically hampered she-pope or some indefatigable sectary in the rank and borrowed garb of Anteros, female in
sex, mortal in condition! Darconville, Darconville, here below in this
dark region is not love's proper sphere—wasn't, isn't, and never shall
be!

"What is love? We meet someone we paradoxically want to need,
call this bum little blueprint 'love' and hoping such a thing means
something when it doesn't are trapped into the fallacy of believing
that irony has meaning. All expectation is temptation! It's a pity at
the heart of life itself, I tell you. A lover is a gambler reciting 'Mori-
turi te salutamus' before his chips. We've all jumped out of a rotten
potato!

"Womanishness! Look at this mother-right society of ours—witches,
woe-men, windigos painted in wode! Universal inchoate sexuality, the
source of all irrationality and chaos in the world! The battle of the
sexes is hardly a battle anymore. It is not even a rear-guard action. It
is a rout. I tell you, degree, priority, and place went out of fashion
with personal privacy and the runcible spoon, and all the brass-titted
Thermodontines in the ascendance now are not simply satisfied to lean
their backs against their marriage certificates and spit defiance at the
world, no, for they haven't appropriated one thing with the spare
cutlery of their loving fingers before they're looking around for more—
and, taking everything, they've set their pugging teeth on edge to con-
solidate their gains and move man to the downside! The bitches are
marching to Spaneria! Have you never heard of the foolish Wanzo
peoples and their women who, frustrated, tied woodpeckers to their
twats and pretended to have phalluses?

"I say they're everywhere. You say they're a minority. Women are
only a minority, my friend, when they are treated as one! Oh, but you

will call them kind, won't you, for thinking them frail, gentle because
having no defenses, and nicer than the fruit of sweetsop, for in the un-
winking vigilance of gentlemanliness what solicitude, I

Concessio   think you suppose he, she, or it feels, can be too great in
the preservation of meekness to refine, exalt, and perpetuate affection? O excellent falsehood! Kind? You mean ig-
nivomous. Nice! It could apply to a dog, a sermon, or a jam-tart!
Gentle, I agree, when their piss doesn't etch glass and defenseless utterly when they're not veneered and secretive as a Venetian demirep
with domino and spiked ring. But frail? *Frail,* sir? Then you admit to
knowing nothing of the female turnix, phalaropus, cassowary, emeu,
and other monstrosities of nature whose maliciousness and size point
to, and are certainly best allegorized by, the sexual turns of habit observed in the black widow spider? And how widows, peradventure?
Why, they are widows in the same context, by the very reason, and at
the explicit moment that they couple—he fucks her, she bites off his
head—and for this and similar reasons I must here plead and adjure
you never to love if only to tell you never to marry! Jobs cost money to
keep, can't you see? There's scarce a thing both loved and loathed.
When loved, *satis, satis.* But if loathed, my dainty duck, my dear-a? O
me! O me, O my!

"I come to the subject of marriage, then, resolved, lest I offend you,
to avoid the rhetoric of exaggeration, which is, nevertheless, not only
inseparable from great oratory but which punctuates information with
the kind of infuriating finality I fear, in this matter, you still show
yourself so deeply in need of being doctored. I shall

Argumentatio   speak to the wound, however. If you find the subject
wearisome, I suggest you seek in yourself the weari-
ness, and if my bouncing candor you can't stand bethink yourself then
of the frankness you once asked of someone in a dress! I have spoken
words, now, dehortatory, expostulatory, and supplicatory, but of marriage, confess, need I heap up here, accumulate, misrepresent on the
side of greater size, or caricature? O laugh it out, you laughsters! O
laugh it up belaughably to the last laughed-out bit of laughter and
then laugh again!

"Holy deadlock? Why, the observation of married couples is a post-
graduate course in pessimism itself! Never mind that hard by the temple of Hymen, in the florid words of Hippel, lies the graveyard of love
—if you must insist, of course, that love exists—the very act of the

male stooping to marry the female makes the mere *concept* of marriage morganatic! And yet can a man actually devote himself to such a trifle? He can. He will. He does. How, you ask? Why, it's easy. The moral misconduct necessary for intimacy, you see, subsequently fosters in the male a desperation for justice in relation to his enemy twin—he seeks to check his precipitancy—and so in a reckless excess of duty-grafted-to-guilt, for next to happiness confirmed misery does well, he connupts for a lifetime someone who, ironically enough, is absolved *by that very act of excess* from the need or obligation to love in return! Marriage? It is a dualism beyond comprehension, the plot of the story of the Fall, the primitive riddle, a ghastly public confession, the binding of the unlimited in the bonds of space, of the eternal by time, of the spirit by matter. The State calls it legal, for revenue. The Church sees it indissoluble, for dynasty—and yet when the deep and ghastly disjunctures of nature native to it inevitably occur, both serve to detain by compulsion such of those who from that oppressive and unpredestined misery would suddenly flee! Marriage? It is nothing more than a slavery to brief pleasure leading to the lengthy slavery of one another. The debate is not closed, only the question. The legend that matrimony is a lottery, in fact, has almost ruined the lottery business! The world's reformers, have they not all been married men? And death on the wedding night, is it not one of literature's immortal themes? The *Iliad*, that bible of war, did it not begin with a wedding? Had Theseus any need of Ariadne's thread to find his way *into* the labyrinth? Didn't St. Peter himself—Matthew 8:14—drop his wife flat in the pursuit of what she clearly prevented him otherwise from seeking? And what that we own, further, have we ever valued as much as what once we didn't have? Aren't possessions generally *diminished* by possession, where even the most fetching person is no longer assured of our slightest concern after we've known her for a simple few months? Marriage? It is a contract, not a commitment, nothing but an act of propitiation by men for first having thought *ill* of women. Women don't marry men, they adopt them—to carry baggage, to hail cabs, to fetch! And to what end does this proprietary institution serve other than to effect the introduction of order into chaotic sexual relations and to establish every assurance in behalf of those sweet little apostles of pairing you so love for the formal acquisition of alimonious funds and a ticket to Rio for a lifetime of comic viduity? Marriage? What is it, finally, but a tyrannous routine of unanswerable female quibbling, enervating habit, and plaguey amorism, no more a warranty of happiness than prison and no more natural to us than a cage is to a cuckoo-bird—a *modus vivendi* that is as incompatible as free-love with the highest interpretations of the moral law, making the remarks of St. Ambrose, fourth-century bishop of Milan, perfectly in order when he asserted that married people ought to blush at the state in which they were living as it prostituted the members of Christ! No, Darconville, remove, remove that marriage hearse! And thus remove that ancient curse!

"Can you imagine what domestic life with a woman must be and still gamble away your life for a mere toss at such a perishable being? It is the single sex for whom marriage for love is so rare that a vow of obedience, arguable antonym of love, is still exacted in the nuptial contract, and what they bring to the hearth must be limited, I'm afraid, to what are their only natural gifts, three in number: deceitfulness, spinning, and the capacity to weep at will. Now, a family's happiness, it's been said, is always in proportion to the cultivation of its female members, but as they're congenitally unable to be satisfied—save only by movable property or the proximity of some male neighbor, mustachioed like a Circassian, to compare you to—the hygienic penalty that must be paid, for woman's denial of her real nature becomes inescapable, is the hysterical self-dissatisfaction inherent in striving to be what, to get, they who weren't once convinced you they were! The saint then—poof!—becomes a scold. The portcullis drops! The more a woman's made an occupation of torturing her husband, you see, the less right she thinks she has to lose him, her hold over him increasing to the measure of her *coldness*. Wanting always comes to an end with having. They nag. They gripe. They breed infidelity. It is impossible, for instance, to speak of one woman with another without her betraying the one who's absent; the Chinese symbol for war is two women under the same roof. They aren't even friends—there is no word in the Latin language that signifies a female friend: *amica* means mistress. No, what they are, Darconville, are born lackeys—the word 'employee,' remember, is always spelled with two e's—serving only to censor. They have no relation to man and no sense of man, but only to maleness. The periods of matriarchy have always been periods of polyandry! And although the Koran says that heaven is at the feet of a mother most men still mutter *Karram Allah* before even mentioning such a worthless subject as women in conversation. And yet how quickly they seek to assume sovereignty, fearing that their husbands will be successful while at the same time insisting they achieve wondrous things and accepting the fruitless but heroic efforts of the poor fools to give them their souls while failing, for want of comprehension, to strive for that same virtue in themselves. And the polluting sadness of it all, as you look to escape, can be neither diminished nor abridged, for no matter where you go or how far you withdraw, there she is—bored, nagging, censorious—peering like a divedapper through a wave! Domesticity? *Happy* domesticity? It's a Victorian pipe-dream! Why, even then when those spindle-and-broom deities performed no more banal an act than merely putting a foot to the treadle the very motion kindled appetites in them they were too stupid to realize they already had! But then what has ever curtailed the sexual frenzy of a woman?

"Don't say children! As no woman is the perfect type of mother—something she shares with the penguin, catfish, shark, and stickleback, among others—how could that be? In fact, the female essentially seeks in the existence of children nothing more than a satisfaction to dominate.

> Girls have mothers
> Upon their necks to bite 'em,
> So girls grab boys
> And so *ad infinitum*.

There's nothing very subtle here, is there? Their daughters are sexual rivals, on the one hand, and everyone knows, on the other, that there is always something sexual in the relationship of mother and son—in fact, the husband of a mother is always a cuckold.

"Sexual frenzy? O, when that itching begins, my friend, how far flung are the perimeters of intrigue and assassination! It's the Bottomless Pit! The Fire Not Sated With Wood! Can it come as a surprise to anyone to see in the Scrovegni Chapel—for there is no wife who has not been untrue to her husband in thought—that Lust is led around on a halter by a woman no bigger than your thumb? Cato believed in fact that kissing among relatives was a custom maintained only to keep women under control in this matter. The natal day of Blessed Pudens —as much a warning as an example—was purposely placed on the church calendar in May, the month of lust. And because of lust St. Pius V had to foliate the genitals of every single statue in Vatican City in 1569. No, Darconville, infidelity is the *mulier puisne* to the *bastard eigne* that is the state of marriage, but there's no stopping it, for when any of these sabre-toothed tarts who has chained herself to someone's bed for a mere band of miniature ice-cubes round her finger decides to act, no longer letting the 'I would' wait upon the 'I dare not,' it's open communion to every passing dunce and dancing master. Nothing can halt it. You can cringe, swagger, weep, or lie doggo. You can motion for an Act of Sederunt or read her passages from the life of Pelagia the Harlot. You can even die. (How many women, however, would actually laugh at the funerals of their husbands if it were not the custom to weep?) But whatever you do to try to dissuade her won't make the smallest particle of difference—it's like trying to rub the smell of nickels off a Jew's hands: an honest woman is unfair to the entire female race. And that applies to the lot of them, whether it be Jane Bedknickers, *Marie Royne d'Escosse douayrière de France,* or this birding-piece new scoured called Isabel Rawsthorne.

"But take heart, Prince Darconville, and weigh well the time—for death comes from life, not life from death. It is but a small step between weariness and hate in a woman, and there is not much to choose between a woman who deceives us for another and a woman who deceives another for ourselves. Reality increases in direct proportion to the length and proximity of contact and when her retractile heart withdraws again—? Look to your sheets, Dutchman. This whore of yours can count beyond two.

"What *is* woman, anyway? A mere collection of similar individuals, each cast in the same mold, the whole forming as it were a continuous plasmodium. Googlies with bisque hearts! Rash, inconsiderate voluntaries with dragons' spleens! Pies with the devil's finger in them! But

all women are at bottom one woman. I mean, you've

Confirmatio been presenting this bechangeable flouter of yours as

if she were the chryselephantine statue of Athena, convincing me then, before all else, that men never want to see women as they are, but if you must insist upon showing in both face and sentiment the grace of the troubadours, you must then coquet with truth after their fashion; the reality, I make free to say, is quite otherwise— men either despise women or they have never thought seriously about them, although the chap who does successfully study them must of necessity be an amphibologist.

"Look at them! The sight of an upright female form in the nude makes most patent her purposelessness—if pretty, briefly pretty, and yet how many abortions for one Helen, how many Gothones for one Aphrodite? No, the caricature of a woman *isn't* one! Their greasy faces! Their buttered hair! Their fucused breasts! My God, they're ugly as dubbs! A very, very woman is a dough-baked man! They were the very last thing God made—evidently he did so on Saturday night: she reveals his fatigue—and the very first to betray him. Their brains, their hearts, are tinier than those of men. Of the one face they've been given they must make themselves another, and, mobbling it, they come flying out at you behind that ill-befitting clownage of false fingernails, chinstraps, mudpacks, padded asses, and toenail polish and then dare to ask man, 'Are you real?' To hear such a thing! To hear anything like it! To hear *anything!* Can you, for example, think of a more re-volting sound on earth than a woman rummaging in her handbag? No, face it, woman is supreme only as woman: 'vapourizing, gesticu-lating, quarrelsome, restless, and oversensitive,' as Carlyle said of France.

"What is the definition of gross incompetence? 144 women! They don't live in the grip of envy only for others—no, most girls, incredible as it may sound, are actually jealous of their own bodies, coming to hate the very tits-'n'-bums superficially used to attract men in the first place. They can't be grateful, conceptualize, or exercise heavy pres-sures with their arms raised above shoulder height. Their acrobatics of excretion could bring a smile to the face of Muscular Dystrophy. And the nap of the female skin? It would vex a dog to see a pudding creep! The sinewy walk is only a condition relating to a built-in instability in the thighbones whereby they tend to lose their balance easily and stumble. Their menstrual flux can sour wine, curdle milk, dim mirrors, and wilt young plants. And, finally, food for her is but a few seconds in the mouth, a few hours in the belly, and the rest of her life on the hip, for, like medlars, they are no sooner ripe than rotten, and when St. Jerome went to Scotland to find cannibals there, it turned out that it was only male flesh that they'd eaten because the female flesh—in-sipid and characterless as banana—was stringy and vile, flowing with unsavory streams. Overbodied? Well-punctured? With small irregular holes? Wherein, for chrissake, does woman differ from a Tilsit cheese?

"It made Byron sick to see a woman eat. Zeuxis claimed he needed all the beauties of Agrigentum to compose the image of a female, and then he died in a fit of laughter after contemplating the face of the hag he'd painted. And then was it not said by the only rare poet of that time, the Wittie, Comicall, Facetiously-Quicke and unparalleled John Lilly, Master of Arts, that if you take from them their perywigges, their paintings, their jewells, their rowles and boulstrings, thou shalt soone perceive that a woman is the least parte of hir self? The rest of them—and it's a good deal—lies on the dressing table! The traditional idea of them being a riddle wrapped in a mystery inside an enigma is a joke! A sphinx without a secret is a minx! It is of course *no* secret that they hate men for the talents they have, partially because they're covetous and partially because they don't know how it's done. Behind every great man, believe me, stands an *astonished* woman! 'Let the vain sex dream on,' wrote Swift, 'their Empire comes from us.' But the more women aspiring to the arts who dominate the women's movement, the more the unnatural and long-frustrated desire for equality—mental, physical, aesthetic—translates into the totally misleading equation of emancipation with creativity. Woman has never created anything, and will never create anything, as beautiful as she has destroyed, for one thing. And then there could never be anything but an ideologically imposed equality of the sexes anyway, for the artistic and intellectual incompetence of women, with the singular exceptions you could name only to reinforce that rule, is the most embarrassing *fact of human history*—an utter void in music, philosophy, sculpture, history, literature, and science for three thousand years! I'm afraid you must look for the book *Significant Women Thinkers* in the same library where you'll find *Great Chinese Comedians, The Encyclopedia of Dutch Etiquette,* and *The Jewish Book of Charity.* But, you ask, weren't they lacking in education? The mind is school. Or wanting in leisure? Vision makes room for vision. Then what about duress? You will argue, reductively, that women were held down, calumniated, and oppressed over the centuries until you stop to consider, with some shock perhaps, that such conditions are more often than not the very linchpin of all meaningful achievement!

"Here, but this is tiring. Have you ever seen a woman try to throw a ball?

"No, nature, I'm afraid, has been very unkind to women—indeed, it perhaps best explains their vindictiveness. They have small sense of humor, less of continuity, and constantly live in the throes of morbidly excitable hysteria—female tear ducts, scientifically, are almost twice as active as men's—the attributive demonstration of which, while doubtless the result of their constitutional irrationality and its *boiteuses journées,* is especially felt in the presence of high-principled, essentially masculine men. They can panic most mightily under such circumstances—and of course when a woman loses her hypnotic power, then what? Of course. She straddles a bike, becomes a religious crank, and proceeds to teach Latin. Their so-called meekness, however, is usually the result of finding discretion more necessary to them than eloquence because, as thinking and feeling for them are in opposition, they have less difficulty in speaking little than speaking well. Mind, in fact, cannot really be predicated of her at all—only the sexual instinct, and yet it is virtually impossible for women, because they are *only* sexual, to recognize their sexuality or the indiscriminate dispensation thereof, for the recognition of anything requires a kind of duality which *they* can only understand, experientially, in the thoughtless and brazen act of cozening two men at the same time. But what of it? By the very nature of being what they are, they consequently need never inquire what they should be, refusing the gambit right out and generously leaving that task to the philosophical speculations of the male, whose uncertainty about it all is at once both the source of his romance and the germ of his malady. Women aren't called whores, you see, in the same way penguins aren't called homely: all aren't only because all are.

"Sex! I hear no echo in this briefest word that could ever make it song. Sex is merely lust—the batrachomyomachia of bunghole and battery from which love, apparently, can do anything but shelter one! It is the lowest form of communication, the vilest expression of need, and the most brainlessly discerptible action in **Reductio ad absurdam** the entire realm of human behavior. Coitus is the price men have to pay to women for their oppression. Their sex organs—a passive pot for fools to spend in—are nothing, emptiness itself, the jar of the *Arabian Nights* into which every Solomon tries in vain to pack his genie. What is their twammy, however, that you need to know it? How value what you can partake of without loving and yet love without partaking of? Who buys a minute's mirth to wail a week or sells eternity to get a toy? Love *as passion* is a scam, the invention of the Provençal knight-poets to justify their verse! There is, moreover, no distinguishing *haecceitas* in the glands: they are all the same, functioning in witless independence of that self we vainly believe to be loved, for any one part of an extended substantive is existentially other than any other part. Leave such things for the sexly sex! The Hindus correctly look upon sexual intercourse as a victory for woman, the degrading passion, in my opinion, by which Adam and the serpent were actually tempted by *Eve,* for, ask yourself, was there any betrayal by the former two until the introduction of the latter? Any contentiousness? Any lack of trust, excess, disobedience?

"No, copulation is abomination—you become susceptible in the act to your own venom like the pigmy rattlesnake that dies when it bites itself on the lip during its frenzy to swallow mice! The violence! It's a biological fact that peaceful matings are nearly always sterile. The vice! Who, in reference to this beastly whingeing, has ever dared admit the crucial and contradictory paradox involved in taking by giving? Then the vulgarity of it! The sparrow stands erect in coition, the hen crouches, whales swoop up vertically, bears hug one another, hedgehogs go at it face to face—only monkeys and women fall into any posture whatsoever! H-o-double-r-i-b-l-e spells horrible! Democritus of Abdera, who plucked out his eyes to avoid the sight of female skirts, called it 'the short epilepsy.' Odysseus refused to couple with Circe on the grounds that his vigor would be impaired. Hector went straight from Andromache's bed to battle—and was butchered! And both Ambrose and Tertullian declared that the extinction of the human race was preferable to its propagation by sexual intercourse. Sex? O, Darconville, it is there in the womb that we have all been taught cruelty and fitted for works of darkness, fed with blood, deprived of light, and blinded and warpled and set upsidedown in the cerements of our burial scene. We live—*inter urinam et faeces nascimur*—between graves! We wake only to celebrate our own funeral cries, perpetually driven to abysses as if instinctively burdened with the true and terrible knowledge that looking into a hole is nothing more than looking into the future we, all of us, must share!

"Stop to think where they are now, your desertrice and her impetrating, impenetrating groom! Who have known each other so briefly must then want each other so well. Lichens liken: about her he disapproves nothing, nor does she anything of him, for to be overestimated is the only real appreciation. And so it is a Dutch concert of lies—and, my, but they do lie a lot! But, here, can castwhores pulladeftkiss if oldpollocks forsake 'em? With relish, my man! But, wait, is it limited to kisses? Cry broom! Were kisses all the joys in bed, why one woman would another wed! No, don't turn away! Look, picture her, there she is noting his

Admonitio

every want and, mad to forestall it, tears away her clothes—she quivers, she pants, she clucks, squealing now in language grown greasier than her pigs and waggling in the air two legs turned to a shape more crooked than a judas tree! Why, a woman, like a cat, could calmly walk over your dead face! And will you still talk to me about ideals, when their ideals, like mantles, cover up their palfreys so that two beasts seem to move beneath one skin? Yes? Than take the fie out of fo and fum for you have paid the fee!

"A new period of history is aborning! I would have you free! Freedom and idleness—Allah's greatest gifts! I would have you join the 144,000 virgin males in Revelations undefiled by women! Why, tell me, must a man's qualifications as a male become identical with that sole and lowly value so esteemed by women? To but acknowledge himself proud in the eyes of a tribe of blowsy she-dowds, repulsive skates, and drabs? The moral sanction that has been invented for coitus, in supposing that there is an ideal attitude to the act in which only the propagation of the race is thought, is hardly sufficient defense. It is no defense. It is defenseless. St. Paul, remember—who was blessed with his vision only *after* the daughter of the high priest of Jerusalem had rejected his ill-considered offer of marriage—says that the single life is the only perfect one. He countenanced marriage of necessity and against his own conviction, and his views on the subject show at best a reluctant sanction, as I'm sure you know, for he knew well the confusion, dullness, and strife apposite to that way of life. Eris is only Eros with an eye. On the other hand, don't be confused. The term 'virginity' when applied to women is merely a geographic expression—to them, little more than a point of commerce—and the outward endeavor on their part to try to correspond to man's demand for physical purity must not be taken for anything but a fear lest the buyer fight shy of the bargain. I hardly think you can be unaware of the view women actually take of virginity, can you? It's the drats! They not only disparage and despise virginity in other women; they are nothing less than terror-fraught at the thought of their own—except, of course, that men prize it so highly. Spry? O yes, they're spry. Spry as a sprint of sprue! But don't be fooled—the Queen, remember, unites the power of both the Rook and Bishop in her movements and, commanding both the straight and the oblique, can get behind you faster than wind. But that's as it is, isn't it? Simply, you must avoid them. Let them alone to sprout up sins somewhence, somewhither, and somewhere else! Take to heart the wisdom of the holy ancient saints, Jerome, Anthony, and Hilarion who, along with your own holy martyred kinsman, left no doubt as to what women really are: obstacles to spiritual piety. Whoever, that lived its tragedies, says that life must be propagated? That it must continue? Why, that's nothing but the worship of *life*, the foulest of heresies! The prophet Jeremiah—16:2–4 of that book—was actually commanded to remain single. Virginity, you'll note, was essential for success in the search for the Holy Grail, and if it comes as no surprise to you to learn, parenthetically, that after the destruction and dissolution of the Round Table all the surviving knights became hermits, how then even in the absence of explicit statement should I ever hope to expect, my friend, anything less of you? The sole purpose of radiators is to *lose* heat. No, I'll vouch you up a chastity, my child, if to it you're disposed, and there shall by a virgin be a viragin deposed!

"Do I seem cruel? Then better is by evil thus made better. Do I seem critical? And yet to tell you little more than would suffice is something in a warning less than either. Do I seem cold? Yes, I'm cold —cold enough, I promise, to take the mother out of crymotherapy, for there's nothing quite like frost to single out the weak **Confrontatio** points in a stone. I'm ugly. I stink. Yes, I can breed in winter like a whelk. But call me a misogynist? Why, woman has hitherto been most despised by woman *herself!*— an assertion that couldn't have been more vigorously confirmed than by the testimony of Madame de Staël when she remarked that what most consoled her in being a woman was that she'd never have to marry one! Who says misogynistic, says biblical! But I needn't cite Paul, sing like a goliard, nor gape back to the gynekophobic 1500s. The Mishmi people will trade one woman for a pig, the Abipona for a handful of glass pearls, and the Island Caribs actually use two languages—one for men, another for women. You can buy a pigmy woman on the Congo border at the *boma* in Bundibugyo for 200 shillings. I've always said that the famous equation of women with livestock—Semonides Amorgos, fragment 7 of his *Elegy and Iambus*— warrants further study. The Chinese don't count girls as children, Mohammed excludes them from Paradise, and the Synod of Macon actually debated whether women could be termed human beings at all! No, I offer no more than enough.

"I see how this modest dehortation on the vulgivaguability of women saddens you, Darconville. If you think it loud, however, it is because you are deaf. If too large, it is because you are blind. If you think it false, then consider the maxim *falsa demonstratio non nocet* which refers to the general rule that where there is a description which fixes the identity of that which is referred to, a misdescription else- where will not vitiate it, mmmm? I could pull the law out of my cod- piece all day. But that's not the question.

"The question is, what will you accept, and in accepting do, and by doing rectify? This late sweetheart of yours—an eviscerating tit- shower between whose yes and no it was impossible to slip a needle— was crooked enough to hide behind a corkscrew. What lived inside her apparently functioned by something outside but let her move about as quietly and efficiently as a bird of prey. Huaman (pronounced 'woman') is Inca for falcon. She simply had *craft,* however. It wasn't intelligence—don't be a fool—only the alertness of exaggerated ego- tism! Those who lack character, you see, must always rely heavily on method. And in the matter of method, nothing shows more of a difference, not one woman from another, but between a given woman and that very woman herself, whether Faustine, Fragoletta, Dolores, Félise, Yolande, and Juliette! Or Isabel, sweet, my coz!

"What pharisee, tell me, ever scoured the outside of cup and platter more assiduously than she? She declined to be alone, I gather, from your very first meeting—a woman refuses the condition of solitude and knows neither the love of it nor the worth of it—and battened on to you, I can see it, with more woeful stories than a Victorian buy-a- broom girl, weeping, like all women, only with those she knows will pity her and so intensifying her self-pity by the thought of the pity of others and then slowly, subtly, forcing you into a détente with her unreserved and shameless readiness to shed tears and to sham love. A spider's silk, you forgot, has a tensile strength greater than steel. You had, in fact, no more reason to believe her than you had to believe that winged game argues in favor of angelology—but you did. You cared. Pitifully, you showed in truth what she shammed which, ironically, unbelievably, allowed the damn traitor who was waiting for that enough courage and self-esteem not only to grab someone else but actually to bump you in the process, for a clever woman never ac- knowledges she has fallen in love until the man has formally avowed his passion and so cut off his retreat—and then virtue disappears like heather obliterated by bracken! The less the splash, the better the dive, see?

"She was forbearing and obliging and yielding like any other fortune-hunting footpad—different, you felt, of course, than all the other earth-reeking soubrettes and dress-envious daughters of instinct you'd known—but you failed to understand that women are always the kindest to those they deceive. You listened to her; you didn't watch. And Miss Poxtakeher? Miss Pennyquick? *Ya zift! Ya sharmuta! Ya sheitan khalida!* She employed sincerity only when she thought every other form of deception might fail, but her intention to marry you vanished the instant it was formed because she had heard those wooden shoes clopping along in the distance. The voice was Jacob's voice but the hands were the hands of Esau! You thought she was an ermine; you didn't know she was a weasel, failing, again, to realize that they're the same thing. And all the while you kept faith. You spent almost four years to be near her in a place that even the Centuriators of Magdeburg would have found dull! You danced, you dipped, you doffed your hat. And although you left for London at one point, you returned to marry her. Birds never limed, you see, no secret bushes fear. But as the argument for loyalty in women is always a hysteron-proteron it wasn't enough for her. A neurotic, she was still dissatisfied—a kind of sloth, *tristitia de bono spirituali,* see?—for in spite of you and all your efforts, not because of you and none of your efforts, she could never be freed of herself. She was both deliberately the maid who serves and instinctively the woman who commands, the shrew in her detesting everything, the servant detesting itself—like the society Jew who in putting on a new nose, a new name, a new servility but proceeds to loathe himself the more! 'When Adam delved and Eve span, who was then the gentleman?' Why Adam, of course; how could it have been Eve? So she chose, the potato cook, what she was—whatever, I suspect, she actually, wasn't, i.e., what she *hadn't.* And why? For purposes of increased security and sovereignty. Perhaps she was bitter that she had to model herself on your estimable image of her for so many years. Perhaps in knowing herself so well she couldn't accept anybody who would have her so readily. Perhaps your genius frightened her; the why is not explained: substantive pauses after verbs of fearing, say? And what did she choose? A family disinclined to risk its middle-class prosperity for ab-

stract, utopian ideas. What did she feel pity for? Nothing. She had
poison in the very knops of her tits. And what does she regret? The
deed, I tell you, only becomes a mirror for self-admiration. The hand
is the whore's second face. O Darconville, Darconville, every woman
has Clytemnestra's address. What change of heart other than the pir-
ouetting bit of fantoccini constant to this sex I admonish you against
believing in ever took place? Isn't the futility of washing an Ethiopian
proverbial? Can you get thigs from fistules?

"This last word—and I shall have done. I urge you to the work of
your left hand! I call upon Lycurgus, Hyperides, Dinarchus, Horten-
sius, Calvus, Chrysostom, and Aristides to inspirit you with the ardor
of my words and to quicken you to revenge! A period of grieving is
also a period of healing and zeal as necessary in every
Peroratio   cause as prudence. What then shall be done? What
sport? How flap this bifarious bitch whose faculties
ran to being in two places at once? She must be forced to remember!
Insensitive people must especially be sent to that kind of hell whose
flames must teach exactly what sensitivity means! Look you, I am here
to inspire, not to gratify. Will you simply pray her to rehabilitation?
Recommend a thatched nunnery? Love those you'll come to hate and
be an ally to your enemies? No, never! Hurl her after the fault to learn
how she likes her own compulsion! Bring justice to Jedburgh! Wax
your black sword, Darconville, and slaughter them all!

"The temptation, of course, is to wait. And how easy to prevail by
doing nothing more than that, for nothing forbids you from reflecting
that with every passing minute she is growing older, fatter, homelier.
You are avenged 1440 times a day! How old is the puffin—twenty-
three? Why, for a girl that's late autumn! She's got two more years to
be loved, ten more to love herself, and the rest to pray to God! But
why wait? Will she not strout? She will. Did she not spitrack you? She
did. Was she not a spot-powdered, downsical-bearing cat of convenience? She was. So, being on land, settle; being at sea, sail. Why hesitate? To suit a natural action to a most unnatural crime? You were
her victim; must you be her dupe? No, my child, the past is the adversary of the future, and past mirth will have future laughter, don't you
see? A few luminous and fervent hours are enough to give meaning to
an entire lifetime, the honor of which is at stake and the outcome
hanging in the balance. The very voices of your forebears cry to you
from the ground, 'My son, scorn to be a slave!'

"Heed to consent! Hearken to comply! Follow not the dictates of a sloven and unmerited mercy but enlist yourself under the sacred banner of justice to play out its ends and prevent the curses of posterity from being heaped upon your memory that both by this trial and its swift redressal we shall be delivered, that we shall have deliverance at last, and until the last shock of time shall bury her memory in ignominious and undistinguished ruin! *Datum serva! Cognatus cole!* There alone shall be peace for you, and otherwise there won't, for what makes a person noble? Not a continued false and smothered love, surely, for love if it's real never refuses what love sends. Neither pity, for that is nothing more than a disagreeable impulse of the instinct for appropriation at the sight of what seems to be weaker. What makes honor? A person brave? Constitutes perfection? I will venture to say that no man ever rose to any degree of perfection but through obstinacy and an inveterate resolution against the stream of mankind!

"I want a platter—listen to me—and I want a head on that platter! Inaction itself must otherwise assume the proportions of a crime. I see a demon behind you standing in the midst of her own noise, the biology of whose shadow cannot and will not be studied! Examine it no further! But there is a reality pitched *above* that shadow. It's yours alone to feast on in ill-will! Stand upon her—and prevail, overcoming the hound that bays and rejoicing only that you've lived to say, 'The dog is dead!' She was your hell in perspective, was she not, and is it not written that justice is the punishment of sin? Rack her soul for it then! There is always more that you can be than what you are! Thaw out thunder! Dun the reality for what it is! *When are you going to learn that Satan isn't a metaphor?*"

LXXXII

The Unholy Litany

Daughters of calumny, I summon you!

—RICHARD BRINSLEY SHERIDAN

THE WORDS were so terrifying that they precluded any possibility of interruption, anaesthetizing Darconville where he lay in a silence of sustained disbelief. Dr. Crucifer's face was bloodless white, like the underside of a sole, his mouth writhing with unintelligible words, when suddenly proceeding to the phonograph he set in a record which came up slowly in the mournful rhythm of plain chant. It was the *"Dies Irae"*—the saddest, emptiest, most melancholy determination of sorrow on earth. He seemed as he closed his eyes to be listening to something beyond him, as if in bizarre and unhallowed colloquy with his inner self, and then he turned, moving now around the ancient relics of the

room, and in the falsetto modulations of that impossible voice began to
recite in a cold drawn-out prolation the queerest litany ever heard:

"—from Eve and her quinces,   *libera nos, Domine*
   —from Jael, the jakesmaid,   "   "   "
   —from Pasiphaë, the Cretan motherlord,   "   "   "
   —from Venus Illegitima, goddess of
         unnatural acts,   "   "   "
   —from Alice Trip-and-Go, who wardeleth,   "   "   "
   —from Dejah Thoris, princess of helium,   "   "   "
   —from Beatrice Joanna, the changeling,   "   "   "
   —from Galinthia, who was turned into a
         cat,   "   "   "
   —from Belestiche, mistress of Ptolemy II,   "   "   "
   —from Fanny Abington and her harlotries,   "   "   "
   —from Lupa, the wife of Faustulus,   "   "   "
   —from Queen Gertrude of Denmark,
         frampold and feak,   "   "   "
   —from Kaulah, the sister of Derar,   "   "   "
   —from Old Mother Whummle and her
         Winchester geese,   "   "   "
   —from Jezebel and her 50¢ womb,   "   "   "
   —from Signora Bubonia and her poxes,   "   "   "
   —from La Dolcequita, *cara de vinagre*,   "   "   "
   —from Umm Kulsum, the hag procuress,   "   "   "
   —from the Marquise de Brinvilliers,
         poisoner and viragint,   "   "   "
   —from Mad Meg and her shittle-witted
         gixies,   "   "   "
   —from Temba-Ndumba, child-eater of
         the Jagas,   "   "   "
   —from all Sirens, Hirens, and Pampered
         Jades,   "   "   "
   —from Agrippinilla, mother of Nero,   "   "   "
   —from Lysistrata and her *antianeirai*,   "   "   "
   —from Hyacinthe Chantelouve,
         the gernative backstress,   "   "   "
   —from the Ghats of the Indian Ocean,   "   "   "
   —from Lady Midhurst, the gongoon,   "   "   "

—from Seraphina Feliciano, Contesse de
    Cagliostro,   "   "   "
—from Linda Ne Touchez Pas, the tit
    of turncoats,   "   "   "
—from Angerona, goddess of melancholy,   "   "   "
—from Unakuagsak, the Great Mother
    of Eskimos,   "   "   "
—from Mistress Libuschka and her
    slit-piece,   "   "   "
—from Urganda, the fairy neckbite,   "   "   "
—from the Fifty Daughters of Danaus,   "   "   "
—from Pudicitia and her mattress
    knights . . ."   "   "   "

Dr. Crucifer deambulated, walking in rogational fashion now, and the drone became perceptibly higher and higher as he moved. He was overcrowing with hatred and disgust, his mouth becoming absurdly puckered and puffed as he began a funeral clap.

"—from Iolanthe the impositrix,   *libera nos, Domine*
—from Sycorax, the black poozle,   "   "   "
—from Venus Calva, who was bald,   "   "   "
—from Medea, the craven sluck,   "   "   "
—from Lady Caroline Lamb, whose
    clicket was ever clacking,   "   "   "
—from Efna Koloi, the Queen of Ashanti,   "   "   "
—from Miss Dubedatandshedidbedad,   "   "   "
—from Lucrezia del Sarto,
    la scapepuzzano,   "   "   "
—from Mother Atkins of Pinner,   "   "   "
—from Mme. Britannica Hollandia
    of Hollands Leaguer,   "   "   "
—from Anactoria the anispix,   "   "   "
—from Cleopatra VII, high-priestess
    of rashers,   "   "   "
—from Rahab the harlot,   "   "   "
—from Melinda Goosestrap, hussy and
    cheatstress,   "   "   "
—from Sue Lozo, the sheela-na-gig,   "   "   "
—from Queen Hatshepsut, *bint al-bazra,*   "   "   "
—from Lambito the pintleless,   "   "   "

—from Khatun, Queen of the Mongols,   "   "   "
—from Isabel Burton, the ballacher,   "   "   "
—from Azazel, inventress of jewelry,   "   "   "
—from Paphian Aphrodite, the pocket
    thief of hearts,   "   "   "
—from Charybdis and her voracious
    mouth,   "   "   "
—from Lady Macbeth, the missing lynx,   "   "   "
—from Jane 'Boo' Faulkner, the nurse
    for a prayer,   "   "   "
—from Eurygale and her fat colworts,   "   "   "
—from Calypso the croshabell,   "   "   "
—from Isadora Klein, the Hebrew
    shortheel,   "   "   "
—from Thuvia, Maid of Mars,   "   "   "
—from Parisina Malatesta, the princess
    of cats,   "   "   "
—from the Maiden All Forlorn
    That Milked the Cow with the
    Crumpled Horn,   "   "   "
—from Gawrey, the flying scrunch,   "   "   "
—from Atalanta the advoutress,   "   "   "
—from Medusa and her forked hair,   "   "   "
—from Lady Bercilak, the baggage
    of babliaminy,   "   "   "
—from Lamia the hellhag,   "   "   "
—from Telesā, the *aitu auleaga* of Samoa,   "   "   "
—from Mother Middle, the factor
    of mediocrity,   "   "   "
—from Sassia, the criminal bimbo,   "   "   "
—from Delilah of Sorek,
    the philoepiorcian philistine,   "   "   "
—from Famiglietta, the Neapolitan
    drazel . . ."   "   "   "

Darconville's heart hammered in his ear as the grotesque incantation, relentless with the music, summoned up a terror in him that wiped his countenance clear of all emotions but the signature of overmastering fear that chilled him up to his hair and down to his feet. Was he asleep: Was this a bad dream?

"—from Queen Endoxia of Alexandria,   *libera nos, Domine*
—from Angiola Pietragwa,
    nymphe du pavé,   "   "   "
—from disc-headed Hathor, goddess of
    Urt,   "   "   "
—from Adnil Notrub, the Falcon
    Countess,   "   "
—from Taitu, the Mote in the Sunbeam,   "   "   "
—from Cressida, the dreadful she-Ghul,   "   "   "
—from Gothone, the shilpit,   "   "   "
—from Frédégunde, the Frankish frisgig
    and assassin,   "   "   "
—from Agrat bat Mahlah, the axwaddle,   "   "   "
—from Kikimora, the objurgatrix,   "   "   "
—from Clytemnestra, the cullisance
    of scabiosity,   "   "   "
—from Princess Aura, lustful daughter
    of Ming the Merciless,   "   "   "
—from Salomé and her shaking rags,   "   "   "
—from Tituba, the human tractatrix,   "   "   "
—from Queen Zinga of Angola,   "   "   "
—from Pasht, the cat-headed woman,   "   "   "
—from Anna Maria Zwanzigar,
    pucelle venimeuse,   "   "   "
—from the Women of Lemnos,   "   "   "
—from Mother Gruel, the elvish shrew,   "   "   "
—from Irene Adler, the immoderatrix,   "   "   "
—from Stheno the Gorgon and her
    wanton franions,   "   "   "
—from Lais the Corinthian snake,   "   "   "
—from Miss Lookingbothways,
    the laiscarpotic,   "   "   "
—from Laverna, goddess of thieves,   "   "   "
—from the Wasawahili Women
    of Madagascar,   "   "   "
—from Shub-niggurath, craftress of love,   "   "   "
—from Sylvia Tietjens and her enameled
    cruelty,   "   "   "
—from Mistress Tomasin, Queen
    Elizabeth's dwarf,   "   "   "

—from Ulrike von Levetzow and her
    organs of increase,   "   "   "
—from Mutter Erde and her foolish
    fecundity,   "   "   "
—from Ann Partridge, schoolmastercide,   "   "   "
—from Cottina, whore of the Levant,   "   "   "
—from Myrtium the frigstress,   "   "   "
—from Ninhursag, the Mesopotamian
    matrix,   "   "   "
—from Black Annis of Leicester,   "   "   "
—from Natasha Rostova,
    the Woman Who Couldn't Wait a
    Year,   "   "   "
—from Eris, goddess of discord,   "   "   "
—from Lulu the Wunderkind,   "   "   "
—from Chrysis, Corone, Ischas,
    and Antycra, the Homeric harlots,   "   "   "
—from Gabrina, the pounding waive,   "   "   "
—from Zenobia, the Arab *magliaia*,   "   "   "
—from Bess Broughton's unbuttoned
    smock,   "   "   "
—from all the Amalekite bitches,   "   "   "
—from Lesbia, titular mistress of Martial,   "   "   "
—from Aphrodite Kalligluttus, the
    strumpet,   "   "   "
—from the Thumblings of Daeumlinge,   "   "   "
—from Gonorilla and her buzzard
    women,   "   "   "
—from Nana the nysot,   "   "   "
—from Mère Guettautrou and her
    chagatte,   "   "   "
—from the Women of Midia,   "   "   "
—from Crobyle the Hairbuckle,   "   "   "
—from Echidna the half-snake,   "   "   "
—from Kwotsxwoe, the Quinault
    Indian quaedam,   "   "   "
—from Decreto the Moon Maid,   "   "   "
—from Sechmet, the Egyptian
    bloodmonger,   "   "   "
—from Miss Funderburk, *la malheureuse*,   "   "   "

—from Skogfrau, the Woman
    of the Thicket,   "   "   "
—from Mistress Birdlime, Moll
    Tenterhook, and Mabel Wafer,
    the loosened drawlatches . . ."   "   "   "

Crucifer, side-stepping the furniture, was traveling as well around the ramparts of his own madness, telling it all in a shower of pain as if he'd stored up such phrases over a lifetime for such eventualities to proscribe the destinies of souls in a vocabulary that pretended to exhaust elements for which even the reaches of uncommon brutality had no interest, no access, and no words.

"—from Asherah of Ugarit,   *libera nos, Domine*
—from Hine-nui-te-po, goddess of death, "   "   "
—from Erzulie Mapionne, voudounist,   "   "   "
—from Mary Baker Eddy and her
    M.A.M.,   "   "   "
—from Trulla, Bradamante,
    and Radigund, warriors of woe,   "   "   "
—from Monhigan, the crow-shaped
    enchantress,   "   "   "
—from Dippthese the doxy,   "   "   "
—from La Belle Ferronnière, *la greluche,* "   "   "
—from Cynara the Scorta,   "   "   "
—from Pontianek the Amboira Witch, "   "   "
—from the Empusai vampires,   "   "   "
—from Mayavel, 400-breasted goddess
    of the Agave,   "   "   "
—from Dinah the gadabout,   "   "   "
—from Rhodopis, the insatiable punk, "   "   "
—from Ishtar, deceiver of Gilgamesh, "   "   "
—from Keres, eater of corpses,   "   "   "
—from La Gambogi and her ivory teeth, "   "   "
—from Phanostrate Phtheropyle,
    Queen of Ceronicus,   "   "   "
—from Friga, mistress of Mars,   "   "   "
—from Izanami, Japanese goddess
    of putrefaction,   "   "   "
—from Dark Anu of Ireland,   "   "   "
—from Archidice the lupanarette,   "   "   "

—from Claria Leonza of Venezuela,
   stupefier of men,   " " "
—from Nut, goddess of the goetic,   " " "
—from Venus Vulgivaga, the wandering
   womb,   " " "
—from Blodeuwedd the Celtic runnion,   " " "
—from all the Potniae, Maniae,
   and Praxidikae,   " " "
—from Marguerite de Bourgogne,
   la pavute,   " " "
—from Louiatar, the blind whore
   of Pohjola,   " " "
—from Manosa, goddess of cobra bite,   " " "
—from Madame Pochet and Madame
   Gibou, beastettes,   " " "
—from Hathor-Sekhmet, exterminator
   of mankind,   " " "
—from Chicomecoatl, the empress of
   devils,   " " "
—from the Danish Ellefruwen
   and Swedish Skogsnufua,   " " "
—from Ignoge, Daughter of Albion,   " " "
—from Mère Castratrice the trancist,   " " "
—from Aphrodite Androphonous,
   the Sodomite vixen,   " " "
—from the Women of Goes,   " " "
—from Lilith, the Woman-Who-Invites,   " " "
—from Archippe and Theoris, the
   spoffokins of Sophocles,   " " "
—from Linda Lubberlegs, the Woman
   Who Never Showed Up,   " " "
—from Tekla Degener, scold,   " " "
—from Sumerian Inanna, the sender
   of plagues,   " " "
—from Cleine, Mneside, Pothyne,
   Myrtia, and all Egyptian gavials
   and rannels . . ."   " " "

The crescendo was ritualistic, an arithmetic of blasphemy and cruelty borne along on the inexorability of its own logical laws made instantly incompatible with any changing, revising, or rejecting opposition that might have been brought forth to prosecute against it and wailed in the sensation of those utterances that were always pitched antiphonally to the musical deathcry as if to deny that evil, without this archabominational chant, couldn't either be recognized or understood.

"—from Mother Cresswell and her claps,   *libera nos, Domine*
—from Canidia, the human dreep,   "   "   "
—from Anna Arkadyevna Karenina,
    the woman of dinge,   "   "   "
—from Maria Grubbe, sadist,   "   "   "
—from Levidulcia and her inclinations,   "   "   "
—from Arachne, originator of spinning,   "   "   "
—from Juoda Hercogienė,
    the Lithuanian bonce,   "   "   "
—from Emma Bridemann, elected vessel
    of the Mormons,   "   "   "
—from Poppeia, the sexual swill of Nero,   "   "   "
—from the Baroness de Nucingen,
    die Alte Hexe,   "   "   "
—from Mathilde Mauté, vaticide,   "   "   "
—from Joan Trash, the lady of the
    basket,   "   "   "
—from Elizabeth I, who died without
    hair in 1603,   "   "   "
—from Miss Fudpucker the fecalist,   "   "   "
—from Eisheth Zenunim, the common
    stale,   "   "   "
—from Ann Hathaway, the wappened
    widow,   "   "   "
—from the 33 Wicked Daughters
    of Diocletian,   "   "   "
—from Aspasia and her four-doored
    womb,   "   "   "
—from Thubui, the happy hierodule,   "   "   "
—from Nyctimene, who metamorphosed
    into an owl,   "   "   "
—from Mother Uphill, underfonger and
    venerilla,   "   "   "
—from Kriemhild and her
    hollowpampered hoors,   "   "   "

—from Linda Maestra, the hag of Goya,   "   "   "
—from Argive Helen, the deceitful
    swawmx,   "   "   "
—from Queen Draga Maschin of Black
    Head,   "   "   "
—from Xanthippe, the conjugal scold,   "   "   "
—from Biddy the Clap,   "   "   "
—from Deianire of Pyrite, the ravening
    prickamouse,   "   "   "
—from Marianne and her caprices,   "   "   "
—from Catherine Earnshaw, the
    bouncing ramp,   "   "   "
—from Kullikrahvinna,
    the Estonian pedicatress,   "   "   "
—from Dame Jinx and her catch-coin
    justice,   "   "   "
—from Mylitta, the Babylonian
    rumbelow,   "   "   "
—from Faustina the spermologress,   "   "   "
—from Aurelia Orestilla, the ginch
    of Catiline,   "   "   "
—from Cina Grofica, the Serbocroatian
    sunt,   "   "   "
—from Suzanne Valadon, the obstinate
    minx,   "   "   "
—from Mère Folle, the cock-brained
    fribble,   "   "   "
—from all Frows, Drabs, Ogresses,
    Ralaratri, and Ponderous
    Nopsters . . ."   "   "   "

The dirgeful hymn of the dead continued as Crucifer, pausing again for breath, could now even ignore Darconville suffering in his bed so intent was he upon the frenzy of names that so hollowly echoed through the room. He only puffed out his cheeks, humped his back, and hissed on:

"—from Joanna of Naples, the nonpareil
    of bawds,   *libera nos, Domine*
—from Praxagoras, the angry bellows,   "   "   "
—from Antonina Miliukova Tchaikovsky,
    the nieve,   "   "   "

—from Queen Cecropia the hypersubtle,   ″   ″   ″

—from the Witch of Endor and her broth,
    menses, and materials,   ″   ″   ″

—from Maria Beadnell, the pinchpin,   ″   ″   ″

—from La Belle Heaulmière, *la catin,*   ″   ″   ″

—from the Sibyl of Panzoult, who spoke
    lies,   ″   ″   ″

—from Valeria Messalina, the notorious
    stew,   ″   ″   ″

—from Dame van Winkle, the whiniling
    dastard,   ″   ″   ″

—from Mother Prat, the fat woman
    of Brainford,   ″   ″   ″

—from all Troll Madams, Titifulls,
    and Tattlers,   ″   ″   ″

—from Glycera, the painted trullabub,   ″   ″   ″

—from Diana Trapes, the walking mort,   ″   ″   ″

—from Lady Fricarelle, the duchess
    of malfeasance,   ″   ″   ″

—from Una the Fairy Queen,   ″   ″   ″

—from Smēraldine and her hairpins,   ″   ″   ″

—from Catherine Alexeyevna Romanov I,
    called 'Figgy,' the *kozlonogaia,*   ″   ″   ″

—from Giralda, the weathercock,   ″   ″   ″

—from Berte au grant pié, *la conasse,*   ″   ″   ″

—from Old Mother Gothel and her
    gamps and slatterns,   ″   ″   ″

—from Elizabeth Bathory,
    the trugging-house truepenny,   ″   ″   ″

—from Hecate the Attic drench,   ″   ″   ″

—from Mahboobeh the slave-girl,   ″   ″   ″

—from Watere Wytches, crownede
    wythe reytes,   ″   ″   ″

—from Fanfan la Tulipe and her
    bumrowls,   ″   ″   ″

—from Empress Agrippina, the orgiac,   ″   ″   ″

—from Notre-Dame des Parcs, the saint
    of the smock-fair,   ″   ″   ″

—from Wjera Sassulitch, the human
    skate,   ″   ″   ″

—from Henda, the wife of Abu Sofian,   "   "   "
—from La DuBarry and her ligbies
    and lightskirts,   "   "   "
—from Lynda Raxa, the rixatrix,   "   "   "
—from La Sorellacia and her sausage
    legs,   "   "   "
—from Dido and all her *dützbetterins*
    and *biltregerins*,   "   "   "
—from Jane Medlar, the Dutch Widow,   "   "   "
—from Pohjola's Daughters,   "   "   "
—from Madame Miracola, the zook of
    hell,   "   "   "
—from Argante, the giantess of
    prostitution,   "   "   "
—from Dame Wiggins of Lee, the female
    mandrake,   "   "   "
—from Venus Pandemos, the queen of
    tarts,   "   "   "
—from Naamah, Noah's crosseyed wife,   "   "   "
—from Senta the spiggot-wench,   "   "   "
—from Paulina Bonaparte, *la pettegola*
    maligna,   "   "   "
—from Queen Aigle of Dreiviertelstein,
    who could fly,   "   "   "
—from Harriet Wilson, the blackmailing
    waistcoateer,   "   "   "
—from the Mother of St. Edward
    of Corfe, the mullipod of villainy,   "   "   "
—from Queen Dollalolla, the slatterpiece,   "   "   "
—from Isobel Gowdie the Strix,   "   "   "
—from Akko and Alphito and all giglots
    and jillivers,   "   "   "
—from My Own Middle-Wicketed
    Mingwort of a Mother . . ."   "   "   "

Stung with anger, Crucifer went suddenly into a full hue and cry, alive with self-inflicted hurt, and he rose up, grey, like Banquo's ghost, heaping even greater contumely on each and every name he uttered with each dart of that sarcastic tongue that looked like a foul pistil issuing from a huge calyx.

"—from Libitana and her dead eyes,   *libera nos, Domine*
—from Dipsias and her flying wheels,   "   "   "
—from Lady Alice Kyteler, virago
    and voriander,   "   "   "
—from Aholibah the aplestous,   "   "   "
—from Miss Farabutto, the quarrelsome
    fratcher,   "   "   "
—from Pythia the oracularia,   "   "   "
—from Ilmator, Creatrix of the World,   "   "   "
—from Cybele, the Phrygian goddess
    of fustilugging,   "   "   "
—from Al Lat, the false idol,   "   "   "
—from She Who Must Be Obeyed,   "   "   "
—from Francesca Bassington, the
    belittling bersatrix,   "   "   "
—from Mary of Brabant, pavior and
    rumbold,   "   "   "
—from Albertine Simonet, *la disparue,*   "   "   "
—from Waila, the Koranic nag,   "   "   "
—from the Wretched Magpies
    of King Pieros,   "   "   "
—from Hélène de Surgères and her cool
    hands,   "   "   "
—from Evelyn Bedstead, the wanton
    bedswerver,   "   "   "
—from Athalie, the child butcher,   "   "   "
—from Columbine, the construpratress
    of all those commode ladies who
    lend out their beauty for hire,   "   "   "
—from Madame Guyon, the gotch-bellied
    tart,   "   "   "
—from Drusilla, the chamberer,   "   "   "
—from Gagool, the evil crone of
    Zimbabwe,   "   "   "
—from Anna Sage, the Lady in Red,   "   "   "
—from Ninon de Lenclos, *notre dame*
    des amours,   "   "   "
—from Elsche Nebelings, the
    Mouse-Maker,   "   "   "

—from Dame La Voisin, philtre-seller
    and whore,   "   "   "
—from Morgan le Fay, the fuxlady,   "   "   "
—from Penelope Devereux, richest
    of bitches,   "   "   "
—from Goody Rickby and her noisy
    forges,   "   "   "
—from Herodias, the jewified bestialator,   "   "   "
—from Mademoiselle de Maupin and her
    pet muggins,   "   "   "
—from Philtra, the money stinkard,   "   "   "
—from La, queen of the Atlantean colony
    of Opar,   "   "   "
—from Acrasia and her bowery wiles,   "   "   "
—from Ethel le Neve, snipe and mistress,   "   "   "
—from Jane Nightwork, the pox-ridden
    fireship,   "   "   "
—from Centectl, maize mother
    of Mexico,   "   "   "
—from Syntyche, the sharny-faced
    scrubber,   "   "   "
—from fierce Camilla, o'er the plain,   "   "   "
—from Omm Jemil, the scoffing bardash,   "   "   "
—from the American South and its
    stinking girleries,   "   "   "
—from Lady Clara Vere de Vere, the
    proud mincing peat,   "   "   "
—from Cunizza da Romano, *la zitella
    inacidita*,   "   "   "
—from Hilde Bobbe, the old witch
    of Haarlem,   "   "   "
—from Mothers Twaddle and Twitchett
    and all weeping culls and drabs,   "   "   "
—from Gara Gertsoginia, the gueuse
    of Gazag,   "   "   "
—from Grička Vještica, the Witch of
    Grič,   "   "   "
—from Laverna, goddess of impostors,   "   "   "
—from Cicely Yeovil, the yawde,
    the yode, the yade, the yaud . . ."   "   "   "

The select and cynically imaginative incantation exceeded by far
the black medieval hymn in conjuring, almost to fantasm, the meaning
of the day of wrath and yet the furious and driving relentlessness of
both proclaimed equally in the full moon of Dr. Crucifer's blowing
face, its morphs of color increasingly going to dark as he droned the
long profanity out in dry arundinaceous whistles.

"—from Atropos and her glittering forfex,	*libera nos, Domine*
—from Empusa the succubus,	" " "
—from Potiphar's Wife, who hadn't even a name,	" " "
—from Linda Pallant, the finished product,	" " "
—from Assma, the sheeny poetess,	" " "
—from Mother Brownrigg, the despicable rudas,	" " "
—from Giulia Farnese, concubine di Papa Alessandro VI,	" " "
—from Zipporah the Desertable,	" " "
—from Kali the Black Mother,	" " "
—from Mesdames Goursey and Barnes, the Abington scrubbers,	" " "
—from Anne Boleyn, the princess of plackets,	" " "
—from Lady Pecunia and her encomium,	" " "
—from Queen Tiy, who did her thutmose,	" " "
—from Marozia, *la grande horizontale,*	" " "
—from La Belle Dame Sans Merci, the terrible frictrix,	" " "
—from Madame la Mort and the xvi gromettes in her stable,	" " "
—from Lady Giacoma Rodogina, the engastrimythion prophetess,	" " "
—from Dame Trot and her basket of eggs,	" " "
—from Aloysia Weber the Unavailable,	" " "
—from the Wife of Bath and her yvel preef,	" " "
—from Franceschina, tanakin of the Low Countries,	" " "

—from Miss Flannigan, the Winnipeg
    Whore,   "   "   "
—from the Great Whore of Revelations,   "   "   "
—from Signora Cianculli, the soapmaker
    of Reggio,   "   "   "
—from Roxana, Countess of Wintelsheim,   "   "   "
—from Mary Powell Milton,
    the troublesome hindermate,   "   "   "
—from Proserpina, Crowned Empress
    of the Nether Clefts of Hell,   "   "   "
—from Queen Athaliah, court wanton,   "   "   "
—from Boadicea, the bullying bubbie,   "   "   "
—from Katherine de Vausselles,
    the wheencat,   "   "   "
—from Aerope the andromaniac,   "   "   "
—from Mademoiselle Maximum
    the maculate,   "   "   "
—from Volumnia, iron-boweled mother
    of Coriolanus,   "   "   "
—from Penelope Whorehound, harlot
    of Bridewell,   "   "   "
—from Madeleine Amalaric, the nativity
    caster,   "   "   "
—from The Red Queen and her scarlet
    queynt,   "   "   "
—from Vidosava, wife of Vojvoda
    Momčilo,   "   "   "
—from Procne, filiocide,   "   "   "
—from Anna Keller Haydn,
    the spoonpinching greedigut,   "   "   "
—from Melusine, the kitchen malkin,   "   "   "
—from Creseide, the cold-hearted
    enjôleuse,   "   "   "
—from Tubby Ursula, the Fatness
    of the Fair,   "   "   "
—from Erichtho the Karcist,   "   "   "
—from bat-eyed Madame du Deffand,
    notre dame de lorette,   "   "   "
—from Vittoria Corombona, the devil
    in crystal,   "   "   "

—from Lucilla and her curious curio,   " " "
—from Mamaloi, the twigger of the
    West Indies,   " " "
—from Athé, heron-thighed goddess
    of peevishness,   " " "
—from Livia Augusta, the leporine,   " " "
—from Mother Laquedem the Yenta,   " " "
—from Niphleseth, queen of the
    chitterlings,   " " "
—from the Phrygian Cybele and her
    eunuch pontifesses,   " " "
—from Mademoiselle Scudéry, the urning,   " " "
—from the Lady Dunya, the land-frigate,   " " "
—from Isis, the female pope of secret
    religions,   " " "
—from the Princess Badroulbadour,
    out of the tomb,   " " "
—from Madame de Maintenon
    and her beavroys and
    ridinghoods . . ."   " " "

Then the "Lacrymosa" began: the grief in the musical flats of the long mournful lament, like fatal heartache, repeatedly sobbing themselves out like ancient questions, and Crucifer now, almost as if turning away from himself, as if now leaving the exequies involved in the burial of a thousand corpses to the unearthly infection of the music alone, revolved, drifted, around the room, almost hypnotized himself, his hands down by his sides as though they were both dead, but he never stopped the murmuring. It was incessant, brutal, eternal.

"—from the Blue Hag of Leicester,   *libera nos, Domine*
—from Asenath Waite, the psychovore,   " " "
—from Queen Hiera, the cuckquean,   " " "
—from Ramping Alice and her riggish
    zooks and mawks,   " " "
—from Aello, Ocypete, and Celeno, the
    triple extract of infamy,   " " "
—from Roxalana, the quean
    of bawdreaminy,   " " "
—from Hélène Kuryagin, the *otorva*,   " " "

—from the Women of the Sidhe,   "   "   "
—from Queen Quintessence and her
    rhubarb soul,   "   "   "
—from Undine, the wayward watersprite,   "   "   "
—from Baba Yaga, bronzestrops
    and blowze,   "   "   "
—from Elizabeth Sawyer, the Witch
    of Edmonton,   "   "   "
—from Alcina, the flatbacker,   "   "   "
—from the Duchess of Wonderland,   "   "   "
—from the bandit Lara and her cyprian
    patrol,   "   "   "
—from Amine, the wicked inquisitrix,   "   "   "
—from Lizzie Eustace, the sorceress
    unsorcelled,   "   "   "
—from Termagant, Mohammed's
    shrewish wife,   "   "   "
—from Julie de Lespinasse, *la liaisonesse*,   "   "   "
—from Europa who diddled a bull,   "   "   "
—from Mutter Frauenwelt, die Herrinnen
    der Herren,   "   "   "
—from the Yakshas of the Himalayas,   "   "   "
—from Thel, the small-souled therne,   "   "   "
—from the Lady Governors of the Old
    Men's Home at Haarlem,   "   "   "
—from Gabrina the jillet,   "   "   "
—from Mistress Alice Arden, stabfiend,   "   "   "
—from Sappho, the silly *gousse*,   "   "   "
—from Lucretia Estense Borgia,
    the lycanthrophile,   "   "   "
—from Alyona Ivanovna the pawnbroker,   "   "   "
—from Yolara of the moon pool,   "   "   "
—from the Comtesse d'Orgueil,
    the Duchesse d'Argent, and Madame
    de Grandes Titres, the unpartial
    daughters of necessity,   "   "   "
—from Gulfora, Queen of the Sabbat,   "   "   "
—from Odette de Crécy and her
    cotqueanity,   "   "   "
—from Ixtab, Mayan goddess of suicide,   "   "   "

—from Minerva and her celestial trollops,   "   "   "
—from Belphoebe, the perforated virgin,   "   "   "
—from Gort à Bhaile, the femina of
    famine,   "   "   "
—from Madame Anima and her firehaired
    procuresses,   "   "   "
—from Queen Draga of Serbia,
    the belly-bumper,   "   "   "
—from Eriphilem, the callat of boundless
    tongue,   "   "   "
—from Mother Waterhouse the Spaewife,   "   "   "
—from Blouzelinda, the princess
    of pillicocks,   "   "   "
—from Dame Hulda and her apparitions,   "   "   "
—from Jeannie Alexander, the wheezing
    arrhenopiper,   "   "   "
—from Circe, the chaterestre, the chevese,
    the chydester,   "   "   "
—from Locusta, poisoner
    of the Roman court,   "   "   "
—from Alecto, Tisiphone, and Megaera,
    the fustilarians,   "   "   "
—from Gnathenion, who pillaged poets'
    pockets,   "   "   "
—from Isabel Rawsthorne, than whom none
    here is more loathsome . . ."   "   "   "

The window had grown almost dark in the dusk, the faintest twilight throwing lengthening shadows across the unlit room. As he heard her name, profaned so familiarly in the mouth of this huge creature built like an oversized marabout, Darconville lost his heart in a downrush of total despair and he looked away, tears now running down his cheeks.

"—from Clepsydra and her hourglass,   *libera nos, Domine*
 —from Mother Shipton of
    Knaresborough,   "   "   "
 —from Beatrice Ambient, the dewclaw,   "   "   "
 —from Umm al Samim, mother of poison,   "   "   "
 —from Mephitis, goddess of sulphur,   "   "   "

—from Juno whose clitoris was
     a thunderbolt,   "   "   "
—from Phaedra, the shameless sot,   "   "   "
—from Rhea and her midget dactyls,   "   "   "
—from Madame Box, the ranting meretrix,   "   "   "
—from Phyllis Grewsome, the
     Washington *protopopsha,*   "   "   "
—from Bathsheba, druggard and drazel,   "   "   "
—from Queen Tomyris, the beheading
     kite,   "   "   "
—from Catherine de Medici, the
     monstriferous matelot,   "   "   "
—from Eudoxia and her equipolances,   "   "   "
—from the Baroness Klara Ungnad,
     weenie-trundler,   "   "   "
—from Maidhdeanbuain and her
     superstitions,   "   "   "
—from Rapunzel the rampish-hearted,   "   "   "
—from Charlotte Corday, hysterical
     virgin,   "   "   "
—from Baubo the Bawdstrot and her girls
     whom none call maidens,   "   "   "
—from Januatica and her horrible old
     sempiternal trots,   "   "   "
—from all the Little Pops of Hoggland,   "   "   "
—from Empress Theodora, harlot queen
     of Byzantium,   "   "   "
—from Mariamne, the dawkin for a dolt,   "   "   "
—from Belides, the dragonian doxy,   "   "   "
—from Actoria Paula, peripole
     and paranymph,   "   "   "
—from Hiberina, the bottomless well,   "   "   "
—from Grognon, the ill-willed
     Stiefmutter,   "   "   "
—from Catherine Bora, the lutheran duck,   "   "   "
—from Penthisilea, the Amazonian bunt,   "   "   "
—from Eryphile, the low betrayer,   "   "   "
—from the Empress Dowager Tsu Hsi
     of Imperial China, the Scourge of
     God,   "   "   "

—from Thais, the trugmullion of
    Alexander the Great,   "   "   "
—from Lady Bertalda and her lavenders
    and leaping-housewives,   "   "   "
—from Typhaon the tallywoman,   "   "   "
—from Guinevere, the spiteful solicitrix,   "   "   "
—from the seductress Phrynne and all
    parnels everywhere who march by
    two and three,   "   "   "
—from Pheretrina, the cruelest of
    connivers,   "   "   "
—from Fulvia and Arsinoë, bumfondlers,   "   "   "
—from Sofya Andreyevna Bers, who
    stole toys,   "   "   "
—from Pythionice the pallaptern,   "   "   "
—from Jennyanydots and her Gumbie cats,   "   "   "
—from Barbara Muehleck Kepler,
    the left-handed jilt,   "   "   "
—from Clorinda, the chattel of sullen
    memory,   "   "   "
—from Ulin, the false enchantress,   "   "   "
—from the Grandmother of Ghosts and
    her woolen effigies,   "   "   "
—from the Princess Papulie with plenty
    papaya,   "   "   "
—from Cytheris, the jade prophet,   "   "   "
—from Miss Emily Faithful, man-hating
    amazon,   "   "   "
—from the Weird Sisters and their
    wheyfaced wirepulling,   "   "   "
—from Anteia the inallegiant,   "   "   "
—from Madame Arcadina, pinnace
    and pythoness,   "   "   "
—from Princess Sumru of Sirdhana,
    the sunck, who smoked her hookah
    over the graves of men buried alive,   "   "   "
—from Solange Dudevant, the deywife,   "   "   "
—from Olympias, the Greek hen,   "   "   "
—from Semiramis the Assyrian punk,   "   "   "
—from Hypatia, pagan philosophress,   "   "   "

—from Fiametta, bastard of the King
   of Naples,   *"   "   "*
—from Dian L. Rotbun, hedonomaniac,   *"   "   "*
—from Ge Panmeter and all the whorage
   of wifkin,   *"   "   "*
—from Marie Duplessis de Camellias,
   la baiseuse, la chouquette, la
   gisquette, la gonzesse, la punaise, la
   travailleuse, la racoleuse, la catiche,
   la petasse, la poufiasse."   *"   "   "*

Dr. Crucifer in one move shut off the phonograph and, caracoling belly-forward, countermarched to the bed with the mouth of a bell and the heart of hell and the head of a gallows tree, but the day of toil for Darconville, his ashen eyes no longer staring into space, had fortunately ended several minutes before when with an inexplicable stabbing in the lungs from a last indrawn breath he passed the threshold of pain now into a deep coma.

LXXXIII

Gone for a Burton

When I loved you and you loved me,
You were the sky, the sea, the tree;
Now skies are skies, and seas are seas,
And trees are brown and they are trees.

—CHARLES A. WAGNER

STILLMAN INFIRMARY was white and antiseptic, the room on
the seventh floor nothing more than a table, a chair, and a high wheel-
footed bed. There was no flourish of architecture, no ornament, only
chrome, silence, and a monotony of windows. Doors, opening, shut.
Lights, coming on, went out. There was no sky beyond the window.
The view, looking westward, was too high for one to see the trees.

The doctors had been worried. They might have lost him, they said,
charging Darconville where he lay, forfoughten, with contributory

negligence not only for excessive smoking but for an acute tension due to some kind of overexertion or apprehension he'd ignored. Where had he been this past week? And how long had he gone without food? The quick hard pulse and convulsive motions had frightened them, along with the obvious weight loss, dyspnea even at rest, and the labored use of accessory muscles for respiration; his chest was hyper-resonant to percussion. He had to lean forward, while sitting, to brace himself. An inept intern, searching for a cardiac murmur (known only to himself), had initially forced him through a valsalva maneuver: the sudden stabbing pain was so severe that Darconville became hypoxic and, past his limitation, fell into hypotensive shock. The intern quickly called an emergency code. Several resident doctors ran in and gave him a saline infusion—wide-open—of 1500 cc's over three hours. They found a bounding right ventricular pulse in the chest beneath the sternum and the sound of wet rattling rhonci on the right but, more ominously, on the left side of the lung only a seashell hollowness. There followed prolonged expiration through pursed lips, profuse sweating, and flailing movements in the chest. An emergency X ray revealed scattered lucencies throughout the lung fields, and now they knew what they had—a congenital condition of bullous emphysema, with an episode of spontaneous pneumothorax.

It called for immediate intervention: one or several bullae had rup-tured, causing air, leaking from one lung, to rush into the chest and being trapped there to increase the pressure from *outside* the lung to collapse it. The harder he tried to breathe, the more the lung collapsed. Quickly, the doctors punched a hole in the chest wall and through the ribs inserted a tube attached to a Gomco machine to suck out air in order to reinflate the collapsing lung, prevent it from closing down, and allow scarring to seal the rupture.

Darconville spent several days on a respirator while being fed intra-venously, and his pulmonary competence was restored to a fragile but stable state. No visitors were allowed—not black Iameth; not Hasmed, angel of annihilation; not Af, ruler over the death of mor-tals. He slept fitfully. When he awoke, the sweat had stenciled his hair to his forehead and his head rocked with conflicting swing and spin, a relentless hammering between the eyes as if, with importunate ques-tions, someone to solve justice yet not knowing how desperately sought release to find and punish the criminal who belonged there instead. He had almost gone for a burton—he didn't care, for it was better to die than live some death too bitter to fear—but he was still alive. He remembered nothing of how he got there, but for all he knew the university had already issued a writ *de lunatico inquirendo,* scheduled as he was, before a week was out, to undergo a required bit of zoopery with a psychiatrist.

"It would of course be taken as healthier—more normal—for you to hate her," the psychiatrist muttered, sitting back and meditatively circling his foot. It was absurd: hate Isabel? Darconville loved her. He wouldn't say it again. But he wouldn't pray for it anymore, either, for God now seemed to him the refuge to whom men only turned to avoid any homage to their neighbor. And then how did Christ expect us to love as we were bidden to do in this life when the very chance for it was taken away? The heavens? No, to seek solutions there—whether of a crime, or a code, or a criss-cross puzzle—was to have your questions not solved but dissolved. To solve it all, on the other hand, he was nevertheless determined (he simply didn't know how!) for love was somehow *inside* him, giving him no rest; it was not a pursuit to which he could turn his attention or not as he chose. In any case, she had promised she'd send him an explanation, hadn't she?—he would wait for it, then. It would help. It must help.

There must be more to love than death, thought Darconville during those long empty days, feeling he wanted only to find something he needed or needed to find something he wanted—to step on the moon and say, to the cagastric night, "Be day!" No, something would come that would save him from hate, and if it wasn't death it had to be love, didn't it?

Darconville told the psychiatrist he missed his cat. Yes, that's right, his cat—because he believed, as he said, that we partially died, all of us, through sympathy at the death or disappearance of each of our friends; memories, even if one wished it, *couldn't* be forgotten. It became a thought that literally upon the thinking brought an ache to his wounded lung, compressing his chest. (Secretly, he began to take the benperidol.) He asked the psychiatrist, describing him, if by any chance he had ever seen Spellvexit. He badgered him to make inquiries. And repeatedly he begged him if he would telephone Isabel on his behalf. Would he? Why wouldn't he? But there was no reply, the foot merely continuing meditatively to circle, now this way, now the other. It must have been a Saturday, at one such session, when Darconville strained across the bed to peer down at the street: the distant marching music, attracting him, was that of the Harvard band escorting a football crowd through the streets below. They all looked so happy, the boys in topcoats and flannels hugging blankets in one hand and beautiful slender girls in crimson tams and scarves waving fishtail-pennants in the other, all of them limber, alive, in the bright sword-cold October air and kicking through autumn leaves toward the grey arcade of the stadium across the river. It made Darconville feel more isolated than ever. Would he telephone, please? Would he call? No, decided the psychiatrist, he must simply learn to forget her; he was worried: the largest number of inmates in bedlam, he pointed out, were people, unresigned to it, who'd been rejected in love. The psychiatrist, however, asked what *he* was going to do, lest he end up among them. (Instantly, Darconville felt an overwhelming compulsion to write a book in defense of them all. I wonder why? he thought. *I?* Perhaps, he thought, there isn't an I at all and we're simply the means of expression of something else. *Wonder?* What is wonder but the imagination seeking what it hasn't. *Why?* Y: the past tense of antique verbs resurrected to predicate present behavior.) His reply was that he was waiting—Isabel was going to send an explanation. But the psychiatrist frowned and continued to express concern, remarking again on the curious absence of a normal heteropathic symptom of improvement: relief by rage. Why did he not hate her? Then Darconville turned to him, not with rebuke, not with ridicule, neither with irony nor sarcasm, but rather with the kind of childlike and simplehearted ingenuousness that suddenly lit up his eyes with innocence as he softly asked, "Do you think she'd believe I loved her then?"

The days passed. Morning brought emptiness, ink flooded the sky beyond the window, and night crept in again, earlier and earlier now, the cold winds outside crying and sobbing like a child in a chimney and blowing out the faraway lights of Boston one by one. Visitors were still prohibited him. Late one night, however, Darconville was awakened when the door of his room, gradually opening, sent a diagonal fan of light across the bed. He sat up quickly and clicked on the lamp. There stood Lampblack of all people—alone—gesturing nervously with a handful of mail he dropped on the bed just before he rushed out. The largest piece, postmarked New York, was an official-looking manila envelope. Darconville slit it open, and an angry blush suddenly filled his head as with a sinking heart he saw what he held in his hands—a photograph of a blond fellow in a naval uniform, the subject's rank and identification below. It was Gilbert van der Slang, himself.

Swiftly, Darconville took up a pencil nearby, crossed out the name with a petulance that broke the lead in midstroke, and shut off the light. The weighty darkness bore in on him in a sudden synathroismus, crowding a million terrible particulars upon him and paralyzing him head to foot, and though he opened his mouth to gasp he was prevented from either calling or crying out under the action of the crippling inexplicable force pressing him to death. He lay motionless in the dark, with tears rippling down his cheeks, waiting for the rest of his life to show him what it would be. Then he could suddenly breathe. Then the darkness began to dissolve. Then he could again discern necessary shapes out of unnecessary shadows. And then he knew that the detective to solve a crime must become an accessory to it. He turned on the light again.

And he picked up the photograph.

LXXXIV

What Is One Picture Worth?

If the Devil did ever take good shape, behold this picture.
—JOHN WEBSTER, *The White Devil*

GILBERT VAN DER SLANG, Ensign (USNR)—it would be a graduation photo—stands at attention in the full dress of regimental commander in the boy navy: white gloves, a sash at the waist, the shoddy-for-broadcloth jacket with its ventral rows of brass-buttons. The subject is stiff as a stork—poker-backed, eyes front, arse tight as a trapdrum—but the martial stance, nevertheless, fails to supply the proper pointing, not for want of high-seriousness certainly—the little chin juts out *niet zander arbijt*—but for the uniform, impressive indeed were it not the type that conventionally attracts ice-cream vendors, doormen, and South American officials. It's the pose of a smugly pretentious deluxe: the Count of Trumpet on maneuvers from the stage of sugarplum opera! The picture, were it hung in a museum, would be entitled, "Are You Proud, Mother?"

The student medals and sigla are very nice, but it's the kind of military respectability with which vulgarity is always on speaking terms, for the white ducks, foreshortened like a clumperton's, are in painful collaboration with those black government-issue shoes—the sort that never seem to be fellows—and the sleeves mooch down too far over the hands. Alongside the left leg, facing oddly inward and suggesting a slight effeminacy, hangs a toy sword with which by optimistic transfer he doubtless seeks to counteract that impression.

It's a sallow face, plain as the way to market, one of those drawn yellow lamplit complexions best exemplified in the work of minor Dutch painters of the seventeenth century. The small blunket-colored eyes, cold as a boomslang's, are looking straight, if unseeingly, toward Cape Disappointment where those who graduate from service academies are of course doomed, for want of imagination, to spend the rest of their lives. He has a bifid chin and the sharp grypanian nose of a logical positivist. The lank hair characteristic of him has always been considered indicative of pusillanimity, enough so to advance by way of suggestion a distinct androgen deficiency—or even possible impotence.

There is a humorless and hard-natured line to the mouth, Protestant in cast, shaped to the possibility of generating inauspiciously vexatious abuse like sending common seamen for non-existent tools (still deemed wit at sea) or ordering a battue of porpoises as a holiday diversion on some dull cruise to the Leeward Islands or the Hawaiian chain of Kukeke Eleele. It would be a high immature voice, slick with alloquia and sea-bop and nautical drunts in the quasi-linguistic bluff of logbook narrative about jackstays 'n' jumper struts 'n' jibbin' the kibber. The head is capitalupine, the hands thin and spidery, deft at small tasks. There is a sapped but inflexible tonality to the general appearance of this brisk little fart, the lack of repose conveyed especially in the adolescent legs, elongating the outline, which run out of the effortfully dovetailed imposture of uniform and down to feet long as kippers—the body actually taking on the appearance of having issued from the feet *themselves!* He is, in fact, quite short.

This is a figure of fun—a cross-grained, long-waisted clockcase of opposability with the generic temperament of a satrap and a talent for extrapolating cues from postures with indefatigable readiness. He loves bandmusic, probably ran cross-country (*les Pays-Bas, certain!*), and would have had the best "cargo project" at the Academy—the kind of officious little pickstraw who'd go into a complete shitfit if anyone in his presence ever failed to refer, for instance, to a ship as a boat. He's a dog to procedure. There is in that bast and Nankeen-yellow mask a sunken and repugnant mood of refusal—spitefully incloistered— showing a person in whom secrecy would erroneously be taken for reserve and for whom everything drops into categories made familiar only by his indifference, as a makeweight to a scale adjusts a gain. An underbutler squats in an esquire: he finds meaningful what he can verify by counting on his fingers, discerning no limit between achievement and ambition, and thus is beauty duly converted by that transubstantiating process of the functionist, once again, to use. There are, however, more wheels and counterpoises in this engine than are easily imagined. His thoughts are executed only to matters of dogged purpose, his emotions but to formulate accumulations—and Either piggybacks Or, the while, for the acquisition of both. Here is Ambidexter, for good or for the time being, whichever comes first.

We discern a sharp composite picture of a prattboy so null in effect —his mind an abode of anything—that in nothing isn't something to which he wouldn't promise all he seemed for everything he lacked. And if a girl? Occasion is his cupid. He is what is his shadow: it is and it is not; he'd strut and fleer and fumble with his hat with untaught fists and with a smile that aches to shield his mouth as glasses would his eyes proceed to peep love ditties in her neck and seek to mirror lies—until such time when promises reflect what's far too malconformed for sight to see he'd turn and gaze inward with the lost half of his double face, and then would turpitude purvey to malice in a flash! It is a photograph of utter vacancy. Vain, pale, fragmentary, silly, indeed almost nothing—wait!—O my God, *but what about those ears?*

His ears are absolutely monstrositous! No, it's not simply that they stand noticeably away from the head—lobeless, horizontal, shaped like eraserwheels!—they actually *shoot* out of the haircut like those xanthodermic warballs made of Hoggland clay with which van Tromp and his sullen brabantois sought to obliterate the English and establish the legitimacy of that cheesemongering, guilder-grubbing, tulip-sniffing, drainage-scheming Gomorrah of the North where people live below sea-level, exact payment from guests, and sport footwear made of trees! His ears?

Are you in quest of comparisons?

LXXXV

A Digression on Ears

> To strike at eares is to take heed there bee
> No witnesse, Peter, of thy perjury.
>
> —RICHARD CRASHAW

THE EARS, which master the face of a dunce, are that part of the head which most publishes stupidity. It was into none other than these, fluting up moronically like foolish squills—*penchant à la réception de suggestions négatives*—wherein was poured, thought Darconville, more venomous lies than even Hearsay of Satinland and all his polyotical side-intelligencers could accommodate! It was astounding: they seemed both to strain away from the cheeks in such vicious inflexions of helix and anti-helix and yet draw up to such devilish points that ugliness was announced instantly and absolutely, as if in those oversized dirt-traps, shutting out all melodies and comprehending only discord, no plot could hatch fouler than themselves. The pinna looked hard and mollusk-shaped, the tragus hemorrhoidal, and the conch darker than the keyhole to hell. There were no lobes.

What is there in the malformed ear that is so revolting? It is the ideographic mark of perverts, penny-simples, and Puritans, and be disarranged in whatever way they might, nothing better indicates a blemished soul. Contour—whether prick-eared, flap-eared, tulip-eared, lop-eared, or jug-eared—does not establish periphery, for what it is is only a poor remnant of what it means: small ones announce madness; flat, brutishness and rusticity; spheroidal, talkativeness; twisted, silliness or imbecility; pointed, cunning, deceit, and that hypocritical kind of lust commonly associated with those face-pulling and dissenting Anabaptists and Allobrogensians with their bowl-haircuts and venereal poxes who were ever ready to club quotations and descant on bare supposals and bantle scripture about in order to preach the dresses off the neighborhood girls, until, you'll recall, King Charles II took the matter in hand—by those twin appendages, in fact, which he found could be gloriously cropped or notched or slit to fit several fashions of contrition. But *large* ears? They are the sumps of rumor and redundance, each a whirlpool fierce to suck in fabrications of a thousand sorts. These are the penetralia of the body, known to every Dumbo, Jumbo, and woebegone basset hound of a detractor who's tripped on them—flags that semaphore treachery—which historically denote flight before spiritual responsibility, natures playing at modesty while working hard at things like ruses, and those meager, choleric, inconstant, and unethical schemes observable from without yet confined within the twisted and grotesque mule-pulleys of people like Wycliffe, Prynne, Calvin, Vickers, Wither, Cranmer, Herr Ludder and other nasal Protestant archdapifers who'd have left the world a far, far better place had they all been immediately banished to the infamous island of Panotiorum where the cruel aboriginals of that place are so monstrously fluked that they live out their lives actually wrapped in their ears! "A long-ear'd Beast and Flanders College," wrote Swift, "is Dr. Tisdale to my knowledge." To big ears we owe our universal death. Eve, the first macrotus, wished to hearken only to what she heard she wanted. Acousticus first brought wickedness into the world.

There is more to the ear than meets the eye. It *looks* awful, for one thing—the asymmetrical non-whorls and misvolutions of its general format showing a factual resemblance to nothing whatsoever on earth, except perhaps for that one striking correspondence to Dutch land-scape. A simile is applied to it as schnaps to a Voortrekker: one is never sufficient. Is it an air-conditioner? A love-lure? A gravity ball? It is a human question mark with a cochlea like a snail, a center like a diphthong, and a rim like a last quarter moon or the symbol for a suffruticose shrub. It never trumpets, though it resembles one. Sound goes through it perforating nothing—as theologians explain the Virgin birth—like saffron through a bag. Its squashed-up shape is a poor ves-tige of the mobile catchment-cup of many other mammals. It cannot be hid. (The contraptions, in fact, contrived for whatever good reason to cover them temporarily—*oreillettes,* muffs, earcaps—are more hide-ous than the ears themselves!) It is the only aperture impossible to shut by itself. It is forever open to fungi, otosis, and the mendacities of talebearers, false delators, and tare-sowing dogs. It cannot discrim-inate between noises it will and will not hear.

It is a vicious circle, like all circles. It has no other one like it. It be-gins to hum for no apparent reason. It aches at simple heights and depths. It cannot move. Insert an insect: there sounds a deafening heavy-footed tread—and yet it is unable to hear higher pitches com-monly available to the lower beasts. It can claim no exact certitude in relation to distance, space, and often time. It cannot determine truth. Of itself it can retain and remember nothing, and nothing produces, save an ignoble dirty mulch called "cerumen" which gathers in the dark like mushrooms and deafens before it disgusts. It is therefore the worst tool to grasp philosophical knowledge. It freezes, it shrinks, it sprouts hairs, it turns color, and, worst of all perhaps, it repeatedly reports—for if one sleeps on one ear, the other can always bring bad news. By our ears our *hearts* become tainted! We speak of being *up to one's ears,* meaning involved or implicated, in debt, or in trouble; or *on one's ear* as captiously or excessively irritated or irritable; or *all ears,* indicating ambitiously opportunistic or vulgarly eager; or *by the ears* as entering into a state of strife or discord. It is a noun with as many contemptuous and derogatory implications in English as has the word "Dutch." The ears of people do not follow suit with the rest of them as they age, remaining not only large, if initially so, but the efflorescence of ugliness until the very moment of death. There is little loveliness, indeed, even for the normal ear, often failing to correspond regularly between the tip of the nose and eyebrow line at the base of the forehead. It is the single tragic constant on the head of man.

But what of those ears of *Gilbert les Grands Écoutilles?* They were goosewings—tegumentary expansions of skin, suggesting the distinct possibility of aerial flight, stretched from head side to the elongated digits of their points as if ready to crow and flap away. It was a comic set of volutes, each proof against each, one slightly forward of the other, like an owl's. They flew up only to be pulled down, ballasted by the priapic weight that wouldn't let them leave and, wallowing unwieldy, enormous in their gait, stuck out while infolding to a flat welt as if not belonging to their bearer. The placement was no better than the spread which was worse than the shape, a contortion best put somewhere between a potato chip and a reporter's logograph for the word "impostor"$= \supset$. It was volume, nevertheless, without bounty, size without grandeur, bulk without any aura of command, an enlargement, though empty, enouncing far more than exceeds enough. They shot up suddenly from ears to shears to sheaths to wreaths! He himself almost narrowed in the competition. He was as if pinned to them, his weak face left in a posture of gawk like a *Doofes Vogelscheuche* seeming to refuse the outlandish ascendancy they simultaneously usurped. He looked like a taxi going down the street with both doors open.

Phrenology claims that certain undeveloped organs of the brain, combined with others abnormally developed, show a tendency toward criminality. The external ear receives the terminal branches of so many classes of nerves and concentrates in such a small space the lines of communication from various centers of sensation that the otyognomist may readily recognize such tendencies. Here, the large circumference where the ear joined the head showed an incorrigible spirit, the coarse and thickened texture denoting destructive tendencies, and the marginal line of the anti-helix establishing an inclination toward rashness. The width at the base of the conch showed a lack of sympathy, with a plane of comprehension very very small. The incisura intertragica, very wide, showed an almost animal covetousness, and the lobelessness, attaching the ear to the face, as it were, made a limitrophe of a complete head. They might have been boxed shut, thought Darconville, but not boxed enough! I shall be called Ukhovyortov!

The memory, according to Pliny, is seated in the lobe of the ear. But these of course were lobeless and exappendiculate—unable then to retain any recollection of that to which, once covetous to hear, they'd been filthily privy—like the barren habitat of two planets sealed off,

mindless and instinctive, from sentient life and reduced to the basic elements of the physical universe which, in fact, they incorporated:
earth (the loam in the conch); water (the endolymph and perilymph
fluids); air (the sonoric puffs that touched the tympanic membrane)
—but fire? Where was the fire?

As Darconville studied the labyrinths of those ears, he assessed
them. They were colossal, he saw, but large enough, he wondered, to
contain the vehemence of my accusations? They provided spatial orientation but balance enough, he wondered, to sustain any gravity
against the onslaught I should mount? They stood rigidly attentive,
but were they vigilant enough, he wondered, against shrieks of destruction that could pierce more wheels of wax than could Odysseus
supply for his men? Finally, they were rooted firmly there but tight
enough, he wondered, to remain when fastened to the tenacious grist-
bite of my hands?

Fire? thought Darconville. O, that could be provided. That could
be arranged.

LXXXVI

The Tape Recording

All that's spoke is marred.

—WILLIAM SHAKESPEARE, *Othello*

IT WAS A GREY AFTERNOON, smelling of rain, several weeks later when the long-awaited explanation from Isabel finally arrived— a primitive misaccomplishment not unrelated, if the truth be told, to a brief telephone conversation Darconville had had with her mother just prior to his release from the hospital when to that solution-proof but suddenly suspicious soul it was quite soberly vouched, and repeatedly so, that though it were the very day of her daughter's wedding, that though the world itself flew off its supports, that though he himself had to crawl back from the dead trawling a sheet of flame, he would have it. And then it finally turned up, in a sealed envelope with insufficient postage, at the Harvard post-office. There was no letter, nothing written down—only a small cassette.

There was a sick color in the sky. The wind was up and the pale undersides of the few leaves left on the trees were layered to windward as, frantically, Darconville set off on the run to find a recording machine—across to Langdell, over to Paine Hall, into the Science Center, and then cutting back through the Yard he found one upstairs on the fifth-floor of the Lamont Library where, conveniently, no one was about. The librarian pointed to a machine. Darconville tore off his coat, clicked the tape into place, and—holding his breath—pushed the button to play. Isabel's voice was cool.

"I found it impossible to write. I'll try, anyway, to explain as much as I can here. You said you wanted the truth, well, I *doubt* that my truth will satisfy you. And you might as well know right now that there's really no point in trying to see me. I guess I can't actually blame you [*sigh*] for the way you must feel now, but it doesn't matter anymore, you see, because I've too long listened to what you've said to me. It hasn't been good for me. I'm afraid I've let you dominate me."

Darconville closed his eyes.

"I don't exactly blame you for that as I suppose, oh, I've let myself be dominated. I can't tell you, I guess, when this whole thing began, but you might say it began from the beginning. There were—little things—always: the trust thing we, you know, had a big conflict over. If you don't know what I mean, it'd be pointless to explain."

"You might condescend to try," said Darconville.

The voice on the tape was assured and complacent, with a touch of weary finality to it implying its wisdom, and the mature pain that informed it, might be just a trifle too incomprehensible to those of less spiritual provision, and yet it bore the stamp of set-speech, typically found in that kind of *parvenu* whose sudden confidence, determining the self-congratulatory tone which adopts clarity of diction to express itself, is so flown with the conviction of its own new respectability that it becomes in itself the worst kind of hauteur, as merciless as it is recent.

"I didn't really trust you. I assumed you were seeing other people, right from the beginning. That's when it began, I think. I mean, I *knew* you lied to me. I didn't blame you, I honestly didn't, I should have been more mature about it all, and maybe it was my own fault for not trusting. But my first year at Quinsy? All that business with Hypsipyle Poore? As you—"

Horrified, Darconville shoved the stop button, pushed rewind, and pressed the machine to play.

"—trusting. But my first year at Quinsy? All that business with Hypsipyle Poore?"

What the devil in hell?

"As you know I was completely taken with you. It didn't matter what you did. Like when you went away, I was completely faithful to you and didn't see anyone, not when you were in England (I don't suppose I can ever really go back there again, you know?) or anytime. And I knew even then that both Govert and Gil, well, I don't know [*audible grinning*], wanted to be with me, you could say."

"Forty thousand brothers could not with all their quantity of love make up my sum," said Darconville, quoting another disappointed friend.

"But I suffered a lot, just like it was with Hypsipyle. I *knew* there was something there—a person can tell. In school people talk. Girls: about your looks, your car, your being unmarried. I didn't believe a lot of it, the rumors and what all. [*yawn*] And of course I didn't even *know* what was going on until I found some of the notes. That was when the doubts came back. And pressures, like you wouldn't believe. You know?"

It was totally unanswerable: *vox, et praeterea nihil*—a piece of faery almost flowing with the lewd heat of anticipation for the third party in whose defense she was forced to reach back four years for an excuse that was non-existent. The habit of lying *did* beget credulity in the liar! She was talking like a tour-guide, perjuring like Epaminondas, but she was so fully pretentious she seemed not to be! Were bad actors, wondered Darconville, only good actors playing bad actors? Yet he couldn't move, so fixed was he to travel along with the words that raveled off with such a routine and premeditated sense of convenience. He could see her: she was obviously lying down—probably at night—feet crossed, speaking her little penny-repentance into the microphone in one hand and maybe eating tiny hard candies with the other, while the slowly turning mobile overhead sent its slow heliocometrical shadows across the cream-and-red bed.

"This past summer those pressures were gone. I was alone—getting in touch with my feelings. Though I needed you, I resented you too. I

know you sold your car, I *know* you were teaching to earn money for
the wedding, I *know* you couldn't get up from Quinsyburg to see me,
still—and you can see I have faults, like anybody else—I resented you.
[*giggle*] It's almost, you know, like a love/hate relationship. It's so
painful, all this reviewing—but [*sigh*] I have to, for you. I see that."

"Trowel on, Mason," said Darconville.

"Then I had my car accident that time. And for you to tell me I
drove too fast, I always drove too fast? I didn't need that then—I
needed a shoulder! That's when it began, I think. That just stripped
away everything that was left and just ruined, *rueened,* all I ever felt
for you, though I can't explain why. That wasn't all. There was the
sewing—the money? you gave me? remember?—well, I never really
wanted to make my wedding dress. I felt confused about that. [*long
pause*] I guess I'm happy with myself—except in the way I've
treated you, which I think you know you caused as much. It's just that
you made me feel small. I would have always felt unimportant if we
were ever—together—that I was, I don't know, *lacking* a lot. You're
probably laughing even now—to be hearing all this, to see how sensi-
tive I can be. I'm just a country girl, really, who wants to live close to
nature and animals and things. [*sigh*] I guess you forced me to look at
myself, to make me see things I didn't want to see. I mean, maybe I
should see a psychiatrist. (Of course I can't afford one.) But sometimes I wonder if it's just not better going through life not so concerned with your faults. I have faults, I admit, if you look closely
they're there. Please don't think I'm making you out to be an ogre or,
I don't know—you know—'cause I think you're basically a good person, as, um, you are well aware of."

It was rhetorical higry-pigry: a language in which Darconville
heard the rude and rustic paratragediations of Fawx's Mt.—the legacy of living down there with all those truckfarmers, sheep-fucking in-
souciants, and raw-wristed moonlings with their flails and rakes—and
from nothing more than the sounds of this meaningless monologue, in
which linguistic incorrectness grappled with illogical inadvertency,
was he able to summon to mind with almost ritual wretchedness those
long wasted years of his life and to see at last the sudden poverty of
those once-cherished memories smelted out of the dross heap of the
past.

"I can be very independent and want to be. I let myself *lose* that. I
felt you didn't respect me. That's when it began, I think. I felt I

couldn't be myself. I always felt I had to be—to *do*—something; it was important to you, I think, even though you told me the opposite. I felt like I had to live up to something—that was a pressure. But, you know, maybe this is good: it points up, like, I'm not what you thought I was. Maybe if you thought I was too good—which I *wasn't*—it'll help you get over this. [*yawn*] You know? I'm not perfect. I know you love me, but, lord, people get over things like this, and you will too. I don't blame you for hating me, I guess. I don't know, maybe you can think back on all the good. I know you'll always resent me— but maybe it'll provoke great writing on your part [*audible grinning*] at the expense, I suppose, of myself. But, who knows, maybe I've given you a motive."

The first side of the tape ran out.

It was a bolus of mendacities. There was no strict line of conciliation to thought or duty or affection, only a post-posited and out-of-sequence rehearsal to *avoid* explanation, *un pièce radiophonique* recorded with an overdeveloped theatrical flair—careless, stupid, and anaphrodisiac—in order to present herself as a sloe-eyed Blakean infant in touch with the dark para-rational world of animals and forests, one of those fake innocenti who'd like you to believe she kissed fog or slept with a felt rabbit, and yet those few sequences not ceremoniously spent in buying her virtue by selling her guilt were squandered in a fatuous half-hour of perfect indistinguishableness, cruelly disregarding any ratio of priority to subsequence and leaving unillumined by the concentrated light of any single defining concern the real facts of her iniquity which she dismissed, typically, by way of the formulaics of heroineism—the "brave" smile in the face of tragedy; the posterosuperior piety; the studio-finish profile framed in modest contrition; and the jolly heads-up tone, making versicle response, that victory will always use in lessoning defeat. It was rubbish. What had really happened? When did it actually begin? Why had she kept up a sham for four years?

Sitting forward, Darconville slapped in side two and the voice continued its disclosures, as hypocritical and excusive as were those of the smooth, deceitful chatelaines of yore. Remembrance fallen from heaven! Madness risen from hell!

"I put off writing to you after you left because I couldn't cope with it. That's one thing I guess I can't be forgiven for: not writing. I started several letters and they just came out wrong, but you'll be

happy to hear, anyway, that it's bothered me; and that's one good
thing that's come out of all this—you remember our talks about it?—I
knoooow I have a conscience. That's almost a relief to me. Yes, I'll
admit, I've been happy, very happy, these past few weeks, it really's
nice now, but it's somehow been tainted, too. I know that because of
me you can never really be happy."

"*Canaille!*" shouted Darconville.

The librarian looked up.

"In June—I don't remember the sequence—that's when it began, I
think. I was really excited about getting married and had no intentions of not marrying. Ask my mother. Then I remember I got scared
—I panicked. It was incredible! But by then, I forget exactly when,
you had left for Massa—"

Stop.

The time-frame? It was crucial! What was the time-frame? Darconville felt an entire period had passed with Isabel waiting not only
for him to leave but to see whether this neighbor of hers would
propose to her! He was certain they had made their rendezvous sometime during the summer, *long* before the fall. She was always a coward and cunning all the time, but while September made her fickle,
July made her a liar!

Perspiring, Darconville quickly tapped the rewind button, pushed
play, and strained with every fiber of his being to listen beyond the
nonversation to the exact words. But she hopped the hole.

"—got scared—I panicked. It was incredible! But by then, I forget
exactly when, you had left for Massatoochits. And, you know, I think
if you had said that day, 'Please come,' you know, 'I beg you,' I almost wonder if I wouldn't have come. I remember *exactly* when I was
thinking that—I was wearing that violet jersey with things, flowers, little ones, on it."

"Resign your purple, Pretender," said Darconville, who knew that a
liar could always be detected by that one ridiculous use of detail.

"When you left I missed you, I did. I worried or wondered—I
don't know—you'd get up there and find—oh, I don't know. I have
this picture of Harvard, all those tremendous people, and I always
thought I was never quite [*smile*] enough. So [*yawn*] a couple of
days after you left, I didn't miss you as much. I wanted to, I guess—
miss you, I mean. But after a week had passed, I just knew. That's
when it began, I think. I just—I don't know—*knew*."

It was frightening. Darconville was almost now unable to recognize actual truth as separate from the violence of her fictions, for she had by her new lights turned revisionary and set upon and savaged fact, like the voracious Terrare who can seize a live creature with its teeth, eventrate it, suck its blood, and, devouring it, leave only the bare skeleton behind. Furthermore, the mode of speech, all borrowed apocalypse, was itself a fabrication—at once, honeyed and perfidious. It was more than a crazy dysphasia fighting ataxaphasia. There was both a fake voice and a real, with neither, curiously, able to hide the kind of *muflisme* that is fascinated with the analysis of itself, but while the former was a sort of mistily gentle babytalk, a canting simulation of virtue spoken as if offered like scented incense to evaporate in this harsh and brutal world not of her making, the real voice, cold as proof, might have been muttered in covens, weaving low in a shuttle of bitter contempt that was full of unseen and unpropitious events in the throat. She had a soul like a jackknife, the kind that opened everywhichway.

There was more, however, and constant observer continued confronting inconstant object.

"I've told you what I remember. And so we come—to Gilbert, and if you *dare* to come down here to try to talk to any of these people, I'll not be here, and that's a promise! I've heard about your letters and telephone calls. I knew in a way they'd be coming. [*cruel laugh*] You didn't think I was very perceptive, did you?"

Darconville found *that* perceptive. In her words he could see her scar whiten and the ugly close-set bullet eyes protruding.

"Well, do your worst! You're mad as a hatter, that's what I think. But it doesn't matter, you and I have absolutely *nothing* to say to one another. [*long pause*] I admit it, look, you were nice—that's not the right word—[*sigh*] gracious, I suppose, about being willing to let me go out with other guys if I wanted to. Well, to be honest about it, there *were* times back in Quinsyburg when I did want to be with someone else—him. That's when it began, I think. I suppose I should have told you. But don't you see? They were neighbors, it was nothing, Mrs. van der Slang was like my second mother. I was close to that family, I knew them so well, but as I think back, everytime I was with Govert—it's funny, really—I actually wanted to be [*audible grinning*] with Gilbert. He was home, anyway, for a couple of days at Christmas and a couple of days in July—"

Darconville, mentally correcting her own emotional appraisal with hard fact, suddenly jerked his head forward. Naked discourse can imply the image it lacks. *Keep talking,* he thought, *stay tired and keep talking.*

"—although this past year-and-a-half he was on a ship, nineteen months to be exact. I *didn't* see him when he came home this summer. He didn't get off the ship until the last week in July and afterwards he went up to New York for—"

He swiftly jammed stop, rewind, and listened to the replay.

"—summer. He didn't get off the ship until the last week in July and—"

The mind whose preoccupation prevents it from grasping wholes, Darconville knew, must sooner or later focus on details, and this one detail, out of the blandest and dullest pantomime of truth he'd ever heard, fairly flew. Again: stop, rewind, play.

"—the last week in July—"

Darconville snapped off the machine and quickly bolted down the stairs of the library, running out across Mass. Ave. and through the dismal rain that had begun to fall dashing over to Adams House. He went to his room, pulled the top drawer entirely out of the bureau, and began rummaging through the assortment of odds and ends. It was a jumble: an old watch, photographs, the inscribed blue cups from England, notebooks, pens and pencils, the bloodstone Hypsipyle had given him, a Cloogy pamphlet ("Glints From My Mirror"), rough drafts of several stories, a missal, and among all the papers, along with that queer illegible manuscript from Dr. Crucifer's library, a pile of correspondence in an elastic band. He sorted out the few she'd written to him the past summer, some four or five, and set aside the very first one—suggesting the postponement of their wedding— ever to broach that subject. His heart fell into his trousers, as every last one of his aspirations and enthusiasms suddenly transferred from the upper to the nether regions. The letter was postmarked Fawx's Mt., Thursday, July 23!

The falcon had come to the fist. Isabel seemed all of a sudden to grow material, a superficies of flesh and bone merely, a creature of lines and surfaces, a language in living cipher no more.

It was goodbye to curtains and crowns, goodbye to the roses of Thalia and the laurels of Melpomene. It was the end of all journeys and joyfulness. Darconville saw her as the very antichrist of deceit, false not through forgetfulness but while remembering, a figment of his imagination with no mercy, no meaning, and no memory. To see the creature who has hitherto been nearly perfect, divine, lose under your very gaze the divinity which has informed her, defined her, given her life, suddenly grow commonplace, turn from flame to ashes, from a radiant vitality to a corpse? It was a sorrow almost literally unable to be borne, a spectacle without measurable dimensions in this world, for in an instant, she became a complete—*complete*—mediocrity.

Through the pouring rain, Darconville walked back to the library. A poisoned taint was on everything: the poisoned air, the poisoned buildings, the poisoned city. He shoved through the doors, the contorted grimace on his face intended to mimic the satisfaction of the discovery he had made, but he of course knew otherwise, as he who by being poisoned does poison know. He sat down directly to the machine again, a hatred in his heart more deadly than the potions of Exili, and turned it on.

"—and afterwards he went up to New York for almost a month which carried him to the end of August practically, getting the license —his second mate's license—and so in spite of what—"

Darconville punched stop and replayed it.

"—his second mate's license—"

Once again he hit the buttons.

"—his second mate's license—"

Darconville suddenly burst into loud ironic laughter, for there are passions the choice of which extend way beyond man's volition. It revved up to such a high comical pitch that there might have been local consequences—the librarian looked up again—had it not as suddenly wept down to vexation and died into the supplication of a long, pitiable, and despairing sob.

He banged the machine and the voice continued.

"—and so, in spite of what you may think, there was absolutely nothing whatsoever going on here last summer, even if you decide to think so, which makes me feel nothing is on *my* conscience. I didn't see him when all this trouble was going on. It had nothing to do with it. That's the truth."

The truth? Pistols without cocks! Helmets without vizards! A damnable lie! It stuck like corruption in her throat and could be recognized under whatever complexion, contour, accent, height, or carriage it might choose to masquerade! It would dog and chain her, invigilate at her deathbed, and be cast into the nativities of her children or else impartial Justice wore a blindfold round her eyes to shield her shame! False spoken! False sworn!

The final words that were heard, as Darconville—his mind a box of cats—reset the machine to play, were now no longer Isabel's, but increasingly the terrible and insistent repetition of certain others from the recent past, drowning hers out, which somehow in their echo awakened more evil than had that hideous falsetto-like whisper in which formerly they'd first been uttered: *if a wrong must be made right, if a way be found, if it should lead you to, could you? Do something?*

"I saw Gilbert, anyway, on September 2, I remember it well, because I asked him if I could come over to Zutphen Farm. I had a real nice time that day, I just had fun, but I've already told you that. (I don't think you really ever paid attention to details, I really don't.) And the next day when I went back over there, there was this horse who had this awful cut, and I'd gotten some medicine—and in a way [*smiling gurgle*] that's when it began, I think. I don't think you understand: I'd known Gilbert *before;* there was no reason to hide anything; we could talk to each other, don't you see, openly? [*pause*] I saw him just about every night after that. We had—fun. Not just fun. Fun, you know, isn't the most important thing in life."*

Those were the last words she ever spoke to him.

The tape, ending abruptly, would stop forever there. There was no more. It was all gone, lost, swallowed like a mineral: his love, belief, time and trust, self-respect, gifts, all efforts and energy, kisses and cares. And neither heaven nor hell, gold nor God, could make it good again. Dreams, he saw, were for devils, not for men. He put the cassette into his pocket and walked aimlessly into the absurd streets outside, the rain-smudged sky overhead looking as if it had been roofed with the oldest lead. He raised a fist. Spirit of the Sky, remember! Spirit of the Earth, remember!

* The value assigned the abstract notation (*Fun*) in this rigorous proposition, while it may seem only putatively factual, actually extends itself here to a philosophical calculus of common truth-functions beyond ostensive definition (*isn't the most important thing*) to the suggestion of an unsubstitutable and immutable absolute (*in life*) by which, had it never been uttered, the straightforwardly empirical protocol established in the pursuit of sufficient linguistic assessment might otherwise be distorted.

When Darconville returned to his rooms not one of the many objects scattered about failed to shriek its scorn at the whole false enterprise. She had lived for years beside him apparently on terms of hatred and incomprehension, but where had been the art to read that mind's construction in that face? He didn't know now and no longer had the chance to see. But the consciousness that the insult was not yet avenged, that his rancor was still unspent, weighed on his heart and poisoned the artificial tranquillity he once tried to obtain by other distractions but could again no more. Darconville was a Venetian. He looked from one empty memory to another and found nothing lasting or loving in them of the girl whose soul once touched them all—a person so free from conviction, so totally dependent on the temptations and conditioning of her immediate environment that to understand her now required nothing more complicated than a look. There was an image of special desolation in the two blue cups that lay on the floor: in them he seemed to locate all his grief. A whole cloud of experience condensed into a drop of hatred—again, he had given her exactly what she wanted—as he picked them up, whirled like a cornered animal striking out, and threw them with a violent curse into that fireplace, above which the Harvard shield now seemed the color of arterial blood, where they shattered to pieces in a sooty explosion of tongs, dogs, and trammels.

The succeeding moments seemed but an imitation of life. Whereas once Darconville had no bond with the darkness for loving alone in the upper light, that changed—radically now, for as he stood in the mess of that room he happened to pick up the strange piece of paper which upon his first visit to that *enfer* of a library had slipped from one of Dr. Crucifer's books. Was it—a code? He turned it sideways, then upsidedown. At first it seemed nothing more than a piece of illogical scribia with lines of miscast letters running on meaninglessly, irrespective of whence or whither. It was written in a kind of bizarre agraphia going right to left, he saw, in looking-glass letters—with the words spelled backwards!

For some reason he suddenly felt the room grow cold as ice.

LXXXVII

The Diabolical Pact

These pacts with the Devil are not only vain and useless: they are
also dangerous and evil.

—FRANCESCO GUAZZO, *Compendium maleficarum* (1608)

WITHOUT HESITATION, Darconville took the sheet of paper to
the mirror and held it at right angles to the glass: it was still unreada-
ble. He tried in vain, as well, to read it through the back of the sheet.
So he began to figure it as it had presumably been written, reading
withershins letter by letter what turned out to be Latin. It came up
slowly in the curial style and seemed to be a formal—what? Suddenly,
his face fell, a witness to malfeasance, and went pale as paper.

alligiS

te mued et reficuL euqretsigam enimoD
erivres ibit roecillop te ,ocsonga mepicnirp
oicnuner tE .ereviv oretop uidnauq eridebo te
te soila te mutsirhC museJ te mueD muertla
macilotsopA maiselccE suispi ainmo te manamoR
tiussop seledif subiuq senoitagor te senoitaro senmo
maicaf diuq roecillop ibit te ;em orp eredecretni
rep alam da erehartta te ,oretop mulam touqtouq
,mumsitpab te mamsirhc oicnunerba te ;senmo
:murotcnas suispi te itsirhC useJ atirem ainmo te
:inoitaroda te iutivres eaut oreed is te
,orecef suispi iem menoitalbo non is te
.maut tucis maem mativ od ibit ,eid euqouq
.ceD sumisecirt ;eid te onna coh iceF
.LMCM
.reficurC
,sinrefni xe mutcartxE
.munomead ailisnoc retni

His eyes forked in comprehension as he read it to the end with a preying ache, moving his head as though punctuating with self-directed nods secret decisions of *sympathy* with it, his fingers twittering with the thrill of such evil, and then shutting it like a clapstick, as though some faculty or prevision in him were unexpectedly proved, he felt something suddenly pass through him—whereupon, freeing his heart, he burst into a cruel laughter of recognition that never seemed to end.

LXXXVIII

Week of the Sabbat

There are certain crimes which the law cannot touch and which therefore, to some extent, justify private revenge.

—SHERLOCK HOLMES,
The Adventure of Charles Augustus Milverton

A GRIM WEEK BEGAN. There was a roar of rain on the slate roof, blown by a wind of such power and purpose as almost to shatter the windowpanes against which the raindrops burst like stars. And all through the first night Darconville brooded, torn between a decision— living for a hating or dying for a love. It was, needless to say, no longer a question informed by any hope, either of enchantment or exorcism, of winning back Isabel Rawsthorne but rather one of related options touching on the summary execution-by-evil of the spectre whose photograph he once again set up on the mantelpiece: the crime that would make him happy or the scaffold that would prevent him from being unhappy. He held up his candle to the photograph as he listened to the wind outside, the whistling, the violent rattling of a window-catch, and his interrupted heart-pulse swam in death: he recognized nothing: it was the face of the Queen of Spit.

To one man in a million dreadful knowledge is revealed. There is, it is true, a kind of psychic poikilothermism when the mind, like the body, must assume the temperature of its surroundings. But Crucifer's black pact with the devil seemed only to awaken in his own mind certain secret knowledge that had long lain dormant, figures of every adjunct to the heavens and characters of signs and evening stars by which the spirits are enforced to rise. There was a harpocratic oath made that night in the silence where, dosed with benperidol, he sat waiting to prey. It would be a revenge Kydian, fierce, and immediate. Darconville chose the way.

* * * * *

Monday. In the morning, he was fully resolved. It would be a matter of diligent preparation, sedulous care, and finally celerity of execution. He would never give up, nothing would stop him. Hunger eats through walls of stone. He first arranged all her letters, photos, the cassette, all the notebooks he'd kept on her. Why? He didn't know. But it didn't matter. He would head her off on fronts both natural and supernatural, for who, he wondered, was so stupid and foolish as to think that all the things done by the body have no effect on the spirit? She could not have found a more ruthless and persequent enemy: he stomped into the haft of his shoe, the heel dropped home snug and positive, and he drew a figure in the air with his finger in front of the photograph which he then turned upsidedown. *"Asmodeus,"* whispered Darconville, *"I utterly forsake thee!"* And immediately he went out and bought a new carving knife.

* * * * *

Tuesday. The weather, turning, brought cold sunlight, but Darconville saw none of it. He pulled the shades, intentionally put his desk out of the light, and, secretive in whatever he did now (for, in the doing, none but himself knew why), spent the morning for some reason compelled to write—facts only—of everything he could remember of her; the estimate of all she wasn't looked fulsome in a list. A bora was blowing up in the Adriatic of his soul, and, patience, the only virtue left there, became a pleasant timekeeper. He baited his fishhooks.

First, he had no trouble learning from van der Slang's grandmother —a boastful and polyphagous old bat who lived near them down there—what he had feared: they were already engaged. (Scarce manumised and already his!) She, however, knew nothing else. And so under false pretenses he wrote to the Naval Academy again for information as to the Dutchman's screwship and its nautical itinerary, hoping thus to determine by logical, if general, conjecture in which month or months in the coming *annus deliberandi* the wedding day might be set. That wasn't all. He wrote to several Quinsy girls in Charlottesville, well-disposed to him, he remembered, because ill-disposed to Isabel, requesting them to monitor the local papers there for any announcements of consequence.

The concrete acts of malefice had just begun. One ingenuity mothered another. Darconville worked with the morbid logic of an inquisitor not only to learn more of this witch and her repeating frauds but also to emperor outrages to serve his pain and so to fright all pity from the world withal where killing the living to regenerate death alone fit the ways of the woes he felt. To know more? To dig more deeply? It was of course folly, reasonless—motus without motive, motive not motivirt!—and yet a wish, the wish a desire, the desire an uncontrollable longing perversely perpetrated upon him because he felt he should *not,* an act soliciting only the absolution of hell unless by sulphuring himself in the sins he learned and so converting to vapor in the heat of his throes to ascend upon her in an infamy unseen he somehow mitigate the strategy of evil involved in the terrible but just equivalence of pain awaiting her. Who would boast a victory that cost no chance of loss? Who would bulletin such success as that which, in the field of mind, took only random memory for an assailant? No, it was too late. No sweet behavior now, no soft minioning could ever hope to turn him from where his appetite was fixed.

I'll draw you to a particular, vowed Darconville, and have you look in a glass! He snatched up the photograph and angrily pressed it flat upon the mirror. There, he thought, *now* bathe your finger-ends and bat your eyes and load your bum with a farthingale! Could it move distraction in the heart of a Minotaur it should find me quartz! What, do you beg for clemency? Resisted, madam! Generosity? Forbearance? Come, I am in haste; be brief. Charity? Kindness? Favor? Pity? *Pity?* He replaced the photograph on the mantel, upsidedown. Card your wool, Eve, thought Darconville—and fell again to writing.

He wrote to Isabel's real father through the district attorney in Little Rock, Arkansas, affecting, with a view to learning of his whereabouts and perhaps more of her, to be leaving them a huge sum of money. He wrote to Mrs. McAwaddle at the registrar's office for a photocopy of Isabel's dossier in which he hoped to descry—it didn't matter what—some irregularity of birth, a reference to family lunacy, any kind of extralegal ganancial trickery in her parents' divorce that might serve as a blocking agent to her marriage. He wrote a handful of vituperative postcards to everyone in Fawx's Mt. whom he suspected of being involved in the conspiracy, composing in a sudden *coup d'essai*, then calling in, one special telegram to Zutphen Farm in which it was warned that, short of an interplanetary cataclysm, he'd appear at the forthcoming wedding in the company of Abaddon, the angel of ice, and sixty other apparitions from the abhorrèd deep. And then he wrote out an envelope to Gilbert van der Slang, stuffing it with duplicates of those of Isabel's letters from the previous year in a nuptial mood—diploid, deceptive, devious—and went out at day's end to mail the lot of them, making an effort as he walked back through the tin-colored dusk to ascertain the location, in back of one of the Wigglesworth houses, of what he marked in his mind. It was a young wild-nut tree.

* * * * *

Wednesday. It was time for further action. Darconville took from his pocket an object that had caught his eye some few days previous, a simple gem, green as jealousy, spotted with blood, that seemed in some kind of mnemonic resurrection both to contain and to conceal the mystery of the whole plot. But the luck? To traverse the world in thought where were swarming, by moderate computation, some five billion souls indifferent to his needs only because ignorant of them and then to remember, suddenly, the deepest accomplice of all who by some strange and inexplicable metonymy not laid down in books *alone* can turn captor into captive and make of the hunter game? How provident was nature in such matters! The chrysalis does not burst until there is a wing to help the gauze-fly upward. He immediately telephoned Hypsipyle Poore.

It has been observed that it's a desperate thief that a thief lets in, but quickly Darconville in his brief conversation with her found a partner whose desires ran before her honor, whose wishes burned hotter than her faith, and when penalties were mentioned so also was a name. Darconville smiled darkly. The long explanation led to the only expectation: as the venality of Vanderdecker, the Flying Dutchman, was legend, he asked, then why couldn't she devise a plan to prove it? Hypsipyle said she didn't understand. (The complexity of language, he thought to himself, lies not in its subject matter but in our knotted understanding.) Why, form schemes, plans, designs! Make him tell the tale anew, where, how, how often, how long ago, and when! *Seduce him!* Then Hypsipyle clucked through the telephone like a wizard and jingled it with a laugh. She whispered an idea. O banquet of foul delight, prepared by thee, dark paraclete! "I love to say yes," said Hypsipyle Poore, kissing him goodbye through the receiver.

Then Darconville put the bloodstone back into his pocket.

*   *   *   *   *

Thursday. But there was more to be done. It required vigilance, for the speed of her moves, elucidating duration, had to be measured in velocity—direction was involved—and yet as Darconville continued to trace out, track, and trip toward the unbroken trail to target, inquiries yielded full-fold. He learned, for instance, with the help of a co-operator at the Charlottesville telephone company—an acquaintance he remembered from the days when Isabel herself worked there—that there had been a spate of phone calls from New York to Isabel's number, with charges transferred to the van der Slang household, between July 10 and August 21. He found out that she had registered in a Charlottesville shop for china ("Kensington" pattern by Noritake) and silver ("Chippendale" pattern by Towle) in *early September!* And then he managed to contact, after an elaborate and roundabout series of calls, several ex-farmhands from Zutphen Farm—three disgruntled, but patriotic, illiterates—who without so much as a question proudly felt it a *duty* to help out the F.B.I.: yes, they said, Isabel and Gilbert van der Slang were together in Fawx's Mt. during July, and, yes, they were *shoot* sure, officer, because it was a small town and—

Darconville put down the receiver. He was, by now, more surprised that he was astonished than astonished that he had cared so much. The darkness that had sat him down despondent in his solitary chair for days together, weaving bitter fancies, dreaming bitter dreams, now grew light and thin, almost as if chased by the sudden desperate longing to be free of this prostitute of figment and fable.

There was a glare of suitable vulgarity in the upsidedown photograph. It was not the beastly eye, weighing one's appearance; it was not the assayer's eye, weighing one's worth, nor even the trading eye, weighing one's purse. It was simply the worldly eye, weighing *position*. Isabeau of Fawx's Mt.! Darconville found that her presence, even in memory, far exceeded his need of her and saw now only a worthless, self-perpetuating piece of fatback—vile, ambitendentious, thirty pounds overweight—who did nothing but in relation to herself and never gazed at a man if a looking-glass were handy, a functor with the heart of a dotbox, a face like an excuse, and a soul as insubstantial as a whiffle-ball. The remorse he felt! It was not only that he had pursued fancy. It was far worse. It was, he reflected, less to have loved someone with a cast of head as apt and artful as the dexterous cast of a trout-rod and legs blown to a size of almost advanced elephantiasis —a condition, making her body so disparate, it seemed to argue the possibility of a bisectional physique whose parts actually moved on separate axes—than actually to have forsaken reason itself! By what incredible fallacy of accident, he wondered, had he ever come to love her? But his interest in the question faded as soon as it was raised, and, putting on his coat, he went out to Harvard Sq. to try to find a wide brass dish.

* * * * *

Friday. There bore so little resemblance in his investigation to what Darconville once loved, however, that a wide and ready interest in the deeper mysteries of his subject sent him to the library where he spent the morning poring over volumes of mystic science and divination, trying, like a sorcerer, to cast precognitive facts out of her bulk and shadow and birthdate.

It was a little hell-hole of black magic and goety up there in that carrel in Widener, but students, peering in, drawn by all the mewing and muttering, so disturbed Darconville that he returned with an armful of selected books to study them in his room and to scrutinize as many as there were of her and all of her as many as there were. He stopped in a stationery store on his way back to buy two candles.

Isabel Rawsthorne, it turned out, had been born on the very day of treachery—Judasmass! The astonishment that Darconville felt could hardly be imagined. It was black nativity (December 30), falling in the decan of those who betray with a kiss and who, according to prophecy, will not be saved at Armageddon. The winter sign, Capricorn, was a zodiacal horror, its ecliptic gloomy, its portents caprice and lust, its symbol in ligature (♑) combining the first two letters of the Greek word for tragedy; and these goats, ridden by Saturn, were, while always associated with climbing proclivities, all of a type: calm and deliberate in method and action, addicted to practical things, and limited in outlook, with a morbid fear of ridicule which often curtailed the expression of their views, making them secretive, procrastinating, and treacherous. The creature was confirmed in her signs.

Then, Darconville cast her numerological chart. First, he found the number of personality—the quickest to disclose its traits—to be *3*, indicating unalterability, fixed position, the need for security. The number of development, riddled out of her name, totaled *60;* he made his reductions, while reckoning up the numbers of both the added (*5*) and underlying (*2*) influences, and came up with *9*. It represented the need for achievement in a chosen object, regardless of the moral issues involved. My God, thought Darconville, the thorn comes into the world point foremost. Here was a bride for Machiavelli!

There's not enough if there's never too much. Darconville meddled and mumbled, probed and pried. He sought to confirm various omens and oddities by applying his wit to the practices of alomancy, rhapsodomancy, capnomancy, spodomancy, sortilege, and especially—for her flesh to him was a map well-known—physiognomy. There was about her, it turned out, a stricter consecution from body to behavior than from lameness to limping: this defect fit that disposition, this flaw that foolery. The phrenological characteristic of a low, comic facial formation meant quarrelsomeness, with slanting eyes and a weak head line indicating an untrustful, petulant nature. Moleosophy assigned a shrewd and petty acquisitiveness to that predominant, dark-colored spot on her clavicle. And metoposcopy proved her trivial in the forehead, the wavy cross lines there forecasting a voyage by sea—a pleasure trip, according to the line of Venus. The chirognomic profile suited her to perfection: the thumbs, indexing the essential character of the hand, were "waisted," disclosing selfishness; the fluted nails, irritability; the knotted knuckles, deviousness; and the hands themselves, large and spatulate, were the hands of mingy pursuers, unusually obdurate ones adapted to the suddenness of the grasp and the snatch.

Night was falling, but Darconville was not quite finished. He went to the kitchen, brewed some china tea, and after drinking it from a white cup he swirled the grouts around three times with a left to right motion—the leaves, he saw, formed a *windmill*. He checked the symbol against the tasseographical values given in the book and read the portent: "a scheme of gigantic magnitude, turning industrious plans into money." Well-pushed, nun, he thought, well-pushed.

Darconville's smile was ghostly as he put on his coat. It was the smile one has in feeling he knows the future by looking at the past. Cracking down all the riddles and fanciful demonstrations was secondary, nevertheless, to other essentials he'd separately but simultaneously pursued all week, undertaken, each one, with an intensity that seemed not only to make claims upon or compel but almost *create* whatever it was he sought. Was he himself aware of it? The answer Darconville left to the mystery of the night through which he now walked, taking the two candles across the dark and empty street to St. Paul's to have them blessed, as he told the priest, for a funeral.

* * * * *

Saturday. The celesta of sweet bells from the Lowell House tower, pealing when Darconville awoke, did nothing to soften his heart. He took more benperidol and went down to his mailbox, pushing through a group of milling students without care. A canting letter from the English department chairman inquiring about his lack of attendance in the classroom he ripped up. The first of the few reports on Isabel— his only concern now—arrived in much the same way she told the truth, not all at once, but gradually, and sometimes not at all. He filed the facts he had; but little changed. The treason had been done, and the clues he found, serving more to sicken than to solve, accordingly were understood as neither here nor there, for what is manifest in a proposition cannot also be stated exactly. A problem is always less complex by nature than the solution it requires.

The story was simple: there once lived a girl who was poor. She was burdened with deep insecurity, hippopotamine legs, and the memory of a putative father who spending but a minute on her mother to get her would spend no more time with either. She grew to hate what she missed: not feeding the anger, however—starving made it fat. The dreams of the riches her family hadn't in the wealth of a family nearby, proving more substantial, alas, than did the attentions of its two eligible sons, led her to temporize with someone else in a romantic *Schmockerei* got of starved vanity and self-aggrandizement-by-association, an amusement by proxy that cost her less trouble than being alone. It was a subterfuge of convenience, with passion its pretext and the mock adoption of values its mask, for she chose what she couldn't imagine to test what she couldn't be, setting out, as it were, not to survey the boundary of ocean but rather to measure the coast. He fell in love; simply, she wouldn't—it reminded her precisely of what she couldn't give to get. But when that particular opportunity arose, she lived to betray what she feared to love and opted to have what she hoped to own. She was *safe* at last. The wedding would not take place in Fawx's Mt., for tripwires had been set. It would be held in secret, very soon, and somewhere else. The announcement would only be made afterwards.

Isabel Rawsthorne! It was a name to conjure with, a creature who fell into the heart of space like a stone in a vacuum, with no attraction and no purpose. The speed of such a fall, multiplied only by the ideal weight, is impossible to measure—in fact, is no longer anywhere. It is noiseless, mindless, nullibiquitous. She would never pine under any regrets, because she had no appreciation of any loss. She would chafe at no indifference, because it was her art. She would not be worried with jealousies, because she was ignorant of love. She who measured her wit by the triumphs of fashion and face-play and smiled away falsity even to herself was silent precisely when she thought and faithfully spoke when she didn't.

She alternated between surrender to foreign influences and a vengeful longing for originality, finding there to be as much weakness in the former, however, as there was futility in the latter. She had no pity in success and self-pity, always, in the case of failure. In victory, her eye was dry and glittering, for repentance of what cunningly she won was rendered moot in relation to an opponent who thereby had no rights. A facile follower, she assumed servility toward the approved and arrogance toward the rejected. She knew, of course, that there was truth and untruth, that right and wrong existed, but did not feel the asperity of such notions because her indifferent and cowardly heart led to a total ineptitude for grasping differences between ideas and values, and if her trouble was due less to positive vice than to the feverish absence of altruism, both nevertheless enabled her to concentrate on any commodity whatsoever—one was like another—and then to appropriate by lies what in the possession, that she might save face, she had to call love, taking it away from one she could not trust and handing it to a trustee whose loyalty she'd see remained assured. Her lack of discrimination—a lack, not a lapse—was accompanied, all the while, by a tenacity that might have been a quality had she any character. But she was characterless. The humane and the advantageous she calmly identified, the teacher becoming the lesson it refused to obey in the face of acquisition. She was hypocritical because empty, clothing destruction in a kiss, feeling hate for love, and was a serpent most when most she seemed a dove. The void was always there. Had it been filled by judgment, she would long since have sat in judgment on herself. She broke her word because it was always meaningless when she gave it, and she broke it so easily that she could never fathom the anger of her dupe. She could veer like a weathervane in a minute. She overlooked significant wholes and yet had that passion for detail that is so often the mark of the small mind and the cankered soul, choosing always what measured to her empty conceit and disposing of what was left like the dramatist who finds a useless character left over at the end and simply kills him off.

With no soul, only moods, she knew not love that kissed her nor indifference that soon walked by: glad, but not flushed with gladness since joys go by; sad, but not bent with sadness since sorrows die. She could do nothing but in relation to herself. Gifts given to her never made one dearer, for the excess of love imparted absolved her of the obligation to love in return. Inconsistencies seldom bothered her. She did not ponder them, but merely denied. Her docility was cowardice. She was arrogant in prosperity and independence but once defeated came crawling to one's feet like a dog, being kept to heel by choice in that faked humility that was only in fact the fear of herself. Determined to stay innocent, however, she who could love so easily because she had nowhere to love from would offer herself indefinitely in this hope, that her takers might know what to make of her and put her to use. Seeking her fortune rather than awaiting it, she had to take every possible chance—and this, of all her fears, became the worst. She had to be loved to acknowledge all she was not and so, winning lovers, was able to dismiss them for showing her so: a self-contained revenge.

Subtlety of thought always tainted her honesty and vanity her friendship. Naturalness she copied and she scorned. She who understood marriage not as the great absorbent of a heart's love and life but as a feasible and orderly conventionality to be played with, bargained for, and finally to be accepted as a cover for her emptiness like the shifting makepiece of a stage scene was herself the model after whom she strove to shape her own life. She had no memory whatsoever. A lethal compound of the plodding and the hysterical, she guided herself by the simple expediency of one forgiving the other. Venal, cunning, constant in patterned deceit, she understood good and evil merely as failure or success. You could tramp as far as you liked into her and still only be marking time, for, though change seemed to characterize her, she never changed and was only capable of what she ever was. A vision, she did not know; a passion, she could not imagine. With no conception of the soul in its strength and fullness, she saw no lack of its demands. Joy was a name; sorrow was another. She exhausted mercy.

The Lowell House bells rang their carillon again, as if to appease, to calm, to pacify him. But poignancy is not so abiding or so cumulative as hate, and the day became cankerous life again. Was it wished for? Or if not wished for, was not the not-wishing wicked? The questions were of no significance now. Forgiveness? I will see her face in the pit of Eldon first, thought Darconville who, without a shred of pity, was only certain before the day was out to secure a stick of red chalk.

* * * * *

It was all in the readiness now. Mistakes, misdates; exaggerations, lies, distractions; all manner of misseeings and misnotings—they were gone. Darconville went out for a walk. And as he walked he thought and, in thinking, could not recall of Isabel a single pleasure with her. It was as true as he'd been told: if people found the recollection of her more pleasing than her presence, something they remembered of her seemed always to be missing when they encountered her again. He muttered various of her phrases in her own voice yet found that language could but extol, not reproduce, the beauties of the sense, if beauties ever there were. He walked and walked, brooding, thinking a thought of wrath and quickening his step, thinking a thought of kindness and fending it aside with his hand. There was a luminous smear of starlit mist over the Charles and the river lights along the banks reflected as mysteriously in the dark water as in the depths of his mind, again, were mirrored figures of every adjunct to the heavens and characters of signs and evening stars by which the spirits are enforced to rise. It had grown late when he returned under the streetlights to Adams House, and, once in his rooms, he lost no time in beginning his preparations. He moved some furniture to the walls, secured the shades, and then assembled—nothing more—his implements of ghostly justice: chalk, dish, bloodstone, and candles. He finished well after midnight, but did not retire, and instead went downstairs. It was Sunday now, but there would be no rest.

With twenty devils at each ear whispering their approval, Darconville played the piano all night with a knife on top of the Steinway.

LXXXIX

Malediction!

There is a foule great cat sometimes in my barne which I have no liking unto.

—GEORGE GIFFORD, *A Dialogue of Witches and Witchcraft*

BEFORE DAWN, Darconville went out and at the exact moment that the sun appeared on the horizon cut with his virgin knife a wild-nut tree that had never borne fruit. Then he returned to the seclusion of his rooms and chose a spot for the operation, placing the photograph of Isabel in the brass dish in front of which he set the bloodstone. He next traced a triangle with chalk and arranged the two consecrated candles nearby, putting the sacred name of Jesus in position to prevent the spirits from inflicting harm on him. Finally, he stood in the middle of the triangle with the mystic wand of twig in hand, spat thrice, and began to chant the great clavicule.

"I, Alaric Darconville, do desire, call upon, and conjure thee, Lord of Evil, Suzerain of the scornful, Depository of cherished hatreds, who dost whisper in my ears thoughts of vengeance and sore retaliation, to appear before me and fulfill what I command thee by spells whose unrecognized traces baffle human reason and by the most dreadful names that shout you honor at the Northern Gates of Hell: Asbeel, Jeqon, Belphegor, Forcas, Gaap, Gadreel, Dagon, Rimmon, Senciner, Zavebe, and Uraka-barameel. Fiat, fiat, fiat.

"Emperor Lucifer, Master of all the Rebellious Spirits, I beg you to be favorable in the invocation that I make to your exalted minister, Lucifuge Rofocale, as I wish to make a pact with him. I beg you also, Prince Beelzebub, to protect me in my enterprise. Come, Iod, Eheieh, Gibor, Eloah Va-Daath, Esytion, Samsaweel, and Atarculph.

"I beseech thee, Evil Spirit, Cruel Spirit! I call thee, who sittest in the cemetery and takest away healing from man! Go and place a knot in Isabel Rawsthorne's head, in her eyes, in her mouth, in her throat, in her windpipe, and put poisonous water in her belly. If you do not go and put water in her belly, I shall send against you the evil angels Puziel, Guziel, Psdiel, Prsiel. I call thee and those six knots that you go quickly to Isabel Rawsthorne and kill Isabel Rawsthorne because I wish it. I conjure thee within this circle. Come hither. Come hither. Come hither, because I wish and will it. Amen. Amen. Selah.

"O Count Astorath, Sataniel, Mastema, Angel of Edom, be propitious and bring it to pass that this very day you include me in your mysteries, wherefore I most earnestly adjure you and by the four beasts before the throne come in this place without noise, deformity, or murmuring and fulfill this pact, removing my sighing and learning my supplication. Xilka, Xilka, Besa, Besa, Besa. Come Aglon, Vaycheon, Stimulamaton, Ezphares, Retragrammaton, Olyaram, Irion, Existion, Mazm.

"Obey promptly or I shall torture thee with the force of the words of power from the Key of Solomon; or I shall constrain you by the power of the Twelve Tables, moon swells, and threads. So come forth instanter! Or I shall denounce you endlessly by the force of unparalleled Jehovam Sabaoth! Come from whichever place in the world thou art and give answers to my questions: answers that shall be true and reasonable. Come, Yomyael, Marut, Gressil, Busasejal, Artaqifa, Moloch, Azaredal.

"I do dance my wand left in the sigils to call thee visibly before this circle to obey me utterly. Each impediment remove thou, and the doorposts move asunder. Bend thou the Creator's castle. Come, come, why stay you? Blow knots upon her, forward and backward, anagrammatized: ENROHTSWAR LEBASI. Leap from hell with hax, pax, max, Deus adimax! Come, Magots, Silphae, Rabost, Salamandrad, Tabost, Gnomus, Esmony, and Fabelleronthou.

"Appear in black and yellow livery, Pentomorph! I will be avenged! Come here, all of you who like the places and times in which duplicity and trickery are done! Deceive those who see things, that they may appear to see what they do not. Ascend alive from hell, ye imprisoned in sheet flame, and scream me promises! Come, Eparinesont, Oriet, Clameron, Casmiel, Sodirno, Premy, and Peatham.

"Rule her with fumigations. Turn her upsidedown and bewilder her with hests of mine, pitchy breath! I propitiate you, Demogorgon from blackest hell, to create ill-will, terror, and sorrow. Oppress, torture, and harass her body, soul, and five senses. Smite her with your left hand and escort her with cruel ministrations beneath the earth and curse in her face with eternal doom! Veer with me! Come, Peunt, Slevor, Dorsamot, Janva, Zariatnctmik, Arios, and Yod.

"You demons, born of black exudings, of black pores, of black skin, of black flesh, blood, veins, sinews, and black bones, howl out from the bottom of all damnation the cries of your signal disobedience. Work for me, Night-Wraiths and Handmaids of Phantom! Come, Tistator, Abac, Iat, Guthac, Derisor, Destator, and Gomeh.

"Ascend alive from hell to where she is and flash out from your fingers jujus, spells, and wails! O Beelzebub, cause her bones to crack and grate against one another, displace her bowels, confuse her, cover her with botches and boils, bulges, and blebs! Come, Agla, Tagla, Mathon, Oarios, Almouzin, Membrot, Varvis, Pithona, and Anexhexeton.

"Smooth Devils, Horned Devils, Sullen Devils, Arch Devils, Shorn Devils, Hairy Devils, Foolish Devils, Devilesses, and Young Devils, all the offspring of Devildom, come with your devilish tricks, quicker than light, and sport with her. May she be smitten down and given a bed beneath some lockjawed hell until the end of time brings eternity upon it and in the doing thereof shall I allow you my inthronization in fire for as long. Aliseon, Hone, Vermios, Erin Catharinos. Galbas, galbat, galdes, galdat, Earl Astaroth—

> "Venite, venite, venite!
> Palas aron azinomas.
> Bagahi laca Bachabe."

He stood there for some time, watching, lost in a fixed and prolonged gaze that seemed to track the smoke's course to his thoughts as the photograph in the dish curled up in fire, its smiling face turning from the smooth color of lawsheep to dark red murray and then to cancer in the accumulation of flames. It seemed, as it burned, to burst forth in a torrent of abuse. Then there were ashes. The room was suddenly strange and solemn and lonely, like an empty but profaned sepulchre after an attempt to muster the disaffected, and in the stink, heat, and cafard he who made that attempt knew he now lived at the heart of cruelty, now lived where the light goes when it is put out. He knew he must seek friends of the darkness now and, with that terrible truth, watching his own shadow sway on the floor with the flickering candles, snuffed them and crept upstairs to Dr. Crucifer's rooms in a stupor of—not of confusion, nor of agitation. And it wasn't remorse or cynicism or fear. A blackness sucked at his heart. There was only one word for it.

XC

Hate

I study hatred with great diligence for that's a passion in my own control.

—W. B. YEATS, "Ribh Considers
Christian Love Insufficient"

"HATE," said Dr. Crucifer, "is love's other face: they are comple-
ments, not opposites. The emotion owes all its meaning, as I've told
you, to the demand for love, each expressing an impulse which exists
only by an antagonism to the fear that oppresses it, for one can never
be a hater without having had this ideal, that one, always loving, will
always be loved in return. There lies not a grain of sand between the
loved and the detested. With everything right, wrong is always somehow involved, and, like bifronted Janus, we love with the dread of
hate in us. Buried in every yes there is a no. It is a Manichean delight:

all the time you hate you steal it from love, its *sole* provocation, for it does not precede the facts that call it forth; it nourishes itself on them. Dichromatism always extends to the complementary colors. You commit in one exactly everything you simultaneously omit in the other. They exist side by side to kill each other, like the heterosporous combination of cedar and chokecherry. What, after all, is the precise morphological distinction between an embrace and a strangulation? *L'amour, la mort:* every kiss muffles a bite. Inside every lover is manacled Taras Bulba. The anagram of 'The heart's desire' is 'hate strides here'—the imperfection in the transposition being the apostrophe you can't cry out.

"Hatred is the appetite which increases as you eat. It is, nevertheless, always in a state of being, a substantial definiteness unto itself. There are many passions which we are condemned to feel only in a reduced form: never love or hate. Both flirt with the impossible, the due practical conceding of each as to inevitability, however, amounting to much, indeed to the sure promise of all. Lovers are half-enemies in the first place, and hatred between half-enemies, often deeper than between opposites, aches for completion.

"The thing confounds scrutinoids absolutely; no more than love does it concern itself with reason but goes through life fixed on delirious hope in order to pledge allegiance to an inverted form of the same ideal. It is not shaped to common recognita nor bounded by the circumvallations of vulgar experience, and the feeble and obvious piety which announces *indifference* to define the essential polarity to the proposition of love I can only assign to the retarded virtuosity of those unguentarians and barely audible paracoits-of-footwork who, fearing to penetrate into other spheres, higher or lower, in ways allowed or forbidden, must live life either on their knees or in a crouch like a dog fucking a football! Hate wears a capital letter. Its colors are as bright as poisonous reptiles. It quickens to bolder action than diffidence or dumbness and chafes as motion conquers cold to run full-tilt at an indifferent world screaming that rather than be less one would rather not be at all! We have long considered views on the subject so general as to be trite, so idiosyncratic as to be useless. We overestimate it and underestimate it. Do you ask why?

"Men, in the mass, are amply content to take life as they're given it, finding the world to be so very comfortable they have no inclination either for its stark ascents and descents. They are a little of one thing and a little of the other and nothing for any length of time: ignoble mediocrities of the Rank and Vile! The common wantwit, further, confines the spiritual world to the supremely good. Mr. and Mrs. Bumb from Main St., America, and all their little tits in mittens at Sunday-Go-To-Meeting? Oh yes, but what of the supremely wicked? Mustn't they necessarily have their portion in it as well? And why not? Why should sanctity alone, and not sorcery, be permitted the children of the earth? I tell you, there are multitudes of us who, thrown head-long into the valley of tears and sightless with rage at the mere premise of creation, eat black pulses and drink wormwood with a joy infinitely sharper than anything within the experience of an epicure! And why? *It is the best way of allowing reality to live up to the imagination!* Hatred, indeed, *is* rare! It is the infernal miracle as love claims to be the supernal, a withdrawal from the mediocrity of things as they're theologically supposed to be, an ecstasy of scorched devotion unavaila-ble to the muddled, second-rate masses with untenanted souls who have no comprehension of the inner sense of things, a transcendental effort to surpass the ordinary bounds and, by so doing, surpassing the common understanding which, nevertheless, still foolishly hobbles after it with notebook in hand to address, then adjudge it imagined. Malevolence! Wrath! Hatred! I hereby muster all the Hierarchs of Tophet to prove them real!

"Hate is old wrath, fire built to correct the inclemency of air, a monodeism of total aversion coupled with hopelessly settled detestation —and the luxury of knowing *whom* or *what* one hates is to experience one of the greatest feelings of elation on earth. It is, in fact, a faith, an intuitive certainty beyond the plane of discourse enforcing an experi-mental right, one which cannot be extended to the common run of mortals without danger, that seeks to renounce in fury what was once expected from others in kindness and locating entirely what, delivered of, alone is cleansed. One hates in order to rob from another a life stolen from himself, for hate not only hates what it lacks, but lacks what it loved, and in its grip—an oxbrake in which you're completely shod of mercy by the very creature you'd swiftly gore to pieces if but freed—the only possible pleasure attains to its secret illusions and in-tentions of *vengeance*. The formula of rupture takes place. Every for-mer excellence of your victim becomes every conceivable fault, every promise an impervestigable lie, and every memory of her a viper eat-ing through the bowels of your benefits, all to set in motion such a fell and deadly hate that through a sea of sins you'd wade to your revenge to drive a rivet in her sconce and hang her up for a sign, reading: '*Obit anus, abit onus!*'

"Hate, like jetsam, sinks. It is proposition, not proposal. It lurks below the rounds of habit wherethrough in any age men canvass and toil, and yet while everywhere the average man when finished will reckon up results, the hater, if no closer to his retribution for his work, feels nothing accomplished, still labors in mind, and with implacable consistency refuses to acknowledge of process completed what is nullified in thought not. How little is achieved by him though other problems be solved! Nothingness is immanent in hatred. Its horrors defy the words of mouth or pen to set it down. Your craw bugles. You become a thermidor of pure pain. Your feet turn to roots, your heart to lead, and yet, while the imagination sprouts more goblins to molest it than the witchlight of night itself, the creative evil at the fountainhead of hate is a lonely and terrible thing, a passion of the individual soul living low and solitary as a bucket in a well, for whereas the lover endeavors to obtain something which he does not have, the man who hates paradoxically tries to *recover* by an act of supreme alienation and anger that which has been taken from him—and which, constantly fleering, mowing, and ridiculing by the very nature of its existence, mocks the mind to murder! Haters vote in the rain.

"The smoldering aspect of hatred, often, is in direct proportion to the degree in which the person's right to exist as a human being has been taken away. And more. It is impossible for a human being to give up his freedom, or be robbed of it, without something coming in to restore the inner balance—something arising from inner freedom when outer freedom has been denied. Now, in conventional circles, in the eyes of the benign, self-contented, ever-poised, well-adjusted bourgeoisie, one is not supposed to admit one's hatred, just as, for instance, for decades past even the admission of one's sexual impulses was considered unseemly. But a few men there are who must remain true to a single extreme character, and for such men, disgusted to insult at the thought of a stinking and cowed *swallowing* of resentment or any like repression, there abides a paramount truth at the core of all hatred— the re-establishing of one's freedom! A man isn't rich unless he's making money while he sleeps. The profoundest urge of mankind is to fly.

"Hatred is that extreme fixation—not, like love, an emotion from those rude and simple times when tall bonnets were in fashion but one predating Cain in the blackness it shares with original chaos—which liquidates the reality of both victim and executioner, for in an absurd irony of contagion the negative qualities it effects in the self become proof positive of the cause; to make your victim undergo the sort of thing which troubles and overwhelms your existence so cruelly is to have to sustain your own hurt. *Respirit domino pro tempore:* the prosecutor becomes star witness for the defense!

"Hate wakens to the actual. You may be accepted for what you are only until what you are is what you shouldn't be, becoming then, in what you shouldn't, what the lover-as-hanging-judge tells you you can't. Provocation—who will deny it?—creates what it provokes! The Law of Talion cries out to its cognate, 'Retaliate!' Enslaved from the start, however, by his very own laws—the pawn of their very enactment—the hater will always be the first among its casualties unless he finds release, and since the only way of ridding himself of the passion can no longer consist in verifying, in experiencing once again, its intolerable character, in spite of the affective presence of what is physically absent, it falls to the purest and most ancient compensation therefore to rectify the wrong, for, as in exorcism, one can never cast out anything but what was first cast in. The best—the *only*—way is to hate.

"Hate! Say the word: how the mouth, shaped to sarcasm, fakes in an adventitious bark what, exhaled, becomes a râle of shuddering repugnance swiftly cut in two by the rapiered T that snaps the entire face shut without one movement of the lips. It blasphemes in a single brief gasp, a respiration incessant and increasing. It is the best verbal equivalent of human ache, thrippling just too high in the throat for a scream and becoming almost a stutter in awe of what can't be spoken, bleaching the heart, darkening the shafts of the sun, and removing the fragrance from flowers.

"The man who hates has lost in the extreme the whole concept of the ideal—or, to put it another way, he has not so much lost an ideal as he has transferred the whole concept of one ideal to the furthest extreme of another—and yet, in either case, exalting, as he must, the necessity of injustice existing in a brutal God, he proceeds to write in his own bitter soul not just a complaint but an entire destructive theology! No man loves, says Aristotle, but he that is first delighted with comeliness and beauty. Now, forbear and listen. As this fair object varies, so does love. There's of course no determining law to love what is beautiful, and the beautiful does not present itself to humans with any imperative to respond to it. Beauty, however, appeals—and yet all forms of beauty which appeal to man, by reason of the aesthetic function, are at bottom attempts on his part to realize the *ideal!* Now, follow whither my finger points: beauty is created by love. It will not and will never have any meaning for you other than the meaning you give to it, a pretext for the expansion of consciousness to beguile the despair you have without it. Sleep is only the bogus we use for dreams, with repose our intention, Eleutheropolis our goal. Man struggles to realize his own ideal, to sound out the highest possible self. Who doubts it? He projects his ideal of an absolute worship-worthy existence—the ideal that he is unable to isolate within himself—and with it crowns another human being, the loss of whom, if and when it happens, becomes of necessity the loss of the ideal, but there is your aspiration as long as there is your ideal and the struggle for it counts for nothing. Mecca is situated in the midst of barren and stony country.

"The ideal! Doesn't it write itself into our weak and insufficient hearts in the wittiest of fictions? Who can say what imp ghosts it, what telchin is its genius? *Quisquis amat ranam, ranam putat esse Dianam:* the blindness of love is precisely the vision of the ideal! O pretty, pretty, pretty but how, you ask, for there grunts Parmeno's sow! The huge hairy smellfungus named Polyphemus won the admiration and love of beautiful Galatea, whiter than the white withy-wind! Venus herself pursued Vulcan, fascinated in the limp of the filthy smith. I could cite the Egyptian salinaries who couched with cadavers, draw parables in the lust for decaying cheese, the poverty of misers, and the gods who are worshipped in silly glyphs. And, tell me then, what strange algebra lurks in the proud father's mind who flashes for approval that snapshot of, what—a vegetable? a wombat? a puffpile of insipid dough?—no, rather his own two-week-old baby, a little puckfisted nobblyblat with forty assorted leaks, soiled buns, and a face like a stump pudding! Love, unlike hate, makes all distinctions void. Every book is about its own author. Beauty, simply, is an emanation of the requirements of love, and hate refuses them. I would give you a wealth of italics here.

"Then the ideal—what does it matter how?—disappears, the provocation to hate we spoke of. So enter hate. (Isn't it odd that this sharpest response to someone occurs just when it isn't asked for?) We once wanted to have what we now abhor—so what we love always tells us what we aren't—but as what we loved wanted us to be what we couldn't be *when* we loved, the haste of departure following the huff of dissatisfaction, it proves by the law of subtraction, if my mathematics is better than your judgment, not only that love wasn't sufficient but that the object of it was nothing but a disastrous splodge not worth the tmesis of what value soever in the first place! Orals, I'm afraid, imply but do not posit aurals. Hate, having entered, now puts its feet up. It becomes a boarder! Then you understand one of the first lessons of hate, that we know each other best, not by strength, but by weakness, not as surpassing but as *lacking* such and such of the ideal —know each other, I say, but do I say more? For example, do I say that weakness makes people kin, creates accord, fosters alliance? The answer is yes when you speak of love. But when you speak of hate? Christ, man, when you speak of hate you speak of hell! *Prevention* becomes the heart of the policy! Swiftly, we do not wish to appear good so as not to be pitied, so, not to be pitied, wicked—why, even as *satisfied* as possible, so that our satisfaction may be truly hateful, the more quickly to ulcerate the soul not only of our occasional or permanent enemy, my friend, but of God himself! Yes, *God!* Have you understood me to say that the hater is an average man?

"Are you then like all the other fools and pseudo-podiospores who'd have indifference the antonym of love? Indifference *disgusts* me! I am what I know and, to prove it, hate what I am—which at least gives me life. Indifference does not prompt us, sir, to unkind actions! You want hatred here. Hatred—if nothing else—is meant to be a provocation to an absent God, a thrust, you see, as though scandalous, frenzied, inexpiable, raging, and unutterable provocations were a way of forcing that God who's let a love be lost to witness his will, with the hater thinking: if there were a God who possessed power, would he allow that virtue which supposedly honors him (even if by means of the shameless and pathetic proxy of it invested in another human being) to be sacrificed to such exotic uncompromising vice? The greater the punishment he feels merited by his action, the greater the value which the hater attributes to his crime! The extreme hater is always a dualist, polymath to ways both good and evil. But which is Sybaris? Which Crotona? Ha! Ha! Ha! No one *knows,* my friend, neither theologian nor thinker nor thrip, for just as once passionate sinners are claimed—according to biographical cliché—to make the greatest saints, the hater's conscience is always activated by the remorse of what otherwise might have been; indeed, the remorse actually provides the energy for the crimes he dreams. He is afraid of discovering that the world is well-contrived and yet constructs the revolution of his abhorrence upon the reason of it, for since he is forced to accept the fact that love, lost, is evil the alternative of hate, found, must perforce be the only good at hand to address it—and so the breach actually becomes the observance in a desperate attempt to settle a matter of contradiction by means of conflicting evidence! There is no better poacher than an ex-gamekeeper. The ultimate profanity is the Black *Mass*.

"It was William Blake who wrote,

> Mutual in one another's love and wrath
> all renewing
> We live as One Man.

"To detest! To abhor, abominate, execrate! To hate! *This* becomes religion: an answer to the pansophistical lie, as rendered in the Gospels, that one must love, for the hater who unsuccessfully has tried now sees successfully he shouldn't have. The astonished reason—if it wishes to articulate the dogma in action which also conveys its sense of scandal—is obliged to substitute the material of *hatred* for the revealed matter of God who in all matters, permissive, if not actually directive, is involved, face it! In that way it gives an exact expression to the impression made by the mystery on a reasoning faculty which has been abandoned, both naturally and supernaturally, to its own resources. All the ills with which God afflicts him can thus be considered as the ransom God—the Ontological Scold—exacts before he allows man the right to inflict suffering on others and to be unlimitedly vicious. To the extent that God, the arch-layer of plots, can be viewed as the original guilty party who attacked man before man could attack him, to that extent man has acquired the right and the strength, even as blind misosopht, to attack his neighbor: 'I am pleased by the evil I do to others as God is pleased by the evil he has done to me.' I mean, if knowledge ends by becoming a crime, what is called crime must therefore in some sense contain the key to knowledge! As a result, it is only by extending the sphere of crime further and further, even to its most inelastic limit—the disposition for someone's utter annihilation—

that the mind, reaching to these extraordinary crimes, will recover not only what has heretofore been prohibited knowledge, that knowledge infinitely greater than that which now we have, but also recover from a long servitude-of-revenge that any Supreme Being worth the candle must be forced thereafter to consider as a simple matter of *res inter alios acta alteri nocere non debet,* the evidence of which in earthly courts—as it then must be in celestial—is inadmissible. *In-ad-missible!* I am with you, impenitent! I spit upon the injustice of the universe!

"But who can speak of the injustice of hatred? O say otherwise! It's almost comical, isn't it, that somehow our sense of justice never turns in its sleep until long after the sense of injustice, nudging it half the night, has been thoroughly roused? What makes so many applied salvationists and advowees-of-nicety think so highly of love is that it hides their defects in the observer's eye. But hate, disabused of such notions, sees those defects—and wakes to act! It douses the fairy lamps! It chooses direct verbs over substantives! It screams for the Lord of the Psalmist who breaks the ships of Tarshish with an east wind to pull someone apart! It multiplies its pain. The very nature of such a hunger is that it's forever unappeased. The morrow of every victory is anticlimactic. It is a step toward reality, a spasm of will, a shout in the face of all violation of rights to *equalize.* Feel no guilt, then, Nestorian. Blows break, that's all. The shattering is only the natural *contre coup* of the strike.

"I have asserted that hatred is only love outraged, for the privation of something presupposes being accustomed to it (*privatio presupponit habitum*), and that between these two natures, so antipathetic, something essential is shared: each remains, by definition, the single and sole reservation of the other without which its own grandeur carries no weight—whom we love more than are indifferent to we are never far from hating. What other lesson can be found in the vine and the bays, the burr and the lintle? But then what is abstractly taught of the two that is ever heard, ever touched, ever seen? How miserably one ignores the other in the passion of what it wants, dismisses the other in the heat of what it seeks! But the tragedy is not that hatred is love outraged, nor that it is love gone by, but that an ideal has been squandered in innocence only to have to buy another to redeem it in guilt. How *mistakenly* can a person have wanted what, taken away, repudiates the meaning of life itself!

"And what exactly does love engender? Self-realization? A shameful paradox. A found ideal? The nature of the ideal is that it is never found. Gratefulness? Why, it is arguable that for a man to feel grateful to a woman is actually injurious to his love for her: he so hates himself for being unable to do for her all he would like to do that he comes to curse himself as small in the reflection of the consequent generosity she, in simply acknowledging as beyond her worth, refuses to blame him for not showing. (We love someone not for what she can actually do for us but for what in fact she allows us to do for her!) No, the spirit is always the heart's dupe. Hatred realizes, finally, that love has its source in the need either to find one so gullible that he can lie to her or to love someone so blindly that she can lie to him. And what best—because most incontrovertibly—does it do? You can prove one from the other by algebra. Love engenders hate!

"You are now so stricken! You lie below in the flashing storm so deep in pain in its violet light the brightness of day seems an ancient dream in perpetual darkness, perpetual night, but blasted, dying, you now perceive a fateful something that is yours by right. All things, however, struck by a thunderbolt fall in the opposite direction! 'O true believers,' says the Koran, 'the law of retaliation is ordained to you for the slain: the free shall die for the free!' Time for you has stopped! Gone is peace of mind! You have become fixed forever—sulphured—in the explosion, alive only in that you would now kill, happily, if only to be given the chance to say why!

"But all will be well! It is the lot of genius, remember, if to be opposed, then also to be invigorated by opposition. Reverence to this! Hatred is meant for those who establish standards, not those who follow them. *Ours* is a Vatinian hate: the supremest. We behold our enemies in an eternal vigil, like the lifeless cobra in whose eye the murderer's image is forever imbedded, and actually crave to hate that constant hallucination of face—whether smirking through the attack it signals or the absolution it seeks—which becomes, in fact, almost a badge of those enemies, for we attribute to them not that state of normal human happiness shot through with the common moods of mankind that should move us to entertain for them a feeling of kindly sympathy but a species of arrogant delight which merely pours oil upon the furnace of our rage. Hate, indeed, transfigures people no less than does love. It boils and concocts into poisonous nourishment all the

facts and fictions it compounds from the lives of its enemies and fuels
the delight it abhors. On the other hand, since it can find satisfaction
only in destroying that delight, it imagines it, it believes it to be, it sees
it in a perpetual condition of destruction—not unlike yourself, for you
are *also* dead! Dead to pardon! Dead to mercy! Dead to harmony,
forgiveness, relief, liberty, and trust! Why, isn't it clear? No living
creature has ever been burnt by lightning without being killed! But,
now, you've become the burning itself!

"Give your enemy no credit, by reflected glory, for rousing the flame
—the passion, the power, the *fire* is in the flint that is struck, not in the
steel that strikes. You alone are consumed. Wherever you go, nevertheless, your enemy is with you. You are baptized now in the Fountain
of Ardenne which has the power of changing love to hate for those
who drink its waters—you are born in it, confirmed in it, devoted to
what can break into open madness even fifty years later in a pain so
absolute and unbearable it approaches the most dizzying heights of
pleasure, for your grief has found the one thing on earth that *ruins* it.
You shall have no peace before its name. Alive, it is your plague, insti-
gates against you, throttles all you are—you must leave yourself, in
fact, to get at it. It is a vice whose name is comprehended in a
monosyllable but in its nature not circumscribed by a world. You're
like the chimera—nothing will satisfy you. You would dwell happily
within the skirts of Jericho and dare the blast of a ram's horn if upon
it depended her death! You would tattoo crucifixes on the soles of
your feet to trample the Savior who has refused your salvation if you
could but barter hers! You become the Dog of Montargis! You would
rip out your own heart to hurl at her! You would sell your birthright,
forfeit an inheritance, and suffer no end of ill-repute simply to spit
forth in the spirit of Juvenal whatever Latin hexameters could tell her
what she was! You would live in a nightsweat and breed horns and
stand a bear and a lion in the way of Assur only to have at her once,
cramping your own fortune to mal-promulgate hers and breathing
hope but to fly into convulsions of joy that the world be destroyed if
only she can suffer in the process!

"The obsession is upon you. You never feel it is accomplished,
killing her always, until you never wish it ever had begun, for while
perfectly instructed in the tribulation there's no surcease of trial, and
though pausing now and then to wonder of the marvelous once flashed
to us and then withdrawn behind black veils and concealments if both

might not perhaps exist less in lars and lemurs than in *another* of our-selves, you are driven hard upon the deed again, and again, and again, until over the waste void that bounds our thoughts and yawns profound between two worlds a bridge of fire has leapt from earth to the unknown shore, and the abyss is spanned."

XCI

A Carthaginian Peace

"There are four sweets in my confectionary—sugar, beauty, freedom, and revenge," said Egyptiacus.

—RALPH WALDO EMERSON, *Journal*

"I RUB A SORE, I see," said Dr. Crucifer, picking a cigarette out of his box, "whose pain will make you mad. I should take heed. You'll bruise her to jelly." He paused, raising an eyebrow, for a moment of exquisite registration. "Won't you?"

Darconville almost smiled.

"You will be forgiven many sins on account of her, let me vouch for it. Now, Al Amin," he said, his left hand feeling to scratch the bottom of his chair with a questioning matchtip, "put me in the picture."

"I don't know where to begin."

"Speak to the problem anywhere you'd like and speak without pretexts. Crucifer can hear."

The cloister lamp was lit. Its eerie glow, however, actually darkened rather than illuminated the large living room; the purple walls became shrouded, and the pieces of black oak furniture were drawn out to such long and forbidding shadows that it seemed as if each was determined to revert in shape to the ghostly length of its original state, while the great sideboard loomed up like some ancient and evil deathship run aground against the obscurity of the far wall. It was, for the medieval panelwork, the dap-joint beams above, and the oddities of acquisition placed here and about, every bit as curious and remote a folly as the creature who habitually kept himself confined there and who now sat back to listen—his eyes closed and directed straight up—in a pose of exaggerated deliberation.

It was without hesitation, having been confirmed to the policy by the speech on hatred, that Darconville now made his disclosures: about the tape-recording, the letters he'd written, and the details—excepting the curse—of what had recently taken place. The front of Crucifer's throat, as he listened, was very long, untenanted, dead white. As he heard his each and every suspicion corroborated, he blew out a ball of smoke but kept stone silent: the conviction he showed by showing no reaction whatsoever made manifest what did not require assertion. Then Darconville showed him the photograph of Gilbert van der Slang.

"The proud wooer?" asked Crucifer, smiling and sitting up. He put his hand in front of his mouth and shook with mirth. He actually took time off to laugh; he devoted himself to it. "A hole in his chin. Ugly beast-ears. Effeminate. But shall we forgive him?" he asked, biting his lip, his heavily lidded eyes mocking his own remark. He spat in sarcasm. "Why, a bat could see he couldn't be a chum of ours if he chuckled. It looks as though he suffers from suprasellar craniopharyngioma—the affliction of having a less-than-thimblesized penis. I am reminded of the featherless White Orpington—this being one, I have no doubt," said he, smiling viciously and puncturing the groin in the photo with the hot tip of his cigarette, "you'll soon caponize." He dropped the photo. "Here, but this is an IQ 60 Epsilon Minus in a circus suit. She's the one you want. The blowing datura-apple! The cozening coypu! The culling spick! The mock-humble, footprintless cvoirth! *Qui facit per alium facit per se:* she who does a thing through another does it through herself." His face went suddenly cold. "But tell me, have you answered the lies on the tape—or the one that allowed a complete lifetime of them?"

"She loved me once," whispered Darconville. "I believe that, first of all. I feel she—"

"You *feel?*" sneered Crucifer. "Then direct intuition is capable of discerning *a priori* truths as adequately as the inductive method of intellect reveals them *a posteriori?*" He sat back. "You outdo the Egyptians, probably the vainest people in the world." He wiped his mouth. "She loved you? She *loved* you?"

"You can't think that a lie, can you?"

"The Monch!" said Crucifer. "The Eiger! The Jungfrau!"

Disbelieving, Darconville just stood there. It was useless to disagree, for, as with all censors, it was impossible to discuss; the only position possible was acquiescence, a mood increasing with the diffidence he felt standing there under that high lamp and its paradoxical light which didn't eclipse the darkness but rather somehow made it visible.

"I'll ask you again: the lies, have you answered them?"

"No."

Crucifer looked away. "Inference: that you listened to it, that you approved it? O, but she'll like that."

"*Approved* it," snapped Darconville, disgustedly. "What do you mean?"

That was better. Crucifer wanted the confrontation.

"What are you talking about?"

"O do *don't,* will you."

"Tell me."

It was simple.

"Revenge," said Crucifer, point-blank.

Darconville slowly walked to the window, stood there a moment, then softly made a vow to his reflection. "I will wait," he said, "I will bide my time. But I will never rest until—I don't care when or how or where—she comes, in seeing what she has done, to have as heavy a heart as I have now."

"*Wait?*" asked Crucifer, puckering his right eye in a malicious wink. "While she gobbles chocolates and makes play with her eyes and fans like the fast women of Paris? Stoicism *is* the disease of young men, isn't it?" He sighed. "Time is on your side, I don't doubt—what there is of it. I've always said that the best reason for disbelieving in God is that he never gave us enough time in life to pursue enough knowledge to find sufficient truth. That we find it at all—as you," he cried, pointing at Darconville and raising his voice to an angry trill in which he couldn't prevent a slight trace of madness from creeping, "apparently *have*—should always be taken, one would assume, as a welcome if miniature surprise." He gulped bile. "But you don't deign to think so, do you?"

"I should explain—"

"Bullfuck!" shrieked Crucifer, pounding out his cigarette and struggling out of his chair in fury. "The only explanation is a bad one! You're at *war!* You will have a cripple's temper until you have found your feet! You think you should ignore this owl's pellet simply because she is low, stupid, and insignificant?" The question whistled out of his nosehole.

"Power is subtle. Fiddler crabs can wear away whole jetties. A pinworm fells an elephant, as Dutch beetles can an elm. The rat flea, not the rat, causes bubonic plague. Cancer chews out the heart of a hero; a kiss in the open air betrays a prophet. And a knife"—he yanked the Egyptian *khangar* out of his academic hood and violently stabbed the air—"a knife flashes and an emperor dies."

"And what," asked Darconville, his voice almost inaudible, "is the lesson here?"

"It's not enough to raise a storm, you poor fool, unless you follow it with a bolt of thunder and a blow of lightning." He gestered to the photograph. "I'd send that Geryoneo down to the house of dole. And *her?* Blood revenge! The Islamic Thar! Shit fire and save matches! '*Hier steh ich treu Dir bis zum Tod*'—her oath, I believe? Then help her out! What goes round comes round. Now is the time your face should form another."

"My face," said Darconville, unambivalently looking at Crucifer, "is facing revenge."

"Yes?" returned Crucifer. "And to be further educated to it is to hazard a loss, in the delay, of the joy of discovery?" He breathed into Darconville's face. "I'd send her disappearing back into her navel like a black hole. I'd huddle her into the wormy earth. I'd quadrifurcate her fat limbs and feed her parts of herself in choice cuts." Darconville closed his eyes. "But I see your position: she's her own worst enemy, that's it, isn't it?"

"Not while I'm alive."

"Then why do you linger with that which you know? It is obsolete. The known is a symbol of the death of the mind! After what she's done to you, will you now sit by until she's a worthless old bushrag in her nineties, some stinking bale of cadaverous goods best consigned immediately to Pluto, and then let death come to her as a *friend?*" His eyes flashed. "We're talking about a bitch here—a word, granted, which hasn't the authority of classical usage, but it certainly has the indubitable authority of fitness, no? No? And safe? Safe? She wanted to be safe?" Grotesquely pursing his mouth into a girlish bow, Crucifer hitched up his robe in a cute little tricot, curtseyed primly, and mocked, "Why, thank you, Darconville, I'll really miss you"—his face fell—"every chance I get."

"I've done something about it."

"Overmuch clack," spat Crucifer.

"I've taken steps. I—"

"What, you've sent a few letters? Is that your idea of revenge? Sandpapering the anchor? Complaining, inactive, and bored like the endlessly munching ungulates I spoke of who know not hot nor cold? You beat the sack and mean the miller. You're not going to act," said Crucifer, blowing disgust out of his great clay cheeks.

Darconville clenched his fists against his eyes and cried out in pain.

"Into each life," said Crucifer, shrugging unsympathetically—and he pretended to lose himself in a fastidious study of the Delville, touching his little finger to a non-existent speck on the canvas and blowing it away. He arranged some papers on his desk. He tidied up.

"I despise her."

"Touching."

"I thirst to see her lifeless."

"A dried sentence"—Crucifer tossed his head—"stuffed with sage."

"I mean it."

"And I'm the Queen of Romania."

"I promise you."

"Oh, to be sure, yes indeed."

Then Darconville dropped his arms, his moist eyes wide open, and desperately confessed, "I am killing her in my mind repeatedly. If I owned a hotel with a thousand rooms in it, I'd like to see her dead in every one of them."

"The mind," replied Crucifer, with a pout of displeasure, "is a hotel room, I'm afraid, where only one person can die."

He began to walk back and forth, then, stroking that huge witcher-bubber of a belly which seemed to propel him forward on a high drift, as if in caricatured pursuit of something elusive and just out of reach.

"I am constrained, I see," he said, turning, "to a seeming digression. It is an indisputable fact, right off, that thought in movement seeks thought at rest in resolution. Beliefs are rules for action, and the function of thinking is to step toward thought's practical consequences, mmmm? Reverence to this! Now you have an *enemy,* my dear misguided boy—a bitch with a rubber heart who in a recent confustication more like a Goldonian drama than a love story used her smile for make-up and her twam for a Dutch bargain all in pursuit of a marriage founded in deceit and against the long continuance of which I wouldn't bet a pound to a pinch of shit! (Of course it won't last: when someone leaves a room, those who remain immediately see themselves differently and always move around to register that difference.) But the point is: you loved her. The point is: she left you to die—the lowest of betrayals of the many there are, the swart crow! A predator, unseen and unseeable, she kept to the night with multiple disguises, using shadow-elimination, outline disruption, and counter-shading all at once! I should have added to my litany Myrionyma, the creature with a thousand names! But, hell, you've heard what she's said, haven't you? And isn't the tongue the neck's enemy? So what could absolve, who acquit, how cleanse this thing who not only hates you but is sitting to virtue in Virginia this very minute as demure as an old whore at a christening? Nothing! No one! Not balsam from mecca, neither musk from the deer, nor civet from the civet's arsehole! But an enemy provides both a stimulus and a lesson, I repeat, and I wish only for the final time to point out—*monstrare*—make clear—*ostentare*—predict—*praedicere*—and portend—*portendere*—what henceforth you must simply no longer ignore: *force destroys enemies!*"

Crucifer paused to swallow his anger.

"Survival is not a desperate affair; it is a natural process! Lost battles," he shrugged, "make not Pompey less. But shall you either by

pointless idling or non-resistance cut off the chance for your own survival in the face of the possibility of it? Forgo justice? Counterpoise
evil by silence? Excuse yourself and accuse yourself? You're standing
in your own light!" Crucifer shook his fist, which grew a warning
finger. "'Tis time; descend; be stone no more! Civilization and
murder are compatible, Darconville. Haven't you read your political
history? Is it not better that a life should contract dirt-marks and
abuse rather than forfeit usefulness in its despicable efforts to remain
unspotted? 'The dead do not praise the Lord,' said the Psalmist, 'nor
any that go down in silence.' Mercy, without retributive punishment,
is sentiment! Worst points to best!

"There is no worse lie," howled Crucifer, wildly waving his arms—
the cloister lamp actually trembled—"than a truth misunderstood by
those who hear it, but, no matter the brand of cant putting it otherwise, reasonable arguments, challenges to magnanimity, and quacking
appeals to sympathy or mercy or pardon are folly when we are dealing
with vile and corrupt deceivers and the beaked and taloned graspers of
the world! I mean, he who doesn't oppose, attack, or even execute
such creatures is as though the *creator* of them! Oh yes, our sympa-
thies are always evoked through *ultra vires* considerations, aren't they?
For pussyfooting? Piety? A pitying tolerance for our oppressors?" He
touched his forehead, wearily. "The ages greatly differ. Your
magnificent relatives—the heroic fashion of them," he sighed, "has
passed away. Wherein lies very obviously a truth: did they lie chained,
subordinate by this world's insult; coerced by the Elizabethan brank
and block; and then go whimpering into their due subterranean
abodes to beat hemp and repent? Or did they walk openly abroad, the
envy of a general valet-population, bear sway, and profess war to the
death with the very dogs who snapped at their heels? *Love your enemies?*" choked Crucifer. "Why, it invokes such a breach with our own
instinctive springs of action as a whole that I take it to be nothing
more than an oriental hyperbole which castrates poverty and pain and
gives over the control of the world to criminal fools, proselytes of capital, and the Set fatuously dubbed Smart! If there be any pretension
more philosophically absurd than another, it is that any person or
thing can act contrary to his own nature. And if there be any pretension more practically immoral, it is that any person or thing *ought* to
act in that manner! Whom therefore ye ignorantly worship, her declare I unto you! *Une Grue! Une Goulue! Une Grognew!* She was

what she was—and so has done what you must undo. Love, lost, breeds death, found. It's the very lesson at the heart of that hideous and twofold penalty of blindness and eviration that we have come to call Adam and Eve! And can you then now admit you shall do *nothing*? Creed love for a foe crippled with miscreed? Believe someone who could perjure through a six-inch board? Can you actually sit there," he screamed in an extended wail of monochromatic denial, "and try to tell me there's to be found a level of emotion so unifying, so obliterative of differences between two enemies, that enmity may proceed to such irrelevant circumstances that one might crawl on his hands and knees to stoop, to kneel, to grovel to kiss the feet of one's eternal *persecutor?*" He gave the word "persecutor" four clear vowels. The echo punctuated the question Darconville, pale as jute, couldn't answer. *"The Trojan Horse has foaled!"*

Dr. Crucifer saw he'd touched a nerve yet waited some minutes for better advantage, his eyes roaming morosely about the room in fake self-objurgation for having gone and wasted his words in an effort that seemed to have fallen on deaf ears. He continued to wait. But the knife was in. So he turned it. "You love her."

Darconville's eyes blazed.

"She is panting for someone else like a cat after seafish," he sneered, "and you positively adore her."

It was intolerable.

"I hate her!" shrieked Darconville, gasping for air, frightening himself in the ultrasonic scream to the point of trembling, and he began to bang his head bloody against the wall. *"I hate her! I hate her! I hate her! I hate her!"* He turned in convulsed supplication. *"I love to hate her. I've cursed her to hell!"*

Crucifer's mouth fell open. With the fingertips of both small white hands fluttering bewilderedly to his neck, he stared in disbelief, thinking: *how you must have loved her.* But he was fast upon Darconville. Had he? Had he, he asked, actually put a curse on her? And unable to contain his joy—he literally appeared to inflate—he rose huffshouldered and victorious, bowling in to overpower Darconville in an awkward and obscene embrace while hissing lewdly in his ear, "You are me!"

It all called for a drink. Crucifer reached into a corner and pulled a bell, as Darconville, shaken, felt for a chair and sat down in silence, the wound under his bandaged chest throbbing. Then Lampblack—

the face that always seemed its own reflection looking out of a lens—
after appearing from nowhere to unwrap and pour a bottle of wine,
was told to get out. With a tiny glitter in his spider's eyes, Crucifer
then made a toast, singing, *"La illaha ila Darconville, Crucifer Resoul
Darconville!"*

Darconville hesitated.

"Shrabt! Shrabt!"

And they clinked glasses and drank.

What however, wondered Crucifer, had yet been established? The
pitch of efficacy, yes, but of what inferential belief? He was not interested in the mere exercise of words, certainly, but rather the very
movement of the spirit putting itself in a personal relation of contact
with the avenging person of which it felt the presence. Now, he
thought, I will bell the cat.

"There," said Crucifer, sampling the winy aftertaste with his
tongue. "I would call it an *amusing* bottle. A touch of smoke, with attractive mid-mouth flavors. Chewy but not sec, hmmm? Apropos, did
you know it is possible to turn Madeira into port in the space of a single night?" He took Darconville in from the side of his fat-encircled
eyes. "Do you follow me? I've told you before, a nice vice is really a
virtue. The blow of a sword and the impact of an idea, according to
the Bhagavad-Gita, reach to the same end and have the same justification in the eyes of God. If a claw be caught, the bird is lost—you can
make pigeon-blood of rubies!" He paused. "Your brows are clouded,"
he asked, leaning under Darconville's face, "when will they thunder?
No, don't look away. The inescapable Aquinas is his best on 'the right
of spoil' in a just war, and St. Isidore of Damietta, in fact, pointed out
that when the chosen lean over from the heights of heaven to contemplate the torture of the damned they will feel unutterable joy at the
spectacle: it's the collaudation of infinite justice. Knowledge that fails
to become action, I've said it before, is bestial perversity, didn't I say
that? I did. I did say that."

He paused theatrically and then picked up the photograph of Gilbert van der Slang.

"Lions 1, Christians 0, is that fair?" Crucifer slowly turned the photograph around toward Darconville and pointed to it with his little
finger. "Shall what poisons you prove mithridate to her?" He paused.
"Or shall I hold the photograph so"—he turned it sideways—"the
way he'd be in bed?"

There was silence.

"Darconville?"

"I am ready."

"*Be Ravilliac!*" charged Crucifer, moving quickly forward in his chair and squeezing its fistclaws. "Have zero pH! Put honor on the top of your tongue and a knife under it! Strangle her with her own tharms! I tell you, men who believe they can do anything they choose to do must presently believe they must do everything they can! What have you come out to see, a reed shaken in the wind? A moral temper has often to be cruel; it is a partisan temper, Valois, and that can be the cruelest! I would have you see her an almanac that you might burn her every *year!* Stab, strangle, burn—what does it matter? Work only swiftly, as aqua fortis eats into brass!"

Darconville followed him with his eyes.

"Don't hesitate. Don't think. God may forgive her, but you never can. The law for her is the law for you—tell me, what most resembles a roast gander?

"Why," cried Crucifer, bounding up, "a roast goose! And, O, what an infinite variety of retaliation awaits us! In the Dantean underworld she'll be whipped by devils as a panderer, for her hypocrisy draped in a leaded mantle, for her simony stood upsidedown in a hole—but first we must get her there! Let it go," he winked, "under the soft name of *satisfaction*. Now," he continued, sticking the photograph as a reminder into a corner of the Chinese screen, "propositions of all sorts must have occurred to you—what, countenance her deceit that by your magnanimity she come to acknowledge her mistake with despair? Ignore her crime that she fatally form the habit of acquitting herself of obligation and die friendless? Refuse her the nobility of suffering by which otherwise she piously seek a martyrdom?" Crucifer drew himself up like a bat, his ears almost growing points. "The trouble with this is it's all insipid pacifistic bilge—and leaves her to make your back her footstool, the spawn's lugs, and to force you to live sick as muck for the remainder of your days meeting circumferences, not angles, not corners, not rest. She *wants* to forget. But opposites—*contraria contrariis curantur*—are cured by opposites. There'll never be a forgetting! And you'll never be at rest! The Palace of Revenge contains every delight but the power of leaving it. Revenge a hundred years old"—he bent over Darconville and siffled under his breath—"still has milk teeth! No, put her to the squeak," he goaded. "A piece of churchyard fits everybody! But be thorough—a little wind kindles, much puts out the fire: she must learn in pain exactly what she's lent."

"Then we agree," said Darconville, surprising himself with the remark as well as Crucifer, who almost squealed from joy. He quickly slipped off his jade ring and placed it on Darconville's finger.

"As coins to Hebrews!"

But the singlemindedness, he thought, was yet to be confirmed, predisposing conditions yet to be, the mood as given not effectively received until.

"What to do now? Be cunning," warned Crucifer, walking with his finger in the air, "for if motion is necessary because of the oppositions which evoke each other, motion must be subtle. Intervene as but a shadow. What I mean is, a lamprey is not killed with a cudgel but a cane, do you get me? Better pull a steady thirty-six than a jerky forty —the old Harvard motto, yes?"

He continued pacing the room restlessly, an uneasiness reduced to the simplest terms of cold reflection, deliberating in an anxious conviction that sifted and tested what he soliloquized within himself of war and cruelty and torment. He stopped suddenly at his desk.

"Stay," he said, "I feel a sudden alteration—ah, lovely girl, trust no longer to your bloom; the white privets fall, the dark hyacinths are culled." He wiggled his dimpled fingers. "Let her paint herself an inch thick, Darconville, to this favor"—he slowly picked up the air pistol— "she must come."

He turned.

"And him."

Darconville followed his pointing finger to the photograph.

"How can you put a hundred pounds of trash into two sacks so that each sack"—Crucifer's hand began to scribble fast in the air—"contains a hundred pounds? By putting," he gleeped, "one sack inside the other! *Figurez-vous?* Go after them both!" He leaned forward in animated receptivity. "Have I not said that when you are lank again, seek the narrow chink where, when lank, you entered? Here." He waved the gun. Darconville stepped back anxiously. "This is a Feinwerkbau E-12 Deluxe, caliber 177, recoilless operation with double piston construction, side-cocking lever, and a fixed barrel set with a micrometer peepsight. It's a classic! The pellets"—he turned his head

sideways and smiled crazily—"have been treated. Never put off 'til tomorrow what you can wear tonight. She can be bleeding six bottles of
alicant by dusk. Take it."

He seemed to turn positively insane.

"Kill her!" cried Crucifer, impatiently. His fanaticism leapt forth
like a sword drawn from its scabbard at any thought now of contradiction. "Where there are no guns, diplomacy must make not butter
but time, not true? Too true. Too true, indeed. But here's a gun!
Shoot her and leave her until maggots are singing in her wounds! Not
a record kill—only a good one-shot kill at twenty yards through her
bedroom window!"

He fired without warning into the photograph: *twaaaang!*

"Kill the Dutchman—the receiver is as bad as the thief—and send
him back feet first to the Straits of Ballambangjang or wherever it was
he came from." He aimed and blew a quarter of the photo away.

"Kill their children, if they should have any! There's to be no pity:
nits will be lice!"

He shot off the face.

"Kill her parents—a murder of total elimination—for the soul of
the offspring, say the Traducians, originates by transmission. Nothing
exceeds like excess! Send them to Azraïl, the angel of death, and let
Munkar and Nakeer inquisition them in hell." He fired: *twiiiing!*
And again: *twoooong!* Howling, he emptied the entire gun into the
screen.

"Kill them all!" he screamed, biting the air in the fullness of his
malice. *"Kill them all!"*

XCII

Revenge! Revenge!

For Rage now rules the reynes:
Revenge, revenge, my Muse, Defiance trumpet blow—
Threaten what may be done, yet do more than
   you threaten.

> —Sir PHILIP SIDNEY, "Fifth Song"

"R-R-REVENGE!" cried Dr. Crucifer, his voice resembling the tearing of a strip of calico. He was almost unable to pronounce the word
from happiness as he pressed the pistol into Darconville's hands. "It is
a wonderful witty word much disliked by those to whom the thing
signified by it is nevertheless dear. Harden your heart. What good is
kindness now? All delight comes to an end, hence the chief pleasure in
the next beginning: spill the thing's blood and water a mandrake! It's
only justice! White, to use the parlance of chess, is always morally

justified in attacking, so let black see to black—remember, in describing a capture only the capturing and captured pieces are mentioned, never slyness of method or means. Say nothing and you won't have to repeat it. But be chaos: fast in action, dirigible in absence. She doesn't have the right to own the area she's in.

"Come, do you hesitate?" Crucifer looked wounded. "Didn't Alexander destroy the oldest cities on earth without a qualm—Tyre, Cyprus, Gaza, Boeotia, and a thousand more? Or Ferdinand Alvarez de Toledo, Duke of Alba, did he shrink from answering with fire and sword the question of Dutch perfidy? And had Louis XIII any doubts about the justice of fitting out Protestant Huguenots as blackbirds and shooting them just for the sport of it as they leaped about and exploded in puffs of feathers? I mean, if you have a problem, and you know the answer to it, isn't the problem immediately eliminated?

"The comfortablest revenge is when you can kill to pardon." He winked. "There's sugar in salt, I tell you. But, here, don't hoard your grief—you have someone to divide it with! It's as easy as witches bottling air! You can summon demons from the hell-light pale! You can appeal to Fornax, god of ovens! You can even pray for it, for in several secret chapels in North Wales you can actually make supplication to vengeance and, with one carnaficial kiss, offer up your enemy to Sts. Llan Elian in Anglesea and Chynog in Carnarvonshire! But you must act! Intense device! Superflux of pain! Nothing is worse for the soul than struggling not to give play to feelings it cannot control. Revenge is a dish best served up cold—have at her swiftly before she tries to make amends! Do it now! Kill her! A promise to do so in the past was not redeemed, Darconville—the thought, I daresay, having too much play in the expression of it.

"All that's real," hissed Crucifer, sitting down heavily on the sofa, "is *rational!* Black magic, with all its grim theatricals, is all very fine and large yet nothing more than exploiting lost angels with impunity. You must not simply cut off from your agony all that is superfluous but necessarily impart a shape to what is left: be avenged here," he pointed, "in *this* life. Scupper her right there in her stained and mousy sheets, rank with twice-dyed blood! Or do you prefer, tell me, other than a pistol?" he asked, taking it and setting it aside. "Are there no longer racks, wheels, strappadoes? Bilboes, feral engines, iron collars? Or pikes, the tyrants of the wat'ry plain?" His face turned the color of craft paper. "I mean, precisely what *are* the other ways to skin a cat?"

Dr. Crucifer's soul seemed to come waveringly forward, like a grey vapor, out of his eye-sockets, until it formed itself into a shadowy double of a person.

"Poleax her! Bang her on the toenails with dowels and mallets as they do to Indian elephants! *Sfregia la?*" he giggled, drawing a finger along his throat. "Death has a thousand doors to let out life!" He threw out a series of short paratactic suggestions. "Scorch her with ultraviolet light! Truss her up in ropes and thraw her jerking in all directions! Slip her a funny-tasting pie! Pick any of the three swords of Mohammed: Medham the Keen or Hatef the Deadly or al Battar the Trenchant! In Iceland"—he clapped his hands—"they beat codfish into powder for bread. Or shall it come as it did for Adonibezec, King of Bezek, who had his thumbs and big toes amputated? How about eserine? Physostigmine? Ovabain? *Bouillon d'onze heures?*

"The quickest poison is the barbiturate thiopentone: one choice intracardiac shot"—Crucifer blew a kiss—"and cheery-bye! Or you might consider aconitine or digitalin, which can't be detected. A more colorful alternative? Try 1000 cc's of scoline, not only swift but the state of horror and intense fear before excruciating suffocation is indescribable. The Borgias adored white hellebore, thorn-apple, and Christmas-rose. Then there's always our old friend curare, which relaxes the abdominal muscles to the point where breathing will just simply stop and, as it's soluble, if the body were then immersed in water—have they bathtubs in Fawx's Mt.?—all traces will disappear. But what? Raw rice, pounded glass, ribstone pippin, Bean of St. Ignatius, fool's parsley, Godfrey's cordial, sesquisulphuret of arsenic—it's God's plenty! Paralysis from buttercups, stupor from buckeye seeds, agony from mistletoe berries! All natural, all nice. In irritant poisoning, the pain usually comes on gradually, and slowly increase in severity. Neurotic poisons, whether spinal, narcotic, or cerebrospinal, of course rarely leave any well-marked traces in the stomach or bowels, and any pretenders to minute analytical accuracy will invariably apply their tests in vain. I personally favor anything, for elegance, that addresses the spinal marrow." Crucifer, smiling, crossed his legs and pick-a-backed his hands. "But I love them all.

"The poisoner is, I must confess, of all others the genius. He must have the confidence of the person he is killing; he must appear amiable; he must be willing to give from his own hand those drops that mean death. And yet all the while," smiled Crucifer, "the victim sits as helpless as an egg about to be tapped! But it doesn't matter how, does it? Death conjugates all tenses. It matters *why*, first of all. Then, it matters when." He paused. "I am an Arab, you forget. Revenge is almost a religious principle among us." He leaned toward Darconville. "The only point is: when you bite, make your teeth meet."

The silence that followed indicated a pause that seemed too much like moral deliberation. Couchant immediately became rampant: Dr. Crucifer fought up off the sofa and, as if his delight in caricature sprang from his own unfortunate condition, played out not only with fists and faces but in terrible detail the rest of his indoctrination.

"There is a various plenty in slaying of constants and parameters. Proficient? Freeze her to death, then thaw her out—the perfect murder. Ingenius? Perform a transabdominal laparohysterosalpingo-oöphorectomy on her, *unsuccessfully!* Historical? Double her up like a small compass in the 'Scavenger's Daughter.' Slow? Try the Thousand Piece Execution: the idea of this is to cut out from her body one tiny square bit the size of a cough lozenge, say, every few minutes or so until bit by bit—all of them selected with discrimination so as to have her live to the nine-hundred-ninety-ninth piece—her whole body has been removed. Amusing? Tickle her to death with the tassels of her wedding card. Suitable? Brank her like a shrew by padlocking a sack over her head—the virtue here being that, unlike a cucking, the tongue is not given liberty 'twixt dips—and dunk her in a gum-stool until she drowns to death. Ethical? Place a lethal snake in one corner of her house and *at the same time* place the exact amount of anti-toxin to cure the bite in another—then walk away. Patriotic? Smother her to death in the Virginia state flag. Metaphysical? Dream her to death in a mind-war and watch her combust in a nasty puff of smoke. Colorful? The Chinese *dai sh'pin* comes to mind, a particular treat where you feed her bits of paper pulp—it's nutritional, briefly—which, absorbing moisture, sit humectant in the digestive tract, making it increasingly more difficult to defecate as each day passes, and in the process renders vain any attempt on her part to try to stick her fingers up her anus to pry out the dry lumps." Crucifer glinked sideways. "Are these yet too elaborate? Too venturesome? Inapposite? Overconceptualized? Explicit? Jeopardous?" He touched a finger to his brow in a pose of self-consultation. "Mmmmm, sad. Then why don't you—"

The expression, as he amassed them, sat loosely on his thoughts.

Then he spoke.

XCIII

"Why Don't You—?"

I'll teach you differences.

—WILLIAM SHAKESPEARE,
King Lear

"STAB HER with a bung-starter! Mail her a poison suit! Employ the scaphism! Hurl her down the Gemonian steps with tincans tied to her ears! Whittle her nose into a dowel! Exenterate her with an oilcloth-cutter's knife! Glume back her scalp and paint the skull with a crimson A! Incrassate her into jellies! Conglutinate her buttocks with hot solder! Bake her a pie made from castor beans, pokeweed, tomato plant foliage, black locust bark, rhubarb leaves, and wisteria pods! Ablende her eyeballs!

"Burn *radix pedis diaboli* in her bedroom! Force her to have buccal coition with a yak! Deliver her over for lewd sport to hordes of ferocious Khonghouses! Snop her, snackle her, smore her in picrotoxin! Tie her down on a nest of dermestid beetles! Pickle her in natron! Replace her nose with a headlight and drive her into a plate-glass window painted the color of money! Inject her with fox mange, nasal gleet, poultry mites! Lock her away forever into the charnel-vault of Montfaucon! Fouch off her buttocks!

"Place Q-wedges in her eyes! Cauterize her cervix with strychnia! Nail her name down with Punic wax and pour acid on it! Sew her up inside a hippo! Bore a hole in her throat and draw down the tongue, for comic effect, to pull it through her neck! Cut the fingers off her first-born and fashion them into a necklace for a cross-eyed pigmy! Grill her on *cashielawis!* Thropple her with your wet hands! Notch her nostrils! Drip plutonium into her open eyes! Roll her tongue up like a bruggioli and transfix it with a mail-opener! Feed her out of a lead footpan into which several Hassidic Jews have just vomited! Plug up her Bowlahoola!

"Beat her senseless with her boiled shoes! Scrobiculate her with a pair of tailor's shears! Hang a wreath of fruitbats around her neck! Put a rocket up her anus and light the touch-paper! Vaginoexcavate her with a hot coal spoon! Put a stone fish into her bathing cap! Baston her with heated gisarmes! Lib off her ears! Shove tacks into her fold of Houston! Upend her into a moldy fust! Crimp her epidermis into artistic sunbursts and slivers with an Eskimo ulu! Sulp her! Feague her! Gaum her! Hamesuck her! Waterzoutch her!

"Strangle her with a numbat's tongue! Coat her with hot creosote, hollow her out, and use her in your garden as a drainbarrel! Beat her into a j-particle! Hang her in a bottle like a cat! Shoot Dutch bric-a-brac off her head with a shotgun! Tack a pocket to her libbard skin! Make stone jewelry out of her distals, terminals, unguals! Give her a felon-wort sandwich! Behead her with a rusty coffee-can lid! Pitch sorb-apple hoops into her face!

"Yerk her on the lip with a gorilla's scrotum-stones! Smother her in her own midden! Force her at knife-point to shinny naked up a locust tree! Contrive to make her feel torment without the luxury of sorrow! Spackle up her mouth! Lay pipes in her you'll scald! Clap her into a pair of hames and take her for a run on a string! Hogcomb her back! Fit a whipworm into her ear! Slingshot a brookstone into her forehead! Stick her toes into Bullivant's Stopper and twist! Roll her in *smilax rotundifolia!* Dunch her in the belly! Duntle her in the teeth! Dub her in the face!

"Raft off her head! Throw her to a Zanzibar tiger! Hire her out to a sideshow where she'll be backscuttled by a Bulgar in a conical hat! Venenate her vegetation! Coat her with meat sauce and release fifty starved Molossian hunting dogs! Send her around Cape Horn in an ill-caulked fat! Reverse her fingers! Thrast her temples with a filter-wrench! Slither a taipan through her bath tap! Hautpin her through the ears!

"Vivisepult her! Snavvle her! Titscrew her! Sheer off her right mammary prominence and throw it to a Maltese spaniel! Snip her weasand! Jackflip her into Appleby's self-knotting binder! Bang her hard on the occiput with a copper stewpan! Saw off the top of her skull and use it as a whistle-tankard from which to drink juleps! Boil her buttocks! Crucify her on the front of a barndoor while wearing a duncecap listing her crimes! Blowtorch her hair off and scald her like a sow!

"Melt her down into a kitty-litter tray! Fustigate her with an eel-ferret! String a zither with her vastus lateralis tendons and play 'A Nautical Man Came By'! Tear out her umbles, reins, and kidneys and replace them with her lying tapes! Give her an overdose of chloral and force her to do unnatural acrobatics! Chop her into messes with an ax-wedge! Fill her calyx with duocide chucks! Place cannonballs on each of her feet and hang her by the tongue from the clock of the Soestdijk Palace! Graft her thumb onto her chin!

"Rip out her temperomandibular joints! Sever her stapes! Brank off her wrists with hoof-nippers! Mammock her into bacon! Bite her on the neck and give her the gleep! Inject her with the Black Formosa Corruption! Grant her the xi pains of hell! Foin off her thumbtips! Suggilate her with night-visits from goblins, bugbears, and tenebrions! Garrote her with corned beef string! Celebrate a mass inhumation with her and her two friends! Duckpop her by grabbing her asshole and snapping her inside out!

"Pack furballs of her own hair into her by suction! Miniaturize her! Decapitate her during the recitative of *Fidelio!* Hand her a bouquet of amanita mushrooms, Persian kerza flowers, Jerusalem cherry plant, pyrethrum daisies, Javanese upas leaves, and tell her to breathe deeply! Snip off her eyelids! Inject potassium under her armpit! Gore her in the temple with a suction trocar! Force her to grab an active propeller! Order her to memorize Zumpft's *Latin Grammar* while bonking her on the head with a hammer! Dye her black! Devil her into a pâté! Dash her against a wall of dolerite!

"Bimster off her flesh! Tap croquet balls down her throat one by one! Feed her the gets of cupped and goitrous Jewgirls! Sit her in a footstool made of Perunite B and throw a lit match at her navel! Suspend her naked from a dree-draw! Fashion a parrot cage out of her sternal ribs! Slip a gluey penny into her glottis! Lower her into filthy sewage! Electroplate her and hang her as a bauble in a burlesque house in Clinch Valley, Va.! Slit her snout! Wish her a case of sheeprot! Fit a barlow knife into her nasopharynx! Crunt her on the skull with a cudgel!

"Sling a schist into her belly! Pewke into her pockets! Thrack her with anvils up to Pantops Mt.! Insert the nozzle of a bellows into her touchhole and pump hard! Pour all over her skin a devouring escharotic! Bombard her with calcium atoms! Turn her upsidedown and let bongo apes depucelate her bum! Split her head with a pike at the lambdoid suture and use them for woks! Upholster your house with her verminous dermis! Whack off her lower lip with an imperfect blade! Attach drawstrings to her and hanfangle her from the vanes of a windmill by 'The Hottentot Apron'! Fetch the rymme out of her throat!

"Adnexopex her! Burke her! Crooch her in the face! Put her to the hot-water ordeal! Roomal her with her lover's dogstones and ropetheats! Hide a spincop in her knitting ball! Drape a mulebell on each of her ears and parade her duck-squatting through the village of s'Hertogenbosch! Whip her about like a bumming-top! Assoil her with rude fists of offal! Thrammle her to a leaking nuclear-reactor! Splashfeed her with phenyl cyanide!

"Glaive off her ears! Hurl Montenegrin shepherds' curses at her through a megaphone! Spray hive-bomb down her throat! Clap her into a casket with a vicious ounce! Mule-pulley off her back from her front! Drop live geckos into her hair! Sproat her through the tongue and lower her into a sharkpool. Cruddle her fibula bones into matchwood! *La plongez dans lessive faicte d'estrons et de pissat de juifvre!* Vault her down the street with a wagstaff inside her! Behead her with a dull thixle!

"Brangle her by the ears! Swage her legs to a perpetual 180°! Afflict her with the scabadoo, dry serpigos, roup, gaffkyremia, and

white diarrhea! Put casting-counters in her eyeholes! Haust her with
higry-pigry! Clap a fistful of Yucatan habañero chilies into her mouth
and hold tight! Depeditate her and force her on a stump pilgrimage to
the Mount of Deceit! Cut her to the rames! Bace her to death with
rubber drubbers! Caboche off her head and use it for a glowball!

"Impissocrapigate all over her! Crosshatch her face with a pie-
crimper! Make her bite down hard on a chunk of Hawaiian coral!
Massage her with a currycomb, abrading the flesh, then rub her with
alcohol, ignite it, resume combing, rub again, and relight! Stuff her
lover's severed cullions into her podex! Jangle puppets who look like
her real father outside her night-window! Set vicious ichneumons
loose at her heels! Sit her in a bed of flaming hot gleeds!

"Comminute her into snuff! Keel-haul her backwards through a
pond of aqua toffana! Dress her up like Satan and walk her into the
Valley of Mina to be pelted by outraged Muslims! Carve a perpetual
pumpkin-like smile into her face! Put a fire-alarm inside her and excite it with a jab every five minutes! Skin her alive and roll her in salt!
Catch her a whisterpoop on the face with a birchrod! Chain her in
gimmaces from a balloon and pot-shoot her with glass bits! Shove her
into a jam-pan! Make her swim into a cave of beach voles! Batter her
with a wanion! Thrash her with a hame strap!

"Acupunctuate her! Swindge her! Thunderstone her! Feed her a
full bag of creep ration! Deartuate her with a pair of calipers! Dose
her simultaneously with huge amounts of Sinequan and Mebroin, Per-
tofrane and Panwarfin, Mellaril and Esidrix! Infibulate her with a
curved seton needle! Pack her bathtub-deep in dough and harden her
into a human Beef Wellington! Tug a sailneedle through her nose-
points! Anchor her down by her byssal hairs and roger her arseways!

"Feed her poison garbongs! Cryogenize her into a glacial dirt-
band! Flame up a hornbeam into her eye! Cripple her and give her a
16th-century larder pan to slide herself about like a *cul-de-jatte!*
Pinch the back of her neck white with a tension forceps! Fuse her legs
together into a tail! Lock her into the Bull of Phalaris! Gamahuch her
with the tip of a pompier ladder! Take out her twenty-eight miles of
intestines and with them hang her parents from the storefront in
Fawx's Mt.!

"Funnel lobster dung into her eyes! Ganch her with razor-sharp
hooks through the clavicles and attach it to a dirigible! Wither her like
Jeroboam's hand! Exoculate her with a spoon and feed the balls of

her eyes to your pet mandrill! Crush the tips of her toes in a *grésillon!* Send shrews skittling up her anus! Stick her head between her thighs —the seat of dishonor—and jab her to death with a firefork! Beat her to death with an elderstick that was cut the minute the sun entered Mars! Roll her about in yucca leaves! Send her wedding veil to an insane asylum in the Tidewater to be used as a volleyball net! Set gongs to work under her bed and when she jumps cut off her ankles! Garrote her with her heartstrings! Pour six quarts of ipecac down her gullet—and gag her!

"Probang her with liquor of ammonia! Blind her with hot pins and place a fat padlock through her eyes! Void on her! Tie her onto the Lowell House bells and gong them! Hang, draw, and quarter her with the tied sheets of her marriage bed! Swing up a hidden steel chungool and swipe off her labiae! Pincer her occicles with pliers! Hamble her in the feet and force her to walk on stilts made out of her lover's bones! Frottage her head with a drill-sander!

"Tamp percussion caps into her ears and explode them! Sponge her in the midriff with sulfuric acid! Turn the killing gaze of a Catablepas on her! March her on the run, backwards, into a forest barbed with sharpened punji sticks! Inflate her with hydrogen gas through a clyster pipe! Squirt burgundy pitch into her ears! Cement her alive into the dungeons of Kasr el-Nihaye! Shake a can of wireworms into her face! Cover her with thistle-seed and unleash seventy-five bags of diseased crows!

"Give her a bath in hot naval jelly! Expose her strapped down on an iron grating in the Dokhma! Puncture her heart with an etching-point needle! Flatten her feet into trays with a spalling hammer! Shoot her with a phosphorus gun and leave a huge circle-burn for a halo on her heart! Take watermelon-sized bites out of her oxter! Tie her with clew lines, furl her, and bash her unconscious into the deadlight of a ship! Fuse her with sulphur into a human candle! Screw an ear-trumpet into her mouth and pour in chloride of zinc!

"Truss her haunches! Switch out her brains! Flog her with a cabman's whip! Nail her face up under a thick woolen drugget riddled with bedbugs! Extract all her teeth and replace each one with a red-hot nail! Allow a candle to burn down in her sphincter! Flay her with a rhino whip tipped with bent pins, knotted cords, switches of heather, and a bull's pizzle! Screw a spout into her mouth and porcelainize her for a men's room in Kabool!

"Request her to play Ἀγχώνην παίζειν! Snatch out her eyes, harden and varnish them, and use them for hacking chestnuts! Ream off one of her buttocks and make her wear it as a fur tippet! Split her lip like a bunny with one snip and make her hop after carrots! Funnel pounds of nephrocatarticon into her and scorch her kidneys! Beat her knuckles with a hickory ferrule! Throw a rabid kinkajoo into her bathwater! Quadrifurcate her and set the meat on four staves in the Rub'al Khali!

"Rowel her lips with scissors! Gavage her in the neck with a dental lancet! Infect her with blotch, fire blight, pink rot, smut, bacterial wilt, leaf spot, black leg, hopper burn, and anthracnose! Pull Christmas crackers next to her ears! Rake her cheeks with a dry rice root brush! Force her to eat a banana stuffed with MAO Inhibitor drugs! Cut her throat with a thrush searcher! Thwack her in two with a whinyard!

"Conculcate her! Bugle her! Stone her with fistfuls of coprolite! Ram the big toe of an ostrich foot into her temple! Scotchtape three-hundred pigeons to her arms and then hurl sacks of popcorn into a rocky gorge! Order her to sew the intricate Peking stitch by remote candlelight in a dungeon for one year! Tip her upsidedown and conquassate her! Punch her with a left hook to the solar plexus, the fiercest punch to absorb! Give her a panclastic sandwich!

"Pound hand-fids into her nociceptors! Tattoo her down the spine with Symmes' Abscess Knife! Rasp her around the neck with a xyster! Enter her in a marathon to run with a silver thimble between her buttocks! Fit her out lodgings on the Mont Saint-Michel sandflats or in Tunguska, Siberia or by the Bay of Fundy! Bash her with a nache! Suffocate her with a wet windsock! Sprinkle seed weevil into her breakfast food! Give her a frightful case of the bots!

"Bash her on the thinkball with Ubaldo's Wand! Remove her cochlea, attach an electromechanical driving unit to the oval window there, and bounce her across the room at will. Hurl her onto a set of maiming caltrops! Pack her mouth with nostrilcress! Knot her around the neck with her lover's cremasters and pull them tight! Snip her psoas muscle and make her run up a slide, sideways! Freeze her in quicksilver and tap her apart into little chunks! Pitch her into a pool of lampreys, and watch them suck her faint! Smyte her in pecys! Langle her by the neck on a leaping-house flagpole!

"Press her into a torture cravat, pump helium into her mouth, and force her to sing, 'I Love You Truly'! Embroider obscene words on her cheeks with red thread! Hammer her into bone ash and round it all into a cupel! Hobble her to her mother and force them to play Wipe the Scut, Donkeyshines, and Sow to Her Pen! Drench her in elder vinegar and chase her naked through the Ragged Mts. in the dead of winter! Frush her! Pertuse her! Bumrowl her! Cuff her! Spancel her like a cow!

"Pickle her as a voucher specimen! Invultuate a waxen image of Beelzebub and with it plug up her jakeshole! Send her an immortelle and develop the obvious meaning! Force her to absterge herself with a swatch of her own hair! Inject her with black mamba distillates until she assumes the nature of a snake! Whip her with the winter branch of a whiffletree! Throw her into a stewpool to fatten up your caribes! Grill steaks out of her baby's feet!

"Shower her with burbolts! Set her impossible tasks, like sorting out an infinite mixture of millet and barley! Make her suck on a musket-barrel, fire it, and send her to hell with her clothes on! Truss her, rub salt on the soles of her feet, let goats lick it off, and watch her die from laughter! Glue a sinapism on her mouth after a hearty meal of drastics and peristalts! Press her between two wheels of gritstone and breccia! Make her peer into the boiler of a steaming locomotive, then nudge her! Stitch her into a sack and wing her into the Bosphorus! Douche her with slacked lime, borax, and alkaline flux!

"Pisk her! Smout her! Minge her! Whinge her! Drop her into a revolving water-screw! Decartilage her completely and make her tap-dance! Reverse her eyes, then place her lover's picture in front of her, and watch her leap for it the wrong way! Sit her in a tub filled to the brim with Dutch Mordant! Swipe open her mouthends with a billhook! Cut a spot in her breast and place a window before her heart as an aquarium for stinging butterfly cods! Sigmoidoscope her with a harpoon, heated white!

"Drop balls of rattlesnakes down her chimney! Sew her ears to her inner thighs and, staring into her anus, let her beslubber her face! Incincrate her alive at 2000° F. and dust a brothel floor in Tirana with her cremains! Scald the bottom of her feet with a candle until the fat drops down to fan the flame! Fill your library with books fashioned with skin provided by her first child! Decapitate her, mesh her mouth, and make her head into a radio!

"Pour hot clay into her vagina and make little ceramic witches of her! Drive a yataghan into her brainbox! Drill holes into each of her teeth, wire them, and drag her over miles of flaming bitumen! Paint her skin with belladonna, morphia, drachms of King's Yellow, thringsene and cause dermal asphyxia! Assault her with Japanese moonchucks! Deploy an *envoutement* and hex her! Pour ice-water into her ear and set massive fans to work! Force her at gunpoint to geek the head off a puffer-fish! Cut her facial cords, temple to jawbone, and watch the character of her face collapse—and, as in all cases of disfigurement, keep mirrors around her!

"Vapulate her! Wherret her! Sneg her! Bash her on the panbone! Thwitch out her innards! Strip off portions of her skin, paint them, and then use them for tiny kites! Abacinate her by placing a red-hot basin near her eyes! Take her first-born infant by the ankle and flog her with it until both are dead! Carve an Eskimo tupelak with her face on it and blaspheme it, scomfitting it with whispers, obscenities, and dark curses! Throw her into a huge thirlpool! Break a needle in her finger and watch her die of lockjaw!

"Estrapade her with jerking ropes! Stuff her every orifice with grain, strap her down, and let her be pecked alive by 117 marabout storks, the ugliest birds on earth! Cut her heart into a thousand gammons! Drop raccoons full of diphtheria viruses down her chimney! Pry off her fingernails with metal *turkas!* Draw off quarts of her blood to use for ink to correct the first drafts of your next book! Stuff her ears with her lobes! Lower her alive into a sarcophagus made of limestone quarried at Asas! Exile her to the island of Pandataria! Send her wandering into the fogs of Exmoor! Beat her to death with mopsticks! Seal her into a room with mygales, bushmasters, and coral snakes and amplify her screams! Hoise her! Souse her! Bounce her! Trounce her! Punch her! Stunch her in the umbo! Pull out her throatball!"

XCIV

Journey to the Underworld

Let it be at last; give over words and sighing; vainly were all
things said.

—ERNEST DOWSON, "Venite Descendamus"

THERE WAS AN END to it only when Darconville, suffering
more than tongue could tell or heart could hold in silence—a ridiculous figure, a failure, a fool—packed that night to leave Cambridge
with complete disagreeable detachment of soul from every earthly sentiment, possession, hope, and desire, for having no proper defense
against the anguish of human relationships anymore he simply turned
away from them, spontaneously writing his feelings in a brief note that
became a minute, then a short confession, and finally an explanation
of fuller statement he could finish only to the point when it was

thrown, despairingly, after a heap of consequential letters, photos, and papers into the suitcase he banged shut.

The demeanor of the d'Arconvilles in direst straits had long been the demeanor of men who had no doubt regarding their own integrity; it applied no longer. He couldn't care again; neither explore; nor feel; and succumbing to whatever doom was now his with no more sense of responsibility than of that meted out to him by a destiny he took to be nothing more than the terrible intensification of chance, he accepted what he thought about no more.

Goaded by insult, heaped by lies, despoiled by injustice, tried beyond his strength, beyond all patience, he left his rooms for the last time and mounted the stairs to receive both a final malediction and the means to carry it out. He reached the top floor of Adams House. As prearranged, someone was waiting for him, someone at the far end of the dark corridor, coming no closer but standing back out of the feeble light, and then the moment, almost interminable in apprehension, was upon him. He hugged his shadow to him like a warm fear. Darconville stood for the final time before Dr. Crucifer. (Of the third he felt in this company? It was a matter God alone understood, if His mercy allowed Him to think about it.)

A sudden and desperate impulse at that moment, a longing to love somebody, anybody, anything not imbued with wickedness overcame Darconville. He stopped. He shook his head. He moved a few steps backwards. There wasn't yet a word spoken.

"He who will not when he may," Crucifer then whispered from the shadows, the voice respirating low in its unsleeping malevolence, *"when he will he shall have nay."*

"Are you talking about me—or G-God?" asked Darconville, his voice pleading as inconfidently he went further forward. But it was too late.

The glare of Crucifer's boiled eyes in their unnatural flush and the severe fat line of his mouth determined to mirror what they themselves wouldn't reflect on, and Darconville saw himself in the corruption: two negatives made an affirmative. They never shook hands. There were no goodbyes. A shadow merely handed him a pistol. And Darconville turned and was gone.

The singlemindedness of love? It can pursue a single aim with a concentration of energy, with a fullness and pertinacity of unwavering will near matchless in power. The wheel of feeling, however, makes an unerring revolution, and, lo, there is hatred. For Darconville, wasted by illness and discredited by disaster, the infection was upon him; his face was like no human face and nearly unrecognizable. Life at its highest and best, such as he himself once enjoyed, offered the possibility of its alternative which as it replaces the other none can escape. Curbed by no limitations, he made no pretensions anymore to the discovery of new and striking facts; out of savage pain, then, out of reckless mockery and loss and long weeks of self-abandonment was wrought a new resolve—and so like the black princes of the Renaissance who would step not a foot in the streets until they had buckled on a sword or sharp dagger by their sides, Darconville set off alone, bought his butcher's ticket at the airport, and began his journey to the underworld where no darkness, however close, could either save or shelter one from that fate in which victim and executioner would alike be instruments. He felt for the pistol: Tartars gave as gifts to the tortured the canes with which they'd been flogged. It would be like the algebra of love, what he was now about to do, suddenness in passion fit to matters of eternal consequence, with one lover firing and another lover dying—shot, unexpectedly, straight through the heart.

XCV

The Night of Power

The Night of Power is better than a thousand months.

—Jacob Boehme

THE WOODS in Fawx's Mt. were wet and cold. Darconville stirred through the leaves, cut through the water-rat-smelling underbrush, and quickly crossed down a dark path, shadowed by funeral pines, that ran parallel to Isabel's street where in a hidden spot he parked the car—stolen at the Charlottesville airport—which he'd spotted from the rainy booth while making a certain telephone call: Hypsipyle Poore, breathing low through the receiver, confided that she *had* managed to sleep with van der Slang, twice, and with words like that of a sweet-natured child drawn into a game it was ready to play without full understanding reported the details to Darconville which he recorded in a little notebook with one hand while the other opened and shut on the instrument as if it were galvanized. He did not pity himself. He did not hate himself. He just endured himself, waiting until darkness fell.

It was windy. The moon was like a golp sitting in the rainy sky, disappearing now and again in the fog, lifting the weight of darkness from the earth while turning the world, the woods, into a place of phantoms and shadows, and finally the pale sickly gleam over the Blue Ridge mountains threw a last ambivalent shadow down the valley to beckon the night he'd been waiting almost all day for, leaving the entire area under the full cloven hoof of darkness. The whipping, but intermittent, rain had chilled Darconville to the flesh, congesting his lungs to the point of actual pain. It didn't matter, he thought, as he ducked, thrashing, through limbs and branches. Hill and valley scarcely seemed to be step and landing for him; rooted trees seemed but as sticks he could smite down. There were only his footsteps— fiends in the fog coming after him—each one nulling the last, as fate overtakes free will, steps past chance toward destiny, and halts at predetermination. He would fix her forever to the very spot on which when last he'd seen her she stood—then *bang!* It would be her last night on earth.

As had been the case all day, hiding in the car, he kept turning over and over Hypsipyle's description of Gilbert van der Slang, which confirmed almost everything—it was astounding with what accuracy —he'd conjectured: pinched nose; scrawny neck; wiry hair; a nasal, airy voice; a motionless cast of features, with rabbity teeth showing when he smiled; and the habit, when making a point, of jerking his mouth in an ugly way, a twitch on the right side as if upon whatever pronouncement to be adding something of force or authority to it. It was, she said, like making love to a broomstick.

There was nobody yet home in the little house where Isabel was living: the lights were out, the driveway empty. Darconville swatted through the brush, rank with patches of scabious knapweed and the mold of wet decaying leaves, crouching along toward the sound of water, and there by a familiar stream, a thing that could barely name itself, he chose a spot. It was a covert in a folding bracket of bushes, set back and out of the way, yet with a direct view through the trees, bare except for the last foliar bundles of late fall, to the conventional little house some hundred odd yards away. A scared bird whistled away. He took out his pistol—and waited, the sound of the ghastly susurration in his chest the only evidence of life in those woods.

It was absurd for the necessity of it: thrilled with the evil of where he was, Darconville could nevertheless exclude himself—out of the inexorability of fortune—from a matter one part of him could not conceive, not acknowledge, not treat as a thing of possibility, never mind reason, and to try to behold himself dwelling in the midst of it, to imagine this was he, became impossible. An assassin? With leaky shoes? In a mottled wood by night? Yet there in fact he was, the claustrophile-with-a-vengeance his students so briefly knew—never intimate, never emphatic, never settled, never in sight. His reclusive disposition was at the extreme. The night brought the forest closer; it was no longer the place where, as lovers, they'd walked a million years ago; it was in the interior chilliness of the darkness, and the moving trees whose every action, travestied by moonlight, almost made him fire proved every time he looked up to be only the wind and the rain whispering in repetitious echo of her, *"You're mad as a hatter! You're mad as a hatter!"*

An hour passed, and another. The covert grew darker about him, and pulse by pulse Darconville felt time grow weaker in his veins. He kept still, not stirring, concentrating on the destruction of her memory and trying to block out all motive, sense, intention, and consequence— for thought is fatal to action—sometimes seeing no ground beneath him and then noticing, suddenly, the serrations in every leaf and every blade of grass. And then whence the smell of sulphur, of burning and smoke, rising out of fissures in the earth? A subterranean fire. It had been burning, like dream into fact, for four years. He blew on his hands. He felt cramped. Where was she? Where *was* she?

He listened. It was getting late; there was still no sign of her: perhaps, he thought, she might never appear. Then he would have to stalk her—who knew?—even to Zutphen Farm and blast her away through a window. Overhead a few dry and shrunken leaves rustled, having points like stars and rising and falling delicately as fingers playing sad music. Along the bed of the slanting ground, all between the stools of wood, there were heaps of dead brown leaves, and sheltered mats of lichen, and drifts of spotted stick gone rotten, and tufts of rushes here and there, full of fray and feathering. Darconville stumbled about, shifting in his wet coat, into several positions until it all became hopeless: the rain came thundering down now in sheets. He was freezing and, unable to stifle the coughing from his aching lungs, leapt away with a train of curses sufficient to poison the light of the moon. The volume of rain beat eastward into the trees, and shuddering—the ice-cold water rippling down his collar and into the bandages—he squelched through the bracken and brakes and thickets of undergrowth, where the moss held the falling rain like sponges. He took refuge in disgust under a huge pine by which, still, the little stream ran like diverted hope and listened to the water brawling darkly along banks napped with that soaked moss, though he was still able to see the house.

It was then that it happened. Darconville, while he squatted there, hunched and inert, his stiff fingers folded around the pistol, was suddenly alert to something in the woods, undeniably like something moving. Turning, he felt his heart shut like a stopper; he froze—and, instantly, it was as if he had come there only to understand what he must immediately come to know he could never learn to forget, for in that moment foreordained his gaze had fallen upon that simple tree, standing alone across the water, upon the midrib of which in thin serifs had long ago been carved a single word: *Remember.*

He stood before it in the pouring rain.

What hand made it? Whose carved? The very hand, he saw without elaborate calculation, that would now mock memory by murder. It was quietly, an overpowering accumulation, in the midst of that storm—with the feeling of what was impending swiftly opening to him in violent contrast the intensity of past consciousness and the idea that it might cease forever—that Darconville suddenly realized that the source of all error in life was failure of memory! A recept, made of many precepts, exploded into concept—and the past, formerly thought adversary to the future, spoke to him. Remember! Remember! Remember the king's words in the old story: which arrow flies forever? The arrow that has found its mark! All forgetfulness, he understood, almost on the edge of exultation, was in itself immoral, for the permanence with which experiences stay with a man is proportional to the significance which they had for him: memory must be preserved *from* time! A thing has the more value, it came to him, the less it is a function of time, and the effort of men to probe the past? Why, it was nothing less than an exertion toward immortality, for the consciousness and vision of the past but pointed to a desire to be conscious in the future, didn't it? And if, he suddenly reasoned, we do not free what we have known from time by memory, can we have any knowledge of remembrance any more than we can have one jot more of time? Memory was eclogue! "What have I got left?" asked Time. "Your genius," answered Eternity.

The moon was dancing in Darconville's eyes through a mist of tears, raining from heaven, half blinding them—and he wiped them so as quickly to obtain the knowledge of what in that small carved word he feared otherwise must fade.

It was a duty to forget nothing! The first of faults, Adam's and Eve's, was not disobedience but failure of *memory*—and the concomitant want of understanding that memory is only another perspective on immortality, for inasmuch as one is without continuity, he can have no true reverence for what of life, in pain or pity, in happiness or hope, he owns to utter and utters to shape and shapes to know if he would redeem the time. Memory, rendering the past obsolete, nevertheless relies on it. Continuous memory was not only the vanquisher of time, the logical and ethical phenomenon saving one, Darconville saw almost in ecstasy, from having to bear the grave burden of living one's own life under the same fault by which, through the very person he'd destroy, he was faulted, but it was also linked to morality, for only through memory were repentance and the rehabilitation of the past possible—the salvation of one's poor self! Destruction? No, there must be preservation! The past! The past! The past, thought Darconville, *was* the artist's playground! The past was the birthplace of the future! He took off Crucifer's jade ring and threw it as far as he could into the woods. To satisfy our now with the memory of then, to shape to know: *that* was how Petrarch attained to Laura in the field of eternal light! And if reality *were* too varied, too abundant, to be mirrored in anything smaller, narrower, less varied than itself? Then?

Suddenly upon Darconville's heart fell one drop of Brahmic bliss, illuminating what it struck and telling him a truth: Rise up, prophet, see and understand, the death of what is is the birth of what's to be!— and instantly the outward circumstances of his life transformed into a consciousness of moral exaltation, an indescribable feeling, invincible to all effects of time and change, an elevation, elation, and joyousness passing the very portals of grace itself as the seraph Uriel, with diffraction lights glowing from his face, stood above him. I hear, I forget. I see, I remember. *I do, I understand.* And he cried out through the woods in astonishment, as if, upon the stroke of creation, he suddenly understood that the occasion is the nothing from which everything comes!

At that very moment, a car's headlights swept across the trees, beamed away, and then the soft crackling of tires coming through the darkness by the driveway was heard no more. The engine was shut off. As the car doors slammed, the very night seemed to hold its breath, as even the sound of wind and rain had ceased. But there was never any noise, for, unable to move, Darconville was facing away into the forest, remaining completely still, his eyes closed to everything but the light that had flashed upon his soul. He couldn't see her again. She didn't exist.

It was done, then, what wasn't, as in the resolution of dreams, and so what can be recorded of what never took place may, for who looked back in another direction never looked back at all and who was given another life never knew how swiftly one was lost (or how close she came to death that night) and what failed of love in time disappeared into the timelessness of love to return never again. He couldn't see her again, who would. She didn't exist anymore, who did. And what had long been done had never been that now would have to be.

XCVI

Quire Me Some Paper!

I'll write, but with my blood, that
      she may see
These lines come from my wounds
      and not from me.

—George Chapman, *Bussy d'Ambois*

"QUIRE ME SOME PAPER!" cried Darconville. "Shear me a
sheep for vellum! Nail me out a desk with the timber of redwoods! A
quill pluperfect shoots from the sky to occupy my hand! Sound me the
Dorian mode! I am alive, O sunset, come back from the dead, and
from Thy crucible dost Thou call me forth, even as I am! All is in
movement! There are angels come to bandage the wounded angels of
battle and bend to lift me from the darkness to the light! *Beauséant!*

Silence is full of execution, and intuition and desire lie undestroyed! I will squeeze secrets through the tips of my fingers! I will bring noses to windowpanes! I am still Darconville, master of my fate, captain of my soul!"

XCVII

Venice

Happy were he could he finish forth his fate
In some unhaunted desert, where, obscure
From all society, from love and hate
Of worldly folk, there should he sleep secure.

—Robert Devereux, Earl of Essex

VENICE is a city of yesterdays. There is in the ancient stone, the narrow and coarsing lagoons, the dark immemorial sea slapping at its very steps an aspect of the eternal which seems to say, in a strange paradox of finality, that time shall endure only if once it comes to an end, a concept reversing the very nature of what it is. There should be no surprise in that. It is a city, in fact, where the natural does not exist, not in St. Mark's glittering dome, neither in the implacable white of the Doge's Palace, nor in the cold churches, old museums, and silent galleries with their ikons and golden mosaics: Byzantine madonnas, infant sibyls with electric eyes, and hierogrammarians standing head downward with their feet folded in prayer.

The city, born of art, has long existed more as a measure of the artist's contemplative imagination than the reality of life in the labyrinth of narrow streets and lanes, smelling of ruin and the sea, might otherwise indicate.

At once conveyed in the deserted gondola stations, however, along the slimy steps, past the empty warehouses and listing palazzi that rise on either hand in the northerly district of the Sacca della Misericordia is a particular destitution, and, leaving the busier, more central quays and piazzetti off the Canal Grande where rows of fantastic façades can be seen with Gothic curved and pointed arches surmounted by circles containing equilateral crosses all rising above grillwork balconies in the Ducal gallery pattern, the tourist becomes suddenly bewildered. The area turns darker, dirtier, more dismal. The water, sucking the walls and welling up in the remotest crevices and steps, is black and foul. The houses on each side rise to great heights still, their lowest stories forming a double line of insignificant shops into which the light of the sun, however, never enters and the dark recesses of which, set so far back from the close rughetti, are poorly illuminated by the flickering rays of the oil lamps which alone are used to serve for light there. Gloomier cells than these are perhaps hard to imagine—being made no less pitiful, to be sure, if viewed through the contrasting light of former days when many of them enjoyed, if not richness of adornment, then at least the comparative wealth of human habitation. Now, many of them were deserted—but not all. Several were still inhabited, by those who, out of either determination or dereliction or both, remained yet undeterred by the dampness, the vermin, or the prospect of a coming Venetian winter.

The old palazzo, for instance—formerly his grandmother's, now his own—in which Darconville was living was such a one. It was a grey narrow house of stone in the Corte del Gatto, a dead-end street set off the Canale della Misericordia which looked across the Laguna Morta on the north side and lay open to its ferocious squalls and winds. All three floors were unheated. There were fireplaces in only four of the twelve rooms. Wood was available in the trainyards at the Ferroviaria, when he could spend the money.

The weather in northern Italy had been bleak, the sudden changes of temperature giving way to a searching cold, and the skies, scarlet in the morning, always turned a dark variegated *africano* by afternoon, leaving the fastlands sunless and the seawater slick and grey almost without exception. The first few weeks in November had taxed Darconville sorely: he had landed as he was with little in the way of provisions, his one suitcase filled less with clothes and personal articles than with notebooks, letters, and papers relating to the book (how long, in retrospect, had been the preparation!) he'd already begun to write in earnest—not, however, before having made a solemn dedication to the task upon the same day of disembarkation before the high altar of St. Mark's. There would be no income anymore, and much of the money he'd set aside for the wedding, along with the few paychecks earned at Harvard, had been spent on rent for the full year at Adams House, several wasted flights south, and the trip abroad. The city had also dunned him for a host of back taxes on the property. The remaining monies had to be rationed for food and fuel and, as ill-luck would have it, several doctor's bills right from the start, for a cold caught in the woods at Fawx's Mt.—one, exacerbated by the dampness of his rooms, he couldn't shake—pulled him down considerably with a sore throat, shortness of breath, and a persistent cough. The doctor, at the very first examination, said flatly that it was worse than a cold, couldn't he tell?—and he fumed at the irregularity of the entire situation. Did no one know where he was? Couldn't he give any other information? Was there no forwarding address in case of emergency? *"Imbecille!"* cried the doctor, who was also worrying about his fees.

The symptoms were indisputable: anemic pallor, coarse wheezing, and a cough that had already scored the larynx. There was further evidence, above and beyond the recent rupture, of chronic bronchial infection, probably acquired from a neglected pneumonia in childhood. He was in a late and aggravated stage of chronic bronchitis with resulting bronchiectasis.

An unaccountable figure in black, unkempt and unshaven, Darconville—fixed to no hope now but completing his book—soon became a curiosity to the neighborhood in those first weeks, before, that is, he retreated more and more into extreme austerity. The children liked him, and he several times took them to the Campo della Abbazia for balloons upon which, to their delight, he carefully inked their faces. He seemed to possess a curious influence over cats, as well, and on several occasions he was seen standing in the moonlight in front of his house and apparently talking to ten or a dozen cats from far and near who were all looking at him. He kept to himself and could admit to no acquaintances save with an old toothless *squalcira* across the way who, remembering him from earlier years, sometimes brought him over bags of biscotti. The rather saturnine and avaricious doctor who periodically happened by for reasons as much inquisitive as professional refused to understand why he was spending the winter there. Why didn't he go to one of the southern provinces? Wasn't he an American? Hadn't he the money? (The doctor, at the doubt, debated further visits.) A good listener only because an intrigued one, he often sat muddled while the young man's extraordinary talk flowed on—talk that scaled the heavens and ransacked the earth, talk in which memories of a curious past mingled preposterously with doctrines of art, comic mimicries, and prevaricating theories about love and hate—and yet this visitor could not help feeling that as soon as he was alone he would sink down, fatigued and listless, with all the spirit gone out of him. The few neighbors in the corte called him *"Il Monaco."* They had no idea what he did, although at night from the top room of that grey palazzo, dimly lit, they could sometimes hear coils of unnatural laughter or the sounds of phantasmagorical tears, a monodrama that seemed, for all they knew, to have its source in some kind of secret and inscrutable theopathy impossible to fathom.

Darconville, in fact, was writing.

The month of November came in and went out in a pitiless drench of rain, decades of days, uncounted and ignored, in which he rarely left that upper room but worked steadily on, hour upon hour, galvanized into concentrated exertion and punching his head hard with resolutions to restrain his nerves against inner warnings of the exhaustibility of human patience. The manuscript grew, quickly. No longer meditating the direst revenge nor passing from one crazed project to another, with each one no less cowardly than extravagant, he wrote down everything he could remember—for victory without blood, he saw, was twice achieved—filling page after page of what had happened to him, not lying, telling the truth, writing to record rather than to imagine, not inventing what never existed by trying to discover the meaning of what had, and as he worked, distinguishing between the impulse to impose a meaning (*animus impotentium*) and the impulse to interpret (*animus interpretantium*), language became the objective of which self-consciousness was the subjective. The bee had fertilized the flower it robbed. Words were all he had left.

The story was simple, a fable about Isabel Rawsthorne and himself: doubt is double. He loved her. He hated her. There was a peculiar agony, however, to this counterbalancing anti-miracle, as if at the precise moment one was well pleasure alone became too insufficient fully to define a man, so one sought pain. The truth of each, incompatible with that of the other, fed from whichever wrong or right was posited by what one had to believe to keep the other real to avoid. What other story in life *was* there?

Darconville's art seemed to rise superior to its own conditions in that Venetian palazzo, endowing even the dross with a sense of mystery he watched to solve. He was perfectly cognizant of the difficulty of the task of writing this book, its unpleasantness, the uncertainty of achievement, but with that awareness he only redoubled his efforts and scratched into his work a useful refractivity of theme and theory out of the very doubts and fears anterior to it—almost unable, always, to control his impatience over, his devotion to, the need for furnishing proof of himself, denied by pain, and to change that pain into considered prose: a prose of love, a prose of hate. This was his perpetual twilight. He retained his inventive powers only by subordinating himself to them, and yet, so fragile was his hold upon his work, he dared not tie himself to any other engagement whatsoever lest even the foreknowledge of it upset a whole day's work. He began to write up to ten pages a day, pausing only for meager meals or to throw another piece of wood onto the fire or to consult his notebooks, rehearsing exact chronology, rifling out a detail, reckoning a fact in the light of delayed revelation. It would be impossible, of course, to understand the fire with which he wrote unless one also understood the passion with which he'd sought that bond of rare and divine love, too rare, too divine perhaps, even for the realization of the one he loved herself. But work he did. His output increased and, somehow, seemed inversely proportionate to his physical discomfort, now a violent perspiration, now a dry and sinister stiffness, but always the ache in his lungs that left a palpable feeling of cavitation there. He determined to leave out nothing of the four years spent with her, and while he lived no more in thrall of what she did or didn't, would or wouldn't, he repeatedly reviewed the photographs and read and re-read all the letters, notes, and messages she lived in once but inhabited no more, a spirit as infinitely far away in time now as she was in space, flash frozen in a past as old as memory was strong, but a past, a memory, calling him back to search and remember what in the knowledge that is revealed at the heart of all violation can be transfigured by the hand of art. The real, engulfed once in the unreal, emerged, and there was rebirth by water. Laurel was the first plant that grew after the Flood.

It was mid-December now, with winterkill in the air. As on every Friday—the only day of the week he stopped working—Darconville set off through the cold-faced city to visit his grandmother's grave. It was a habit he had formed from the first week of his arrival, initially with only the complication of money spent he couldn't afford, later against a doctor's orders. He faced away from the wind and hurried across a few blocks to the Fondamenta Nuove, paid the rampino, an old silent scaramouche there who, recognizing the black muffler and familiar black coat (threadbare now), unhooked the gondola from the steps, and they sloomed out in long lateral pushes toward the island-contained graveyard offshore, the Cimitero Communale.

The gravestone was a simple one, crowded into a shamble of sunken burial plots and old blackened tombs, many of them with skulls on the entablature and inscriptions relating to both plague and poison, open all to the melancholy requiem of wind and water. A spiked iron gatehouse, set in the circular wall, gave entrance. Darconville walked to the grave and, standing against the rapacious gusts of wind, tried to settle his thoughts around her memory. He tried to offer up a prayer, an attempt that became only a self-conscious reflection defeated by the hypocrisy he found in himself—in his failed love—which required forgetting to overcome and forgiving to absolve. *I can't forget, I can't forget!* he thought. No! No! No! And what of forgiving, he thought bitterly, wasn't circumscribed and so contravened by reinventing the imagination to acknowledge in art the questions life refused? He whispered to his grandmother but realized that the condition of our nature was such that we lived only to see those whom we love drop successively away, our circle of relation growing less until finally we are almost unconnected with the world. All union with the inhabitants of earth must in time be broken, he realized, and all hopes that terminate here must end in disappointment in spite of what by the desperate intercession of the heart we seek to keep.

The impossibility of being able to discover the results of prayer by any merely human test plagued Darconville. How, he wondered, could one determine when a true prayer was offered? If so much depends on the character and spirit of the suppliant, how could anyone who is unable to read the heart tell when the request which a seeker presents is such as God can approve? And how could any external observer take cognizance of such spiritual considerations as those which must enter into the determination of the questions whether, and in what form, a prayer has been answered? Where were the delicate instruments to measure the results in the suppliant produced, sometimes by the denial and sometimes by the granting of his requests? There were no answers given that didn't force one to have to *find* them. And so he walked for hours into the darkening afternoon, the winter light disappearing abruptly as if the cover of the universe had suddenly banged shut, and he brooded over the questions interrogating him by the echo created in the void of his poor prayers.

The strong winds, snatching at his coat, almost took away his breath. He ducked into the chapel of San Michele to get out of the weather, overcome as he entered by a severe tetany of coughing, strange in the silence, and he sat down in a pew and tried again to pray. His prayer became dreams, a slow wandering to an upper level of consciousness beyond the preteressential candlelight and scent of wax, and the dreams in their measurelessness showed him by way of his failed effort in what form a prayer might be answered: yes, he thought, I will make the ultimate confession! It must be the story of *all* lovers, with the ethical and aesthetic sense in the work leaving no means of reaching the truth uninvestigated. Not a simple reproduction of the sensible appearance of things but a representation of their inner reality, embodying and illustrating the truth by the laws of general validity! No, I shall write, thought Darconville—but to forget, and so by forgetting, forgive. It was almost as if he had never known what a certainty was until that night. Prayer, he realized, is utterance! The answer was in itself. Art creates the Eden where Adam and Eve eat the serpent.

Suddenly, Darconville was bending over, almost motionsick, with something fluttering in his chest, and, dizzy, his arms drawing in, he caught himself over a cramp, coughing violently from the lungs—and a spattering of black blood dropped onto the marble floor. It was the first sign of his indisposition, a second new truth to cope with but ignored, fatally, by the splendor of the one that came before.

The gondolier told him to hurry—it was late enough, he complained, to be asking double the fee—for the sea had grown choppy and a nightfog had blown in, ominously closing down over them. They rowed back to the city over the ebony swells, the bluish watery lights of Venice showing dimly through the vaporous night, and the clanking of invisible buoys, with their pitiful lack of resonance, sounded more lost and lonesome in the obscurity of the sea than ever could be imagined. The city from this approach had an aspect of death, as livid as a drowned person. Washed, undermined, and long worn by the lapping waters that rose each day with the powerful flow of the tide, working as a prisoner files his chains, the north side was being slowly eaten away. The façades of the palazzi, their rough coats faded and discolored by the salty air, were many of them blacked, the stucco astragals crumbling off them like sugar. The slick cobblestones under the lamplight shone and were strewn here and about with dead bits of calamaretti and scampi which had fallen from the boats, sails unfurled now, cordage stacked, all jerking in their moorings. The Merceria clock struck ten. It was late and the streets were nearly empty, except for a few old women wearing black shawls who hobbled through the shadows with bread and produce in net bags. There was the rattle of a descending shop shutter. A herring-gull screeched.

Darconville walked back over the narrow and acute streets and sudden bridges to the Corte del Gatto, a tired gallery of ancient chimneys and leaning walls: dwellings of different styles and epochs and states of preservation all jostled together but comfortable enough, he remembered, to have made him happy years ago. What had happened? Had he changed or had they? Now it was all an appalling, proliferating entrapment of hulks, with no interruption of line-building, haunted by class disability and poverty and fetid contamination, a phantom street of oppressive silence, a *rioterrà* of dark mysterious doors that once opened straight upon the water but now crouched down behind the dwellings on the dockside of the more respectable Corte della Misericordia, blind to them on the other side.

The grey palazzo—Darconville's—stood at the very end, the sottoportico, bolted by a door, once having led straight through to a walled courtyard at the back where now could be found only broken statuary, weeds, and several metal pergolas, rusting away. The voices of orphans out there, once raised in play, had long gone into the stone.

He let himself in, to a rush of dampness and Roman cement; the door, booming shut, echoed through three floors. He stood down in the antichiesetta, looking up. The walls were cold and thick and bare. The rooms were empty, long ago having been despoiled of their furniture and drapes and wall-fixtures, along with the beautiful desk on which, it seemed so long ago, he'd first begun to write. The lofty windows, half-covered with pieces of linoleum, could only be secured by renewing the cross-irons that had been pulled away, and the stone arches, with open fissures, had been clumsily buttressed by poor plastering. He took the flight of stairs, by cornices carved with flowers and broken walls open to brick facings, to the second-floor landing—where the rain had found its way between the arch-stones and was there arrested by the frost, operating like a wedge and dislocating the stones—and climbed to the upper floor. He quickly built a fire and cut up four lemons to add to the boiling water in the huge kettle hanging in the fireplace, an old massive chimney grate with half-dogs for wood or coal. By the feeble light of the fire, after drinking the weak toddy, he wrote until three in the morning, his inspiration dying with the last embers in the hearth. The manuscript had by now grown to more than three hundred pages, much of it taken directly from his notebooks, and what had already been done, a kind of commitment, gave him strength to do more, although this particular night's work he couldn't re-read for want of energy and a terrible ache in his diaphragm. He felt feverish, so drew a pile of blankets onto the bed of gamy old wood got at a priory, and slept.

That night he had a frightful nightmare; it was as though someone were handling him secretly, locating the place to drive a knife into him. The touch seemed to spread lightly, fluttering over him delicately, until it gripped him in the small of his back. Darconville woke up shouting, snatching at the point on his back where the hand was—and then leapt up, shivering in horror. It was a rat.

Unable to shake off the frisson, he dragged the blankets to the window and sat up, beside himself, searching the floor. The wind that had earlier been howling outside as if it would tear the very festoons off the pediment had died down. How long had he slept? He rubbed the window. Then he noticed for the first time, falling beyond the cracked and dirty panes, the light flaughts of snow.

XCVIII

Wear Red for Suffering

The soul's dark cottage, batter'd and decay'd,
Lets in new light through chinks which time has made.

—JOHN CLARE

THE WINTER settled in hard, descending in ice and sleet that chilled the waste of snow around Darconville's palazzo, looming spectral in the feeble light like the last human dwelling at the end of the habitable world. It was a place uncheered by a touch of changing light or a solitary ray of sun, where the gloomy vault of darkness above and beyond the fire in his room seemed in collusion with the dismal recollections, distinct in ferocity, he wrote with unrestrained gratitude to be free of. There was no relief in the weather; the days were brief, dark, and frigid. He stopped up the wide chimneys, reinforced cracks where he could, and closed himself off in one room.

It was with some pains, initially, that Darconville placed before himself the undeniable advantages to be gained by way of novel occupation for his senses from the coldness of the room. And yet he scarcely made the adjustment before he realized the terrible depth that could be reached by such penetrating cold. At a pace adapted to his waning strength, however, he continued writing morning and night, alive, as time passed, to this new possibility, that figures, originating in the disease of delicate nerves, actually ministered to functions of the imagination unconscious of one's affliction, and whatever he dreamed of, when lethargy got possession of him, something importunate in the pages underhand called *out* of those dreams and made use of, like the infractions of a law that are dragged in only to prove it. There was often dreadful loneliness. Still, the loneliness was not the old loneliness, because there was a term put to it, however long to look forward to—and while his poor thoughts constantly reverted to those remote but rapturous early days spent with Isabel (the kite-flying, the engagement on London Bridge, the kisses and cares of so long ago) he found them briefer than the beauty of trees that only blossom to fertilize to reproduce, and so he shook out of his wasted hands every miracle of memory ever beheld or thought of, as if, instantaneous in passage, it might otherwise disappear and never come back again.

Christmas Day was, perhaps, the loneliest of them all. He walked out into a morning that was so cold that one could have cracked it with one's fingers, the first breath taken coincident with a sharp feeling of diffusion and dilation in his chest. It seemed to him that he could see his past in the ornateness of the palazzi and his abandonment in other dead romances of that city as he made his way on foot to St. Mark's for Mass.

The whiteness of the huge piazza, as he entered it, hurt his eyes, and the cold sun, refracting off the snow and houses of whitest stone, somehow cast a cruel objective light onto that dark disheveled self, shaped to shadows, walking into the pitiless glare. The pigeons flew double, bird and shadow, against the Campanile. He stood a moment before the great cathedral, its façade flat as a drop-scene, golden with old mosaics, the four fantastic horses in gilded bronze galloping over the five byzantine domes into the winter light. There was almost no room inside, the close air dispelled only in the extremity of sudden drafts from doors opening and shutting. The enormous crowd of people, visitors and tourists, reached all the way back to the atrium where

Darconville, listening to the anthems, prayers, and then the solemn chant of the *Puer Natus Est,* thought back on a Christmas three years before, tears filling his eyes as he looked up at the thirteenth-century vestibule mosaics on the small domes overhead and portentously focused on the first, the Adam and Eve group, with Eve, a curiously forbidding figure, summoning to mind in an instant of phantom paradox the terrible machinations of Dr. Crucifer. Remorse flooded Darconville's soul. His throat swelled with a cough he couldn't expel. He suddenly heard the constant pushing and pulling of his own breath in the crowded darkness there and, turning in panic, quickly staggered outside where he was overcome with an attack of violent hemorrhage.

There was no question whatsoever now that Darconville was chronically ill. Repeated infections, in destroying the bronchi, essentially left only arteries and veins of the lungs encased in scar tissue, and because a constant stream of mucus ran through the bronchioles to the mainstream bronchi, swollen now, no longer clear, and almost useless in terms of elasticity, particularly severe episodes of coughing threatened to rupture the already frail bullae. He had grown accustomed to the situation, however—with almost every day during the month of January being spent over basins and slops—and would accept nothing but the most random and cosmetic attention (often, with threats to the doctor) lest greater distractions prevent the work he was almost maniacally driven to finish. Time! He wanted only more time!

It seemed less important, somehow, to be well than to write well. To require two things, he felt, was to have them both undone. So he was inspired to feverish activity, and his forsakenness brought a renewed flowering of language when nothing of sickness could make him stop and nothing could swerve his pen, the very one, he could not forget, of which in the dramatic boast of his youth it was said *no other hand dare touch*—"The Black Disaster." He felt in his fingers that magic pen which, explaining the void, filled it, and taking it up repeatedly returned to work. In pages of violent beauty, slashed across with fierce bitterness, he poured out his threnody. The worse he grew the more furiously he wrote, the words of love and hate snapping into place about this girl—deceitful, common, infantile, cruel, and yet utterly necessary to him—who, in fact, was herself the formal cause of the entire, unpremeditated enterprise, an action she hastened as did Penelope, who supplied the weapon for her suitors' downfall, for although it was Odysseus who took on the more than one hundred able-bodied men it was she, not he, who remembered the big hunting bow that had been hanging in the inner room. And of method? Darconville only kept fixed to his desk—like Odysseus, again, who sent each bowshot through the holes of the ax-heads while *seated*—triumphing over the pains of the living to discover thoughts trembling to be born, a situation, oddly enough, that rendered only time for him, not health, the single want in that room.

The month of February, its skyscape dark as thunder, brought no relief. A storm in mid-month left Venice to the mercy of the bitter northwind, the wind-chill factor plummeting temperatures to below zero, splitting brass, stiffening clothes, and forming ice across the pan of the faces of those who dared to try to make their way out over the blast-broken crusts of snow, gelid streets, and ice-choked canals where mere sounds in the air were as sharp and crackling as artillery.

A snowstorm followed. It was a blizzard of incredible dimension, the white winds blowing in havoc and flooding at the crest of the tide and driving monstrous drifts into houses half-tilting into the sea over the battered seawalls. The shrieking winds, rattling windows, blew down every corte and calle, with great drifts rolling and curling beneath each violent blast, tufting and combing with rustling swirls and twisting up into vertical spirit-spouts that tore down chimneys, rang bells, and shattered glass. For days the storm wreaked havoc, snatching little whiffs from the edges of the sea, twirling them round, and making them dance into the chines and chinks of the piles of the old city, pointed with barbs of frost. Darconville was almost unable to control his patience in the maddening cold. Blowing smoke, suffering severe headaches, he worked on steadfastly with a kind of desperate courage, clinging to the thing whose worth, increasing, could now only be realized through the knowledge that it would soon be taken away, and, finding a degree of force and enthusiasm that is given alone to the doomed man, he never gave up. A death sentence concentrates the mind wonderfully. He knew he had no time to lose.

The room got colder and colder, its mold fusty in spite of the fire, and the black east wind, having changed, was now striking off the raw Adriatic. By now, the lattices were quite blocked up with snow, sifting in where the lead in the iron-frame had failed, and water stains spread down the inner walls. Darconville began not to be able to bear it. His feet, freezing, began to sting. He rubbed oil into his leg joints. He covered himself with blankets and went through the house, trying to walk

the stiffness out. Downstairs, he saw that the frost had pierced through the ribs of the old house, striking to the pith of hollow places, and in several places the frost-blow had burst the walls. The windows, coated with ice like ferns and flowers and dazzling stars, were opaque where they hadn't fallen weakly inward from the weight of the snow against them, and in the empty front room a mere whisper of wind through the chimney had come to the old kettle upon the hearth-cheeks and cracked it in two.

After five days, from over across the Lido the sun burst forth upon the world of white, but what it brought wasn't warmth, only a clearer shaft of cold from the violet depth of sky. The temperature never rose a degree outside, and the sunless rooms of the palazzo thawed not a whit. Darconville, utterly frail, his body almost attenuated to pure spirit, looked more like a forpined ghost than a living man, his face thin, the long hands once so full of power now drawn and pale. He sought to distract his mind by several quick excursions from priory to priory for wood, begging for fuel to stay alive. The icy air made him giddy and lightheaded, his feet feeling like weights as he plodded through the thick snow. As he walked the streets, it seemed to him that passers-by looked at him malevolently or suspiciously, and each step somehow became a step toward the sharp edge of the grave, each corner more unreachable, and every bridge a bleak wicket to Elysium. But of all things the very gravest to his apprehension was that he wouldn't finish his book, the completion of which, he felt, waited now on less than several weeks, possibly sooner. And so driven, he would get his necessities, return, and immediately go back to work.

The body's distresses often made Darconville restless and irritable, and yet, while gathering ills assailed him, he found serenity of spirit in his writing—no longer an attack now on the nature of someone who, three thousand miles west of his writing hand, was so wayward she was without peer but a cosmic perspective on love and hate which, while relating to a personal subject, reached to the nature of man himself. The quest overrode the goal, in fact. The manuscript had changed, developed, and the death of every tender sentiment in him, as brought home by the mute but marshaling evidence he was forced to discover about her in retrospect, miraculously gave birth to a freedom *from* her—a release to see that ends touch beginnings, for if a necessary function of the imagination is to imagine its own absence, that absence allows one a glimpse into a world even more excessively

interior than even fancy can devise, a desert of contemplation, a retreat, in which, with one's senses atrophied or impoverished, truth is
no longer created but divulged. The familiar is too familiar to know.
And so living in solitude as he had been for so long, he saw with increasing amazement that universal thoughts were infinitely richer to
reflect upon than the particular people who engendered them were to
study. Every word is a metaphor for a deeper truth that sign hides.
Description is interrogative.

The old lady in the Corte del Gatto, guessing the serious nature of
Darconville's illness, came to increase her visits and toward late February, shocked at the extreme disorder of his condition—a wasting diarrhea had begun and the room took on a noticeable malignancy—no
longer felt she could leave him alone. She carted firewood up to the
room, left him various nostrums, and scolded him apprehensively,
muttering with various but incomprehensible signs of resignation. His
moods changed. He became impatient and fretful. When she considered how ill he was and what allowance should be made for the
influence of sickness upon his temper she tried to indulge. He went
from seeming imperturbability to sudden explosions of anger to bouts
of sighing. Then on February 27 he had another frightful hemorrhage
—one might have tracked his path from one cold room to another, the
bleeding was so profuse. She immediately notified the doctor.

There was nothing to be done anymore to dissuade Darconville by
argument from further exhaustion, and the imminence of dire peril
only increased his resolve to work down to the last pages, but then all
this went over as, vomiting blood and yellowish-green sputum, he
could no longer muffle alarm with still another effort. The doctor,
wailing in impatience, forced him by compulsion to his bed, adminis-
tering some old tetracycline pills which, having lost their effectiveness if
not their color, he'd found in the musty reaches of a samples drawer
and pressing him, all the while, to go immediately to the hospital on
the Rio dei Mendicanti as the weather would be getting worse. Darconville refused. The doctor asked him where he would be willing to
go, to Kreuznach or Soden? Bagnères-de-Bigorre or Luchon? Bour-
nemouth or Brindisi? Darconville, coughing, struggled up and banged
the bed. "I will stay *here*," he cried, almost in tears, "in this Capharnaum! *In this Capharnaum!*"

The winter days, darkening early, seemed interminable, and all the
following week the feeble light, swallowed up in swift successive shad-

ows, left the sloping snowdrifts machined hard against houses frozen to the inner stones. The skies looked sick, and at the end of the week the soft and silent snow again began to fall.

Darconville's bed, to stem the chill, was pulled around to the fireside. A salamander, filled with oil—sitting next to a pail in which, repeatedly, his poisonous effusions were spent—had been secured to supplement the loss of heat that seemed to evaporate so quickly through the cold-packed walls. The wind whistled through rags stuffed into the windows. The air, confined, was unwholesome but worked somewhat against the night air, the damp bed, and the swelling in his feet and legs, lately come to a continuously aggravated condition. He would not stop writing. Nor would he permit himself to be undressed out of apprehension of the pain he would have to suffer in being dressed again. He felt cold and then complained of a more than usual degree of heat, a pain and oppression of the chest, especially after motion; his spittle was of a saltish taste and sometimes mixed with blood, especially after long fits of coughing which were all invariably proven dangerous now, with increasingly severe hemoptysis. He became hoarse. Water was steamed in pans to foment his lungs and ease breathing, and yet all the while, in spite of the cold sweats, the nausea, and the apostemes which appeared in the lower body, he shaped his last and best efforts in a shaky calligraphy around the work at hand for yet another page. Another page. And another. *Un altro, un altro, gran' Dio, ma più forte,* thought Darconville, *ma più forte!*

Paper is patient. The creative pen kept to the receptive paper—it *leapt* to use, through every phase of perception, with thoughts, unsummoned and unannounced, pensioned out of the blandishments of common reality, constantly stealing upon him for inclusion, transmitted down through the memory of those who lived in ancient times, races illimitable, to be resumed across the years in all the emotions, passions, experiences of the millions and millions of men and women whose lives of love and the loss of it insensibly passed into his own and so composed it. The room *itself* was a lesson compacting his goal: there was absolutely nothing else to do but write. He wrote doggedly, stopping only to rotate his wrist to relieve a graphospasm or to try to press an ache out of his diaphragm. He wrote desperately, searching the past, as fear picks out objects in the dark, to identify what would otherwise forever loom as phantoms to his sight. When there seemed to be nothing left, he slept, then rose again to write—no, not with an elevation available at will, but through the whispering of innumerable responsive spirits within him that stirred like the invisible motions of the mind wavering between dreams and sleep to remind him that out of fatal mortality could be snatched something in the life of the world that did *not* participate in disintegration but could transfigure it. The end, indeed, was near. And then one night, alone, with only the Holy Logoi standing above him in a thousand diaphanous shades of ether, Darconville looked under his hand and found that from disorder—from the spectacle of order that was so vast it only resembled disorder—a civilization had emerged. Future became a fiction. The work was finished at last.

It was March by now. A deep peripneumonia had set in, causing pooling of secretions in Darconville's lungs, the exudation of pus, and the dissolution of already scarred mucosa. Small blood vessels were rupturing, sending up viperish clots of black blood in remorseless acceleration. The inadvertent swallowing of clots produced nausea and retching which the doctor sought to check by drastically limiting his food. At first, he thought he would utterly go mad from hunger, but soon he could eat nothing solid without suffering immediately, neither the loathly bowls of milksop which appeared at every meal nor the whimsical remedies—jills of broth, lac ammoniacum, and the mixtures of vulnerary roots of plants—which the old lady credulously hoped might overcome this terrible illness that by now had set all medicines at defiance. He lay silent, flushed with fever, the only sound being his labored breathing and the clup-a-clup of tongue upon arid palate. Curiously, he kept the manuscript by him, as if reluctant to surrender it, sometimes reaching weakly for a page to add a note, to turn a phrase, to knock off the waste marble. Suddenly the fever, denominated ardent and inflammatory, rose higher, ushering in a bounding pulse and a hammering pain in the head. There was a coarse twitching of his muscles and impossible congestion. The manuscript was placed in a black tin box.

Darconville had now come under the shadow. His body was completely extenuated by the hectic fever and colliquative sweats which mutually succeeded one another, the one towards night, the other in the morning—and then he was cold, a chill creeping over him like another emotion sent to temper one already there, too absolutely there, a terrible and unresolvable complementarity in which radically opposed but equally total commitments to the meaning of life seemed to coexist in what became a single phenomenon that, irreconcilably, was also and was at the same time nevertheless the secret at the center of all truth. Under his bedclothes at night he shook like jelly, unable to think for cold. He was no longer able to turn in the bed. An unpleasant odor, like dissolution itself, emanated from his cold sweat. His mouth was cold. His cheeks were cold, hollow, withering into themselves. He could feel an inrush of bitter cold from the window through which, silently, he watched the night-by-night movement of the moon eastward through the stars. Distance was a mocking vision to his fever-lurden eyes, but he said nothing, for when a person's trouble comes down to the final intimacy he gives no one access to it. *Custodi nos, custodi nos,* he thought as he lay there awaiting the resolution of the mystery, for the lights of heaven itself were dim. The very stars wandered.

It was a windy, whispering moonlit night in Venice, the frost-fog looping around the lower sky in mid-March when Darconville was hit with a sudden eruption in the forepart of his chest, a slam that gave him such violent pain when he sprang up to gasp for breath that he quickly drew in his bowels to prevent the motion of the diaphragm. He screamed out in agony, as his back seemed to break. The old lady, praying the rosary in a corner, crashed over a chair spilling a posset of tea as she rushed to wash his mouth of spittle, at first thin, then becoming grosser and streaked with blood, now filling his throat as infection eating through the weakened wall of a bronchial artery tore through a rupturing bulla, fragile from repeated coughing spasms, and boiled into his lungs. He clutched for the old lady's hand, impossibly trying to say something—but, heaving, vomited up a tremendous rush of bile and blood and, completely beyond himself, incapable of explanation, he suddenly couldn't speak. Confusion, utter and horrible, surrounded him, because confusion was complete within.

Astonished, he leapt to his feet in the grip of massive shock.

It was as if, evacuating at every step—his wild protesting hands streaming with blood—he were being driven backwards with each violent convulsion. But the hands were reaching out as his brain, fleeing the onrushing hypoxia, was rapidly flashing images he was unable to control, and with memory distorted in the replaying reflexes of acute cerebral damage he for an instant actually looked into the *past!* He seemed to be struggling out of the hematosis in an attempt to describe or call upon something he couldn't yet see, and then with a terrible snorting noise which seemed, as it rose through the phlegm filling his throat, to burst his nose in a lethal explosion of bright blood that spattered all over the bed and sheets and cold floor, he tried to speak— mouthing words that wouldn't form. Groping blindly, he made a motion with his hands as if something were coming towards him and stumbling forward, just before he fell, reached up in a last fatal moment of blindness to cry out inexplicably and desperately and loud, *"My cat! My cat!"*

Then something came towards him at last.

XCIX

The Black Duchess

Like as it was with Aesopes Damosell, turned from a Catt to a Woman, who sate very demurely, at the Boards End, till a Mouse ranne before her.

—FRANCIS BACON

The Black Duchess, a 15,000-h.p. tanker built specifically to carry liquid cargoes, was meanwhile steaming back up the Atlantic with Gilbert and Isabel van der Slang on board. They had been married, on deck, by the ship's captain on March 13 with no relatives in attendance and spent their honeymoon on the island of St. Maarten by the Virgin Islands. There had been no announcement of the wedding beforehand. A small notice of the event appeared one week later on page six of a Charlottesville newspaper with no other details, no mention of witnesses, and no accompanying photograph.

C

The End

Attired with stars, we shall forever sit triumphing over Death and
Chance and Thee, O Time.

—JOHN MILTON

IT WAS FIVE O'CLOCK in the morning, the earth's shadow still
undisturbed by dawn, when a municipal traghetto took Darconville's
body across the grey Rio dei Mendicanti to the mortuary of the
Ospedale Civile for the post-mortem examination. The chimes of the
Campanile sounded the hour through the fog. The burial took place
after a fortnight's delay on the cemetery island of San Michele in a
reused gravesite, dug out of the frozen ground when the sketching of
clouds on the dismal horizon, after that interval, blew in a cold rain.
There were no mourners, no rites, and no funerary exequies other

than that of a recitation over the coffin by a Capuchin friar who read from a simple hymn:

"Veni, Creator Spiritus,
Mentes tuorum visita,
Imple superna, gratia,
Quae tu creasti, pectora . . ."

The official report was filed of fact-finding, documents' inquiry, and the medical investigation performed within the limits of the state, with several questions, stemming from the lack of information of the papers supplied, unsatisfactorily answered. The palazzo was locked and boarded up. The deceased's clothing, including a black coat faded and soiled and ripped more or less at intervals of its seams, was burned. A pen, a watch, and a suitcase of papers were confiscated by the proper authorities, while the black tin box containing a large manuscript was suborned by the doctor, in the stead of due fee, with a view to adding a penny to his competence.

There alone was epitaph.

There was nothing more: only the transfiguration of a soul, in memory remembered, lying buried in the ink that writes. But memory had its birthplace in those words, not the other way round, for creation is to memory what resurrection is to death, reversing pain to send it back again to ask of the momentarily incomplete idiom of that which prompted it—that feeble analogue, called reality, overflowing itself in every direction—what is meant in the terrible paradox at the heart of that truth which has two forms, each of them indisputable, yet each antagonistic to the other: loving and hating. The question stops on the threshold of what cannot be investigated. It can only be felt; felt, then faced; and so faced, redeemed in the work of art that, taking the hint nature suspended, proceeds to detach itself from, and then maintain, the past against the influence of the present, which is only another approach to immortality—to make an *image* out of the force with which one has struggled to survive where finally one, transformed, has been created by what has been endured and mastered in the past, the fashioning of an incomprehensible beauty that slowly but finally emerges from the endless ceremonials of sadness. The confusions, misunderstandings, and mistakes, wafered on your forehead, will never disappear. One perishes from cold, kneeling for illumination outside the bed, in order to give life to the artifice of prayer.

But the survival is in the art—for *there* the heart begins to measure itself, not by its constraints but by its fullness, its poor baffled hopes dim now in the light of those infinite longings which spread over it, soft and holy as day-dawn. Thus it must be while the world lasts, the very misprisions against the spirit coming only to test and reveal the power of exaltation. Sorrow is the cause of immortal conceptions.

West Barnstable, Mass.
1978

Alexander Theroux was born in Medford, Massachusetts. A professor of English Literature, currently writer-in-residence at Phillips Academy, Andover, he has taught at the University of Virginia and at Harvard. Dr. Theroux is the author of essays, short stories, poetry, plays, children's books, and novels. His portrait of Darconville appears on the jacket of this book.